CHRISTINA STEAD was born in Australia, and went to Paris in the late '20s, where she worked in a bank. From that experience she drew much of the information that she utilizes so skillfully in HOUSE OF ALL NATIONS, first published in 1938. She has written eleven books, including DARK PLACES OF THE HEART, THE PUZZLE-HEADED GIRL, and the highly acclaimed THE MAN WHO LOVED CHILDREN (also available in a Bard edition).

D1285637

Also by CHRISTINA STEAD

THE MAN WHO WAS NOT WITH IT

HOUSE OF ALL NATIONS

CHRISTINA STEAD

BARD BOOKS / PUBLISHED BY AVON

Note: This is a work of fiction. No real persons are represented in the story. Any resemblance to real names or attributes of persons occur accidentally, without the knowledge or desire of the author.

AVON BOOKS
A division of
The Hearst Corporation
959 Eighth Avenue
New York, New York 10019

Copyright 1938, © 1966 by Christina Stead.
Published by arrangement with
Holt, Rinehart and Winston, Inc.
Library of Congress Catalog Card Number: 72-80210.

First Bard Printing, April, 1974.

BARD TRADEMARK REG. U.S. PAT. OFF. AND
FOREIGN COUNTRIES, REGISTERED TRADEMARK—
MARCA REGISTRADA, HECHO EN CHICAGO, U.S.A.

Printed in the U.S.A.

Sequence of Scenes

ON est dédommagé de la perte de son innocence par celle de ses préjugés. Dans la société des méchants, où le vice se montre à masque levé, on apprend à les connaître.
—DENIS DIDEROT, *Le Neveu de Rameau*

Credo

No one ever had enough money.   —JULES BERTILLON
There's no money in working for a living.   —IDEM
Of course, there's a different law for the rich and the poor:
otherwise, who would go into business?
                                          —E. RALPH STEWART
If all the rich men in the world divided up their money
amongst themselves, there wouldn't be enough to go round.
                                          —JULES BERTILLON
Woolworth's taught the people to live on nothing and now
we've got to teach them to work for nothing.   —IDEM
The only permanent investment now is in disaster.
                                          —MICHEL ALPHENDÉRY
A self-made man is one who believes in luck and sends his
son to Oxford.   —IDEM
There are poor men in this country who cannot be bought:
the day I found that out, I sent my gold abroad.
                                          —COMTESSE DE VOIGRAND
It's easy to make money. You put up the sign BANK and
someone walks in and hands you his money. The façade is
everything.   —JULES BERTILLON
Everyone says he is in banking, grain, or peanuts, but he's
really in a dairy.   —HENRI LÉON
If there's a God, he's more like Rockefeller than Ramsay
MacDonald.   —WILLIAM BERTILLON
Patriotism pays if you take interest in other countries.
                                          —DR. JACQUES CARRIÈRE
With the revolution coming, there's one consolation—our
children won't be able to spend our money.
                                          —FRANK DURBAN
Here we are sitting in a shower of gold, with nothing to hold
up but a pitchfork.   —JULES BERTILLON
Every successful gambler has a *rentier* sitting at the bottom
of his pants.   —IDEM
A speculator is a man who, if he dies at the right time, leaves
a rich widow.   —WILLIAM BERTILLON

Scene One: He Travels Fast But Not Alone

THEY were in the Hotel Lotti in the Rue de Castiglione, but not in Léon's usual suite. Léon's medicine case in yellow pigskin lay open, showing its crystal flasks, on a Louis XV chair. The Raccamonds, man and wife, bent over this case and poked at it.

"He always travels with it: cowardice of the lion before a common cold, eh?" Aristide reflected.

Marianne sniffed. "He's afraid to lose his money, that's all."

The white door opened a few inches and an immense head, with long black hair carefully brushed over a God's acre of baldness, appeared in the crack. Clear brown eyes sunk in large sockets searched them, forgave them. "Hello, Aristide! Just having a bath," said the head. "Wait a few minutes, will you? Sit down, Marianne. Ring if you want anything. Excuse me." The door shut. In a moment, it reopened. "Excuse me. How are you, Marianne? Do you want some tea, some—a cockta', sherry? Ring, on the telephone. I'll be with you in a minute."

The door shut. Water was running behind several doors. Marianne fingered the curtains. "Why did they give him a suite at the back this time?"

"Perhaps they're full up?"

"So early in spring? No. He must be economizing." They waited. The water stopped running and they heard distant splashing. Persuasively came the edged voice of a woman. Marianne pricked her ears and looked at Aristide. "Then Mme. Léon is here?"

"No: one of his women, it must be."

Léon's traveling library was on the table: three dictionaries; Cook's handbook; *Winter Sunshine;* the *Revue de Transylvanie,* and *Polish Up Your French*.

"She must be taking a bath, too."

Aristide shook his head vigorously. "Léon never lets his women use his bed or his bath: modesty."

Beside his bed was a faded breast-pocket photograph

13

of a solid woman in ostrich plumes and kid gloves—his mother.

Marianne laughed. "Fear."

In a moment more the door opened and Léon appeared, fully dressed and very fresh. Behind him was a dazzling young woman, a Ukraine blonde, with a long plump face, a complexion of radishes in cream, hair in page curls. Her eyes, large as imperial amethysts, roved in an indolent stare of proud imbecility. For a full minute after the sudden splendor of her entrance, Aristide Raccamond found himself bathed in her glare. In the exalted fashion of Paris whores, she singled out and courted the husband in the presence of the wife. Henri Léon waited for her a moment and then hurriedly introduced her: "My friends, Mr. and Mme. Raccamond, old friends, good friends: Mme. Vera Ashnikidzé, an old friend of mine."

She advanced with studied insulting vanity. "Charmed, I am sure." Her manners were perfect, that is, she flouted the Raccamonds outrageously, stirred the eels in their souls, while she went through the polite ritual minutely and coaxingly. Léon allowed them another gasp at his swan and then spoke to her in Russian. With a little frown and a lascivious smile, a short cooing broke out of her throat and she passed to the outer door, wallowing in the swelling air, not giving a second glance to the Raccamonds.

Léon came back from shooing her off, with a bashful family smile. "What do you think of her, eh? Eh, Marianne?" He flushed. "I value your opinion, Marianne."

"Russian, eh?" asked Aristide, somewhat embarrassed.

"Very beautiful: I admire your taste," croaked Marianne.

Léon made a wry face, recovered himself, expostulated, "She's a lady. I met her with Paul, Paul Méline, with a little friend, a Mme. Something, on the Champs-Élysées, Café du Berry. There were two of them right there at the little table. Méline was with me and I had a bet with him that they wouldn't speak to us. He got them into conversation and he won. I didn't pay him yet. He got the other girl. A lady, too." He begged, "She's a decent woman, Marianne, married. Have you ever seen a girl like that, Aristide?" He exulted, checked himself immediately out of respect for Marianne. He grinned at Marianne. "Marianne doesn't mind if you speak up. She knows you're

14

faithful. Don't you, eh, Marianne?" He became earnest. "I can tell you one thing about that boy, Marianne. I've known him ten, fifteen years, I've tempted him." He bubbled over with the confession. "I've tempted him." He sobered again. "No disrespect to you, Marianne. That was before I met you. Since I met you, never! Never, I swear to you! You're a fine type of woman. I respect you. But I've got to say it: he never fell! He's faithful to you, Marianne, I've got to say that for him." He ended with a shade of regret.

Then he laughed, "Listen, Aristide, there's too much talk about how good the pound sterling is. I want to see that banker you were telling me about. Berty? Berty— Bertillon? I've got an idea. Never mind—" He lowered his voice. "The other girl says she's a widow. She's quite a lady. Méline had breakfast with her. She's just gone, I think. Poor girl—" (He was evidently thinking of his own girl again.) He confided to Marianne: "A beauty like that. That's surprising, isn't it, Marianne? What do you make of it? And she lives in the Rue de Valence, near the Gobelins. Quite poor! Miserable! That shows she's honest." He looked dubious. "I saw her room last night: two rooms. Her husband's a naval lieutenant—comes home every three months. It's not much. She hasn't heard from him for three months. She's had typhoid fever. Some little trouble between them, I guess." He said lustily, "I should worry! My profit, eh! He, he, my profit." He clouded again. "I didn't like her telling me about the typhoid, but she says she comes from Transylvania too. Says she's a country girl. Shows she's honest. Eh? Eh?" He meditated between them, convinced they were absorbed by his affair. "She seems unhappy—I don't want no sympathy tales though. Imagine a girl like that living all alone. Can you?" He became gigantically sunny. "If she does. Well, who knows? Well, where are we lunching, Aristide? How's the son at Oxford, Marianne? My boy— not satisfied at all. Wants to be an archeologist; what's that, eh? Old ruins, eh? No good. Well, wait, wait, we'll see."

They went towards the door, Léon affectionately grabbing Marianne's arm and murmuring, "What do you advise me to do, eh? You're a mother. You've got brains. What can I do? Well, where shall we—here, here, down-

15

stairs, I've got some telephoning to do. Here, here, this way."

They had resigned themselves to Léon ten minutes before. Now, they let him waft them to the lounge, where they were supposed to wait for him respectably while he skirmished with his own business. They drifted to the bar of the hotel, waited, standing, awkwardly. "Let's have a drink," said Marianne.

"What for?" Aristide asked. "We don't know if Léon is going to drink."

A handsome, slender, middle-aged South Russian, with that mottled dusky-and-olive complexion often seen in underfed Negroes, leaned across the bar to a young woman whose silver curves resembled those of the chromium. He said in a conversational tone, "What beautiful nipples you have, Mademoiselle! I'm mad with enthusiasm. I should love to bite your splendid breasts."

Aristide started. "There's Paul Méline! Let's go and speak to him before Henri comes back."

The barman laughed. "I'll introduce you to Mademoiselle, Mr. Méline, so that you needn't be so formal: but you must behave."

The young woman had flushed, but looked at Méline without resentment. No woman had ever looked at Paul Méline with resentment.

"See how beautiful my wife is," said Méline, getting out a leather billfold and extracting a bundle of photographs. "Here she is—that's my little boy." Whereas Léon had an old, dull story and began by telling girls that he was unhappy and misunderstood at home, Méline always showed a picture of his wife and raved about his domestic happiness. It put everyone on the right footing and kept him out of scrapes.

"Good morning, Paul," said Marianne. She took the photograph and looked again at the heavy Russian beauty whose dress was dashingly but comfortably draped over her, like a shawl over a grand piano. Méline got up, bowed, ignored Marianne's plainness, seemed to enter it in large figures in her credit sheet that she was cherished by someone (Aristide) if not by him. Then he took the photograph back rather hastily. It was not intended for Marianne. "Let's have our drinks in the foyer," he said. A waiter saw Méline a long way off and floated rapidly nearer.

16

From their seats in the lounge, waiting for their drinks, they could see Léon at the desk. A black-coated manager with a set face appeared to remonstrate with Léon. Two clerks looked distantly preoccupied till they moved round the corner when they began to smirk in an unpleasant gentlemanly way. The revolving door turned and blew Léon's voice to them, brisk: "No, no, no, no, no. You quoted me one price. I've been here for months. You made me one price. I don't pay another. Next time you tell me beforehand, see." His voice faded again. They heard Léon commanding, "Send someone to fix up the room. Did Mr. Méline come downstairs? Where, where? Is there a lady waiting tor me? Where is she?"

He came springing towards them with his sturdy step, a short giant, five feet three in height, a great skull, bull neck, prizefighter's shoulders, gorilla's chest, thick waist and fleshy limbs, in a suit with too swagger a cut. His arms were short and thick above the elbow but of normal size in the forearm, so that they swung as he walked with an exaggerated sweep. Everything he did, even his sitting still, betrayed a violent will. He turned and rushed back to the desk with a swirl of coattails, to give the groom a message. He called peremptorily, "Hé, boy!" Another groom approached with the self-respecting scuttle of a great hotel. When he dispatched the second, both grooms sneered and grinned behind his back. They were taller, and were slender, dark young fellows, wearing white collars and the hotel livery. They thought Léon a bounder and themselves the tailor's dream. Besides, Léon had an all-in rate at the hotel and did not give any tips.

A pale blonde with large hat, pointed chin, thin toes, thin neck but a good figure, sat and scrutinized them steadily. She also observed Léon with prepossession. Léon's bossy back, bright shoes, and malacca cane at an angle of forty-five degrees performed at the telephone switchboard. The telephone girl smiled her sweetest. Now he came towards them again. "That's right, Aristide, having a drink? No, none for me. Well, where shall we eat?"

"Griffon's is a good place: I've been there a lot since you were here last," Aristide informed the air.

Léon recovered himself. "Yes, yes, is it good? I've got a lot to talk over with you, Aristide." He turned to them, "Excuse us, Marianne. I want to go over a lot of business with your husband. We'll both make a profit.

You don't mind, do you? I must look around. I'm expecting someone. A lady. I want her to come to lunch—er, I want you to run your eye over her, Marianne. I think a lot of your opinion. A very fine business head. I don't usually go in for business ladies—" (the sudden sunrise which was his smile) "—one of the smartest I ever met." He frowned slightly, shook his head vigorously into his collar, and pulled back his chin with a rebellious pout and a somber roll of the eye. He thrust at Aristide, "How's Bertillon? Jules?"

"As usual. I'd like you two to meet."

"He does, eh?" he said vaguely. "I want to meet him, too. Saw him only a second. Heard about him. Smart feller. Must see for myself. Can't believe it: a *goyisher Kopf*. Old Amsterdam family, isn't it—Antwerp? Family in diamonds, something?"

"The grandfather. The only non-Jew," said Aristide priggishly, "in the business."

Léon's laughter rumbled in the seven mountains of his mind, "And *he* got out. He, he, he, ho, ho. When can I meet him?"

"This afternoon. Whenever you like. What hour? I'll be there."

"No, no. Not this afternoon. No. I've got some business. Yes. Business. Be occupied until late tonight. This woman's introducing me to a cotton planter and a man with an oil-royalties business in Mexico. Very smart girl. A cotton-picker, she says: revolutionize the southern states of the U.S.A. I hope it's one hundred per cent. I don't trust women's introductions. I'll see. At any rate. When can I see Bertillon? Tomorrow morning early? First thing? Eh, early? What time's he get in, eight?"

"Nine-thirty," said Aristide.

"All right: late. I'll be—where is it?—39, Pillet-Will, nine-thirty." He wrote it down. "All right. Come along, Marianne. Wait, I'll look round. She must be here. Smart woman. She wouldn't come upstairs. Nice woman."

Léon frowned. "No, no, no, no: she doesn't want me to put up—nothing like that. If she does, good-by: nothing doing. But—I'll see. You'll give me your opinion, Marianne," he said coaxingly, but without conviction.

He bustled into the passage, came round through the winter garden and the writing room, energetically shuttling his haunches, enumerating the women. Halfway, he saw the observant blonde and, hooking his stick over his arm, rushed towards her. She sat still and when he bent over her, smiled a pearly smile. The great impediment in her career was her expression: she looked as calculating as she was. She had a sweet smile and had brought out with care the lights of her soft skin and pale blonde hair, but the gray-blue eyes looked out sharply still from between her pale lashes and the California sun had drawn early crow's-feet in the corners. Léon held her pear-shaped small hand with its diamond and platinum bracelet for a minute, patted it, devoured the jewels. Méline lost nothing of all this. "Will she?" said Léon's attitude. "Won't she!" replied Méline's.

She rose, and they approached. Aristide stood up. Nothing distinguished him from hundreds of Paris stock-exchange runners but an extensible melancholy, indicated by a gloomy bend of the head, feet firmly placed, and eyes bent down as if he were forever in a struggle, torn between pleasing others and doing his duty to himself. He was a Mediterranean, pallid, with large mistral-shaded eyes, glossy like the polished woods of ornaments: the hairs of his large head had moved aside to form a Suez Canal in the center. His sensually rounded, great-bodied, sulky, sloping frame was almost drowned in a tidal wave of flesh that had struck him two years before, at forty.

"Mrs. Weyman—good friend," said Léon, "from Hollywood."

Marianne took a fancy to Mrs. Weyman while Léon was introducing her. She appeared to be as clever as Marianne herself; physically she was her antithesis.

Léon left. In about a quarter of an hour, he joined them at the table, with a wink at Méline and a smile as big as an oyster in each eye. His mind was elsewhere. He cheerfully threw an observation into the conversation, "Alfonso XIII will fly if he loses, eh? It would be pretty cowardly, eh? You expect a man with Alfonso's salary to show more manhood. But he won't. They sent a bull into the arena and found it was a cow." He laughed, looked round the table, blooming and nodding, like a great peony.

Raccamond was a little more talkative than usual, from the wine and the presence of "personalities" and money. "When the bull doesn't fight, they say, Go home, cow!" He laughed under his breath. "You know," he looked at the American, "that is the worst thing you can say to a bull." His voice became confidential, almost as if they talked about sexual matters. "And the worst thing you can say to a man is to call him a *femmelette*, puny woman: did you know that?"

The restaurant manager came near at this moment and, seeing his client Aristide fat, prosperous, and conversational, he bowed his old head to him, "How do you like the sole? Is it good today? I believe so." Aristide resented this familiarity, was furious at being interrupted in this rare imaginative vein, and scolded, without looking up, "Wait till I've tasted it: then perhaps I'll have something to say." The manager moved away with bitterness. Méline threw him a posy of smiles on the way.

Léon was intensely impatient, hardly listening even to what Mrs. Weyman had to say. His ideas had reached a certain heat so that sitting down, eating, thinking, reading the menu, even the appearance of light streaming on palms, even the sound of water splashing and the orchestra playing, were impediments to his will. He wanted to be gesticulating, calling attention to himself in a very grand manner. When they made remarks to him, he drew them into his eyes thickly, with a somber look; his eyes snapped away from them, he drew himself up and looked at them all from under his monumental lids as if they were enemies who would insult him in another minute: but he was ready for them.

"Have you been to the zoo in London?" said Mrs. Weyman in passing.

"Eh, eh? Animals? What is there in animals? Do you like animals?" he said desperately to Aristide, thrusting his Adam's apple across his plate. Animals were, God knew, quite another thing from himself and his affairs. "No animals!" He looked round and perceived the waiter serving fish at a side table. He snapped his fingers, "Hey, cigars!" He stuck a large cigar in his mouth and rolled his head around the restaurant, Jovelike. "Hey, *allumettes!*" he called. The waiter, ruffled, took no notice. "Hey, hey" (snapping his fingers) "—I don't think much of this restaurant," said Léon to Méline. "Not as good as the Criterium in Antwerp and this—in Paris—not as good as the—you know, you know the—" He snapped his fingers at Aristide. Aristide cravenly replied, "Rôtisserie Ardennaise in Brussels?"

"No, no Ardennaise! No!" He looked furiously at

20

Aristide as if he had committed the most stupid mistake. "No—hey! Hey! *Allumettes!*"

"Rocher de Cancale," said Méline, flirting with Mrs. Weyman the while.

Léon noted this and muted his pipe for a moment. "That's it: Rocher de Cancale: not so good! Much better! No taste!" He forgot his manners and looked round impatiently.

Marianne said sagely, "I think they have finer flavors here."

Léon thundered, "No! *Allumettes!*" The headwaiter was now quite near, side on, endeavoring to make up his mind to obey, trying to hide his chagrin.

Méline brought the scene to an end by saying sweetly to the waiter, "Would you kindly bring some matches for Mr. Léon?"

Léon rumbled, "Very bad service here—no good, like the other—bad—" When the cigar began to run through his veins, he melted somewhat and began to take notice of Mrs. Weyman, leaving Marianne to her own devices. He patted Mrs. Weyman's silky arm and issued an ukase: "Paul, Aristide, Paul—Marianne, what do you say? Tonight we'll make whoopee." He blushed and smiled like a small boy. "I mean fun, by that." He patted Mrs. Weyman's hand. "I feel like making whoopee, we'll rejoice. We've got—" he hesitated, looking at Marianne, "—beautiful—" he swallowed with embarrassment and cheered up again "—beautiful woman, Aristide, you must come, make Marianne come, no excuses, you haven't got an engagement, have you? Put it off! Put it off! Méline!"

Paul Méline excused himself. Léon frowned for a moment, bit his cigar at the unperturbed Méline. He began clapping and looking round. "The bill! The bill!" A flustered and irate waiter arrived with the bill. He planked down some notes, got up before the women were ready, helped Mrs. Weyman brusquely with her furs and marshaled them all out, like some sultan, decent fellow, who has taken his wives and flatterers to a restaurant for a mild birthday. The women tried to keep each other in countenance. Outside, Léon dropped behind and asked Méline, "Did you see him, eh? Achitophelous? He's in there with Henrietta, his daughter. Pretty girl. Wonder what he's here for? You know what he's doing here? Have you seen him?"

Méline looked through the curtained glass which separated the lounge from the fountain court. "No. Henrietta? She must be nineteen. She's a raving beauty, isn't she? He must have difficulty keeping her at home at night."

They both peered like conspirators through the curtain. "Maybe he's come down to fix up a wedding," said Léon. "I heard he was after Rhys of Rotterdam's boy. But where's the mother? Are they on good terms still? My, what a beauty! Let's get rid of the girls for half an hour and go in, see what he's up to." "Mrs. Weyman?" said Méline. Léon laughed uneasily and looked inquisitively at Méline. "I'm looking for romance, you know." Méline knew then that Léon really believed in the business Mrs. Weyman had proposed to him. Léon saw his twinkle and clouded a little, "I don't know if I ought to go in there when he's with his daughter. What's his game?"

Méline said without malice, "I thought you and he weren't friends since the diamond deal."

Léon looked at him directly, divining how much he knew. "Never mind, never mind!" he finished vaguely. He went to the desk to ask if Mr. and Mlle. Achitophelous were staying in the hotel. They were. Much pleased, he came back towards the women with Méline.

"Got to run," apologized Méline.

"Are you going to Bertillon's?" asked Henri Léon with sudden suspicion.

"I might run in. I'll have a look at what the market is doing. See you soon." Méline went off, cheerful in the thought that Léon would spend the entire afternoon wondering what he was doing in the Bertillon Bank and what his game was in Paris.

Léon looked through the glass again at Henrietta Achitophelous. She was a Southern beauty of Assyrian cast, with a long pronounced nose and jaw of perfect mold attached to a small rounded skull, low forehead, brilliant sensual eyes, brows like plumes, a bisque face framed entirely in small black curls. Her shoulders, upper arms, and bust swelled from the slender parts as if formed by the gust of some longing potter. Léon was overcome for a moment by a fragrant intoxicating cloud, peculiar to him when he saw a passionate female beauty. Achitophelous, his great friend and enemy, was dining discreetly in a corner of the farther court. He could see him accidentally between the players in the orchestra, but the cold light from the glass roof fell straight on Henrietta's face.

Marianne had tried for several years to contact Hollywood through the actors and American moneyed men going and coming in Paris in the stock-exchange houses and in the Parisian theatrical world. While Léon was still footling round the lobby as if he had affairs with invisible beings there, Marianne bent to Mrs. Weyman. "Do you like Paris, Madame?"

Mrs. Weyman tossed off a laugh. "Oh, I come here every so often: I knew Paris as a young girl. I like it in a way. I have roots everywhere. Or none."

Her eyes glittered towards Aristide. "Are you interested in getting foreign accounts, say in the U.S.A., for your bank? I have many friends among novelists, Hollywood artists, and the planetary rich!" She laughed a hard laugh. "They've got the big money of today. I can put you in touch certainly with some of them. Paris attracts them. You can do me services. I'd like to meet the head of your bank: I hear he's the white-haired boy of society here." She leaned forward nervously, vibrating with the thought of business.

Aristide was intent: they wandered hand in hand through a desert of stock-exchange conversation. Aristide and Marianne exchanged glances which said, "This is a valuable friend: we'll make up to her."

They all at once saw Léon dialing numbers out of the tiny memorandum book in which he kept the names of women, houses, and streets. He came out slapping the book into his vest pocket with a satisfied air and approached with a rapid military swagger. He grasped Mrs. Weyman's arm. "You've got a beautiful figure, Margaret."

In the end Léon succeeded in bundling them out of the hotel into a taxi, which sailed off, headed for the Scribe Bar, leaving him unexpectedly standing on the mat. He turned quickly into the hotel. The manager at the desk, watching him, frowned. Léon had sent four girls up to his rooms in twenty-four hours. And on an all-in rate: not even a market tip to the manager.

After Mrs. Weyman left them at the Scribe, Aristide had his notebook in his hand. "Hotel Westminster. I'm to have lunch with Mrs. Weyman tomorrow. It looks like

23

business." He gave Marianne a marital glance, full-bodied with meaning. Marianne said in a lower tone, "Well, I saw Mme. Quiero."

Aristide frowned a query. She leaned forward. "You know, the handwriting expert that Mme. Bertillon uses? She said your handwriting shows you have a difficult temperament but this will be a lucky year for you."

"Lucky in money?"

"Lucky in money, advances, and favors from friends. She said a blond man (that's Bertillon evidently) will make your fortune this year and a dark-faced man next." She hesitated.

"Well?"

"She said you run in cycles—always the same, beginning to end. She said what you're afraid of will come about."

"Did she mean war? Perhaps it means the officers of reserve will be called up. Did she use the crystal, too? I don't believe in them unless they can do that. Did you ask her about stocks and currencies? Did you ask her about the pound and the dollar? I suppose nothing on that—they're worthless for exact figures—" He drooped. "Who knows if they're not just police agents? They don't seem to know much else."

Marianne recited, "What is secret will be found out within the twelvemonth."

Irritably Aristide knocked on the cab window, saying, "Can I sell or buy the market tomorrow on information like that?"

Marianne smiled a little, her self-reliant conceited smile. "She said you would lose old friends and make new enemies."

"You pay the taxi," said Aristide. "I have no change."

"Neither have I: I'm just going in to cash a check."

Raccamond paid, giving twenty-five centimes for a tip. The chauffeur looked up at the bronze doors of the bank, standing inwards. On each leaf shone Mercury's staff, in bronze. The chauffeur spat.

Scene Two: A Check Technique

ON ONE side of the doorway was a brass plate with the name BANQUE MERCURE and on the other side, facing it, the name BERTILLON & CIE. S.A.

A woman went into the bank before Aristide. He plunged forward, bowed: "Good day, Princesse." She smiled cozily, went in chatting. Raccamond followed doggedly. Marianne restrained him in the square entrance and murmured, "Who is it? Tell me please, Aristide."

"Princess Delisle-Delbe," he whispered. "I've taken over her account. Let me go, Marianne: I must go."

He unhanded himself and fled after the Napoleonic Princesse, a young widow with a large estate who put plenty of money into the American and English markets. He intercepted her before Urbain Voulou, the elephantine, smiling blond chief customers' man of the bank, had reached her. The three stood together a little while, until Aristide with his dark atmosphere of earnest insistence drew her eyes away from the smile of Voulou; and Voulou, saying, with good sad simplicity, "Things don't look too good, Princesse: I think things are going down, Princesse," withdrew.

Aristide went on as if Voulou had never been there, "The figures for the first two months of 1931 show a decline in trade: an increase in tariffs is sure. Mr. Alphendéry, our technician, you know, thinks you should sell about half of your long position in U.S. Steel and Air Liquide. He says he calculates Air Liquide will lose eventually about one-third of its value. There are queer rumors from the U.S.A. The banking situation is bad. We recommend selling short rather than buying."

The Princesse, settling the pretty little black hat on her black hair, said, "Is that Mr. Bertillon's opinion? I think Mr. Jules Bertillon is a genius in markets. Is he in?"

"Not yet, Madame. Yes, I believe that is his opinion. He and Mr. Alphendéry are generally of the same opinion."

"I just want to sell a foreign check," smiled the

25

Princesse, dismissing him. "Will you see if Mr. Bertillon is in?"

"The telephone, Mr. Raccamond," said Jacques Manray, the stock-exchange clerk, respectfully.

On the telephone, Aristide heard, "Aristide! Are you and Marianne coming out with me tonight? Sure? All right. I'll be round. H'm. I put off the business dinner. Is —is Bertillon there now? I'm coming round."

In ten minutes Aristide heard a garble of laughter in the quiet green murmuring entrance hall. Somehow Michel Alphendéry had got downstairs and introduced himself to Henri Léon. They had got on to Spain. Léon, as usual: "Because I have confidence: I believe in Spain—don't you think that counts, eh? Don't you think that counts? I don't mind doing business in the country of Garcia or Hernandez: that country appeals to me."

"Fermin Galan and Garcia Hernandez," Alphendéry emended.

"The revolution began in Spain already with Fermin and Garcia Hernandez on the border: that's a great country. I'd put my money there any day, when it quietens down a bit, if those boys look as if they can hold the—reins of power," stoutly continued Léon. "Any day. My boy!"

Alphendéry began a conversational oration: "A country that's entering into revolution is a great country: stocks fall, landlords sell, dowagers shriek and depart, squires fly, but the land continues to bear in the old, golden way, olives grow, there's electric light to sell: socialist municipalities need whitewash for the cabins and stones for the roads, there's medicine, cosmetics, hairwashes, Woolworth dodges to sell. When the permanent moneybags fly, there's the place for new wealth. When others go like this" (he stuck out his absurd little hands and shook them violently), "that's the time I move right in.

"You're right, Mr. Léon: your instinct's perfectly right. Supplies are cheap, consumption is never as low as it seems, and a new market is worth a ton of money today. The Spaniards have nothing: then you have everything to sell them. It's the new colony. Life goes on, doesn't it? Everyone has an infinite capacity for consumption. Especially the Latins!"

26

Léon nodded energetically, his face drawn a little from a too fatiguing day and night, his eyes no longer dancing, but serious and absorbed. Aristide saw this close attention to Alphendéry, and approached with his solemn authority. "Léon, I—" Léon waved him aside. "Léon—"

"Wait, wait, Aristide: this is—" He actually held Aristide off with his large hand, made a half-turn to shut Aristide off from the colloquy: "Interested!" was the word that tumbled out of his mouth.

Alphendéry went on instantly, "Life goes on! Life went on under the corruption of the Roman Empire. These ages look like acts of a historical drama to us, but they were sewed together by the little Andrés and little Maries who set up house together, had children and bought gadgets for the home all through the Dark Ages and today. A few go revolting but the girls buy rouge to attract the boys and the mothers look for cheaper zippers to put on François' pants."

Restlessly Léon egged him on to the more serious part: "And, yes—and—but the—Coty—"

Joyfully, Alphendéry took him up, "Life went on under Attila, went on in the Dark Ages. These will be the ages of night looking back from the days to come, but we're alive: we can't go dead dog. This is a new Napoleonic age, a new Commune age. Revolution! Why, it always produces new markets! All new money is made through the shifting of social classes and the dispossession of old classes. Today we have it. Property is changing hands, losing its old owners all the time. This is the time to move in."

Léon rolled a fierce look round the people scattered near, wanting to get Alphendéry away to privacy.

At this moment, a fragile, tall, elegantly dressed young man, with a bowler hat, a fur collar, and an antique Dutch face, with long nose tip biting the air, approached nonchalantly.

"Jules," caroled Alphendéry, "meet Henri Léon, a grain—"

"We've met," said Léon.

"Hullo, Léon," said Jules Bertillon. "What have you been saying, Michel? That now is the time to make money? It is."

"I was saying that few old fortunes survived the war:

27

you must make new money to swim through a social crisis. The old goes rusty."

"Like the General Strike," said Léon. "In the General Strike I—did I ever tell you that story, Aristide? I must tell it to you, Alphen: the same thing. Everyone sitting round wrapped in their coats like corpses, waiting for the last day, red flag over London: I get an idea—I get an idea." He looked around, for some spot to talk business in.

Jules said, "Every crisis is a storm of gold: most people run under an awning to get away from it. Do you know how to make money, Léon? If you do, spill it. Here we are sitting in a shower of gold and nothing to hold up but a pitchfork!"

There was a wash of laughter, but Léon stood and looked at Bertillon, now moving harmoniously towards the stairway, pale marble and green-carpeted. Léon looked as if he had been faintly smacked. In another moment he was walking after him. He took two steps, then turned and called, "Mr. Michel? Mr.—er—er—are you coming up?" Alphendéry started and hurried after him. Aristide Raccamond strung out last, following the other three upstairs, dubious, but on the job. "Mr. Alphen?" called Léon.

"Alphendéry," said Alphendéry, "Alphendéry."

"Nice furnishings—" said Léon "—looks good. Respectable: looks businesslike but elegant."

"Jules Bertillon did it all himself. He has superb taste! He always says that money should live in the Ritz-Carlton."

"Did he say that?" inquired Léon hastily, in a confidential tone. "A nice feller, has charm, hasn't he? Eh? He has charm. Gets people in."

"Oh, the bank," said Alphendéry easily, laughing, "is a sort of cosmopolite club for the idle rich and speculators of Paris, Madrid, Rio, Buenos Aires, New York, London, and points farther east and west. And Mr. Bertillon gives the best exchange rates in France. People appreciate that courtesy—it's the one thing that tells in a foreign city. A little paring of the rate of exchange and the client has big confidence."

"Right," said Léon, settling back his head and eying the back of Alphendéry's small, square head with augur look. "And charm."

"Charm is a cunning self-forgetfulness," confided Alphendéry.

"I like the looks of it," declared Léon.

They followed Jules into his own room, a large room overlooking the general entrance and the cashiers' windows and booths downstairs. It was furnished grandly, if somewhat gloomily, in the best Amsterdam taste, with walnut paneling and bookcases, a beautiful French desk, a high-backed carved Italian chair in which Jules sat, flanked by two branched upright Italian bronze candlesticks, six feet high. Facing the desk and Jule's great chair were three large, deep, and superlatively soft green armchairs. In those chairs people were at their very best. The walls were olive green: on the green carpet were several Persian rugs. The glass-cabinet bookcases lining two walls were empty except for several rows of blind backs.

"Sit down," said Jules. At Aristide, who entered with some diffidence, he frowned. "Do you want something?" Alphendéry interposed, "Baron Koffer's man will be downstairs at two-thirty: you know him, don't you?" Aristide started and hurried out.

"The great Belgian financier?" inquired Léon hotly.

"Yes."

"You better go and see him," Jules said crisply to Alphendéry.

"He's not there, yet," Michel explained. Jules smiled coolly. "I thought you said he was. Sit down, Michel. Mr. Léon, I want you to go over with Mr. Alphendéry the idea you have about the pound. Mr. Alphendéry is my exchange expert."

"Yes?" Léon looked at Alphendéry with interest. "What do you think of sterling? Will it hold? Will it go off?"

"How long ahead are you looking?"

"This year? What's the secret of sterling? Do you think it will go off? I figure—sterling, gold bloc, Belgian franc, Swiss franc, French franc. What's the secret? That's just my instinct."

"Perfect," laughed Alphendéry. "You mean, will the French withdraw the balances they have in London? Will it pay them to, or will it pay them to hold them there as permanent blackmail? Can they afford cheaper wages in England?"

Léon poured out a confusion of ideas, declared to

Jules, "I think sterling will go off this year, or early next. That's what they think in Amsterdam. (It doesn't matter who thinks it, you can always make money.) It's an open secret that can't be used. They will hold off. They have to use money. You can think money is going off, but you've got to do business. You can't hold up payments: if you don't pay, they only wait to pounce on you—credit's no good. In the ordinary course of business you pass through checks on Saturday morning for cashing on Monday. Nothing suspicious in that. Suppose it goes off over the week end? Eh? I've got an idea. I want to know, Bertillon: I have a technique. Infallible. Will you endorse me? I give you ten per cent."

"Do you get it, Michel?" asked Jules offhandedly.

Alphendéry leaned forward, his eyes glossy with his personal passion, exposition. "Certainly. Mr. Léon will pass through checks selling sterling for X francs or X guilders, say. To prove he is not selling short, which requires margins, you, Jules, will give your guarantee that Léon actually holds in your bank the amount of sterling he is selling. Léon can say, I have sterling credits to my account in the Bertillon Bank in Paris and can turn over the sterling at a moment's notice. If they call you on the telephone, Bertillon, you say the sterling's here. You will give the accommodation to Léon, in that case, Jules. If necessary, you can transfer the amount of sterling necessary to Léon's name, under release from him, on the books."

"Check technique," said Léon.

"That won't be necessary," said Jules impatiently. "You better open an account here, as from today, though, so that it looks O.K."

"Yes," Alphendéry answered Jules. "A couple of thousand francs: nominal."

"I can do it anyhow, I think," said Léon, "but if you want to do it that way, I'll let you know. I have an arrangement with—a friend, with—you know, Grosshändler in Switzerland, of the International Quayside Corporation? Him. He knows everything that goes on in Zurich, Geneva. The Federated Cantons Bank knows everything a couple of days before. They generally go off over a week end. Now if I can know on Friday, say, or even early Saturday morning—you see—I ring up, say, anyone, Meyer, I say, 'Wolff, listen, Brandenberger, I'm selling sterling, are you a taker?' 'I know what you're doing, Léon,' he says, 'but I need the sterling, anyhow: I can't help it and perhaps you're wrong.' I sell, he takes the check: Monday morning, the banks give me half an hour —I'm in, say it will go off twenty francs in the pound over the week end. Say, I have a hundred thousand sterling—it's a little profit, but it will cover any losses in a bad grain year."

"If you get the information from this Grosshändler," said Jules.

"Oh, we're thick, I'm in deep with him."

"But do you think sterling will go off this year?" queried Jules. "I don't."

"If I'm wrong, I don't lose anything: I have my sterling, I sell it, I have my francs: a few francs one way or another. It's—certain, certain: it's one of the few safe investments!" He laughed round at them. "Well, what do you think of my check technique?"

"You ring me up, Léon, and we'll fix it up," promised Jules.

Alphendéry went out with Léon. Generously Léon said, flushed with having spoken, "You get percentages out of accounts here, don't you, Alphen-phendéry?"

"Oh, yes."

"I'll put in a small account, how much? Fifty thousand francs! You'll get the percentage: there you are, that's what I think of you," said Léon, beaming into Alphendéry's face.

"Jules will be anxious to work in with you," said Alphendéry modestly. "Don't worry about the percentage. I work here—I work here on a different basis, do you see?"

Léon's face fell. "He wouldn't give it to you? I don't put it in usless you get a percentage." He became absolute, "No, I don't put it in otherwise—I want you to get it, my boy. That's to show friendship. I can sense we're going to work together." He leaned back and stared at Alphendéry's forehead, seriously. "You're a—" he shut his mouth strictly. "We'll do business, my boy." He patted Alphendéry on the back and began to stride towards the stairs. He stopped at the stairs for Alphendéry to catch up a step. He went downstairs impulsively and when they reached the ground floor, he planted himself in the fairway looking at the well-dressed crowd of clients. They were cosmopolitans interested in speculation in the bourses of the world; in the stock and commodity markets as well as in exchanges.

"What do they take positions in?" asked Léon, staring quickly at them all: "Any grain, maize, barley: or just shares? What shares? American? There's no money, only trouble in America now. England, eh? The market's up. What do they come here for? Who's Bertillon? Has he got big money? I hear he hasn't so much. A one-man bank. There's a brother, eh, eh?"

"They're here," laughed Alphendéry, "because they want big profits in a little time: this is the same crowd you'll see at Biarritz and at Deauville and at Le Touquet. This is the International of the Upper Ten Thousand. Some of them believe in Jules's luck. So do I. Some of them hope to divide the profits of his careless audacity. So do I. Then he has branches abroad: they keep their accounts and clip their coupons there and avoid income tax here."

Léon's eyes had brightened, his voice dimmed. "Yes, is that so, is that so? Some lad, eh? Smart boy. Has he got brains, eh? He's a genius?"

"I think so."

Léon nodded and considered Alphendéry. He nodded again to himself.

"A mercurial money crowd," laughed Alphendéry. "It flows, it registers the temperature, it never freezes."

Léon's great laugh: "You'll do, my boy, you'll do." He looked around. "Beautiful: he has taste: it's the finest bank in Paris, and little—you could hold it in the hollow of your hand. A hollow jewel. Perhaps not hollow, eh?"

"Not hollow for Jules or us: it represents hollowness," said Alphendéry with a touch of sorrow.

Léon started. "How?"

Alphendéry said, "You know the lines of Shelley?

There stands the Tower of Famine. It is built
Upon some prison-homes, whose dwellers rave
For bread, and blood and gold: Pain, linked to Guilt,
Agitates the light flame of their hours,
Until its vital oil is spent or spilt.
There stands the pile, a tower amid the towers
And sacred domes; each marble-ribbèd roof,

32

The brazen-gated temples, and the bowers
Of solitary wealth—"

Alphendéry's resonant and variable voice gave the lines full beauty. Léon had swung round slowly to face him and come close to him, like a freighter swinging at its mooring in a harbor. Léon's face had softened and his eyes had misted.

"The tower of famine: for the people, you mean? Is that what he meant? A poet. My boy, if I don't see the people win, I'll go to my—I'll see the end of my life, unhappy. I don't care if they expropriate me. I used to be a poor boy and stand in the snow waiting for a plate of charity soup. I don't like that to go on."

Alphendéry bit his lip, nodded his head, his eyes shining meanwhile. After a moment, Léon said, "So they're all society butterflies, eh? And Bertillon's a bit of a playboy, I hear. Doesn't he give a cup for racing, or something? Does he spend money?"

"Jules is as full of ideas as a hive of bees. He goeth along like a dancer."

"A dancing hive? And honey? Honey on thorns, eh?" He laughed, his eyes showered merriment. "Alphéry— Alphendéry—you're an inspiration to me. You ought to come and see me up in Amsterdam soon. I'd like to ask you about my investments. If you—can give me—you can advise me, perhaps. I've got Argentine bonds—you'll tell me. Not now. I've got fifty thousand sterling in South American bonds."

"Sell them," said Alphendéry promptly.

"You're a bear?"

"I'm a bear on everything. So is Jules," said Alphendéry. "That's our opinion on the world."

Léon patted him on the arm with finality. "I think you're right, my boy: by James, if I don't think you're right. Well, come up and see me. We'll work together." He looked at Alphendéry's forehead seriously again, stuck on his hat, and strutted valiantly out. He jumped into a taxi, stuck a cigar into his mouth, and gave an address. Closing the door, he peered into the obscurity of the twilight entrance to the bank, and waved gaily to Alphendéry.

Aristide Raccamond came up with an air of portent to the straddling Alphendéry and said, "I just saw the agent

33

for the Baron Koffer. If you will talk to him and give him some views on the market I think I'll be able to swing the account: at least, he's promised to make a deposit here of bonds and gold."

"What good is that? You mean, as collateral?"

"No, no: just to give us prestige. We would have to give a receipt for the numbers of the bonds and the gold: but if we give him the accommodation of our vaults here, he might swing us some of his business later on. We ought to give him a small commission."

"For what? Is he going to give us stock-exchange orders? Is he keeping a drawing account here? No. It's not business. I mean, we'll accept the gold and bonds if he wants, for the sake of the prestige and of having the Baron's man about, but no commission unless he gives commission business. That's flat."

Aristide frowned. At the same moment, Jules Bertillon appeared on the gallery above, walking from his own room towards the staircase and casting an eye over the bank and its human contents as he did so. When he got downstairs, Aristide Raccamond was sitting at the desk which lay between the staircase and the front door. Alphendéry was standing near the front door observing the transactions at the tellers' windows.

Jules Bertillon stood still at the desk and looked at Aristide Raccamond, who raised his eyes and said, "You see, Mr. Bertillon, I am here."

"How did you get here?" said Jules without anger. "I told you I didn't want you working for me."

Alphendéry, observing the conversation, approached.

"Ask Mr. Alphendéry and Mr. William Bertillon, your brother," said Raccamond, most seriously, neither impudence nor triumph showing in his great solemn face, only a great sense of personal dignity and worth.

Alphendéry began to explain with hurried, light accents, "You see, Mr. Bertillon, this man was brought in to us by the Comte de Guipatin and by Légaré. The Comte de Guipatin vouched for his moneymaking ability. He has a list of clients. After you threw him out, Raccamond came to William and said, 'I'm out of a job due to the failure of Claude Brothers: why don't you give me a chance? I don't ask any salary. If you'll take me on for six months without any salary, or any claim from me afterwards, I'll work for you for nothing for six months and show you I can bring money into the bank.' "

"I said that," said Raccamond.

"You had no right to do that: neither had William," said Jules acidly. "Michel, send Constant to London about sterling. Come upstairs, will you? And tell William I want to see him."

Jues went lingeringly about amongst his clients, smiling and inclining his head to several of them. Their heads turned after him, smooth as gold, sweet as diamonds, supple and secret as a rope of emeralds. He glided between the pillars, passed through his own board room almost without being seen, and went upstairs to his own great room by a hidden staircase, without passing along the upstairs gallery.

Raccamond detained Alphendéry. "I am afraid Mr. Bertillon does not like the arrangement. Will you plead my case? Will you ask him to speak to the Comte de Guipatin? The Comte de Guipatin will explain to Mr. Bertillon that I know a great many society figures, distinguished people—I know the artistic people and the racing folk of Paris. It would be very rash to get rid of me. I like Mr. Bertillon and I want to be with him. I like this type of bank. I could go to a big bank but what would it profit me? My own way would be more difficult to make. Then those distinguished people do their big business with the big banks, but with a small personal bank they do their small personal business. And that is the most profitable. It can be made exceptionally profitable. You see, there is even smaller, entirely intimate business which I can do for them, in my own person, and so they begin to grow on me, I on them, I mean, and thus I can draw them in to your bank. Surely Mr. Bertillon will reconsider the case, if he sees this. I can be of infinite service to him. . . ."

Alphendéry patted his arm, smiled into his face, said obligingly, "Surely, surely, Aristide, don't you worry. I'll put it to Mr. Bertillon as well as you do yourself, and I can do it better, for I am not you: I am a friend. I hope you think of me as a friend, Aristide. I believe in you, Aristide. I believe in you. You seem really to have excellent connections. Don't worry. I'll do all that can be humanly done."

"The Comte de Guipatin," said Aristide with the same

rigmarole sobriety, "will vouch for me. He saw how I organized Claude Brothers."

"I think, if you'll take a little bit of advice, Aristide, that we'd better leave out Claude Brothers. Philippe and Estèphe Claude were—are—intimate friends of Mr. Bertillon." Aristide frowned formidably. Alphendéry rattled on, with the bells of benevolence in his tones, "Not your fault they went bankrupt: Oh, we all heard the rumors long before. But businessmen, especially bankers, are superstitious."

Aristide raised foggy, absorbed eyes to Alphendéry. "Yes, yes. Thank you."

Alphendéry ran upstairs and found William already there, tall, blond, lazy, plump, staid, leaning against the bookcase and talking in a low tone to his youngest brother, Jules. Jules raised his voice crankily, "Who told you to let that hard-luck into my bank? I don't want him, do you hear? He must go. I don't want guys who work for nothing. I don't like them: it sounds unnatural and I think it's funny. What is he so anxious to clamp himself onto me for? He's got to go. I won't have him. He's bad luck. He was with Philippe Claude and he went bankrupt. I don't want the odor of bankruptcy round this place. Send him away."

"Now, Jules, Jean de Guipatin—"

"I don't care what Jean de Guipatin thinks. He doesn't know a bank draft from a fly in the ointment. He's twenty-five and this Raccamond is a man of forty. Jean's a nice fellow but he's a gilded youth. Anybody could take him in."

Alphendéry interposed, "Jules, he's got really imposing clients. He's a remarkable fellow, I think. Overpompous, very Germanic for a Frenchman, unusual temperament, but he knows a lot of rich society folk: he knows the Comtesse de Voigrand."

"I know the Comtesse de Voigrand," shrilled Jules: "I don't need this hard-luck monkey to introduce me to her. Why, Jean de Guipatin knows her as well as his own mother: you're crazy. I won't have this Raccamond and that's all. He smells wrong. I don't like that type. I know the type I can't do with. That's all. Now tell him to get out. And stay out."

"Listen, Jules," said Alphendéry, persuasively, idiotically rash, simply because of the promise made to Rac-

36

camond, downstairs at the desk: "I don't like Raccamond, neither does William. No one likes him, but he
knows how to smooth, and flatter and lick boots: he
says himself, in so many words, that he does private services for these ginks—and you and I can well imagine
what he means by that. Well, you know how you get
these rotten corrupt rich people: by serving their vices.
He does that. What else can he mean? And if he's on the
inside of the bedroom and bathroom secrets, as he says he
is, then he's really got money up his sleeve and he can
shake it out into your pocket."

"What's he so anxious to get in here for, though?" Jules
worried. "I don't like people to suck onto me: it makes
me feel ill and I suspect it. I don't like the chap, I tell
you. I wish someone round here would do what I want
done."

"Look, Jules," continued Alphendéry, still fanatically
faithful to Raccamond, "what harm can he do you? If you
don't like him, throw him out after three months: but
give him three months. It's not his fault Claude Brothers
went into liquidation. Nobody knows why they did. The
liquidators, in their usual way, will be liquidating from
here till the time their sons graduate and their daughters
marry leading barristers. No one knows anything about
it. There's no reason for supposing Raccamond did. If
we're going to guillotine everyone who's ever been near
a bankruptcy—"

"I would," Jules said, but petulantly. Alphendéry saw
that he could not be bothered objecting any more at that
time. "Let me answer for Raccamond, and William here,"
said Alphendéry, "and if you've still got the voodoo
blues—because you're frightfully superstitious, Jules—"

"And I'm right: it's instinct," pouted Jules.

"All right," Alphendéry laughed, "if you've still got the
superstition blues after you've given him three months'
trial, then sack him. . . . But I want to tell you one
thing I found out today: he's a sort of unofficial flunky
of Dr. Jacques Carrière."

"What!" Jules rose in his chair. "Throw him out. I
don't want that bounder's flunkies round me. I hate Carrière."

Alphendéry laughed. "Don't you see, you big sap, that
Aristide is probably on the outs with Carrière and he'll

be willing to sell out Carrière's games for a small consideration?"

"I don't give a damn what are Carrière's games. I know what mine are. That's enough. I don't try to figure out anyone else's games. It's all I can do to guess my own. No more Raccamond. Tell him he's got the sack—the invisible sack, since he's not employed. But you tell him, Alphendéry. Go on."

Alphendéry's face looked blank. He had overplayed his hand. He was quite crushed by the thought of having to go back to Raccamond to tell him his embassy had failed.

Going out, William said, "With Jules, you should never give too many reasons. I know him of old."

"You're right," said Michel humbly, "that's true of all willful men."

William went down and found Raccamond talking earnestly to one of the rich charitable ladies of the sixteenth *arrondissement*.

"Isn't she a friend of Mme. Citroën?" said William, very low.

"I've heard that. But lots of people are."

"Doesn't matter: we'd be mad to kick out that fellow. What do we care about his morals? I'm going to let it ride, for a few days at any rate. Tell Jules I couldn't find him. Let him tell him himself. I know Jules. He won't. We've got a man to buy tickets for the bouts for clients: I don't see why we can't have a man who knows the prices at the House of All Nations!"

"If we didn't have any toilets, our clients would leave us, too," said Alphendéry.

Scene Three: Blind, Instinctive Love

HENRIETTA ACHITOPHELOUS, flushed and at the brightest hour of her dazzling young beauty, threw herself back rebelliously into one of Bertillon's great green armchairs. In this posture she was completely hidden from view, unless one stood in front of her. Achitophelous, handsome in the beak-nose style, yellow, with deep-sunk eyes and thick eyebrows, completely bald, fifty, sat in a straight armchair, leaning forward on his elbows, his plump yellow hands clasped. The nails were finely pared and shone. He seemed to chuckle sardonically.

"And then, what does she do?" he inquired of Jules Bertillon, who smiled at the young girl. "What does she do? She goes round spreading the most frightful scandal about the schoolmistresses—a little boy is not half so dirty."

Henrietta exploded. "I couldn't stand their rotten old school and I wanted them to expel me. There was no other way. Of course, I could have said I was pregnant, but they would have made a doctor come and find out."

Jules's carillon of laughter filled the upper air. "Oh, Henrietta!"

"I come from Constantinople, where I had a big business deal on, and I find what—she had flown, run away. Where to? To Paris. And before she went, she told the headmistress she was a Bolshevik and that she was going straight to Moscow. Naturally, I am almost hysterical. I cable everywhere. . . . And all the time she is in Paris, laughing at me. . . . Next, she threatens to sue me!" He threw up his hands limply and elegantly in a well-worn gesture and shrugged his shoulders.

"What for?" asked Jules, laughing.

"What for? For trying to get the police to export her —throw her out, expel her, you know what I mean."

"I was keeping myself," cried Henrietta rudely, "and you had no rights over me."

"Keeping yourself! H'm. How; that's what I should like to know. We'd all like to know. . . ." He turned to Jules Bertillon. "Her poor mother was nearly frantic."

Henrietta mimicked him cruelly, "My poor mother was nearly frantic! The ladies came in to tea. 'And where is dear Henrietta now, darling? In Paris, how charming. And is she at school there? No? How odd! What can she be doing in Paris? She has gone into the theater! Oh, my poor darling: how terrible you must feel. But do you *hear* from her? And—where does she live, dear? Are you —are you perfectly sure—but how *worried* you must be!' Yes, poor mother. Poor mannequin."

Achitophelous leapt to his feet. "There! You see: is that a way to talk to a parent, about a parent? It's no daughter, it's a monster. A mannequin. Her mother is the most beautiful, the most charming, kind—I wish you could know my wife, Mr. Bertillon."

Henrietta jeered, "Beautiful! She's ugly: her life is one long frustration. She is a wax figure of repressed impulses."

"This ridiculous language," cried Achitophelous, pressing his hands to the side of his head. "You hear that! That's the way she talks day and night. She thinks she knows everything. Frustrations! A little frustration would have done you good, my lady."

With splendidly curling lips, Henrietta declared, "This is an age of revolution: children cannot know their parents any more—their parents represent all that is old, hideous, and repressive. The old shell must be cast aside: the new race must spring to the light like—h'm, like—butterflies do."

"Thus," said Achitophelous, with deep irony, "yes, I am a grub. I work for you, rear you, keep you in luxury. Your mother gives you milk, she puts your hair in curl, she looks through your laundry, and she is a grub. You see, Mr. Bertillon. Have you got any daughters, Mr. Bertillon? No. It is a good job, a very good job. I bring her to St. Moritz last autumn to see a very nice young man, young Rhys of Rotterdam. It was all settled. Two hundred thousand francs I was giving her at the wedding and eight hundred thousand when she became twenty-five. He has his father's business. What does she say? I won't marry a bourgeois. A bourgeois!" He sank down into the chair again.

He leaned forward, with heavy sarcasm, "And what will you marry, may I ask?"

"The man I love," said Henrietta, "and perhaps not once but many times. I am beautiful. Anyone would marry me."

"You would live with someone perhaps, like any little servant-girl."

He was shocked when she answered, "Of course: and I don't have to worry about babies: anyone at all would marry me."

He took up the tone of the sarcastic pupil again. "And who would keep these illegitimate babies, may I ask? Not me."

"My husband."

He laughed cruelly. "Yes. Bolshevism to you, my lady, is illegitimate babies. That is all you think about. Sex."

She cried indignantly, with tears in her eyes, "I am much more worried about the Kuomintang and about the wicked oppressions in Indo-China than I am about sex."

"The Kuomintang!" Achitophelous pounced. "It has been crushing your Reds. Why? No discipline. Life is discipline. All my life has been discipline. Look at your hands! Filthy. Look at your nails. Not polished. Look at your hair: all out of curl. You haven't been to the manicure for a month. Is there anything in Karl Marx, may I ask, which says, you mustn't go to the manicure? The Kuomintang is nails, the Kuomintang is hands, the Kuomintang is rebellion against parents. Li-Li-Hsian is scurf-in-the-hair, dead Peng Pai is sex. They didn't worry about their particular job. This is what you have to worry about, and you don't. Look at me! Do I like to clean my teeth in the morning? No, I don't." He smiled comically, at this confession. "But I do it. Why? Because I know that success is discipline, whether you're a—bourgeois," he shook with laughter, "or a Bolshevik. Pah!"

Henrietta spoke in a cool voice, from the green depths of the chair, "All you say is only aimed at getting me to give up knowing Adam Constant the teller and I won't. You would rather have me marry a rich, stupid boy who can only think of profits, profits—" she caricatured richly the flung-out hands of the expounding businessman; "You are perverted by profit. You might have been a fine man," she said with great sadness, "but look at you! The new world will never see any more such human sell me. You want to sell me to Rhy for his son's pleasure."

She folded her hands, with considerable satisfaction.

Achitophelous looked very grave. "What can you know about such things? I do not want to buy and sell you, Henrietta. You are free to marry the man you love, if he is a decent fellow. You must not say such things. You know nothing."

"Adam and I know about everything. We discuss everything. We know more than you and Mother will ever know. We discuss everything because we want to be free."

"You mean free love, that's all."

"There is nothing wrong in free love if it suits you. I don't think—" she began to speak more slowly, with less

41

assurance. She smiled with a childish pathos at Jules Bertillon. "I told Adam all about it. I won't give myself to a man until I have a true and deep affection for him. But I have needs, too." Her voice was troubled.

Achitophelous cast a quick glance at Jules Bertillon, frightened at this admission. Jules Bertillon knew half the likely bachelors in Paris. He started forward.

"Henrietta, what do you know about sex? Answer me that. Do you know anything about it? Are you still a virgin? Can I give you to the son of my friend without being ashamed of myself?" He looked at Jules, in despair. "You see. I am afraid she will go to the dogs. She will be a bad woman. She is too like myself." He bit his lip.

But Henrietta was not listening to his asides. She answered his question. "I am not obliged to discuss this with you. I am a woman. I can only discuss such things with my lover."

Achitophelous was receiving shock upon shock. He was Oriental and had an Oriental view of women. He wilted, and said sadly, "With a stranger you discuss it, but not with your father." He sat up. "Before you love a stranger you have to show that you can place your love firmly at home with those it belongs to. You are not yet nineteen. Love your father and mother. Show them blind, instinctive, unquestioning, perpetual love. I bring you up and in return I only ask this one thing. But I insist on it—blind, instinctive love. If you can't love me that way, you are no good to me. You can get out. You are no daughter. You are anybody's girl."

Henrietta sneered, "You brought me up, with money. I was an item on your household-expenses account. Item: two roller towels. Item: three new saucepans. Item: an apron for my wife. Item: schooling for Henrietta. Mother and I furnished your home rather nicely. I hate all things that are bought with money. I am not grateful for them. You cannot buy any sort of love with money."

"Oh ho?" said Achitophelous slyly, a smile stealing into his face. "Well, does Karl Marx say that, too?"

Henrietta flushed, in confusion. "What I mean is—"

Achitophelous became businesslike. "I won't argue with you. You're in my power. You must learn discipline. The workers have a right to protest. They worked for it. They worked at what they didn't like to get their bread and they can say to any man at all, 'I demand my

42

rights.' You're not like that. You never worked. Would that appeal to Lenin?"

Tears were in Henrietta's eyes, tears of shame and anger. She knew she had been foolish and could not bear the ridicule. Achitophelous drove home his advantage, blow after blow. "When you can come to me and say, 'Father, for three years I have done everything you asked me. I have gone to the dances you asked me to, I have met the young businessmen you asked me to, I have gone out riding, driving, flying, whatever it is, with them. I have gone to Deauville, Biarritz, the Comtesse de Voigrand, and the Ritz-Carlton, with them. I have got myself properly dressed at Molyneux and had my hair attended to. I have looked after myself. I am a virgin. I have passed my examinations. I can keep house. I can give a big dinner to businessmen.' Then if you say, 'I have a nice young fellow with a good position, willing to marry me,' why, I'll let you marry him. I don't want to force you, I want you to marry for love, if you can. And if you've told me the truth, if all that is true, I'll—I'll, well I'll let you marry anyone—a taxi driver even. I'll buy him a fleet of taxis and put you in business, if he's such a handsome fellow." He laughed roguishly, leaned over the arm of her chair. "Why, why—even a grocer. I'd buy him a stand and say, 'Here, be happy. . . .' You can marry the—head of the Communist Party, even."

Henrietta said, "All this is to stop me seeing Adam Constant. You don't get me with that drivel."

Achitophelous turned to Jules. "Mr. Bertillon! Mr. Bertillon! What am I to do? Rhys wanted very much for his son to marry her. He was willing to give him a million francs himself right away." He shrugged his shoulders hopelessly. "Only one daughter and that one an outlaw, almost a criminal."

Jules straightened himself and said gently, in a judicial tone, "Mr. Achitophelous, I can, I think, settle everything to everyone's satisfaction. No, I can't forbid Adam Constant to see your daughter. He is a teller in my bank and I cannot tell him anything about his private affairs. I didn't know he was a communist, but even if he is—"

"You can dismiss him," pleaded Mr. Achitophelous. "Don't you see? She's ignorant." He dismissed his daughter with a supercilious shrug. "If he hadn't a job, she wouldn't love him. If she had nowhere to go with him."

Henrietta cried in indigation, "I go nowhere with him."

"No," said Jules. "You see, he's a very good teller. And I don't mind communists. I think they're nuts, that's all. But decent nuts. Because they're not serious. I pay them good wages. And the women clients like him." An expression of anxious astonishment crossed Henrietta's face. "That is something in a society dump like mine," smiled Jules. "The girls are the very dickens to manage, in money affairs, and a nice-mannered youth with genteel sex appeal like Adam Constant is an asset." Henrietta smiled faintly. Jules thew her a cool glance and went on coaxingly, to both of them, "I'll arrange it. Leave it to me. You will both be happy."

Achitophelous looked pleased but still dubious. "If you do, Mr. Bertillon, I will—er—I—er, you will have my eternal gratitude."

"You take things too seriously, Achitophelous," ended Jules. He got up. "If you'll just wait there, a moment, I'll go and get one of my directors, Michel Alphendéry. He's a very fine fellow, knows more than a university professor and is very humane. He sees everybody's point of view. He's much better at human things than I am. And—" he smiled broadly at Henrietta, "he's a communist, too."

"Yes!" cried Henrietta with childish glee. She lay back in her chair. At the door, hidden from Henrietta, Jules turned and winked at Achitophelous. Achitophelous composed his features and took a turn up and down the room. Jules was away some time.

"Nothing," said a soft voice from the depths of the armchair, "nothing will prevent me going to the Salle de la Mutualité, with Adam Constant."

After a moment, Henrietta laughed, "My eyes are wide open."

She opened her splendid dark eyes wide and looked at him. He gave her a thunderous look, by no means paternal. "Eyes opened by Adam? Nice conversations you must have, about—pah!"

Henrietta said, "We talk about nobler subjects. The cause of the people. And how *detestable* it is to be the spoiled daughter of a rich man!" She was egging him on, having had a very good lunch.

Achitophelous laughed offensively, "Oh, he is worried about that, is he? He seems smarter than I thought."

Henrietta cried, "He is, but not the way you mean, the horrible, criminal way you mean. Oh, such degradation! My father can only think foully. It's possible for even a capitalist to be refined," she told him severely. "In fact" (she sighed), "as Adam Constant says, that is our great weakness: we have neither art, learning, science, nor refinement yet on our side. You have them all. We have nothing but history." She broke off, looked at her father. "Do you want to hear what he said yesterday?"

"It won't make me a penny, but I should very much like it." He smiled and put his hands behind his back.

She pouted her breast unconsciously and recited, "The earth parched by privilege will be planted by our seed."

"Well," said Achitophelous, looking at her speculatively, under his eyebrows, and taking a promenade, "well, a nice prospect. That's what he offers you? Let me tell you, sentiments like that are cheap as dirt. He can't keep you on that sort of literature. You're a fool. A young fool. One of you is a sucker."

Jules came back with Michel Alphendéry. "Achitophelous, are you at it again? This is Mr. Alphendéry."

"You are a friend of Adam's," said Henrietta trying not to be shy.

Alphendéry said, "Well, Jules has told me all about it —or not quite all, I suppose. Now, have I got to convert the father or the daughter? I can do either."

"The father."

"The daughter!"

"I'll talk to your daughter, Mr. Achitophelous," said Alphendéry cheerfully. "Can I take her to lunch tomorrow?"

Achitophelous shot him a suspicious glance, but after a minute's study, said, "Yes, why not? With pleasure."

Henrietta bridled at being the center of attention and became a little fatuous. But Achitophelous turned to Jules. "Well, that's done. Have you got a man called Mouradzian round here?" He stopped in the middle of a sentence when Henrietta took her leave, and shook his head. "A son," he said to Jules, "is a gilt-edged security, but a daughter is goods that have to be given away with a bonus. Have you sons?"

"Four," said Jules carelessly, "do you know Henri Léon?"

"Not much," said Achitophelous, troubled, "he's all right. Sell, he can. He can sell last week's bait for tomorrow's halibut. He's all right. Is he in business down here then?"

"Oh, he's a friend of mine," said Jules. "You want to see Mouradzian?" He reached for the telephone. "Tell Mouradzian to come up here."

Achitophelous sank into a chair. "My wife is pure as an angel," he said heavily. "Where did Henrietta get such traits? Her mother is like snow. Such a temperament!" He flushed and giggled. "She gets it from me, all right."

Scene Four: Whoopee Party

IN THE evening the women had their war paint on and Léon was in fine feather. He had spent a couple of hours at the Turkish bath with Paul Méline. They sat late in the restaurant of the Café de la Paix. Léon liked its loaded serving tables and gilded pillars. As a poor boy he had dreamed of fleshpots like this one: this was his way of telling himself he had arrived and that he was really a rich man and everything his to command. He was showering questions on them, interspersing questions with anecdotes of his career.

He seemed to be carrying Mrs. Weyman off at a hand gallop. Once he even burst into song, a Roumanian folk song, in his sweet fluted voice, at the request of Raccamond. The married pair were of use to him as a social screen, in case anyone turned up who knew Mrs. Léon.

Aristide tried to speak of the bank, said slowly, "Comte Jean de Guipatin is working with me there: he's related to the Bourbons; there's Comte Hervé Lucé, a fifteenth-century family; Prince Julius Campoverde, an Italian aristocrat—all customers' men."

Alphendéry strolled into the café. Léon called him and asked, "Who are your customers?"

"Our money comes from South Americans who make money every two or three years in some new mining grab or nitrates steal or currency flop, and a few old Spanish land hogs, a few Hollywood skyrockets, a few Eton playboys, a few Theosophist bankers, a spa owner, a hotel speculator, a German steelworks heir, and the like. Not a bad little collection: we can survive."

Léon settled back his head in his collar, threatened, "Seems nothing but a society outfit: rich young yellow-bellies. No good. These counts: are they kosher? Do you think any of them have any real cash you can sound on the counter without bending it?"

Alphendéry spoke energetically, "Some new, some old: consolidated squirearchies, new political money wedded to the U.S.A., conserved Napoleonic dough, society figures who remember where they came from and how far: not too rusty, not too incautious. Opportunist, clever, unscrupulous, and talented money. People who eat their cake and have it. The best for business: steady income, new sources, no baccarat, no scroungers, no expectations, no frozen funds. A few Chicago streetwalkers with packing-house fortunes, married to phony counts, a few French hereditary bankbooks, a few postwar youngsters, motordrome and flying aces, born in a bedeviled world, crazy to make a fortune, amoral, playing for big stakes: the latter hang around Jules Bertillon as if he were their long-lost brother. That sounds shaky, but it's sounder than you guess. Jules says, 'I can work with any ace: he understands me. If I'm ever held up, it will be for speeding.'"

Léon laughed but said thoughtfully, "Birdmen: *Luftmenschen?*" He seemed to believe Alphendéry's tale. He mused, "But no big money. Not related to Morgan's? I heard something. You have a cousin of the Rothschilds in one of your branches, Aristide tells me."

"Have we?" said Alphendéry: "Perhaps. Everyone has. The Rothschilds have given up keeping their second cousins."

"That's bad," said Léon. "I wouldn't keep them if they wouldn't." He laughed suddenly. Alphendéry said, "I have to go. My old mother's leaving for home—Strasbourg—tonight. Good night, ladies. Good night!" He jumped up. They all saw that his clothes were good but his hat was shabby.

After he left Léon was thoughtful. "Well, I don't want to talk business. But I don't object to its being little money. Means you can make a graceful exit in a crisis. If France gets any poorer, you'll have socialism here and they'll gun for the big fellows. . . ." He shook his head. "At the same time, it's small. It depends on yield. You make your money how? That's what I don't understand, Raccamond. Can't figure it out. I've been worrying about it, all the afternoon. You don't give loans, you don't give commercial credits, you get no half-commission back. Isn't that what you told me? Then how do you make money?"

Aristide said, "I'll find out later on: I'll work it out."

"Well," commanded Léon, having exhausted the subject, "don't let's talk business. We want to make whoopee, don't we? No business." He clapped his hands and stared round at the pillars. "Waiter, where's the waiter? A bottle of wine. You want some more wine, don't you, Margaret? Of course. Marianne? Aristide?" They all licked their lips and agreed under their breaths. Aristide alone said in a businesslike tone, "We've got enough, Henri."

"Enough? Enough! Two bottles of wine for four people. You're not going to go back on me, Margaret? I want to have fun tonight. I come to Paris to have fun. Come on, darling, say you'll drink some more wine? You will. Waiter! More wine. Another bottle."

"Certainly."

Léon looked round the table grandly, with satisfaction. Aristide said, bending over his plate and cutting a great hunk of meat, "Bertillon makes fortunes for himself at Deauville and on the stock exchange: he's lucky——"

"Don't talk about Bertillon," commanded Léon cheerfully: "let's talk about me. I want to be with my friends tonight. What'll we do afterwards? Eh? A cabaret. The Scheherazade? I've got four tickets. A girl there gave them to me. Four tickets and champagne free. She gave me four. We'll go to the Scheherazade."

They ate dumbly while he looked round, searching for fresh horizons to beam upon. He leaned forward. "Ah, I tell you, Marianne, Alfonso XIII has to go. They all have to go: all the tyrants. That's what my heart tells me. No oppression. You can make more money under socialism. And if you couldn't, I'd still want it. . . . Moneymaking isn't all of life. My life would be empty if there were only money-making in it. I tell you, Margaret, if I thought my life was going to end like that, I'd go and throw a bomb at one of the men who are oppressing people. A man can't go out like that. You light a gas flame, it sings and suddenly it goes out. There's no more money in the meter. Do I want to be like that? I get sad,

48

Margaret, when I think that my life is empty." He got gayer. "No, Margaret, I can't end like that. I've got to be famous, Margaret: by James, I'll be famous, I'll make my name known, even I have to throw a bomb and kill— George V—no, he's too gray—kill Mussolini and free his people." He looked tenderly at them all. "Eh, Marianne, did you know I felt like that? No, Marianne, I can't just be put back into a box after having been out all over the table, like a pack of cards." He looked around. "My, what a pretty girl! Don't they have pretty girls here. *Hé*, Miss!" The girl smiled and approached with her tray of cigarettes. "What do you want, Margaret? Abdullas, Abdullas, Marianne? I'll buy you all cigarettes. Have you got any small Abdullas, Miss? These, these, no these, haven't you got any smaller—there you are, Margaret. You're too pretty to be working here, Miss. Bring me some cigars, will you?" She went off smiling. He whispered gigantically, "I say, she's a pretty girl: um, isn't she? Isn't she a pretty girl? What do you think? Say, they're pretty smart, aren't they? Nothing but pretty girls here. Look at the other one: not so bad. Poor girl, I bet she has to work hard."

They smiled suitably. The girl approached again. It must not be forgotten that theoretically Margaret Weyman had approached Léon on a business proposition. Léon said, "Hey, Miss, what's a pretty girl like you doing here? You ought to be in the chorus. Aren't you in the chorus? Why aren't you?"

The girl dallied, with aplomb but without conviction. "Why, I never thought about it, sir."

"You're too pretty to be working here. You work pretty hard, eh? When do you get off?"

The girl said with a quiet dignity, her eyes having summed up the other women, "Oh, late. It depends. I get off at seven and then I have to come back at eight and don't get off till eleven."

Léon shook his head. "Eleven! No, that's late. Young woman mustn't—unhealthy. And what do you do between seven and eight?"

The girl didn't even trouble to smile but said in a cash voice, "We stay in."

Léon was all consideration. "You stay in—here, ugh? Upstairs, ugh?" He shook his head, said to Margaret Weyman, "It's long hours, isn't it?" He asked the girl,

"And then you have to go home: how long does that take you? Is it far?"

The girl cast eyes at a handsome Balkan man, as she answered carelessly, "It's quite a way. Near the Place de la Nation. I often have to get the all-night bus."

Mrs. Weyman, annoyed by Léon's raw style, got up and asked her way to the ladies' room. Marianne sat on, ghoulishly enjoying the scene. Léon felt somewhat relieved by Margaret's exit and made haste to bring things to a head. He finished his canvass in a flurried warm tone: "It's a shame, a pretty girl like you. Would you like to get into the chorus? I know someone in the theater. This gentleman here knows Henri Bernstein, almost all the actors and managers of Paris. Don't you, Aristide?"

Aristide was sullen, but Marianne said instantly, "Certainly: that's true."

Léon nodded his head like a good little boy, "I'll see if I can do something for you: should you like that, eh? See me after work some night and we'll fix it up. What do you say, eh?"

The girl yawned. "All right: I don't mind."

"When do you get off? Eleven tonight? Tonight?"

"Later," said the girl.

"I've got a car. I'll take you in a taxi home. I don't like to think—pretty girl. You'll be tired at night. I'll get you a job, depend on me."

The girl smiled sweetly. "What have I got to lose? . . . Tonight, perhaps." She went off lingeringly, and with some misshapen gratitude, it seemed, in her heart. Perhaps she was lonely.

But Léon triumphed and puffed out his chest. He bent to them. "Eh? How was that? I don't waste time. That's what I say. Do something for a poor girl and she's grateful. You give a poor girl two and six, and she says thank you and means it. You give a girl you pick up in the Scribe Bar a couple of hundred francs and she hardly opens her mouth. She never reckons it means more than a week's wages for a miner. She never thinks of the miner working for his wife and children for a week for less than she gets. You've got to take working girls to know real gratitude. How did I make out, eh? You think she likes me, Marianne, eh? Yes, I think she took to me." He spied Margaret Weyman coming back and finished quickly. "Shh! Don't say anything to her: she's a nice girl, she's a nice woman. You know American women —not sophisticated, not European."

Margaret sat down. He put his hand on her arm. "Margaret—another bottle of wine!—Margaret, did I tell you what I did in the General Strike in 1926? I was in London, see, staying with Strindl and Company, with Taube, he's a fool, but old Elster is his uncle and let the boy run the business—boy, I say, fifty he is, but Elster is seventy—I was staying with Taube in Hampstead. I wake up in the morning. I eat breakfast at a quarter to eight. There's no breakfast! There's no gas to cook me an egg. There's water running: I can wet my face. That's all. There isn't even a tin of salmon in the house. And no grocer boy. All right, I think, I'll go downtown and get a cup of coffee. I call my chauffeur Corbin. 'Sorry, sir: I've got no petrol. I can't even get down to the gas station and at the gas station they've no deliveries.' What's the matter? A general strike. Misery! All right, no tube, no taxi, no car. I must get downtown: see what's doing. So I walk. All right. No coffee downtown, I go to the Baltic:* the janitor opened it but who was there? Almost no one could get there. The Post Office was open but who was there to run it? Almost the telephones weren't working. I walk round. Everyone is gloomy. I go to the Western Union. There are two boys who lived in the city alone working. An American company. 'Tell me what's the opening Winnipeg and Chicago.' Terrible. . . . So it goes. I go home and I think. No business. If business could be done! I come down next day. Some more people are on the Baltic but no business: everyone is walking round gloomy thinking the red flag will be over London. It nearly got by. They nearly got the red flag. And still a terrible market in Winnipeg and Chicago. By the third and fourth day, no one thought of business, people were only wondering if they could get the price of a boat fare to Antwerp or Paris. What a pity, I think. No business being done and the market so low. I get an idea. It looks like revolution. The markets are starving. Not an order out of England in three, four days. They'll just wolf down any order. So I go to the Western Union and I calmly telegraph to buy half a million bushels wheat in Chicago in Strindl's name. They had the credit: their credit was still good. . . .

---

* Baltic: Mercantile and Shipping Exchange, London.

Well, I calculated: if it really is the revolution, they can't dun me in a soviet Britain, can they, for wheat bought before the revolution? And if it isn't the revolution, if we can sell short on the red flag yet, then the market will go up and I'll make money. Perfect. I couldn't go wrong. And I could say, 'Who telegraphed? Not me.' I signed Strindl or Elster or Taube. I had a right: don't forget they were my partners in Amsterdam at the time. No swindle. No. Well, was I right? That's how I made ten cents a bushel. The market had had a tremendous bust. I plunged. No harm. Fifty thousand dollars—ten thousand sterling. I took a risk. Ha? Margaret, what do you say?"

"I wouldn't mind being your partner if there were two of me."

Léon took this as a great compliment. "You're great, Margaret. Well, let's go somewhere. Say, say, look at that girl. What a beauty! Fancy her sitting there like that waiting for men: isn't it a shame. I'll tell you what, Margaret, Marianne: let's ask her to go with us? Yes. Look at her, poor girl. A beauty too. What do you say?"

He looked eagerly at them.

"I'm a sport, Henri," said Marianne, "but Aristide and I are rather well known in Paris, and doubtless this woman is, too. What will be thought of us: Aristide's clients may—no, certainly will see him in the Scheherazade —you can't take a woman like that with you to the Scheherazade where everyone who counts in Paris may see us."

Léon looked crestfallen, but his eyebrows rising took in Marianne's dowdy black evening dress and sequin-scaled jacket, her badly curled hair, her thick rouge. The handsome woman waiting for men on one of the padded seats had caught his eye by this time and knew he was discussing her: she looked the two women over with superb insolence, and they crumbled and fell to dust at her glance, while she continued to glitter and even grew in beauty like a sea gull letting fall sea drops from wings shaken by sun and wind. Léon dismissed Marianne with an unconscious but careless curl of the lips and nose and turned abruptly to Margaret, took her arm in a brotherly fashion.

"Margaret, come on: we'll all go along and have a good time."

Margaret was recovering from her astonishment enough

to look down her nose. This disgusted Léon. He snapped
his fingers, smiled at the woman, cried, "Madame." He
said with a sudden malicious inspiration, half intoxicated
and half in anger, "Margaret, why didn't I notice it before? This is Mme.—I forget the name—this is the intimate friend of a friend of mine, a grain merchant: why
you know, Achitophelous, Marianne, why this is an old
friend of his, poor woman: she had a bad time. He isn't a
nice fellow to his women. Poor girl. Imagine her waiting
for men in this café. Madame. . . ."

He had left them and energetically gained her side.
With mocking and brilliant looks she was splendidly flirting with him and sneering at the others. Aristide had
pushed a heavy and irritated look towards her, taken her
in and now sat with his head bowed over the table, until
he had the presence of mind to say, "Marianne, Mrs.
Weyman, we need not stay: if you like—"

Mrs. Weyman dryly replied, "I think I will stay. If this
is really a friend of Mr. Léon, how can we leave him?
He is our host. Wouldn't we look rather ridiculous, suddenly getting up and scuttling? Let's wait. He's only doing
it to annoy us. . . ."

"Is he?" asked Aristide sardonically. "I hope so. Let us
wait and see."

But now Léon came towards them, leading the dark-
browed houri by the hand. She was dressed in black,
low necked with silver fox furs. An exceedingly smart
hat with evening veil set off the black brilliants which
were her eyes. Her hair appeared to be done by Antoine: she had platinum and diamond bracelets and silver
and ebony bracelets on her arms. She was so much better dressed than either of them and so much grander,
silkier, and stranger in manner, like polished ebony, that
they were at a loss. She seated herself and Léon said,
"This is the friend of my old friend Achitophelous, Mme.
Verneuil."

The women, like two clucking schoolgirls, bowed and
felt dowdy. As if forcing them against a background by
sketching her own personality in more brilliantly, the
alleged Mme. Verneuil lit an opium cigarette, after offering one to each of the other women, showed off her
carmine nails and diamonds, and said in a saccharine
coo, "And what shall we do, Mr. Léon?"

Léon looked round, said, "Let's get another friend:

let's see if we can see another of my friends. There, on the *terrasse*."

Mme. Verneuil gave a faint start, but came quivering back to the leash, like a black greyhound. "You have some more friends here, then, Monsieur?" She laughed.

"I am looking for more friends. I want all my friends. Eh, Margaret, don't you want to meet all my friends? I know Paris so well. All my friends have friends in Paris. Let's take them all out. Poor girls. Such beauties. Such houris. It is practically paradise. You do not mind, dear Madame? Are there any of your friends, here?"

"No," said the black-browed Parisienne, slowly, "none of my friends is here. I do not think, in fact, I have any friends living or dead, except you tonight, Mr. Léon."

Léon frowned at her for a moment, but she only responded with a salon smile. He sawed the air with his hand. "Waiter, *hé:* bring some more wine." The waiter looked faintly pained but hurried away. The headwaiter advanced with a real smile and saw to the nesting of the bottle himself.

"I can sing," said Léon. "In the Seven Mountains, where I was born, everyone can sing. But not here. Do you believe I can sing?" he said turning suddenly to Margaret and quenching the light in the houri's eyes.

"I should like to hear you again."

"You will, you will: but I must have all my friends. I don't like this female exclusive game—do you, Aristide? Listen, Marianne: Aristide will have four girls and I will have four. We will take out ten girls and two men. That is a dozen. I feel like a dozen, or even a baker's dozen, tonight. It was remembering the one hundred and twenty-five thousand guilders I made in the General Strike. Ah, Margaret, I was walking down the street this afternoon: I looked in the gutter and saw an empty purse. Think of it, I said to myself. It is a month since I was in love; since I felt in love. That's a terrible feeling, Margaret. Do you know what I mean? I need romance. Let me have romance tonight. Be nice to me. Bear with me." He begged so nicely of them that they all softened and even Aristide left off toying with a coffee spoon and his foggy eyes smiled for a moment, or at least lightened faintly. The women even settled themselves more easily and accepted each other.

"Love is usually a caricature and a bad joke," said Aristide.

"I have gypsy blood," said Léon: "I went to the White Rabbi in—my home—last year, and he said to me, 'Olim (my name), you're a wicked man, but your star is lucky. You are rich and you will go on getting richer.' It is my gypsy blood: it is with me. There is a rose in my blood: wherever I go, stones glittering underneath my shoes. Did I ever tell you my first experiment in agriculture? No. My father died. My poor mother lived by herself with four children. One day my uncle came and drove his cows into our yard. After that we sowed cucumbers. We always sowed cucumbers. We make wonderful pickles," he beseeched Madame Verneuil, who was bored but pretended to devour him with interest. "Pickled cucumbers, what do you call them? When the cucumbers came up, the whole yard was covered with cucumbers: you couldn't walk without mashing them. I never saw so many. Good, we thought: the yard is good for cucumbers. But next year there were no cows; when we sowed, there were only two or three stringy things. My first lesson in agriculture, you see. At first I thought it was perhaps our gypsy blood, luck. My grandmother—" he stopped abruptly. "Waiter: Aristide! See that girl over there! Aristide: go and get her. It's a friend of mine. I met her—in the Westminster Hotel. She is a very fine lady. She was worth—millions." His eyes danced. "Millions of—pesetas: her husband was a Spaniard. Now look at her. Isn't it sad? We'll have a good time. We'll drink the wine and then we'll go to the Scheherazade."

Aristide sat up and said, "I really think we have enough company, Léon. The Scheherazade is really very small and the company is small; you can't take a big party there unless you arrange—"

"Nonsense. You're afraid: don't be afraid, my boy. Go and get the girl. She's a dear old friend of Mr. Rhys of Rotterdam. When the Spanish husband died, Rhys was very kind to her. Poor girl. Do me a favor, Aristide, and go and ask her."

"What is your friend's name?" said Aristide sternly.

"Ask her! She's probably married now. You don't want to offend the ladies—wrong names? You can make mistakes, eh, Marianne?"

The two women who had started the evening with a

good lead were perspiring with embarrassment, irritation, and doubt. No one could believe Léon's tales but here he was chattering in a sort of French with the Mme. Verneuil and there was no telling that he did not really know her. Besides, the Scheherazade was a first-class cabaret and they rarely had an opportunity to go to it. Marianne decided to hold out for the sake of the champagne which they would presently get.

Léon cried, "And afterwards we'll go to Mitchell's on the Rue Pigalle and have bacon and eggs, four o'clock in the morning. First to the Brasserie Moulin Rouge, then to Mitchell's: first an omelet, then a raft of eggs. Good, eh? But first we'll have some fun. How are you, Madame? What is your married name now? This is Madame Verneuil."

"I am Mme. Saintspères, then," said the girl throatily. She was a strange-looking woman, neither young nor old, or both; her bugle eyes popped as in childhood or senility; they were large, blue, and exorbitant. Her pink skin was deeply flushed and it might have been fever or natural complexion. The mouth was formless, the teeth white and protruding. She laughed gawkily, showing the teeth, and yet she showed no embarrassment or fear in the presence of the splendid Mme. Verneuil. Her dress was bizarre to Continental eyes and took after the American or English unsophisticated adolescent pattern, a cut between Kate Greenaway and a Burne-Jones heroine. They had all seen her round Paris for years and marveled at her persistence in living a life for which they were convinced she had no talent. And here she sat in the Café de la Paix. She took her seat next to Margaret with composure.

Another girl, seeing the gathering, came nearer with hesitation. Léon looked her over, recklessly beckoned her. The other women of her profession now began to understand what Léon was doing. A good and kind man in his personal relations, his drunkenness was bringing to sudden flower some secret malices and acute perceptions of personality which in his sole passion for money and his merchandising even of love had been dried up, like peas of Pompeii, perhaps, which can still flower after centuries of being buried.

This new woman was also well known to all frequenters of Paris cafés. Some said she was Russian, some, German. She was tall, ugly, plump, dark, and heavily marked with sadness and poor living, but well built and with a great pride in her manner as tall Russian women often have. She had on a round cap which did not suit her heavy square-built features, a poor black dress which muddied her spoiled olive complexion, black gloves, large feet in low-heeled shoes. She approached with dignity, as if she was meeting the acquaintances of some close friends of hers. Her stone-cut face smiled. She sat down and began settling herself as if richly dressed. The other women feared her for her great poise. Although poor, strange, and ugly, she had many lovers and although she would whore for a piece of bread or to pay her rent, she had lovers for long intervals. Some said she was formerly the Baroness So-and-so of Vienna and her history indicated that she had some secret attraction of history or station, above her present looks. Léon, however, when she came near perceived that she was not the type to amuse him vastly, although he murmured, leaning back and eying her fast, "What a woman! Magnificent, eh? Look at her?"

Aristide looked at her with immense distaste. Léon noticed this and began to laugh. "Well, Aristide, speak up! See if you can't see any friends here. Haven't you any friends? Why, you live in Paris; and look at me, in ten minutes, look at all the old friends I see here! This is Mme. Verneuil, this is Mme. Saintspères, and what is now your married name, Madame?"

The noble ogress shook all her teeth in a wide laugh and said sweetly, "Anna, that's all; never mind the Madame. I am your old friend Anna. Don't you remember I never had any other name?"

He looked at her vividly, appraising her great proportions, startled. The meeting had now become interesting for all the women, who for the first time, no doubt, had an opportunity of measuring each other's talents and learning the method and attractions of the others. The waiter had begun to smile, relishing this treat offered to all the hungry women who had been waiting round the café; for although they belonged to a world to which his wife, sister and daughter did not, and although he found them parasitic, the waiter at least liked to see money spent on other than these plump and self-satisfied married women. Léon took a drink of wine.

"Here are we making whoopee and the Red Army is

fighting for civilization in China," he said sadly, shaking his head.

The dark-browed Parisienne bridled at this, blew smoke from her cigarette. She had turned her back towards the whore who sat next to her.

"I would spill my last drop of blood against the damned Reds," said she. "There is civilization, the family honor, self-respect over here. What must it be like over there? I pity the women when those bandits pass over."

Léon laughed. "You are a great fighting woman!" He broke off, and looked serious. An improper idea had occurred to him and he was a decent man: he disliked obscenity. He shook his head and looked round. "Lady, lady! Come over here. There is a friend of mine," he announced shamelessly to them, "what a woman! Why, I met her when Kratz and I were over last March." He frowned. Kratz had played a lot of dirty tricks since then.

They were presently twelve sitting at the table. Then the ogress said, "Now, we are sufficiently fabulous, Monsieur: let us go somewhere else."

"The bill!"

One of the girls began cadging for cigarettes. Another took her place by Aristide's side and began coaxing him to come in "their" taxi. The two women who had begun the evening with Léon, Marianne and Margaret, now stood huddled aside, ruffled and astonished, trying to look dignified.

Léon suddenly noticed hovering with curiosity in the distance the cigarette girl he had previously courted. This reminded him that he would never have time at this rate to return and take her home in a taxi. So he suddenly bundled them all out to the sidewalk and as the girl passed near him on his way to the cloakroom, he said, "Tomorrow evening, sweetie. I met so many friends tonight!"

She laughed at this. "All right. At eleven."

He went out, extremely pleased with his new appointment. He was losing interest in the bevy of girls. He thrust them into two taxis, taking Margaret and the prettiest with him, and left Aristide with Marianne and the others to the other taxi. Aristide and his wife felt shoddy when they found themselves, by Léon's generalship, in this position.

Léon made Margaret talk and when the hetaerae found

out that she lived in Hollywood and knew intimately all the great stars, they were wild with enthusiasm: they really fell in love with Margaret, flattered her, and drew her out in long silken threads with questions. She began to have a better time and Léon decided that, positively, he loved her and perhaps she would be the Great Romance of his middle age.

"Margaret," he cried, "will you come with me to Russia? To the Ukraine? I will buy grain for the people of Russia. What do you say to that? I will have a function: I will do some good. By James, if I can't do that, don't you see, I'll have to do something, create a scandal, set the town hall on fire, kill Mussolini."

"Could you keep your fingers out of the plum tart yourself?" joked Margaret. "I am sure you couldn't."

"I could, I could: you don't know me. If it was for the people—"

The female merchandise cackled hollowly at this and the slow, ugly Russian—doubtless she was Russian, after all—said in her deep cracked voice, "Why, you don't understand anything about that country; they don't believe in private property! Women are even common property: not cattle like us, but all women: good women, pure women, mothers."

There was a bizarre silence.

"Who would you be without private property?" laughed Margaret.

"Who? Well, tell me who I am with it." He laughed, himself again. "Let's forget it. I have money on me tonight. I'll throw it away: spread it round thickly a bit. Driver, don't go first to the Scheherazade: stop at the first bazaar—night club, I mean."

They began the round of the night clubs in their two taxis. They stopped in the Rue Pigalle. Léon had a system all his own for visiting cabarets. He liked music sufficiently, and he loved dancing. He liked to see the tango very much indeed, and often went to El Garrón to see the drum-dance. His object in visiting cabarets was to add a string to his long chaplet of handsome women. He was not impressed by the luxury of the cabarets, but was very exigent and easily bored by their shows. Their shows were pretty poor, in fact, for they were really places for the sale of women and champagne. If he paid for a bottle of champagne in a cabaret and found no pretty women, he did not even look at the floor show and considered himself sold. For one of the most brilliant grain traders and option placers on the Continent that was not a nice position. Therefore, to get past the theatrical Don Cossacks, Argentine and Andalusian dons, Montmartre apaches, red Indians, porters in evening dress, and black-satined coat snatchers who stood at heavy portieres and painted doors, to get an eyeful before venturing his party in, Léon left them standing on the pavement, with the chauffeurs of the taxis fuming and suspicious, cried, "Wait!" and muttered to the doorkeepers who tried to induce him, engage him, push him, entice him, seduce him, inside the great maw of pleasure,

"One moment! I'm looking for a friend of mine: Mr. Guinédor."

The curtains would droop reluctantly aside and Henri Léon for a few minutes would be able to sample the entertainment, the women in attendance. He did this as a matter of course, without consideration of the women already in his company. This evening they sought Mr. Guinédor high and low. They even went into the Caveau Caucasien, sat uncomfortably amongst its half-gilded demimonde, the scurf of Paris that thinks itself the jewel in her ear. The Cossack dancers, of whom one was a prince, of course, performed very skillfully the traditional sword dance, while a blonde Russian woman, junket-white, in barbaric velvet décolleté, sang "Black Eyes" and "All Russia Is Under Snow." Beautiful Byzantine paintings covered the wall, very suitable to the Byzantine culture these relics of a better order lived in. Every section of the room was decorated by long Persian and Turkestan rugs and tapestries. They ordered two bottles of champagne. Pop! Glouglou. Léon and Mrs. Weyman drank little. Marianne and the dark Russian woman finished two glasses each with only a slight leavening of their heavy black flour. Henri said impatiently, "Let's go! This is slow: don't you think it's slow, Margaret? Eh, Marianne: shall we go? It's slow."

He snapped his fingers, swept away the anxious captain, nodded blindly to the owner, whom he knew (and who had once partaken of a girl that Léon himself had unsuccessfully desired), and towed his party ungracefully, ridiculously, out of the place, so that a ripple of smiles lighted up that gloomy, respectable place of off-color entertainment. He stood at the door calling for his hat and coat, his back to the company, masterfully discontented. Aristide helped some of the women with their hats and coats. They stood jostling each other and nicking out the collars of each other's coats like a party leaving after an auction. Out on the pavement, he breathed again and brushed away the cabaret runners and pullers-in and the voices of hungry taxi drivers.

"Let's all walk." They all walked. "No women," declared Léon.

"Haven't you got enough?" Aristide was in a rage: he was being made a fool of in public. A French woman passing, said aloud, "Six each: *formidable!*" His eyes smarted: he cried easily. He walked along moodily imagining a knife stuck into Léon's muscular back. It would rend a lovely suit. A pity.

"Paris is dull," Léon cried back to him.

The women had begun to laugh and were billowing all round Aristide. Marianne puffed in the rear of Léon, heroically resigned to public disgrace.

"A Russian girl told me there's a place up this street, a new place which is very high class and has beautiful women there, exiles, real aristocrats. I know they're all aristocrats, but these girls really are, princesses and the like down on their luck, since the revolution." He laughed. "I'd rather see them here working in a night club than oppressing the people drinking and rolling under the table in St. Peters—Leningrad."

The bizarre girl with the American get-up and the bugle eyes said in her high voice, "They take the bread out of French mouths, don't you see? I am not for revolution. One set begins to steal the bread of another; let us all stay in our places and know where our bread is coming from."

"She sleeps with philosophers, apparently," said a female voice.

They laughed ghoulishly in the night. "She's only fit for that."

"Let them whore at home, that's right," said another.

"Is it their fault?" asked the dark Russian, Anna.

"Ah, you're Russian: you don't understand patriotism," shrilled the dark Parisienne, first picked up.

They entered an intimate Russian "aristocratic" cabaret. Léon complimented the hostess.

61

She passed quickly on to other subjects. Léon was the richest man, by far, in the room. Everything he did spoke power, wealth, and the ability to make money any day. She addressed herself particularly to Marianne, and then moved off. Aristide danced stiffly with Margaret, whispered doubts to Léon that he could make the highborn hostess.

While the women were getting their cloaks, Léon showed Aristide a card, but not long enough for him to read the name and address on it. "Her card." He rolled his eyes ominously at Aristide, then smiled. "She's a sweet woman. Listen, we'll go for a bit of onion soup, Rue de la Grande Truanderie." As they went out the door, Léon suddenly contracted and hid himself among the women.

"Who was that?" whispered Aristide.

"Nobody: what do you mean?"

But Aristide turned this way and that and presently observed standing in the doorway they had just left, Léon's school friend, onetime crony, and now bitter enemy, looking at them. He was showing his false sharp teeth in a smile intended only for himself. Aristide smiled to himself likewise. He drew close to Léon.

"Aren't you taking a cab?" cried the Parisienne dark-browed girl.

"Oh, it's coming on to rain," cried another.

Even Margaret drew in to the wall. "Henri, my twenty-five-dollar shoes!"

"Walk or stay behind," said Léon, and marched off in front where Aristide joined him.

"I just saw Julius Kratz: we passed him in the doorway."

Léon was silent. Aristide murmured, "You are enemies now. I have seen a lot of these unfit but fated friend—fellowships, Don Quixotes with their Sancho Panzas, Don Juans with their Leporellos."

Léon quickly raised his smoldering eyes to his face. "He came from Kronstadt: I came from Hermannstadt. We met at the age of twelve in the soupline of the same relief society at London, on a bad, winter day. We were with four other families in an apartment in a tumble-down house in Black Horse Yard and Jack was in a house, all bulging out, used by pullers-in, thieves, and street-walkers just near St. Mary Axe. I made money. I took

62

him with me. There's no Leporello in it. You know that as well as I do, Aristide."

"A Leporello just the same," murmured Aristide seriously. "You can't get rid of him. See how he crosses your path. He'll try to do you harm."

Léon was dubious, frightened, "How do you know?"

"I know the animal," declared Aristide.

"No, my boy, no, no." But Léon was not the same. They heard Margaret talking about her shoes. "There were my twenty-five-dollar shoes speckled with mud——" Léon exclaimed with sudden impatience, "Where did I pick up that cow?" He was restless now and fell on his onion soup before anyone else, handed round a few hundred-franc notes, and stood up suddenly with his hat on his head before anyone was ready. Insulted, angry, feeling their evening wasted, and these men washouts, the women were very slow getting on their wraps. Léon kept looking at the clock. Then he said, "Listen, Aristide, you're an honest man, you're going home with your wife, you go to sleep legally, and I don't blame you, on the contrary—I'm busy, I've got to go to the station to meet a friend, Rhys, who's coming in from Brussels——" While talking he had dragged Aristide out of earshot.

"I'll meet him for you," Aristide said avidly.

Henri Léon smiled his broadest jolly-boy grin and clutched Aristide's arm, "Listen, I'm going back to that Russian place: I've got to make that girl."

"You'll never do it."

"What do you bet? Go on, my boy, do this for me. I'll do something for you any day. My wife and daughter get in tomorrow morning at eight. I got no time to waste."

"I think you're wrong," Aristide said sullenly. "I think I know women—as merchandise." He said it not obscenely but with bitter coarseness. Léon drew down his brows and gave him a close look: instinctively he took a step back. "What? Well—you don't happen to know the Rue Navarin, do you? I think she said she lived there but I don't know the number."

"What do you want me to do? Start them walking, I suppose?"

"Nicely, my boy, nicely. Now, when they come up to the corner, I'll say I just remembered I have to go to the station to meet Mr. Rhys of Rotterdam. You send the others off. You know what I want."

"I have no money," said Aristide. "Not for that, Henri."

Léon threw back his head, looked round, "Hey, taxi, taxi!" A taxi wheeling round the street, drew in. "Get another: get two others," commanded Léon. The driver, with a quick glance, climbed down off his seat and got two others who were coasting round looking for nightlife stragglers. "There!" said Léon. "Girls, I'm terribly sorry, time just passes like water in your company, sweet company. I have to meet a friend of mine, Mr. Ganz of Amsterdam. Got to go now. This gentleman, old friend, will take you to the Moulin Rouge, get an omelet, wonderful omelets there . . . see they get it, Aristide . . . nice red wine. See you get omelet, very good after champagne: make you sleep. See you have it. Marianne, you go with Aristide and see they get it. You're a good sport. Margaret! Darling, sweetheart!" He took her hand, fondled it until she withdrew it. "Darling," he said urgently, drawing her off a little, "my wife and daughter coming tonight. Very unfortunate: I telegraphed them to stay another day or two but it's this marriage of my daughter's. Tell you all tomorrow. Just meet them and take them to their hotel. They leave tomorrow evening. It's all right, darling: trust me. You understand."

"I'm tired," said Margaret firmly. She got into a taxi.

"That's right," said Léon climbing in after her, "jump in, I'll take you home, Margaret, myself. A bit of penance. I need it, eh? Ho, ho. Hotel Westminster, driver. Wait, wait! Jack's is the restaurant: not Moulin Rouge. Omelet. All have some. Here, Aristide, here's some money. Here. We had a good time. Made whoopee. Here, girls." He handed some money to the tall Russian. "Give them one each, one hundred francs each. Had a good time. I enjoyed it. Good night, girls. Here, Aristide, here's for the omelet—not enough—taxi for you and Marianne. If it costs more tell me in the—h'm. Never mind. Don't waste money. Driver, Hotel Westminster. Good-by. Marianne! Good night. See you tomorrow. Very sweet of you to come, Marianne."

"Au revoir," called the girls.

"Good night," he snapped. He had already forgotten all about them.

They drove off leaving Aristide and Marianne on the curb with the women. Aristide looked at the money thrust into his hand—four hundred francs. Léon had short-changed him, as usual. He looked at the girls, only nine of them.

"Here," he said in a curious bullying tone to the Parisian woman in black, "go and get something to eat!" He gave her two hundred francs and got into the taxi. "Driver, Rue du Docteur Blanche."

"Hey," said the woman, "hand over the other two hundred! I saw he gave you four hundred to take us out to supper. And there's the taxi waiting. Something of the piker in you."

"Drive on, what are you waiting for?" cried Aristide savagely. The chauffeur shrugged his shoulders and turned the wheel.

"What about me?" cried the third chauffeur. There was a shower of insults and reproaches from the girls waiting on the pavement. Stretching her neck, as they turned the corner, Marianne saw that the tall dark girl was paying out and the chauffeur was leaning out of his cab, giving them advice: "They are dividing it, all right," said she.

Aristide said wildly, "Horrible." He struggled for a reason. "I don't want my wife to be seen out with a party like that. Suppose we had been seen. He has no sense."

Marianne reflected, "Things whizz when Henri's about. Has he really gone to the station?"

"No. Of course not."

"The chit in the restaurant, I suppose?"

"No. The Russian woman."

"Well, well. Well, she has class, at any rate."

"Léon stinks of money," Aristide said rudely. He wrestled in an agony of envy. "Eleven hundred francs to those whores, about one thousand on champagne—they sold him nine bottles of sixty-franc champagne at one hundred and ten francs apiece. Mme. Ashnikidzé got five hundred francs. He'll probably give this woman a thousand, that's about her rating. And this evening when I asked him about the twenty-five thousand gulden he owes me, he made a joke out of it. Why shouldn't they go for him? He bought me for less. I don't know as much as they do."

Marianne asked with circumspection, "Did he make you any offer at all, any settlement?"

"No! Said the market had been up and down, his accounts weren't fixed up for that year because that was the year the books were lost—the usual story. Oh, you know it's hopeless. He made me a proposition: he wants to become a baron in Belgium. If I act as his go-between and write the proper letters and if he gets it, he'll see about giving me my twenty-five thousand gulden."

"And he gave you nothing?"

Aristide admitted with shame, "He gave me—one hundred and twenty gulden—ten pounds in sterling he had on him. I took it. Why not? Anything from that fellow is cream. I didn't expect that."

There was an embarrassed silence. Then Marianne laughed. "The deposit technique!"

"What he calls the deposit technique: yes."

Scene Five: Small Kratz and Great Léon

LITTLE Julius Kratz, friend of school days and soup kitchens, clung to great Henri Léon as he zoomed upwards, lent him his advice, the advice of a wasp to an airplane, told him his defects with peculiar truth, listened to his inspirations with more asperity than a wife, and devised plots against their friends. Sometimes, in pure mischief, they wrote anonymous letters to friends in business, mentioning magic words: *Scotland Yard, the Parquet, the Crown Prosecutor;* or sent telegrams worded as follows, *All is discovered, fly to the Continent;* or *All is discovered, fly to England,* which usually resulted in their receiving postcards from Bruges, Milan, or Chester! They studied the lists of donors to the Established Church in the wealthy suburbs in which they lived, and directed income-tax inspectors to these pillars of the church. These little scherzos occupied odd crannies in great Léon's mind but kept Julius Kratz busy from morning to night. He was forever lounging into some somber and pompous office got up by Léon, with some new joke, over which they would both laugh like hyenas for ten minutes. At the end of the morning, Léon would take Kratz out for coffee and ask him when he was going to pay the next installment due to him, Léon, on the mortgage of his house and Kratz would invariably reply something like this, "A fine friend: yes, a mortgage is the gift of the rich to the poor!" or, "You're

66

a vulture, wait till I'm dead: then you can pick my bones."
By a law of nature, until they were both forty, Léon always had a mortgage on Kratz's home.

Henri Léon, always mindful of the misery from which he had sprung and to which he was determined never to return, had labor sympathies. Further, he aspired to political honors, and seeing England as the country in which revolution came slowly and respectably, he got himself naturalized, with the words, "England has always welcomed immigrant genius!"

If he had had more theory and less cupidity, he might have been a great leavener of the masses, a sonorous revolutionist, a meteoric careerist, a second Garibaldi or a Mussolini, perhaps; but he had two fiery passions which stood in his way. The first was love of money and the second, love of women. The first took him to Liverpool and the second there settled his fate. At the age of fourteen, his second talent, proclaimed before, besides, by his brilliant roving eyes and great trumpet nose and that parallel lift of the long shadowy brows and mouth, declared itself in a lively style. He was that creature, rather rarer in the West than in the East, supposed figment of the darling dreams of men and women, so rare that the masters of dreams go looking through history for traces of him as a "race concept," a Don Juan: a Don Juan in the grain trade. He was the inexhaustible suitor of innumerable women; an insatiable curiosity led him to desert the fair who had once proved frail.

Henri Léon, settled in London with his lady, was often called abroad. On these trips he was accompanied invariably by Julius Kratz. Kratz provided an alibi for Henri Léon in his gallant adventures in public places, and was a companion in private. When Henri Léon's ladies, sniffing a little coolness in the air, decided that the time had come to realize their positions and demanded silver foxes, minks, leopards, and other guerdons, it was Julius Kratz who would announce that Henri Léon had just had serious reverses in the stock market. And when some of these ladies took up arms, it was little Julius Kratz, the weasel, not worth shooting, who interviewed them, soothed them, cracked a nasty joke at Léon's expense, and pocketed the pearl-handled revolver at the psychological moment. In return for this, Henri took Kratz into the cabarets, gambling circles, theaters, follies, bars, restaurants, and whorehouses for which Kratz had the most passionate thirst. He sometimes gave Kratz a little to gamble with, he put him up at hotels, paid for his mistresses, champagne, his wife's operations, his children's schooling, his clothes. He took it out in mortgages. He sometimes helped him by writing to Labour members with whom he was intimate (for Kratz often went skulking in fear of the shadow of the Home Secretary), and he took this out by lending Kratz money at a rather high rate of interest. But he lent him money and a man will do anything for that. And Léon seemed to think it only fair, that since he held him in a vice, he should let Kratz insult him, spit venom at him, and talk scandal about him behind his back.

In the last ten years Léon's greed had led him into the bad affairs of the Diamond Syndicate (with Achitophelous), the New-Art Furniture Company promotion (with Leverwurst), the Restaurant Refuse Company (with Jake Neunkinder), the Artificial Indigo Company (with Schwartzperl), the Color Process Company (with Paul Méline), and several others. In the last ten years, Kratz's greed had got him into the messes of the Happy Hearthside Company, (with Jakie Neunkinder), the Reformed Rubberized Fiber Company (with Schwartzperl), the Glass Insulation Company (with Leverwurst), and the Good-Little-Larry Toy Company (with Benny Hobogritz). Léon had financed Kratz's partnership in all the latter, and Kratz had gone in with Léon in all the former.

At forty, Julius Kratz looked back over his career, decided Henri Léon had all the luck and all the mortgages, took a ticket for Australia for himself, his wife, and children and set sail; but not before he had sat down and written a long letter to Henri Léon, a letter of the most hideous, cruel reviling, touching him on all his soft spots, mentioning that death was just around the corner for him and that the White Rabbi of Botoshani had called him a wicked man and a sordid soul and prophesied his ruin. He saw to one or two other things, too, in between packing his few trunks. He referred all his creditors to Henri Léon, transferred his debit accounts to Léon's accounts, cabled his friends on the Continent and in America that Léon had ruined him and wrote to the income-tax authorities in England, America, and the Continental countries in which Léon was engaged in business, telling them the true state of Léon's fortunes and revealing to them where he kept his private trust accounts.

Scarcely a week had passed in his life, in which he had not made Henri Léon tremble by casually mentioning the Angel of Death; strangely audacious himself, and no doubt thinking Azrael would scorn to stoop and pick up a bug so mean and small as himself.

When Julius Kratz left so suddenly, Léon felt relieved and then subdued. Then Scotland Yard called upon him and he found out that "an anonymous person" had told them he had four or five passports. Immediately after, the favorite son of the head of Bang's Grain Company, for whom he was working, ordered in the accountants and made a thorough examination of the books. Léon was forced to take an airing on the Amsterdam quays and hire an office boy to drop some of the books in the Thames mud by accident. When he returned, he found that Marian, his wife, long neglected and at last enlightened (by Kratz), had taken a lover. Following this, laws were introduced in a certain neutral country in which he kept the bulk of his money, threatening him and others like him with heavy taxes. Then a book which had been written for him by a professional "ghost," and which was the darling of his career, was savagely attacked in the press, as a frost. Within a week of this the minister he had most cultivated in the English cabinet, on whom he had spent the most money, to whom he had written the most artful sentimental letters, and in whose name he held, in his vault, a bundle of photostated checks, died suddenly. Following this, the most admired of his casual mistresses married and wrote him a long moral letter.

Henri Léon took a cure at Schuls-Tarasp. He took his shroud with him in his trunk. When he got back, with his hair half gone and his face drawn and grayish, he wrote a letter to Julius Kratz in Australia, enclosing the money for the return trip for him, his wife, and two children, and told him to cable the name of the boat and the date of sailing. He was firmly convinced that little Kratz was his scapegoat. When Aristide Raccamond, therefore, told him that he had seen little Kratz or his double in the entry of an apartment house in Montmartre, Léon had shivered and also rejoiced. He felt that his luck had turned and he was on his way to a second fortune. And yet again, he shuddered, when he thought what he must go through to have that luck, little Kratz's snickerings, harpings, whinings, his insults, threats, and dark warnings.

He had observed the luck sign in Alphendéry's head with hope and had begun to think that if he took on Alphendéry, he would not need the detestable scapegoat. He therefore, for the first time, wished that Kratz had stolen the money and not sent him a cable and not taken the boat back from Australia. He determined to employ Alphendéry in his own business, but purely as a mascot, and at as low a salary as possible. He saw at the first glance that Alphendéry would not drive any sort of bargain.

Scene Six: Limen of Honesty

JULES said to Alphendéry, "You'd like to be an agitator, but you're too kind to your dependents and so you've got to keep on working for a high salary and it's a good thing. It keeps your head cool."

This conversation worked Alphendéry into a fit of discontent. He was very brilliant, fitful; spent some time walking up and down the corridors, with his hands in his pockets, murmuring yes and no to people or ignoring them. Everyone knew this was a sign of the greatest distemper in him and left him alone. Presently, he went into Raccamond's room and gave him a review of the market and political situation, which Raccamond retailed to all his clients as soon as he went downstairs. But on the way down he went in to see Jules Bertillon and presently Jules came after Alphendéry, irritated because Raccamond had once more implored him to give him some sort of rough balance sheet or interim report to show to clients. "I could get ten times the business," Raccamond said. Jules had given him a flat refusal.

"The man is a donkey," Jules exploded. "If I had gone bankrupt yesterday and also embezzled, I'll guarantee I could get business again today and get people to believe in me. You don't need a balance sheet to get business. If you're as antipathetic to money as that, you won't get business, even with a balance sheet. What does he think a balance sheet proves? Hasn't Kreuger got a blance sheet? He's got a forest full of balance sheets. And what does Wallenberg say? He's got a balance sheet and I don't understand a thing in it."

"Why don't you do it, Jules?" asked Michel. "If people believe in black scratches on paper, give it to them. Make them happy. What do you care?"

"No: it commits me. Anything in black and white commits you, even if it's the truth. The more mysterious the business, the handsomer it seems. People are all bush lawyers: give them a few facts to chew on and they won't be satisfied till they tear you to pieces. Everyone slanders his banker every time he has a toothache. But you give them no balance sheet and what can they do? They can only imagine vast operations that are beyond their imagination. That's ideal. Then your whisper is as good as the next fellow's. Then it is all mystery, secret gold, and high finance. Why, Michel, 'Write nothing down'—I thought that was your maxim! I've taken it over. Many a promising career has been cut short by a conscientious typist and a bookkeeper with his books balanced. Surround me with dullards and loafers, O Lord: spare me the office boys who study bookkeeping and the bookkeepers who study banking and the office managers who read pamphlets on will power. I don't want those who believe in my game. I want those who don't—I pick them out quickly and sack them—and those who can't, like yourself, and those who don't know there is a game. The best people for a man like me are dopes and communists."

"Why?" Alphendéry was restored to good humor, finding Bertillon delightfully ridiculous.

"I'm not joking. Dopes are grateful to you for keeping them because they're dopes and communists because you know they're communists. But the ambitious dull guy that's found you out wants to punish you for the good years he wasted learning a game that didn't exist! Poor dopes! Why, it's as plain as day, from the first day—" he laughed, gay and free. "Look where you stand with me, Michel. You are a sort of limited power of attorney; you have the right, also, to buy and sell stocks, bonds, gold, commodities, transfer them in or out as you wish; you sign checks, you accept accounts, you make decisions. But you're not a director, you haven't got a contract, and I could turn you out tomorrow if I wanted to. And without even the regulation six months' salary, because you're not on the books of the bank! You are responsible to no one and everyone is responsible to you. You could clean me! But you're not ambitious, you don't want a partnership. You hate to sign letters. You don't try to make me divide, you don't steal a ha'penny, you even take me out to lunch once I've taken you out to lunch. It's fantastic. Why is it you're not ambitious and you don't try to steal my job? Because you're a communist. You despise me. You wouldn't let your friends see you standing in my shoes. If you stole money and the police got after you, your Red friends would never talk to you again. And that's what you can't bear! You have ideas outside the business and they're your real life. Don't you see, I'm a hundred thousand times safer with you than with a budding De Wendel? You wouldn't even steal the money to give to the Reds. I call that real drama, Michel, don't you? Most people would be glad to take all I have if they were in your shoes. But I'd trust you with this bank, if I had to run, and I'd fully expect to get it all back at the end of the year. And then you wouldn't ask for a reward —you'd just hang around, rather quiet, with a hurt expression. Oh, Michel, Michel, Michel, my dear boy."

Alphendéry laughed. "You'd trust me with sixty million francs? Do you think any man can resist that amount?"

William had come in and was standing against the door. Jules said cheerfully, "Yes. Am I right or not? Eh, Michel? Would you steal it? Tell me. I'd like to know. You wouldn't. I know you. You couldn't."

Alphendéry said slowly, with some regret, "I'm afraid you're right, Jules."

William laughed shortly. "And no one's making him try it out."

"Would you, Michel?" Jules was curiously persistent.

"I'll make a deal," said Alphendéry: "thirty million I'd be honest, sixty million and I'd be a crook."

"If you gave it back, even the thirty million, you'd be a fool," said Jules roughly.

"He wouldn't, you needn't worry," said William; "and I say that, having as much respect as you for Michel's honesty and principles. A man with thirty million doesn't have to be honest. Honesty is another word for an empty pocket. What is honesty? It's being too poor to buy yourself a ticket across the Channel where they can't catch you. You think you'd get the money back out of Michel because you think he's soft and a neurotic, don't you, Jules? Well, that's where I know him better than you. The hardest man to break is the softest. People know that, by instinct. Everyone suspects Michel of having dark designs round here and of being in the thick of something. Only because he's so nice and sweet. Could you argue Michel into giving back the money? Michel can argue you into a cocked hat. Ah, haven't you got something else to think of?" He stretched his legs, his contented chops set firmly as if he had said all that needed to be said for evermore.

Alphendéry harked back to their own conversation. "I don't like stupid people to work with. They don't know what you're driving at and they get angry and sore."

William said sagely, "The only reason you don't want smart people round you, Jules, is that you don't want to work."

Jules only laughed at this brotherly candor.

Scene Seven: Jean Frère's Garden

ALPHENDÉRY was filled with longing. He wanted to see people who "spoke his language." After work, he waited for the teller, Adam Constant, and strolled with him down to a little bar, near the offices of *l'Humanité* where they usually saw some of the workers. Constant was somber.

"What is there to live for in France today?"

"I thought you lived for your poems, your workmen's classes, and *The Workers' Almanac*."

"It's not enough—for me."

"You're young to feel that."

"Twenty-four!" Adam laughed bitterly. "I don't know enough to write. That's the trouble."

"What do you want to do?"

"Go out to China, maybe," said Adam.

"To join the Red Army?"

"Yes. You see Chiang Kai-shek has started a new campaign against them. The first Congress of Chinese Soviets opens in November."

"With a little alteration of the muscles, you could pass for some brand of Chinese."

Adam Constant laughed cheerfully. "I was born in the East, although I'm pure French. You see," he added, rather shamefacedly, "I feel I cannot teach till I have learned. And I have my way of learning."

"And so you'll go?"

Adam nodded. After he had finished the *apéritif*, he said rather confusedly, "You see, I'm not very happy here. I still have the feeling that all communists ought to be angels and work together singing psalms. Ridiculous, isn't it? It's like asking them all to be virgins before you go in with them: something like that. Oh, I suppose it's some troublesome heritage of my Protestant ancestors. It leaves a mark on you to be born a Protestant in France."

They were both silent, sipping a second small vermouth, when some husky-sweet vocables exploded in Alphendéry's ear. Only two men had that voice, Henri Léon (who was in Belgium) and Jean Frère. Alphendéry spun round, with the ardor of Jean Frère already in his entrails and his throat, his limbs, even before he visualized his face and form. This was how Jean Frère appeared to everyone: first, like the warm and vigorous somnolency that precedes healing sleep, a period of shadow redolent with the most splendid blooms of the imagination; and again, in the same breath, like a seasoned barge captain particularly good in the grain, with a slight sea roll, freshly rank with the cargoes in lighters, one who sings our frank but not lewd compliments to all the girls along the banks.

Although he was forty, with his youthful, vigorous, and engaging aspect, his well-knit walk, he could have been twenty-five or twenty-eight. His variable, unaffected voice had the low-pitched rich, somber, or sentimental tones of an old-fashioned oboe, or became fresh and hopeful as a schoolboy's. He had a dark, broad face, smaller and shorter than Léon's, a dark rosy skin, shining dark eyes and a rather large, but well-formed mouth, with the lower lip pouting often. He had not the compressed mouth of adults, but there was often about his lips that slight damp pout that children have who are under two years old.

One of his great characteristics made him very different from the bald Léon: he had extremely thick long curly coarse brown hair, growing low and irregularly on the broad forehead. When he smiled his eyes went into slits the shape of snowshoes and his mouth elongated like a longbow over his regular white teeth. He was thickset with a short thick neck, a large widespread nose, with a faintly Negroid air. His hands were firm, wide, and brown as a farm laborer's.

The clothes of Jean Frère also merit description more than those of most men because he wore the very same, summer and winter, year in and year out: they were therefore a part of him and painted themselves in any point on the memory as well as he did. A suit in heather-mixture sports wool bought ready-made for the type "broad stub," too large for him, unpressed, so baggy at the knees that chickens could have been hidden there, worn unpolished brogues, an old cotton shirt close round the neck, and an old shoestring tie were in no way concealed by an immense old rough tweed overcoat two sizes too large, in the great patch pockets of which some dozens of newspapers, manuscripts, and periodicals were stuck. Precariously on the decidedly uncombed hair an exceedingly old soft hat hung sideways. When anyone looked too long at this hat, Jean Frère took it off, turned it round on his hands, and with some bitterness spoke of having it "renovated." On occasion he wore a large workman's cap. The dark, curly hair fell down from under the hat in a wild, unchecked style of its own, sometimes over an eye, or ear, sometimes in the middle of the forehead. Nevertheless, Jean Frère always looked engaging.

Two suns rose in his eyes when he saw Constant; he threw an arm round the shoulders of each. "I'm going to take you two boys out to see my garden! A Pernod! It rained yesterday and now it will be good to dig. They threw me out of *The Almanac* and so I'm going out to let my garden nurse my sorrows. Michel, you will come! Adam's coming, aren't you, Adam?" Michel flinched and drooped.

"You are coming tonight to see the garden?" said Jean, seeing this and rightly interpreting it. "Look—my second Pernod. I've been off it for three weeks. I—I saw a doctor. He told me to lay off cigars, cigarettes, and strong liquor. Of course, I have that small wine at home. I didn't feel so good . . . I'm getting old," he said with a faint breathless apology and smile.

75

It was strange to hear it. Alphendéry had to say to himself, in so many words, every time he met Jean, "This boy is over forty: he has been through the War," and then he always had a contraction of the heart. But Jean did not worry over the prospect of growing old: he was sure he would be killed in a street fight one day with the police, and so avoid the long agony.

After his two Pernods, Jean Frère wanted to eat. "To-day I'm as hungry as a bear because I'm not going back to the office this afternoon. Gee!—" he shook his head a long time.

"What was all the trouble about?"

"An article of mine. I was after Levilain for the way he attacked the new playwright Bonni. Why do they have a man like Levilain for dramatic critic? He hasn't got even a hair of the hide of a dramatic critic on his—hoo!—skinny—hoo! I think skinny people are naturally jealous."

"They're hungry," said Alphendéry, with sympathy. Skinny he had never been.

"Yes. Jealous and hungry. Everything—chimney pots, loaves of bread, moneybags, pillars in art museums, big gilt frames round masterpieces, rolls of carpets, horses, women—all bigger than they are. They want to bite the sides of houses. Bite, bite, they never get enough!" He laughed ruefully. "And Bonni, to make matters worse, has a juvenile *embonpoint* and is the handsomest man that ever rose to take a bow, not handsome, downright beautiful and soulful. And Levilain looks like sin, injustice, and poverty in one person." He shook his head. "Let's go. We'll have a bite in the little Spanish dump, shall we? And then we'll go out home. My garden! Judith's out there. She'll be terribly pleased to see you."

Alphendéry made a last faint attempt. "Are you sure there are enough beds?"

"Oh, of course: why, there are lots of beds!"

Alphendéry immediately had a grim vision of what sort of beds those lots of beds must be.

But Adam suddenly said, "I'd really like to go, Jean. I stifle for the country. I've been wanting to see your garden."

"Neither of you has ever seen my garden," said Jean joyfully. "What does it cost to eat here? I generally have a plate of soup in the bar along the street. Let's see. H'm, h'm. Well, we can stand it. I'm hungry. Hey, comrade" (mumbling). He said aside to Alphendéry, "I don't know whether to call him comrade: I suppose he must be at least a socialist? I suppose so. Hey—er—have you got a special daily dish, anything like that?" His face was suffused with laughter, as if he and the waiter had spent their boyhood tumbling about the roads together. When the waiter went away to get the card, Jean said, "He's a nice fellow, isn't he? Eh, don't you think he's a nice fellow? They look all nice here. I like it. I often look in here but I never came here. Do you like it? See, the pretty pots of flowers and things. Shows genuine taste, doesn't it? I generally take onion soup at lunchtime down the street. I like it! They make it wonderfully down the street. Sam Convient he calls himself!" He laughed, full of glee.

"Sam Convient, Sam Convient!" They all laughed, in fact, shook with fun. Alphendéry had not had such a good time for weeks. "Have you see that café opposite the cemetery of Père Lachaise: *Ça roule.*"

"Not bad! H'm—when they come out of the cemetery —a philosopher."

Even Adam Constant cheered up and they all began to look forward to the night in the country.

Everyone who knew Jean Frère had heard about his garden but very few had seen it. Someone had murmured rather darkly to Adam Constant at one time, "Wait till you see it!" Jean Frère regularly reviewed the garden annuals and agricultural handbooks for *The Workers' Almanac* so that he could have the books for himself afterwards. He always found them excellent.

After a dinner they enjoyed intensely and several carafes of wine—for each was under the impression that he was treating the others—they took a bus to St. Germain-des-Prés and after waiting for some time for the tram at the terminus there, started on the long, long ride to Fontenay-aux-Roses.

Ineluctably they reached Jean Frère's home in the country.

A little clean wooden staircase ran up through the ceiling of the front room. "I can sleep up there," said Michel, "certainly, why not?" and he ran upstairs, bumped his head on the ceiling, stared over at them a moment, with an expression of surprise, and with another step brought his head level with the attic floor. He had no words when he saw it. A mattress lay on the floor, with a candlestick and a half-used candle next to it. Tobacco had spilled out of a little pouch, matches lay on the wooden flooring. There were low bookcases, books half opened lying face down: a discarded pajama suit lay near the bed. Clean new rafters came so low to the floor that there was no standing upright: two skylights looked out sideways to the black skyline, where he saw dimly the waving tips of trees. But the attic was very dusty. Nothing had been moved since the last scurried Monday morning. The rumpled army blankets lay as they had been thrown back in that hour of alarms.

"Of course," said Michel loudly and cheerfully, still standing at his post, so that they could not see that his face was not composed, "I can sleep here: it's just the very thing." His eyes were fixed on the candle and matches standing on the naked wood.

But Judith Frère insisted on installing him in the bed-room, in the proper bed. There was a built-in wardrobe of unpainted wood, a box at the bedside with scarf, lamp, and book. Jean, his wife, and a square-built girl installed Alphendéry in the bedroom with the most amiable generosity, asked him if he would like some coffee, and all smiling, went out, shutting the door. But first Judith showed him the bathroom and the various little compromises with recalcitrant plumbing that had to be made, and showed him how to wedge his door to, and where to get coffee if he got up first in the morning. And Jean said, "If you get up early, just go straight out into the garden and get some fresh air." It was a long time since Alphendéry's sleeping had been attended with so much love and good will.

He wedged the door and with a stricken look sat on the bed. He felt very sick, not morally, but physically. The floor was uncarpeted and not even planed. It was covered with sandy loam, brought in on the shoes of enthusiastic gardeners of the previous week. The walls were unpainted, the bed coverings thin and rumpled, and the bed linen was the sort one might expect to find in a boy's shack. Michel found that he could not sit upright. His head swam and even the sweet air did not attract him. At no time in his life, perhaps, had he wished more passionately for a loving, decent, quiet, intelligent wife. "A working girl," he

78

said to himself. He visioned, in a moment, what "a working girl" would make of this room in no time. He lay on the bed in the bedroom so kindly given him and closed his eyes, pale, mortified, ill. And he was ill.

Adam Constant, a silent and rather tenderly smiling witness of the previous events, now poked his sharp nose and chin through the door, which was not very tightly wedged, and looked at Alphendéry lying there with closed eyes. He came in, took off Michael's shoes, hung up his waistcoat and coat, and covered him with a blanket. Then he tiptoed out and shut the door carefully. He had observed what would scarcely have been conceivable to Jean. All the rest of the house was quiet. Adam went and sat for a long time on the veranda, looking across the wide stretch of garden, over the trees, into the hills and the distance. He was thinking of his own fate. He was convinced his life would be a short one. But the thought of where he was going and how he might die, as well as the soft night air, filled his lungs with an almost divine gust. Into his thoughts for the future stole a recollection of a moment just past. He had gone first upon to the veranda, to meet Judith, as if he had some message to give her. But he had none. She came forward and said in a low, secret, urgent voice, "Did you come? I thought you said you could not come so far and get back to work. It does not matter. I am glad. There is room. There are a few others here, but it doesn't matter."

That was what she had said so secretly and rapidly. And he had answered her, in the same quick, hushed voice, "Yes. I know. But I needed the country so much. And I have never seen Jean's garden."

He thought ths incident over for a few minutes and smiled faintly in the dark and nodded to himself. He muttered to himself, "There are moments when the air is rarefied."

Judith, on her pillow, on the mattress beside Jean, in the now dark attic, was thinking, "How bizarre was our conversation! What we said and what we meant—why, the voice was the whisper and the thought was the voice. I am happy."

But now Adam Constant was thinking once more of China, and Judith began to dream that she was telling Jean, her husband, all that had been happening all day.

When Alphendéry woke in the morning he heard sounds all round him and knew it was late. He had tossed and turned, expecting to smell fire at any moment, and had only fallen asleep when the night began to pale. The sheets and pillow slip were also witness to the love the Frères bore their garden. He saw Judith pass the window, dressed in a shirt and trousers and marveled at the girl's becoming *embonpoint*. Adam was rearranging the white little stones that stood round a pond in the middle of the lawn. Someone was moving round cups and saucepans in the kitchen. The hungry animal, Alphendéry, got up, and putting his things on without washing (he secretly blessed the country for this) followed his nose to the kitchen. Mme. Lucide, the girl guest, gave him coffee, cheered him, and sent him out into the garden. He picked his way quickly through the house, which looked as if a wild wind had passed through it that very morning, and out on to the veranda.

A great shout from Jean Frère greeted him. Jean was digging on the other side of the clay path. Alphendéry had the illusion for a moment that he had gone blind. He blinked. Where was the garden? Jean Frère's eyes shone. He smiled his golden infant smile at Michael, let his spade fall into the tussocks, and said, "There, do you like it! Gosh, I feel a different man out here. There is my garden!" He pointed without any self-consciousness to the tangled weeds, grass, shrubs, and lumps round him. Then scrutinizing Michel's expression and hearing Adam laugh, he explained, "My two brothers dug it up a bit last year. Now it needs doing again."

Two or three square yards of ground showed the color of earth and were drastically heaved about. The earth was sandy loam and very stony. Behind and round this a wild half-acre stretched away to a flat marshy spot where water still shone. The half-acre went up and down, a vale of a thousand knolls in miniature. The pasture grass was thick, high and knotted, while along the side of the path were old garden shrubs gone to seed and choked in weeds and rubbish. Round the house, however, Judith had planted soft-leaved herbaceous plants, mostly lifted from the grounds of a deserted burnt house. They spent the morning now, picking out the best plants from the encroaching weeds, and even Michel was able to distinguish a few good-looking plants which he indiscriminately

80

named "lilies." Jean was so extravagantly happy all the morning and Judith and Adam seemed so cheerful that Michel could not help feeling that he had missed one or two good points which might be urged for the country.

Adam finished his job arranging the stones and then began to break up new ground in the wild half-acre. He found some mint and this brought Mme. Lucide out, to hunt for plants for salads, poultices, and infusions. Adam knew these things as well as Mme. Lucide and got on beautifully with her. Alphendéry could not help feeling a little hurt that his friends treacherously possessed all this agricultural learning, away from him.

Jean appeared, yawning, mooched round with them for a bit, and then gave up work and sat on a tuft. He showed no disposition to come and sit by Michel and talk politics. Jean only wore slacks like Adam. His rather long, robust, and youthful torso lent more light and youth to his broad sunny face. Adam, too, looked different, above his naked body: he looked more the frail earthly first man hearing the strains of sun music in one of William Blake's dawn pictures.

The ground broke open, brown, odorous, faintly moist. Adam drove the hoe into the matted strong grass roots which held the earth together. Judith watched them occasionally and smiled and called from the veranda.

"It's heaven here," called Jean blissfully. "How grand you look, Judith, by Jove! You must live in the country: you were made for it. You look ten years younger."

"I don't look fourteen," protested Judith, glancing unconsciously at her developed figure.

"Women always look better in the country," said Adam in quiet, affectionate tones. "They understand Mother Earth." He looked up at Judith and gave her a smile. Her clothes were tight-fitting because she was growing out of them. She was the perfect wife now, wedded to the earth, functioning with it, secretly fertile. The two men felt free and happy. But Judith, though alive with joy, was seen in many reflective poses round the house that morning, absorbed in some idea, perhaps not entirely pleasant. She was feeling the buffets of a battle taking place, not only in her heart, for it had long moved out of that cramping corridor, but all through her body, in her chest, her muscled waist, her broad hips, her thighs, even in her ankles. It seemed that this conflict had started up suddenly

81

the moment Adam Constant had come last night and said, in that quiet voice, "I needed the country so much. I have never seen Jean's garden."

Alphendéry, seeing all this silent activity about him, got up and took a walk up one of the dried mud ruts. They saw him in the distance, patroling by some decayed-looking shrubs and trees, twisting his handkerchief into knots, a habit of his, when alone, and probably talking to himself. For talking was his great amusement. Alphendéry had been walking up and down more than half an hour when he glanced for the first time at the shrubs along the paddock track. He recoiled and his heart flopped stickily around. They were loaded with swarms of small black caterpillars, living for the most part in communal cocoons, very large, white, and flossy through which, though, imprisoned they could still be seen, moving sluggishly. This vermin had attacked a great number of green things in the neighborhood. They ate up the leaves and covered the bare branches with their horrible black masses and their giant white cocoons. They confirmed Alphendéry's worst suspicions about the country. He hurried back towards the house. No one was about. He knew what had happened. They had all gone off to pick "dandelions" (which with "lilies" completed Alphendéry's botanical universe). They had deliberately left him to walk near caterpillars and gone off to collect dandelions; probably at this moment they were indulging in that raw laughter that degraded even the finest men, even communists, in the country. He met Adam and said, "I begin to understand fellow feeling here, because there is nothing between me and the earth."

"Yes, it's the beginning of fellow feeling all round, the birth of a curious feeling, that brotherhood is not just an idea, or a fear of loneliness, or a need for telling other people your ideas; the feeling is, this is a piece of the very same flesh, as one piece of velvet and another from the same robe, but, I mean, the texture, the grain, the folding —no, I haven't said it! When you see a lot of wounded in a hospital, covered with bandages, you are just part of a roll of gauze, like the others: you are gummed together with sticking plaster out of the same box. When you see another person and, though you have never held his hand, you know you are planted in him and he will be obliged to explain you away and stand by you, his life

82

through; and you know he will, just as likely, ask you to die for him, as to lend him a franc, you feel very pleased: you take the sharp knife out of your belt and throw it far away, into the middle of the Luxembourg at night, you scuttle it in the Seine: the sharp knife which we call ambition, or what you will. For, what can you lose, if you die the same day: why shouldn't you go and fight, for example? You have already touched with your finger, lightly but sensibly, the living clay, you have been at the heart of life and seen invisible life. The clay of all living men is on fire, after that, with the same life. But there has to be one, perhaps not your lover, who has to be the door to the house of the living. Do you understand that, Michel?"

"No," said Alphendéry, "I never experienced that. Perhaps I never will."

"It is quite an accident. It happened to me: the odd thing is, I have not much wish to live now."

"Why?"

"I don't know." Adam shook his head and went on cheerfully putting in the little plants from the burnt house. "It was a woman," he added; "an ordinary woman."

For lunch they had aromatic dishes of plants mostly taken from the wild "garden." They praised Mme. Lucide, teased her, and she caught them out on agricultural and country matters. After lunch, Alphendéry went for a short walk and climbed a knoll with Jean Frère. There were tins and rags about: Jean snuffed the air. In the distance, a hill covered with trees stood up.

Scene Eight: J'Accuse

THE visit to Frère's garden strengthened the acquaintance between Adam Constant and Alphendéry. "When is your book of poems coming out, Adam?" asked Alphendéry, coming in from lunch.

"In about two months. They are slow. They have always been slow. They are the fruit of seven years," said Adam.

"It has to be that way, with poets, perhaps?" said Alphendéry.

Adam's ragged black-and-white face, with its traces of fire and desolation, grew smaller and younger as he smiled. "Well, I hope it won't be always so. I put it down to solitude. I always think if we could rub shoulders with a happy people we'd be throwing off poems all day long. I don't believe in conservation. A real poet would be a waster, not a conserver. He'd scatter his fragments everywhere, along the roads, in an automobile, passing a manured paddock, saying Cheerio to a girl in an apron outside a country pub. Oh, I think when the people are free a great harvest will come up and the poet will be the first to eat from it, with the stealing birds and the harvesters at noon. To feel the hard meat, the reluctant milk of the heavy cream grain! What is more beautiful on earth than the land under wheat and barley? It takes all the shades of the sky like a thick pile. All the voices of the air gather in it to sleep and stir and sleep. It gives comfort, it gives wit, it gives peace. So is a land heavy with well-watered and round-ripened people. I wish I could see that age."

"Well, you will: you are young enough," said Alphendéry.

"No," said Adam, "I don't think so. I might. But I don't want to see it when I'm too old. I want to see it now: I want to see a harvest now, even this year! It's silly: the world won't begin to roll faster for my sake."

"You had lunch with Henrietta Achitophelous?"

"Yes. She is beautiful. Full of the hairsprings of her secrets. But she doesn't know them. She never will." He laughed questioningly. "Platitudes and vain health go together: you see it in new colonies, virgins, and humanitarians."

"How do you like working here, Adam?"

"I like it well. Financiers are great mythomaniacs, their explanations and superstitions are those of primitive men: the world is a jungle to them. They perceive acutely that they are at the dawn of economic history. It is fascinating living among the Cro-Magnons. . . ." But his face suddenly became drawn. "I am patient," he said evenly: "what I have in mind is to write a book of poems new even for today. It will not be much but it will be bitten as deep and plain as the words on jail walls. For life as it is is a concentration camp for Man. And in one corner sits the poet, snarling if he is touched, chuckling over a little dirty bag that contains his life's savings. Out of all his experiences, he sedulously lays aside his conclusion, his aphorism, his extract of sentiment, his pellicule of profit. A love affair leaves nothing behind but a pair of glossy eyes; five years of life are reduced to five verses: the day lost in fruitless brain-racking becomes a bitter aphorism at night: that is the profit poet, the superfluity poet, the luxury-tax poet, the bank poet, poor wretch, the limited-edition, gilt-edged, signed-copy poet, the poet who gives himself a gilt-edged invitation to a small select party of kindred souls and one by one sheds them, disappointed, confused, betrayed——"

He tried to go on but there was a racket just behind Alphendéry: Henri Parouart, a humble barnacle of finance, a stone who got into the shoe of every stock-exchange dealer round the town, was figuring on a scrap of paper and explaining something to Abernethy Gairdner, the American short-story writer.

"But I don't understand how they make money, according to this process," Gairdner explained. "How does it pay them?"

"Look," Parouart began as if his life depended upon it. "Say I buy an American stock, say U.S. Steel at 100. The broker sells it out at 100. U.S. Steel goes to 200. Then the broker owes me 100. I buy three shares at 200. On the books my account stands—owed $100 + 3 \times 200 = 700$. My equity is the first 100 now plus a profit of 100 equals 200. I owe the broker 500. If the market drops so that my equity is no longer 700 but 500, that is a drop of twenty-eight per cent, that is, my account stands debited 500 on the books, and nothing paid, then they owe me nothing and I owe them 500. Meanwhile, they have taken no risk. Their profit is 500. Clear?"

"H'm," said Gairdner, "of course."

"Now," said Parouart, "I say, tell the bank to buy one hundred U.S. Steel or Royal Dutch, it doesn't matter. But the bank has already got two hundred U.S. Steel that the client has bought for himself. And now he has his doubts about Steel. He thinks it might go down. So he doesn't want to have my one hundred Steel on his books as well. He sells a hundred U.S. Steel instead of buying

85

it. So he only has a hundred U.S. Steel altogether on his books."

"But why should he do it then, just when you want to buy it? Why can't he sell his own?"

"This is all part of a process, a long process, don't you see?" cried Parouart, hopping from one foot to another like Rumpelstiltskin, in his anxiety to spread an idea that had been eating into his nights. "It didn't start today or yesterday. It is just part of a balancing process."

"Yes, I see. It gives him the cue, that's all. It helps in bookkeeping. Is that your idea?"

"Yes, you can put it that way. Bertillon sends me a chit: 'Bought for your account one hundred shares Hokum Company at, say, '$100 a share.' He debits me ten thousand dollars. The market goes down. Hokum is $75 a share. I've lost twenty-five hundred dollars which I owe him. Theoretically! But he never bought those shares. It just cost him the ink. I pay him the twenty-five hundred dollars which is his clear profit."

"That's simple. But," said the writer carefully, "supposing the U.S. Steel Corporation comes along and says, 'We're paying a dividend of $1 on every share.' Then the broker would have to pay you $100 out of his own pocket. Would it be worth while to take the risk? Because the market doesn't always go down twenty-five per cent, it often goes down only one-fourth of one per cent. It's a big risk. And then, think of the bookkeeping: think of the organization. Think of the risk! It's a good theory, but is it practicable, for any one?"

"Yes," said Parouart testily. "You're assuming that the bank always has to make a profit. But suppose it loses! It pays you out of reserves. How do we know what is the bank's financial position?"

"Now," said the American slowly, "don't you see it's different over there? You see, there's no matching books over there: everything is done right on the floor of the stock exchange and there's an exact record, second by second, of every sale made, so you don't have to stew about this: you can look it all up and see if the transaction was done."

"I buy a hundred shares," cried Parouart, "and every other sucker in the country buys a hundred shares and who is to say which was mine? Who can tell whether my hundred shares were ever bought? A big day on the stock exchange, thousands of shares every minute: who can tell? We French call that balancing, *contre-partie* operations."

"Well," said the American, "you may be right: in fact, I think you're probably right. But you can't prove it. So what are you going to do about it? Why worry? As long as you think he's good for the money."

"Who says he is?" demanded Parouart cunningly.

"Another of those grateful beggars," said Alphendéry, as they moved away, "who use our bank for a café and then spit on the *terrasse*."

"Warn him off," said Adam dryly.

"You can't run a stock-exchange department without these little sacs of venom: they are not men, they're exudations of the money world. They're galls: a shriveled little insect of a man is working away somewhere inside them."

"There are no men in this bank," remarked Constant, "only money galls of one color and another shape: only an infection of monsters with purses at their waists that we wait upon and serve. . . . My dream is, that one day I will get them all down, I will leave them on record. I want to show the waste, the insane freaks of these money men, the cynicism and egotism of their life, the way they gambol amidst plates of gold loaded with fruits and crystal jars of liqueurs, meats pouring out juices, sauces, rare vegetables, fine fancy breads, and know very well what they are doing, brag, in fact, of being more cunning than the others, the poor. I'll show that they are not brilliant, not romantic, not delightful, not intelligent; that they have no other object but their personal success and safety. Although, of course, there are plenty of living intelligences among them, sidetracked talents, even warm breasts, perspicacious men amongst them, but all, all compliant and prostituted. . . .

"I'll show another thing," he said lower, putting his face nearer to the grille, to reach Alphendéry's ear, "that there are some of them, and those nearest the top, who believe absolutely in what the revolutionaries teach, who know that the ones they call 'the agitators' are only speaking plain truths, buttressed by every known fact, by every fact that they alone know and that they keep from the people. . . .

"It follows that the denunciations they utter, and the prosperity tomtoms and the strokings and the dulcet tones, the flames of hell drawn round the Reds and the pale sainthoods lithographed round cabinet ministers are only a gigantic, monstrous masque put on the boards to fool the people. 'Knowledge, money, real love, power,' they say, 'are too good for the people. These things are divine, we must keep them all to ourselves.' And they debase learning, coinage, sex, democratic control to fool the people. . . .

"But they are haunted. They fear the numbers of the people and their inevitable revolt and all they can think of is how to employ agitators for themselves, *provocateurs* to head off the crowd, disappoint the believing, betray the courageous and frighten the right-thinking asses and the liberals: and for the little fellows they have the distractions of war at home and abroad, when things look too lively. I'll write down how they meditate for hours together on how to excite political passions and make civil war simply to affect the stock exchanges and aid their own speculations in currencies. I'll show them for what they are, bestially selfish, true criminals and gangsters, who admire particularly gangsters in their hearts and comment at length, with love, on the exploits of bandits, armament sellers who sell arms against their own country, great exploiters who kill hundreds of men, women and children under them, apaches of commercial life, profiteers of war, rapine, and fratricidal slaughter, and all those who make their fortune by no matter what means. I'll show their 'society' made up of princesses in whose blood runs the blood of ten thousand miserable shopgirls exploited and prostituted for them; of comtesses who are women of the basest lives, drunkards, prostitutes for a title, or for a cocktail, who dispute, blackmail, play the Sarah Bernhardt, yell and faint for a couple of francs wrong in their account; of young women of good family who sell themselves, of women who sleep in any bed; of husband- and lover-pimps; of *provocateurs,* spies, stoolpigeons, homosexuals, drug dreamers, boxers, actors, and cinema actresses swollen with unhoped-for success and lunatic with power; of fine violinists destroyed by a passion for gambling and great singers whose voices tremble with tears, but only because Phillips Glow-Lamp has gone down from 263 to 249 between the first and the second

88

acts—all the rascality of Europe, Ethiopian princes come to Paris to sell their country, princes of Morocco come to taste the pleasures of a capital that, if they were patriots, they would detest, dubious nobles from old Russia hunting bed and board, the debile, crooked, or vulgar aristocracy of England, Spanish grandees and South-American feudal landlords, inavowably ferocious, luxurious, and sensual.

"I'll tell what I know, that the lobbies of great bankers that the poor workman fears to enter, and that he comes into twisting his cap, swarm with gunmen, gangsters escaped from the American police, bankers from beyond borders with their swag about them, mayors from stripped municipalities, kings in exile who had the foresightedness to exile their money ahead of them; of all those who pour out a tale of banishment and poverty and who are rich in millions, and of secret agents preparing *coups d'état* in foreign countries and of their political enemies already preparing to secrete the estates that would be snatched from them; also of the friends of those in power, who send abroad gold for the day they will fall and negotiate the purchase of yachts which lie waiting, polished and under steam, in harbors along all the coast, men who buy doubles to front the public fury and private vengeance and keep unoccupied apartments in frontier towns.

"I will tell how they exchange a daughter for a mistress and a mistress for an automobile, how they spent ten thousand francs on a mistress and grudge their stenographer a ten-franc raise, and how they send their daughters to school with the daughters of leading swindlers and distinguished hetaerae in order that they can learn to wipe their mouth on a serviette without taking off the rouge, their baccalaureate! In other words," he said, flushed and laughing with embarrassment, "the low-lives of high scoeity who go to the Opéra and drink at Fouquet's."

"And read the market quotations in Bertillon's," laughed Alphendéry. "Yes, this is a great experience for you. And I imagine you never expected to see that!"

He pointed at Raccamond, at this moment hurriedly threading his way through the groups in the lobby. They were chatting while awaiting the opening quotations of the American stock exchange, which are relayed by telegraph and come through to Paris every day at three o'clock.

During the morning and just after lunch, the majority of these idlers had put in orders for the purchase and sale of stocks. They were well preened, and fluffed-up, cheerful, expectant, full of interest because the game was about to begin again. This was the third inning. The London market opens at ten and the Paris market at twelve. Stock gambling is thus an all-day occupation and—for those who care to see the New York market close—it saves the expense of evening entertainment, too.

Raccamond saw nearly all his Paris clients there. He was very much ashamed of a guitar which he was carrying, and had to deliver on behalf of a South American client, to old Richard Plowman, former head of the Timor and Arafura Banking Corporation, and now closest and most faithful friend of Jules Bertillon. Plowman was a man of sweet and obliging nature who made himself messenger-boy for all sorts of private commissions of clients and friends. He got pearls restrung in Paris for London ladies, and French rejuvenators for London gentlemen, and Kruschen salts for John Tanker, Sr., the oil millionaire. He read cuttings, smoked the best Havanas, wrote letters, and read best-sellers in the great room on the third floor which stood over Jules's own room.

Raccamond, in his great hurry to rejoin Richard Plowman, and give him the wretched guitar, did not notice a heavy Scotch terrier smelling at the corner of his desk, at the end of a taut leash; and he went sprawling over it, while the guitar flew down the staircase which led to the vaults. There was a flutter and a round of laughter through the bank: heads appeared at the three circles of higher balconies. They concealed their laughter as he rose. Jacques Manray, share clerk, strode over, flushed and manful, to help Aristide. The culprit, charming Mme. Mimi Eloth, mistress of Achitophelous, a great favorite and *grande dame,* genteelly twinkling, was at his side. "Oh, a thousand pardons! He is so *wicked!* MacKenzie is so stupid! MacKenzie, apologize to Mr. Raccamond! He will never stand still. But you're not really hurt! What an idiot! It is because he is a champion! Next time I will get a mongrel. Come along, MacKenzie, I'm furious with you. I will tell Mr. Jules all about you."

With insulting insouciance, she smiled and turned from

90

poor Aristide towards the lift. Etienne, the old porter, closed the gilded door of the lift cage and bore her aloft into glory to the first floor, surrounded by flashing mirrors, serpentine brass, and electric bulbs concealed in cinquecento blooms.

Old Richard Plowman was quite pleased to see the guitar. He took the guitar, laid it on his table, and in the great dark-green room, filled with blue smoke, he softly tweaked the strings. And he began to think of the Timor and Arafura Banking Corporation. But Raccamond was already downstairs, burbling about stocks and dividends to the Comtesse Rosy de Cousse, his latest acquisition, called by some "Dishonest Rosy" and by others "the Milwaukee Pavement Pounder," but who remained a countess and one of the bank's biggest accounts, for all that. The Comtesse was drunk.

"I inshist on sheeing Mr. Jules," she kept saying. Aristide, in a panic, led her upstairs. The Comtesse flopped into Jules's great chair and said, "Jules, Jules, you are a shwindler but I'm not going to let you get away with it."

"What's the matter, Rosy?" Jules asked, with enchantment. "You know I wouldn't swindle you."

"Oh, yesh, you would, oh, yesh, you would. But you can't get away with it. Rosy ish a tough—baby. Here'sh my first monthly shtatement: you owe me 293 francs."

Jules took the account and read it through. He lifted the receiver. "Alphendéry, come here!"

"Shright," said the Comtesse, "make a riot: tell them I'm not a sucker. You're a good boy, Julesy, I like you —I'm going to stick by you. Tell the boy to bring up 293 francs. I want it now. Put it on the desk right now. I don't want any—finagling."

"Alphendéry," said Jules severely, "there's a mistake in the Comtesse's account. We owe her 293 francs. Will you ask the bookkeeper to put it right."

Alphendéry took the account and glanced through it. "Comtesse, you've made a mistake. This account is in order. We don't owe you anything."

The Comtesse fell into a fury. "You're a liar: careless accounting. You plank 293 francs right down here or I walk out of the bank."

"Now, Comtesse, let me explain how you got this idea. We don't owe you 293 francs: as a matter of fact, there is a mistake here and you owe us 301 francs."

"All right, all right, Comtesse, we'll call it square."
Jules lifted his pen and was about to alter the account,
which Alphendéry had put in front of him.

She sprang out of the seat and seized the thick tough
piece of paper. "No, nothing doing." She turned to
Alphendéry. "You heard what he told you: tell your man
to pay me 293 francs."

"But Comtesse," Alphendéry deprecated her pose, her
manner, "Comtesse, if you'll cast your eye through this
again. . . ."

"Tell this man to leave the room: he's insulting me,"
shouted the Comtesse. "He's trying to make me out a liar.
Tell him to get out."

"Get out, Alphendéry," said Jules furiously, for he had
hoped to get the drunken Comtesse out in a minute or
two.

"But Jules," said Alphendéry.

"Get out, Michel!" shouted Jules.

Alphendéry bit his lip and walked out. He went round
to William's room, hesitated, turned back, went round to
the door of the second brother, pushed it open and found
it empty, as usual. When he returned, mortified, silent, past
Jules's room, in a few minutes, he heard the Comtesse
giggling and retailing scandal: "The little Comtesse Lelgarde is a mad Lesbian: she was drunk and making up
to Aline, and Tony looked stony. Then Lelgarde and Aline
went off together to fix up their hair and when they
came back Tony was sitting admiring the bracelets of
Caro de Faniul. Then Jacques Carrière came in—"

Spilled on the desk in front of her were three hundred-
franc notes.

"How can you humiliate me like that?" asked Alphendéry. "I am always loyal to you, Jules."

"Oh, you've got to humor the girls. I get on fine with
them. But if I could get a law passed keeping women
out of banks, I would." Jules shrugged and went on about
other affairs, in a cold, brittle voice. He detested Rosy
but she was one of their set. The telephone rang; Jules
lifted it. "What you say? Tony and Aline? Go on. Rosy
was just telling me. O.K. Ask them over for dinner."
He rang off. "Tony's divorcing Aline because of the little
Comtesse Lelgarde. At least, that's the latest. I don't
believe it."

At this moment, Aristide Raccamond went past with the Baron Koffer's man, saying, "Something is hanging over markets: some great disaster seems to be hanging over our heads. People are ready to question the giants of finance. We have not yet seen the bottom. The history of business may be down, step by step, and crash to crash, from now on. Don't buy yet, Mr. Broeck. Tell the Baron that is our considered opinion. We are constitutional bears."

"There goes Raccamond wearing your tail feathers," said Jules gently, to Alphendéry. "He seems rather smart. Perhaps you and William were not so wrong, after all."

"I think I know men," said Alphendéry. "He takes orders, he's a hard worker."

"I asked him what he thought he should get. He said ten thousand a month."

"Wow! He isn't picayune."

"I gave it to him. What the hell."

"Well—he'll make it or he won't make it."

Scene Nine: Jules Bertillon

A ROBBER by instinct, sharpshooter of commerce by career, nourished by corruption (one of his grandfathers served his time), child of his age, Jules Bertillon was born to profit greatly by it, without understanding it in the least. He had only one interpretation of history and politics, an economic one; he saw in altruism the perspicacious self-interest of cunning ambition, imagined that philanthropists are good jolly souls who can't bear to be afflicted by the sight of the misery of men, but this also, by a side glance of self-interest, and he was persuaded that the great saviors and leaders of men are ambitious men who, coming from a wretched cradle, hope to succeed quicker by demagogy. As for the martyrs and agitators who remained in these roles, they were simply unbalanced men of small talent, brought to lunacy by physical defects (because of the evident morbid sacrifice of self), and by perceiving that they could never succeed with their temperaments in the swarming life of men. He admired the successful and was cheered up by all success of any kind in any sphere of activity, gangsterism, revolution, politics, roguery, or even the arts, because art, he said, was a way to get oneself fed by the rest of mankind without working or with little work, by reason of an inborn capacity. He regarded it as a rather delicate little trick for getting jam, as well as a sort of evidence of the smile of the great god Luck. He admired artists, for example, even more for this favoritism shown them by the stars, than for their works, because he regarded art as a rather old trick. In fact, he was a careerist of a very pure type, and admirably adapted. Besides, this, he was full of a fantastic, ingenuous, and disarming charlatanry, and of a delicate, wise charm which knew how to simper, do a ballet step or leap strongly and agilely like the best of dancers. He was a proud man and always approached the swing-doors of his various offices whistling or singing softly to give warning to his employees, since he found it unworthy of himself to scold people for wasting time. At the same time, it gave him an opportunity to listen at doors in complete tranquillity!

Jules loved to be known genteelly and in his own world and he would have preferred above everything else to illustrate his name by grandiose acts: therefore he moved about splendidly, spent money fabulously, gave tennis, polo, racing, aviation prizes, and he loved to have his name in all sorts of transactions, for instance in gambling and speculation, where it would have been more prudent to hide it. His losses and the attacks made on his name, out of jealousy, came from this love of glory which he could not subdue.

He thus let everyone know that he was a great speculator in exchanges, stocks, and at baccarat; a lucky gambler, he gave out. When dining out with some rich man, or with the representative of one of the great old commercial and banking houses, he told his secrets, bragged, and gave free rein to his fantasy, lying, and vapid cynicism, making a thin, hollow, despicable thing of the extraordinary charm that was the man entire. His judgment was limited, he never troubled to find out the background of other rich men's lives, he pretended to himself that they were all like himself, part of Ali Baba's band, and thus he was able to lose overnight ground which had taken him and his friends months to gain. He knew, really, nothing, and nothing of the world he lived in, worked in, made money in: monstrously ignorant, he succeeded because he had recognized at once that in the financial world there are no dignities which cannot be questioned or facts which are not given out for someone's interest.

He hatched thousands of projects, but was unreflective and disdained the law too easily. He knew that the great financiers disregarded the law completely and bought counsel and judgment, but he did not observe well enough that the big men in his game use the laws to punish and get rid of little men who threaten them. He was brave, full of go and gaiety but he was frail. His will was short-breathed and he was volatile. He detested all detailed work and long study which he called "slavery." He always cried impatiently, "I pay you for that. I don't want to be bothered with details. I've got the ideas, eh? I pay you to carry them out."

Apparently very polished, kind, and egalitarian with his employees, he easily got angry and began to shout, throw himself about, and scold. He was irritated by meticulous discussion of details or theories and if anyone spoke seriously except about money, he shook himself, jumped out of his chair, walked up and down, became arch, began to sing, tap on the desk, make unpleasant comments and ironic asides, or, in a sharp, cunning tone suddenly break in with, "What are the figures for all that?"

He had a vocabulary just adapted to his needs, disliked slang and commonplaces but misunderstood and mispronounced a good many ordinary words and elided more sounds in speaking than anyone else in Paris. He didn't know any foreign languages, except a little English, and then he preferred the American cinema expressions and a little Yiddish which he had picked up and which he used comically to salt his style. The few foreign expressions he knew he prounced with a perfect intonation and accent but without any reference to the spelling.

He wanted to see all his friends succeed and was always thinking up bizarre ideas to help them, as, for example, that Abernethy Gairdner the short-story writer, who confessed that he could only turn out one short story a month, should copy all the stories out of *The Arabian Nights,* change the names of persons and places, and send them in, seriatim. He was devoted to *The Arabian Nights* and took the entire unabridged edition with him wherever he went. He wanted to put Hervé Beurnon, the sculptor, in touch with all the deputies in the Chamber so that he could do all the war monuments for their various districts; tried to get eligible bachelors for the young women of fortune; even (because Alphendéry was a communist sympathizer) thought up a few schemes by which the Communist Party could make money.

When provoked, he thought immediately of direct action, gunmen, scandalous arrest, anonymous denunciation to the police, political influence, whispering campaigns, injury; but he was mercurial and often lethargic and fought with one hand tied.

He was wholly superstitious and defied science. "What's wrong with superstition?" he asked saltily. "Get me together all the bankers of the world and I'll ask them one question, Where are you now? Another, Are you one hundred per cent solvent; are you fifty per cent solvent? And this with their mathematicians, statisticians, crooked parliamentarians, with their journalists, go-betweens, and Moon Hopkins calculating machines, with the game built for them, the wheel fixed by them and the cashier paid by them and with gunmen at the door to flatten anyone who gets away with anything! And still, where are they? I'd rather gamble on the color of Alphendéry's hat: it's just as satisfactory and a big reduction in overhead." He said that again and again.

But whether laborious or lazy, Jules's brain was never idle a moment. When not making money, when actually losing it, he would be occupied in gaily and convincingly whispering about legends of his wealth, designating countries, banks, and vaults where his assets were safely planted "against currency depreciation," hinting at his luck in speculation, filling the ears of his own believers, like Cornelis Brouwer and Pedro de Silva-Vizcaïno, with the stories of his winnings at Deauville; so that at a certain time when his pyramiding in various markets had cost the bank nearly two million francs and they were running on the day-to-day deposits and were obliged to send out margin calls strictly, conservative clients of the bank were saying that "Jules Bertillon could not be worth more today than about fifty to seventy-five million francs, because he must have had losses lately." Almost all other bankers and speculators, like Méline, Léon, and Claude Brothers behaved humbly and alternated between gloom and bragging, when they were short of money, but Bertillon must have always believed in his genius: he never lost elegance or his translated, cool demeanor. In this way, he laid the foundation stones of a house of legend in which he lived safely for many years. Years after, when he had not a cent, people were to believe that he had pots of gold buried in Spain, Hungary, Switzerland, Scotland, and Weiss-nichtswo, and he was always too gracious to undeceive them. He was, in fact, a man gifted from birth and specially destined for his business.

This was the man, this hummingbird of rumor, fancy, and adventures, to whom Alphendéry, Richard Plowman, Adam Constant, Aristide Raccamond, and many other diverse natures attached themselves. They hoped as much from his speculative daring as from his unexampled generosity. To very few he revealed his true self—that he was daring because he was ready to fly at a moment's notice and regarded his imposing, wealthy bank as a joke, and that he was generous because he was handing out "gambler's gold, fairy money," as he always said. "I give it because I can make it: why should I hoard it? I can always make it."

Scene Ten: Why the Police Pursued Pedrillo

WHEN Raccamond entered under the stone acanthus leaves at 39 Rue Pillet-Will in the morning, cheerful, he had an unpleasant surprise and felt his heart hop gluily in its cavity. Sitting in one of the armchairs by the desk he had taken to himself, with the habitual nasty glance which betrays him, sat a plain-clothes detective. Aristide retreated to the doorstep and looked along the pavement. There were two more plain-clothes men there.

"Now, I'm finished," thought Aristide, "that damn Claude Brothers business. Haunted all my days by that bankruptcy! Now, I'll have to go to Lallant. How can I escape? But wait! They saw me come in. Perhaps they don't know me when they see me!"

He nerved himself and walked sullenly towards the stairs. He felt as if he were made of badly jointed planks.

The detective saw him go past with a steely glance but made no move. Aristide went into the board room, through it, with lowered head, and up the private stairs which led to Jules Bertillon's door. Behind Bertillon's private room was a second door, concealed by a bookcase, where one could gain access to a passage leading to the general staircase in the next building. This arrangement arose naturally when two old buildings had been thrown together and reconstructed and Bertillon had seized upon it for its convenience.

"Better," thought Raccamond, "throw myself on the mercy of Bertillon, a good sort, than fall into the arms of the dicks." He had to go through Bertillon's room to get to the private passage. It took him a minute, though, to make up his mind to knock.

"Who's there?"

"Raccamond!"

"Oh, come in, Raccamond," said Jules Bertillon amiably.

Jules was sitting behind his great desk, pale, merry. His eldest brother, William, pale, plump, was grinning from ear to ear, his leg slung over an armchair. Hidden from view, except for one impeccable cuff, someone sat in one of the great chairs, his back to the door. Comte Jean de Guipatin, of bobsleigh build, tall, handsome, and softly nubby, like a puppy Great Dane, was smoking a cigarette and speaking Eton English to the person in the armchair. A beautiful white Dandie Dinmont bitch lay on the floor, its sweet eyes trained on the cuff in the armchair. Aristide, in his distress, realized that the cuff was also a good sort—Pedro ("Pedrillo") de Silva-Vizcaíno, dashing young Chilean, a madcap, baroque character, charming, very rich. Aristide's heart which had been overworking now failed him.

"Come in, Raccamond," said Jules, "come in: good news for you. Comtesse Rosy wants to see you about C.P.R. *Hé*, did you notice a couple of detectives hanging round downstairs? Is there one still sitting in the armchair?"

"Yes."

"Cheer up," said Jules briefly, "they're after Mr. Silva-Vizcaíno. Listen, Pedro, you'd better go. Raccamond, no one will suspect you. Go down and get a taxi to wait outside the scent shop on the corner. Tell him he's to drive immediately to the Gare St. Lazare when the gentleman comes down. Mr. Silva-Vizcaïno will come out from next door, and get into the taxi with you. Drive him to the Gare St. Lazare, get out, go through the station, and get another taxi in the Rue d'Amsterdam and tell the chauffeur to drive to the Gare du Nord. Get Mr. Silva-Vizcaïno a ticket to Brussels, first class, put him on the train and wait till the train goes. I've just telephoned to Constant to bring me up some money."

The teller came respectfully through the door and laid ten thousand francs on the table. Jules gave it to Pedro, who was sitting in a state of quaintly self-engrossed trepidation, seeming not to hear these remarks.

"Now, Pedrillo," coaxed Jules, "leave Tiqui to me. We'll let her parade up and down the balcony a bit after you've gone, for a decoy, until Raccamond telephones to us from the station that your train has left. Then I'll send her home and Claire-Josèphe can take care of her."

"No, I want to take Tiqui," said Pedro, "I must take Tiqui: I'm very lonely at night otherwise."

"Go on, Pedro: you're never lonely at night. Everyone in the world knows Tiqui: she'll give you away in a second. Tiqui! Tiqui! You see, she knows me."

"She can only eat the sausages I grill her at night," complained Vizcaïno.

"For God's sake! I've got two butlers, I don't know how many cooks and maids at home. They can grill sausages as well," said Jules. "Here, Raccamond: here's the money for the ticket. Now go out and get a taxi in the Rue Lafayette, will you?"

Raccamond, mystified and a little grudging, turned to go.

"Mr. Bertillon, my friend the grain merchant is coming in this morning."

"You mean Léon? Good, I'll see him. Lively boy. Now go along and come back as soon as you can."

Raccamond did not at all relish these messenger-boy trips: he believed one only got on by being a stickler for status. However, he went. Jules recalled him at the door.

"Hey, Raccamond, don't look so miserable. You see, if the Comte de Guipatin goes out, they'll know he's getting up some getaway for Mr. Vizcaïno. We're all his friends and we would all, severally, be followed. But you're not his friend and you're safe. Don't be afraid, Raccamond. Mr.

99

Vizcaïno just tried to abduct a lady, that's all. A little Latin fun."

Raccamond was faintly relieved. Vizcaïno laughed reminiscently.

"A wonderful girl, marvelous black eyes! What a shame! She wanted to come!" The others all shouted with laughter. Smiling softly to himself, the discreet shadow of a smile, Aristide went downstairs and into the street. The detective in the armchair, his eyes full of strictures, watched him go, but never suspected him.

In the taxi, Pedro said, "What's all the fuss about? The Paris police don't understand the Latin temperament at all. They're cold northerners. I was walking in the Parc Monceau. I see a beautiful girl walking along the path and I suddenly put my arms round her so that she will not run away and kiss her. She does not cry out, so I think, 'It is all right,' and I kiss her again. She looks at me with such soft eyes! Women are so beautiful. The air smells sweet, the evening is coming up, and I try to get her to lie down on the lawn. Just then the policeman comes up and tries to arrest me! 'Don't dare touch me,' I say, 'it is an insult to this beautiful young girl. She does not object. Besides, I am the son of Don Alvarez-Garcia de Silva-Vizcaïno.' He said, 'A lot I care.' So I run away. The beautiful young girl begins to cry. I begin to cry myself when I see her being taken home by the policeman. I run and hide in my flat. This morning I hear my concierge talking to someone. I look out and there is a policeman. So I go down and run out past them before they have time to look at me. I come to the bank: I say to Jules, 'Jules, I am being persecuted.' The Paris police are absurd. They all are recruited at Dunkirk probably." He looked round anxiously. "Oh, they bundled me out without Tiqui. Didn't you take Tiqui? What is your name, man?"

"Raccamond," said Aristide somberly.

"Raccamond, will you please look after Tiqui? Will you see they don't neglect her? Will you see, personally? Tell Richard Plowman to take my guitar to London and get a new string put in it. He must take the guitar, pack it very carefully in tissue paper and corrugated cardboard and carry it himself and take it to them in Piccadilly, so that they can get the right string. It is the best guitar

100

I ever had. Will you promise to do that for me, Rac-camond? Oh, what will I do in Brussels? It's cruel to send me there alone."

Once he evinced a desire to get out of the taxicab and go back to Tiqui. Then he proposed that he should wait in a café while Raccamond went back and got Tiqui and the guitar. It did not worry him at all that he had no change of clothes, no hat, and no purse. He had plenty of friends in Brussels and they would all keep him, lend him money. He had wads of money in banks everywhere, but he never troubled to draw it out, unless one of his friends took him along. He was very miserable. However, when they got to the Brussels train he saw a dark young girl, with a swan's droop of the neck and harem eyes, walking up and down between stern mother and fat father and he became very happy that he was going to Brussels and thanked Raccamond profusely for bringing him along. Aristide went and sat in the Pullman with him for a while listening to a complaint. Pedro had to walk three miles every day to a certain shop that alone in Paris kept the kind of sausages Pedro and Tiqui liked. He did all his own shopping and had never let a woman shop for him. "Women have no taste of any kind: God gives them divine beauty and no human qualities. They don't need anything else." He had to walk because it was uneco-nomical to take a taxi. He spent a few minutes explaining to Raccamond how much each sausage would cost him if, for example, he took a taxi to the shop and back again.

Pedro as he walked and talked had a flitting, sweet dark smile, the quick dusky gestures, the bright obser-vant eyes, nods, and flirts of a tropical bird. No woman passed him without getting a quick, unconsciously affec-tionate glance from him. He was of medium size, very dark, slender, and delicately formed, looked about twenty-eight and was ten years older. His movements were unstudied, quick, grave and graceful as those of any animal which follows its own wild will all its life. He was full of airy wildness.

Raccamond thought him congenitally mad, but since he was an aristocrat, he treated him with great respect and even found his weaknesses something very proper in a gentleman. Besides, Raccamond had another reason for handling him with silk gloves. Pedro's brother, Xesús, had killed a waiter in a café in Rio, for an accident which

101

Xesús had taken as an insult (and the waiter's family had killed Xesús). Manuel, another brother, had lost an ear, in an inopportune meeting with an outraged husband, in Madrid. Pedro told bloodcurdling tales of the cruelty of his eldest brother, Antonio, and of his father, Don Alvarez, on their estates in Chile. Their peons were no better than slaves and these savage dons burnt their lives up like straw. It was well known that Pedro carried a fine knife with a curved blade somewhere in his pale-blue monogrammed silk shirt.

Raccamond lifted his hat and wiped his hair, when the Brussels express pulled out. Pedro waved to him genially from the window.

Scene Eleven: Why Léon Is in Business

WHEN Aristide telephoned to say that the train had steamed out with Pedro on it, Jules answered him, "Good work, Aristide, hurry back. Your friend's here. Léon, Léon, of course."

Aristide tumbled into a taxi and sat there in a heap of anxiety. If that elder brother, William, sulky and irresponsible, or the man of flash and intrigue, Alphendéry, got hold of him, Léon, who disliked intermediaries, might begin to think that Aristide was of no importance in the bank. And Léon only gave money to money. He didn't waste anything on commissions and "manipulation taxes." When Aristide got upstairs the door stood wide open in Bertillon's room and there was no one about. In the distance he heard Léon shouting. He strode round the corridors. Yes, in Alphendéry's room Henri Léon's voice was shouting, with a rising inflection, with frequent weightings, "You see, you see?"—his characteristic cascade of hesitations, gropings, then suddenly the clear apposite expression, sweet as a bell and the harmonious rush of words. The padded swing-door was locked on the inside.

Crestfallen, Aristide walked up and down the corridor trying to listen, but finding it impossible, as there were other persons in the room putting in their words and their words were inaudible. He presently went round to his own room, some five hundred yards away round two sides of a long U corridor. What a morning! And he had come in, feeling sure to pass in some good stock exchange orders, in the wake of the balanced French budget and its promised surplus.

In Claude and Company, at least, everything had been conducted in a respectable way: clerks in their places, the chiefs respected and staying in their offices, not scurrying round as if the bank were a maypole, not cracking jokes with everyone about the essence of banking, for example: there were no *police des moeurs*—well, the Parquet came at the end, but so it does always: no rushing crazy Chileans to the train. Aristide looked out the window into the Rue Pillet-Will and across into the corner of the Rothschild garden. It took some minutes for even this inspiring sight to cheer him up.

With Henri Léon, ten years ago, life had been a circus. Living with Léon was like living with a waterspout in a carafe; uncork it to get a drop of water and you were drowned in half the ocean. But Aristide was ten years younger then, just demobilized, sure of civilian success, a lieutenant with the military medal, full of bloom. Then he had married, not for love, but on a basis of mutual respect, Marianne Marcuzo, sister of Dr. Marcuzo of the Czorvocky Bank and through Paul Méline had got to know Henri Léon. He was thinner then, no press of blood. What a misery it was to make an honest crust! Léon let him down, of course. When the parent firm sent from Mannheim to examine the books, Aristide had no time to think. Léon was in Amsterdam. They came down on Aristide as office manager and company secretary. How to explain the state of affairs? Aristide Raccamond had seen at one shocking glance that Léon had removed whole sheets of the journal. Paul Méline's operations and his own remained. Méline knew how to force Léon to take him into partnership in his own firm later on, but Aristide had believed that Léon was really bankrupt. On that occasion Marianne's instincts had been right and his own wrong.

"I swore I'd pick my men carefully after that," thought Raccamond. "With what result? Claude and Company? Still, bad as it was, that was a workout. This time, with that back of me, I can't fail. This is my great chance to create something of my own. . . . But I must keep Léon. He's still my friend. He wouldn't let me beg my bread. He has genius and he's four times a millionaire in guilders."

The street was very busy at this moment.

"We Jews—" continued Henri Léon, "I'm really in business now. This is not like when I was with Strindl's and I was an iguana sucking out the eggs they laid, day and night. They kept me then. No! I'm working now. I'm not swindling."

"Go on," said Jules Bertillon, "you know damned well you made a couple of million dollars for them in New York and you built up the whole of their business in Mannheim."

"It's this," cried Léon, disregarding this, with a jerk of the chin, "it's a wonderful scheme for the wheat business. Alphendéry just said a good thing. Take over the food-buying for Britain! Yes. It's this. The wheat-buying for Britain should be taken over, not nationalized, not a government department, the buying left free and over what periods the buyers like. You see, do you get it? A millers' buying committee with government approval. It looks like muddling through: the English public will worship it. It looks like a lukewarm amateurish stab at nationalization: the Labour Party will think it's enough of a compromise even for them."

Alphendéry's clear, schoolboy-debater voice was on the air. "I analyze it like this, Jules. *A*. The scheme is excellent because it takes the buying out of individual hands and exploitation; but, *B*., it is elastic, and *C*., it is under government control, but it is not uniform. It avoids the fault of uniformity which the English hate. It can be manipulated, it can conform to machinery that already exists. *D*. Its machinery is not stiff. *E*. It binds the individual talent and the taxpayer to the service of the government, in competition with the grain merchants who are now struggling against each other for everybody's disadvantage. *F*. It is controlled by the taxpayer. *G*. It leaves the way open for nationalization (this is a sop for the Red element). *H*.—oh, you can think up a hundred and one reasons. Some form of public control of food-buying is so undeniably good that everything is in its favor. And then the Great War left the form in people's minds. It is all nutty and unscientific, but it will appeal to the English, just for that reason. It's cunning makes the English so indirect and so, indirectly, so stupid on plain matters. It's their position in Europe. The Americans are Anglo-Saxons but they haven't that."

"They're cruder," said Jules.

"No, no," said Léon. "Get on with the *schematism*, Alphéry—Alphendéry!"

"Well, here's Léon's schematism, as he says, that I worked out for him." He was one wave of laughter. "I only met him two days ago, but we get on like a house on fire."

"Yes, yes," said Léon. "Now, for argument's sake, for argument's sake—a company, the manager owns fifty per cent—"

"Well, here it is," broke in Alphendéry with sobriety. "Léon wants to quit business, but he's afraid to give it up altogether. He'd go to seed, or the girls. And he still wants to make money. Also, he's having difficulty with the combines. He goes to the British government—the French government would do equally, but they're smarter—and he says, Why should your all-essential flour be bought at the hazard of the markets? Let the millers be protected by a buying committee, a government affair, composed of government servants, which will buy from time to time according to the markets and hand out the stuff to the millers as they need it. There's no question of storing it and of the expense of silos. There's no fear of the government committee's being held up by the combines or by foreign sellers. Because you have on the committee an experienced merchant who has his ear to the ground and immense foreign experience and who is above suspicion—a man who belongs neither to combine or private business. Léon will only elaborate the plan, which has a strong socialist dressing, if they give him this position. Then, while they're setting up the board, he liquidates his businesses abroad and he lives on his capital, which he has taken to England, and on the government salary. Léon, expert to the Government Buyers' Council! Good. The millers know their requirements and the Council fixes a price at which they will buy. Léon buys for them. He alone knows the buying price.

"What am I doing meanwhile? Meanwhile, you, say, Jules and Méline and I form a wheat company. I have an office in Paris, say in this bank and am the manager of the wheat company. I take over Léon's buyer, who will be out of a job because Léon is going out of business. We'll call it the Société Financière de l'Exploitation des Blés. I own fifty per cent of the shares; Léon owns the rest privately. Actually Léon, knowing the price the committee is prepared to pay, will buy the wheat cheaper in advance and will sell it to me. I sell it to the buying committee at one farthing less than the price they are seeking. 'How do you get it so cheap in a high market?' they ask me. 'I'm a good buyer,' I say. I only do this in ten per cent of the cases, though. So it looks good. Only ten per cent of the cases. They cannot suspect. Or how Léon made a business out of retirement. The beauty of it is that the English public benefits and the bread is cheaper —and, wow, are they going to need it! And we're going good. A profit out of altruism!"

Léon irritatedly stared at Jules with half-closed eyes. Alphendéry rippled all over with laughter again. Jules tipped his chair back on to the back legs and balanced with a dreamy expression, while he repeated the theme of his life music.

"You and I both believe in altruism, Henri, because altruism is selfishness out with a pair of field glasses and imagination."

The sinewy, slower timbre of William's voice followed. Aristide called him "the stupid brother." William gave a faint hiccough of laughter. "Imagination! Hey, you don't want imagination, you want a credit balance! Let the other chaps, on the outside, imagine. You can't draw checks on imagination. Or if you do you soon find yourself studying geology. Imagination is making little ones into big ones and its end is the reverse."

Aristide arrived behind the door at this moment, knocked, and was let in. Léon was walking up and down hastily, with his hands in his pockets, his short-tailed coat flirted over his hips. Jules was leaning back in his chair, slim hands in pockets, looking like a star of the Russian Ballet, playing bank manager in some goblin set. He was as thin as spun sugar, with spun-sugar skin, large clear eyes, set wide in a narrow skull, a long, voluntary nose with prominent nodule and irregular fleshy tip, the gambler's nose.

Léon was withdrawing an impatient thunderous glance

from William. Jules looked at him with patronizing, smiling irritability. William, unperturbed, threw his last dart wide of the mark, "Imagination is the first stop on the road to the nuthatch."

"Ah, shut up, William, we're trying to do some business."

William went on in the same level voice, "Business? Poker, you mean. Stay out of commodities, Jules; it isn't your game. Only doctors and opera singers punt on commodities."

"Even a Mussolini, in his half-blind miserable way," Alphendéry erupted, "a confused, nineteenth-century tyrant, sees that there has to be a semblance of socialist organization to keep the people contented."

Léon slapped his hand down hard on the table. "Yes, you've got something there! Perhaps I see that because I've dealt in grain futures all my life and I see in Russia great grain futures, and a giant, unhindered consumption. People free to eat as much bread as they want: when they get to that day," he said solemnly, facing them, "we can make fortunes on the bull side. And the bull side is the side it's natural to take." He nodded at them, then shouted, "She'll pay her debts. Her paper's good. I'll take it!" His golden humming began, forerunner of a clap of laughter: "I'll take it!" The vortex of laughter. He took a turn up and down, his head thrown back. Then he came back to them, elfishly, "At the same time, if we can get someone else to take it instead, it will be one move ahead. That idea of yours, Bertillon, German paper was a pick-me-up. I immediately thought, Now, what's everyone bearing? Not only German paper, but Russian paper. Surely we can work out something for the two. Now, let's set our minds to work. With your brains and mine, Bertillon—we'll work out something. With this boy here," he put his hand on Alphendéry's shoulder, "we'll make money." The clap of laughter. "I'm only in business (I was telling Alphendéry) to keep myself from getting into trouble with women, but while I'm in, I'll lead them a dance. When I find a girl that can give me real romance, I'll get out." His merriment dried up and he began to look for his hat and stick.

"I'll go with you, Léon," said Alphendéry hastily. They went out, leaving Aristide weaving gloom uncertainly in a corner of the room. At the door Léon turned round,

"It's good! Luther—wit's end: get 'em purged—Russian paper. Russian gold. Ha ha! The Reds get Russian gold. We get Russian paper."

"With our great wits, ha ha," Alphendéry seethed behind him, "with our great wits—with our great wits—and the Reds in jail get gold. They say. They, they—ha ha—with our great wits. H'm."

"They seem to hit if off," said Jules genially to Raccamond. "Léon put fifty thousand francs in the bank and insisted on its being put down to Alphendéry's account. Michel doesn't want it. Anyhow, we'll make it up to you, Raccamond."

Aristide went out meekly. He had lost Léon but gained the bank.

Scene Twelve: The Revolution

"Do you know what I did with the two per cent commission you gave me on Léon's account?" asked Michel Alphendéry, the next morning.

"Went to Auld Reekie and got a suit?" suggested Jules. "No."

"You should have then," cried Jules, with one of his unexplained tempers.

"I bought myself fifty German communist books for my library."

"Hey, I thought you knew enough already," said Jules, just as suddenly restored to good temper. "I'm surprised at you, Michel, being such a mooch for the Reds. Stalin found out that the workers don't know what to do with money. That's all right. It isn't the Stalins that bother me. They know their game. But a man like you, Michel! A guy makes the money he can. Anyone who doesn't is a bit crazy. If there were the difference of a hair in your brain, Michel, you'd be batty: you'd be standing on soapboxes. That's a tomfool idea to want to try to make everyone rich by confiscating from the smart guys who knew how to get out of the tangle early! Why, if all the rich men in the world divided up their money amongst themselves, there wouldn't be enough to go round! It all proves there are constitutional dreamers—they're sick; you're sick, Michel.

"I say, don't you realize if you gave everyone the same amount of money today, in a fortnight, somebody, some Citroën, some Oustric, some De Wendel would have got half of it back! You're too intelligent, Michel, not to see that! Why, types like me only think in money. Why, take me. When I take off my pants I'm thinking up a gag, when I make water, what the deuce! I'm asking myself why I didn't take a crack at the cheap crook who tried to do me in yesterday. I dream all night and I get up at three o'clock to write down all I've dreamed because there are some good schemes among them. When I wake up, I think of a check with a big figure, if I'm good-tempered, and of petty cash if I'm out of my humor: big or little, but I only think of money. How can the workers beat a man like me? They think of all sorts of things, what the boss will say if they're late, how much he's going to cheat them at the end of the week, whether they're too tired to go to the Trade Union meeting, whether they ought to knock the block off the blackleg fellow, whether they can get their wife an abortion. And all the time I'm thinking of money, money, money."

His face clouded. He looked irritably at Michel. "Michel, it's not the Stalins or the Lenins or the Hitlers that worry me. They know the game. They'll play along with us once they get to the top. It's the fanatics that follow them. They're nitwits and when they get themselves warm with thinking up a few slogans, they think the rest of mankind has got central heating that way. It's dangerous to give guns to a lunatic. And these nitwits do that. Then they can't control them. Because they're dreamers. Now these agitators are smart men, but it's cheaper to lock them up than to employ them, because they're unbalanced."

William was in a good temper. "What do they get up a constitution for, that's what beats me? They ought to just put in one rule: I have the right to jail anyone I don't like. It all comes down to that."

"With a constitution you fool all the people all the time," said Jules. "Listen, Lenin and Stalin know just as well as you and me, that all the rebelling in the world wouldn't get men to work for monkeys. Why? Because we've got guns and we've got organization. And we've

109

got something to fight for. Well, compared with us, the workers are monkeys. They talk, they speak our language, but it doesn't mean the same thing. They live, but as far as we're concerned, they only live from the time they punch the time clock in the morning till the time they punch it in the evening. In between those times, they're only moving pictures of men to us. Why should we worry about what they think? But you're a puzzle to me, Michel. You take them seriously."

"Listen," said William, kindly argumentative, to Alphendéry, "you know, Michel, it's a racket, too: it must be. You don't tell me that if a chap in Arcos is offered a commission in London or Paris, he won't pocket it behind their backs. Why shouldn't he? What harm is he doing them? It's human nature. Why are they running it otherwise? Why do they fight that way to hold their jobs? What's the incentive? Of course, it's some sort of a racket. Only the Russians are smart Orientals. It's not so easy to catch them at it. And they know how to advertise. They've got the Genghis Khan technique. You know, glory. And if they did catch them at it, would they advertise it?" he asked with intense cunning. "Do you mean to say they'd do all that for just the same wage as a carpenter? Did you see the latest, eh? Piecework is paid for! Ah, they're wonderful advertisers. Better than the Boches. They know the trick better. Isn't their line the same as this Adolf Hitler's, or Mussolini's? What's the difference? Isn't it a dictatorship too? Only they add 'of the proletariat'! I don't want to live under a dictatorship. I want to make money without being fenced round. If it isn't a dictatorship, why don't you see Stalin getting down occasionally and saying to some carpenter, 'Comrade, you take the job'? You're just a sentimentalist on Russia. You don't know human nature. You judge everyone by yourself. I bet if you offered Stalin a million bucks to go and live in the Engadine he'd do it, wouldn't he? Blum has money, hasn't he?" William shrugged and lighted a cigarette, having used up all his usual arguments in one breath.

"What about Lenin?" said Alphendéry, peacefully.

"Oh, he was just a fanatic; he wanted power. Power's —well, you can't talk about that. It's like loving a woman. You can't predict what a man will do once he wants that."

"What about William Z. Foster, the American leader: he was offered a position in industry and he refused it."

"Oh, well, a man like that's just a madman. Most men aren't like that. What's the matter with him; has he got anything wrong?"

"Naturally, like most men, he's not perfect: and in fact, he is a great sufferer. . . ."

"You see! What did I say? You see!"

"Listen," said Jules sharply, "don't go telling Léon you're a Red. These Central Europeans are funny."

"I like your knowledge of human nature," said Alphendéry with asperity. "Léon's a follower of Mac-Donald in England, Blum in France, Louis de Brouckère in Belgium, Fritz Adler in Austria—Fritz Napthali—all the great beans of the Second International. That's your conservative for you! You boys are comic in your ignorance."

Jules, at ease in his chair, spouted one of his ideas. "The world's getting down to a Woolworth level. Woolworth saw that what we've got now is a pauper economy. Dress them up in colored shirts, give them grass slippers or wooden sabots, get them to work for nothing, and sing at it, too. What does it matter what they sing? The 'Internationale,' or 'Horst-Wessel,' or 'Hallelujah' down in the swamps of the U.S.A. That's the only way profit is going to be made from now on. The history of everything is down from now on. The only investment now is in a crash. I saw that in 1929. Everyone else was wringing their hands. I was short a few stocks in the American market. I made a bit of petty cash: but the next day I figured it all out to myself. I said to myself: I won't weep. I won't cry. I've got the hang of this—first the Russians started to smash the works and then the Americans had to. That's it! The history of the world is down!"

"You're a superb natural economist, Jules," said Alphendéry, "although you don't realize it."

"Don't I!" cried Jules.

"You have hit the nail on the head. There are going to be three quick sweeps between the last war and the next. The expropriation of the Russian bourgeoisie on October 30, 1917, the expropriation of the American bourgeoisie via the stock market, October 29, 1929, the smashing of the German bourgeoisie, if a type like Hitler ever gets in. But a Hitler will never get in in Germany: they've got to do it some other way."

"Yes. You see what it is?" went on Jules. "We've got to get ready to make money in a declining economy! Now, I think Léon sees that, too."

Scene Thirteen: The Bank

THE telephone rang. Jules said, "All right. Send him up!" To Alphendéry, "It's Jacques: Jacques Carrière. He's trying to sell the brewery his uncle left him at Burton-upon-Trent—in England, isn't it? He's very worried about the payments. He's afraid the pound won't hold. His payments won't be completed till 1933 or 1934, according to the plan they're working out. I told him the pound wouldn't go off. There's India, isn't there? While the maharajahs rally round, the Bank of England can still clear petty cash without inflating it. . . . I wouldn't mind being on the inside of a game like that, would you?"

Alphendéry said, "Germany probably won't be through till next year, neither will England. I wouldn't bet on it. Perhaps Britain will see Wilhelm II or his son back on the throne before she permits the rise of a pseudosocialist regime in Germany. No one knows what her game is. She doesn't herself: that's why it's so deep. If you ask me, I don't think there's fifty per cent of the gold they allege there is in the vaults of the Bank of England. If a private company can cook its accounts, how much easier it is for the Bank of England, synonymous with security and the credit of the State, in England and throughout the world. Who dares question it? Who looks over its accounts? In London, lots of people think the Old Lady finds her purse half empty, but she can be kept going on prestige and on the new financial business of the world, the balance of debit-paper. That's her new game. So far, she's done nothing to discourage Hitler and as Hitler, representing fascism, represents nothing but an empty treasury—for it's a last expedient, everyone hates it, including the reigning bourgeoisie—that's a bad indication for Britain. Still, it's a long bet. In Germany, too, the masters, powers, thrones, dominions, are watching carefully, watching their step. . . .

Go slow with Jacques Carrière. . . . You may laugh at me, Jules, for being romantic but I wouldn't do business with a man of his private habits. In doing business, you should bank on the one sound spot a man has: Carrière has none."

Jules waved his hand, wading in his own speculations. "All right, Michel, thanks. I'll see you after? See if Carrière is coming up, will you?"

Alphendéry looked over the balcony and saw a sprinkling of clients and visitors downstairs. Carrière, a dumpy red-haired young man, showily imperative, wearing upper-class mannerisms like a toga, was talking to Aristide Raccamond earnestly. The room, a sounding-chamber at this point, carried up the tones of their voices. Mme. Marianne Raccamond stood waiting for Aristide to take her to lunch and had got into conversation with Fred Pharion, the new cinema star, a loose-limbed, weak-jawed young man with curly brown hair and large brown eyes, handsome and gay in general appearance and towards this woman gentle and receptive.

A brilliant middle-aged society harridan in black talked sympathetically with Ignace Dvorjine, a cashier, a Russian exile, formerly proprietor of a small estate in Kharkov (he said) and violently anti-Soviet. Although his personality, made up of airs, a frozen reticence, and bitter pride, was unpleasant to many of the employees and some of the clients, he drew White Russians to the bank and was a very able accountant. His son, Arthur Dvorjine, an *émigré* at the age of five, had been reared in a poor apartment in Maisons-Lafitte with children of French socialists and was himself "a Red" as he said, although actually a Left democrat.

Next to Arthur, who was idle and reading, stood Jacques Husson, a Quaker, a small, thickset, rheumatoid womanish man of forty-five, who loved to chat with the women clients, told them his backaches, asked their advice and always had a long line of "fans" at his window. Beside him was André Ribot, the pale, tubercular, young teller and beside him Henri Martin, a man of superior intelligence and experience who "knew what the game was about" in their cant phrase, who had been a high officer in the secret service during the war and had sent more than a dozen men to the firing squad in the time of his service. He considered himself superior to the commis-

113

sion men and even to William, the elder brother but junior member of the firm. He had got out of hand when he first entered the bank, and had begun to do peculiar business for himself on its books, but Jules had brought him up short and since then he had had a clean record. After a long period of sniffing and superiority he had decided to work in with Alphendéry, regarding him as the leading, the only mature intelligence in the bank. He looked up and smiled at Alphendéry now. He was acutely conscious of every person in the bank at the moment.

In the end booth stood darkly twinkling, like a sweet ferret, a debilitated, polished youth of dark complexion, François Vallat, the clients' secretary. He attended to the little personal wants of the customers without charge by the bank. He ran messages for them, got them opera seats, seats at the boxing matches, took their passports and identity cards to the *préfecture,* knew people in embassies who sent the long-winded identification papers through like lightning, gave advice about triptyques (automobile permits for the Continent), knew addresses, recommended restaurants, and in general gave the advice that a private secretary of Mr. Bertillon would give to Mr. Bertillon's friends. He was well dressed, sensitive, servile, and had perfect taste.

It had often been noticed by Jules Bertillon that the more generous he was, the more his moneyed clients expected for nothing. Nevertheless, he loved the idea that his bank was sleek and that its servants were as perfect as those in a rich mansion of high respectability. And, in fact, the bank quietly breathed out his own air of teeming wealth. Along the other side of the square downstairs hall were tellers' cubicles, also. In the first of these, seated on a high chair, her rosy beauty always framed in that green air, strange behind gilt bars, like a madonna materialized in prison, sat the customers' mail girl, Mlle. Armelle Paëz. She watched and meditated, smiled and got invitations to dinner from all the high-stepping male clients. Adam Constant was in the next booth. And after him, was occasionally to be seen Jacques Manray, the stock-exchange manager.

At that moment, a tall, dark young woman in a coat of the silkiest sable entered against the light. Marianne at first only saw the lilting step and the sheen of the fur. In the light she recognized the brilliant hairdressing, the irregular, dark, merry features of Claire-Josèphe, wife of Jules Bertillon, an heiress in her own right, of Spanish and French parentage. She surged forward.

"Good day, Madame." She said this in a loud voice, but Claire-Josèphe, young and nervous, involuntarily withdrawing herself from the crowd of furious stock gamblers and rich plungers in her husband's bank, went quickly through them all, with a faint smile to Jacques Carrière, a childhood playmate. Marianne flushed faintly and looked out to the curb where the Hispano-Suiza stood with Jean, the chauffeur. Claire-Josèphe chattered girlishly with the fascinating inanity she had been taught at finishing school, with Jacques Husson, and then whisked back through the throng to her car. Marianne smiled once more and said with emphasis, *"Bon jour,* Madame!" this time finding herself face to face with Claire-Josèphe, but too loudly so that Claire-Josèphe certainly got the impression she was talking to someone over her own shouder. She looked at her blankly, with a little surprise, dipped to get out of her orbit, and swept on. Marianne went to the writing table where Aristide usually sat now and pretended to be writing out a check. The mail girl, Armelle Paëz, sat, watched, added up details of personalities in her imagination.

Marianne looked up and saw Jacques Carrière bowling along behind the screen on the balcony. Fred Pharion was smiling oafishly to himself—at what? The Bertillon door shut. Aristide, at a loose end for the moment, came looking for her through the crowd. He detected a pallor in her ruddy complexion.

"What's the matter, Marianne?" There was fear in his tone, as well as solicitude.

"Nothing, nothing." She recovered herself, grinned. "I don't suppose she recognized me: we just met for a moment—Mme. Bertillon. She just treated me rather shabbily—made me look pushing."

Scene Fourteen: The Collection

WHY, thought Raccamond, were the employees allowed to be so free and easy? Mlle. Annette Gentil, the head stock bookkeeper, a smart girl, but one whose chatter was like a tap left running all day, was standing by one of the pillars upstairs looking down on the population of the ground floor. He began to push his way through the crowd towards the stairs to ask her to look up yesterday's purchases and sales for the Princesse Delisle-Delbe, a very important account he had rescued from the paralytic clutches of Jacquot de Machuca, a spineless aristocrat, and which he was now setting to rights.

He found that Mlle. Gentil was talking to a tall red-gold youth with a small head and large feet. Aristide patiently trod water for a few minutes, then, with a certain glance that Mlle. Gentil caught, swung the door of his room. "Old" Berthellot waddled past them in his white waistcoat and stock, going to lunch although it was only eleven-thirty. Aristide was buttonholed by the senile millionaire, John Tanker, Sr., who asked with an insistent, tinny cackle. "Is that you, Whittaker? I've been waiting a long time for you—such a long time. I can't see Bertillon at all. What do you hear about Austria sevens, 1943? I'll sell them. What time is it? Whittaker? No, what's your name, man? I didn't get down till ten-thirty this morning. It was so hot. I have no time for business at all. How are you, um, Raccamond, that's it: pardon me. . . . Shall I sell? That's what I came to ask. I need your advice. No good holding a portfolio full of dead paper. You see, I've got to think about getting my money affairs into final shape. I'm an old man. You'll be very good if you find out for me about the following: Austria sevens, '43, Belgian sixes, '55, Australian fives, '57, Cuba five-and-a-halves, '53, and I want you to sell Argentine sixes, '59, worthless, practically. . . . Can I leave that to you, Raccamond? I'll call back."

Raccamond was obliged to go and get the bonds book

and ask Alphendéry's advice, meanwhile Mlle. Gentil poured talk endlessly into the invisible ears of the corridor. Half an hour later, when Tanker was still sitting there, sucking the head of his cane, and politely rambling on, there was a knock and Armand Brossier, the confidential clerk, his pale curls for once falling over a lively pale expression, said, "Pardon me, sir, I'll come back—"

"No, no: what is it?"

The man, who looked like an ailing adolescent, came in smiling with a little chamois leather bag in his hand, one of the bags, in fact, in which he stored away gold.

"Mr. Raccamond, Mlle. Gentil, the bookkeeper, you know, is going to be married, as you have heard perhaps. We're taking up a collection to buy a wedding present from the whole staff. As she attends particularly to clients' stock accounts, we thought you might like to make one. Mlle. Gentil has been with us twelve years, in fact, long before we were thought of," he said with deference.

"Does Mr. Bertillon know this?"

"Yes: he gave me permission."

The old man's hand went towards his pocket, clung there for a moment, then he took it away, shaking his head. "No, no: I wish the young lady luck. I don't know her. Gentil? I don't know her."

"We're taking the hat round in an unofficial way, but if you like I'll give you a receipt to be in order," said Brossier, innocently, to Raccamond.

Raccamond flushed. "No, the whole idea is most unpleasant to me. I can't contribute. If Mr. Bertillon is making—some provision, it ought to be considered that that is, as it were, from the bank: individual members of the staff should not be asked—it resembles gouging, a holdup. It's unnecessary. It means that every time anyone leaves or gets married, we have this mendicancy. I have a sense of my—what is expected: one expects to give presents to friends, not strangers. No, Brossier. I'm not going to apologize. I dislike the idea. It's foolish." The flush had receded, but two brownish spots still lay under the white lower lids. Brossier looked furious. Raccamond went on, impatiently. "The idea of seeming to supplicate a contribution from clients is—so repugnant. A client must never be asked to give money for nothing. They are not in the bank for that. This isn't a benefit society. And—who knows Mlle. Gentil?"

"She has looked after their accounts for twelve years," said Brossier, angry.

"We must never give them the impression that we expect anything of them. The client is—almost a sacred person in business."

Tanker had hatched a scheme—they did not come so frequently now—for an oil-royalties bonus public company and wanted to see if shares could be sold in England. He had a letter in his pocket from his solicitors at the moment and from Paul Méline, chief motor, though not chief name in the Kirkonhill Trust. He thought the business could not be done in England but there were ways of marketing such an idea. "I must get into business again," he said to himself, without paying any attention to Raccamond, though he nodded politely. "Whoever uses his reserves and deludes himself into thinking that it's income, hangs, smokes, and eats his own bacon while smacking his lips and saying, 'What a fine pig!' Yes. I must go to work." He got up and walked to the door. At the door he realized he had left Raccamond in the middle of a sentence. He said, "Pardon me: I must go to London. Here there is little information on some matters. Yes, my banker. Good day."

Raccamond had wasted half an hour on the old man and the only result was a humiliation. "Old imbecile, why does he cling to me?" The door opened: Tanker's brown hat came through the crack. "Thanks very much, Raccamond," he said. "You went to a lot of trouble." The door shut. "I get no commission out of thanks," said Raccamond aloud. At that moment, he saw Brossier with his wash-leather bag going into the large directors' room which was given over to the machinations of Cambo and Dreyer and the divagations of Plowman, all unprofitable livestock.

Daniel Cambo whose personal fortune ran to half a million guilders, while those of his mother and sister added another two million in Swiss francs, said in his teasing, goodman voice, "No, sir, I never give presents. Only when they pay me a profit. Ha, ha. Eh."

The genteel voice of is partner, old Dreyer, polished with a silk handkerchief and dusted off like his silver and waxed furniture, murmured, "I always do a mitzvah, Daniel. What's the proper thing, young man? What do the others give? Is ten francs enough? Tell her *Mahzeltof*, young sir. Do you know what that is?"

"Good luck," rattled Cambo, "good luck for me, too." Then his warm voice shaded darker. "Here, this is all the loose change I've got, not much, but it'll help, won't it? I say, young fellow, how do you like these? Just samples. If you don't let on to the others (it wouldn't be nice), if you want anything for yourself, or a young lady, you can have them cost price. I got them to show the Galeries Lafayette. Nice dressing cases, mirrors, everything; if you want to—say, for that wedding present— I'll give you a couple of samples at—very cheap, just to throw them away. I've finished with them. Don't you think that would be nice, Ephraïm?"

"Perhaps, yes, perhaps," said Dreyer, softly.

"Come round after you've finished collecting," said Cambo heartily: "There, *Mahzeltof*, eh? A young lady, you know, a young lady likes those things. It was lucky I had them here."

A directors' room, thought Raccamond angrily, and no directors. Madness to give that beautiful room, with banqueting-hall windows, free to anyone. He himself could have done with it. It would give him a great air of dignity. The Princesse, for example, would just as soon come and see him as Bertillon, in a room like that. But two hucksters had to be there, and a cracked old man who cut out pictures from *The Tatler*.

Well, let it rest, though Raccamond: let the prologue go on. Time will show who are the actors with the best parts.

The snow-headed doorkeeper ambled upstairs with a slip of paper fluttering in his hand. Raccamond advanced, "What is it, Etienne?"

The old man combined respect with independence. "Mr. Bertillon," he said firmly.

"Let me see."

"Mr. Bertillon," the old man said, rising to his full height. Raccamond was reduced to following him towards Bertillon's room and hearing Bertillon read the names,

"Franz Rosenkrantz and Franz Guildenstern . . . sounds like a comedy couple."

"No one walks in for your good," scolded William (behind the scenes). "Tell them you're not in."

"What are they like, Etienne?"

"They seem two very nice men, sir."

Jules's shout of laughter: "You go and take a peek at them, Alphendéry."

Raccamond skipped into William's room, skipped out in a minute. Alphendéry had gone back and was saying, "Typical Berlin high-pressure businessmen: probably something to do with German defaulted bonds, one of those export businesses, no good to us. You might see them. They probably have a little money. Maybe they're shifting their business: there's a lot of that going on."

"Sharks?"

"I don't think so: they're taking stock of the bank with efficient but pleased expressions, expensively dressed in the hard Berlin style. But all that proves nothing. Germans always get the externals right."

"Don't want them," laughed Jules. "I'm against them. Etienne, tell them I'm not in."

Etienne saluted and reverentially crept out. Alphendéry followed him and came back fizzling with laughter. They've gone off in a pest of a disappointment: they'll come back. Etienne said, 'Mr. Bertillon says to say he is not in.' You're not much of a crook: you picked a cherub for doorkeeper."

They telephoned for Etienne and with the old white-headed workingman standing in the center of the three, Jules said, "Now, Etienne, a lot of people come into the bank who don't bring business. They come in to get my money. They want me to lend them money, chiefly. And usually they don't want to pay anything for it. They have good suits on but they're charity cases just the same. The better the suits they have on, the more they expect to get for nothing. That's a rule of business. . . . Now, Etienne, I've had a lot of experience and I can tell the ones who want money, by looking at them from the balcony. If they know I am here, they will try to buttonhole me. They will wait four, five, six hours. So I have to say I am not here. It is a lie, Etienne, but I must say it, otherwise I cannot run a bank: I'll have to open a waiting room and give up business. And you must lie for me Etienne. You must say I am not here. Because then they wait and they annoy me. Do you understand, Etienne? I know it's not the truth and I'm sorry for it, but you must lie for me, Etienne. Just say, Mr. Bertillon is not there and leave it at that. . . . Now, you see, those two fellows are coming back and they are annoyed, into the bargain, because they know I am here."

Etienne blushed at the idea that he had done wrong. "I am sorry, Mr. Jules." He loved Jules, whom he regarded as a young boy, a miraculous child. "Did I do any harm?"

"Not a bit of it."

His soft old eyes nodded to Jules. He went out.

"Isn't he respectable!" cried Alphendéry. "I'd deposit money with a bank that had Etienne, myself."

"Sure," said Jules. "You must have decent people round you: a bank is a confidence trick. If you put up the right signs, the wizards of finance themselves will come in and ask you to take their money. Show a man a marble column or Etienne's soft brown eyes and he goes frantic and sheds money for you: the way he sheds blood for you if you wave a flag. A man is just a cheese, he sweats and sweats until he shrinks and cracks and goes moldy. He lives on milk, you put him in a round pot and he goes round, or a square pot and he goes square: you collect the milk he sheds and then you eat what's left! . . . Did you ever think, Michel, that even a pirate or a gangster puts his money in a bank? They stick up one bank and put the money in another. They wouldn't be a bank clerk to save their lives, but they give their money to one. That's the mystery . . . Lord, what nitwits!" His whole peal of bells rang out. "All suckers—even me."

"I could stand being such a sucker," said Alphendéry mournfully.

Jules was emphatic (he seemed to regret his last words "even me"). "Pah, you'll never have a cent, Alphendéry: if you wouldn't sell your mother's womb for tripe, you won't make money."

"Yes, I am too softhearted," regretted Alphendéry.

Henri Léon sat impatiently in one of the deep leather chairs, studied with violent attention the richest of the clients, returned to his present preoccupation (viz., would he get a Belgian decoration for a letter he had written to the Food Ministry, or would he have to pay real money for it?), put a sudden rude question to the clerkish boys, probing the intelligence of the lackadaisical customers' men, came back restlessly with the sudden rushes and calms of leashed energy, sitting down again, taking out his notebook, and writing in it, "Send Rhys, Rotterdam, book on Bismarck," looked at his telephone book, watched the

121

beautiful mail girl through her bars, tried to estimate the cost of the sculpture on wood and stone on the doors and windows, saltily scrutinized the tellers, wondering what was the matter with such insects that they didn't skip with the cash, and fixed with the start of the stallion any beautiful luxurious women who walked about, passing over the workers who slid through the crowd, with a walleye.

Henri Léon pretended not to see Armand Brossier with his wash-leather bag and obvious intent, and when he came near, he simulated profound sleep or meditation. Then he opened his eyes surprisingly wide, swept the room to see if he was observed, noted Jacques Carrière and made a dash for him, to ask him if he knew anything about currencies, in view of his relations in ministries and banks. There, as luck would have it, Armand Brossier pursued him, not for him, but for Carrière, who for years had held quantities of stocks and bonds in accounts at the bank, especially in its branches abroad. Mlle. Gentil was the girl who held the secrets of all his income-tax evasions as well as those of the other great clients, "Old" Berthellot preferring to remain officially ignorant of all that. Armand Brossier, therefore, with that simple blackmail that is no more than justice, expected Carrière to give something relatively handsome to his bag for the wedding present.

Léon extracted a ten-franc bill and gave it, smiling delightfully to the young man with a friendly "Good luck. Where's the young lady? I must see her and wish her good luck myself. A wedding," he said tremendously, "always gives me pleasure: I like to dance at weddings." He insisted on going upstairs to see the bride-to-be.

The pale Brossier, silently absorbed, lit the staircase like a ten-candle-power bulb on his way down. At the bottom he collided amidships of a tall, powerful man, black-haired and bronzed, with a broad, produced forehead and chin, snugly dressed in black with white hair-stripe, in the richest South American dude fashion, who was consulting a platinum and ebony wrist watch while taking the stairs in a bound. A diamond pin stuck in his black-and-red satin tie; he had a frilled ivory silk shirt and red socks. There was a fine gold chain round his ankle. This was Zucchero Zurbaran, an Argentine millionaire of great strength, a sweet, savage, uncivilized nature, who owned herds of steers no wilder than himself, to whom his servants, peons, and boundary riders were men-dogs to be lashed, to be trampled down and shot at will. Of him the usual legend was told that, having invited a young worker who sang and played well into his home, he showed him the pictures of some of his ancestors and for no reason suddenly drew his revolver and cried, as a wild lark, "Shall I shoot you or not?" The worker, a young Aesop, saved by instinct, humiliated himself, pretended great fright. The wild bull, appeased, put the young man out of doors, then, saying "Think yourself lucky," he shot instead at a dog running round the garden, laughed, "But there's more pleasure in shooting a man: it takes longer to breed him."

Zucchero had been purposely trained to uncontrollable passions, gambling, whoring, killing, and South American bullfighting: his race trained to waste and terror. He belonged to the highest South American, Paris, and London society, appeared at all the grand crushes, fancy-dress balls, charity banquets, broke duchesses' hearts with his magnificent male beauty, was a friend of the then Prince of Wales, a great lover of country life. He was a member of the thoroughbred club to which Jules belonged and greatly admired the audacity and disorganization of Jules. He felt at home in Paris, the capital of the Latin race, though keeping to the resorts in which his idiosyncrasies were passed over with the tolerance accorded to vast landed wealth. He only went with the wilder young men, shunned contact with the reasonable portion of the French population, alien and cold to him. At home he buzzed and boomed, belonged to the small species of giant meat flies in bronze mail, who eat off the sweating brown backs of the natives: his power over human life gave him a grand fling and satisfied animal beauty. In intimate society with Jules and other chic young fellows, he was sweet as a robust broad-faced child, full of unprovoked horseplay as a Rhodes scholar, wild and senseless, but cunningly ferocious in his rages.

The bag flew out of Brossier's hand and scattered over the stairs. Zurbaran laughed, but at the money, not at the clerk. For him the clerk no more existed than the statement of account he sometimes received, never read, and always lost, in the wind, the sweeping, the waste-paper basket, something that the world sent his way but entirely out of his cosmogony. The black-diamond eyes

123

of Prince Hal of the desert shot out a flash; he scooped a handful up, laughed, put it in his pocket. The clerk said, "Please, Mr. Zurbaran" respectfully. But Zucchero had filled some of those bags of gold coins in the safe and never withdrew them. "That is for a wedding present."

"Is that so?" Zurbaran plunged his hand back in his pocket. "I don't know how much—take it all, there!" He flung half his pocketful of change back on the stairs, turned and bounded upstairs.

Raccamond stopped him on his florid way: it seemed a bloated goat-cheese merchant trying to sell his goods to an Oriental despot whose diamonds and daggers jingled.

Zurbaran was oblivious of people but when spoken to showed that he was aware humanity existed. In this he differed from a certain section of rich South Americans who, sent to English snob schools, combine the cruelty of their own system with the cold-mannered sadism of England. Zurbaran stopped and tried to collect his wits, sketched a smile, a rock-salt cleft in the dark sand of his face, his eyes, like splendid and voracious eagles, perched in niches in the cliff-forehead, above which dark plumes grew.

Urbain Voulou, great, golden flabby-dabby, lounged out of the customers' room and benignly looked over his chicken yard. Aristide gave him a man-eating glance which he did not see and would never have appreciated. Urbain Voulou still got twelve thousand francs monthly, the salary he drew in the days of the American bull market, when fortunes were won and doubled in their board room weekly. Jules was too kind and believed too much in his grand coup to take it out on the customers' men yet. But Urbain's customers had mostly died out, been pauperized, been sold out through lack of margin, been repatriated by their families or their embassies, taken to sponging, art. Urbain was humble now, whereas in the old days he had been lordly; his commissions had shrunk to hundred-franc notes. He did not know what had happened. When the market went up a couple of points for a couple of days, Urbain began again to unfold, roll in and out with sea-gait, laugh at pessimists, recommend everyone to buy—the corner had been turned; but when the market went down, he relapsed at once into his credulous, helpless humility, was nice to everyone, contradicted no one, said in a humble deep voice, "Things are bad, Comtesse: you oughtn't to invest."

He had a few clients who stuck to him for his goodness and his belief in the benevolence of nature and his ability to drink everyone to a standstill in any of the smart, sporting bars. His little wife was saving bank notes meanwhile against a rainy day.

Aristide saw him take out a fifty-franc note and give it to Armand Brossier for his collection. "Calf's head," he said between his teeth.

Hastily threading his way through the crowd, with a loose cloak, a bowler hat, and a black leather bag came Maître Rodolphe, a lawyer he had met on another day in his career of vicissitudes. He came about the Wades' case: the Wades were Urbain's clients in the palmy days. They were now involved in a suit and countersuit with the bank. The bank was suing Wade for seven hundred thousand francs odd, an overdraft run up progressively, because Wade was rich and smiling, lived on the Côte d'Azur, ran a yacht, dressed his wife at Schiaparelli. He now refused to pay entirely. But Lucienne Wade, the wife, once a cabaret singer, had one hundred thousand francs in an account in the bank. She demanded payment of it and when Jules Bertillon refused to pay, she brought suit against him. They found (what they should have inquired about in the first place) that Lucienne, having had a heap of money when Wade married her, had had her marriage contract drawn up with a separate dower agreement.

Jules, too lazy, too sanguine, had always refused to get a release on Lucienne's account: they were so unbusinesslike, they would never cheat him. Wade's letters showed how unbusinesslike he was in fact—friendly scraps written on paper from here, there, and everywhere:

Madrid: "DEAR JULES, I have your letter asking me for the money. I am up a tree just now but you may be sure I'm thinking of you. *Yours ever,* DÉDÉ."

Pontresina: "DEAR OLD PAL, You have been frightfully decent to me. I'm expecting my ship to come in any day and then I'll drop you a note. *Yours ever,* D. W."

Aix-les-Bains: "DEAR JULES, One of these days I may need your friendship, so you may be sure I won't let you down. *Yours ever,* D."

And another from the Negresco, Nice: "DEAR JULES, I'm flat broke, if you want the lowdown on your old comrade Dédé. You couldn't send five hundred francs, could you? You can take it from me, our accounts are always in my mind. *Yours ever,* ANDRÉ."

A specimen from the Westminster, Le Touquet: "DEAR JULES, Making money hand over fist: you come along and break the bank in your usual style. Lucienne is dying to see you. *Yours ever.* (P.S. Lucienne wants about five thousand francs. I haven't bothered to stick in a check. Be a good fellow.)"

When Jules's lawyer saw these documents, he sighed and said to Alphendéry (who conducted Jules's legal business), "Never, never in my life have I seen an institution run like this: it's lunatic! What's the object? It would be so easy—well, what can one do? I'll do my best: I'll write him a letter but I'm afraid you won't get it. Wade is a thief, with intent, of course, but there is only the letter of the law."

Maître Rodolphe, a man with the precision, cynicism, and sophistication of Talleyrand, came up.

"The whole suit is based on fraud and iniquity," Alphendéry in forensic ardor declared, standing in Bertillon's room, legs apart, under the great luster. "How can a man of your professional stature, Maître Rodolphe, urge it? How can you argue such a cause?"

Maître Rodolphe was a bullet, five feet, one inch, one hundred and eighty pounds, head a bullet, body a bullet, fat, so neatly dressed that he seemed one piece, talking in machine-gun style.

"It is an unjust claim," said Maître Rodolphe. "I can admit it here since if you repeat it, I can deny it. I am a blackmailer, my clients are blackmailers. But there's nothing you can do about it. You can't plant shame in my heart. No, sirs, one and all. To allow the overdraft without a guarantee, without a release, was an act of folly. . . . People like my clients live on folly. I live on them. There you have it in a nutshell. . . . If equity and human, natural reason were allowed there would be no law, there would be no lawyers. Anybody who tries that is hounded out of our profession, I assure you! Oh, I assure you it has been tried! President Magnaud, for example. . . . I know, Mr. Alphendéry, that Mr. Wade borrowed nearly three-quarters of a million francs from Mr. Bertillon. I grant he borrowed it without the intention of ever paying back a centime. I submit that my clients are persons who live on just such technicalities. I have seen them at work. But I assure you they usually have to work harder for it!" He was not laughing: he was putting his views seriously.

"I know, Mr. Alphendéry, as you have eloquently said, that Mr. Bertillon is a good man, a kind man, an amiable character, who advanced this money, as he has advanced a great deal of money, out of the rash geniality of his nature. But, sirs, Mr. Bertillon behaved like a philanthropist, not like a banker, like an impressionable humanitarian, not like a man of sense, like a friend, sirs, not like a man of business. In other words, he opened a bank and behaved like a benevolent asylum. And I've seen benevolent asylums which—oh, la, la!—in short, he behaved like a fool. There is no other word for it. What do you expect me to do? No, you cannot beat me! Believe me now and save a lot of time and money. Your time, Mr. Bertillon, ought to be devoted to banking, not to lawsuits. Your name appears too often, I tell you as a friend, in law lists. Stick to banking or take up litigation as a profession. I tell you this, which is naturally against my interests, because, sir, I think you will be perpetually robbed otherwise. Not that it is my business. The contrary. But here and now, I will beat you. You will lose the one hundred thousand and another sum besides."

"What Maître Rodolphe says is only sense," said Alphendéry. "Then, let us buy you off, Maître Rodolphe. What will make it worth your while? Twenty-five thousand francs? That is what you are going to get from the Wades, I calculate. And then—are they quick payers? We'll make you out a check now. It will pay you to take thirty thousand—in notes, say, rather—and save your time and trouble. What do you say to that?"

"I would rather do it," Rodolphe smiled. "It is a petty case, although it is quite watertight; you haven't a chance, sirs, against me. I am inexpugnable, my dear sirs. But what does it benefit us in the long run? I will then have to work on some other case equally nauseous from the purely human viewpoint. The Wades will divine that I have been bought and will go off to another lawyer. They don't lack here. They'll insult me, injure my reputation—for I work mostly among such persons, they are no worse, rather better, than the average. And think of me, Mr. Alphendéry. The Wades (I can admit it, you know it) are immensely rich—villas, yachts, Madame in the great Rallyes, at the Bal des Petits Lits Blancs, et cetera. She's a pretty whore, he an elegant ruffian; they drink, dance, sleep with, are seen in, the world. . . . And you will keep on buying off lawyers at thirty thousand? No, it is cheaper to let me run the affair on for a few months. I'll sting you as hard as I can, for it's my business, but it won't be so expensive! Permit a remark as a friend: I am astonished at the way you do business. Protect yourselves, my dear sirs. Thank you very much, gentlemen. Good day!"

"You see," said William: "Jules the lawsuit king scores another triumph. Another wash-leather bag gone to glory. Let's set up our own legal department."

"Not so bad," cried Jules, "and put Alphendéry in charge; it'll be cheaper."

"Nothing doing," protested Alphendéry. "A legal department and you'd sue the whole day long, on the principle that once you have a letterhead you must have a company incorporated to fit it. I know you, Jules. You take on a legal department and I resign."

Small in the sight and dreams of godlike men, Armand Brossier crawled about below with his wash-leather bag. Abernethy Gairdner smiled like a bloodless angel, declared in his pure voice whose echoes could be heard rolling round the building, "Of course, with pleasure. Good luck to the young lady."

There went the Hallers. Brossier smiled at the little trotting pair, one blonde and one dark, amiable, fat, pleasant. They had been to the bank for thirteen years to partake of its bourse services and now considered it only right to contribute something. Raccamond loved the Hallers in his unsmiling tormented soul for their solidity and their confidence in him and the way they valued his opinions which they had gratis, except for the dinners they gave Marianne and him, once a month, ever since he entered the bank.

A delicate figure blacked itself into the great bank doorway, advanced with small weaving feet, a figure of negligent youthful elegance in light gray, with (as he came under the central glassed roof) a dark blue shirt, yellow tie, a figure that advanced rapidly but as in a dream, pushing its way through unresisting crowds. It stopped to speak anxiously to Armand Brossier and then,

the light falling on the profile, Aristide remembered who
it was, Pedro de Silva-Vizcaíno, forbidden entry to
France, but once more in his old haunts. Aristide was
startled and looked at the front door expecting to see the
little capes of police agents already silhouetted there. A
man wanted by the police, three times denied entry to
France, walks freely into his favorite bank in Paris at
midday, with all the world to see! But wealth, like
genius, is to madness near akin. Pedro came upstairs by
the secret stair, reached Bertillon's room at a point down
the corridor, walked into Jules's office.

Aristide heard the first words. "I went to your house
first, Jules, and Tiqui is not there. Where is she?" Where
was Tiqui? Where, the guitar? Aristide erased himself
from the frescoes of the upper story. God knows, the
servant and bootlick of rich people should be more careful and cherish canaries, sick grandmothers, family ghosts,
tombstones, pot plants, collections of butterflies and rem-
edies for gonorrhea, if he is to succeed, but Aristide, in
his troubles, had forgotten it entirely. He felt most depressed, saw himself a failure. "But," said Aristide to
himself, "if you know men's foibles, they have the foible
of thinking you know them too well and they are weak
with you."

Where was Tiqui? "The man on the way up," said
Aristide to himself, "has to kiss not only every step on
the ladder but also pinch in the trouser creases of the
one on the steps above and also wipe off with his
whiskers the droppings of their dogs. Nothing but envy,
backbiting, sneers from the idle, lies from the spineless,
petty jokes at his expense, hate, that was the internal history of every success. Nobody but the boss counts in a
small affair like this: he has the money, he can withdraw
it in a day (frightful thought), the reins are loosely held
in his erratic hands and the general feeling is, 'Go to
hell, you're only a rich man's whim, the same as me!' At
first I remembered every act, attitude, allusion, and at
night rolled up mountains of such sand grains that took
the breath from my lungs. But now—who can get back
at them all? I was foolish. It is a question of who is
the master. The *canaille* worship a master. A radical I
am, but the royalists are right when they say, 'Without
a chief, no beauty in life, no order.' Would I obey a
committee, stand rebuke and recall from a whole de-

129

partment? But with a single head I can grapple, breath to breath, hand to hand. Yes, that's the secret: if you are head, they hate you more, love you more." Downstairs he saw a Spanish grandee pacing about. Aristide reflected, "Gold from Spain placed in Paris and gold from Paris placed in London and gold from London placed in a hole in a mountain in Switzerland and gold from Switzerland transferred to Oslo—and Bertillon was the clearing-house, a sort of little London on the Seine. . . ." A smile crossed Aristide's face. . . . Bertillon is a genius, fortune smiles: the golden hand of fate is on the tiller.

"Always happy to know of a marriage," said old Richard Plowman, laughing and putting his hand in his pocket. "Here you are. My daughter's only been married a few months. Perhaps you know the name. Johnny Arpels is her husband. You've heard of my daughter Anita? I suppose that soon—well, we won't talk of that so soon. . . . I know Mlle. Gentil very well—charming girl. Very intelligent. Remarkable. And who's she marrying? I must see her. Which is her room?"

When the count was made, Brossier netted one hundred and one francs from the clients (mostly due to Zurbaran's lunatic broadcast), three hundred and fifty francs from the employees, and five thousand francs from Jules Bertillon. Alphendéry gave an Encyclopedia and was invited to the wedding. The wedding was held in the church at Senlis (although both bride and bridegroom were atheists) to please the parents on both sides. But it was years since either of them had been to church and Alphendéry, the Alsatian Jew, student of ethnology, was the only one who knew the service: they followed his lead when it came to kneeling, rising or making a response.

Scene Fifteen: The Man with
Cunard-colored Eyes

It was a variable day, starting chilly and damp, with smoky-blue interludes and a midday warm and gray. There were bitter communist May 1st notices posted on the hoardings and fences, immediately covered up by

130

moderate C.G.T. notices in pink. In two days there had been two arrests of alleged Soviet spies and there was general trouble and anxiety in the air. All the morning the desultory conversations in the bank had turned round the bad U.S. Steel report received late the night before (after the close of the market) and the two brokerage failures of the week, and the usual rumors were flying round of two bank failures expected within the succeeding few days. As many of the clients in the bank had small money interests in numerous countries, there were doleful faces about and Aristide Raccamond traveled moodily round the corridors looking for Alphendéry to give him his philosophy of the day. He had on a new pair of spectacles, large bridged over his large tapir nose, and he looked like a whole face of dough depending from the bridge of the glasses. Presently he came down and began earnestly persuading Dr. Jacques Carrière who had dropped in.

"There have been recurring declines in American business since 1850, still more bad years since 1900. The monopoly capital system of production will reach its final stage in the U.S.A. towards 1938 to '40 probably. The best thing for anyone with money to do is to lay out a five-year-plan in the stock market, say, first 'bearing,' then watching for a small rise, then flurries of rises, then artificial 'dope' rises, the market pumped up by the interests, then preparation for inflation."

"Interesting," said Dr. Jacques Carrière, "a five-year-plan of investments! Good idea. I'll think it over. Come out and see me at home."

"There goes Raccamond giving my advice," said Alphendéry with good-humored regret. "When will I make money and a reputation for myself? I must start some time."

"A five-year-plan in investments, is that your idea? Not bad," said Jules.

"Why not: modern finance is what medicine was in the stage of necromancy. We ought to take a hint from the Soviets and steal a march on the interests."

"If we knew what was going to happen for five years ahead!" Jules shrugged.

"We do. The only thing that can happen to the British Empire from now on is trouble: she's had everything. The only thing that can happen to Russia is prosperity

131

if there's no war. For America, a lot of trouble, then inflation, a temporary boom. For Germany, some desperate attempts at fascism—the German people won't take to it, but the bosses may try it—and then a restoration, aided by Britain, when they see fascism is breaking down. For Italy—secret alliances and present aid to the highest bidder. For France, preparation for war with Germany, a Soviet alliance: an attempt at fascism, which will doubtless be defeated, certainly be defeated. For China, a long struggle resulting in the eventual triumph of the Soviet system over the greater western part. . . ."

"That's what you want to see, not what will happen," said Jules: "the powers will see to that. America won't have that. . . . And how are we to plan for five years on that, may I ask?"

"For England, the bet is on inflation, either of currency, of commodity prices or of both: the Government must resort either to taxation on a scale never before seen, or issue more bonds or devalue the pound or print currency. The only alternative that great capital actually fears is increased taxation since it is no longer possible to pass very much of this load on to the shoulders of the workers or middle-class consumers. Wages and middle-class receipts have touched bottom. The standard of living of any group may yet be slightly reduced by wage slashes or exploitation, especially in the shape of increased efficiency of the worker at the point of production, but there is a curious resistance to exploitation by heavy taxation. The wage-slashing technique is only restrained by the fear of reducing the physique of the nation's manhood below army acceptance level: that is marked, in their opinion, no doubt, by the dole figure. (Of course they are wrong: but the advance of mechanical warfare is such that they have no longer to depend so much on route-march power of the national riffraff: they have their trained bodies of well-built men for flying, the key services. But they are dead wrong.) You see it is true basically that the extent to which labor can support taxation after the boss gets through with it is small, and the bosses therefore are afraid of increased taxation. Now all such fears are translated by the stock market into depressions, even panics and lower valuations of stocks. On the other hand, inflation enables the capitalists to defer the burden of the government deficit on to the future accumulations of capital, and it increases profits here and now by raising the value of manufactured articles at a rate faster than the comparatively halting increases in wages, after inflation. Because the prices can be altered from here to tomorrow, but the increases in wages have to be wrung, penny by penny, from the bosses, through strikes and collective demands. And it would not pay the bosses to grant them any other way—despite their cries about lost profits—because they gain time thereby. Therefore an inflation program permits a stock market to capitalize increased net profits, higher prices for goods sold and a lagging increase in wages as against the prices at which the products of labor are sold. . . . Therefore, my dear boy, it pays the British capitalist class to inflate: they must inflate. And they will make a profit out of it for a few months. But that profit cannot last and after that you will have a depression and a social awakening among the lower classes, much worse than any that is taking place now."

"The English will never revolt," said Jules: "they are too meek and mild."

"A social awakening doesn't mean revolution; and starvation wages, dole, or outright starvation do not mean revolt. If misery spelled revolt, we should have had nothing but revolt from the beginning of time. On the contrary, it is quite rare."

"But what do I get out of this?" queried Jules impatiently.

"This," Alphendéry proceeded sagely: "there will be big increases in stock-market ratings among especially the cheap, worthless, gaudy, spectacular, and flimsy minor promotions and corporations: an increase in paper money suits them as sound money never could. They can't pay their way so well on a sound-money basis, but this momentary lag of wages, this increased exploitation of labor, gives them their chance. For an optimistic stock market such as you see after inflation is merely an investment in the lowering of the real wages of labor. And is that a pure pleasure for the little profiteer, apart from anything else! Now, my scheme is a simple one, Jules. Let's work out our share-guarantee scheme to cover only the little tawdry shares that banks won't lend on. When inflation comes, as it undoubtedly will within the next two years, we can line our bathrooms with gold."

"It's good," said Jules. "We'll send a man to England at once. We must get an Englishman, someone who looks honest and won't ask too many questions. But we must have an English company, don't you see? The English won't put their shares, even tin-pot ones, with a French company: with the perfidious French, good God! So we must get a couple of public-school men with the farseeing Cunard-captain sea-gray eyes, and square jaw and no brains, put them in a nice, worm-eaten, dark-green office with heavy furniture and a picture of the Bank of England in 1866 and of the South Sea House, and send them round the country talking to country bank managers and family lawyers. That's the thing to do. It's a great scheme. Now, who speaks English? You: you jabber it all right. Raccamond? Adam Constant? How about him? Would you take him along with you?"

"He speaks English perfectly," exclaimed Alphendéry with enthusiasm.

"Good, then send Adam Constant to scout round for offices and then you can go over and engage some men. Now, the English are funny. They won't look at a firm that was set up yesterday. What we've got to get is some old title that's been lying round in solicitors' offices for the last twenty years and buy it. What would it cost? Twenty pounds?"

"No: the cost of incorporation and the tax on the capital: probably about one thousand pounds."

"A hundred and twenty-five thousand francs. It's a big sum."

"Not in English units," said Alphendéry. "It all depends on the unit you count in."

Adam Constant came up, sat uneasily in the big arm-chair, and looked at Bertillon dumbfounded. He had not from Bertillon's description any idea of what was wanted of him, except that he had suddenly to go to London, a place he had never seen, and sign a lease for some offices, buy furniture, and engage two English public-school men, and make sure they were not hangers-on of the secret service. Many more details were added which seemed to him bizarre and fantastic.

"I'll explain it all to you, Adam," said Alphendéry. "The essential thing is a man with Cunard-colored eyes."

Scene Sixteen: 'Ware the Bank

"You see, Adam, most men are constitutional bulls: I'm a constitutional bear—I can only win when the tendency is down. But the history of the world (our world) is down now. I can only see pessimism for capitalism: if it has any spring left in it, I will be wrong. . . . The stock market doesn't understand alibis.

"Jules Bertillon can only make real money in a dissolving world: If they ever get the jigsaw puzzle together even for five minutes, Jules will have to live on his reserves. We're in the phantom buggy with him. We're riders of the storm: all of us together with him in this phantom bank, built on misery, shining out of mire, solid in an earthquake, soundproof in thunder, a living lightning conductor: an accident in capitalism. So—take your first-class ticket: it may be a long time before another comes your way."

"When one survivor comes to shore after a wreck, I can't believe in him. I can't believe in myself now," said Adam. "I feel we live in a dream world. What do we produce? What service do we give? Who are we, whose cousins, whose employers? How can we extract food, drink, and Pullman seats from looking through gilt grilles all day and handing paper money backward and forward. It isn't real . . . it's Katzenjammer Castle." He shook his head and laughed delightfully. "But of course, I'm not saying no. You have a heart of gold, Michel, the only gold thing you'll ever have." He looked ruefully at the frayed edges of Michel's trousers. Michel drew his feet in hastily and went on, "The only thing I regret about a bear market is that Jules makes so much money that he begins to want to expand in all directions. You know he wants to open a branch in Berlin and one in Shanghai. I imagine old man Richard Plowman, who used to be head of the Timor and Arafura Trading Bank, put him up to that. But I really believe there is a chance out there. They must be speculating wildly. The world is so unsettled and no one puts money away in chaotic times. . . ."

"If there's a chance of sending anyone out there, Alphendéry, send in my name, will you? It's my chance: there's a power drawing me out, it's so strong that I know I will go one way or another."

Old Richard Plowman, "the perfect Englishman" with small, long oval face, gray hair, kind blue eyes, was born in the British consulate at Caracas, worked in British banks in Sydney, Shanghai, Colombo, Alexandria, and Old Jewry and once had ventured into foreign lands and worked in Chicago. He became head of the Timor and Arafura Trading Bank, made money, and retired. The year of his retirement, like many another modest Englishman, he went to Paris. There he met Jules Bertillon. He was captivated by him and saw in him the sort of young man he would have liked for a son.

He was one of Jules's first believers: one of those who first saw his star rise. He now regarded the marble, mahogany, silk, and plush of the bank as the furnishings of his spiritual home and was always in and out of the bank, at any time of the day and evening. He knew all the employees, canoodled with the clerks, accountants, and typists, loved especially those who had special rooms—he would drop in on them, about tiffin hour, through old habit—and had an immense room of his own, as big as that of Jules, in which he spent long pleasant hours smoking and talking with Jules and old Paris friends.

Whenever he vacated this room and went to walk on the Champs Élysées or by the Seine, or to eat or visit ladies, or do little commissions for them, the two busy restless associates moved in, spread out samples, wrote letters, concocted guarantees and agreements, looked up tariffs and completely changed the stage. Daniel Cambo was now in general merchandise and his uncle Ephraïm Dreyer in knitted goods.

Dreyer was a charming mid-European Jew, with old velvety skin and fine hands and nose, and Cambo was the energetic, muscular Balkan Jew of the same type as Léon but less Napoleonic, because issued from a very rich family. When they packed up their papers and notions and went out to do business with someone in London, New York, Kharkov, Geneva, Vichy, or Constantinople, old

Richard Plowman came back with some book of memoirs by sea dog or friend of the Aga Khan and sat there again in the great green-painted room, bringing with him all the old air of eternal security, eternal self-content.

He often lived with the Bertillons, for all of whom he had an unquestioning affection; he knew all their friends and lived in a happy world in which the pearl necklace of Mamie, the divorce of Tony and Aline, Poppo's racing car, Pedrillo's peccadilloes, William's salt soup, Claire-Josèphe's new dress from Worth, Anita and Johnny's new maid, what Tommy said to the attaché at the Mexican embassy, and the new thoroughbred of Jean de Guipatin were the chief characters, and creatures of absorbing interest. He had forgotten how he made his money and had returned (because it was simpler and made Jules seem even more charming) to the innocent credo of a schoolboy of fourteen.

Plowman had just come back from London. He had brought eight ounces of best smoking mixture from Fortnum & Mason for Dr. Jacques Carrière, Pedro's guitar with the new string attached, a cribbage board for an old English crony (married in France) of "Old" Berthellot, the head accountant, an iodine locket for his housekeeper, and the English style of Kruschen salts for François Vallat; he had an old tattered Charing-Cross-Road copy of *Sweeney Todd* for William Bertillon, whose imagination had been fired by a chance reference to the demon barber, a pound of Ceylon tea (gold-label) for Mrs. Haller, one of the clients of the bank, and a pair of socks, two and six, very cheap, English style, for Mr. Haller. Nevertheless, he felt shamefaced because he had failed to get a real (cheap) Dunhill pipe for Jacques Manray, who coveted this particularly. On his way to get some pearls restrung for Lady Bobbie, a young acquaintance of his in London, he had picked up Claire-Josèphe to take her to the pictures and to lunch and here they were at the bank, where Claire-Josèphe had to cash a check.

"Oh, Jules," cried Claire-Josèphe in her fashionable babble, "the most awful thing happened to Richard on his trip to London. Tell him, Richard."

"Yes, I was quite cut up," said Richard. "I lost eight pounds, one five-pound note and three ones in the Burlington Arcade. I am perfectly sure someone picked my pocket. Such a thing has never happened to me before,

137

I've never lost money. It's most upsetting, I assure you. It's not so much the money—although, you know—but it's the idea: I have eight pounds in my pocket and someone can come along and slip it out without my feeling it. And not in a crowd. What was I doing. Was I standing gaping, without knowing it? It makes me feel so—bad: I couldn't sleep all night. That's what made me come home earlier: I felt London had turned on me."

"You can leave the smoking mixture here," said Jules. "Jacques Carrière rang up to say he would be in. He's interested in the fate of sterling. What did you hear, Richard?"

"They'll never go off: it would mean the crash of the sterling area."

"Any big selling?"

"Yes, but mostly foreigners. Frenchmen, Dutch. They say."

"The French should know: it's all a question of whether they continue to withdraw their funds from London. If they're selling."

"We'll squeeze them, my boy: the old game. Why, we couldn't afford to go off gold: London is the world center of foreign deposits. Our reputation is that we're solid, we don't waver when the rest of the world is a jelly. It would ruin our banking business. We couldn't afford to do it, dear Jules. Don't you bet on it. Don't listen to the hotheaded plungers here: Paris is so feverish compared with London. You know it's a tangible difference: in London everything is silence, calm, quiet: we're well balanced. You ought to go to London, whenever you think of selling, Jules, dear boy, and you'd think twice about it."

"H'm: I often prefer to be rash. You make more money that way. . . . However—well, look who's here! Frank 'Rhodes' Durban!"

Richard Plowman's lifelong crony, bronzed, broad, and sixty, with a breezy expression and waterlogged gait, hove in sight. He had been tubercular at twenty, gone out to South Africa, and made a couple of million sterling out there.

"Hello, Jules! Don't believe him: he's a Little Englander, although he was born in a consulate. She will go off and it won't be her ruin: she'll stagger and right herself and you'll see a regular wave of prosperity carry her homewards about 1933 to '34 and onwards to 1938. Then we'll see what we shall see."

"Rhodesia makes everyone a pathological optimist," said old Richard with regret. "He only comes to London to say the opposite of everyone in the club."

The two old fellows presently trotted out.

"You haven't got too much money in this bank, Dick, have you?"

"Yes: quite a bit. Why?"

"It's too nice. Where's the bill department? Where's the loan department? Where's the business done? I don't see any banking."

"It's a rich man's club: a gambling, deposit, and tax-evasion bank, don't you see? It's just the rich man's section of a big bank taken out, polished, and set rolling on its own wheels. Very good idea. Jules always had such chic ideas."

"Don't believe in it," said "Rhodes" Durban stoutly. "Take your money out: I don't care if he's your own son. I like to see property, freights, loads of grain, sugar, leather, dates, asphalt, something, behind a bank. I don't see it here. That's wrong."

"No. Now I'll explain it to you: this is very comparable with another idea of Jules's that he had last night and is going to start straight away. He's going to get a big ocean-going yacht like Virginie Henriot's. He'll institute a gold-bar, bond, and stock transport between say Cherbourg and New York, or say Bordeaux and Buenos Aires. This yacht will only carry such goods required for quick delivery. No waiting for mail boats, customs, taking on passengers, all that. And it can sail any time: no waiting for schedule. Everyone will take advantage of the special precious-stuffs yacht."

"Yes? I should like to be the captain. You mean to say people are going to put their fortunes on a private yacht—"

"A company will be formed: nothing of that sort."

"Oh, a company will be formed. That will be very different, of course!"

"You're used to those bluff South African types," scolded Richard Plowman. "You don't understand a delicate intelligence, a man who instinctively thinks in finance and precious goods; his grandfather was in the diamond trade. It's in the blood. He belongs to one of these old

European families in whose veins it is not so much blood as some rare old liqueur that runs."

"You're crazy, Dick: I pity you. If you put a ring in your own nose you can't expect people to resist the temptation. But I'd hate to see you lose a lot of money: you couldn't stand it as well as you think."

"I'm a simple man, Rhodes: I have the tastes of a baby. No one can get at me. I'm safe."

"When we have everything naturally we desire nothing —therefore we have simple tastes. That's no riddle. You'll get a surprise one day. You've got to the stage of playing with dolls: one doll is Claire-Josèphe and one is Jules. Take my advice and go back into banking yourself. You've forgotten what the human race looks like."

Scene Seventeen: In Praise of Gold

THE word "gold" spoken by those who have seen it, had it, lived with it, has undertones of sensual revel and superstitious awe and overtones of command and superhuman strength that excite the greatest hostility and indignation in those who have not got it, have never seen it, or have not lived with its beautiful invisible presence— invisible, because it is always socked away. This joyful sensuality comes not only from its brightness, softness, purity, rarity, great specific gravity, nor from the designs, head, crowns, olive branches, men with staves, lions, unicorns, escutcheons, arms, and legends printed on it, nor from its finely milled edge in coins, nor wholly from the worship value of a very small bar of it, nor from the soft jingling it makes in a leather bag, nor from the way, like a little sun it can bring light on to the face of everyone who regards, and reverence, as Ra to his admirers: it comes from all these things, but also from a life-long association of the word "gold" with the idea ultimate wealth, perennial ease, absolute security. It is an absolute and in its presence the anxious heart breathes sweetly and the blood laughs and the toiling brain sheds its dew of agony. Sweet gold! It has in it everything that man desires in a wife, that cannot, precisely, be purchased with gold. Beautiful gold! It is cosmetic: it makes a girl handsome and marriageable in a moment. Virgin gold! There may be suspicions and shades of jealousy clinging to those whose all is paper and participations, but there is a sun-colored cloak "Sir-Galahad" model for those who own gold. Fetish gold! But that's an old one: we know what that means: it means "I've none."

Armand Brossier lived in the state of mind of a pure and pious choirboy who has the happiness to serve in a cathedral. He it was who took up the gold coins deposited each day, who doled them out to clients who were hoarders, who counted them and saw with religious ecstasy the number of little chamois bags increasing, and with foreboding their decrease, as rumor came and went. Jules had taken him into the bank and found him tubercular. Armand had got into the war in its last year, been gassed, had pneumonia, and come back in health completely ruined. Jules found his coughing ghastly in the echoing white walls of the hollow pearl that his bank was, and had sent him off to Chamonix and the hills behind Nice to cure him. For him, he had opened a little office in Juan-les-Pins—and made money by it. When Armand seemed cured, he brought him back to Paris, gave him the key and combination of the safe, and left his duties at that. The relations between Armand Brossier and Jules were those between Abelard and the most impressionable of his students. Armand slept soft and dreamed sweetly and had halcyon days. When he wanted to marry he went and told Jules and Jules raised his salary one thousand francs a month, because he was always rash and he believed in treating well the sprite of the combination.

The foregoing will explain (to those who don't know) one of the reasons, apart from reasons of speculation, why the question of "going off gold" fretted so many nations, so many individuals, for so many days: why some took it as a world-without-end calamity and some as an unnatural blessing. In the old days those that sought the absolute tried to make gold: our own conception is not very different.

Scene Eighteen: The Bet

"I DON'T know where you get your information, Carrière," said Michel Alphendéry, "and you may be right, but the pound sterling has stood up so well to attacks from outside and in that I wouldn't bet on its going off now: that's all. Nor would I bet on its staying on. I like to bet on fixed horse races. But here you simply can't know what's going on behind the scenes. Perhaps you do." He looked with meaning at Carrière, who was the crony of most of the young Radical-Center deputies. He got up, dusted his knees, showed some intention of going back to his room.

Jules was leaning back in his chair looking at the shade-somber olive walls of his room that never saw the sunlight, staring at the crystal luster, looking at them all rather impatiently, smiling and rocking in his chair.

Carrière stood in the center of the room, one foot forward like an orator, balancing on the other. His hand was stuck in his jacket. His powerful small head thrust back brought into prominence his forehead, Roman nose, broad chest, and early *embonpoint:* it also emphasized the roll of fat at the nape of the neck. His left hand was on his hips, his feet were in shiny handmade shoes. He was tall, with solid bones, had a late-Roman look of arrogance, self-confidence based on boundless vice, astuteness, and corrupt waywardness.

His shining blond poll turned from one to the other. Will Bertillon stood, tall, plump and fair also, against one of the bookcases, an athletic figure grown too fat, too young, a slight graying of a fresh complexion due to too many indoor hours and soft sitting. He rang his own little peal of bells, in a faraway meditative tone: this he did by gently sifting the coins in his pockets, gathering them all up again and once more rhythmically letting them chink down. He chuckled now.

"When even Michel thinks they won't go off, I'll trust the British to pull a fast one. They'll go off overnight some week end, you'll see. Some day we're not expecting it. How are they to make money otherwise? And there'll be a tight squeeze first to shake out the shorts. You can't outguess the other chap's game. You know—who—is going to give us the information when he gets it from Grosshändler of the International Quayside Corporation. If *he* knows it. Who is really on the inside of the inside of the inside? How can you guess the other chap's game. I don't know a quarter of what Alphendéry really thinks and yet he spends his whole life explaining what he thinks. And you mean to say we're going to scrape out the inside of the Chancellor of the Exchequer's brainpan? Let's keep out of all Crime Club guessing competition: they know the answer and you get a prize if you deduce the murderer from the facts on page 143. That's where we stand with sterling. . . . It's bankrupt they are? And is that a reason for going bankrupt? Bankruptcy is nowadays the normal method of doing business with your creditors—why, if they're really bankrupt, they can blackmail the world with— What are you going to do if the sterling area goes off gold? What are you going to do if there's a panic in Lombard Street? Are you going to put your money in America! With every bank shutting its doors? Are you going to invest in China? In France, which is going to be losing her man power and money like water in about three years from now. . . . You make me laugh: bankrupt! They don't worry."

Carrière swung round, pointed the finger at him,

"Bertillon, you'll never make money with that philosophy: you can secrete, but never produce, a male hedgehog. To make money you've got to outguess even the crooked roulette wheel."

"William's right: sterling won't go off. You have nothing to worry about." Jules looked dogmatic.

"You feel as confident as that? I almost think you're right. Would you like to make it a bet?" Carrière moved up to Jules's desk, his dark blue eyes glinting intently through the long lashes. "How much do you bet, Jules?"

"Anything you like: what do I care: I'll take you to any amount. I've just got a hunch sterling isn't going off this year. It's an old trick. Everyone's counting on it going off. Why shouldn't they squeeze the shorts? Let me stay on through this crisis and all the money in the world will pour into London. That's how they live. There's no other reason for planting your money up there in the fog."

William, who had been playing nonchalance all through this, felt his nose-for-danger twitch. "Jules! Even Alphendéry says he can't understand a thing in the Bank of England statement."

"It's just like Kreuger's," said Alphendéry: "they smell the same to me. True, there's a statement but what's the good of a statement in Aramaic. I don't read Aramaic."

William, struggling for Jules's financial soul, became easy again.

"Why," said Carrière, "a matter of foreign relations: would France allow her to go off; France has gold. Why wouldn't she lend it to England?"

"She won't," said Alphendéry. "She's so busy lending it out to make a ring of roses round Germany. . . . You see, Jules, there is a likelihood, that's all you can call it."

"The Bank of England," laughed Jules, "is just like Bertillon Frères. . . ."

"With this difference," Michel rushed in, "with this difference," he laughed softer and repeated, "with this difference though: we've got a cover of one hundred and ten per cent or something like that."

"Yes," said Jules: "now what would I do if I were Montagu Norman? But, it's my bank. I'd kill myself with laughing to see the whole world selling me short and I'd let them mortgage the last foot of Uncle Tom's farm and then I'd snap down: I've got the dough—or, I've got the power, or the backing. No, my bet is he won't go off."

"I'm glad I never took up banking," said William. "They say it requires so much brains."

Jules silenced him testily. "You don't help with those funniments. I am in banking."

"Banking?" meditated William. "Don't call it banking. Call it a raffle or *rouge-et-noir* and you'll know what that is you're doing. Every time you hear a man say, or think, 'I'm a Napoleon: you're just mud on my spats,' or 'One day you'll be able to see my star without the aid of a telescope,' or 'I bumped my head on the moon last night, I must remember to stoop tonight,' or 'Things are going on and on and up and up,' or when he calls a janitor a building supervisor or a crapshooter a banker— you know that tomorrow you'll have to buy a box of matches from him outside the church. . . . Know what you are: you won't lose any money, even if you don't make the grand sweep. I've heard about one but not seen it yet. . . ."

He pulled out one of his eternal cigarettes, did not offer it to anyone, lit it, and kept his eyes on Alphendéry, for he knew both Carrière and Jules were furious with him. He went on in an intimate conversational tone as if he were opening his secret heart to Alphendéry. "That's how they all come a cropper. The little ones throw dice on the zinc counter, the middle ones buy Snia-Viscosa, the big ones go to Deauville. You go in the office sweep-stake and go without lunch all the week to punt at Auteuil, to get two hundred francs to buy ten shares of Dummy-Gummi Incorporated and put a mortgage on your house and buy a false identity card to be able to get into Monte Carlo and get to the point of putting a bullet through your head, because you want to have the right to sit with crooks and order hot hors d'oeuvres at Philippe's. You begin with a postage stamp and end with a post-mortem."

"Speaking seriously," began Carrière, deliberately turn-ing to Jules, leaning on the desk, compellingly balancing on both hands, with a brilliant, persuasive, old-school-friend intimacy, "Jules, are you taking any chances on the pound?"

"Why, the Americans have to keep the pound at par. Your money's safe. Any boy would be crazy not to take you on. It's a little safe money."

"Would you guarantee such a contract as mine?" said Jacques, friendly, detached. Jules flopped down on the two front legs of his chair and brought his hands down on the blotter, in a whirlwind of good humor.

"I'll guarantee you to pay your whole contract on that brewery in Burton-upon-Trent at not less than one hun-dred twenty-two francs to the pound. Tell them to send the sterling drafts to me. I'll pay them."

"Every three months?"

"Every three months, whatever——"

Alphendéry spoke. "Jules, aren't you rather rash? How long a period do the drafts cover, Carrière?"

"Three years from this month," said Jacques briefly, with a touch of scorn.

William pleaded earnestly, "Jules, if you want to throw money away, throw it in the street: think of the fun you'll get out of seeing Marianne Raccamond burst with indignation when she sees a couple of street cleaners in Rolls-Royces."

"I woke up this morning knowing I was going to make money," said Jules. "It's all right. I'm sorry for you, Jacques, but I can't stop you: you're wasting your money. O.K. It's a deal."

"What's the consideration?" asked Alphendéry coldly.

"O.K. We'll just call it a friendly bet," said Carrière coolly. "We'll have a letter, one from you, one from me, countersigned. That's sufficient, isn't it? No documents. It's enough."

"What's the consideration?" said Alphendéry.

"Certainly," said Jules. "You send me your letter, not a lawyer's letter." He was restless however, and got up, stretching his legs. William and Michel Alphendéry said nothing more, both having one idea in mind, and that was to make Jules go back on the bet as soon as they could get him out of the sight of Carrière. Carrière picked up his hat and stick and looked at them with that smooth, bursting expression which was almost a smile.

William stood up.

"And what's the consideration? If the pound should go off and we had such an arrangement with you, we should be liable for any amount—there are no buffers for runaway currencies. You ought to do your banking with us, Carrière, on the strength of a deal like that. You ought to pull in some of your friends in the Chamber of Deputies, and tell Larue to give us carte blanche. Or would you rather have an overdraft? That would be more in our general style of business. I'll write you a check now. How much? Jules is giving away the bank in the morning. Be round early and see if you can't get a slice. If you know anyone who wants a bank tell him to drop round."

Jacques laughed, and had a twinkle for William.

"Oh, I'll give you a deposit, Bertillon. Jules, write down two million francs on your books for me: I'll send it round. Now be sure to write it down to my account. I've got a little account of two million over at the Crédit. I'll tell them to transfer it. . . ."

"Keep your petty cash," Jules said languidly, grandly. "What's two million? I don't want your deposit. I can rustle up business without you putting up earnests. Don't be a fool."

146

"Well, I'm still saving up," said William. "I'll take it, Jacques: so just send it round to my account, will you?"

"I'll tell them to transfer it before closing this afternoon," said Jacques, negligently magnificent to Jules.

"I'll tell you what we'll do," said Jules, on whom common sense was slowly gaining. "We'll pay one-half per cent of it into Raccamond's account. It will give him confidence and he's your man in a sort of way, isn't he? Ten thousand will cheer him up. He's still so blue about that Claude Brothers business. He still has to go down to give testimony and he's one of these neurotics who want to bang their heads against the wall every time anyone says 'You're a crook.' "

Carrière looked at Jules in an odd way. Jules laughed. "Oh, don't mistake me: I know he's all that's crooked. But that makes no difference. He's out for himself but he can't do without me. And ten thousand is a nice present. . . . Well, I'm having lunch with the Comtesse de Voigrand. I'll tell her I've seen you. How's your mother?"

"The old buzzard got back to town yesterday. That reminds me. I must ring her. I want her to advance me some cash for those vineyards I want to buy near Lyons. Everyone says it's a bad investment, wine is gong to be used for irrigation one of these days. But I'm banking on the Eighteenth Amendment being repealed in the U.S.A. With the people getting no jobs and no dole, they've got to give them some pleasure in life. She always behaves like a hellcat but she usually comes across." A spasm of hatred passed over his face. He said, viciously, with a raw, rich tone, "I hate her."

"Why?" said Jules carelessly. He didn't care for his mother, either, but he had no emotions about her.

"She knows I'm waiting for the pleasure of sending roses to her funeral and she gets heartier every year. She enjoys making me crawl for the few million francs I want for my ventures. She knows what I could do with half—just half—six hundred million francs."

He looked at Jules with hatred: Jules calmly, penetratingly returned the look. He knew what fly was stinging ambitious Carrière's mind. Jules and he were abreast, in the figures of their reputed fortunes—about one hundred and thirty million francs each. Jules had a little family money behind him but Carrière's inheritance when his mother died and two of his uncles died would be colossal, counted in astronomical numbers. But they were all healthy and Carrière, fretting and rotting away his youth, was just as likely to die as they. When he left, William commented.

"He's got to gorge on dead bodies, fermented juices, and living men to keep alive. His right is three fat corpses—his mother's, his two uncles'—and two million francs. That's the way he sees himself when he's normal. As I never dream I don't know what he sees when he gets outside a bottle of champagne. . . ." William turned to Jules. "Forget that Mickey-Mouse sketch about the bet. I won't pay him a farthing even if you do sign anything with him. What do you let him get under your skin for?"

"I know, I know, I never intended to," said Jules. "A verbal arrangement is one thing: a contract is another." William went out: they heard his coins jeeringly singing their tune into the distance. Round the corner they fell into silence.

"His ideal is to put gold coins under a board and live along with his Chinese nightingale," said Jules.

"He's faithful to you, Jules," came the voice of Alphendéry, behind his back. "Will's always narking you when he's with you but behind your back he won't hear a word against you. You know how he puts up with insults: everyone is good enough to sneer at William and he gives that round, white, pleasant look and laughs at me, 'What do I care, if the bank gets on?' And the bank, Jules—what is it but you? It's a rare thing. Whatever happens, your brother William will stick to you: when you're getting on, he jibs, snorts, cuts across, but if you're ever in trouble, he'll be the last one to leave. You ought to see how he frets when you're sick. 'My baby brother —that fool youngster.' The way he worries about you, Claire-Josèphe, and the children, I'd swear, if I didn't know, you were all his children."

Jules said nothing for a few minutes, turned over a yachting monthly, looked into the shagreen-bound, gilt-edged diary with ivory leaves in which he had only made one entry in the three years since William gave it to him. Then he got up, took his hat, smiled affectionately. "Got to have lunch with the Comtesse. . . . By the way, Claire-Josèphe says why don't you ever come over to dinner? We never have anyone. . . ."

"Don't be too cynical at the Comtesse's." Alphendéry

was solicitous. "These aristocrats are friendly but they're always watching you to see whether you fit into their game."

"She thinks I'm a riot," said Jules. "I don't mean a thing to her: she just gets fun out of me. Don't forget one thing. Everyone adores a successful thief: he's the only thing on earth can guarantee them twenty per cent on their money. Ha, ha!"

"And the bet?"

"Oh—oh, I'll ask the Comtesse what she thinks. She detests Carrière and Carrière's mother. How did I come to make a crackbrained bet like that? However—I think I'm right at that."

He was no longer there. Urbain Voulou going out to lunch saw Jules Bertillon, slender, arch, and very beautiful, driving off in his Hispano-Suiza with his stalwart chauffeur at the wheel. Urbain took off his hat and, watching Jules's courteous smile, let his hand fall till he seemed to be covering his heart. Jules looked like fine wax: and gold-dust stuck easily to that wax. Urbain Voulou, great soft lummox, was happy every time he saw Jules Bertillon and from then on till he met the crowd of bourse runners and clients' men he had once known, when they never failed to make him miserable by recounting all the tales told in town on the score of Jules Bertillon.

After lunch, Alphendéry walked a bit, then dropped into the old Café de la Rotonde, opposite the Galeries Lafayette, for coffee. William was there eating a Welsh rarebit. He was hunched over the little plate. He looked up when Alphendéry sat down at his table, grunted, and when he had swallowed a burning mouthful, said flatly, "If the worst comes to the worst, we've got a million pounds in gold in London and we can go. Shut up shop with profit. There's more money in a decent bankruptcy than in working for a living. But I won't let him get away with any such nonsensical contract with Carrière."

"He won't sign it: nothing's done. He'll think it over. He's going to ask the Comtesse and you know what she thinks of Carrière. He'll come back with a clear brain. He can't undertake a contract running into possibilities of millions of francs loss without consulting us. What's his object? To annoy Jacques. What's Jacques'? To annoy him.

Do you realize—if the pound went off and began to slide? Well, we could pay it, I suppose. But I don't want Jacques to take his pound of flesh every month. . . . Not that I care. One day everyone crashes. That's why I'm a bear. It's a twenty-to-one bet on the facts. . . . You're betting on a funeral. Everyone's sure to pass out. . . . My philosophy is, every day you make your expenses is a profit. You eat that day and you eat one day less out of your reserves. That's the only advantage I see in being in business: to live. But—Jules!"

Alphendéry lowered his voice, looked around. "William; how much have you, honest to God, cut and dried, that you can lay your hands on? Gold bars, gold-dust, gold coins, notes, Liberty bonds, *bons du Trésor*, Treasury paper, War loans: are we liquid? Are we solid, that is?"

William wiped his mouth, flipped for the waiter. "I really don't know exactly how much, but there's an awful lot there, Michel! There's at least one million pounds in gold in London, there's a vault in Geneva with gold bars in it. Claire has put away about twelve million in *bons du Trésor* for the children, and Jules has a lot of the sort of stuff you could sell at a moment's notice without moving the market more than a quarter of a point. I've saved my salary: what do I want out of life? It's enough if I go home and hear my Chinese nightingale sing. Nightingale seed is what I want out of life!" He laughed fully, content. "Jules has a couple, perhaps more than that, of little companies incorporated in Luxemburg or some such place, darned if I know what he does with them. I think they snooze and do nothing. It's impossible to get an answer out of him, but I can't imagine that he hasn't got cash soaked away for hard times. In general—there's a whale of a lot of money in the place, Michel, and don't you lose sleep. Don't get nervous. You don't want to be like this Raccamond. . . ."

Alphendéry opened his eyes wide. But all he said was, "I'm not curious, William: if you tell me it's so, it's so."

"What do you care? You're always with us: you'll be provided for."

Michel said casually, it seemed, "And the clients?"

"Supposing we were eighty per cent solvent: that would be more than any other bank in the world. And we've got no widows or orphans."

Scene Nineteen: No Retreat

THE butler poured out of a giraffe-necked crystal carafe. The Comtesse de Voigrand, a virile old woman of seventy, was a beveled, electric-lighted showcase of those salon virtues and porcelain graces that characterize the French woman from six to eighty-six and from the table in Maisons-Lafitte to the table in Passy. She smiled at Jules with that healthy worldliness and practiced friendship which brings out the best in all social souls. They formed a triangle of Louis XV chairs. The second was Jules Bertillon, very gay: the third, Mr. Armand Lalmant, former professor at the Sorbonne, now retired to be the Comtesse's librarian and personal savant-in-fetters.

Jules was always so pert that it took a thimbleful of liquor only to set him bubbling entirely; he declared, to the Comtesse's amusement, "Certainly, I understand the idea of the class war. There are those who know what they want and those who want it when they see the other fellows with it, but don't know how to get it themselves. We steal from the pigs: the pigs know they want truffles and we want truffles when we see the pigs with them. Money is truffles. Are we going to grub up their truffles for them? Porkers fish for truffles and then bring home the bacon; what a pig's life! First the Morgans see it, then the little spry fish like me, then the gangsters, then the manual workers, then the clerks, and it takes twenty-five years to get from the top to the bottom. It's the time lag that gives us our profit! . . . I like Marx, Lalmant. If the rich ones would follow Marx's idea and stick together in a class, they'd never lose a cent. Look at the Army: even when a chap lies and forges, it sticks by him. . . ."

"If there had been honor and loyalty among thieves, society would have wiped them out long ago," said the Comtesse.

Jules ran on. "Just the same, as every imbecile will say some bright things in a lifetime, if he gossips enough, Marx, who was a sort of lunatic, had some bright ideas. No, the class war is a good idea. I suppose he really

151

wasn't mad, just one of these—h'm—er—journalists." He eyed the professor and smiled.

"I'm not surprised," said the librarian, a tall muscular, severe, gray man with an arid tone that made the tongue of his listeners swell, blacken, and cleave to the roof of the mouth. He smiled unpleasantly. "Nowadays even the richest is convinced that a revolution is coming—the day after he dies. And they don't mind."

The Comtesse was becoming mellow. "Money is a hard master: it takes no excuses, it flies from a false economics."

Dryly her secretary replied, "Comtesse, all this isn't romantic, it isn't due to the intelligence of money: these people see the revolution because it is here, as we are at war often before the outbreak of hostilities. But we are entering upon a new state of war: war without the paraphernalia of the old history books, war without costume, without notes, ultimatums, treaties, war in which peace is but a truce. So with revolution. Revolution has been with us since 1917 . . . 1919! . . . 1926. . . ." He laughed. "But it isn't only that! All rich men are haunted by a more personal fear—they are all persuaded that they will die in penury!"

"I assure you, Mr. Bertillon," said the Comtesse, with her ready laugh and energetic mien, "I am quite worried about it: formerly we had town and country houses. But now we all have *pieds-à-terre* in town and hideaways from the Reds in the country and all the uninhabited islands in the world are being dug up and planted with gold bars. Thank goodness, Scotland provides so many, and then there's the Aegean. Think of the treasure-island stories there will be for the ages to come. Happy children!" She turned the talk. "They say Jacques Carrière is becoming a Roman Catholic again after having been fearfully agnostic for years," insinuated Loïse de Voigrand, with a twinkle.

Jules was a Catholic, of course, but never gave a thought to the Church except once a year at Easter, when he went as a matter of habit and because the whole world went. Lalmant explained. "In ages of disaster people turn from the Church, and it turns from the people: it becomes a chief's superstition and mummery again. They are all second-rate men to lick the shoes of the bosses when they could serve the people! Can a man of wit eat his bread

152

in an atmosphere dried with errors, forgeries, stupidities, lies, and mountebankery? As for the people—the physics laboratory provides wilder joys in the matter of transubstantiation, the dissection table, better anatomies!"

The Comtesse looked at him with respect: he was able to knot her into his skein: a steady fire burned day and night under this pedantic exterior: the Comtesse knew him to be one of the first intellectuals of France and also one of the first to join the new revolutionary movement. She knew his eternal flame and it warmed her old bones.

"True," said the Comtesse, "but the Church can no more retreat gracefully than the rich can. We have to march towards another slicing of heads. The only thing we can do, stiffening, is to develop towards a final liquidation. Yet, when the last day comes," she made a little *moue*, "what does it matter how clever we have been, with your bank or any other, Mr. Bertillon? Paper, gold, houses, orchards, mines? A crooked sixpence in a little crooked house on a little crooked island—if we fly in time. What a commerce between countries in rulers: their only invisible imports. You take my king: I'll take your queen. . . ." She shifted and pressed a bell. Her firm, well-stocked, manly mind wanted something more solid to bite on.

The butler appeared. "Madame is served."

"Well, Mr. Lalmant, I'm so old that the society I was born into will last my time, but it won't last Jacques Carrière's! His mother is worrying about him spending ten million in three years. He'll never get back the money he spent on the futurist theater in the Rue Delambre. That's what comes of being a liberal, hereditary bank-book—quandary—squandery. Remain a tough old aristo like I am and know where you stand and when not to stand there!" She cackled. "Jacques, forsooth, an entrepreneur! He'll be running for Ajaccio next. As for Mme. de Morengo, she's made up her mind to see her son has a fine funeral. Did you hear he had syphilis? Silly parrot. That broke up his first intention to marry. What a dowry slipped through his fingers! I'd made up my mind to marry him to Toots Legris for old sake's sake and to kill off dear Inès de Morengo: for naturally she'd die of chagrin to see him tobogganing in the Legris Dolomites of gold. Do you know what is his weakness, Jules?"

"What, Madame? I mean what do you think? I know a

153

hundred weaknesses he has: and I hate every one of them: even his virtue, relentless spite, is execrable to me." The syllables chased each other head over heels like jelly-boned puppies: he was laughing, drinking, smiling, covered with blossoms of light from head to foot, as if fairies stood off in the clouds and shuttled the reflections from a thousand fairy mirrors on him: he was nearly drunk.

"Oh, Jules!" laughed the Comtesse. "Mr. Lalmant, look at Mr. Bertillon. Jules, you are not drunk by any chance? Is your head so full that one drop spills it over? He's a magnum of champagne. No, Jules, if I told you all Jacques' weaknesses now, it would do you no good and I only wish your good. . . . The first is, he's pompous and thinks he can think. Now, you're born naked of theories and you're shameless: you're such a reckless, hand-to-mouth boy that I love you. Look at the charming, self-indulgent get-rich-quick foppery that it is! And how is your star, Jules, how are your pictures, askew, the ravens on top of your house: what color is Alphendéry's tie today? Oh, he thinks he's of the race of Morgan, but he's independent of their solid grasping qualities."

"You're right, quite right," babbled Jules. "I'm a gambler, I'd gamble in sawdust if I didn't have chaff and in chaff if I didn't have barley and in barley if I didn't have International Harvester. Quite, quite right. . . . But what sort of a gambler, dear Comtesse? Ah, ah, that's what you don't know. A special sort of gambler: the one that dies rich. I have the secret: everyone's a gambler, but he dies rich only if there's a *rentier* sitting at the bottom of his pants. Ah, ah! And what is Luxemburg for, I'd like to know, if not to sit at the bottom of my pants? . . . So I only get money to throw it away: no, I'm an international harvester: it's the chaff I throw away. Take my advice, Comtesse, and you'll die rich."

The Comtesse held her sides and even Lalmant smiled irrepressibly. "And what is it then?"

"Bet on disaster, Comtesse," said Jules solemnly, waving his finger at her. "The world's like an old pope: it's dying with a hundred doctors in attendance. It's dying of everything at once, because they kept it alive too long. . . . Bear everything! Take my advice."

"But not sterling, eh?" said the Comtesse. "You don't think that's going down, eh? Not from what I hear."

"Sterling." He sat up and looked at her cannily. "No. So. You heard it from Jacques?"

"Yes. . . . And I wonder myself if you're right."

"Of course, I'm right."

"Yes, I think you are. . . . But of course, it's not serious. You're rash, Jules: very few men in Europe would take that chance today."

"I will: it's against my principles and so I'm hedged."

Abruptly, she changed the subject. "Jules, I should like you to send Alphendéry to see Professor Lalmant and me for lunch one day. Alphendéry is a Red and a brilliant man."

"Don't you bluebloods do anything but invite Reds round to see you, these days?" grinned Jules. "What's it for?"

"Boring from within, dear friend," said the Comtesse, with a high giggle.

"They'll never make a punched franc with their crazy way of thinking," said Jules, suddenly cross. "They put you out of joint. We should keep away from them. They see what's what, but they see it in the wrong tempo: march time instead of jazz time. They ought to be organized. . . . Alphendéry often jangles my nerves with his abracadabra. It's only a new religion. It's newer than planchettes."

The Comtesse laughed to see him so discontented. "Jules! The bet with Jacques: the bet with Jacques. Don't forget. His mother is furious with him. She's heard of it. . . ."

"Then I'll do it," said Jules. "She's always saying I'm flimsy. . . ." After which he became chaotic, worried, and hectoring, and the Comtesse said no more about it.

"I heard that Pedro climbed up a drainpipe somewhere in Brussels and attacked a young heiress of seventeen. He was scared off, sent her a note, and made a rendezvous the next day in a teashop. She was late at the rendezvous and he raped the tea girl instead: she was so furious when she came in and found them that she got her father to turn Pedro out and now he's in London! That's what Stéphanie de Changford just telephoned me. Don't you think he ought to go back to Chile, Jules? He's so irresistible! But they understand those things better in Chile."

"Why should I? I like to have him round the place. His

155

father will die soon enough. They say the old fellow's off his rocker and rides round building chapels."

Scene Twenty: Roundshow

JULES got back to the bank cheerful but in a fragile state of mind and could not bring himself to sign the letter on his desk. He wandered round the corridors whistling under his breath. He whistled his gay way into the third room where he found Aristide Raccamond talking to Richard Plowman and John Tanker, Sr., who was sucking the head of his cane. John Tanker, Sr., that well-known oil owner from Texas and Mexico, was now in his dotage. His fond children hourly expected his death. Richard Plowman got up and took Jules affectionately by the arm. "Did you lunch with the Comtesse?"

John Tanker looked at Jules. "I'm very worried about my accounts in Swiss francs. They say the Swiss franc is going off."

Raccamond looked up, slightly dazed, from his earnest attitude of compelling intimacy, and after hugging with a glance the two brown-eyed old men, said, "Mr. Tanker is thinking of selling all his stocks and taking a short position. I've told him we consider it wiser."

"Or perhaps I shouldn't," said John Tanker, Sr. "Perhaps your information comes from a pool. What am I to do? I don't want to lose my money. I mustn't lose any more money. When I was younger I did nothing but make money. Now, every turn, I lose money. What do you think of London, Bertillon? Do you think it's safe to keep a balance in London? Will they confiscate gold, Bertillon?" He shook his head, his hand trembled on the cane: "I mustn't lose any more money."

Raccamond said, "You won't, Mr. Tanker. Mr. Bertillon himself is selling short all the time, except in London."

Passionately the trembling old man asked, "Are you, are you, are you? Tell me: where do you get your information? It all depends on the source. In the old days I could smell a pool a mile off. I'm an old man. No one

156

will look after me but myself." He murmured some string of words to himself.

Jules was sympathetic: "Why, Tanker, what do you want to make more millions for? Why don't you get married and have a good time? Get someone to look after you. Where will be all of us in a few years? You can't bank on eternity any more, John. I'm not worrying and look how many more years of poverty I would have than you—then why should you worry, John?"

The old man shook his head long. "You are young. You have time, strength. When I was young I shouldn't have worried. You can make more money. No one else will bother about me. My money—" He looked closer at Raccamond. "What's your name, eh? You're new, aren't you?"

"Raccamond," he said, startled: they had conferred so often!

"Yes, yes. Perhaps you're right but I don't know if you know. I must ask Alphendéry: that's who I must ask, Alphendéry. Jules, what about my S.O.N.J.? If there'll be a war, I shouldn't sell. Do you think the Swiss franc is going off, Bertillon? Do you, Plowman?" He looked at Raccamond. "Do you, Whittaker?" Aristide started. Jules, standing behind Tanker, Sr., shook his head. Raccamond answered, "No, no, Mr. Tanker, you needn't worry."

"Ah, pah," said the old man, "you don't know anything about it. I don't know. It's a dangerous time. I must think about it myself. Perhaps you're right. Don't sell yet." He looked closer at Raccamond. "What's your name? Eh? It doesn't matter: you had a man a little while ago, Bertillon, Légaré: where's he? Bad policy to keep changing your men. What about my S.O.N.J., Bertillon? Whittaker says to sell. You can never tell with these customers' men: what do they know? Stock-exchange rats: run about after dark, pick up the grains that fall. Rats!" he said loudly, fiercely to Raccamond. "Never make any money themselves. Don't know what money is." He nodded to Bertillon. "Money is a mystery—an open mystery: you and I could tell them a thousand times what it is made of and they wouldn't know any better. No good asking their advice. Now, Alphendéry—he's secret: he looks seedy, but they say," he lowered his voice and quizzed Bertillon, "they say he's made millions for you, Jules, and has socked

157

away half a million dollars in America. Is it true? Eh? Where is he? I get my advice from moneymakers. . . . Have you ever made a fortune, Ratisbon," he asked Raccamond, cunningly. "No, eh? Then why should I take your advice. He says to sell, eh?" He began to lift himself out of the chair, cunningly laughing at Jules. "I must see someone about my Rio Tinto and Anaconda: I'm very worried." Without looking round he went out: the swing-door padded gently on his back.

Plowman said, "Where are his children?"

"Oh, they don't care twopence for him. He divided up his money with them about ten years back so that they wouldn't be sitting round with their tongues hanging out for his funeral: the result is they live ten thousand miles apart and they've all got lawyers waiting briefed, ready to fight his will, whatever it is."

The felted swing-door opened of itself, a little slit: then Tanker, Sr.'s old brown felt hat peeped through the crack. He surveyed them carefully and came in.

"Bertillon! I was looking for you. I think I ought to switch, really." He looked at Plowman. "Hullo, Richard." He sat down. "Everything costs so much. I can't afford it. My sister has no sense of responsibility. Nothing but spend, spend, spend: waste, waste. A woman of her age to be gadding about! She eats downstairs in the restaurant! I tell her, 'Why can't you do what I do, eat in your room?' No: money, money, money. I told the hotel clerk to put a table in my room so she could come and eat with me. Company. She doesn't have to make it. I make it. I boil it two hours. It's on now. When I get home, it's done. What can I eat but porridge, at my age? My digestion. I like those other things: I like them. But my digestion! They put me in a little burner. I told them, 'It's all in the service.' They don't expect anything. She gives, she gives." He rubbed his knee. He held up his hands to Raccamond, showing the knots at the fingers. "Look at that!" he said with mournful vanity. "Rheumatism. Aix-les-Bains. Hrmph! 'It's old age,' I said to him, 'you can't cure'— Aix-les-Bains! That's it: money—they want you to spend. Old age you can't cure, so why should I spend the money, I ask . . . spend." He laughed, had a flash. "No one on earth could make money if everyone thought the way I do—I did—" he stopped a moment to grieve. "Let them criticize me. God bless them. They don't know. If I spent

158

money would I have it? Ha! My sister is an ignorant woman. . . . Steaks, blood, blood, ugh! She'll be sorry for it. Let her eat porridge with me—restaurants!"

"What do you eat for supper though, John?" said Plowman, kindly and even with some interest.

"What do I want, an old man? Nothing, nothing, nothing. I don't eat—to keep me going—nothing, a little of this, a little of that: nothing. What can I eat? I hate to have a lot of people round me expecting tips. . . . I said to her, 'I'll cook the porridge: you've only got to eat it. It's not asking much. Surely you can eat with your old brother.' You'd think—human kindness—alone! Who cares? Now! Now! It's a tragedy to be old," he said, looking imploringly at Jules Bertillon, "No one to look after your money: the least chink of a coin and their eyes full of greed, snatching, murdering greed!" He brought his stick in quickly to his chest. He shook his fist and looked at Raccamond.

Raccamond leaned forward with a spasm. "Mr. Tanker! Are you going to buy the Anaconda?"

"Eh? Anaconda? What about Anaconda? Buy? Sell? Who knows? Do I want to sell? I'll see: there's no hurry. I'll let you know. Thanks very much for taking such an interest in my account. I've got to be going. Good-by, Plowman. You see, it takes me forty minutes to walk home." The felted door swung.

Jules walked to the window and looked out. "Don't worry about John Tanker, he's no more gaga than you or me. His head is screwed on tight when it comes to Anaconda. What do you make of it, Richard? How much of the porridge act is a gag? I know for certain he really lives on porridge. He made a settlement on his sister twenty-five years ago. He's not a bad old duck. He's been very decent to his family and they've all turned sour on him, except his sister. They're in agony trying to get to his cashbox. They tried to shut him up three years ago. . . . Are you coming along, Richard?"

"No, I'm going over my account with Aristide, here."

Jules laughed. "What on earth for? Ask Mlle. Gentil in the next room: she's got the whole bank at her finger end. . . ."

"I was. Raccamond and I were having a little chat," said Richard pleasantly.

159

Jules laughed. "O.K. Claire wants you to supper to-night, don't forget."

The door shut, Jules felt dissipated, ill at ease. He looked for comfort somewhere. In the next room was the aged accountant, ten years past retiring age, Jean-Baptiste Berthellot. He was dressed in a loose, greasy black coat with tails, low-cut waistcoat strained over his belly, white shirt, and stock, and sat sleeping, his hands aground on his fat legs. He had just got in from lunch. His thin hair, not yet gray, lay in streaks across a bald patch. A minute after the door opened, he opened his eyes and smiled placidly at Bertillon. "Good day, Mr. Jules." He struggled vaguely, pretending to be about to rise in his chair, but Jules patted the air with his hand. "Sit down, Berthellot. Anything new?"

Berthellot smiled broadly. "No, no nothing, nothing at all!"

"Don't you want to retire, Jean-Baptiste? You can have your pension any time you want it."

"Thanks very much, Mr. Jules. I know. Not yet, no. . . . Mr. Jules! I entered a monthly meeting of the Five Brothers Simla (Luxemburg) Corporation this morning."

"Oh, good! You look after that, Jean-Baptiste: it's mechanical."

"I drew my usual director's fees." There was a sort of malevolent twinkle in the folds of the old man's eyes.

"That's right."

"And I entered an extra meeting of the Delaware Blue Dome Holding Company, Inc.," murmured the old man with a crisp suggestiveness.

"With the usual director's fees," said Jules, grinning. "O.K. . . . Well, don't overwork, Jean-Baptiste. At your age, too many directors' meetings might make you liverish." He let the door close softly behind him and grinned to himself in the green dusk of the corridor. "Old horse thief!" He stood thinking a moment. Should he retire the old creature by force, or not? He wanted him to train someone for him before he went. Jean-Baptiste Berthellot was the only one beside his eldest brother, William, and himself who had any idea of the real income and outgo of the bank. Alphendéry didn't know: twin brothers, Paul and Francis Bertillon asked nothing as long as their bills at Pyle's were paid occasionally; Claire-Josèphe was only concerned with the fate of her marriage portion. No one else counted.

Berthellot was eminently trustworthy because he was so vain of his self-perfected little system of inoffensive blackmail: he was "director" or minority "shareholder" in several inactive companies which Jules had incorporated in Luxemburg, England, Scotland, and the State of Delaware, U.S.A., both to dispose of assets and to scatter responsibility, and he never failed to roll up for his director's fees, although naturally no meetings were held but were only entered formally on the books to comply with the laws regulating such companies.*

Jules shrugged his shoulders and laughed it off, compliant, lethargic. "Microscopic graft! One of these days the attractions of growing radishes in Juvisy will be too strong for him." He walked off and after an abstracted moment spent looking over the balustrade and considering the "lambs" he had gathered in his "sap basket" downstairs (his private terms for clients and the open court with glass roof in which business was done), he walked into the next room whistling. An open file case, an unoccupied typewriter, a green carpet. Jules went to the window and looked out into the street. Tanker, Sr., who must have been dallying downstairs over the blackboard, was just struggling across Rue Lafitte. A taxi swerved away from him and the chauffeur indignantly gesticulated. Jules laughed. "The spines of all the Tanker lawyers must have crawled." He yawned and looked round the walls. Jules Simla Bertillon, citation for bravery, military medal; for having brought down four enemy planes singlehanded. Jules Simla Bertillon, Chevalier of the Legion of Honor; Jules Simla Bertillon, certificate of the Racing Club of France; the same, member of the Thoroughbred Horses' Club. He kicked his heels round, much bored, and came to the squat green strongbox that he was considering when Armand Brossier, gold clerk, came in. He almost saluted Jules. "I beg pardon!" He had just taken a bunch of keys out of his pocket.

"Got some money there, Armand?"

"Yes, sir: some gold Mr. William just bought—some American gold eagles and a Persian gold piece someone brought in for curiosity, five krans. He bought it at once."

* Books of minutes, already made up, may be purchased.

He proceeded to twist the mechanism and unlock the secret drawer inside. Jules looked in.

"How much have we got in there, Armand? Mr. William didn't tell me we had so much. Why, you've got twenty-five bags thereabout, haven't you? What's in them?"

"Different coins in different bags: here, gold eagles and gold half-eagles; here, twenty-five-peseta pieces in gold; here, some German gold twenty-mark pieces; in this bag, odd coins, like Japanese ten-yen pieces. The rest are all sovereigns, half-sovereigns, and gold louis . . . roughly, about 1,625,000 francs in here. Mr. Bertillon, about one hundred thousand francs per bag, as well as I have been able to divide them." He was very earnest. He exhibited the bags, each about the size of a goose egg, as passionately as if he had dug it up himself.

"That's all right," said Jules calmly. "You like that, don't you, all that gold?"

The young man smiled palely. "I suppose I do, in a way: you cannot look at gold as filthy lucre."

"When people are collecting gold they aren't doing business," said Jules, with a note of irritation. "Gold is constipation: even bankruptcy is more fluid. Gold isn't wealth: positions in markets are wealth. Don't be taken in." He smiled. "But you're doing no harm. They'll take it out again soon enough, don't worry, and bury it in some other hole: dogs always are digging up their bones."

Brossier regretfully closed the drawer and the safe. "Yes, Mr. Bertillon: I understand." But he looked downcast. Jules was irritated. He had had no idea that William had bought so much gold. He went along to William's room and as he was opening the door, cried, "Say, you've made me costive in gold. Why keep gold? To pay a debt to a rich man is a waste of money—he'll throw it to his brokers or his whores in a couple of hours and to pay a poor man is a waste of time: he'll pay his rent to some gangster who'll be across the Spanish border tomorrow with the general funds and the chap you pay'll be on the bread line tomorrow, however you look at it. Keep your money. It's all right to give confidence by gold, or as a bet on inflation, but don't spend so much money on it. It's a commodity, and we're not in commodities, William. We're in grapples, clinches, blackmails, plunges, lucky breaks, long odds, lowdowns, big gambles, and secret bookkeeping. . . . You and I are trying to run two different sorts of banks on the same premises. I wish you'd do what I want. I started this bank. . . ."

"I know you did," said William mildly, "but gold is virtue: one double-eagle crushes four shady rumors. And gold has no name, it licks the hand of anyone who has it: good dog! It's better than stocks and bonds; it's always valid; and it doesn't have to be changed into any other value. It is value. You let the Comtesse de Voigrand know you can pay out a demand for, say, fifty thousand francs entirely in gold, and she'll bring you back the next day half a million: gossip harvest. . . ."

"What's the use of reserves in a time like this: have the Germans reserves? We have and we're picked on by all Europe: blackmail is what pays," squealed Jules. "We've got out of the gold age, that's all. Gold is only good because it's portable . . . the governments have learned a thing or two: they won't be letting us hold gold and let it sweat profits in failing currencies, the way it does at present. . . . Not too much of it: I need funds. . . ."

William was laughing in his sleeve. "Say, Jules: you know the Swedish baroness used to be here? She left an account of two hundred and fifty thousand crowns: I thought she'd forgotten about it. You know she's always soused in akvavit. Last week she sent in a letter demanding the transfer of two hundred and fifty thousand francs (not crowns) to her bank in Stockholm. I forgot about it, I've been so busy. Today I got another letter insisting on the transfer at once of her two hundred and fifty thousand francs at the current rate of Swedish crowns—about 41,666 crowns. So I did it. If she finds out her 'mistake,' we'll transfer the rest. . . ."

Etienne, the venerable doorkeeper, appeared in the doorway, his faithful eyes on Jules.

"Mr. Jules! Monsieur Aristippe de Partiefine would like to see you."

"Send him up. Poor guy," said Jules, "I suppose he wants a loan: his last wife only gives him petty cash."

Aristippe de Partiefine was one of the fabulous figures ,of little Paris—a penniless Casanova; so charming, so rich in love, and so empty-headed that four rich women had married him and deserted him.

"Aristippe must be forty-five now, you know," said William in a melancholy tone.

163

He came up, tall, broad, very swarthy, well groomed, bowed a little from his excessive height, modest-speaking, mild. His features, though well formed, had a disproportion that caused people to say, "Why, the man's quite ugly!" His eyes were set rather close together, but deep enough with richly folded lids that disappeared in shadows at the outer corners; his jutting nose had a slightly thickened end; the long mouth with perfectly formed, dark swelling lips, broadened to smile a guileless, kind, confiding smile, whenever Aristippe turned from the person speaking to him, to some other one standing by, as if to confirm this silent person in their first impression: "I am your friend: count on me." Women immediately felt that they had happened on an affinity, a natural intelligence, a deep harmony, a grand devotion. Aristippe smiled at Jules.

"Jules, I have a little scheme for business. I just wanted to know if you knew some good stenographers, male stenographers I should prefer—I want some copying done. . . . I have a formula I want copied out. François Legris said he would back me. It's a good formula—for reinvigoration, much better than the Titus pearls."

"Oh, I'll get one of my girls to do it."

"Oh, no: I shouldn't like the young ladies here to do it . . . you don't know some public stenographers. You see, they are used to all sorts of work. And then it has to be translated from the Polish. It was sent to me from—a man I know in Warsaw. It is used by him and his family. It is a sort of family secret. It is all in Polish. There would have to be so many words to look up—you see," he smiled his smile at William and went on to Jules, "Your girls couldn't do it. Besides, I must pay for it."

"Have you got it?" asked Jules. "I can read Polish. I was in Poland one time."

Partiefine handed over the formula. It was a typewritten document about fourteen pages long, giving the formula, the complaints it was supposed to cure, the happy results obtained by its use, a short history of the family that had originated it, the method of distribution, its cost. . . . Aristippe smiled once more sweetly at William to show that no favoritism was meant by showing Jules the formula first. . . .

"It looks fine," said Jules.

"I have some chaps going round the pharmacies in the

sixteenth and seventh and fifteenth *arrondissements* and the pharmacies have agreed to take it, but I've got to get up some diagrams and publicity. Do you think François Legris will really put up money?" Aristippe had a rather timid and deprecating manner which showed Jules that he hoped the Bertillons would back him, too. "I thought a few, downstairs—" he hesitated and smiled at William, "might like to back me," he said softly. "I showed it to a couple of them. Your manager, Urbain Voulou, said he would put a couple of thousand francs into it. I think it should—interest—the pharmacies seemed—quite interested. Of course, there are other—other kinds—being sold. I thought I might call it the Polish Formula: it's attractive, isn't it? Or the Viennese Formula. . . . Will you give me the address? . . ."

"Ask Alphendéry," said Jules. "He knows everything."

Aristippe soberly thanked him and moved out with the gait of the leaning tower of Pisa walking.

"I'll give him a couple of thousand, if he brings it up again," said Jules. "Every guy when he's out of luck invents a contraceptive, a reinvigorator, or a purgative: why I wonder? That goes in the petty-cash account. The Comtesse told me to take Carrière on: she thinks the pound will hold, she thinks it's just a scare."

"Yeah? Well, I'd rather start fooling with the pound a few months from now: why is he anxious to run you in on this? Keep out of it. Carrière is poison."

"Oh, I won't do anything. I don't trust that fellow." William walked out.

The door opened and Jules came in with Dr. Jacques Carrière, the famous young society bachelor, and Aristide Raccamond. Carrière was a head taller than Raccamond, Raccamond a belly wider than him; Carrière was flushed with wine, conceit, and impudence, but the secretary, Lucille Dalbi, thought him handsome. "I don't need you, Aristide," said Jules insolently. Aristide lowered his head, looked at them all like a cornered bull, and left. Carrière sank down and his knife crease and florid shoes emerged more opulently.

"To begin with, Jules, I'm a bit overmargined and you've got about 275,000 francs of mine here: you can make a book transfer of that, before I send you the rest round from the Crédit. By the way—the commission:

I'd like to have a half per cent paid to Comte Hervé Lucé, poor chap. He's a friend of Jean de Guipatin's and I thought I'd make a bit of money for the poor fellow."

"Why not?" agreed Jules. "You know I don't want the money. . . . What's the matter with him? Dope?"

"Dope. I know the chap that sells it to him. You've got one of them here unless I'm mistaken: I've seen him hovering about the passages and back streets, pressing the hands of funny-looking gentry—that miserable little huckster-fellow that wears a bowler hat, a Belgian, isn't he? Looks like a bankrupt private detective, never shaved in the morning. Quite a cad, I should say, but—in cahoots with the drug squad."

"You mean Henri Parouart? He's a chiseler, petty blackmail artist. Catches us up by one minute on an execution in New York and a quarter of a point in London. . . . Blackmail doesn't interest me," said Jules with more emphasis: "a blackmailer and a denouncer always find themselves on the pavement. They do no more than beg their bread in a peculiarly slimy fashion: at the first breath of big business, the ranks close and we chuck them out. . . ."

"I've heard a Paris Napoleon is behind Parouart," suggested Carrière with malice.

"In those shoes? Let him ride: I'll get something on him, sooner or later, when I have the time. Well, Jacques, we're going to have Spanish royalty with us in Paris. Do you really think he's got all that dough here? I think we'll get fat with all the revolutions going on. They all come to Paris—everyone from the Aga Khan who sells his bath water, to Don Jaime de Bourbon, who only lives by divine right, gets here. . . ."

"Shall we write a letter to each other about this pound-sterling business? Or let it rest. Do you care? Perhaps an informal letter."

With confidence, foxily, Jules agreed, "Sure, I'll write a letter: what do you want? Mlle. Dalbi, ask the telephone girl to get Comte Lucé up here: he's going to get a half per cent, he may as well witness it."

166

Scene Tweny-one: The Letter

THE letter in its final draft was so full of erasures and reconsiderations that Jules said, "Listen, Jacques, I'll send it to you by tonight's mail, or tomorrow morning: you send me yours in the same mail. That'll settle it. Hervé will be my witness. . . ."

"O.K. . . . I must get along. I want to drop in at the Chamber to see the debate. The future of Briand has got them all excited."

"Good luck: why don't you run for the Chamber? You could get big support down in the Dordogne, a native son. Must be lively down there. I'll bet the border towns are flustered with grandees, jostling each other, their coats all out of line with concealed duros. . . ."

When Carrière had gone, Jules called up his crony Pierre Olympe, a lawyer fabulously ignorant, but extremely fashionable. Between them, they concocted the letter about the bet on sterling and posted it off to Carrière. It read:

I agree to pay you in francs, at the rate of 122 francs to the £, any sterling demands in the sum of £25,000 each, the first demand payable on May 10, 1931, and succeeding demands every four months thereafter, until the sum of £250,000 shall have been paid, on this basis. On the other hand, should the £ continue above the rate of 122 francs at the dates of such demands, the difference between 122 and the prevailing rate shall accrue to me, Jules Bertillon, on each occasion.

Carriére read this carefully and laughed aloud the next morning at breakfast. He looked across at Caro de Faniul, with his suffering white face and long scarlet mouth. The youth's hands, long, firm, white, and ringed, tapped impatiently: he was scowling frightfully and forcing his face into a wrinkled mask because Jacques was reading the mail in his presence. Jacques smiled. "Read that, Caro."

His lids drooped and he tossed it back. "You know I don't understand anything about business!"

Carrière was even more expansive. "Why, he says 'sterling demands,' the fool, not 'drafts.' Thus, without any brewery at all, he has to pay me the difference in exchange on any demand I send through: he hasn't mentioned the brewery, for example. Well! . . . Of course, the pound will go off: it will give him a stitch in the side trying to keep up with the pound, and it may ruin him. Not bad!"

"You are filthy, Jacques."

"That sort of boy, self-centered and ignorant in a world of quicksands, if he gets something done, thinks he is a genius, something mystic and superior to us other men: he has never seen a snow crystal or the hair of a fly through a lens, for example: if he did, he would believe in demons! It's so easy to break him—it's no more pleasure than splintering a match, really."

"Then don't do it, Jacques: it's so vulgar."

"To realize anything is vulgar," said Carrière. "When you've done it, you ask yourself, 'Why did I bring it out in the light of the sun?' like the mother of an ungrateful son. There's as much difference between the image and reality as between the joy of conception and the chaos of childbed." Caro looked at him coldly, drank the last of his coffee. "But why is this so?" asked Jacques Carrière, with the slow grinding tone of one who is forced to talk although he knows he is boring his partner. "Because I am myself formless and cannot conceive properly. You see that, don't you? You should. If I could grow up, entirely, I would not be so vicious: I am an unhappy myth. Jules is endlessly, primevally fertile. But he isn't human! He doesn't even try to be a man."

"He is charming," said Caro. "You know, when I met him I said to myself, 'Who is he? Where have I seen him before? Long ago, very long ago?' And later in the evening, I found myself saying, 'Hermes, Hermes,' again and again, muttering the name like that. Why (I thought) Hermes. That's Jules. He would be at home in ancient Greece, crooked, modern, plausible, argent, endless coiner, stamping images of himself on wax hearts, his own fraud, currency." Jacques studied him carefully with an aged expression of craft and understanding.

"A king-thief!" said Jacques Carrière.

Scene Twenty-two: "Weltanschauung"

FRANZ ROSENKRANTZ looked in the mirror all the time he talked and this gave his conversation an added polish, a reflective elegance of mood which matched well his polished fingernails, eyeglasses, white collar, and smooth thin black hair. A few gray hairs in tufts over each ear fell in with his mid-European color scheme of balanced black and white. The responses that Alphendéry made to him were only legatos in the sonata of his reflections: he heard what was said faintly as an echo and he bound these musical echoes into his theme.

"I was at Verdun," said Alphendéry. "I saw five years of war and I really am still alive."

"Undoubtedly: then we never faced each other—I was in the division that occupied St. Quentin in 1917."

He looked into the mirror, half smiling to himself, but at himself. "One would say that time is a river in which we turn over and over like logs and blades of grass!" He held his wineglass to the light with a gesture from the old gay dramas. "I prefer the purple mantle of dark Burgundy! The French put all their *Weltanschauung* into their wine! Our wine is clear, reedy, piquant, reasonable, and we put our *Weltanschauung* into our music, literature, and philosophy! Judge which nation has chosen wisely."

Alphendéry, whose efforts at conversation, or rather at brilliant monologue, or apothegmatic reply, had been silenced several times by the man in the mirror, now tapped on his knife with his head down, a very rare thing for him: his conversation usually flourished to the accompaniment of profuse, meaningless gestures. He said automatically, "There isn't a Frenchman alive who doesn't try to make himself a picture of the universe, and a remarkably well policed one (too policed)! But there isn't the background of Grimm's fairy tales, marvel, dread, and illiteracy that is the basis of much of the profound thinking from over the Rhine. The troll wood, the Black Forest, dragon rocks, river maidens, the Lorelei: it produces a beautiful and confused effect of torrents and thunder in

German music. The vast barren stretches, like Courland, produce your German categories."

The man in the mirror was thrust into the background. Another legendary figure arose, the racial theory. Captain, now German citizen (in exile) Rosenkrantz, said, "It astonishes me to hear you defend the two-dimensional thinking of the French. You are French, in a way, by birth, but your father and mother came from that very region, you say, from the Black Forest! You yourself were born in Strasbourg. Except for a territorial convention, that is Germany. And then, more important, you are, like me, a Jew! The Talmud has given us a rich, medieval background, even if we don't go to the synagogue, which makes us friendlier to the splendid complexity, the grand subterranean instincts of German thoughts. Germany is the true home of the modern Jew."

"Are you in Paris?"

Rosenkrantz shook his head. "Economic necessity. New forces arising are alien to the German soul, the German-Jewish soul. The Marxists, the National Socialists. Both Jews and Germans understand that social organization is founded on the family: the German has the tribe father, the Jew the father as King in Israel. The Frenchman has no sense of family: he habitually keeps two ménages, he has illegitimate children, brings venereal disease into the heart of the home: he has no sense of true organization. Tell me one thing, Herr Alphendéry, would you have your children brought up in France?"

Alphendéry laughed. "You keep on forgetting I am French."

"But you are a Jew. You must yearn for a deeper, truer sense of living."

Alphendéry suddenly became excited. "I know I am French and forget everything else. Compare Diderot and that ass Kant. Diderot was a mind that adorned six universes of knowledge—without him the social history of his time could not be written. Kant? A monstrous pedant, a colossus of ignorance, who never went thirty miles from his home and never had sexual intercourse. Is that a man? That's a mummy. I don't believe in your pure reason. The only philosopher for me is the one who is ostentatiously physiological, and whose brain only overworks, because all his other functions overwork: a true giant of a man, not a beetle."

Captain Rosenkrantz, retreating before his man's choler, shifted to more familiar ground: "Even the German needs a little fermentation to produce the perfect metropolitan type. Between ourselves, there is too much of the Slav and the peasant in your ordinary German."

Alphendéry bit off a chunk of the conversation, like a hungry, healthy man who bolts, and whose digestion is nevertheless unimpaired. "Yes, in fact, the Jew has been hammered on the anvil cobbles of cities for many generations, long before the ancestors of most of the Germans had learned to cook the roots they dug with their nails or their stones. But that does not make him a Jew. It makes him a metropolitan. What is the Jew? Just a bourgeois. The soul of the burgher. The reason you don't like France, Herr Rosenkrantz, is that you can't pick out the Jews here: they all look Jewish, everyone. You don't like that. You want to sit in a tribe, don't you? And then the French are as smart as the Jew, they have all he has —a head for finance, money monopolies, learning, family organization, love of law and medicine, rationalism, democracy, a complete organization of property round the family. But what were we, Herr Rosenkrantz? The wireless telegraphists of the Middle Ages? By carrier pigeon, or grapevine telegraph, or messengers, or mails, we got to know the prices for which goods had been or could be sold in the central markets; we were the exchange men. Where are we now with the radio? The peasant in the wildest parts of Bessarabia, once he has a radio, knows just as well as you or me the closing in Winnipeg and Chicago. No more Jew: the radio wiped him out. Let the Jew become a citizen. But no. The Jews howl against the Soviet Union which frees them from pogroms, from the sweatshop, from rabbinical graft and superstition. They cling to Germany which detests and insults them, to the British Empire which is using them as does a jackal, as a cat's-paw. And we think we're clever. . . . What is it the Jew doesn't want to lose? Not Judaism, my dear Herr Rosenkrantz, but the bourgeoisie, of which he is the archetype, the most concentrated example. That's my analysis of the return to the synagogue by the overrich members of our congregation. A defense against Bolshevism? And what is Bolshevism? It's Izzy, Jakie, and Manny forming a labor union in the sweatshop. So the

171

boss runs back to Judaism. . . . Let us forget the Jew, Herr Rosenkrantz, let's remember humanity."

Rosenkrantz had an intelligent, flushed, and insincere air, with something of patronage. "You are one of those who put our racial history in a nameless sepulcher because it has been unpleasant. But that is where our wary intelligence comes from! From fight, from oppression, from loopholes. Forget that and we become like the Gentiles, ignoramuses, bumpkins: we have lost our patrimony! And will the *Goyium* ever let us forget it? Perhaps for a liberal generation or so, but it returns. And the French! The French cunningly wish to submerge our rival intelligence by absorbing us, making us lose our identity. At one time, they said, 'Your race or your life!' That's it now. I prefer the Germans and the old Russians who hate us, imprison us, lock us in quarters like lepers, but respect the integrity of our race. Yes. We suffer, but the essential, the dignity of the soul, and the race soul remains. We are men, being dogs."

Alphendéry's reply was like a trumpet: people in the restaurant turned to look at them. "We suffer and live in the best hotels, eat in the best *brasseries,* travel in the luxury expresses, spend money at Le Touquet, dress ourselves in the Rue de la Paix, ski at St. Moritz, own châteaux from here to Tokyo, have our paws on all the credit and commercial banks: we reign and we are oppressed, too. We suffer the way my broker in London, E. Ralph Stewart, with a house in the country, a house in Mayfair, and a leased shooting lodge, is a follower of the humble despised Christ. I am tired of those fairy tales."

He looked tired. Rosenkrantz sneered politely. "But you believe in socialism, if I'm not mistaken! The theory of a man who put his own children in an orphan asylum, for example. Karl Marx who drank beer with the roughs on Hampstead Heath and assaulted policemen. Refined company. Their socialism is a sort of bureaucratic tiger-eat-tiger. Where else do you have such corruption as in France? Imagine the possibilities in a more democratic or, as you say, a proletarian state. What virtues has the common man?"

Alphendéry was cool with rage. "May I ask why you left your paradises then? They still pogromize Jews in Roumania, I believe. You ought to go there if it's so fine for the soul and for business."

"We, in international business, are never in a foreign country. The market place, the exchange booth is our home. Am I dealing with France? Are you? Are we dealing with Rotterdam, the Ukraine; telephoning to Bucharest, London, Liverpool, Dublin? And whatever country we're in, we're telephoning those places; it makes no difference. France is just a foothold to do business in. What is there in it to hold the soul of man?"

"There, you see," said Alphendéry calmly, "our greatest weakness: we have no gratitude to our friends. And we kiss the foot that kicks us, abasing ourselves, as no living man should, while winking to each other and telling ourselves how smart we are, fooling the *Goyim!*" Alphendéry started laughing like a diamond. "They make wonderful pastry here."

"The French are good cooks," said Rosenkrantz with a faint sneer.

"And Paris is farther from German aeroplanes than Antwerp," Alphendéry put in with rebuke.

Rosenkrantz smiled to himself, spat out a cherry stone, wiped his fingers elegantly, and looking round for the waiter, clapped his hands.

"Coffee?" asked Alphendéry. *"Un café noir."*

"Demitasse," corrected Rosenkrantz in his old-fashioned phraseology. He put his serviette on his knees and looked at Alphendéry who was replete, rounded, and smiling in his happy digestion. "Mr. Jules Bertillon is a charming man. A little—faunish, shall we say? It occurs to me that he has no ideology at all. It is impossible, of course, but one would say—almost irresponsible."

Alphendéry smiled. "He likes to give that impression."

Rosenkrantz half closed his eyes. "Brandy? Waiter, two *fines maison*. It's easy to caricature oneself: to play the part of oneself, I mean. Many people do the same. It's a double role. They are at liberty to be themselves, they sense a masquerade. This may be one of those cases."

"He has a vivid financial imagination: that I can testify to."

"Has he financial intelligence though? Instincts, I should say, but not much real financial *Weltanschauung*. My impression. I don't want to underrate him. That would be quite an error. It is well to know men's distinguishing characteristics before you begin to work with them: then

173

there are no surprises, you can determine your plan of campaign beforehand."

"Bertillon has one distinguishing characteristic, his make-up is solid, his bank is liquid. It's a whim, of course, in these days, but he is like that. His own system. He is not so light as he appears."

"If I didn't think that, I wouldn't do business," Rosenkrantz lifted his clean cuffs to light a cigar: through the smoke his gleaming teeth smiled at Alphendéry. "Herr Alphendéry, as between brothers-in-the-credo, you can tell me your real impression, your own private summing-up of the situation. It will go no farther."

Alphendéry's beautiful, resonant voice was sharp when he said, "My private impression is that Bertillon is a financial genius who is bound to live and die rich."

Rosenkrantz said in an undertone, "I hope so." Alphendéry could see him studying him through the smoke, with some doubt. Alphendéry, used to racial confrontations, due to his frontier birth, knew what was in his mind, viz., "This is a Gentile-loving Jew . . . he's a hard nut to crack. Or is he holding out on me for some private bargain?" He knew that in Rosenkrantz's view of the world there were no motives in men but those of personal gain. And yet Rosenkrantz was an exceedingly well-educated, relatively humane, and widely experienced man. He said, "You think Mr. Bertillon will work with us? It costs him nothing and adds a department to his bank. We could organize the same in his other branches, especially in the Low Countries. . . . We have our own correspondents. Only we can't afford to pay for cable service, quotations —a serious cable service, quotations—a serious handicap. . . ."

Generously Alphendéry offered, "But why can't you get it from us? We get it automatically and we really have no use for commodity quotations, except as a check-up. Our boys wouldn't mind a bit telephoning them through to you, either here or in the Netherlands. . . . You're strangers here and you will need your path smoothed till you get the hang of the city. . . . We don't mind at all giving you the service. I can help you personally: I know my Paris as few men do." Alphendéry, who had been out of tune all the evening, warmed up in the spirit of his generosity and beamed at Rosenkrantz.

Rosenkrantz feared in him the "rationality of the

Frenchman," which he regarded as a slick, apish, mental trick for avoiding the profound problems of the universe. He dropped something of his *Geheimrat* manner and they discussed diverse manners of co-operation between the little office in the Rue Boissy-d'Anglas (Rosenkrantz's office) and the Banque Bertillon in the Rue Pillet-Will. Alphendéry recommended him to Maître Lemaître, in his opinion the leading lawyer of Paris. In leaving, they bowed to each other with German courtesy, Rosenkrantz with courtly elegance, Alphendéry with something more of roundness, jollity, and affection.

Rosenkrantz immediately telephoned to Guildenstern. "Alphendéry, the alter ego of Bertillon, is partially with us. He began hostile but he is coming over. It's a Jew, after all. I don't think we need worry on that score. Now, what I figure is this: either Bertillon is really rich, in which case we can get in through Alphendéry, eventually, or, being broke, they won't go down for six months or a year, because, naturally, they won't plunge: they'll arrange things carefully, and we will inherit a good proportion of their clients, by that time. And if it's longer, we can, by that time, dig in to the other branches and have claims on them: we can be there before the receivers. We'll get a contract out of them for six months or a year, say, and we can word it—Bertillon has the reputation of being rash and ill-advised. His lawyer is Pierre Olympe, an absolute fool who married money. An ex-airman. No, I didn't get a lawyer. Alphendéry, who is quite a talker, one of these soft liberals, recommended a lawyer, but naturally I don't want one he's too friendly with. Besides he seems to be some jurist of international repute: we don't want that. We want a man with business *nous*. A Jew, of course. . . . Bertillon's a harlequin, and Alphendéry's a socialist; the three other brothers—pure zeros, of course. . . . There's a very smart fellow, Maître Lallant, was in trouble, but he knows everybody, taps all the pipe lines: he's the one, evidently. Alphendéry kept on insisting that Bertillon is rich. Selling line? Like most liberals, he's blunted: do you think the *Goy* has pulled the wool over his eyes? Tomorrow morning in the Select at eight? Good night. My respects to your gracious lady."

Alphendéry walking up and down his room, twisting a big handkerchief bought for the purpose, for two francs fifty, was laughing to himself and saying, half aloud, "The

Jew has been polished on the . . . Jew has been polished on the cobbles of . . . anvils . . . long before the Saxons learned to cook the . . . ha . . . the roots they dug." (He didn't know whether to be pleased for the Jews or angry for the Germans.) "Ha! The French put their *Weltanschauung* into their wine. That's good! Rosenkrantz is a man after my own heart . . . cultivated, Germans very cultivated people—no doubt, no doubt. . . . In a way." He walked up and down two or three times, waving his handkerchief into more knots and horns, his lips moving, smiling to himself: his expression became stern, the invisible auditor, the air, heard, "Judaism: I'm tired of their Judaism. A lever to bigger and better business. Degrading. Degrading . . . is making money such a passion that? . . . Degrading. Good day! We're all Christians together: let's put a piece of orange peel under Smith's boot. Yes, good day, brother in the covenant, I want you to steal your boss's account books: he's an infidel. No, you won't? Then—no sense of honor, no honor . . . no sense of, no sense of. . . . It's my own fault if I . . . money —their class . . . we serve two: *their* social system to keep up which we need money and work for it. Degrading. Our own fault. Break our backs to pay tribute . . . for our dream and hope. We all do it. All those who are not ambitious do it. Get ambitious for them, for *them*—we do it! We do it! Not ambitious."

In the morning the concierge stopped him and showed him a letter that had just come by hand. He opened it and read, with stupefaction:

DEAR MR. ALPHENDÉRY,

I confirm our conversation, in the restaurant Ruc last night. You remarked that Mr. Bertillon was wealthy and the bank liquid, and that both could be relied upon. You agreed that Mr. Bertillon was anxious to enter into business with us. You offered further, that it would cost us nothing and that it added a department to his commission business in commodity contracts and that if you get offers of such contracts you turn them over to us as a matter of course, you having no organization to deal with them and it not paying you to set up a department of your own. You admit that our collaboration would be of great use to you in gaining accounts and, for example, stock-exchange business in London. You say you will ask people in centers abroad to send commodity contracts to us and you will put us in touch with important persons you happen to come into touch with. You agree that we should have a quotation room and on your suggestion, are to ring up your bank and get free service from them on quotations that interest us. You further agreed to help us in all matters pertaining to our business, and offered to recommend us to a lawyer. I think we are in agreement on these points. Pray do not trouble to acknowledge this. We take silence for consent. Greetings!

FRANZ ROSENKRANTZ and FRANZ GUILDENSTERN.

The concierge hurried from her lodge to see why Mr. Alphendéry was laughing his head off in the mute white entrance hall. "Ah, Mme. Mercier, ah, ah. What a joke! Read it . . . never in all my born days . . . read it."

She took it with great eyes, devoured it, handed it back with a stubborn expression; then she said in the wifely manner of concierges who like their clients, "Mr. Alphendéry, I know nothing about banking, naturally, but listen to my advice: like the Corsicans, they sound fierce and they have nothing; they have stage manners and they seek a vendetta. I know, Mr. Alphendéry. I regret to say I have a Corsican brother-in-law."

Alphendéry sobered, folded the letter. "My word, you may be right, Mme. Mercier. Many thanks."

Jules and William put their heads together over this exhibit. Alphendéry was laughing again. "I don't think they're dangerous; such pompous prigs can't be dangerous."

"And they can't bring us any money," said Jules nastily. He detested pedantry.

"Listen," pleaded Alphendéry, pleading foolishly, because it was his nature, for the man who had enlisted him, "That's just German. It doesn't mean anything. We can laugh at them and still do business with them. What harm can they do us? None. These letters will make them a laughingstock if they were ever mad enough to bring them out in court. And did we ever receive them? . . ."

"I don't know," wheezed William, "these artists strike

177

me as being like the government; they may be lacking in substance, but they've got the classic style. The judge can understand that. Let's go gently with them. . . . But they're oversmart. They're making passes at Alphendéry because he's Jewish. Let them do all their business with Alphendéry. When they come, Jules, don't forget, leave it all to Michel. He's not called Bertillon."

At that moment Etienne Mirabaud, the doorkeeper, came up with their card. Jules said, "Our birds are downstairs! . . . Etienne, bring these gentlemen up to my office. Let me see them first, Michel. I want to see what tricks they'll try on the Gentile. Go down by the back door and have a coffee, and then come in with your hat in your hand. I want to have some fun."

"I could do with a coffee."

"You've just had one."

"What difference does that make? . . . Twenty minutes —is that right?"

"Yes. Hurry!"

Alphendéry, on his way out, peeping through the almost closed door of the interior staircase, saw them arrive—small, assured, dignified, stalwart, like government envoys, preceded by the porter. Rosenkrantz, who spoke the better French, began by imposing himself. Bertillon's language went by fits and starts, in an idiom of his own, broken and allusive, but with these he was different.

Knowing that they secretly feared "the *Goy*" to the same extent that they slighted him in private conversation, Bertillon had on his suavest manners, the manners of an old family of merchant princes. Alphendéry laughed to himself all the way downstairs. He sat in a café down the street, feeling luxurious, read the papers, and finally came in through the front door, got his hat out of the cupboard, and went to Bertillon's closed door. The voices had fallen to a steady hum, impossible to hear anything through the oak door. He knocked.

"Come in!"

Bertillon sat in the center of his large desk, upright, delicate, smooth, his capacious and beautiful hand spread out on the empty blotter. A gold pencil had fallen out of reach. A small piece of paper containing two or three items lay in front of him. Rosenkrantz and Guildenstern sat in two armchairs brought forward. Guildenstern leaned forward. He belonged to an old family of wheat

178

merchants from Poland: wheat was in his blood. He was more energetic, not quite so plump, grayer, older than his partner, less polished, and his French had holes in it. Rosenkrantz leaned back, quite the captain, quite the messroom hero. He had just been interrupted and looked round with distinguished rebuke at the intruder. He changed to compliment when he saw Alphendéry.

Alphendéry shook hands warmly, explained to Bertillon that he was late because he had to call in at the Banque de l'Union Parisienne: they interchanged a scarcely perceptible nod. He said to Bertillon, "I just saw two dentists downstairs as I came up: it looks as if the commodity business is picking up."

"So?" said Guildenstern.

"Two dentists: there won't be a grain of wheat obtainable by tomorrow," said Bertillon carelessly. The two Germans were mystified and ill at ease. Bertillon explained to them that an American dentist had cornered the cotton market.

"How is it possible?" asked Guildenstern.

"Oh, in America they pay dentists as much as the President."

Rosenkrantz was irritated, thinking they were being smoked.

Guildenstern said, "I think we may say then that the business is done, Mr. Bertillon. We will get our lawyers to draw up a temporary form of agreement, a trial form, should I say, and we will submit it to you this afternoon, or tomorrow morning: as you wish."

"Tomorrow morning or afternoon," substituted Rosenkrantz.

Bertillon appeared to be about to rise. "Very well, gentlemen: tomorrow or the next day, when you wish. Mr. Alphendéry will go through it with you. If he wants any change, arrange it between you. I will leave it to him. He has full power to act for me, for us."

He looked straight at Alphendéry. No one said anything. Then Rosenkrantz said, in his best voice, with a slight touch of the saber there, the saber cut more visible on his cheek, "Then we are to deal with Mr. Alphendéry, not yourself: with him as your agent? But you will sign it?"

"No, Alphendéry will sign it if I am not here. What he

signs is all right! He knows more about it than I do: his grandfather was in wheat, for example."

They were taken aback. Unexpectedly Bertillon's laughter rang out. He stood looking at the three of them with benevolence. One could see the slight movements of the two Germans tending towards each other. They were clearly perplexed. A moment later, their resolution taken wordlessly, Guildenstern said, with respect but curtly, "We regret very much that we cannot continue these negotiations with yourself but we will, of course, arrive promptly with the draft agreement and discuss it with Mr. Alphendéry."

"Mr. Alphendéry will sign anything that is to be signed," said Bertillon unpleasantly.

"Understood." They hesitated.

Alphendéry appeared to be raining smiles on the room. He landed in the forefront of their dubieties. "I got your little note this morning. Thanks for the memorandum, without prejudice, naturally. You have the Germanic method. We are more free and easy here. After all, even a contract is no good if a man is determined to do you, is it?"

They looked uncomfortable. Jules had risen and come round the table.

"We always confirm our business conversations: we eliminate error," said Guildenstern clumsily.

"It's human to err," said Jules laughing.

"Then, I don't see why you don't carry a dictaphone," Alphendéry suggested.

They both started, doubtful whether this was an insult or not. But no, Alphendéry was laughing in the most amiable way. Rosenkrantz shot a glance round the office. He said stealthily, "So! Is that your method? That is quite American in efficiency."

"Oh, no," said Jules, "not always. I should have my vaults full of records, instead of gold. . . . Will you excuse me? I have an appointment for lunch with Mr. Emile Moreau." This was the name of an important personage in the Banque de Paris et des Pays-Bas. The eyes of the Germans glittered. They were ceremonious and Jules escaped. At the door he smiled at Alphendéry, "Sit in my seat, Michel."

The two produced a memorandum which they had already shown Jules but which he had not read. It covered the note sent to Michel, but asked for estimates of cost, noting the manner of confirming to clients, etc. It was by far the most efficient document that had been seen in Bertillon Frères for a long time. Michel saw the slip of paper which Bertillon had left in his place. It said:

1. Hold-up merchants, but business getters.
2. Alphendéry must sign anything: 6-9 months: no more.
3. Kaimaster-Blés, S.A. Agence—Bertillon Frères.
4. No guarantees. We cable, confirm. Half-commission?

The conversation he had with them was, of course, confirmed that afternoon by registered letter. Everyone began to take it as a joke. Rosenkrantz and Guildenstern put off drawing up the agreement and the signature, now, for a day or two, hoping that they could get Jules Bertillon's signature and waiting for credit reports on the Banque Bertillon and on Alphendéry. The reports they got were, as usual, diverse.

Scene Twenty-three: Credit

THE Banque du Littoral du Nord wrote:

The Banque Bertillon Frères has with us a satisfactory deposit account. We have had relations with Mr. Jules Bertillon and his brother, William, for a number of years and as far as these have gone, they have been satisfactory. The bank, being a private one, does not publish a balance sheet.

The Northern Counties Bank of London wrote:

In our opinion Bertillon Frères is a speculative institution run chiefly to cover the operations of its head, Mr. Jules Bertillon. We do not feel that it is run on sound banking lines: they do not give credits, discount commercial paper, or make advances against securities. But whether its policies conform to those of the general habits of French banks we, of course, cannot say.

The Scheldt en Doggerbank opined:

This bank, a private bank with unrevealed funds and sources of income, profits, and associations, is said to dispose of large capital almost entirely derived from speculation. These speculations are said to have proved extremely profitable. It does not perform ordinary banking operations beyond foreign exchange. It does not seek credit, and does not solicit savings accounts. We are unable to give an opinion of its worth.

"In sum," said Guildenstern, "excluding the compliments from the business rival, it is satisfactorily mysterious. Do you smell money or not? Franz, you say you spoke to some of the customers' men. You didn't tell them we were going to do business?"

"No," said Rosenkrantz, "I dangled an account before their eyes. I saw their chief clients' man, one who is attached to the direction, Aristide Raccamond. Here's his card." On the table it lay, sharp, startling,

ARISTIDE S. RACCAMOND

(with the military medal, the academic palms, and the sign of the knight of the Legion of Honor)

Attaché à la Direction   39 Rue Pillet-Will
Bertillon Frères   Paris IXᴇ.

Rosenkrantz went on, "A big flaccid pale-green watermelon, one of these overfat Mediterraneans with a nose from Carthage, shoe-black melancholy eyes, the melancholia of obesity. An energetic fellow though, steaming with sweat and ambition, envious. He cherishes the bank like an orphan child: seems to be quite intimate with its position and pretends that Alphendéry is not the shadow behind. It may be anti-Semitism, that. He would like to be in Alphendéry's shoes. In this Raccamond I smelt a mixed aroma of simmering injustice, self-interest coming to the boil, and possible blackmail, with plenty of lickspittle . . .

all pickled. This Raccamond has run about the Bourse for long years. He tells me the bank has always had all sorts of unfavorable rumors about it. . . ."

Guildenstern sat immobile in his chair. "What's that? For twenty years? The Rothschilds spread a rumor too, that they're on the downgrade . . . perhaps to avoid jealousy from the big banks? Who knows? Who knows?"

"I told him I was going into business here and might do my banking through Bertillon Frères. His mouth was watering. Shell him out and then kick him out. A no-good type."

"You only saw this Raccamond?"

"No. I was in the board room this afternoon. I sold a hundred shares of Atchison. That's business. . . ."

"That's money," shrugged Guildenstern.

"No. The clients' men are after me now, ready to be affable, and the manager, Jacques Manray, took a liking to me. I'll buy them back tomorrow."

"Well," said Guildenstern, "I, for my part, saw Paul Treviranus. He used to be in Louis-Dreyfus, now he's —he says Alphendéry has two million francs, Bertillon told him so, one day at lunch when he was somewhat shicker. Bertillon, William, has about ten, and Jules has about three hundred million francs. He's positive about it! Ha? I tagged it on to our New York cable this morning. Response: Bertillon has been a bear in several markets since 1929 and is rich in many millions. Alphendéry's fame has spread to Berlin, Amsterdam, New York, and is thought to be the *éminence grise*, running big accounts for other houses, for which Bertillon's is a blind. Epstein of Mulloney and Moonsteyn, London, on the telephone, says that Alphendéry has all the power, the man behind the throne, but it is because he is a great juggler and smart as a snake charmer, for he has no money and actually the only money the Bertillons have is clients' money, but some of the big names have accounts in the bank. I don't pay much attention to Epstein—he says what he thinks you want to hear. Loewenstein says 'without prejudice' he doesn't believe they have a sou beyond what their clients are fools enough to leave them. 'Isn't it true,' I asked, 'that at times in late years a relative of the Vernes and a relative of the Schneiders'—I didn't give the names, just probing, you know—'had accounts with them?' He was troubled: 'Yes, yes, I don't know.' That's a clue.

Who does he really work for? Evidently an enemy of theirs. Now find out the rivalry there and you have a clue to the real power behind Bertillon. I don't believe for a moment he's sitting up there by himself, a lone hawk. There's no such thing nowadays."

"I say, yes," said Rosenkrantz. "I wonder what his real game is."

"Let's think about our own," recommended Guildenstern.

Scene Twenty-four: Against Michel

"I DON'T see, Jules, why with your assets and your relations in society, you don't go into real banking. You act like a man who has read the first page of a book on banking and then threw away the book."

"I never read a book on banking," flung out Jules, carelessly, his eyes on the opposite walls, his fingers drumming on the desk. William's silvery coin dropping came from behind. The twins sat and faced their youngest brother, in the two great armchairs, occasionally putting in a trivial word, apparently preconcerted.

"I did once open a book on banking . . . I read the first page, and threw away the book," amended Jules in a conceited tone. "It cost twenty francs. To vote in the General Assembly of the Banque de France, you've got to have about two hundred shares . . . two hundred shares at, say, seventeen thousand francs is—"

"Is 3,400,000 francs," said Alphendéry: "you figured the 3,400,000 francers wouldn't tell you the game for only twenty francs. Correct. Now, Jules, you've got a lot of bonds on deposit, haven't you, even from shareholders of the Banque de France? A good many of them are abroad, I know, but a good many of them are here and you do nothing with them. You give a certificate of deposit but you get nothing out of it. Why don't you and Jean de Guipatin and a few of the other silvertails form an omnium of your own?—I'm sure the Comtesse would help you—a lot of people have confidence in you and you've started in the right end, not like Oustric and that meteoric sort that pooh out. Get the shares together, get a say in the general assemblies. Everyone does it. With your affiliations you can build up an important private bank in no time. Why don't you try it?"

"I don't want to play along with them: I want to sell the whole works short from now to kingdom come. I'm not building any great private bank. What for? I wouldn't put my sons into banking. I don't hang on till I get wrinkled, fat, and raucous. I don't want to marry my sons into the Union Artistique and the Jockey Club. Say, one of these days, those Reds are going to get some sense and start a gunpowder plot at the Jockey Club and the kidneys of the omnium engineers will be found sticking to the Eiffel Tower. I thought you thought a revolution was coming? I'm not one of the Comtesse's crowd who think the revolution is coming the day after they die. If the workers knew what I know about myself, I'd leave for Vishnuland tonight: and one of these days, some Michel, or some other fellow, is going to put them wise."

"They have already been put wise," murmured Alphendéry.

"No! Let the guys in high finance put machine guns on their garden walls," said Jules. "I'm a postwar man. I live from day to day and I'm doing no more fighting, even for cash. I'm just a gilded pickpocket and, believe me, a pickpocket has to have twinkling ankles."

There was a sound from the door of the interior staircase, like linen being torn. Richard Plowman walked in boldly, went to Jules, put his hand on his shoulder. "Everyone is depressed: things will change. In a month or two you'll see that Michel's theories don't sound so convincing," urged he.

William surveyed them all, calmly, with his fair round face. Michel was contrite, anxious, but he said, "Plowman, you've forgotten how you made your money. Did you read about Wiggin."

"There are such men," said Plowman, worried. "It is most unfortunate."

"The world's always rotting somewhere," said Jules cheerfully, "and I have a nose for decay."

The others all went out and Plowman settled down seriously, to undo all "Michel's influence."

Scene Twenty-five: The Friendly Touch

LÉON, for a reason he would not tell, was staying in the Hotel Scribe. When Alphendéry rolled in, he called, with peremptory habit, to the waiter, "Another coffee, quick!" Léon mumbled, "You know Mrs. Weyman?" and then began to shout lustily, "Well, Alphendéry, how about taking a trip down to Gibraltar? They say all the rich Andalusian women and girls from Seville—flying there— say the town's full of beauties: no husbands. Oh, boy! Would you and me—excuse me, Margaret, a little fantasy. Well, how would you like" (gigantically) "to go to Gibraltar, Margaret? Give you a little color. Plump— well, you've got enough. You're pretty, did I ever tell you that? You've always been pretty since I've seen you, but after this lunch—it was a good lunch, eh? Eh? I'll make you happy, Margaret, and want nothing in return. Alphendéry's getting to know me: sometimes I'm generous. Sometimes, only sometimes." He chuckled and drank all his coffee at a gulp.

Alphendéry laughed, "Spanish money is flowing in Biarritz like water." He leaned towards Mrs. Weyman. "The Americans are sending over old boats out of Charleston harbor and doing a regular ferry trade between Spanish ports and Hendaye."

Léon said in a gay storm, "Margaret, I'm for the people. If they look like putting any sort of order down there, I'm going down. I'm going to buy an estate there. Not too big. And I'll go to the government and I'll say, 'Friends, I'm friendly to your cause, I believe in you: I want to put my money in your country. It's a grand country, and I like the women.' (That'll move a Spaniard's heart!)" The genial gust blew round them. "How would you like to be in olives, Alphen? I'll buy a small olive plantation down near Málaga. And I've been looking into the perfume business. I'm going to send my Antwerp manager down to look into it. There's only two, three firms in the business. Very bad perfume. I'm going to give the Spanish republican girls a new Coty. A fortune:

186

and I'm no Corsican. I'll stay out of politics. Yes! Those boys are running it well enough for me. Where there's a republic, there I know how to make money. I'll see the widow or the sweetheart of Garcia or Hernandez, those boys who died for the republic, and I'll say to her, 'Sweetheart, I'll make you happy. I love the republic too.' And I'll look after her, give her everything she wants, make her forget. She'll be grateful to me." His face clouded for a second. "If one of them's pretty. If she's got revolutionary fire. Fire." His face cleared and he looked with a thrill of pleasure at Méline. "They wear roses in their hair still in Andalusia, don't they?"

"And follow the bullfights," said Alphendéry, with excitement.

"No, sir, no bullfights, don't like them. The beautiful girls still go; they still hang their shawls over. But with men. No, a factory girl, a working girl, they're more tender," he said tenderly. He looked happily at Mrs. Weyman as if he expected her to share his tenderness. She smiled at him. He grasped her arm, said, "You've got a beautiful figure, Margaret. You'll go along with me: come along, come along, Alphen. How's Bertillon? Making any money?"

"We made some this week."

"How much, how much?" queried Léon. "All right. Come along."

He steered them to the writing room, planted Margaret Weyman in a chair and exhorted Alphendéry: "Have you got a piece of paper, my boy? About my private matter—I have an idea." He became coyly confidential. "I brought Honfleur, the socialist leader, a piece of Wedgwood china last time I came from England. You know, he collects. He's a socialist. You can't bribe him. You've got to flatter him; not too broadly either. He invites me to dinner and says to me, 'I think we will take power within two years and I hope so: supreme power is a great experience for a man.' Oh, boy! Can you imagine that? Such a mental cripple! He was quite touched by the china. Original, you see, simple, the friendly touch. Just a little friendly thought between old socialists. I told him I was a socialist in Roumania, I applied for French naturalization papers the day the war broke out, but I wrote a letter to the minister, Viviani, the old socialist, telling him I had always been a Frenchman at heart and a socialist by instinct and that in the meantime I was joining the French colors, though a foreigner. It looks good, Alphendéry. I think I made an impression on Honfleur. 'Look up my record,' I told him. 'Five years of war, Honfleur, and not touched. I am not only patriotic but lucky.' Ho, ho. I tell you, he seems to like me. And when he gets in, I think the officership of the Legion of Honor is a certainty. I've got to get my foot in." His voice sank lower and he flushed charmingly, "My ultimate object is— the grand cross. I'll get it, my boy: I'm lucky." He struck a Napoleonic, somber, prophetic tone. He raised his thick, short arm, his eyes smoked. "Michel, let's write a letter. 'Dear Mr. Honfleur, or, 'My dear Mr. Honfleur'? He called me Léon: then he writes me a letter, 'My dear friend.' I can't call the hoary revolutionist 'My dear friend,' not yet. Michel, this is where you and I can work wonders: we compose a letter to him, just sentiment, quite amiable, expressing admiration. An old socialist like me is deeply touched by—that's the point, Michel! By what? We got to think up something—touch him on his soft spot. You help me. It's our business: you go into the private matter with me and I'll do you good, my boy."

"You want to get it free?" asked Alphendéry dubiously.

"Not free, my boy, not free: but—*deposit technique:* no lump sum. Work it up. Get him involved on the side of sentiment, then charity, then check to him for gift to old socialist in want—something like that. Involve him. Lay the foundations now when the socialists are out. He stuck to us when things looked black, they'll say after. It'll look genuine. I am French (along with four other naturalizations), I do love France, I did fight for France. See! They make a coalition. They put me in the Legion of Honor lists. You can't pay for it then. Why? See how I figure it, Michel? See if I'm right. In this I'm dead right. When they're in power," he lowered his voice, "prices for Legion of Honor will be high. Question of honor, political opponents. Of course, the conservatives are corrupt. Who pays attention? So Legion of Honor is cheap. But the socialists got to be honorable. Principle; muckrakers. So Legion of Honor is dear. I hedge. See? I come in on clean government and high prices for the Legion of Honor and I pay dirty government prices in advance. Smart, eh, a *hochem?* What do you say, Michel?"

188

"Sounds all right," Alphendéry acknowledged brightly, "but you might have to wait some time."

"I'm a socialist: socialist government comes in, sets up wheat commission. Will they give it to Léon? Léon got his Legion of Honor from Tardieu! No, no, no, my boy. These tories won't have me: the others will have me. Got to play their game. I'll wait. Besides, ho, ho, besides, my boy, I like to get an option: no fun in buying outright. Ho, ho. He, he, you think I'm a bizarre character, don't you? I like to play the game though: any ass can buy it—plunk! Make a donation! Smack! Legion of Honor! No."

Alphendéry said patiently, "All right: what do you want to write?"

"That's the problem! There's nothing to write. What to write, eh? What excuse?" He exclaimed excitedly, "I have it! Galan and Hernandez! Recognition first by sister republic— Ideal, my boy."

"What?" asked Alphendéry astonished.

"My dear Mr. Honfleur, it gave me a great deal of pleasure to dine with you the other day—h'm— It was indeed an honor—h'm, honor, my boy, honor, eh? That's better: flatter: bigshots like flattery, lot of flattery, lot of kicks. Read it back."

Alphendéry was mortified but mildly complied, " 'My dear Mr. Honfleur, It was indeed an honor—' "

"An honor," Léon meditated dubiously, "a bit greasy, eh? Banal? I was immensely gratified—"

"Egocentric," Alphendéry put in, sharply.

"You're right, egocentric, no good. My dear Mr. Honfleur, I look back with the greatest pleasure—"

"Greatest and most intimate pleasure," supplied Alphendéry.

"Greatest and most intimate pleasure: h'm! Ho, ho! Sounds like a—love rendezvous: so it was. I made love to the *Goy:* I cooed to him. Oh, boy—well—most intimate pleasure—no! Too literary. He knows me. My dear Mr. Honfleur, Your kindness in receiving me—no: out with it: it grovels. Let's see. Got to get the right word. He's a writer, sensitive to— Here, here, here! Write, write! Alphendéry! My dear, etc. Since our delightful meeting the other day, I have pondered over your words, and been guided by them in my studies of the present situation. H'm? How's that? Long and limp, eh? Never mind. You see, there's the dinner, an allusion, no bowing and scraping for a dinner: then, his words of wisdom. Go on, Michel: a socialist worrying about the present situation, you see? Write. There is only confusion beyond the Rhine; we watch Russia with sympathy but we are—no, no, but—and we are moving towards an understanding with Russia and this any French patriot who is also a socialist views with enthusiasm. Nevertheless, nevertheless, Michel—" he shot his thick arm up and down, "nevertheless," he looked Michel sternly in the eye, "those of us, and you first among us, who have spent their lives working for socialism, must see in the Spanish Republic the beginning of a new day for western Europe. That most concerns us!"

Alphendéry said crossly, "Too much like a stump speech: he belongs to the welling-eye brotherhood himself."

"Too much like a stump speech? Is it? Let's see: read it over."

After sweating for an hour, the two literary artists had produced a page of text in which every word had been erased, underscored, and rewritten three or four times. It then read:

My Dear Mr. Honfleur,

I am obliged to leave Paris to attend to my business in the Netherlands, earlier than I had planned and thus, to my great regret, will miss the debate in the Chamber of Deputies on the recognition of the Spanish Republic. I had especially wanted to hear your voice, not only because to an old socialist and humanitarian like myself, your rich understanding and mellow statesmanship are an illumination of our present problems, but also because I know that you are for the immediate recognition of Spain and that is what I wish to see, both as a French patriot and a republican. As we have bound forever to ourselves, with ties of respect and affection, the American people alien in race and language, we should bind more closely the Spanish people, our kin. Amongst the preoccupations of a copious commercial life, this is still my first hope. They say that this will

190

be a somber year for our side, but it will be lightened
by the new day in Spain: I cannot despair. I will wait
upon you when I return from Amsterdam and trust
that at some time, you will have a moment for me,
when we can go over some perhaps quite elementary
problems that are disconcerting me. Need I say that
our meeting the other day was to me one of the
most pleasant occurrences of my life? The very
manner in which you state a dilemma is for me a
flash of light and I have since pondered over the
present situation from a new angle.

Yours respectfully,
HENRI LÉON

"It's good," said Henri Léon rubbing his hands. "Let's
think it over. You do me a favor, Alphen: you ask your
girl to type it out double-space and we'll look it over.
My boy, you and I are partners in this. Don't you see,"
Léon wheedled, "perhaps—" he murmured mysteriously,
"when I get sick of the grain business, I might go into
politics, French politics. Now I couldn't do without someone like you, a brilliant scholar, a good head, good language sense, good sense of men—now, I'm very poor on
sizing men up. You see? You're in along with me. The
moment I saw you I said to myself, 'This boy looks like
luck!' And I'm luck, Michel, I'm your luck. I'm grateful
and when Henri is grateful he shows it. Ask anybody.
Well—h'm. Don't ask anybody." He twinkled. He became
pressing, "Now—" he mumbled quickly, "got to see a
man for dinner, from Bucharest, just come from London,
Paganin, dinner," he smiled affably. "My boy, meet me in
the Scribe at half past nine. We'll have coffee, a good
time—we'll finish this letter. Eh? You'll do that for me?
And I'll look after you, my boy."

"Well, you can give me five thousand francs and I'll
do it for you," said Alphendéry.

"Five thousand francs? Of course, not much, not much
at all." He hooked his stick over his arm, settled his hat
on his head, straightened his back, "Well, got to get
along. See you nine-thirty. So long. Thanks, thanks, my
boy." Alphendéry got up and they bustled to the door.
At the door Léon held him mysteriously. "I hear you're
going into the commodities business with two Germans.

What is it? Can you trust Bertillon? He wouldn't take my wheat schematism."

"It's just commission business," explained Alphendéry.

Scene Twenty-six: No Money in Working for a Living

"WELL," said Michel Alphendéry to Jules, "Léon had one good crack last night: he says prosperity by repudiation is the new economics."

"Do you realize how rich we would be," Jules asked thoughtfully, "if we repudiated, Michel? The Dow-Jones average of New York prices is down to 121 as against 383 at the top of the boom in 1929. We've been selling short all round the world markets for six months. I've just been going over our entire position with William. Guess how much we're worth."

"You mean bank deposits, clients' equities, our gold abroad, the money we've cashed in recently, our equity in brokers abroad, guarantee funds in banks abroad for our branches—everything?"

"No, not guarantee funds abroad. Do you know how much we could skip with?"

"Do you mean everything in *sight*—without paying out the clients at *all?*"

"Ah ha."

"Let's see: let me figure." After a few minutes' penciling, Alphendéry ventured, "One hundred and fifty million francs—I'm not including clients' bonds."

"Very close: 161,000,000 roughly. I say, Michel, that's fair enough—if we had it clear and away! You could hide in some South American country, or South Africa or one of those places for a while until the shouting died down and then come out large as life. Everyone worships a successful thief. Why wait? We've got what we were waiting for!"

"I don't want to spend my life in hiding," said Alphendéry.

"What do you care? Money has no country. Change your name and become a Chilean and join the Chilean Communist Party if that's what's worrying you. I'm serious,

Michel. I've been figuring that it would pay us to just jump. What are we working for? There's no profit in working for a living. We won't always have this amount of money in the kitty from now on. Days will come when I'll lose it in the market, clients will withdraw it. Perhaps a moratorium will come; war. Something will clean me out. Fellows make a fortune and end up with their pockets hanging out. Because they don't know when the bell rings. The bell is ringing now. We little fellows can't survive too long. The government wants to bleed us for taxes. We're the goats when the deputies throw a sacrifice to the lambs. A raider has to get himself into the service of some big robber, like a Rhodes, or know when to retire if he's working for himself. One of the two. Mercury himself would have to work for De Wendel today. De Wendel hasn't a fifty-year run! I'm darned lucky to have survived twenty years. It's because of my great streak of luck. Why shouldn't I run away with the cash register while I can have the best fun out of it?"

"Yes," said Alphendéry, "did you ever hear of extra-dition laws? You want to make another one hundred million in Chile? Under what name? People will inquire into your antecedents."

"No, People ask no questions of a profit."

"Yes? And you're so nondescript! No one would ever recognize you! And the South Americans who come round here like flies in summer! How many people in France are afflicted with this particular bright idea every year—lawyers, petty bankers, trustees? Our countrymen have damned long memories, Jules. If you come back after twenty years, they'd have you in custody when you touched Marseilles. There's no statute of limitations here for principals. What makes you so dumb, Jules?"

"I'm not stupid, Michel. I've been thinking this thing out for a long time. I've been in business twenty-five years, ever since I was fourteen. I've always known this day was coming. I never had to learn: I *knew* when I started. Now the day has come. This is the highest I've ever been and perhaps ever will be. Who knows? Things may turn upwards. I can only make money when the rest of the world is going to pieces. I'm like the pickpocket who gets his big chance in an earthquake. I've got to slip away before the buildings fall in on me and before the police are reorganized. They'll never let me make the

193

final scoop, don't you see! They'll close the stock exchanges first. Say, if we want to make money for ourselves, all we want, you and I, is one room with two chairs, one table, and a telephone. We'll take a little room somewhere, change our names and speculate for ourselves. Perhaps—we could even take a room with a chap like Léon, or across the corridor, call ourselves a grain firm and make money. No one would look for us there in a thousand years. Léon would never give us away: he'd like to be in the conspiracy. You read up all the dope and we get to work and make money. Say a year or so of that and then we can take a holiday. We'll work out a plan of campaign together. I don't want to take the risk of business any more. Why the overhead? Why the façade? We've got their cash, haven't we? Who wants to be in high finance? How long do dynasties of dough last? Let's be rich and safe."

"That's against nature," laughed Alphendéry. "You mean you wouldn't pay *any* of the clients?"

"Not if I slid out. They'll start the hue and cry anyhow, whether you take one per cent or one hundred per cent. Why should you leave anything lying around for the liquidators? Pay the employees six months and they'll stand by you. They know I'm a good boss."

Alphendéry tapped his lower lip, considered pouting, dubious, not wishing to push Jules to an extremity. "It's not worth it, Jules. We have enough lawyers around the place to be able to stage-manage a normal bankruptcy. You can pay off the biggest clients, Plowman, the Comtesse de Voigrand, the Princesse Delisle-Delbe, the Comtesse de Marengo—especially that type, they're the most dangerous—Carrière, anyone likely to be vindictive and after you've got enough abroad for yourself, say, fifty million francs, you can pay the smaller clients so much per cent. You see, the smaller clients are only keeping small accounts here in any case, sort of courtesy. Then no one will be after you. You won't necessarily have to live in exile. You can always buy off the cops or the judges for a small bankruptcy; there need be no tom-toms and you won't face Devil's Island if you go away and return. Another thing, you can't be made a political stunt, for you are neither a big crook nor a robber of widows, orphans, and concierges. That's infinitely more sensible. It lacks drama; but drama is expensive."

"If I only get away with fifty million!" said Jules disappointed. "Only one-third! Ph!"

"Don't forget," warned Alphendéry, "that no bank could stand an inspection of its books and so they're only too glad to cry 'untouchable' and make you an example."

"And we lose one hundred and ten million francs, for them," complained Jules.

"It's true that's not much for a man, his wife, and children to live on," lamented Alphendéry. "It's only the monthly salary of a ticket collector on the AB bus line on the boulevards for fifty-two hundred years. What you need is enough for sixteen thousand years; or are you going to live as long as from four times pre-Glozel to now? I can see that. Couldn't you tighten your belt and draw in the life line and go through a decent form of bankruptcy and try to live on sixty million francs? I'll meet you for ten million. Now, for a man in your profession, at your age, the expectation of life is—say thirty years, maybe longer, but say thirty years. That gives you two million francs a year if you just live on your capital and don't invest it. If you invest it in *rentes françaises* three per cent at seventy-five, you will get four per cent net yield or 2,400,000 per annum while preserving your capital intact . . . ."

"It's not enough," said Jules. "If I only took sixty million and left all that cash lying round the place, they'd investigate me from here to doomsday because they'd be convinced that a chap who could leave fifty million behind must have ten times that much put away. It doesn't pay. The only thing is to clear the shelves. I pay the employees six months' salary each, or, in other words, I simply give them the sack, because I'm going out of business. They get a chance to get another job and the working-class sheets can't howl, either. I just worked out with William what it would cost, say, at the rate of one hundred and fifty thousand monthly in the main office, bright day, dark day. Leave the branches to themselves, all the branch managers—they're all rich sons of guns—and I'm willing to take the moral blame—'that pirate Jules Bertillon let us all down'—you know. Every investigation committee—if it came to that—would exonerate them.

"Well, salaries here, about one million francs, not more. Of course, I'm overcalculating. Raccamond gets twelve thousand monthly, but you could pay him half of that and then I'm a fairy godmother to him, he's only just come in. And he can't yell, because he arranges his salary so that he seems to get six thousand francs monthly, only, here: the other six thousand he draws, on overdraft, from a little company he's formed for himself abroad—or he had formed before, from the time he was with Claude Brothers. I don't know. At any rate, his official rate is six thousand, and if I pay him six months at that everyone will say he's well treated: so his is thirty-six thousand only. Then our golden parasites, Jean de Guipatin, Arturito MacMahon, and so forth: those ginks owe us money. We've got money coming to us from the estates of old Comte Lucé, Hervé is overdrawn sixty thousand francs, Tony owes us some money, Pedro de Silva-Vizcaïno probably owes us money, Zurbaran owes me twenty thousand francs. Partiefine owes me a couple of thousand, there are the little businesses I support, say twenty thousand owing to me in all, on I.O.U.'s. In all about three or four millions of francs, which I won't collect but which will be counted as credits and can serve as a sop for the liquidators. You would have to lose that."

"Don't forget, Jules, one black mark: don't forget what you owe for income taxes. You've been buying off the inspector for ten years. When they get on to you they'll be ready to serve you up Guiana smoking hot. The government as a first claimant would have no mercy on you. The clients' shrieks are going to be nothing to the government. The government is the meanest of creditors. You owe them, for ten years that you've been dressing the returns, with taxes, interest, penalties, about eight million francs. You've got to leave the government that amount, Jules."

"Do you think I'm crazy?" asked Jules, in horror. "Eight million sous is too much. For what? For a rival bunch of gangsters who are always trying to put tacks under my tires? Don't be soft."

Alphendéry considered for a minute. "Jules, it seems a pity. You have a big pull with the moneyed immigration. Rosenkrantz and Guildenstern are only the first forerunners of a wealthy German immigration, especially of Jews if things go bad in Germany. Jews don't forget that France was their liberator, despite the Dreyfus case. With me here you could get their money. Why, you're only just beginning! Let's look at the branches in the Côtes d'Azur *et* d'Argent, in Monte Carlo, in Zürich, in Brussels, Liverpool, Antwerp, Amsterdam. You've only had them running a few years, some only a few months—like the Antwerp one. They're not on their feet yet! With war coming there will be immense speculation in commodities: there is a fortune to be made in all those cities —with immigrant money, scare deposits, commodity accounts, speculation in American shares (when things go up), transfers to London. Now is the time for a great, but solid, pyramiding. You have only begun, Jules.

"What will you do, if you quit now? You'll go and stew for a few months, then you won't be able to bear the tedium and you'll start again in some tinpot way, after wrecking one of the finest networks in the world. We get a freshet of alien money here every time there's bad political news in Germany and America. Perhaps America won't get any of it. Europeans are funny people. America is, in the minds of most of us, a land of gangsters, racial terror, strike war. Now London looks shaky. Who would invest in Germany with the threat of the National Socialists? Confidence has been shaken in all the good old institutions. Rothschild no longer means florid money, incalculable foresight, the Bank of England no longer thrills bank clerks, the Rock of Gibraltar will get malaria next. You're going against your own principles: this is the age to make money in. Look at your situation! You're one of the few men in the world who had the courage to say, 'This is an age of going-down and I'm betting on disaster,' and who actually went and pyramided on disaster and who has won! Why give up? You are born for this age! You are brilliant, Jules. You can be another Rothschild."

Jules turned restlessly, as if with a small fever. "I think you're arguing for respectability, Michel. I've always known that, at bottom, despite your communism and all, you're very respectable. The Rhineland counselors, lawyers, and writers you come from are rustling stiff and starched in your blood. Admit it: you don't like to go bankrupt!"

Michel vigorously nodded. "No, it's not that. Why don't you go away for a week and think it over, Jules? You're not strong. Paris in spring is getting you."

"I'm all right. But I have a hunch."

197

"It's not that I'm respectable, Jules. But I have to earn my living and this is the only thing I know how to do. Who will employ me if my name's associated with a scandalous runaway, a dubious bankruptcy, or a notorious embezzlement?"

"Everyone!" said Jules heartily. "People only give money to thieves; they respect them. If you ran away you'd be courted: they'd only despise you if they found out you didn't steal any money. If you ever do skip, don't forget to let everyone think your old overcoat in moth balls is really lined with ill-gotten gold. You'll get invited everywhere. Besides, who says you're going to look for a job? Won't you be with me? You're not thinking of leaving me, Michel? You wouldn't do that? We're together in everything, aren't we? You're not really serious about this socialist boloney?"

Michel wanted to evade an answer, for he did not intend to run away with Jules. He did not intend to leave Adam Constant, Jean Frère, and his other friends. The idea of leaving them and of having them despise him was something he could not face. He fought for them.

"But Jules, I don't understand! Only the other day you were full of sparks, bringing in a list of really brilliant schemes and now you want to throw the works in the fire! What has happened? Have you lost on the Paris bourse? Treviranus, Cristopoulos are always around here. I saw them this morning. Have you lost money?"

"No: I've been making money. It's unreal. That's why I want to scram. Now is the time to shut up shop. The Credit-Anstalt is gone, Rothschild is bunged, everyone expects war every week, Léon is talking of selling his business and retiring to Spain or the south of France, even America doesn't seem to be able to collect the money owing to her: she hasn't the power any more, or she's afraid of putting the whole world into bankruptcy. Don't you see the time is close when they simply won't let us make money any more? When creditors can't collect debts—"

"It's a good time to get into debt," laughed Alphendéry robustly. "You haven't thought of that! You own money. You ought to owe it too. Why don't you go and take out mortgages on all the apartments of your family, on your yacht, airplane, and Gauguins? Mortgage everything you've got up to the hilt, if you *must* jump. Make a real

198

clean sweep. Why, your ideas of a cleanout are picayune. Owe money, when you jump. In the first place, you will have more; in the second, they'll think you're really bankrupt, that it's all gone down the drain, and they won't be so vindictive! Common sense. Go to the Banque de Paris et des Pays-Bas, go to Morgan's, go to The Guaranty Trust, go to the Société Générale and get an overdraft! Then gird your loins and fly! Your credit's good. You can easily get up to fifty million francs in overdrafts. That will give you two hundred and ten millions and you can pay off all your employees and say, Richard Plowman and a few like that, without any loss of your good name. People will say, 'He did his best to pay those who trusted him.'"

"Good name!" cried Jules irritably. "You can't get a passport on a good name, you can't so much as pawn your wife's ring on a good name. Good name is a bee in your bonnet, Michel. But that's a good idea. I might do that."

"And if you've got two hundred and ten million francs, why shouldn't you really go into business in a big way?" asked Michel.

"Listen, Michel, do you know any real toughs, assassins, I mean?"

"No. What makes you think I do?"

"Oh, I thought you might. You're always running around to those Red meetings, at the Vel d'Hiv' and what is it. I thought you might know a couple of thugs out of work who'd polish off Carrière for me. The air wouldn't be so thick if he wasn't around. I'm always running into him. . . ."

"Why, what's he done now?"

"Only I don't like him. The proper way is to get rid of someone who is laying for you. I just want to skip to annoy him."

"But you're not going to take him on his quarterly sterling drafts payments. Or are you? Jules, tell me the truth. Did you write a letter to him, about the business?"

"No, I didn't write that fox any letter. Still, I don't want him to say I welched. Let him walk into the trap."

"What trap?"

"I've got up something with Pierre. . . ."

"You think he has no information?"

Jules's manner became flighty. "And at the same time I got the feeling that everything is getting phonier and phonier in the bank, so why not forget it? Half a million a year for that apartment in the Porte de St. Cloud. Lapage and Company suing me for the decoration; seven hundred and fifty thousand sunk in original paintings I can't get back anyhow. Why shouldn't I move to Switzerland? I'd be near the children and I could live on *rentes*. My children aren't like me. They can't tell a one-thousand-franc note from a tram ticket except the youngest, and why should he get into this game? I'm going to make him a professor. William's only dream is to dig himself a hole and fade from human activity. You're a philosopher, Michel. . . ."

Michel broke in laughing. "I'm not a money type: if you are money sticks to you, as if you were covered with bear grease."

Jules hung his head. "I'm tired, Michel." "Yes, I know you are, Jules. Do go away for a while and leave William, the twins, and me to run things. We'll be circumspect and your dough will be intact. Don't act hastily. You're a great and a good man, Jules. I don't want you to ruin yourself."

Jules muttered, "Why the dickens didn't I get a gun and blow up that assassin yesterday?"

"Who? Carrière? Jules, you are in some trouble . . . you're concealing something from me."

"I'm not. . . . Last night I dreamed of a hen yard of thin chickens. A dog howled from four o'clock on. I couldn't think of anything, gold, silver, or checks. I've got always to be thinking about money or I feel life isn't worth living. Hang the dog! What do I care or . . . what else is there to live for, Michel, tell me?"

Michel braced himself, clean as to face, collar cuffs, and spectacle-shine, said with his air of upright little professor of law, "There's mankind to live for—"

Jules murmured drolly, "Oh, mankind, Michel: be serious!" But he listened with some gay curiosity to Michel, tipped back in his chair, remarking the sincerity and energy of Alphendéry's traits. Michel went on with fire, "Your own sense of futility, Jules, shows what it is for men to live and work for themselves alone. You just find yourself the owner of a great fortune, a thing men dream of all their lives long—you have, in one direction, reached the summit of men's desire—and suddenly you don't want to work any more, you don't want to live: I don't think you even really want the money."

"Oh, yes, my word, I do: don't make any mistake about that."

"Yes, but you are a creative man: you want to build and what have you built? What is all that money but counters? You have long ago lost the sense of money that a poor man has, when a hundred-franc note means relief from pain, a thousand-franc note means marriage. That is money. What you have are counters. You might as well have matches. Suddenly you find that you hardly want to count it, for there is no joy in that. Money has flowed to you, but your joy has been in inventing schemes and you can invent them as well when you are poor. Meanwhile your money goes bad, begins to stink, vultures wheel round you and you are unhappy and discontented. But that is all you know, spoiled artisan. The corrupt fairy tales you have been told, the carefully whetted greed that has been lured out of you has made you build in counters and ink scratches in an account book. You see, because you are fine and fertile, that it is not enough. You think if you increase it suddenly with a great swoop of villainy, steal from everyone that confided in you, make a great scandal, see your money grow overnight from a bean to a beanstalk, that you will catch the hen that lays the golden eggs. But if you do it, Jules, I warn you, you'll be just as unhappy as before. You've built a hothouse here to force your fantasies in. They'll parch outside. No one will care for them. They'll grow twisted, leaves will turn into flowers, stalks will broaden into leaves, potatoes will grow on stalks, peanuts will hang from calyces, the world will be monstrous and topsy-turvy, you'll gamble, be spendthrift, melt your money down in liquor, cover women with it, your happy marriage will be broken, your children will drift away from you, your brothers will desert you, no one will care for you: because you are without a function. And you can only work with this machine you have built. You don't know how to dawdle, Jules, if there is no bank waiting for you to come back to. You can only enjoy yourself now on the Côte d'Azur, at Le Touquet, because the bank is here to shape your fantasies to. I know you so well, Jules. Don't give up this solid universe: don't float back into the air. Your feet are winged: unless you chain yourself by a golden chain to something on earth, you will join the worthless, fleshless creatures who float round our enterprises, our tenements of commerce, trying to get in. I know you: you don't exist apart from your bank, just the same as it would decay, until one could put his fist through the walls, if you were to leave it. Someone might buy it up, true, but it would not be this bank, this strange palace of illusion, temptation, and beauty. The beauty of this place is you, Jules. Its soul is you. And you are it. Don't leave it. You couldn't stand disgrace, for all your wise saws. Listen to me. You see, I'm not preaching humanity to you. You have to be born to love of humanity, and trained to it, the way you have to be born to money love."

Jules looked at him with a bright eager smile.

"You think the bank would collapse without me?"

Michel said, "I am only thinking of you, now, Jules: not that making money is not creative: that it employs no one, gives no one work—"

"Now, Michel, I employ forty people in Paris alone."

"Yes, you money-makers try to fool yourselves that you are of some use to mankind! You would be benefactors, too. You see what I mean?"

Jules shuttled his legs, laughed, "No, I don't give a hoot for them. Why should I be mean? No reason. And why should I be generous? No reason. I do what pleases me."

"What is the secret attraction of this money you so fanatically build up. You're a fanatic yourself. Why money? Why not sequins? Why not candied apples? Why not pebbles? Because the figure in your bank balance is a tally of counters, counters invented by your sort, and passed among yourselves in secret recognition of your right to, and power of, robbery."

"Oh, now, Michel, you're getting fantastic," said Jules charmingly. "What would I do if I didn't rob? Let someone else rob? Why? Will robbing stop if I stop robbing? No. It's human nature. Look at Rothschild and those culture hounds. They know all about music, art, and philosophy. If there were really anything in it, they'd stop making money and study art. Who ever did?"

"Then I'm practically an idiot," laughed Michel.

"Oh, you're a bit off center: you've got the brains. You could transfer a couple of hundred thousand francs, a million francs, a couple of million francs, any day, into your name and you don't. Now, that's just lunatic. There are guys in the world who don't care for money. There are people born blind, too. They don't count. You think

202

like a logician, a mathematician; but the world isn't syllogisms—it's grab and graft."

"In any case, the theory that socialism consists of dividing up the money was invented by millionaires to flatter themselves with an absurdity," said Alphendéry. "Socialism consists in putting the means of production of wealth, land, railways, mines, etcetera, in the hands of the people, or rather of their seizing these things from those that now have them. It is your system truncated, grab without graft."

"There's no such thing," pouted Jules. "You're just an idealist. The people who can't make money invent a theory that those who do are thieves. Without us there'd be no money at all. We make it: the smart people. Listen, you revolutionists are *crazy!* People don't want to make money. They want to rest and listen to the radio. Stalin is a smart one. He runs the state and lets the workers get tired out building dynamos and then he teaches them to sing songs about Lenin. I'm not one of those superpatriots who can't stand the sound of Russia—I think they've a smart gang there, a lot smarter than we have here. Every country's got a right to its own system. And naturally they try to sell everyone the idea that they've got the ideal system: it makes the other countries green with envy. I wouldn't go and shoot the Russian worker. His mouth's stopped for another fifty years. But if I didn't know you, Michel, I would shoot men like you, who go round stirring people up, while their own brains are confused about the world. . . ." He looked at Michel, laughing at the provocation.

"Jules, why do you say those things? You don't believe them."

"I do. I don't have to shoot my workers: generosity is gamblers' luck, you know. I'm not in business: I'm a sheep shearer. The lambs eat grass and grow wool and I clip it."

He stopped, having lagged and grown thoughtful during the last few minutes. "Well, Michel, what do you think of this idea of skipping? I'm serious. I want you to go and see Maître Lemaître and see how much he can do it for. If you're really dead set against a simple walkout."

"I suppose I'm old-fashioned or timid, but I love you, Jules, and I don't want to see you end up this way. Why can't you pay off your clients? You've got the money."

"Wha-at? Don't be funny."

"Then why can't you wait till we form this consortium you were talking about? You can pay off your clients and put the residuum into the pool and make money on your own with no overhead and no liabilities. Just one room and a telephone: you and William and me. We'll plant the twins abroad or keep them."

"The residuum! I'm not in business for any residuum! What consortium? The Banque de France is a better consortium than any I can get up. No, I'm cashing in. When I get another streak, I'll go back into the market."

"Why be in the market at all? Let the suckers guess for you and you bet against them: our old line is the best, wisest, most innocent."

"I'm not an old maid playing patience. I want big money and what have I got round me? Savers, hoarders, go-gentlies, abacus gentry back in the carpetbags of the Middle Ages, squirrels, ants, census takers, penny-bank campaigners—installment-plan robbers, shilling-a-week shortchangers, Saturday tillshakers, busfare embezzlers, dime defalcators—you're as bad as Etienne. You're honest. It's no good hiding it. All your philosophy hasn't got you farther than scraping and pinching like the knife-grinder's wife. If you start little, you remain little. If you start with bells on, you end with bells on. I know what I want. I only want to hear from you how it's to be done. You're my technical expert, Michel. I employ you for that. Go to Maître Lemaître or Beaubien and find out how to do it. That's all I'm asking you."

Michel stood up with dignity, still pleading. "Jules, you can't make real money without working at it. There's something queer about gamblers' money: it doesn't sound on the counter. And are you just a gambler? You've seen enough at Deauville to know what a breed that is. Are you just that?"

Jules turned his back impatiently, rudely drummed on the edge of the long bookcase, pretended to look at the backs of the books. He turned in a minute, smiling brightly. "Ah, Michel, you'll never understand the likes of me! I've never done a stroke of work in my life: neither did my father, I'm glad to say, and my grandfather didn't wear out the small of his back with toil: grinding diamonds isn't exhausting. I come from a breed of men who have harvested, for generations, what others have sown,

204

or dug, or made. Not by the sickle, but by magic. I'm a magician. You can't wonder that I'm impatient with all the sicklers and hammerers of the world. The hammer and sickle! A good sign for a nation of peasants, country Jacks. I'd pay your fare to Russia if I didn't want you here. You'd find an upper class there, and commission men just the same as here. Even so," he frowned, "they paint their propaganda up too red and yellow. Listen, Michel, your father was a lawyer, wasn't he?"

"Well?"

"Where did you get these crazy ideas from then, that money comes from work?" He laughed. "Well, Michel, unless we can think up a really good out by tomorrow, I've decided to blow up the bank. Hey, how about really blowing it up! Get the dough out and put in a stick of dynamite! Say the Bolsheviks did it! Say, that's brilliant. We'll transfer everything to—Oslo? Some can go to Antwerp in William's name, some to Geneva in yours? What did you say was your limit of honesty? Thirty million francs? All right. I'll trust you with fifty million. That'll be in your name. We'll have a consideration. You can sell me a factory in Schnippezoc. We'll claim it afterwards. When the lawyers and the sleuths fade out, we'll go and get it and start business in Australia, South Africa, Mexico, or Kansas. Antwerp? No one's interested in a bank scandal in Paris: they read them in the papers every day. There's a street there—last time I was in Antwerp I saw a little street, near the Leopoldstraat, full of quiet old houses, and private banks with grilles: dressed gray stone, brass plates with initials; not a sound; respectability at home in the family vault, discreet as a high-class house of rendezvous. No questions asked. Take the name of one of my companies. They look it up; in existence for twenty years! And it's a monarchy and a potty one: no fear of socialist big-game hunting among the bankers. Ideal! You'd like Antwerp, Michel. It's not far from Brussels for gaiety, and there are swell bookshops full of arty books. It's only a quarter of an hour from the Dutch border in case of another German invasion. Let's shift!"

"Back to your grandfather's stage!"

"Yes. Thank goodness, everyone is losing confidence. The central banks have to publish pictures of their vaults with a sample of gold ingots: they have to run feature stories on the mint. Let's get hold of their trash paper, before they use it to light their fires, and give them a modicum of hard cash. When you're round at Lemaître's, get him, or one of your other legal pals, to think up a watertight blanket guarantee."

"What's it to be? New business or no business? If you're going to collect people's securities, you want a solid name and a good façade. You can't go bankrupt and then expect people to hand you over their only insurance against sickness, old age, and unemployment."

"In a time like this, people will hand you anything for cash. It's a hold-up. They're trapped. Um. Let's see: how does this sound? National Credit and Securities Nominees?" He scribbled, "How's this? Antwerp Consolidated Securities Assurance, Limited? Good, but not good enough. They're mad on the Congo, aren't they? How's this: Ruanda and Urundi Gold Trust, Consolidated? Leopoldville Gold Corporation? What about Amstel Securities Corporation? Amstel Nominees. Solid and plain. I seem to have heard of it for years, myself. Amstel Banking Corporation? Have you ever heard of that?"

"I might think so, if you popped it to me," mused Alphendéry.

"We'll see. Hello? Give me Mr. William's office. . . . William? William, what do people think of the Amstel Nominees Corporation, Leopoldstraat, Antwerp? Didn't Léon mention it?"

. . . .

"It's a small, private affair, isn't it, rather old-fashioned?"

. . . .

"What do you think we can buy in it for? Find out, will you?" He put down the receiver. "Yes, William has heard of it. Let's try someone else. Raccamond, that's the guy. . . . Get me Raccamond at once. . . . Raccamond? You know the Low Countries, don't you? Is the Amstel Discount Corporation, Leopoldstraat, Antwerp, solid? Is it a good bank? . . . It is? You're sure? . . . Thanks. No, don't trouble yourself. Very interesting." He put the receiver down with a broad smile.

Michel asked, "He knows about it?"

"Certainly. It has a few branches. It's worth about a couple of a million guilders (that's the Amstel part of it). Worth a couple of million guilders already and we only invented it two minutes ago. . . . I saw a nice suite of offices in the Rue Tronchet, by the way, yesterday. We might take them, if we don't go bankrupt and work a business there for ourselves, just William, the twins, you, and I, maybe Mlle. Gentil with her husband—just speculate for very big accounts: sift out the small fry: a rich man's securities and speculation outfit. Plowman, Zurbaran, the Silva-Vizcaïnos and all that crew. We don't want any pikers. . . ."

"Are we going to bankrupt or not?"

"I'll see. . . . Hello? Get me our printers. No, tell him to come round at once: I've got a new letterhead for him."

"What letterhead's that?" asked Michel, anxiously.

"The Amstel Discount Corporation, of course. When you go round to Lemaître's, ask him to look up Belgian law and find out what incorporation fee, and what rules for directors and all that. . . . Hello? Get me Maître Olympe. . . . Say, that bomb idea is the best. We'll pay an old anarchist to throw a bomb, then we'll hustle him out after he's dropped a few clues, and we don't even have to move from Paris. Or he can sit for six months and we'll make it up to him. . . . Say, I've got a better idea. Let's get 'Old' Berthellot to falsify the books—Hello, is that you, Pierre? Say, have you been to see about that lease in the Rue Tronchet? Well, hurry up: I want it signed. I want to get the furniture in. Did you tell the brass-plate makers to make the name plate yet? Well, why the deuce didn't you? I told you the name, Geneva International. . . . Well, get it done. Good-by." He slammed down the telephone.

"What about 'Old' Berthellot?" asked Michel.

"Get Berthellot to falsify the books, you see and make believe to run off with about ten million francs. He has always wanted to live in the Channel Islands. You find out, Michel, where there are no extradition laws, and we'll pay his passage. While he's falsifying the books for his ten million he can cover up about—well, the lot: we'll send him round to 'inspect' the branches. Then I'll pay the Parquet to forget it. Don't want to crush dear old servant, loyal for many years, etcetera."

"Berthellot mightn't like to end his days under a cloud."

"Don't make me laugh. 'Old' Berthellot. Old thief. He's the only one of our paper directors who turns up for his monthly director's fee. But he's sane. He hasn't got the neurosis of blackmail, like all the accountants and petty

207

clerks who suddenly think they've found out a great scandal and run to the police: your-money-or-the-police breed. Berthellot will see in it a chance to insure his old age. That's better than blowing up the bank. Or could we combine the two?"

"Will I get Lemaître on the phone or are you just blowing off steam, Jules?"

"Of course, I'm serious. I say, if I'd thought of it on May first we could have got a bunch of toughs to break into the bank, scare the customers and say they were communists, and loot a few filing cases: the government would adore a chance to search all the communist quarters for stolen cash."

"We didn't have the money on May first. Besides, communists are known better than other citizens: they have party cards. This is just scatterbrained, Jules. You're writing a comic-opera scenario."

"Couldn't we forge party cards? Give it to some toughs? You've seen what they're like, the cards, I mean, haven't you? Could you remember? Or you could get one for a sample. I say, Adam Constant has one: let's get him up."

"Listen, Jules: you know this is moonshine. This is a bad year. If you want to put on a first-class show, let's conserve the money we have and wait till some really bad crash occurs, another Credit-Anstalt, a currency going off (the pound perhaps), a war, and then we can go futt with the honors of war. We can show that we lost our investments, were long of the pound, or had strong commitments in wheat or something of that sort. I have several friends—Léon, for instance—who would help us out in that way. Ephraïm Dreyer would: we've done much the same for him. We've helped a hundred of the extra-rich evade their income taxes for years."

"I don't trust the bastards: no rich man is a patriot, no rich man a friend. They have all only got one fatherland —the Ritz-Carlton; and one friend—the mistress they're promising to divorce their wife for. Dreyer? The police have examined his books twice already; his books are too well known. Léon? Maybe."

"Antedated contracts in wheat. That's the formula. Lemaître will tell us how exactly."

"Léon? His *quid pro quo* would be usury. I don't trust that boy."

"Well, we'll think something out."

"We can't stand still! To stand still is to go backwards in this business. Tomorrow the clients guess wrong and if we're out of the market ourselves, we lose a couple of millions in equities. Are you going to lunch? Have lunch with William and then you two come over to my house tonight. The whole family will be there. We'll all talk it over. . . ." He laughed and sauntered out.

Alphendéry looked in at William's door. "Going to lunch? O.K. I'll wait."

William nodded. His hands in his pockets he was looking out the window at some rats running on a neighboring roof, and occasionally he dictated a letter to Mlle. Dalbi. He was a blond personable figure, in the pink of condition, with a baby-skinned rosy face and never a wrinkle. He looked as if he had never been troubled by a thought in his life.

Scene Twenty-seven: Snapshots

"A SPECULATOR is a man who, if he dies at the right time, has a rich widow," William stated at lunch. "Everything is a time technique. I know Jules. If he wants to make a getaway, he had better make it. No good making two bites at a detonator. No good waiting till the barricades come, either. I know it's coming because comtesses are going red, the Raccamonds are turning tables, and whores are getting conservative. Well, if you know that —it's all a time equation—why wait? It doesn't matter what country we're in: all we do is to lease out the open spaces in people's heads. What have you and I got to worry about, eh? We've got enough to live on. Now, every day we work is a double saving: we pay for our food and we save another day in our reserves. But if it comes to going, we can go. Why wait? We've got the money. Profits in a stock market are like raising a boy: it takes twenty-five years to rear him and put him through college and one second for a taxi to mash him up when he's rolling home drunk. Profits are like love: you spend a year waiting at the gate for Katie and it takes you three minutes to get over it."

He dipped his face deeply into his beer. He came up like the gamboling porpoise, "So what do you care? Why worry? I never worry! Go to the pictures. Forget it. Don't dream. I never dream. What is a dream? It's a lunatic idea. I never had one."

"That's interesting," murmured Alphendéry. "Janet said he came across authentic cases in psychopathology of people who never dreamed."

"Pathology!" cried William wrathfully, suddenly emerging from his beer, "They have nightmares and *I'm* crazy. Look at Jules: everyone knows he's as crazy as a bedbug, he comes in yellow every morning from dreaming. Look at me. I'm fat. He eats nothing."

"Yes, Jules dreams a lot," murmured Alphendéry.

"Awake!" He shrugged his shoulders and plunged again into his Pilsener. "All right, for a playwright: he can use them in his plays. Not in a balance sheet."

In the afternoon, Jules was in hoplà temper. One of his old friends, Xesús Maria de Huesca, a poor Spanish nobleman of a junior line, came in with one of those perfect selling ideas which occur twice a day to the rouseabout geniuses of Paris *boulevardiers*. He was a man-mountain of about fifty, partly bald, with black eyes, suiting, hat, and shoes, and a gallant tie of various colors. Xesús Maria required a loan from Jules of twenty thousand francs with which to finance a sure-fire invention, a pill made of ingredients named in the Spanish *Catholic Encylopedia,* under the heading "aphrodisiacs," to heat the blood in female hearts. Most of the money was needed for the printing of pamphlets, leaflets, and diagrams. Señor de Huesca had a middle-aged friend in the Place des Ternes who would compound the pills for him; and he intended to place them himself with the assistance of one or two indigent but intelligent compatriots. Jules refused this attractive proposition.

Cornelis Brouwer, manager of Jules's Brussels branch, came in and spent one hour and twenty minutes talking about the *Aryan Path* and ended by withdrawing ten thousand francs in cash to go to Deauville for the week end.

Claire-Josèphe rang up to say she had just seen the

210

famous medium, Ras Berri, who said that before Claire-Josèphe and Jules were pavilions and pillars of gold; and that Jules, Jr., had colic and they had better call Dr. Dupont in the Boulevard Malesherbes. Jules advised her to call Dr. Dupont in the Avenue Victor-Hugo, who was frequented by the *Etat Major*.

Pierre Olympe rang up to say that Tony and Aline had finally decided to divorce each other and were now living together in perfect harmony.

Richard Plowman came in with Frank Durban, and Durban said, "I don't think you're going to last long, Jules: I've advised Dick to take out all his money." Plowman laughed and hit him on the back, "You should have advised me not to go into the Burlington Arcade where I lost twelve pounds in notes, last time I was there. That rankles. It's so silly." Jules's face lighted up, "What makes you think I won't last, Frank?"

"It's the drawing-room atmosphere," said Durban.

"He just yearns for the veldt," said Plowman foolishly.

"I don't think your feet are on the ground," Durban ended, but amiably.

"Of course not, he's Mercury, he, he," giggled Jules's old friend. "He flies through the air with the greatest of ease." His thin voice essayed a song.

"Sit down, Richard," said Jules, taking the old man by the arm showing him a deep, soft chair.

Richard Plowman took a cutting from his pocket, "You remember the octopus we shipped in the Mediterranean last summer, Jules? Here's something extraordinary." He said to Durban, "In 1875 an extraordinary number of giant octopodes and squids were found either dead or dying on the surface of the sea. On the average they must have weighed half a ton each. Their long arms reached a length of forty feet. Remains of them have also been found in the stomach of the cachalot. They are found on the coasts of Alaska, Japan, New Zealand and on the Pacific Island of St. Paul. Think of the sudden disease that overwhelms a whole tribe of these fearless behemoths in a night! 'The desolator, desolate.' Probably invisible microscopic misery! So we are attacked where we least expect it, eh?" He went on in a calmer tone, "In warm waters at this season, the *Loligo vulgaris*—"

Jules leaned back and dreamed: let them go on talking. The two rich peaceable old men were like household gods

211

—one on the right, one on the left—that assured him all was right on his hearth. When they went out, Durban stopped at the door and said, "Do you hear, Dick: you must take your money out. Or at least leave a few thousand francs only, for old sake's sake."

"You're frank in name and nature," said Jules, smiling.

"I never stab in the back," said Durban.

Plowman smiled, pulled his mustaches, trembled with a sort of shining pride, "Frank, I've staked Jules since the very first day he started a little exchange shop: I believe in his star as I believe in—the Thirty-nine Articles!"

"So do I," said Durban.

Plowman laughed and, putting his hand in his arm, dragged the old atheist out.

Scene Twenty-eight: Posters on the Bank

WHILE the others prattled of segregations and holding companies, Claire-Josèphe, with her hair beautifully fixed in the manner of the *Atlantide*, and looking more like a debutante than a wife of ten years' standing, battled for her own rights and those of her four children. She insisted on Jules providing for each member of the family, from mother to youngest son, separately, and on the bankruptcy taking place some considerable time after so doing, so that it would resemble neither collusion nor any other kind of fraud. She was in her rights. With the same delicate, virgin air, she produced documents that she had been working at all day with Maître Pierre Olympe, their crony. Jules accepted these with a twinkle but without a murmur. Alphendéry had spent hours of the late afternoon with Maître Lemaître, a leading jurisconsult.

"Maître Lemaître thinks you are right. If you move now you will save money. He foresees greater severity on taxes and a tightening up perhaps of the banking laws, and severer penalties. If you move now, say, within a year, when the judiciary is still susceptible to certain kinds of persuasion, you will get out with your skin whole. Lemaître calculates that the bankruptcy will take fifteen months to arrange, and you begin now. You must keep on making investments which lose money and buying contracts in commodities on which you lose money. This Guildenstern and Rosenkrantz combination might even help us!" He laughed at his cleverness. "Naturally, you must make a little, too: but on the whole, the picture will show a man who has lost his touch and his nerve. But it must be stage-managed, this decline from multimillionaire to pauper! Otherwise, irate clients will chase you for mishandling their affairs. You must work up a background of misfortune and pathos so that those you steal from will pipe their eye every time they think of you."

"Impossible!" Jules's large handsome white hand cut the air. "A year? He's mad. I want to take the next boat, if I'm going at all, as it were. What will happen in a year? Perhaps long before that, there will be a panic and everyone will want their money."

"You can't suddenly have a one-hundred per cent bankruptcy in any case—it wouldn't look convincing," said Michel. "And then there's Plowman."

"I don't know." Jules looked worried. "This morning I had my ideas straight and I was all for going clean out. Now you fellows have got me so confused with your Lemaîtres and Plowmans—why can't you fellows ever think straight? If I have to, I'll pay out Plowman. But it's a waste of money. What does Maître Lemaître know about business? His family has always been rich and always been in the law: naturally he thinks in long legal mazy exits. No punch to them. I don't want to have a book written for me on the art of going bankrupt with fifty subsections. Any little peddler on a side street with all his brains in his cockeye can go bankrupt overnight and I've got to be a prince and take a year at it! I won't do it that way."

Alphendéry leaned back and eyed Jules with patient scorn. "Every little cockeye spends six months at least cooking the books, and working up antedated claims: that's why they're so thin and mangy: they stay up at night working seriously at it, the way they do their business, too."

"All right," cried Jules, exasperated, "all right. Let's forget it. We'll keep on in the same old way and one of these days we'll go up the chimney in good and earnest: that will be honest and kosher—the books will please

213

your Lemaître, but he won't get his fee. Dick Plowman can pipe his eye but he won't get a sou back. William and the twins can go and drive milk carts and Claire-Josèphe can teach school. I'm with you all—you ninnies! Is that banking! The Comtesse won't have her money, I won't have her confidence, the State won't get its taxes, and our landlords won't get their rent. . . . Ugh! Ptt! You haven't got an ounce of money brains in your heads. People love thieves."

"That's so," said Alphendéry. "Léon has loved Méline ever since Méline stole about three hundred thousand guilders from him. Only death will part them."

"And so," said Jules, now master of himself and of the scene, "I don't have to go through all that *mishmash.*"

Claire-Josèphe's sweet, frail voice broke in: "Jules, darling, you must fix up the children's futures: then you will know how much you have left."

"Now," said Jules, "you boys have nothing to worry about, you know that. We're all together. We'll scatter and then we'll meet again at a fixed place on a fixed date. We can fly. William still has a pilot's license. Alphendéry gets air-sick but he's necessary because he can hand out the flapdoodle to passport officials and he looks like a Bulgarian or a Spaniard or something. By the way, Michel. Your friends down in the Communist Party must know a lot about faking passports. Why don't you go down and get us a wad of false passports, for Claire and the boys and the twins and William, you, and me. I don't mind paying a lot for them. They can use the money to stick posters on the bank denouncing the golden octopus after we've gone. And good luck to them." He laughed consumedly! "Oh, I'd love to see it. Like a man who wants to see his own funeral." He forgot the notion.

Their talk lasted till two in the morning. Michel was driven home by Jules. They were so exhausted, one and all, that the bankruptcy was beginning to take on the face of a deliverer. Michel particularly kept saying to himself, as he paced the floor of his apartment, "The waste of life, the waste of life!"

The telephone rang: an airy voice said, " 'Lo! I'm in bed. I say, Michel, let's form our own Bertillon Bank Creditors' Protection Committee. You can head it."

"That will impress everyone. . . ."

"No: you know the rumors about, that you represent

214

God knows who, Alsatian high finance, Gros, Hartmann, Herrenschmidt, Mieg, and so forth?"

"Yes. I've heard I represent everyone from Deterding to Oustric. You mean pretend three-quarters of the bank belongs to my correspondents. You can't arrange that in a night. And I'd be on the stand: I don't think I could stand the strain after all these years, frankly, Jules."

"Couldn't we sell the bank on its goodwill to someone in the Netherlands, or some American; on the ground that all that money was placed in by your interests?"

"I think that kind of sucker has withered away some years since. But you might be able to sell the bank. That's an idea."

"Yuh, and then clear out—that saves a lot of mess."

"Whatever you like. We'll discuss it in the morning."

"Yes, you're tired. O.K., Michel. I'm not tired. I guess I'll have this figured out by the morning."

"If you put that energy into business, you could double your fortune, Jules, instead of behaving like a wrecker."

Jules laughed gaily, "Oh, you're a puritan still, Michel. I know what I want. I don't want to join *the great families*." The accent was a sneer. "High society. High banking. Grand marriages. *Tout-Paris*. . . . Up the raiders!" He hung up.

Michel smiled to himself and went on pacing the apartment. "A gambler who knows when to quit, when to quit, a gambler who—break the bank! That's it! Break the bank, break the bank—that's where it came from—came from."

He habitually repeated phrases to himself aloud while his thoughts raced on in the same strain, a way of weaving thought and word continually, his chief pleasure.

Scene Twenty-nine: Man Without Luck

LÉON's wife and daughter, beautiful, small, buxom, both unenterprising harem women, sat at tea with Méline and Léon. Everyone was in high spirits for Méline had been flattering the women and Léon was pleased with the display of wit, charm, and manners they gave. His

215

wife, some years discontented and cranky after she had found out some of his infidelities, had now taken her parents' advice and resigned herself to it with some show of cynicism, making Léon pay tribute in the shape of bracelets, furniture, new boudoir arrangements, and trips to spas whenever she wanted them. She had also quietly taken a lover herself and conducted the affair in a decorous manner. The result of this arrangement was that though everyone was miserable, the estate remained united and intact, the family was socially acceptable, Léon had no more scruples about his lady loves, the rabbi called regularly, and Hélène, sensible and charming girl, was on the brink of an engagement to young Rhys of Rotterdam, a youth already rich in his own name and whom the romantic young Henrietta Achitophelous had let slip through her fingers.

To reward himself for this bright turn in his affairs, Léon was taking Méline to Amsterdam to look over a property that had fallen in through the bankruptcy of the leading estate lawyer. In this house he proposed to establish Mrs. Margaret Weyman, who was now beginning divorce proceedings against her husband. He had worked it out with one of his layers: he ". . . even went into romance on a basis of yearly returns," he told Méline. He had a contract drawn up ready for Mrs. Weyman to sign. He and she were to share the cost of the property: for the time being as an evidence of good faith on his part, he was to advance Mrs. Weyman's share of the money, at a rate of three and one-half per cent per annum. He gave the money for the furnishing up to two thousand guilders; she was to pay the remainder. The furnishing was to be done by Mrs. Weyman. Mrs. Weyman was to repay him out of rent received from the letting of one or two apartments in the building. The other two apartments were to be used as follows: one by Mrs. Weyman to live in, one by Léon and Méline, co-lessees, as a *pied-à-terre*. This arrangement saved Léon's face and gave Méline a home in Amsterdam when he did business there. The two partners meditated warmly over this project while they pieced together small talk with Mme. and Mlle. Léon. Méline had hitherto had difficulty in eluding his wife's friends, even in Amsterdam. Léon congratulated himself: up to this epoch he had had several thousand women, but never one with the "class"

216

of Margaret Weyman—brains, good looks, sex appeal, ardor, and responsive love.

"Bertillon only sells short," Méline was saying. "I couldn't place a share with him. Downstairs, that was another story. North Atlantis, Consolidated Tin, Bats, Imps, anything. Your old partner Raccamond is in a good spot there, believe me. Only I believe he's second-rate. It's a pity. If a real salesman were in a place like that—" He laughed. "Alphendéry said he'd do business with me, however: he can throw me all their business if he wants to. They say he's the power behind the throne. What do you think?"

"Power behind the throne!" Léon said irascibly. "Who knows? I don't know, my boy. He's a nice feller. Raccamond: no. When a man loses his luck," he continued sentimentally, "no use—good-by. Whatever he does is no good. Not only that, Méline, the boy has no constructive ability. Bricks without straw. All grab, for himself, for his boss, no joy in building. Grind, grasp, graft, but no imagination. I knew when he muffed the deals he did for me."

"Did you see Aristide?" queried Méline, disbelieving Léon. Léon avoided the question, and continued philosophically, "A man without luck. That boy's bad luck. No good." He shook his great head and fleshy chin in his tight collar, loosening up, "A head as big as the Sorbonne, nothing in it: no *nous*." He lifted his finger. "He brought bad luck to me and to Claude Brothers. He went into the bank for three months without pay, Alpendéry told me." He shut his eyelids over the threatening globes, half opened them. "What's got for nothing isn't worth having. No, sir: if I were Bertillon, I'd turn him out. I spoke to him myself yesterday. I said to him, 'Aristide, you're a fool, put a price on yourself. If you don't mark yourself up, who will?' He's sentimental, got principles. Says coming straight from the Claude Brothers failure, he couldn't have got into Bertillon otherwise, they're all so superstitious. He went round the stock-exchange houses of Paris—naturally, they turned him out, laughed in his face: he had to come humbly, hat in hand, groveling, where he used to be respected before. And the customers of Claude Brothers after him, 'Where's our money? You must know—we know what salary you got. Our dough went into your salary—' It wasn't easy for him, so he got sentimental, figured he could get into Bertillon's if he laid low. He was desperate—a customers' man tarred with bankruptcies. Of course, I think, with Raccamond —something about him, the bully, the—h'm—don't know —something queer. I told him, 'What can you do if you don't price yourself?' Result is—either they give a man too much or too little. At first he got nothing: now he gets fifteen thousand francs every four weeks and commissions. They must be—hand-over-fist—coining money. What do you think? What does he make it out of? I figure bucketing. Alphendéry says no. Their man. I'll get it out of him: but—figure it for yourself.

"Well: I spoke to Aristide yesterday. 'There's destiny for me in the house,' says he. Napoleonic! Yesterday cheaper than dirt, he now wants to be king, emperor, a big banker. No sense of proportion—in everything. Méline, I sell myself dear and I buy others cheap, I know they've put up the price, they saw me coming. Every man has his price and will take sixty per cent off for cash. I take 'em on the time-payment system, deposit technique—that basis: sometimes give 'em a bonus to take themselves off—me too. Ho, ho, ho, ho." He threw back his head, laughed clearly, looked cunningly at his wife and daughter, laughed a little laugh. His wife and daughter looked deeply, irreparably bored.

He seized the young girl by the shoulder. "Hélène, come some day and see how Papa makes money? Eh? You'd be surprised, my girl, you'd be surprised, you'd be surprised. You don't know me."

The girl looked faintly interested and smiled: her mother politely sneered. Méline rushed in, "Oh, I assure you, they are all terrified of Léon on the grain exchange: no doubt of that. They'd love to throw him off, but no chance. He's kosher: too good for them. You should really see," he wheedled the wife.

"I have an instinct, Paul," said Léon, wagging his finger. "Aristide will come to a bad end, constructive ability but all—straw and no bricks. Eh, not bad, eh? I'm not bad, eh? I've got him, eh? Paul." He lowered his voice. "And a police record: something against him. He went white that day— You know the Claude Brothers affair was a bad business for him. Aristide knew about the swindling all right: tried to blackmail, then insisted on his cut. I know, I heard— A swindler with no sense of humor is lost. A two-timer must see himself as a monkey on a stick, a Punchinello, a fraud, an actor. An actor knows he's an actor and knows when to act. A ham puffs and blows, no *diminuendo*. Aristide only sees himself as a very deep swindler. Ha, ha! And now a Napoleon with destiny: a bank with destiny. You know what destiny I think." He looked at the women and flushed, pulled himself into shape smartly. "Still, I got a *schematism*. Ho, ho. The *Goy!* Jews," he said in broken German to Méline, "have one talent, both the pushcart man and the prince in Israel. What is it? We laugh at ourselves. H'm. Not always. The *Goyim* believe in their destiny. That's where we're one step ahead: we hedge on destiny."

Léon knew no Yiddish. Coming from the Balkans, he spoke various Eastern tongues and the Ladino of the Jews exiled from Spain. To speak familiarly to Méline (from the Baltic) he used German, which he hardly knew outside trade phrases. He half shut his eyes now.

"A man without luck!"

The women had begun to whisper intimately to each other. "That Alphendéry," Léon continued, leaning closer to Méline, "seems a bright boy. I'll give him a chance—"

"You're employing him?"

"No, no—just a little job, see what he can do: no guarantees. If he's good, I keep him hanging on. If he isn't, I turn him back to Bertillon with Raccamond and the other—Schlemihls. I think he's good, though. Good secretary."

"What do you want a secretary for? To write, 'We confirm having shipped this day'? You're getting flighty. Do you want to impress the grain trade?"

Léon was ruffled. "Maybe, maybe." He twinkled good-humoredly. "I don't know myself yet." He lowered his voice. "For my private matters: smart boy, good negotiator. Like him."

"They say Alphendéry's pretty well off, that he controls big private accounts in the Netherlands."

Léon frowned. "Don't think so. That's what I have to find out. Instinct is—maybe. But I can smell dough."

"A good disguise, perhaps," Méline laughed.

"Yes, yes," Léon shouted with conviction. "A brilliant fellow, remarkable. Yes. I believe in Bertillon when I see that feller."

Scene Thirty: Mme. Achitophelous

"I SAID to him" (said Achitophelous from one pillow to the next), "this is not commission business, this is pillage. You will handle it with me and before you go to Belgrade you give me a letter. Now, Haidee, I can't make up my mind; I have another idea: I could say to him, I am going to ask you to work on joint account and I want Leo and Korb to get one-quarter per cent."

"Oh," groaned Mme. Achitophelous, "I feel terrible; I am in agony, Dimitri. Will you stop chattering? It's three o'clock in the morning and I haven't slept a wink. I am in the most awful agony. I am sure there is something wrong. Please get up and get the clyster, Dimitri. Ever since that awful child ran away to Paris my digestion has gone to pieces."

Achitophelous brought the clyster.

"You ate too much halvah," said Dimitri, but with decent alacrity prepared to act the family doctor. "You are in such a state that you don't notice how much you're eating. You're getting quite plump, Haidee; I mean, plumper than before."

"Acute indigestion is very dangerous," cried Haidee. "You've got the digestion of a horse. How would you know? Look, put the lamp on that table. Hurry."

"You know, sweetheart," said Dimitri, after a few minutes, "you have been rather cold to me lately."

She laughed, "At least you can do one thing, Dimitri! Cold? Everyone but you knows I have a lover, you lummox."

Dimitri stopped and wiped his head. He looked at her pitifully. "Haidee, this is rather a shock to me, you know. Who is the man, Haidee?"

"Let me up," she said scornfully. "Everyone in Constantinople knows it, they even know it in Cairo and Athens. Everyone knows it but you, stupid. Munychion, Thargelion's cousin. And now that you know, you had better think about my getting a divorce. I am going to marry him."

Achitophelous sat down on the bed and looked at his Turkish slipper tops. When she came padding back to bed, rosy, round, and beautiful as Henrietta's mother should be, he said, "It's not like you to do this behind my back, Haidee, and make me a laughingstock. Is that nice?"

"It's better Munychion than some fat businessman, the sort you bring to dinner. You'd like me to sleep with them and get you a better percentage, wouldn't you?"

"You're not dutiful, Haidee."

She laughed, a long, silvery, independent laugh. "Ring the bell, Dimitri: I want Suzette. I forgot to write to Konstantin (that's Munychion's name, darling) to tell him to come at eleven and take me for a drive! It must go off first thing in the morning before I get up. I never telephone—it's so coarse!"

"Don't go out with him publicly, Haidee."

"Naturally, I will. I have every right to. He's my lover."

"No wonder your daughter thinks about nothing but sex."

"Press the bell again, darling. She must be snoring her head off, the lazy devil."

Dimitri pressed it and hung his head. "What sort of a home have I?"

She laughed, got up very sprightly. "You've a five months' home here and a seven months' home in Paris. I threw in four children for a bonus. How many has she got? You've only spent ten thousand pounds on your Paris girl. She's economical! You've spent one hundred and forty thousand pounds on this home in the last twenty years, for running expenses. I've still done better because my marriage settlement is intact. Suzette! Bring me some tea and some writing paper: I want you to take round a note to Mr. Konstantin's house as soon as it is light."

The maid, a pretty young Greek girl, laughed, "Yes, Madame. And Monsieur, some tea?"

"Yes, bring him the cup with the pink roses that Mr. Konstantin likes so much!"

"Yes, Madame."

"I was going to divorce you, Haidee," said Dimitri severely, "but now I find this out, I will do no such thing. Have you running round the Mediterranean with Munychion a few weeks after the divorce and everyone pointing at me: the fat old businessman. No! You've gone too

221

far. Now you'll get no divorce. And I'll cut off your allowance. You'll have to pay for yourself."

She had a self-satisfied chuckle. "Then Papa will sue you for the twelve hundred pounds you stole from him when you were in his office. We shall see with whom I will be riding and who will be handing me clysters, you mildewed meat pie! I tapped all your telephone calls the last two years. Ha! That surprises you!"

Dimitri had gone red and then pale. "You did that?"

"Yes."

He suddenly began to laugh, "Ah, ah, ah—that's a joke, that's funny. Ah, ah, ah!"

"What's so funny," she said sharply, "it is funny, old coal sack, the way you run out with fifteen waitresses in one month."

"Ah, ah, ah," he cried, with tears in his eyes, "and I was tapping you, Haidee: for the past eighteen months I was tapping your telephone, too. That was why I was so surprised about Munychion."

She sat bolt upright. "I knew very well you were tapping me: I found the receiver in your collar case. I just fooled you, darling: I just faked all those calls. All the time I wrote to Konstantin!"

"It is funny just the same, ah, ah, ah!"

"Yes, it really is funny: ah, ah."

When Suzette came back she found them both in the merriest mood and she put the rose cup down in front of Dimitri, laughing too, "Ee-ee-ee."

"And then you slept with Suzette on the fifteenth of May last," laughed Haidee.

"Oh, yes, it is too funny," said Dimitri and pinched Suzette on the arm.

"Suzette," said the lady, "run along, now, my girl. Get your sleep. You must run off to Munychion first thing in the morning."

Dimitri stopped laughing. "No, now that's going too far."

Haidee kicked her ruby velvet slippers and wound the edge of the silk bed sheet in her fingers. She looked gravely at Dimitri. "Old man, you don't know how far I'm going. I have sent a book of poems to the publisher's, and they are coming out in two days: they have Konstantin's name on the title page. You will be forced then. I knew you, you coward. I have given Konstantin

222

jewels too: he gets nothing, the poor, sweet darling, from that boat company he runs."

"You should see," said Dimitri sitting up, "what I gave Mme. Eloth: five diamond bracelets, all in one night."

"Oh, indeed! It's too much, you miserable fellow! Five! You gave me a pearl brooch for my birthday! Go to the devil with your disgusting Eloth. I'll kill you. I won't stand that. Oh, you misery." She rushed to him, took him by surprise, laid him out and so kicked, pinched, cuffed, and scratched him that he began weeping and saying weakly, "Don't, Haidee, don't, darling dear, don't. You're hurting me, Haidee."

In the morning Haidee rode out with Konstantin Muny-chion dressed beautifully and modestly in black, with diamonds and ebony ornaments. Konstantin's emerald bracelet flashed in the sunlight. Haidee's dignified carriage and sweet, melancholy smiles made everyone feel she was only doing the right thing. A woman has to protect herself in this life.

Scene Thirty-one: Poor Pasteur

Letter from Mme. Mimi Eloth to Dimitri Achitophelous, in Constantinople, June, 1931

Hôtel Baur-au-Lac, Zurich

DARLING,

THANKS for your letter from the 17th and I think already thanked you for you letter to Paris. I am very sorry you still have troubels with you daughter and you are so lonely with no one to love you: but for one thing I wouldn't take the responsibility to force you daughter to wedding with a nice boy yet if she is unwilling. As for you newphew: do not worry about him: he wants nothing but money. Do you not realize, darling, that all these people only troubel you so much because you give them a handout? You are the richest of you family: that is a curse. They do not respect you more for it, darling. I see these peopel with the eye of you good friend, like a man. Do not take you wife so soon to that doctor about indigestion: perhaps it is not a cure. If it *was,* the world would know about it. Indigestion is not an uncommon troubel, after all. But still, who can tell? If you read the great Pasteur's life you feel what scientists have to go *through* before they gat *acknowledge.* I know this now myself through bitter sorrow—I mean what peopel have to go through to get knowledge of the world. I have written different letters to you about the bonds which are mine and about the annuity of which I have usufruct. My lawyer tells me that different letters he had addressed to you concerning all this have not been answered: I do not know if you got these darling, or if someone else got them. If it is not interesting to you any more, I can do no more. All other things with me develop not favorable. But what can I do? It is not my mistake and yet my mistake. I should have stayed in my homeland and settel. What is there to do for me now but to commit suicide? I could go to the Midi and live in poverty in a littel hovel for £20 monthly and my expenses for dresses, etc., down to ten thousand francs yearly, for whom have I to dress for? or I can take out life insurance for 100,000 guilder in your name and my poor mother's name and after three years is up suicide. I go to the hairdresser, make up, laugh but underneath I am a mummy. I am certainly home at our home in Paris the 10th July to present you with a birthday cake and wish and fifty-one candles. I am the only one you say who ever geb you a birthday cake. I am terribly down and depressed: my tears really don't stop a minute and I feel a big fool in life. Please make enquiries about the life insurance and the limit for suicide as I begged you above I think it is three years. Saturday I leave for *Rome,* then to Zurich again, then for Berlin to see my friends. But though I travel and travel, I know I have fail in life. You have shown me this. Why is this? And I thought you promised me so much! How fate makes us a great fool, all of us. Love, M.

P.S. I am sorry I cannot find the diamond bracelet you ask me for back to get altered. I move so much,

I mislay things. I will look for it. I am so sorry you have business losses. This was the only thing I love most and what proves it is the other things I have put in a safe-deposit in my mother's bank, also the lovely fur coat you geb me. But if you want it back, I will get it and will not mind been a little cold if my darling has had business losses.

M.

P.P.S. Forgive, as always, my *Greek:* I learn it but recently because I think I am going to preside at dinner-table of my darling. But now it is not so and really I am so sad I cannot write good Greek. M.

From Dimitri Achitophelous to Mme. Mimi Eloth, June, 1931

Constantinople, June, 1931

MY OWN SWEETIE,

I have your letter, my darling. Business is very bad. I will be in Paris on the 9th for our party on the 10th. I am so worried about business, sweetheart darling, and about my troubles at home that I cannot think about anything else. I cannot make out how your lawyer's letters to me went astray. I look in every post for letters from you. We will look for the bracelet when I get home. Do not worry about me. When I have made another million I will get out of business and solve our life problems. And so I must work!

D.

P.S. I was too bullish and I lost some money this week. D.

Scene Thirty-two: Real Romance

HENRI LÉON was very happy. At the age of forty-three he was once more head over heels in love. He was full of love and gratitude for Margaret Weyman who so unexpectedly unsealed the fountains of his earliest passions and thrust him out into a deafening wind storm of desires with a few stars above, the Venus of adolescence, the early twilight globes of hope, content, and fresh blood, the rare warm rain of love given again. Léon called himself a Don Juan and Casanova indifferently, but for the greater part of his life he was no more than a great cock, calling on compliant women, getting and giving little joy, arousing no love.

He had good looks, lustihood, power. He smiled and sang sweetly, spent money freely on women, pursued them relentlessly. But his obsession was money-making and his great appetite degenerated into a petty satyriasis: he picked up the women who were in the love business, because it saved time, and muffed the few affairs that sprang up spontaneously with pretty, plump, respectable, middle-class women, the kind he really admired, because he wanted the consummation as quickly as with café women and because, taking advantage of their respectability, he gave them their fare home instead of large presents.

And even the splendid women that, with a sultan's eye, he picked out occasionally in the great hotels and on the fashionable boulevards, like Mme. Vera Ashnikidzé and the so-called Russian Princess, he treated no better, except that, as they were in the thousand-franc class, he gave them a thousand francs where he gave some poor girl frequenting the dark corners of the Place Vendôme at night, one hundred.

But Léon was at heart still the village lad who rushes the village girls and likes to count the number of his triumphs. True, he only counted them over to himself, but his chief satisfaction in venal love was, as in money-making and bondholding, the *number* of women he slept with. He was modest. Still like a village lad, he feared and rejected the multifarious arts of the great strumpets.

For years Léon proclaimed to all his friends that he was looking for a love affair. He regularly regaled Méline, Raccamond, little Kratz, with stories of Mme. Léon's stupidity and wept over his misfortunes, even though his eye would stray during his stories and he would note with swelling bosom every pretty leg that came within a hundred yards. His children, he said, didn't love him (but he was never at home), his wife never talked to him (but he only talked about money and she had enough of her own.

On the chapter of his love conquests it was that little Kratz was able to make the most biting comments. "You a great lover! Huh. You buy your women like a grocer. You have a lot of money, so you buy more than I can, that's all. Don't make me laugh."

"Listen," Léon would answer good-humoredly, "Kratz —it's true I buy them. But look at me: a great dome, a great tail, short, thick, and forbidding, the money type, not the love type. There are a hundred dandies and grenadier guards and Rudolph Valentinos hanging round every night club. But they all go for me and I get them for the same price as the Valentinos. So? So I must have some winning ways."

"You buy them," Kratz shouted in malicious triumph, "you buy them. They go for you because the dandies look like monthly allowances and you look like the king of the stock exchange. You sound, talk, look, smell fat money. When you're out to get a whore you buy the dearest champagne, you bring out that million-dollar wallet of yours, you command, unwrap a roll of domestic and foreign bills of the largest denominations, you snap your fingers rudely like a man used to ordering a clutter of miserable clerks about. You fool, you look like big vulgar money."

"Not vulgar," Léon would say in a softer voice, disappointed. "They know men. They know I spend freely on them. I'm not mean."

"You buy them," triumphed little Kratz, "you buy them. Look at me, thin, rat-faced, poor: obviously your hanger-on. I get women for nothing." Léon would frown. Kratz did get them for nothing, but he was a mean, poor-spirited fellow—he only went out with hopeless nurse-maids, servant girls, and ignorant poor lonely women, timidly trying to help out their miserable fare given them in the kitchens they inhabited, too fearful and too stupid to put a price on their favors.

This insult, repeated and stuck on to others, was one of the reasons for the separation of the old cronies.

Léon had been looking round for some years and had begun to feel really pathetic, when Mrs. Weyman appeared, told him he had a challenging personality and a handsome face and refused to go to bed with him. Instead of angling for flowers and scents, she gave him a swagger cigarette case of ebony and chased gold, with his initials inset. This was the first time Léon had received any gift from any woman but his daughter.

Léon could not sleep without the gold cigarette case, looked at it a hundred times a day, drew it out as often as he could: besides being his unique present, it had cost Margaret Weyman, he calculated, fully eight thousand francs! Léon fell in love "at first sight."

Léon therefore prepared to go into his love affair in the style of a pasha. His little house was one of the most charming in Amsterdam, in a rich and progressive district. He had drawn up a maintenance agreement between himself and Margaret. In the meantime, Mrs. Weyman had united affection and interest and fallen in love with Henri Léon and there was talk of divorce and marriage. Mrs. Weyman had, in fact, already instituted divorce proceedings against her husband. When Léon asked her to sign the contract that he had prepared, she became thoughtful. To tell the truth, she was disappointed. "Be honest with me, Henri. If you're not going to marry me, tell me, and I'll make other plans."

Léon was intimidated. "My dear, I swear to you, look, I never swear unless I mean it—I swear to you that in five years we will be married. I can't do it at once, because Hélène's marriage has got to be put through decently, and I couldn't divorce her mother in her first year of marriage. It would upset the young pair. But after the first year, I'll divorce my wife, put my son into business and we'll live in Amsterdam, Antwerp, Paris or even New York, if you wish."

Margaret had several long parleys about the agreement. Mrs. Weyman and Léon now formed a trust, the Margaret Trust of which she held fifty-one per cent and Léon forty-nine per cent of the shares, into which Léon put one hundred and fifty thousand American dollars, and Margaret nothing. Léon was to operate the funds of this trust every year for the next five years and distribute the profits pro rata between himself and Margaret. He calculated that he would make up to fourteen per cent yearly. Margaret had about a hundred thousand dollars of her own invested for the most part in three-and-a-half per cent bonds. Léon contracted to pay her the difference between the yield on her money invested in bonds and stocks and seven thousand American dollars as well as give her ten thousand dollars yearly for living expenses and a dress allowance. "You are," explained Léon, "my wife, at least to me: and you must be properly established as a wife would. You and I will be known as a couple and we must do this thing in style or we will be despised and our relation despised."

To mark the signing of the contract Léon brought Margaret to her apartment in the house in Amsterdam, three bracelets in platinum, set respectively with diamonds, emeralds, and amethysts. As Margaret hesitated between them, Léon cried, "Here, keep them all, my darling. Why should you have to pick? Keep them all! After all, they'll be mine again soon, because we'll be married."

Léon and Margaret Weyman were now in their prenuptial honeymoon. Léon was quieter than usual, went away earlier from work, was not at his wife's home for months at a time, only turning up when some arrangements had to be made for his daughter's marriage. Léon began to run the funds of the Margaret Trust with exemplary brilliance: he had put a hundred and fifty thousand dollars on ice for a woman and he now had to make them pay him something. He was staggered at his own magnificence. What a woman! Only a woman like this was fitted to be his wife.

And for the first time in years he began to think of his dull and now decidedly malicious little wife, with pity. In observing her in this new light for the first time, he suddenly saw that during his long absence she had blossomed again, the grayness of years had vanished, and she had become one of the prettiest little women in Switzerland. Léon was glad that the divorce must take some time. "It must all be done without hurting her. It will be a great shock to her to realize I don't want her any more." He became quite tender about his wife at times, thinking that when she was divorced she would look back and regret her rich and brilliant Henri.

Scene Thirty-three: Mamma

ALPHENDÉRY received two letters, in the same mail, from his mother.

Strasbourg, June, 1931

MON BIEN-AIMÉ,

Your letter made me the happiest old girl; I was very worried. I thought you are now becoming a revolutionary. I am happy that you have improved since last year. I hope you get a complete cure. I have felt lonely not seeing you on your birthday. About the delay of war—owing to the splendid advance of the Russians it is not definite, it may be a change may take place, a surprise party. Let us hope for the best. Do you remember when I used to wake you up saying, "The Czar is killed," or, "The Kaiser is assassinated" to get you up for school? I was looking for a room near Cousin Kitty, but it is impossible to find one—the people are quite wealthy and roomers are not desirable. The trouble is I cannot look myself for a place to establish so I got to suffer. It is a pity of my being for a few years in Paris with you, not knowing the right place where to get relieve from my physical troubles, Aix-les-Baines and Vichy and Vittel it was not worth while. So we make mistakes in life and suffer useless and you, my poor son, lose money. Please, *mon fils bien-aimé*, write me as soon as possible. You letters are the best medicine for me write me all; keep well and cheerful. Take good care of yourself, don't go too much with the revolutionaries, it is all right for young men, but you are a family man. You have your troubles. Don't forget your old girl with love and thousand kisses.

MAMMA

Strasbourg, June 1931

MON CHER FILS,

Your welcome letter and the 2,000 francs cheque received. You cannot imagine, my jewel, my happy moments of reading your charming letter. I am well provided with my living expenses. I possess 3,000 francs in cash and a 800 franc balance from the 2,000 francs cheque you sent me May. I am very worried of your going with revolutionaries now with all war-clouds, riots, revolutions and this Adolf Hitler, though they say he is not German and the Germans are a great socialist people, they will never listen to that race-talk but he says he is going to make the poor little shopkeepers prosperous and that is something. Only he wants votes, that is all. You have one life, my treasure, you never can tell what may happen any moment, try your best, if it is only possible to keep a steady position and make connections and you can return here and if things go bad we can fly to another country, perhaps America. Living is cheap but to pay with the life for, it is not advisable. My best medicine and recreation will be of seeing you my sunshine. Lately I am feeling very often giddy, may be it is due only to old age and weakness. Thousand kisses and take good care of yourself, my dove.

MAMMA

A week later, Michel received another letter from his mother.

Strasbourg, July 1931

MY DEAR MICHEL,

Your welcome letter received: don't worry too much about me. I am only a guest in this world and my time soon over. You have plenty of worry and expense, to cover all your expenses is not fun, nobody lending you a hand to relieve your burden. You should only be able to endure your troubles. It is all over with me. What can't be cured must be endured. If I am to die alone, in misery and poverty in my old age, that is my burden: complaining won't help it; you know I never complain. What is the use? Who cares for the sick and old? You don't

231

write how is your health, my treasure. Are you in good shape. As to your plans, you say nothing: you know best what is to more of advantage for you. It is my destiny to drag myself alone all my last days in this world without son, daughter or grandchild. I would not mind to put up with all the unpleasant troubles only to hear you are doing well and happy and not going astray. If you had only taken my advice. Revolutionaries are not for you: I am glad you have given a speech at Juvisy for Jean Frère and he is a good man, but that is for workingmen, not for you. He came from the slums: he has something to fight for. Not you. You cannot ask a woman of good education to live poor with you in a little place. Your old mother is different, but not a young pretty woman. Of seeing you I have little hope. A man needs a woman. I am so frail and sick. I am eating solid food but cannot eat much and my friends are afraid to come and see me, I look so bad: it is all due to my chronic weakness. I believe what I see. My dear son, you go to so much trouble to get nowhere: you are sure there is no fear of war I hope. There is difficulty getting identity-cards for foreigners in this part: they are calling up the military service for Alsace-Lorraine. If the torment comes again where will I go? As long as you do good for yourself, but when you are in sickness and live alone, who will look after you? I am wishing you luck and glad you get to know poets but you cannot write poetry, my son, you are from different stock: don't forget your grandfather was the first lawyer in Mannheim. In meantime stick to your job. Please write me often and all. With much love and kisses, old sweetheart.

MAMMA

Alphendéry, in terror, got leave of absence for three days and took the evening train to Strasbourg. He arrived there unexpectedly the next morning, coddled his old mother for a few hours, took her out, and in the evening the two spent a gay time in a restaurant listening to a German band. She was feeble, through the overthriftiness and loneliness of the old, but otherwise in good health. Alphendéry left the same night, promising to make her a home in Paris. He was afraid to stay away from the bank for three days, because he alone knew the technique of balancing the short and long positions and William Bertillon and Jacques Manray, who took turns at it in his absence, always muffed it and caused great losses. These were, in general, bad times for him: he waked far into the nights and when he slept, slept and groaned. When would his slavery come to an end? He was bound to the bank by money needs and affection for the Bertillons, as well as inertia.

Scene Thirty-four: Five Cents and the Million Dollars

KÉZÉBEC, the Breton painter, Abernethy Gairdner, the American writer, and Garrigues, the Gascon sculptor, were seated together in three green armchairs in the stock-exchange clubroom looking earnestly at something that looked like a geological cross section of the Dent du Midi with its escarpments, but which was really a two-line graph of American railroad stocks 1921–1931 and American industrial stocks for the same period. Kézébec had been nearly a week constructing it with the greatest care. Kézébec was explaining.

"The market must reach rock bottom again, after another fall in which I will sell short, the market will begin another long rise and then we can look forward reasonably to a period of boom."

The writer added his gem: "There should be a stock-exchange committee ruling to prevent undue booms and then we would not have these crashes: the stock market would be more predictable. After all, the broker loses as much as the client who can't pay, doesn't he?"

The sculptor, who had dropped every penny he had earned on war monuments for the past three years: "You see rails are not nearly so speculative: the rise is much more even, but whenever you see a long rise in prices you should drop out. I've had too much bitter experience. If I had any money now, I'd chisel to make my bread, that's all."

"And so," jeered the American writer, "if you had got

233

out at the beginning of that Alpine climb in the middle of 1928—"

"Will history repeat itself?" asked Kézébec, with caution.

Alphendéry leaned over the center chair in which sat Gairdner. "You still here, Gairdner? Why don't you go off, as you promised me, and write those masterpieces the world is crying for? I told you I'd throw you out if I ever saw you in our stock-exchange room again. I don't want your money. Go and write."

Gairdner, little, blond, delicate, kind, flushed. "I know, I did promise: but what's the use? I don't believe I'm so important as you say. If I could make about twenty-five thousand dollars I could retire into Vermont and get the peace necessary to write. If I don't have the money I can't do it. I know myself. You see, I'm not really a healthy personality: I'm a sort of multiple personality. My personality is a kind of earthworm in sections —it would take years to grow together. A man like me needs a lot of money to write. I suppose that shows I'm worthless." He looked pallidly sorrowful like an ailing child.

"And what are you doing, Kézébec?" Alphendéry continued. "Why aren't you out in Brittany leading the back-to-Brittany movement! You believed the French language is tied up with French imperialism; don't you believe that the price of U.S. Steel is tied up with American financial imperialism? I thought you were a revolutionary socialist!"

He glanced quickly at Garrigues who was sitting, as always, voiceless and neurotic, and went on to Gairdner. "You sit there," and there was a note of patient scorn in Alphendéry's voice, "and think the capitalist class is going to hand you out strawberries and whipped cream the rest of your lives. . . ." He laughed. "Did I ever tell you how to make enough money to retire for life in three days?" The three of them started and looked earnestly at him. He waved his hand in a white gesture of disavowal. "In Chicago I buy a one-day option on a million bushels of wheat, put up ten thousand dollars— there's a variation of one to five cents, say it goes up five cents, fifty thousand dollars. The market favoring me, and renewing option with my winnings, by next day's closing, $40,000 becomes $160,000: next day, the third

234

day's trading, that is, I'm up to $640,000: the fourth day, I'm up to $2,560,000. . . . That's enough for me to retire on. In fact, making money is easier than playing marbles: you've only got to guess right twice. You've only got to guess right three times to break the bank at Monte Carlo. That's why it's so common. . . . But Levi Z. Leiter did it!"

"Supposing it goes down a cent," said Garrigues, heavily.

"You've got to have the ten thousand dollars to start with," said Gairdner wearily. "You can't play the market with two cents and that's what I've got."

"You've got two thousand dollars," smiled Alphendéry.

"I may as well throw it in the Seine for all the good it is to me," said Gairdner.

"A mere song! Fifty thousand francs is a mere nothing to this nabob," cried Alphendéry, lifting up his hands. "Man, come back to earth: you don't live in the Age of Gold. Why don't you take your two thousand dollars odd and move out of the bank into Meaux or Nevers or Louviers, live like a French scholar on bean soup, and write your guts out. The market has made a ghost of you. You're not a man."

Gairdner flushed very deeply. "You're right, but I can't do it: I will either make twenty-five thousand dollars or commit suicide."

Garrigues sat by and bit his fingernails. It was three months since he had sent up an order, over a day since he had had anything to eat save for one coffee which Urbain Voulou had given him. He followed Alphendéry out of the room.

"Mr. Alphendéry!"

"What, Garrigues?"

"You must replace my shares. I am wiped out. You stock-market sharks have taken everything. You must give me an overdraft to help me recoup myself."

"Have you no money at all?" demanded Alphendéry wretchedly.

"I am starving," said the sculptor fiercely. "You ought to know: you swindlers have taken everything."

"There was no swindling—you can look through the cards yourself."

"Cards!" He threw back his head and laughed tragically. "The whole office is yours, isn't it? You've bought them all. Everything fits your story. If I had every book in

235

the place, it wouldn't do me any good. But I know the truth. You must give me an overdraft to trade with, or credit me with one hundred shares, or I will blow my brains out."

"Come upstairs to my office," said Alphendéry quietly. "I'll see Mr. Bertillon."

"Emotional blackmail," said Alphendéry. "We'll have to give him one hundred shares."

"Do what you like," said Jules.

"Why didn't you let him?" asked William. "We could easily get a cleaner in and he'd be better off. He's insane. He'll never do another statue in his life."

"Isn't this a terrible business we're in," said Alphendéry, "that drags writers away from their books, sends men insane, induces men to waste years of their lives in a stuffy room looking at figures, intent on gorging more and more and more money, until they've forgotten how to count, or what money is or comes from, until they don't even want what's bought with money—as, leisure, fine tailoring, good food and drink, round-seeing, books —but just want to sit there in the stock exchange year after year. . . . There are the Hallers, who are stuffed with money, coming in day after day. They're free, happy, have enough of everything in the world and could spend their lives traveling. But they sit every day all the year in the green armchairs in Jules's board room looking at rows of numbers changing, and when the market closes, they go home to sleep. There is nothing else to do—in Paris, the bull's-eye of desire—until the markets open again the next day. It's an insane asylum you run, Jules. I can't stand it: how can you?"

Jules came down on the two front legs of his chair, long in the air, and said soberly, "People of my class pay an awful lot for mental specialists. If I didn't get them, some Freud or Fraud would. . . . What do you care about these poor squibs of men, Alphendéry?"

"I love men, Jules."

Jules raised his eyebrows, surprised. "That's a prejudice, Alphendéry. Most people don't get on because of some old prejudice. Drop them and have a couple of crazy superstitions like me: you'll make more money."

Scene Thirty-five: Field Day for William

HENRI LÉON'S dome was refined and diminished by
the pinched felt. He lunged briskly into the bank at eleven
o'clock in the morning, twisting this way and that to espy
someone of importance in the cheerful springtime crowd
now filling the small tellers' den, the lobby, and the stock-
exchange clubroom. A rapid fire of laughter rang out in
the stock-exchange room where someone was saying he
had just gone in with Aristippe de Partiefine in his Viennese Formula.

Mnemon Cristopoulos, red-haired, middle-aged, suavely
exotic as to suit, socks, and tie, with a fine gold chain on
his wrist and ankle, serpentined muscularly through the
crowd, avoiding contact with the women, delicately ac-
knowledging and sizing up the men. Near the beautiful
lift-cage, made of fine wrought iron somewhere gilded,
stood Aristide Raccamond, his head characteristically
thrust forward between his fat shoulders, using his hands
as best he could to gesticulate, while holding his usual pile
of folders and newspapers under his arms. His expensive
new clothing was pendent from his great body in extrava-
gant loops and flags. He did not see Cristopoulos in time.
Cristopoulos looked at him with revulsion, edged away,
and pointedly avoiding him mounted the staircase to the
balcony. Aristide watched him upstairs with nostrils
pinched and mouth open. He got out his heavily initialed
handkerchief and wiped his always livid forehead. But
he felt safe: Jules Bertillon was no homosexual—detested
the breed, in fact, and Cristopoulos, who had a great
affection for Jules but would always have to love him
from a distance, would never tell tales of this particular
sort on Raccamond. But only a year ago, when Raccamond was procuring for Carrière, Cristopoulos had said,
"If you cross my path again, you stinking flesh thief, I'll
ruin you." Cristopoulos, strange fellow, elegant, busy,
secret, had no public scandals about him, and he had a
large and respectful clientele in commission business.
Cristopoulos represented what Aristide would like to be,

on the second plane. On the first plane, he wanted to be a great banker, a great force, someone who sat "with the gods": someone who always knew what Marthe Hanau would put in her next issue.

An English broker visiting Jules Bertillon both for personal and bank business, cool as a cucumber, in appearance like a gray, superfine badger bristle in a Piccadilly shaving brush, seeming to despise faintly but wholesomely the excitable Gaul, bared his small red lips over his rat teeth and passed upstairs.

Léon hailed him, "Hey, Stewart, what are you doing in Paris? Is the market going up? Is it good for a rise? . . . What do you say to Mulloney and Moonsteyn's new promotion, North Atlantis?"

At this moment William Bertillon moved upon them with the swift immobility of a ship of the line. "What's the news from London? What's the latest ramp? Those boys are still turning over thousands I bet. I hope you get some of it, Stewart."

Léon looked quickly from one to the other: Stewart's mouth became smaller and tighter, then it opened to let out the voluble rat-bitten reproof: "In my opinion, North Atlantis is a perfectly good gold mine, not overvalued: the rumors have been spread either by the promoters themselves to interest the public, or else by the short-sellers trying to provoke a slump."

William spoke out of time, feeling gay in the good weather. "Why should they? It's probably rotten anyhow. . . . No offense, Mr. Stewart. Look at the record of all business. According to Dun and Bradstreet ninety-five per cent of them shut up shop for some damn reason inside of ten years. A bear market is a twenty to one bet on the facts. It's all a time equation. You're betting on the morgue—but Jesus, what tricks they go through before they land there! It's like chasing a fox—he jumps, he doubles, he gets his mate to run for him, he swims a creek—" Stewart was looking at him as if he was ready to pop like a lighted cracker. William was in his most annoying mood; he buttonholed Léon. "England's such a Christmas tree for share pushers: noble lords will sit on the board of any company for a couple of quid a sitting. And the public. Loco or idiotic. God, I've never heard of such a people, except perhaps some peasants in Bessarabia, or the niggers in the Cameroons, who believe in what they believe in. Magic. Put up any sort of business that sounds utterly impossible and they'll gulp it down. Because—why? Because life has always been handed to them on a silver platter since they conquered India and South Africa. Now a real, solid business doesn't appeal to them, like a sixpenny bazaar or cheap machine-cut dresses. Nothing that is any good to the working people. I wish we were there. I've always said to Jules you could make millions there. . . ."

Stewart's and Léon's eyes opened wider and they showed a faint interest. "Gold mines!" said William. "Brokerage is the true gold mine. No labor troubles, no accident insurance there. Frankly, Stewart, I don't give a damn whether you execute the orders I give you or not! As long as you can pay me! If you work on the other side of the book from me you're more likely to be able to pay me! That's the way I see it. Business is business!" Stewart, extremely irritated, darted looks round to see who was listening. Abernethy Gairdner was listening and drank it all in, politely, with bowed head, as if lost in calculations for his desired twenty-five thousand dollars.

Stewart said crankily to Léon, "What do they think of Hitler up in Antwerp? You people must see more of it than we do."

"Hitler," William started off again. "Hitler looking for votes is like a man making love to a woman. 'I'll give you a bracelet, I'll give you a fur coat, I'll give you a motorcar, I'll give you an apartment, I'll give you an annuity'— then he puts on his hat and asks for change of a ten-franc note. 'My dear, there are two sides to every deal. Thanks very much. So long.' The German people. Idiots! Once a Heinie, always a Heinie!"

"They won't listen to Hitler, no, no!" said Léon violently. "What's he got to offer?"

"He's going one better than the goose step: he got the goose-step arm, too," jeered William.

Stewart determined to break away. "You've got a big crowd here, they seem to like the place," said he.

William laughed long, a luxurious laugh; he stretched himself and yawned. It seemed to him that fine morning that his Chinese nightingale was chirruping and whistling on his shoulder. He looked round, pink under the eyes, his eyes round and clear and his snow-white teeth smiled broadly. He was completely indifferent to Stewart's irritation and also to his hate. He said lusciously, "The suckers: they're always here. They never take their money. That's how we make money. You may think this is a bank, Stewart, but it's just a casino with letter drops on the front door. And we make casino money. Did you ever hear of a man who won money in the market and took it out, Stewart? No, if the suckers win, they double; if they lose, they put more money in to try to recoup. If they're gamblers, they plunge; if they're amateurs, they whipsaw. And there are people who ask us how we make our money! . . . . The stock exchange is a tout, only in one case you're betting on a real horse. . . ."

Léon listened intently, for this problem had been absorbing him for some minutes, ever since, in fact, he had seen the white, stone face of the bank in the morning light. It had come back to him, struck him with an ache: how did they make their money? At the end of William's remarks, therefore, ignoring Stewart's pained and disgusted face, he gave a shout of laughter and putting his head between them, said earnestly, "You're right, William. We all say we're in broking or grain or banking or shoelaces—but the real business we're in is milking. . . . Good! Where's your brother?"

Near the door to the stock-exchange room, watching them and the other groups, stood Garrigues, the Gascon sculptor, sulking, his large country frame bowed, his poor suit sagging, his great forehead with beaded brows clouded. Gaston Garrigues, having nothing with which to pay for bed and bread, naturally could not answer a margin call and his account was closed by Alphendéry. Now, after desperate figuring, he had persuaded himself that the bank had robbed him of several hundred francs. He had complained to the criminal division at the prefecture of police and his complaint had been dismissed, for the police were used to the pleas, whether insane or justified, of miserable stock gamblers, against the various banks of Paris: they came in at the rate of two hundred a week when the market was wild. After this, Bertillon had called him in and credited him with one hundred shares of International Mercantile Marine, a reasonably quiet stock which he expected to go up. But this had only convinced the obsessed Gaston that there had really been something crooked in Bertillon's handling of his account and that the one hundred shares was in the nature of hush money. He knew very well that big gamblers were ruined in the market in the course of nature but did not see why he should be.

"I only want it to live," he said to himself, "so that I can work without my stomach cramping from hunger. There's no danger in that. I must win."

He had just now borrowed five hundred francs from his father, a poor share farmer near Bergerac, and was watching for Aristide Raccamond so as to offer it to him to put on ten shares of Tubize. He divined, with his sick intuition, that Raccamond was a force opposed by nature to Alphendéry in the bank, and as the one had brought him bad luck, he hoped Raccamond would restore his fortune. When the order was sent upstairs to the telephone room, Jules Bertillon had just come in and was lounging there. He tore up the order and sent down a message that no orders were to be taken from Gaston Garrigues, except for the one hundred shares of I.M.M. and that the five hundred francs was to be returned to him. He telephoned for Raccamond and Garrigues to come up to his room.

Raccamond, standing near the lift, got the message first and rushed up the stairs, pleased to let the lobbyful of people see him on business intent.

"Raccamond, I told you not to take any more orders from Kézébec or Garrigues."

"He brought in the money——"

"I won't have him. If he tries to gamble here again, I'll have him thrown out physically. Remember that!"

His voice was a whip and his manner scorpions. Raccamond shrank, retreated, bundled along the corridor. "I don't understand him, I don't understand the house: what sort of a . . ."

Garrigues got his share too and, of course, imagined a persecution, and that Jules Bertillon, alternately, feared him and his accusations.

"I'll bring suit against you!"

Jules jumped up. "Get out of here, Gaston: go back home and help your father on the farm if you can't work. I don't want you here. I won't take your money. I'm not interested in poor men. I can't make money out of them. Now, that's what I really think of your business, Gaston. Get out. Thank you and good-by."

Gaston looked at him furiously, seized the bundle of

papers he was carrying—reports of American day-to-day trading, Dow-Jones averages, charts, and the like—and rushed out of the room. "I'll show you up," he cried, in the voice of an animal that rarely speaks. At the bottom of the staircase, still footling round the lift, he saw Aristide, hangdog, waiting for clients. "You've done me dirt— I'll pay you for this," said Gaston and pushed him as he started past. He got to the door of the bank and there hesitated: then he turned and surveyed the crowded lobby. No one at all had witnessed his excitement, his departure. He slowly pivoted, took a step, came back, tussling with himself. Then he stood again near the door of the boardroom. So the matter was to drop. Gaston, like a dingo, walked up and down, round and round, chewing the rag, but helpless, waiting perhaps for a miracle to happen, for the pillars to split open and drop money into his lap. He ached to see the place and ached to leave it, this citadel of invisible gold. The stock-exchange workers, the clients suffered him: they only once in a week gave him a passing thought with, "That sculptor with no cash, a nut . . . has some sort of a grudge. They all have when they lose. Those artists have no guts. Why don't they stick to their arting?"

"Well," Jules was masterfully gay, "Michel, I chucked out two of your sob-story boys this morning. Garrigues and Kézébec. I can't throw out Gairdner yet because his family still may cable him a few thousand dollars: also when his mother dies, he's coming into something like fifty thousand dollars. We ought to make a rule never to take in anyone who works for a living: they can't stand the gaff."

"Let's do that hereafter," agreed Michel. "But how? You can't make them show their identity cards the way they do in Monaco."

"By smell," said Jules, "by smell. And tell that fool Raccamond. He's so hungry for commissions, that he even took an order from François Vallat yesterday. I don't want my men in the market, unless they're seasoned, like Jacques Manray, or are so much in debt to me like Urbain Voulou, that it doesn't make any difference, anyway. I don't want the small fry. Big gamblers know they're punting; little fellows think they're selling their souls to

242

the devil into the bargain—they all turn into Sarah Bernhardts in consequence."

Stewart had moved away. He never failed to be astonished at the flurry of clients who gathered in Bertillon's lobby. In England, not even in a broker's office, let alone a bank, do clients gather to gamble in the stock market: this is because the fixing of prices is done through jobbers and the London market is settled fortnightly. But wherever the American stock market is concerned, because every trade is (supposed to be) done on the floor of the exchange and the price of every trade is recorded, speculators find an intense fascination in the flashing in and out of the prices: they seem to picture to them not only the wild scramble in the exchange so many miles away, but also the heartbeats of Dame Fortune herself. And with them stock-market luck has become one and the some thing as fate.

"Look at Garrigues, that damn sculptor," said William, still in his detestable vein, "he's a failure. The theory of art is the bunk: an artist who knows how to sell himself can always sell his pictures. A bad artist has always a thousand excuses why he can't sculp or paint. They naturally become gamblers: art is a gamble. They don't ever work. Artists are basically people who get paid for amusing themselves. They're all dreams: they don't exist if no one takes notice of them. They're invented by other people. What's the sense of art anyhow? A photograph gets the details down better than a painter; a *procès-verbal* or the archives of the criminal police give you conversation and plots better than a writer; an automobile is a lot more difficult to get right than a hunk of stone. They're out-of-date and when they try to catch up they find they're out-of-step; then they're more wronged than a left nancy, touchier than a retired Indo-China colonel, more sniveling than a school telltale . . . they begin dupes and end rogues. If I had my way I'd only let in here the ones that know what game they're in, the scenarists, film stars, and radio warblers, artists of photo-montage, voice doublers, and cabaret decorators. Those old-timers—Jesus, I get a crick in my neck trying to see them crawl round my ankles, they're such petty cash!"

Léon's eyes followed Stewart with regret: he was pining to get some tips from Stewart. "You annoyed him," he said to William. "He's touchy, like all Englishmen. What do you want to offend him for?"

"He's coming here for his health, not for mine," said William in his stark style. "I can kick him in the teeth today and he'll come back tomorrow with a new false set to smile with, if he needs the business. And we don't need him. Say, I know what's the matter with him. I never saw a fruit merchant that liked you to cut bits out of the inside of his melons to sample them, even when they're good. You know the English: a nation of window dressers."

Léon shook his head. "Stewart is good; he's a good businessman. He's got the place full of Jewish boys. He likes the Jews. He's made a lot of money." He edged off in search of Stewart.

William went in search of other prey. "Asking the stock market to make your living expenses," he said, when he collared Jacques Manray, "is like going to a whore in the hope that she'll give you money to buy your wife a dress. She'll take a special pleasure in picking your pocket."

Scene Thirty-six: Ralph Stewart

"Who is that talking to Mr. Léon?" asked Raccamond of Alphendéry, from the balcony.

"That's E. Ralph Stewart, of Stewart, Murthen, and Company, one of the biggest brokers on the London Stock Exchange: one of our brokers. Stewart is a very smart man . . . started without a shilling. Don't be taken in by his bumptious, testy, all-England manner. He knows more about the London market than any ten men— although he won't tell it to you, because he's more patriotic than a German Jew cheering for King George. You've got to dig through a double-coat of Up, England! to get any meat out of him. I'll introduce you; you ought to know him if you're going over to England any time."

Stewart began to blink, swallow and stutter inaudibly when he saw Alphendéry. He almost brushed Racca-

244

mond aside and had obviously an important subject that he would not bring out in Raccamond's presence.

"Glad to see you, Stewart; coming upstairs?" queried Alphendéry with joy, as if Stewart was the man he most wanted to see in the world.

But Raccamond bumbled along. He had fluent English, with a broken musical southern French accent. "I want to introduce my clients especially to the put-and-call market." He devoured Stewart with his great, round, fringed eyes.

"Yes," Stewart was milder than before, "Mr. Alphendéry can explain it all to you."

"I have personal clients," said Raccamond, his tone heavily weighted.

Stewart looked at him rapidly and spat out in his most incomprehensible style, "I-understand-of-course-you-mean-clients-of-this-house. Mr.-Alphendéry-is-their-specialist-in-the-London-market. I-take-it-you-are-working-with-him. Consult-him. Good-day."

"I beg pardon," said Raccamond, contritely.

Stewart tossed his head and repeated the sense of his inquiry, biting each word as if he loathed to have it pass his lips again.

Raccamond sprang at him. "No, no. I am working up a special business myself. There are types of operations unique in London which this house does not particularly— er, push: there is the hedging of international shares— arbitrage—I feel we have neglected this side of the business." He perceptibly grew and was more dignified. "A private business—doing business almost entirely on the Continent—" Stewart looked at him with contempt, but it might have been a mere tic Stewart had.

"—We should be half-English, half-French. Mr. Alphendéry is—a remarkably able man, very able, but he thinks towards the Continent—towards Berlin even. I've had experience elsewhere, you see. I worked in Buenos Aires. I want to divert a lot of business towards London with a view to establishing myself—the bank, a branch of the bank—there. I went over this with Mr. Bertillon when I first agreed to come in with him. . . ."

Stewart looked impertinently up and down Raccamond while he was speaking. As soon as his voice dropped, he rushed out with, "I-must-say, I-don't-share-your-opinion-of-Mr.-Alphendéry: he's-a-remarkable-arbitrage-man.

Amazing-understanding-of-the-terrific-stutter-stutter-it's-
ever-been-my-pleasure-to-meet. However, Mr.—what's your
name? Eh?—"

"Aristide Raccamond: I—"

Stewart waved his hand impatiently. "If your clients
are thinking of English stocks, they're right. There's the
beginning of a big rally on now: spring rally; it'll go
on right through the summer. No doubt of it. Who would
put their money in America now? After all, England is
still the home of finance . . . No doubt of it. All the
money is pouring into England. Only place where people
have confidence. Only place for investment. Tell them,
everything's sure to go up and up all the year. I see no
slump ahead at all. I take no stock in this bogy talk.
England's the world's banker. Never failed yet, never
failed yet. She keeps her word, that's why." He added
crossly, with contempt, "None of this, none of this—
speculation you get in the American stock market. Every
Tom, Dick, and Harry trying to make a pile—like in
France! It's our system . . . eliminates crowding . . .
spreads the takers. Excuse me!"

He had seen Alphendéry beckoning from the balcony
and rapidly climbed the stairs. Aristide looked after him
with envious affection. Old Thomas Sweet, Stewart's man
in Paris, was falling behind the line. In due time, Raccamond thought, he would like to install himself in old
Thomas Sweet's lucrative job. Thomas Sweet was an old-
timer with the manner of the Wilhelmstrasse, 1900, dull
proud official old gent and altogether a dud in modern
Paris. Murthen was established in London for three hundred years: Stewart had the active, irritable, unpleasant,
insolent brain of a young animal: compared with Murthen's history, very young he was and the red blood in
the firm came from him.

Mnemon Cristopoulos came down the stairs, bland,
secretive as ever. What a detestable pink shirt! thought
Aristide, but at any rate it served as a pilot light—for
others. What was he doing here? Always here. Jules must
certainly be doing some business with him. But why didn't
he place his orders through his own customers' men, like
himself, Raccamond? This bank, though it would absorb
his energies for a year or two to come and though he
would absorb it slowly (and surely) as the python—nasty
beast, as the earthworm, petty beast, as the python, nobler

beast, absorbs the antlered stag (but what does it do with the antlers?)—this bank would be only a sort of ante-chamber where he would meet the men necessary to him. In school he was head in mathematics and in Latin lyrics, too. The son of a tailor.

His dark-lashed lids wide open, round the swimming whites of the pupils, watched Stewart stop and laugh with Alphendéry. Alphendéry was a valuable man—personal charm, living wit kneaded into him, a likely, valuable man, with something feminine, compliant, winning, re-sponsive that attracted men—old, Jewish, Central Euro-pean blood? A man who loved men's company and knew how to bring out the best in them and who suggested ideas to them, so that they felt richer through him; he got a lot of affection and a lot of business, purely through his affectionate behavior and encyclopedic information but rather a light intellect, a pessimistic, cynical, skating, skim-ming, inverted, scholar's intelligence, due entirely to the lack of a great urge in him.

"The urge is everything," thought Raccamond to him-self, standing there lost in the gay press of the money-making crowd. "It roughens the road, but it makes it longer and higher. Now an Arab horse galloping—he has no need to gallop, but he becomes incomparably stronger than the one that fattens in the rich dowager's stable. Fantasy is needed to draw a man out of the rut." Chateau-briand, his favorite author, remarked, "A little madness is needed to get a man out of some situations."

"As to Alphendéry," thought Aristide, "he is willing to attach himself to anyone: he is a good third mate. All he wants is a salary large enough to let him buy books, to pursue the even tenor of his way. He will work but won't push." Raccamond did not intend to lose sight of him: he would gradually supplant him and show Alphendéry that he was the man he should attach himself to. At the very first he had heard of him as the man who stood nearest and dearest to the Bertillons, even at times as the *éminence grise* of Jules Bertillon, and he had picked up all the information he could about him.

One disquieting thing: Aristide had bribed Madame Fur-ness, a corn-yellow blowsy girl in the accountant's office to get the salary list of the employees, in order to picture the hierarchy. But Alphendéry received no salary: there-fore he either drew at will, according to a verbal agree-

247

ment with the Bertillons, or received commissions from these foreign richissimes. He also drew on a foreign corporation called Lollard and Company and signed the checks as a member of that foreign corporation. The whole thing presented a prospect of months of sapping to Aristide and he was quite happy. This sort of thing appealed to him above all. Perhaps, Aristide reflected with a contraction of the gullet, Alphendéry was not quite so guileless and influenceable as he appeared!

"No man ever made enough money," said Jules. "I like the London market and among other things I'm going into the business of selling C.P.R. and Royal Dutch short. A chap in Fleet Street is sending me memoranda about Royal Dutch. He knows the inside of the inside and he's convinced I'm working for Gulbenkian, and a great personal enemy of Sir Henri Deterding, so he gives me the true oil. I know enough about them to sink a battleship. The point is—when? The whole British system is backing them up from what I can see. That's the only weakness. Do you think you can pick the moment to sell Royal Dutch or any of its subsidiaries, Stewart? Say, I had my boy over there looking them all up at Somerset House, a shilling a time; but I don't care, I'm willing to sell Threadneedle Street and Throgmorton Street short, if necessary. I don't give England five years. Where would they be without India? And do you think if the Five-Year-Plan goes through the Hindus will continue to pay through the nose to keep Lancashire alive and all that? It's a regular Bastille you've got there, isn't it? Deterding, Bearsted, the Samuels, the Ionides, all the Alliance Assurance crowd, the Church of England chief, the Sebag-Montefiores, the steamship high mucky-mucks, the Big Five. It's too perfect, Stewart: it's the one-horse shay . . . they'll have to all go down together. I'm willing to bet on it."

Stewart pursed his lips and looked as prim as if someone had said, "It's profiteering" during the collection in church at Virginia Water on Sunday. "I hope you won't, Mr. Bertillon. Everyone was selling England short, as you say, before the war and no one thought she'd come through the way—especially the Americans," he said with peculiar distaste, "but she did and then money flowed into England because everyone thought, if she can weather that storm she's good for a long time yet."

Alphendéry laughed. "1919 and 1926 were sad blows at that happy idea." Stewart stiffened, took no other notice of him. Jules started at another straw and careered off, "And say, I told my boy, Adam Constant, to find out about silver. Do you think silver's a good bet? Deterding's interested in it, isn't he? Of course, if India gets a silver basis that'll remove the chief cause of discontent and then you can't sell her short, as part of the British Empire. Constant writes to me," he said with some malice, for he knew Stewart was very angry that Constant had been getting information from other sources in the city of London, "Constant writes to me that one of the big metal brokers considers silver a good speculation. Deterding is not dealing through them and no one knows anything of his movements and if he was dealing through Montagu's or Handy and Harman, people would know. He says," Jules's eyes gleamed with fun, "there is not much business being done. It's probable, they say, *he says*, that it's a newspaper campaign."

"I'm all for silver," chattered Stewart.

"Don't say that, Stewart, or I'll think you're in debt," teased Jules. "Anyone who wants to go off gold is in debt: that's an axiom."

Stewart was furious: "In Manchuria there has been a bimetallic system for twenty-five years: when the Japanese occupied Manchuria they thought of introducing a gold-standard system, but they found it wasn't necessary, wouldn't work. And that's another thing, they've got to buy silver for their new unification system in Manchuria."

"I'm on the gold standard, I don't care who goes off," said Jules, unreasonably, for he did not care for argument; he simply got an idea, by suggestion or intuition and stuck to it.

Recklessly, Stewart asked a question that had been hanging on his tongue for a quarter of an hour. "How long is your young man going to stay over there?"

"Oh, I want him to sound opinion, generally."

Stewart began to splutter, "I-heard-he-went-to-Lord-Drogheda-and-started-talking-about-the-interests-of-world-capital . . . created ridiculous impression . . . no good sending these young clerks with their ignorance of our point of view."

Jules looked resentful. "He tells me what I want found

out. Who's Lord Drogheda?" Stewart clamped his mouth shut.

William strolled in at this unfortunate moment and clamored, "Did you see that young man Constant, Stewart? We sent him over to try to settle that shady affair with Sedeba, Roda, Jones . . . afraid there's nothing doing. Of course, they bucketed but we can't get them to show their books unless we can get them into court and we haven't got enough to go on. We can't say they bucketed? . . ."

"He came in," whirred Stewart, "he came in. Sedeba, Roda, Jones are hard to catch; they work through shadow firms . . . get orders placed by ghosts. Not the first time."

"Oh, you bet," caroled William, "they're all bucket shops. No firm could live a minute if it wasn't. If you take the same risks as the suckers, where's the percentage? You've got to run a book. They may get you one time in a hundred but the whole stable can never win. The stock exchange is like Duggie Stuart, only he has to deal with real horses: that's the snag in his business."

Stewart went almost purple, but he could not turn his back on the eldest and weightiest of the Bertillons. Alphendéry burst out laughing and sprang into the breach. "This is William's field day. What he means is, if you stand still in finance, you go backwards: you've got to be advancing, taking risks, taking positions. How to take them? Bet against the majority. Everyone knows that. Isn't that how the casinos run? You don't need to crook the wheel. Not one in ten thousand can do the hat trick. You won't get two men in a hundred to win on the same throw. A scatter diagram: that's all. That's what William means. I say, Jules, Léon is here; he wants to talk to you about wheat. Mr. Stewart, will you come round to my office? I want to go over those puts with you. Let's see, when's settling day?—"

They both went out. Jules scowled at William. "What's the matter with you, spouting that hokum when Stewart's here? Why should I encourage him to bucket me?"

"I love to stick a tack in the inner tube of his hypocrisy," said William.

"Why don't you get a job in vaudeville?"

William became angry and lost all his good humor and Jules saw, with relief, that he would not be ready to drop any bricks for at least half an hour.

Scene Thirty-seven: Spring Fever

Léon made mysterious signs towards William, but Jules said, unexpectedly, "Go ahead, Léon."

"Bomba, your man—Berlin—came to see me, German bonds . . . insurance technique. Don't know whether I can do it—good idea though. I told my man to work on it. Where's Alphendéry? He knows about German bonds."

William pricked up his ears and looked suspiciously at Jules. "What's this? I know nothing about this: I thought you had sacked Bomba."

"Oh, he was coming back here and I told him to come back via Rotterdam and see Léon. Idea is: there are lots of German bondholders scattered throughout the world; they've held on to German bonds, out of affection, superstition, Germany's the coming great nation. Now, they're broke—everyone's broke—get them to give us their bonds on promise that our consortium has agreement with German government to market them in Germany. Germany looks hopeless. I have a hunch German bonds are going to rise for a time. We'll give them a two-year, five-year deposit agreement; before five years are out German bonds will have gone to hell. In the meantime we can market them on a rise, sell them short, because we have the supply. Or, if they fall very low, and we see the German government is secretly buying them in, we can hold out. If they repudiate, probably the government will still try to buy them in, *sub rosa*, the way the Russians do, and we can get something for them. In the meantime we have them to manipulate. Idea is: the owners receive an advance from us based on present price; we credit their coupons: they pay us loan interest, or we agree to pay the unpaid interest, from now on, till maturity. What does it matter? The world won't be here two to five years from now; or there'll be a war and no one will want German bonds, anyhow. Good scheme, eh?"

William considered. "Yes, it is a good scheme. How are you going to get the bonds?"

251

"Supply is the question—always the question. How?" Léon rushed in.

"Circularize!" said Jules languidly. "Get an organization, form a new company, get a lot of good fellows, not on to the game, give it a good name—I thought of one—German Bondholders Overseas Insurance Company—how is that?—give it a big capitalization (on the books)—get some German banker out of a job, or some statesman or prince, and write all over the world, everywhere, Abyssinia, Australia, everything down to Zeeland. They'll pour in. Look, I got up a letterhead." And like a magician, Jules, who had been meditating this quite privately produced not only a letterhead but a pompous, serious, pathetic letter from one Jan Witkraan, formerly of Antwerp, now out of a job, who would willingly organize the new insurance company of Mr. Bertillon at a reasonable salary.

"I've engaged him," said Jules carelessly.

William's face was a study. Léon said, "Good. Where is he? We must see him at once and get the letters out."

Jules spoke, "There's a surplus of everything in the world from German bonds to wheat. What's the problem? Market it. That's all. Wheat reminds me—Léon, couldn't we do something about all the wheat that's stacked up everywhere with the mice eating it? You're a wheat merchant: can't you figure out something? I'm not satisfied to sit here on a cardinal's chair and look grand and old-Flemish: I've got to make big money; I'm not satisfied with pulling the ears of the stock market: that's millet seed to an ostrich, I want to make grand money. What do you say to the two of us making a clean sweep and getting away with everything, Léon?"

Léon laughed, twinkled, "I'm with you, Jules. You're good luck, my boy—I feel it in my bones."

William slumped against the bookcase, "Spring fever!"

"I might do something in oil," said Jules modestly, "only I'll wait till the conference next year. We're right on the spot here—the town will be buzzing."

"Be a lot of phonies about," warned Léon.

"Well, want to go in with me on the German bonds business?"

"Hm, think about it, hm . . . see Alphendéry," said Léon. At the approach of a partnership with the mercurial Gentile, Léon's assurance fainted: he feared to cross swords with a Gentile. As a result he had been mulcted entirely by Jews. He now grew uneasy, changed the subject, and finally strode out into the corridor, dishonestly stretching his neck left and right, making a show of looking for Alphendéry in a great hurry.

William grumbled, "This is not a bank, it's a merry-go-round. Do you have to have your finger muddying every pie?"

Jules grinned, "This isn't a bank: there's a sign outside saying BANK and when they see it they come inside and drop their cash on the counter. If I put up the sign BARBER they'd come in just as automatically looking for a shave. It's all in the sign. This is a stage I've set and filled with supers for the great act of Jules Bertillon, multimillionaire, and when the climax comes, I ring down the curtain. In the meantime, *they* pay to see the show."

Scene Thirty-eight: The Five Brothers Simla

THE Five Brothers Simla Corporation was a Luxemburg corporation, an assets-holding company which William used for the deposit of gold and bonds earned in trading and general business by the Bertillon Bank. He knew his brothers' natures well, and regarded himself as the keeper of the Bertillon flock. He wanted little money himself, he never intended to marry, he wanted no children, and his ideal was to retire to a little farm and keep a couple of horses and beehives.

But his twin brothers, Paul and Francis, Claire-Josèphe, Jules's children, Jules, Jr., Charles, Edmond, and Simla, were all used to luxury and seemed to expect to live for ever on velvet. The Bertillon brother whom the few people in their intimacy called "the silent brother" or "the mysterious fifth brother" was Clément-Nepomuk, a year older than Jules. When Clément-Nepomuk had been born, no one expected any more sons and when Jules was announced, everyone was sure the baby would be a girl. Jules arrived, out of all reckoning, a boy and immediately became the most auspiciously favored, the brightest, most cunning, and mercurial of the five brothers.

In the female line in Jules's family there had been four

253

sons for four generations. Jules's grandmother was called Simla and thereafter it became a family name. Each of the sons was called Simla as a second name.

As Jules grew, the original fourth son faded in significance and now he seemed several years younger than Jules. He lived in Germany, sat in cafés, dribbled strange, delightful, unclimactic, and endless tales to any who would listen to him. He received an allowance from Jules and blackguarded all his brothers, weaving extraordinary villainies round their names, accusing them of doing him out of his inheritance. But actually he had spent all his inheritance, and now was just as happy living from hand to mouth. He did not really believe that his brothers were unfair to him, but once the idea had occurred to him, it grew, like all his other ideas, into an epic.

William never spoke of Clément-Nepomuk Simla Bertillon and only once had mentioned him, and that to Alphendéry in a sentimental moment. He was convinced that he was the bad luck of the family and that sooner or later, the twins (who were halfway there) and Jules, the forehead and diadem of them all, would display some strange weakness, some beachcombing trait, in a line with those of Clément-Nepomuk. Thus, in long-sighted preparation for that day of wrath, he had founded the Five Brothers Simla Corporation some fifteen years ago and this was his paternal nest egg for the family. Not even Jules had anything but a faint idea of the deposits in this company; even "Old" Berthellot did not see all the books. Perhaps it was this that was at the bottom of William's ineffable calm and staidness. At the back of this all, though, was an infinite tenderness for Jules: he was quite unaware how often he nagged Jules; he nursed the illusion that he only spoke gravely to Jules once in a long while, in order to keep Jules from going too far off the track. But he was in every way prepared to see Jules go up one day in a grand conflagration, and then William would quietly succor the whole family and start Jules on his way again somewhere else, or somehow else. His utter disregard for everyone's feelings also arose from his single-minded affection for his brother.

In the last five years he had also carefully put out tendrils and communicated some of his sentiments and safeguards to Alphendéry: he held Alphendéry in a true affection because Alphendéry was so loyal to Jules and never tried to rob him. Very often Jules, tired of his "games," lightly tossed the reins into the hands of William or Alphendéry, and went off for a week end, a week, a month, three months, to spend the life of the idle rich. During those absences the bank was quiet, silent, unblooming and as if closed, like a heliotropic plant when the sun is away; there was a sterile air upstairs and the familiars of the bank, Richard Plowman and others, had a half-life, moved more like a frieze, continuously applied along the walls with a rubber roller, than living creatures. Nevertheless, a quiet continuum of life was there: Alphendéry worked for Jules's account, transferred gold and stocks in and out, followed his own devices in the foreign markets, watched over the clients' accounts, was master of the money-making departments of the bank, while William managed the whole of the banking routine, and Jacques Manray and Urbain Voulou the downstairs office. A man of a predatory sort would have found his golden opportunity there, but Alphendéry did not. The brothers were convinced that this was because he was a "scholar" and an "idealist" and a "Utopian" and therefore readily listened to his ideas on Marxism, Russia, and the history of socialism even when they saw no immediate profit in it. But Richard Plowman was against all that: he preached against Alphendéry's socialism, he fretted about it, and was sure that it was bad for the reputation of the Bertillon family, and when he heard what Adam Constant had said to the Irish lord about "capitalism," he literally wrung his hands and begged Jules to "speak very strongly" to Michel. Jules laughed him away. "Don't you realize we're all keeping our pet socialists now? The Comtesse de Chamfort, the Comtesse de Voigrand, Carrière's mother, Guipatin's father —they're all living with or associating with, or keeping, pet socialists now. It's their insurance against the revolution. And it's their weather donkey. When the tail twitches too hard, they get their umbrellas, and when it falls right off, they skip to the Isles of Gold."

When Léon had gone for good, Alphendéry returned with a scheme he had been worrying about for a fortnight. "Jules, we should change the wording on our customers' forms. For example, instead of saying, 'We have

255

bought for your account,' we should say, 'We have credited to your account,' or 'You are credited with.' "

"Why not," said William, who acted as Alphendéry's rearguard on these occasions, "why give excuses for quibblers?"

"All right," said Jules, "what does it matter?"

"When we get new forms printed we can say that and no one will notice the change," Alphendéry carried on.

"The judge is only looking for you to give him a way out," remarked William.

"Oh, let it ride," shouted Jules, suddenly irritated, "I'm going to make big money; you two fellows sit there all day thinking up new wrinkles like two college boys writing notes on Molière and I've got to make the money. You don't make money out of codicils, riders, and word shifting. I'm going to the pictures. I've worked too hard. . . ." He jammed on his hat, walked out, and came rapidly back. "I won't have that form changed, do you hear? I want it as it is."

Scene Thirty-nine: Daniel Cambo

DANIEL CAMBO stretched his long thick legs and reveled in the luxury of telling the boys how devilish clever he was. There were half a dozen of them gathered in Jules's room to discuss his bazaar venture. He was already "turning money away," for his fame as a get-rich-quick-slick had reached every client of the bank months ago. Every real money-maker feels that he was born a Machiavelli with footnotes and that he has improved himself into a Napoleon of strategy and a vulture of iniquity. When he has any time off, he shakes hands with himself for his genius, chuckles with himself over his inspirations, pats himself on the back for his bigheartedness, gets wistful over the child poetry in his heart.

"Did I ever tell you how I got a shipment of novelties from New York for nothing?"

"No, how did you do that, Daniel?" Jules stretched himself also and gave himself up to the pow-wow. William stood lolling against the bookcase, as usual clinking the

256

coins in his pockets, pretending to take no interest in anyone, but intent as an ant gathering together bits of information against Daniel, who had the reputation of being the sharpest chiseler of them all. But William, of course, thought himself a pretty good crook, too.

"How did you do it, Daniel?" Francis asked. His twin brother, a perfect replica of himself, eyed him coolly. They were sleek gentlemen both and thought Cambo a great liar and rascal, but his reputation for quick-slick money and immediate turnover had lured them both; they had made it up between themselves to invest their savings with him, unknown to William or Jules, if he gave a convincing sales talk.

"It was easy, easy. I go round to the bond division on the wharves, you know. I give the man a couple of dollars and he tells me what merchandise is lying there, on drawback, or consignee can't pay and when I see something I can use, maybe I go and see the consignee. Maybe not. It depends. This lot, these six cases—there were two boys who wanted them for a novelties business in Twenty-third Street. But fashions change so quick in America. They got them from Czecho and by the time the shipments got there, the fashion had changed. So! no good.

"In America you can get any amount of job lots for nothing. But you got to go carefully, otherwise they think, 'Quick, here's a sucker from Europe.' I brought over a pattern of knitted goods once to America, I showed it to a man and said, 'Look, do you think this would go in America?' 'Yes,' he said, 'it would go good, very good, but it's too expensive; the process is too slow; you got to put hop into a process to get things out here: it's no good.' So I got a pattern of a machine from Lyons and brought it over to America and I showed it to an engineer. 'Look,' I said to him, 'can you make a better model?' 'Yes,' says he: 'sure I can do it. Give me four days.' And in four days he brought me back a model of a wonderful little machine. That's American. Ha! I had it made and while it was being made he thought of a couple of improvements. I got twenty made and put the girls to work. They turned out goods twenty times as fast as back in Lyons. I didn't let anyone into the factory . . . no fear. But a boy in Chicago worked out the sort of machine it must be and next week he had an improved machine on the market and a coupla fellers went into business and beat me hollow. I had to shut up shop. That's how it is in America. It only pays to buy the hash.

"All right, it makes a big waste of machines and goods. All right, bring them back to Europe. Go into the business of waste. Eh? It's the best-paying today. Well, everyone's gone into the fire-sale, mill-ends, shoddy business, but this is something different. A real smart bazaar business with regular lines and disappearing lines: not dreck so much as sample lines, odd lines, sample shipments from Japan, Czecho, Germany. Buy everything below cost from people whose capital has been lost. Like me in the machines. See: deal in human dreck, not dreck goods! A man's bankrupt: he'll sell for anything. A man dies: his heirs are damn fools, don't know the business—they sell for nothing. A man starts in business, no capital, he is dying for enough to eat: he's glad to sell and he goes back on the unemployed lines. And you got to know how to bargain. See! And it's nice business."

"What about the goods you got for nothing?" asked William impatiently.

"Listen, not for nothing, just for warehouse charges, and I got them back." He laughed, winked, and expanded, so merrily it was a pleasure to see him. "Well, I went round to those boys in Twenty-third Street and I found them working out a bankruptcy. I could smell it. They didn't want the goods. No one in America would touch them. They were too good to ship South. And for the North, they were out of fashion, just rubbish and they couldn't even pay the warehouse charges.

"I went round to the warehouseman and I said, 'Look, those boys won't take those goods; they won't pay the charges; those six cases are going to lie there messing up the place for months. The consigner won't take them back so easy. You'll have to sell them at auction and what will you get out of it? I don't know that I want them, either. Maybe, though, I can sell them to some connections of mine in France. I'll see. I can't pay for them myself, not on the spot.' I slipped him a couple of dollars, see. I said, 'Those goods are on drawback. Well, you send them back to the original consigner telling him they're refused. All right, at Le Havre my man calls for them and takes charge of them. It's not your fault. Wrong address. I get the bill of lading from the boys. Then I see if I can sell them to my friends in France. If I do, I pay the ware-housing charges and something for you, see. And we'll do some more business, some other time. I'm in that line.'

"He said to me, 'Buddy, what do I care who gets them?' So he ships them to Le Havre with the wrong address, I call for them, I sell what I can, what I can't I put back in the cases, then I fill the same cases up with a lot of stuff I can't get rid of and I send the stuff back to the warehouse in New York. 'Refused. Wrong address.' I sup-pose the chap in Czecho got back a lot of funny stuff and he sent it back again. Maybe they're still going backwards and forwards. But you've got to be smart. I didn't pay a cent, only a couple of dollars."

"You've got to nose around," said William, thought-fully. The twins, Paul and Francis, looked like two chick-ens who have seen the same worm.

"There's a little chap down in the Place des Vosges makes swan's-down powder puffs: they're washable. But what girl is going to wash her powder puff if she can get say twenty for five francs, say four for one franc? You see, they're just manufacturing in the void. You got to manufacture for a market. It would be like a story writer saying, 'I don't write for *Vanity Fair* or the *Mercure de France* . . . I write for anybody, everybody' " (Cambo said innocently). "Now, there are thousands of these poor little birds: and I'm doing them a favor: I'm a natural market for them. Say, these little fellows can't make a cent anyhow. I'm doing them a favor if I take the stuff off their hands below cost.

"Now, I want to show you one thing. It doesn't pay me to go into business manufacturing things. It pays me to buy only from the one-horse shows, the attic factories, wom-en who knit in parks while they're watching their babies, unemployed men turning out little gadgets. You save rent (because the homeworker is paying his own rent), you save installation, deterioration of machinery—all that's washed out with the one-horse manufacturer when he goes bankrupt. You don't have to bother about factory laws, installing W.C.'s, hours and wages and overtime. And you're doing them a service: you're giving them work, you're giving them a market.

"Now, they sometimes put in machines when they see you coming back; they save you the expense. You say, 'Give me the exclusive supply,' and they're willing to borrow money and put in the machines. Well, if the goods don't please, and they're overextended, they can sell to your competitors for a bit (but you've already broken the back of the market) and then they go bankrupt! If there's still a tag end of market, you buy the bankrupt stock cheap. They were bankrupt before: they're bankrupt again! They've always been bankrupt. And so you've done no harm; you've given them something to eat for a few months. Say, these little fellows can't last. They're not adapted to the wholesale age."

Jules put in sharply, "And what do you do with the stuff that goes stale on your counters?"

Daniel laughed, threw out his hand with a vast gesture. "What do you do? Why, I send it to the country, little dead places like Sens and Senlis and—anywhere—and then to Morocco. Now that's where the real jewel of my scheme is lying. You see? You go to the receivers and you say, 'These goods are old-fashioned: I know. I was selling them six months ago in Paris, now they're done. You can't sell them except in some dusky paradise. I don't know if I can sell! Maybe in Patagonia, in the Solomon Islands. But if you want to sell them to me for almost nothing, I'll do you a favor, I'll take them off your hands. You see, my competitors won't look at the stuff. But I'm different: I've got, maybe, someone I can write to . . . factors.' Then they ask around, they don't take too much trouble, why should they? They give it to me by private treaty. I slip them a couple of ten-franc notes. Well, what can you do? You've got to earn your living. You can't go to sleep standing up." He smiled his open, good-natured, boyish smile that split his great honest face with a neat strong bite of white teeth.

Daniel was busy from morning to night, like a prodigious hummingbird, flitting, hovering, quick as a flash of light from one store to another, from giant wholesaler to poverty-ridden private home, from small artisan in the Faubourg St. Antoine or the Place des Vosges to miserable mothers knitting and doing gross filet lace for a living in the park of the Buttes-Chaumont. He also observed, without any need of a notebook, the prices in department stores and working-class bazaars, the first necessities as well as the first luxuries of the poor: men's shirts, children's shirts, socks, kitchen utensils, kitchen silver, cleaning powders, rag flowers, cosmetics, buttons, lamp shades, electric fittings, wedding rings. . . .

The clients of the bank were divided sharply into two camps, immediately—those who saw in Cambo's scheme the big new racket, and those who said, "The French will never buy goods turned out wholesale to one pattern; they are a petty-artisan nation, and care for the curious and individual; they understand quality." The ladies especially (those who six months later were buying knitted shirts for nephews and nieces from Cambo's stores at twenty francs) sustained the thesis that Frenchwomen, even working girls, were too elegant "by nature" to buy things to cover their delicate individual skins in vulgar bazaars. Mme. Mimi Eloth, Mme. Berthe Yves, Mme. de Sluys-Forêt, and Mme. Raccamond led these insurgents: they appeared to take Cambo's proposition as a personal insult.

"He is, after all, a Smyrna Jew: he does not understand the essentially French," said Mme. Raccamond and they all agreed with her.

But Jules, and almost every moneymaking male in the place, was with Cambo. Alphendéry said, "Frenchwomen! Those that come from the Gare de l'Est at seven o'clock in the morning aren't Frenchwomen, they belong unwillingly to the international of flour-sack home dressmaking: of course, they'll hail Cambo as a savior if he puts out twenty-franc dresses."

"Sure," said Jules, "slaves. Everything comes back. We're getting back to slavery. They've got to learn to like mass-production goods. We've got to sell them something. Say, Mussolini and Woolworth are the giant minds of our age; Musso got them to wear mass-production, nonsoiling shirts; Woolworth extended it to everything they want. They both succeeded, didn't they? Hitler will get on, mark that, you boys. He's got the mass-production idea. I bet you anything you like some smart fellows in Germany now are behind him, only waiting to sell brown shirts, by the million. Say, Daniel, it would pay you to organize a green-shirt movement or say a red-shirt one, for the Reds."

"Why don't you, Jules?" Daniel asked with a certain hope.

"Oh, I don't sell anything visible." Jules lay back and

indifferently began playing with his paper knife. "You shear the white lambs; I'll take the black sheep."

They grinned at each other, flattered by the notion that they were all infinite blackguards. Ephraïm Dreyer pondered: "Will they let you get away with it, Daniel? Won't they try to shut you up? You'll undercut them all."

"And what am I doing all that time?" asked Daniel. "I hold them off a year or two and then I sell out. Business today is climbing up the corridor of the avalanche, before the avalanche. Let it pass. Climb again: Look, Morocco's not a French colony; it's only a protectorate and has its own laws. French goods don't get any preference, but pay twelve and one-half per cent ad valorem like those of any other country. So the French interests there have no advantage. I dump Yankee goods in Morocco, that I buy the way I told you. Do I pay twelve and one-half per cent? No. You don't have to pay in money in Morocco: you can pay twelve and one-half per cent in goods, in kind. So you pay the customs one-eighth of the goods. Naturally, I pay them in goods I don't want particularly, whatever has deteriorated in sales value. Then I give the customs officials a couple of ten-franc bills, and when he auctions the stuff off, my stuff that I paid over to him, I buy it back at a bargain price. Before anyone catches on, I've made my money and I sell out."

Jules was about to speak but Daniel held up his hand and walked with one restless pace round the corner of the table. "But what's the beauty of my scheme? Everyone can think up the one-eighth ad valorem in goods, can't they? But I go a step farther. I form an American company, a Delaware corporation. I have nominee American shareholders; I'm the director—William and I represent Americans. Under the capitulations, I can demand protection for my Yankee friends; I get extraterritorial rights! You get preference as a foreigner. Let the Galeries Lafayette or any other French concern try to compete with me, then! The Yankee consul has to protect my interests. It's beautiful. Watertight, till they see through it and then —we will have sold out. So I buy for nothing in America, I pay my duty in bad garters, and I get special protection against French competition in a French protectorate. It's beautiful." His honest, sanguine face shone with enthusiasm.

"How much do you think you'll make?" asked Jules.

"About half a million francs the first year. About a million in all . . . then a quick sale. Maybe more. Sell out for seven and a half millions on a five-year basis. The cow will be milked dry by then."

Jules was inspired, as always, by the display of acumen. When they had dispersed and Daniel had gone down to the stock-exchange room to receive the homage and questions of the client-cronies, Jules wandered into Alphendéry's room, musing.

"You know, Michel, I just had a brilliant idea. How about getting into touch with Sournois, the deputy who is Carrière's friend and get him to start a movement like that National-Socialist one in Germany, a fake one. We'll form a consortium and take over a shirt factory and manufacture colored shirts: black, the French are Latins and like black. We can sell them to Daniel in his bazaars. We'll make red and black. Get in touch with the *Action Française* and see what color they'd like their men to wear."

"Jules, there's one thing you must understand: we must keep clear of these reactionary movements. If I ever find you in any such thing, I leave you right away. I'd rather make my living selling *L'Humanité* on the streets than work with you."

Jules laughed. "All right, I'm only dreaming."

Jules was wafted out on his own good humor. For a few hours after that, however, he sat in his room or drifted about the bank scheming like a spider and the subject of his dreaming was the manufacture of badges and uniforms. He telephoned Daniel. "I've got a good idea. Come up. The Arabs are madly superstitious! Give them astrological readings free and sell dream books along with them! There's a little hand token they think brings them good luck. Why don't you give them a little hand with every two pair of braces?"

They were closeted together a long time. By the end of the afternoon, there was no weakness of the human race they had not made provision for in the projected popular bazaars.

Scene Forty: Adam's Return

ADAM CONSTANT presented to Jules and William Bertillon and Alphendéry, as soon as he got in in the morning, the newly printed articles of association of the Leadenhall Securities Guarantee Corporation, Limited, which he had just formed through the bank's solicitors in London, Ledger, Ledger, and Braves. The association had an office in St. Mary Axe, an office manager who had just departed for a tour of the provinces, to sound provincial family lawyers, and a stenographer who did nothing with dignity all day and was paid two pounds ten weekly for it. The manager, Dacre-Derek Caudal, sea-blue-eyed was immensely grateful to Bertillon and to Constant. He came to them from a desert of unemployment two years long, and he vowed everlasting fidelity to them.

The corporation lent out money to indigent *rentiers*, received their negotiable stocks and shares as security, and had the right (section seventeen of the agreement signed by him, close-printed in pearl type, gave this) to sell out the shares, replace them, and manipulate them exactly as if they were the property of the corporation. At the end of two years, and not before, the *rentier* was to claim his shares and pay up the loans he had received.

"Not only," laughed Alphendéry, "will they not come back to reclaim them, but they'll be in hiding for fear we'll be after them to make them pay. For what those two-penny shares will be worth in two years is no one's business: they will read like the bear's pipe dream. And we don't give all the loan right away; we give a small advance now, a stated amount and so on. Poor devils! There must be plenty that would give us their shares, even if we explained the whole thing word for word."

"Don't be so sure," said William unpleasantly. "They like to live on bad Ceylon tea and keep their Aunt Emmy's heritage in paper. Perhaps you won't get any offers."

"You keep in touch with Caudal, Constant," Jules said,

264

calmly. "I leave this end of the business to you. When it's going all right, we might be able to use you for Shanghai."

"Are you sure it's the right time to open a Shanghai branch?" ventured Constant. "I can see this three-cornered fight going on in China for ten or fifteen years. Perhaps the international settlements will be wiped out."

"Certainly, I know. But I'm playing for five years, not ten," Jules explained.

Scene Forty-one: Thargelion

Paris was lovely now and yet Alphendéry left it almost every weekend to go to Touraine, Normandy, Burgundy —any spot that could be reached within two or three hours. He had no car and he traveled alone by rail, carrying no luggage, putting up at the best or second-best hotel of the town, eating pasties, fish dishes, chickens, and drinking local wines in chill dining rooms, going rapidly by foot round all the points of historic and romantic interest—then returning on Sunday evening, tired but refreshed. He was always going out like a honeybee to other scenes to bring in a store of sweet for the dark hive in which he lived. He disliked the bank much more than he admitted to himself. He had half a mind to go back to Alsace and live with his mother, become, as he put it, "a poor scholar." But that did not attract him very much, either. He had seen too much also of the men at the bank: he inwardly had little sympathy for their money passions; their range of wit and learning was that of an eight-year-old boy. Some like Jules, Cambo, and Léon were interesting but suffocating personalities, planets circling with their satellites, self-sufficient, dark planets with their own motion, but absorbers of his wit. He struggled on because those he supported were not used to poverty and because since the age of fourteen he had seen the weekly pay checks coming in. If it had suddenly stopped he would hardly have known how to face the day.

Alphendéry had many friends, strangely assorted friends, clients of the bank, who came into his private room during the week, partly to enjoy his wit and economic learning, partly to spy on him and try to discover what he did alone all day in a room, this man of resource and ability, who was publicly said to be a "stock-exchange clerk."

Thargelion, with a dark bloom like Mediterranean night, tall, mellow with the beauty of many generations, a sort of Aristides turned society tobacco runner, came in softly, elegantly, daily to court with his discreet perfumes, suave poses, and snatches of exotic verse the unsuspecting Alphendéry. The son of a famous modern statesman, sufficiently rich, he was always occupied in Paris in missions for some opposition party ready to make the assault of power in Greece. He also had a wine business, a fig business, and had divers other small sources of revenue. The past winter Alphendéry, sick, gray for want of sun, said to Thargelion, "How can you be here, away from Greece? How can you stay so long away from the blue skies that the whole world turns linger-longer glances on?"

Thargelion said in that bright melodious accent, which is the sign of his class, the rustle of polished steel, the cooing of ball bearings, the jingle of arms in deep bottoms sliding through the flood tide at night, "That Greece is an illusion of tourists: I do not want you to care for Greece in that way, Mr. Alphendéry. I detest it. A cousin of mine sells tickets to tourists, vulgar creatures, to see the ruins of the Parthenon: it is nothing but a couple of split stones. I would rather see the American Radiator Building: it is modern Greece. . . . Oh, do not speak to me of that aspect of Greece, it is repulsive, like a salvaged wreck covered with green slime that the salvagers bring up for prize money. . . . Greece is—strikes, fights, treachery, blacklegs, democracy, even the Red International now. I do not want to see it . . . I detest it. . . ." He softened. "But if you would really like to go there, Mr. Alphendéry, I would arrange it with only too much pleasure, on one of my cousin's ships, or in the company of a friend of mine: you would be well looked after. For a vacation cruise, perhaps it is not so bad. Besides, you are not like those who go and gape, you understand these things." At this word, he lowered his voice and spoke so exquisitely, so tenderly, that Alphendéry felt his skin prickle and his diaphragm gulp. After Thargelion had gone downstairs, incomparably urbane and sleek, Alphendéry went and looked into the mirror of the men's washroom, at his odd masklike face, enough to make Goya start from his Bordeaux grave and grab him by the coattails as he went by. Then he smiled.

He went into Jules's room, sank into a chair, and after some idle talk, said, "Thargelion has been making love to me."

"That's good," said Jules. "Egg him on. We'll get Paleologos's account. He and Mouradzian can swing it between them. . . ."

"By the way," interjected Alphendéry, "did you write anything on that bet with Carrière? You didn't, did you? It's too dangerous."

"Do you think I'm crazy?" asked Jules, dismissing it.

"There's no harm in it, but it's fiddling," said Alphendéry. "Every rich man has a fiddling department and if he doesn't put cotton wool in his ears, it ruins him."

"Ptt!" blew Jules.

"Trouble with my brother," said William who had lounged in behind, "is he thinks he's a banker but he's still an office boy figuring winners, behind the filing cabinet."

"You two wisecrackers make me sick," said Jules, put on his hat and walked out.

William frowned. "Once in a blue moon he goes so crackers that he does the right thing: that's what saves him." He sat down in Jules's place. "He looks funny, though. I wonder what he's been doing."

William continued, "Banking isn't dreaming, it's having enough in the kitty every morning to pay those who won't come back tomorrow. You don't want imagination; you want a credit balance."

"Do you think I could get six weeks off to go and see Athens?" asked Alphendéry.

They compromised on a week-end trip to Rambouillet.

Scene Forty-two: A Stuffed Carp

THE old question came up, "Is it the fourth floor or the fifth?"

"Sometimes I think it's the third."

"Last time I'm sure it was the fourth. They're all like peas in a pod."

But they got out at the fifth and walked down to the fourth, as the little gilded lift did not work in reverse. All the pale gray paneling and coconut mats were the same and with the constant walking up and down, Marianne and Aristide had begun to forget even whether it was the Bapur Tea Company, the Mouriscot Hydraulic Company, or the Assam Carpet Company which had its quite exotic offices opposite the Hallers' flat. But, tonight, as usual, it proved to be the Bagpur Tea Company. They rang, settling their papers and parcels, undoing their gloves, smiling confusedly at each other. There was an uneven, heavy step, a key was turned, a chain rattled. In the crack of the door now grew a pale lump face with iron-gray hair, brown eyes, and hairy warts. The pale purple mouth laid open like a stale knife incision was mute but unrebellious.

"Good evening, Anna."

The maid opened the door wide. She ruggedly seized their coats and one hat, covered the coat-tree with them and speedily lumbered down the dark wide hall to another door, where she said something coarsely, in a foreign language—Hungarian, no doubt. A mistress voice answered. She closed the door, came back, took the long-proffered hat from Mme. Raccamond and, ignoring the gloves, pushed open the door of the anteroom, looked at them like an impatient sheep dog.

"Oh, good evening, dear Mme. Raccamond. How delighted I am to see you and Mr. Raccamond! You look tired. Please excuse my husband for a moment. He is telephoning the newspaper to get the latest on the Briand crisis."

"Good evening, dear Mme. Haller. How pretty you look!"

"Do I? No, you're kind. You have such a pretty dress on, too, Mme. Raccamond. Very pretty!" The little dark plump woman touched Marianne's sleeve lightly, like an affectionate cat. "Such good taste. You look so young, too! But why" (whispering) "does he look so tired?" A nod of complicity. "Yes, they are very busy at the bank. Poor man. . . ." (Brightly) "You must not work so hard, Mr. Raccamond. Mme. Raccamond is quite worried about you. No business worries, now, I hope." An arch smile to Marianne. "Let us go into another room."

The ritual went on. Mr. Haller now appeared smiling at the intermediate door, little golden hands outstretched, little golden head thrown back in welcome, little paunch neat, tight, and muscular. "Well, Mr. Raccamond! How are you? And Mme. Raccamond?" At once Haller drew Aristide apart near the Indian silk striped curtains. "I was just telephoning Havas. They tell me . . ."

"Come away, Mme. Raccamond, let us go into the other room for a minute—I will show something—you know what" (whispering). "Mr. Haller doesn't like me to" (a little gay glance). "We will leave the men alone for a while" (softly). "Eh? Yes?"

"What lovely crystal!" Marianne cried.

Eagerly, softly, Mme. Haller: "Yes: do you like them? It is real. Hand-cut. Feel."

"Oh, how heavy!"

"Yes—see, see! Feel the edges. Hand-cut. Can you tell hand-cut, Mme. Raccamond? It is easy."

"Such a size. Like diamonds, like vases in pure diamond."

Her solid, feature-encrusted face thought, What a price! Eagerly, intently, Sophy Haller: "Yes: really, like a diamond. You are right. I keep these two here. Georg wants me to put them away. Don't you think it would be a shame?" (Whispering) "He wants me to put everything away. He says it isn't nice to display them."

Marianne looked at her, silent with a confusion of protests and amazes.

The men moved nearer the doorway, standing still in the bow of the large window which overlooked the Rue Madame and the Luxembourg Garden. "Tardieu will over-reach himself, " said Haller, invisible. "He's been to the dry cleaners too often. The super Bel-Ami of every great swindle in the country."

"Yes, but look at his relations: he has all the thorough-breds in his stable. . . ."

Haller's manly, fine-woven voice, "Too many lawyers in the Chamber of Deputies: no one loves them."

Mme. Haller looked round, drew a little closer to Marianne. "Mme. Raccamond, do you know, I am weak. I like to look at these things. What harm is there in it? I think they're beautiful, don't you? Do you see any harm in it? I am so glad you agree with me."

"What are beautiful things for if not to make our lives beautiful?"

"How beautifully you put it, Mme. Raccamond." An estimating glance, a nod. "Yes. Look at this powder jar from Florence. See the glaze! Do you see it, Mme. Raccamond? Do you understand glaze? See the wreath of roses! All done by hand!"

"Ravishing, unique!" Marianne had a breathless moment. Mme. Haller looked at her in gratitude. The heaven-blue little jar was a museum piece. She said deprecatingly, with upward glance, "It is said it was made by Benvenuto Cellini."

"Really?" Doubt in the air.

"Of course, no one can guarantee—but they assured me—" (Oh, please say that it might have been made by Cellini.)

Marianne conceded, "It is a Cellini *design*."

"Oh, yes? Do you know—do you *know* Cellini, Mme. Raccamond? Oh, I always felt you were so artistic." The little golden hand of Sophy Haller was laid on Marianne's green silk sleeve. "Mme. Raccamond! Should you like to see some other pieces of crystal? I have many, many pieces" (mysteriously) "but Mr. Haller likes to have them in the cupboard."

"Oh, I love beautiful things. Let me see them. Do."

Coaxingly, "Mme. Raccamond, I know you love beautiful things; I can see it. I knew it from the first. I said to Mr. Haller, 'Mme. Raccamond is very artistic.' That is a pretty dress, Mme. Raccamond. Where did you get it?"

"At the Galeries Lafayette."

"Oh, do you get your things there? They are nice, aren't they? And not dear. Now this I paid two thousand francs for." She exhibited with satisfaction the dowdy little creation which did not flatter her milk-drop form. "I know someone there," she whispered. She became self-conscious, blushed, and darted to the immense polished walnut cabinet which almost covered the wall at one end of the room. "There! Look, Mme. Raccamond—all that—" Standing on three shelves inside were several dozen pieces of crystal, jars, vases, plates; occasional diamond gleams darted from the stuffy dark of the shelves. Excitedly, looking behind her, and whispering, she opened

270

a drawer very softly. "He would be angry with me! Look, look, Madame——"

She drew partially out of its nest a magnificent encrusted piece of linen, with drawn-thread spiderweb lace and lace insertions, a lifetime of enwoven headaches and blind eyes. Underneath, in the gloom of the deep drawer, appeared the fold of another and yet another. "Six of those," whispered Sophy. "A woman in China has been working for me alone all her life and now her daughter helps her." Her face fell, her eyes looked like two tears. "They have never been on the table, Mme. Raccamond. They have only been out in the light for examination, for renewing the tissue paper." She shook her head, a tiny shake such as would not break a drop of water. "Don't you think it is a pity?"

She became reckless, opened both doors and all the drawers, one after the other. A cascade of pleasure waited for Marianne's view. There were eleven fur coats of various skins and cuts, a pelisse of fifty skunk skins, a splendid sable which had never been worn but twice made over into the fashion, a cape of twenty-four silver foxes. Marianne had to blow the hairs, feel the skin, examine the dyeing, feel the silky, silky feel. She was beyond words. Never had she imagined a fur so fine and costly. She examined Mme. Haller as a desirous coquette examines a little burrowing, busy animal, all unconsciously showing the silver of its pelt in the sun.

Mme. Haller for the last few months, ever since she had known her, had worn to the bank a poorish bearskin, mangy under both arms, and an old felt hat. Marianne lost heart. She realized what she had missed in her striving, ambitious world, never caring for the things of the flesh, laughing at people who were annoyed by her coarseness, resolving to show them all, to make her way, competing with men on their own terms. The display went on. What for? She might become famous at fifty. But look back at the silver pelted years, the warm, odorous years, when her thighs were white and firm to bear great twilight furs, the russet years when her hair was black and sleek to show up diamonds, the milk-round years when, though she was hard-featured, the gold patine of youth shone dully when she laughed! At the bank Marianne had actually patronized Mme. Haller for her worn, mangy little "trotter." Here, she had fourteen slips, all hand-embroidered by a Hungarian girl, whom she had found in a village and sent abroad to learn the art. ("Her eyes were now going, poor girl. But she still sends me something year after year.") The slips had never been worn or washed; hand-drawn thread, hand embroidery, hand-made lace, tulle inlets, a very herb garden and rockery in Madeira work. A bedspread, never used, embossed and drawn, a tea cloth too rich and fine to use, curtains for summer use, hand-filet, to go up this week. (It shows you never can tell, thought Marianne: a little body with apologetic manners, caressing, unassuming, in old clothes and dyed hair and this veritable Open Sesame at home. Ah, ah, the simplest people have the greatest secrets.)

Bokhara carpets, Turkestan, Daghestan rugs—silky ancient Persian carpets. "We use them on the floor because that is the best way to keep them. Look at the lead seals. Do you know how to tell a Persian carpet, Mme. Raccamond? Look here, you see the other side? Didn't you know how to tell a real Persian, Mme. Raccamond? No? How surprising! Mr. Haller doesn't want them out, but I say" (briskly, sharply) "there is no sense in our storing them. They might substitute them. Of course, they are insured." Carpets, curtains, door drapes, piano covers, silk shawls, Chinese mandarin robes. "We have no room for them: they must lie in the chests. We have five chests inside" (in awestruck tones, she made a step towards the door, recalled herself) "all full. Don't you think it's a shame? But they will always be worth something. They will never lose their value, even if gold were to lose its value. With these things the value cannot be lost because the workmanship is there, don't you see? Do you see, Mme. Raccamond? All value is in workmanship! You use these rugs, a generation, two generations, more: the shahs housed them for centuries and they are still good. You do not have to protect them from the sun. They did not fade in the Persian sun."

Old silver, two whole services. "This is all solid silver—feel it, Mme. Raccamond!—and can never be sold at less than the price of silver. Do you think silver will be remonetized in England? I don't think so, Mme. Raccamond. What does Mr. Raccamond think? No, no, I don't think so. But there is the workmanship. Look." (Low) "It is very good. There was a gold service, ten pieces, but I would not buy it. It is a bad thing—a bad thing—"

she whispered and looked round. "My husband—and my father was just the same—says we should never exhibit our wealth: it is bad taste and it arouses envy in the working people. Look here, Mme. Raccamond! Brussels lace, do you know Brussels lace? One day, my mother drove into town to buy some embroidery frames at the big shop. My father came past and recognized our carriage waiting outside the shop. He was on foot. He crossed the street and ordered the coachman to go home. We had to hire a coach to go home. 'Why did you do that, Ernst?' my mother asked in the evening. 'It was most inconvenient.' 'It is wrong to exhibit wealth, it engenders envy,' my father said. You see! Quick, quick, come here, Mme. Raccamond: I mustn't show it to you, but come quick. This we picked up in Rome. They say it was made in the reign of Hadrian. What do you think?" A gold fruit dish; a plate of gilded silver, the rim designed in bas-relief with a wreath of dancing loves and ribands; an onyx sirup jar, mounted in gold filigree in which small cameos were encrusted; a ring that opened with a little shrine to the Madonna inside the jewel.

Marianne felt faint. "But these things are priceless! It's a sin to hide them away. What are they for?"

"Even in case of trouble, some museum overseas would buy a thing like that," softly and eagerly said the little lady. "You see, it's much more useful than money, really. Come." She shut all the doors. "Let us go and join the men. Look, do you think I am like my portrait, Mme. Raccamond? A friend of ours did it. He has always painted pictures for us. We are a regular customer. Your hair is pretty tonight, Madame."

They sat in their usual seats in the far corner of the great salon, with half the lights in the luster turned on. Haller discoursed upon alternating and direct currents. In a minute Mme. Haller would return with the usual Indian grass-linen cloth, the usual teaspoons, the usual hand-painted service, the usual pearl-handled fruit knives, the usual old silver sugar basin which they always must admire. Above Aristide the second portrait of Mme. Haller, in a ball dress and pearls, smiled its rosy mediocrity.

Above Mariane, who sat next to Aristide, but on the settee, hung the paintbox-bright but execrably mediocre oil painting of a peasant girl, resembling Mme. Haller. She

273

wore a red kerchief, by a blue river, in meadow grass decorated with yellow flowers. On the other side of the marble mantelpiece, decorated with great empty crystal vases, empty of flowers, hung another of the court painter's pictures: a barnyard with a peasant girl in a red blouse, strewing corn for chickens and a cock with a red comb. Between the Turkish drapes in the great windows was a portrait of a gypsy girl, her head in a red silk shawl.

"Mr. Raccamond—a glass of Cordial-Médoc is what you need. You always have it." He took it unresisting. Haller had gone back to his telephoning. Sophy, waiting for the servant, sat down and smiled pleasantly at them both.

Marianne sat wedged in by a little round solid oak table, battered by feet and tea trays and time. Aristide's large dark eyes, roundly throned in his starch-white cheeks, rolled fearfully about the room, Marianne thought; the hall empty except for one cheap hat-tree; the salon empty save for this table, settee, chair, and Mr. Haller's desk. And not misers. Fearful of the revolution. And in the rooms beyond, doubtless, their furniture stored as were their treasures in the walnut cabinet; nothing for show. Mme. Haller had told them the first time they came that "all their furniture was stored abroad, including most of the carpets and a piano."

Mme. Haller patted Marianne on the arm. "You two are still such lovers, aren't you?" Her girlish, protected laugh. "I never told you that we first wanted to have you because we saw you walking arm in arm in the Rue Lafayette one lunch hour. I said to Mr. Haller, 'Those two love each other,' and then we saw it was you—although we had not found out your name, then." She confided, with a glance towards Haller, "We do not want people who have troubles because it upsets us too much. We cannot help them and they disturb us. You know how it is? I had a very old friend who came to see us for years! I did not see her for some months and then when she came she told us she had lost her husband!" (Whispering) ". . . he ran away from her." A shocked expression. Marianne had that uncomfortable rustling that women have on this announcement. "With another woman! Poor woman. My dear. At first we liked to let her come because she was so unhappy and she seemed to have no new friends, but she did not get over it. She always wanted to talk about it; she used to be here for hours crying and making me so upset. At last, Mr. Haller said, 'You must send that woman away, Sophy. I know she is an old friend but she is upsetting our whole life: it is getting to the point where our whole life is devoted to her and we can't get her husband back.' So I stopped asking her. You have to keep yourself strong so that you can face your own troubles. This is our home. So we only invite cheerful, happy people who love each other, like you and Mr. Raccamond." She nodded rosily at them both.

Marianne, who had a horrible feeling of cold when she heard the first part of this speech, and who was less complimented by their choice of her than shocked by the idea that she would certainly lose their friendship if they found out that, Aristide, for example, had an old mistress and a son by her and that Marianne's own nephew was little better than a thief and so forth, said, with perfect composure, "You are perfectly right, dear Madame: it is your refuge against the world!"

Mr. Haller, coming from the telephone with a list, called like an earnest father, "Sophy! Sophy! They will have further news at ten-thirty."

Aristide, who had been brooding, doubtless on the same subject, now asked eagerly, "What do they say?"

"There is no doubt the foreign loan market in England is dried up; they're lending nothing abroad, either in Berlin, London, or Paris! J. Henry Schröder have urged foreign loans as an aid to world business. I have no confidence in the pound myself."

"Would you sell it?"

Mme. Haller pressed the bell impatiently, after a frown from her husband. The door in the far corner wobbled with some independent sign of life and she called, "Anna! Anna, hurry up there!" and some sharp command in Hungarian.

The door was kicked open. Anna rushed lopsidedly into the room with plates, cruets, a great oval dish of chicken livers and eggs chopped up and arranged in the shape and size of half a hen, a biscuit barrel with dry biscuits, a glass of rusks, a plate of round breads, and a glass of celery. Marianne knew what all these things were before they were brought to the table, for the dinner at the Hallers was a ritual. Mme. Haller began to arrange these

275

things on the table and to set round the plates. Haller said sharply in German, "Sophy! You have forgotten the liqueurs. We must have them first." He looked consolingly at his guests, said in French, "Mme. Raccamond would like a liqueur. You will have a liqueur, Mme. Raccamond: we have yellow and green chartreuse."

The time was long past when Marianne or Aristide would have fought off liqueurs *before* meat at the Hallers'. Aristide was already a little pale. The ordeal of the meal had to be gone through, themselves fighting off the rich, relentless, noble food as best they could.

"Yes, thank you, Mr. Haller."

Once they had attempted to have the wine set before them, before the liqueurs, but the Hallers had been so wretched at this topsy-turvy order, and so sure that the taste of the expensive food was spoiled that the Raccamonds had never had the heart to fight the fight again. Mme. Haller had tripped off smiling and twinkling with the knowledge of good things to come. Now she returned with three bottles, green, yellow chartreuse, Cointreau.

"I know," she whispered, smiling to Mme. Raccamond, "Mme. Raccamond will have a little Cointreau. Ladies prefer Cointreau." Sharply, she reproved Georg, "You know that, Georg; I've told you ten times."

He said in German, placid, eying the food, "Softly, softly. This is very good, Sophy! I don't get dinners like this. Perhaps Mme. Raccamond prefers the yellow chartreuse."

"No, the Cointreau is older, it is more mature. And it goes better with chicken liver."

Georg bowed to his wife's superior wisdom and explained, "The Cointreau has been eleven years in our cellar. It is sure to have a wonderful taste. We have not opened it before tonight."

Sophy was pouring the fragrant transparent oily liquor into their little glasses. "Taste it, Madame. Eleven years," she said with awe. "Do you know that, Madame; that if you put wine into a cellar it is better for the keeping and the longer you keep it, the better it is? We have been buying them for years. They become very valuable after they have been kept. Do you know that? Take a little Cointreau, Mme. Raccamond. Drink it up, Mr. Raccamond. Oh, you must take more than that."

They were plying their forks and knives as fast as they

could, drinking the liqueur, raining compliments on her, for that was the sweetest thing in the world to her. All day she prepared one of these dinners and dreamed about the compliments she would get in the evening when the "friends" came.

"Is it good, Madame dear? If I only hear you say it is good, then I am rewarded."

"It is wonderful," said Marianne, good soul, for the twentieth time; "no one can make it as you do." This was true, besides. "It's inexpressibly delicious." Actually, Marianne was hungry. They always fasted on the days they were to go to the Hallers'. As soon as they arrived, about seven in the evening, after a little preliminary chatter, this prodigious gorging began and went on for an hour and a half.

"There, it's delicious, you hear that, Georg! You don't pay me such nice compliments."

"I do indeed, Sophy. It is wonderful tonight; never have you made it better."

"Oh, Mme. Raccamond! Do you hear that? I have got a nice husband, haven't I? He is still a cavalier." She repented of this coquetry and immediately coaxed, "And does Mr. Raccamond pay you compliments, too? I am sure he does. Mr. Raccamond is *very gallant*. Are you a good cook, Madame? Oh, I am sure you are. I will ask your husband: he will let the cat out of the bag. Don't be afraid, dear Madame, whatever he says, I am sure you are a good cook. You are so intelligent." Her eyes searched Marianne's face and her expression became that unconsciously cunning one of a pretty woman flattering a plain one. "A little more Cointreau! How is it? Do you notice the difference in flavor?" Unaccountably her expression was suddenly dubious. "Do you really notice the difference?" She said sternly, "You know it is much better than the ordinary Cointreau you get in restaurants." She shook her head severely. "Georg and I never eat in restaurants. You don't know what you're eating. Mme. Raccamond, would you and your husband eat in restaurants?" As Marianne and Aristide ate in restaurants every day of their lives, Marianne was forced to say that they did—in good restaurants, of course. "Good restaurants!" Sophy looked too polite to say what she really thought.

To turn the tide, Marianne murmured, "This Cointreau is far, far better than anything I have tasted before."

277

Sophy shone, "You hear, Georg? You hear that?"

Georg emerged from his third helping of chicken liver and egg to beam gratefully on them both. "Sophy, perhaps they prefer Benedictine. I think it goes better with chicken liver myself. It is a question of taste, of course. If Mr. Raccamond, Mme. Raccamond prefers Cointreau— but that is a ladies' drink—"

"Ann! Anna! Benedictine! Benedictine, fool," she added in Hungarian.

"Perhaps we have enough," reconsidered Haller, in German.

Sharply Sophy replied, "We must give our guests a choice, Georg. What are you thinking of? Anna, do you hear me? Hurry."

Anna, who was standing in the door, as if stunned, half-bumpkin, half-menace, turned in her rapid flipflop and bundled out. Mme. Haller had to go and presently came back with the Benedictine, round, bright, smiling as the bottle itself.

"You see, the seal is unbroken. Fresh from the cellar . . . eleven years old. Anna" (she looked at the door and lowered her voice, even though Anna did not understand French) "does not understand anything about wines. She would serve the wine with the chicken liver if I let her. She objects to them, I *think*, and she pretends not to know which ones I mean." Her voice went still lower: "Anna's very bizarre. She objects to us having guests. She thinks we use too much light." Marianne involuntarily looked at the luster. It was a handsome affair and Marianne could see that the history of it would soon be on the boards again. It was a beautiful piece of wrought brass, just the same; they had found it, finally, in Rouen.

"Oh, Mme. Raccamond! Look at her, Georg! Mr. Raccamond, look at your wife!" Sophy pointed in despair at her empty plate. "You don't like it, Mme. Raccamond— oh, I'm going to cry." Marianne protested that, on the contrary, it was so much better than anything ever got in the restaurants of Paris that she was ashamed of her eagerness for it and was intentionally holding herself in; and, as a reward for this speech, found herself with another helping. Aristide was very pale by this time, but still a natural pallor, and not that horrible green to which he would advance before the feast was through.

Already the smell of the liqueurs and the great helpings of chicken livers had gone to their heads. Happily, little Mr. Haller lay back in his armchair, looking at his little liqueur glass. "We don't get this every day. She doesn't make it for me," teasing Sophy. "You must excuse me, Mme. Raccamond: I haven't eaten since five o'clock this afternoon. Sophy wouldn't let me eat."

"Georg! Some bread, Mr. Raccamond."

"Mr. Raccamond does not take bread, Sophy, don't you remember?"

"This bread wouldn't harm you, Mr. Raccamond: it is very good for you." Haller began to explain, taking a large piece of the roll and holding it up for inspection. "See, how it is baked! See the fine crust! You don't get that anywhere else in Paris. We looked all over Paris till we found this bakery. The trouble with most bakers is that they are dishonest and they use synthetic yeast. I insisted on examining their kitchens myself till I found one that uses real yeast."

"Did you know that, Mme. Raccamond?" Sophy asked accusingly, for she now suspected Marianne of entirely neglecting her husband's health. "Most of the bakers use paraffin in their cakes!" Her voice fell to the most shocked tone she had at her disposal. "Real yeast takes longer to raise but it is better for the digestion. Did you ever ask your baker what yeast he uses, Mr. Raccamond?"

"No," said Aristide. The little round couple were horrified, protestant, although they had eagerly awaited this answer.

"No! No! Oh, Mr. Raccamond; perhaps that is what gives you indigestion! They are so dishonest. It makes me so angry," cried the lady.

"Sophy, you forget that Mr. Raccamond does not suffer from indigestion; it is overweight he suffers from."

"Never mind." She was hot: "Yeast is not so fattening as paraffin. Mme. Raccamond," her voice was now a trumpet call, "do you ever buy pastry in a street pastry cook's?"

"Yes," faltered Marianne, for she very much relished little cakes in the afternoon, "yes, I do quite often. There is a very good pastry cook near me; very good." They were pleasurably scandalized.

"Mme. Raccamond!" High, and then low, "Mme. Raccamond, it is really dangerous. Do you know we never" (very low) "buy any cakes in a pastry cook's. I make

Anna cook everything here and the fine cakes I make myself. I get the butter, flour, everything specially. One day I was walking with Mr. Haller and I saw a little cake in a nice-looking pastry cook's just near here, so I bought it, although he told me not to, and brought it home. She looked such a nice, honest woman. And I was sick all night. I ate it and after I had to go to bed. We sent for the doctor! He said there was something chemical in the cake that upset my digestion." She finished with a slight hysteria, "They're all dishonest, Mme. Raccamond."

Marianne said humbly, "This is very good bread! Where did you get it, did you say?"

At this the Hallers exchanged significant glances, smiled a little beside their noses, and Mme. Haller began with embarrassment, as if in the presence of vulgarians who asked questions that no one should ever ask. "Well, we looked all over Paris, you see it took us months. And one day—"

"A little place, down near the Marais," said the husband.

"Near the Marais," Sophy chimed in, gratefully. "Just a little place. I go there myself."

"Eat more chicken liver, Mr. Raccamond," recommended Georg at this point, the good host, taking up the great silver spoon. Unresisting, Aristide, the ameba, let him heap the plate. Aristide knew quite well what was to follow and he allowed his appetite to be carried out on a stretcher, with a mortal wound, at a first encounter like this. Marianne's strained glance reconnoitered his chubby chops. Would he hold out?

"You are not eating, Mme. Raccamond! Georg! Don't you see that Mme. Raccamond has finished all her Cointreau?"

At any rate, the burning, too-old or badly housed Cointreau made her throat and palate insensitive for the time being and she was somewhat prepared to shove down something of another dish. It was an endurance test.

Mme. Haller pressed the bell. Mr. Haller cheerfully wiped his mouth and remarked to Aristide who was sitting back, fat pale palms on fat gray knees, his round large soft mouth slightly open, that he thought the chemical fog lately tested at Lincelles, as a defense against air attacks, infinitely more valuable than the poison-gas drill, and that at the first sign of war they would, of course, pack up their few things and fly to America. Aristide was able to reply that he thought poison-gas drill very salutary and could not understand the action of the radicals in opposing it as it was most particularly to their advantage to know what to do: the rich, who cooperated, for example, would either not be in Paris for poison-gas attacks or would have their own gas cellars.

Anna pressed open the door and looked in with her habitual affronted unease. Mr. Haller slipped off pleasantly into a political discussion with his guests and the lady of the house excused herself to attend to a dish, with a good many nods, becks, and wreathed smiles, with a little self-conscious trotting step and a little coy smirk to Mme. Raccamond, at the door, which, they knew, indicated that the stuffed carp would be the next thing on the menu.

Anna, clearing away, gave the two visitors unfriendly, surmising, lowering looks, as if they were intruders who had been brought forcibly into the house from the entry, under police guard and upon whom she would presently have the pleasure of closing the front door and bolting it. She was about fifty-five years of age, of middle height, loosely built round the middle, with a sallow, impasted face, graying thick hair, a sloppy gait, and a manner which suggested mute rebellious and resentful submission. When they saw her, each of Mme. Haller's friends got frightened and counseled her mistress to send her away quickly. Not until the Raccamonds had come four or five times did Anna's manner relax towards them, for example, and then they had the impression that they were only admitted for inspection and were closely guarded all the time she was in the room. By this time she had once said "Good evening" to Aristide and she would even consider Aristide front on, for a minute, without embarrassment. As for Marianne, she got a cataloging glance when she arrived with a new blouse, pair of gloves or bag, but never a glance of recognition or an answer from this savage creature.

Haller had been an engineer and he exposed his view to Raccamond, at this moment. "This is what I think, Mr. Raccamond, that in calculating political chances, we have to do the same as when we are putting up a bridge or a skyscraper: we have to ask ourselves, not only, 'Do the individual parts of our scheme fit together'; not only, 'Will they stand up on paper'; but, 'What invisible forces have they to withstand, what stresses and strains, what winds, traffic on holidays and at eight in the morning, the nature of the erosion, the type of subsoil': you see? To build a politic, Mr. Raccamond, we don't want a man of any particular party so much as a fine architect. I regard it as a problem in society physics, social geology, social climate. New countries develop new formulae to suit their conditions. Without fantastically evalued sites would the skyscraper ever have developed even in Manhattan? One had to have the conditions of overvalued real estate in Manhattan to produce the skyscraper, after that the traffic problem, the bridges, etcetera, etcetera. Now, no doubt in Russia they have their own unique conditions, no doubt, they are producing their own characteristic solution. We should here. I am not one for imposing a cut-and-dried solution. No. I am willing to consider the Russian experiment on its own data." He formed an ogival arch with his hands, let his clear, serious, blue gaze begin digging an answer from the mountain of China clay which was Raccamond's face.

"Yes, yes," Aristide's voice from its well, "but where is that architect? We cannot always have the best in the world: we are not Americans with their dollars. We are only looking for someone to keep the bridge in repair. Skyscrapers are not for us, any more than Le Corbusier houses. We have not that money yet. Some day, when our stock market is like the Americans—but even then we are not in the same position. There is the fear of war. Why should we build to give targets for German planes?"

Haller, with hands still poised, had the air of an engineer, working out his own style by using someone else as a sketching block. "New models are always possible." He laughed: his stomach was in a state of happy digestion. "For instance, there was the old Brooklyn Bridge, one of the wonders of the world when it was put up, the work of genius of the Roeblings, but now it is no longer useful for modern transport, although it is charming to the eye. How do we know the Third Republic, pleasant enough to look at, can't be superseded by a better model? Why can't there be a Fourth Republic? Naturally, it is to the interest of people who have invested in the old model, not to change." He stopped smiling. "If you want to know what I really think, Mr. Raccamond, I have been reading his works for five years and I have

282

formed my own opinion. No man will live longer in the mind of man when the history of today is screened down, than Lenin!"

"Lenin!" they both cried out.

"An *arriviste* of genius," said Marianne with her sure touch for agreeable commonplaces.

"I can't agree with that," stoutly held Aristide. "Why do you say that?" (*Mon Dieu*, and the man is rich enough . . . it shows they get fantastic and whimsical when they get idle, these ex-capitalists.)

Haller replied, "Because he's got the engineering view of society. Look how he organized production in a wasted, undeveloped, antiquated society like Russia's! What man has done so much elsewhere in so short a time?"

"What has he done?" asked Raccamond, meanwhile. "What do we know? Everything we hear from Russia is propaganda, prepared in Leningrad. A friend of mine who was in Russia, on business, said that everything is impossible. His suitcase was stolen at the railway station. He went through with a party and they were supposed to go through according to schedule, parks, factories, all the routine. But he said to himself, 'Just the same, I want to see for myself.' So he pretended to misread the schedule and stayed behind a day. When he came down to breakfast the next morning after the party had left, all the good food had vanished. There was nothing but black bread and stewed tea, as the peasants drink! Stage dressing! And the hotel was full of bugs. And he said the people in the streets are in rags! His heart bled for them, and I assure you, Mr. Haller, that he is not a particularly philanthropic man. I don't think we should base our ideas upon what the press agencies hand out, Mr. Haller. The venality of the press, we know. And in a one-voice country. With a pinch of salt, at least. Then don't forget, the Russians are a very backward people: they don't know how badly off they are. It's easy to fool them. Things are better! Yes, indeed, I should like to see it first, with my own eyes."

The liqueurs working in their stomachs and the conversation, the interest aroused by the introduction of Lenin, one of their favorite topics, and their apparent victory, also habitual, made them begin to wonder when the next dish was coming. Sure enough, the door opened at the psychological moment and Mme. Haller trotted in,

283

jolly, bearing a larger dish, on which was a huge stuffed jellied and nobly decorated carp, the *pièce de rèsistance* of the Haller feast, a dish Mme. Haller invariably spent the previous twenty-four hours preparing. Behind her, Anna was perilously toting red-bordered Sèvres plates, silver, a little crystal dish with extra pieces of roe, jelly, and stuffing, and a small dish of macaroons.

"There!" said Sophy, with a blush of triumph at them all, especially at Mr. Raccamond whose eyes opened and who quite openly licked his lips.

"Did you do it all yourself?" Marianne exerted herself to please, as her own eyes were pleased. It was the most delectable of dishes and Mme. Haller's masterpiece. She knew that Mme. Haller only made it when Aristide and she came to dinner. Some strange feminine instinct prompted Mme. Haller to feed that great mountain of flesh till his eyes popped. She passed the fish out more sparingly. It was very good. With less ceremony than before they downed the helpings of carp and Mme. Haller pressed them less to convert the good great delicate fish into Raccamond meat, for it was a particular delight of Georg's and she knew he would go foraging, at night, after the Raccamonds had left, in the kitchen, hoping for some remnants. Nevertheless, one way and another, with their exclamations of pleasure, with Haller pressing and she herself pressing, from habit, they got through the carp and several glasses of chartreuse each and there was no time for talking at all, except for asking occasionally, "Is it good, is it really good?" and exclaiming almost with tears in her eyes, "Oh, I am so glad! If it pleases you, I am most happy." But, strange thing, the tears were there as much for the vanishing of the carp which had taken so much labor, thought and love and delicacy and experience and money, and for the vanishing of all the dreams and desires of praise that had grown up round it in its brief afterlife, and for the astonishing end to which so much hard work was directed. Nevertheless, she was not wholly conscious of this last feeling: it would have been unworthy of a good hostess. Strangely enough, there was something displeasing to her, embittering almost, in seeing those two good, fat Raccamonds engulf her tender, kingly fish, surrounded by so much perfumed shining jelly and dressed in so many little sprigs, and bits of lemon, and olives and fancy bits of gelatine. This time

284

she had really surpassed herself and there was not an ounce of the fish left. Leaning back a little, she therefore comforted herself with liqueur ("I mustn't take very much, my head turns, I haven't a strong head like you, Mme. Raccamond") and presently the slight shadow had disappeared. She had the pleasure of hearing the great blubber of voracious male, Raccamond, whose appetite attracted her dreadfully, almost sexually, say, "You are the best cook I ever knew or heard of, Mme. Haller. Isn't she, Marianne?"

"Oh, wonderful, wonderful, I wish I could cook like that."

"Oh, is it really good, then?"

They both cried out, "It is the best carp we ever tasted." Haller looked at them with a smile between gratitude and derision.

"You fatten me, really." Aristide shook a playful finger at her, ludicrous gesture in his solemn demeanor. Marianne, breathing a little hard to cover up that absurd gesture, rushed in, "Yes, you go to too much trouble for such poor folks as us: it is a shame, Mme. Haller. You ought not to."

The little thing's face clouded. "Oh!" She looked quickly at both of them. "You don't like it! Is it bad? Oh, how dreadful!"

"No, no, no." The boulder of Sisyphus to roll up all over again! But they came to it with willing, if exhausted shoulders again. "No, it's a delightful, wonderful fish." Aristide looked at her with a husbandly, tender admonition. "Only, we don't want you to go to such preparations for simple people like us. Why, it is fit for the President of the Republic."

"Simple people! Oh, how can you say that? You are people with such good taste. If you praise a thing I know it's really good. Then the carp is really good?"

"Yes, yes, indeed."

"Then I'm satisfied."

Mr. Haller was still picking bits of roe and jelly out of the second dish. Impulsively, gratefully, she leaned forward and helped Aristide to another piece of roe, one of the last titbits she had been reserving for Georg's night hunting. "There, eat that! It's nothing, not a featherweight."

"Oh, no, I beg you."

"Not if you like it! If you don't eat it, I'll know you don't like it."

Aristide ate. His ears had flushed. He helped it down with a half-glass of chartreuse, not quite knowing any more what it was, only that it was an alcoholic drink which whipped his gastric juices into action.

"I am a bear on principle, you see, Mr. Raccamond," said Haller courteously, harking back to another part of their conversation, "because money is limited on the bear side: shares can only go to zero. But on the bull side the theory is that it can go to infinity simply because we can go on adding up. That is why, on general principles, the bulls are always wrong because there is no mechanical factor to limit their dreams. Ignorant people, with a limited knowledge of how money is made, like to bull. But money is really only made through bear operations, through put and calls, and through arbitrage, protected to a limited extent, through stop-loss orders, although they are unsatisfactory. You have to let money out on a checkrein."

"Unless you're in a pool," said Aristide, for this was his dream.

"I'm talking of the independent money-maker." Haller shook his head.

Marianne was talking aside to Sophy, rash because the carp was finished to the last crumb of the roe. "How did you learn to be such a wonderful cook? Did you learn it at home?"

She lifted her little dimpled hands in the air, delighted. "Oh, no, no, no, no. I knew nothing. When I married—Georg, I was eighteen! I knew—less than that," a tiny piece of fingernail. "My mother never let my sister or me into the kitchens. When I got married, a favorite uncle of mine wrote to say he would come and visit me and see what a good housewife I was. He loved jellied carp and I decided to make one for him. I got a big book, I went down to the market myself, and bought a very big carp. I've no idea what it cost me! Do you remember, Georg? Well, that was thirty years ago. Could you believe we have been married thirty-one years? The book said, 'Savonnez bien!' so I scrubbed it with a scrubbing brush and soap. When my uncle came I put it before him and told him I had done it all myself. He put one piece in his mouth, for it looked beautiful with jelly and everything, just like it did, tonight—and you said it was good tonight, didn't you?—and spat it out. Oh, my dear Mme. Raccamond, oh, my poor Mme. Raccamond. I burst out crying. 'What's there in it?' he said. 'Stuffed with soap?' Well, Georg, you have eaten all the fish."

She rang the bell while she gazed round at them, pink. "I am very happy tonight: you liked it." Georg looked at her, content, and then went back to his dispute with Raccamond. Sophy whispered, "Never mind, he left his estate to my sister and me, just the same; he was childless and loved us very much."

Marianne saw in the Hallers the sump of a large childless family. Sophy nodded at her. "Your son is doing well at Oxford, of course? It is so charming." She nodded to her, congratulating her. "Anna! Hurry up!" (The rest in Hungarian.) "Try a little more Cordial-Médoc, Mme. Raccamond. We laid in a big stock just after the war, for Mr. Haller was sure there would be another war within fifteen years!" The Cordial-Médoc, like the other drinks, had sharpened and lost its original flavor by bad cellarage but they both cried out they were all excellent, superlative.

"Dear Madame," Mme. Haller again said, "I prefer to eat in my own lares and penates. Restaurants cheat you."

"Sophy! You ought to see what Anna is doing!"

She answered sharply in German, "Georg! Why do you always order me about?"

"A hostess," he laid down, as if repeating some basic assumption of physics, "should always make her guests' comfort her first care."

"Excuse me," she said to them both, blushing. She went and stood behind Georg. "Georg, you are naughty this evening. You command. You order." She laughed girlishly, still the nineteen-year-old bride, conserved, put her hands a minute on his shoulders. "Naughty, disagreeable Georg."

"Go," said Georg, gently. She tripped off at once. "Yes," continued Georg, in contented repletion, "Russia will one of these days be the most modern state in Europe and in perhaps twenty-five to fifty years will be better off than America. Look at the anarchy that reigns in America!"

Mme. Haller came in with a deep fruit dish in which large half-peaches swam. Behind her, Anna, bearing a

287

dish deeper and smaller, full of whipped cream; nuts and nutcrackers and sugar. She returned to the kitchen and brought back a plate of cakes, while Sophy nipped out and returned with a bag of chocolates and a jar of honey. "Georg, come and eat."

Georg had been looking through his engineering text-books to illustrate some point to Aristide and now came back slowly, with his eager, sunny, blond face turned to him. "If the government has the foresight to form a trade pact with Russia, France will ride the storm in the next few years. Russia is making herself felt. France was boycotted for years after the French Revolution: statesmen all fulminated against her and those who supported her were treated as ragamuffins and tatterdemalion intellects, but it became impossible to neglect her. You see!"

"And she, of course," said Aristide nastily, "needs an outlet for grain. She'll ruin the little grain producer in this country." He himself reaped a few bushels yearly on a little place down south.

"Mme. Raccamond, will you help your husband to peaches and cream?" asked Sophy. Marianne did so, putting only one peach on his plate. This caused a frightful outcry from both the hosts and Aristide's plate was heaped with peaches and cream, which his doctor had told him not to touch. "Just a little . . . it won't hurt you!" Sophy nodded confidentially, "This is better than you get anywhere in Paris; a man brings it in specially for me twice a week from the country. Just taste it, Mme. Raccamond. There! Eh?"

"No system can support compound interest," said Georg. "I will show you a little calculation of my own. Do you read propositions in algebra easily?"

"How would we run the state without it?" demanded Aristide, whose dream was to insure his old age by a great quantity of War loan, Treasury bonds, and so on. "Why, colonial expansion has only been possible on compound interest. My customers wouldn't buy stocks or bonds if they didn't expect compound interest on their money. Money can't lie sterile, Mr. Haller."

"Eat, eat, Mr. Raccamond; you are eating nothing." He ate obediently, saying between mouthfuls, "I know it's a burden on the mortgagee, but that is the only way you can encourage people to save and to hold property. Mort-

288

gages and rent are really a sort of compound interest on your saving and foresightedness."

"Georg, don't talk to Mr. Raccamond: he wants to eat. Look at him, his plate is empty. Help him to some cream, Georg. You see, Mme. Raccamond, these are tinned peaches, but I only get the very best. They are the Australian brand, Yanco . . . do you know it? There is only one place where you can get it. You don't know?" She bit her lip, almost irritated: the Raccamonds were really no connoisseurs. She felt it her duty to save Mme. Raccamond from poisoning Raccamond by inches. "Mme. Raccamond, I'll go and get the tin."

"Sophy! There's no need to do that."

"Georg, don't speak so sharply; you don't understand that they don't know the brand!" All this in German. She hurried out. At the door: "And after, some tea, some coffee? Yes? A little tea with wine in it, surely."

They were glad to see her go, being anxious to plunge back into the interest discussion again. Marianne especially, who was slowly accumulating an income from bonds, was heart and soul for interest.

"Interest is sound arithmetically, but unsound and revolution-producing politically," Haller set out, placing a little slip of paper with algebraic symbols on it, between the peaches and the chocolates. "Interest is unsound financially and revolutions are necessary to purify the financial system; revolutions lead to a revival, the dead weight of indebtedness is thrown off: repudiation is necessary to liquidation and this to optimism and new hope. Nothing arouses hate for the ruling classes like excessive taxes and an excessive burden of internal debt. Lenin saw this. He acted as a cathartic; the ruling classes in Russia had stuffed themselves to bursting on interest. You see, the financial papers enable the people to see the Fat People eating."

"You mean the financiers?"

"Yes, I call them the Fat People. Now, human nature teaches us, we know by instinct, that there is something wrong when five per cent of the people stuff and ninety-five per cent have almost nothing to eat and no money to put into interest-bearing bonds at all."

Aristide said cloudily, "Perhaps, there are thieves, my dear friend, amongst the rich, but what about the sound bourgeoisie to which you and I belong? The sound bourgeoisie—the workers don't realize this—are hard-working, intelligent, saving, modest, liberal, the only good people. The best intelligences are found amongst them, the highest positions in the State. The workers live from hand to mouth. If they ever seized the State, it would be a fearful thing: the State would live from hand to mouth."

Marianne nearly nodded her head off at this and looked positively Chinese with grasping and avarice. Not that the Chinese are grasping—this is just the way she looked. "We go out on the road on Sunday in our little car which we have just been able to afford, out of our savings. We can hardly get along the roads with working-class people in cars too. Secondhand cars. God knows they can't afford them. And there they go racing past us, jeering at us, using up oil, destroying the roads, risking human life, not only their own lives—they can do that, with pleasure, but ours too. They have no idea of economy. I shudder at the thought of the money that must be poured out in Russia: every sou is gone. No wonder the country is breaking down. It's a detestable thing. It's because they were a nation of animals and personally I don't blame them so much as the old aristocrats. They were very charming people in themselves, but they didn't improve the country and now they have to pay for it: a nation of animals and pack mules have got hold of their estates and their factories. When the landed people and the capitalists get back it will take them twenty years to repair the country."

"You are wrong, Mme. Raccamond," said Haller, in his deliberate manner, intending no offense though. "A backward economy eventually proves more economic than an excessively hurriedly modern one. Do you know thread at all, Mr. Raccamond? Look at the thread in this shirt, it is made of six strands; it won't wear out in forty years, probably. I was getting some very fine thread from a place in Lille, but only a little of it, some years ago. Finally, I went to see the man, thinking I would buy the place and improve it, make a big business out of it. I found him in a side street and his machine a tiny old-fashioned thing, more like a bedstead than a modern filature. I sat down on the floor with him and he told me his brother went into business, put up a modern spinning factory, and has been bankrupted because of the

290

constant need for modern improvements in machinery. The buyers demand it. Then the slack time comes, he is left with it on his hands, weeds grow in the courtyards, dust falls from the walls; in five years when business picks up, industry has got far ahead of him. He has used up all his capital, he owes everything to the bank, and he has nothing to start with again.

"Meanwhile new competitors are starting from scratch with the latest thing in machines. You see the waste? America, for example, has spent all this time, labor, money, lives, has seen bankruptcies and suicides, to learn how to build modern buildings; and England has now only to take over the latest designs and profit from American experience, without bleeding for it herself. The expense of experimentation is enormous and I assure you, Mr. Raccamond, that thousands of profitable, time-saving inventions are throttled in their cradles, even in America, to save money. Now Russia was saved all the elementary struggles of machine capitalism. She is that much to the good. She can start right off now, with her first tractor factory the same as the best tractor factories in Germany or America. She need count nothing for depreciation. But in an old-fashioned economy, like England's, the profit lasts only a short time. The preservation of antiquated styles by tariffs and loss of trade by old patterns eventually disabled the country. It cannot be done artificially. Only in the revolutionary way. And Lenin saw that, too. He was a great economist!"

"That is very well for men of our cultivation," protested Aristide, with a blank expression, "but workers cannot understand these things. We have had a university education. I once tried to read Marx and found it quite impossible. I didn't understand even the first page. How can workers then?"

"That is a comfort to me," Marianne peaceably put in, lapping up her peaches. "Even if the Reds continue to govern in Moscow, which I don't believe, it will take them fifty years to acquire any culture, a hundred and fifty years to produce a Velasquez, longer than that to produce an El Greco."

Mme. Haller returned with the opened peach tin which she had rescued from the garbage box. She was flushed. "You see, Mme. Raccamond! This is it. You will recognize it by the label? It's a pretty label, isn't it?"

"They are the very best," Georg explained. "You see, they get so much sun, they are unusually luscious. Otherwise we would not eat tinned things at all. The ordinary brands are unhealthy. You don't eat tinned things, do you, Mme. Raccamond?"

Marianne's eyes brightened at a recollection, "Yes, we do . . . not much. But we do get a simply marvelous *pâté de foie gras* from the Dordogne, the best I ever tasted; it is made by a little firm down there. Do you like it, Mme. Haller? I would get you a tin."

The Hallers were pale with astonishment. After a moment, Mme. Haller managed to say, in a stricken voice, "Mme. Raccamond! You know—" (very low) "how they are made, *pâté de foies gras?*"

"Why, yes."

Almost tonelessly, she questioned, "You know they are made from" (a shocked look) "the diseased livers of overfed geese?"

"Of course."

The two couples exchanged glances of complete incomprehension. Almost stonily, Mme. Haller said, "No, no, we never eat them. We could not eat them."

What was so particularly shocking to them in the sluggish livers of lazy, overfed geese? But Mme. Haller had managed to convey a feeling of cannibalism. Briskly, Haller broke the spell, "Some wine, Mme. Raccamond? Do you like Burgundy or Bordeaux, red or white?"

"Oh, Burgundy, thank you . . . red." A pleased look, "I didn't know you had wine." She began to think, after so much liqueur, ugh! but I need a tonic.

"Tell Anna, some Burgundy, Sophy."

"I'll get it myself. And Mme. Raccamond, did you taste the butter? I must show you the box we get it in. We get it specially from a place near Mulhouse. It is sent up every month."

Yes, and now it is rancid, thought Marianne. "Really, I used *beurre d'Isigny,*" she said with confidence, mentioning the best domestic butter in Paris.

"*Beurre d'Isigny!* Oh, Mme. Raccamond, do you buy it from the butterman like that? But you know that they *mix* it! You get nothing *pure*. You must get it yourself from the producer. You don't know what you're getting."

Marianne flushed. "We don't use very much . . . we eat out most of the time." She dared him to go back to the ground of restaurants. He eyed her for a moment and turned courteously to her husband.

"The reason I have built up a reserve of goods as well as gold is that gold itself is sterile and the holding of it sterilizes not only money-making capacity but even the mental faculties all round. It stultifies its holder. You see, even me—Mr. Raccamond. I was able to retire at forty-five, and what have I done the last ten years? Nothing. When the depression came I realized that not only was the world sterile, through overproduction, but I was sterile. I want to go back to my home town and become a doctor. I regret that five years ago I did not start my medical course, but there is still time. I think I will do that. I fear the sterilization of gold. I hold it in so many places, England, Switzerland, Canada, for example, that even traveling has no pleasure for me any more. I am afraid to disturb my gold reserve. You see, how it is with me? Do you understand, Mr. Raccamond? And so the only thing for me to do is to go back to earning with my bare hands! . . . Do you remember when you were a student, Raccamond? I was happy when I was a student. I was a prize student. I thought I would be building machines all my life. . . . You know, we are lazy, Mr. Raccamond. The government should force us all to do some vulgar labor, like weeding gutters, or cleaning sewers, for a month every year: it would act as a purgative for our laziness . . . . Yes, indeed, Mme. Raccamond, we have to be forced. Working people too must be forced; to do the dirty jobs, they will have to be pressed to obey hygienic regulations! I had some peasant girls once who would not bind their hair in handkerchiefs to save their hair from the looms. I had to be very strict with them. . . . I would not mind going to a new developing country myself, say, like Australia or Palestine and showing the people how to work."

Sophy returned with the butter box and behind her, Anna, carrying a plate of sausage and a bottle of red wine.

Aristide was spilled in his chair, his mouth half open, his eyes bulging and his pendulous cheeks some pale shade between French blue and mauve. When the wine was poured for him, although his head was reeling, he grasped the glass and drained it, hoping to combat the nightmare indigestion that had already set in. He looked

293

with bitter astonishment at Haller, breathing freely, cheerfully, cutting up the sausage, which (of course) came from a special, though nameless, shop, brought specially in a basket by Anna, the only shop in Paris free from bacteria, poison, and pollution, according to both the Hallers. Anna, at the door, surveyed them a minute. She knew, of course, very well, what they came for, the two black pigs: they came to snuffle and grub in her master's dishes.

"A little port wine?" asked Sophy, and getting out a special glass, put the purple-mantled port, not a particularly good one, by Aristide's plate. He pushed it away a centimeter, "No, please." But with the usual protestations, he drank.

"If Hitler or some demagogue like that insisted on everyone going to a labor camp for a month a year," said Haller, "even I would say there was some good in him. But he's a weak fellow."

Aristide shook his head: he had quite lost the thread of the conversation; he blurted out feebly, "You, Mr. Haller, pay your own debts. Where would the sausage maker, the bread baker be otherwise? You wouldn't get your butter from Mulhouse."

Haller laughed and ate a big piece of sausage with relish. "Yes, but if it were a question of paying them compound interest forever on a sausage, if I had to mortgage my bread to them as well and keep on paying through the nose, I would run away and remain solvent and honorable in another country where such fantastic practices didn't exist. I would even run away to Russia. . . ." He raised his eyebrows, looked seriously at them. "The little harmless bourgeois, with little homes, haven't been touched. They respect them. I would keep my money abroad. . . . Take America," he went on, not remarking that Aristide was past taking anything, "in America the increment of wealth is three per cent per annum, the increment of population one per cent, but the Government gives four per cent which is more than reason allows, and most people casually expect to reap six to ten per cent on their money—in the stock market even more. All that should be purged from the system, industry should lose that dead weight, the common people should have all that shifted off their bread and cheese. . . . We take laxatives, Mr. Raccamond; the system should, too."

"There would be no confidence," Aristide said slowly, with a death rattle in his voice, a choke which made Marianne blanch, "if such things were said publicly."

"Aristide," cried his wife, "what's the matter?"

"Oh, what's the matter, Mr. Raccamond?"

"Air—a little air . . . I'm faint."

"Oh, dear. (Georg, you hear!) Air. Open the window."

Georg got up and went to the window, with precise haste. Aristide rose and hung trembling to the arm of his chair. Marianne darted anxious looks round, wondering if he would have the courage to go outside the room. But their tiny hostess was struggling on the other side, already heaving him towards the window. "Oh, Mme. Raccamond, your husband . . . help him, look!" At the window, Aristide collapsed into the window seat. Georg stood by him and spoke to him in murmurs. The curtains flung themselves out into the room again and again as the blessed zephyr blew in. The two women retired once more to the sofa and sat talking, Sophy commiserating with Marianne. Poor Mr. Raccamond worked so hard. These rich clients were so exacting: the market turned for a day and plop, down they came on the customers' man. The men had left the room.

Pale, but himself, Aristide now returned, took his place, and Georg, relieved and content, sat opposite him. "Sophy, is the tea ready? Mr. Raccamond needs some tea."

She pressed the bell. Meanwhile the clock had been going round and round and Aristide, with drops on his brow, had watched that dreadful minute hand dragging itself with malevolent slowness to the half-hour, to the hour. They had now been here gorging two hours and ten minutes, and it was by no means finished. What a man goes through to keep customers! And this one, too, who sometimes passed a hundred shares in a month, and who paid himself ten times ten per cent interest by getting the Raccamonds to dinner and pumping Aristide about the bank, about the market, about Bertillon's position in the market, about Alphendéry's relation to him, about the great goldbugs who had their bonds with Bertillon and about a thousand other things, upon whose details he fed in his long idle hours of the day and night. But

Aristide knew that engineer or no, mathematician or no, one of these days Haller might require a "private service," some transferring of bonds, or gold, and that it was just possible he would get it for himself. . . . He looked at the little rubicund blond gnome with his mountains of gold and despised him; him, once a leading spinner of East Prussia, now a frog in a giant bell jar predicting the political weather!

"The tea, Sophy! The tea."

"I suppose she has gone to sleep. When I went into the kitchen, she was singing and she would not answer me."

"Then go out yourself, Sophy." (In German) "Don't show yourself so incompetent in the management of a servant." She trotted out.

The door opened. "The tea!" said Sophy cheerfully, ushering in Anna with a tray on which stood handsome glasses full of a transparent orange liquid. "Now, Mr. Raccamond, you will feel better. You need a little stimulation."

"Put a little more wine into it than usual, Sophy. Mr. Raccamond is tired, he needs it."

The tea became the color of blood.

"Moderation," said Haller, "is a wise use of liberty, a wise limitation of plenitude. There must be a redistribution of goods."

"Some of these chocolates with your tea, Mr. Raccamond; they are the best chocolates in the world and come from Switzerland. Lindt and Sprüngli. It is amusing that when I was at school in Switzerland," said Mme. Haller, "I was told to be most careful not to acquire the Swiss 'li' for 'lein', and once when they asked me what chocolates I had bought (they were very careful of our diet), I said Lindt and Sprünglein."

"Ha, ha," said Georg. "Well, Mr. Raccamond, moderation is a thing financiers won't hear of and so we have revolution, their own fault. They can't be moderate, and so neither can the ninety-five per cent disinherited. It is inevitable."

Marianne said tartly, "There have been a lot of revolutions already and no one is satisfied."

Sedately Haller shook his head, as he put another macaroon on Aristide's plate (he assumed that as Aristide was no longer suffocated, he could eat again). "No, where the redistribution goes only from five to ten per cent of the people, that is not a revolution. You see, Russia is the only revolution that concerned ninety-five per cent of the people. That's why they like it."

"But the worst elements are on top," cried Marianne, in real distress. "Look at *L'Humanité!* Look at the way they criticize the theater and literature. 'The impact of dialectics.' Bah! How can they use such barbarous words!"

Haller pleasantly sipped his wine-filled tea, "Ah, my dear lady, they are not trying to please us . . . no! They will do away with us. Entirely. They don't need us! A shoemaker, Madame, can make shoes: he doesn't need our executive ability at all. It's sad, but it's true." He laughed sunnily. "I would love to go to Palestine, for instance, and knock some sense into their heads."

"Whose heads?"

"The workers' heads . . . teach them how to work."

Aristide said, "Would they listen to you; they're obstinate brutes."

Sophy fluttered gaily, "Oh, we had a communist and an unemployed man up here to talk with us, at dinner, on two separate occasions; we know just how they think."

Georg flushed, looked extremely flattered, boyish. "Yes, I quite agree with the communist, a most intelligent man and not a bit grateful for the dinner, you know."

Faintly Marianne asked, "What was he? The secretary of the party or something?"

"No, just a tramman Georg found down at the sheds. He wrote a letter to our paper about it."

"What paper is that?"

"The *Frankfurter Zeitung.* It is the only liberal paper. It is the best paper in the world. We read it every day. The literary criticisms, my dear Mme. Raccamond: you would be delighted to read them. So very refined, modern, too."

Georg, on the point of revealing his naked soul, said to Raccamond, "Why do you work for Bertillon, Mr. Raccamond? It is (don't laugh at the old-fashioned phrase), it is rather sordid, isn't it? Why don't you free yourself and—better yourself. You are the slave of great capital, aren't you?"

Aristide looked displeased at this admonishment. "I hope to get on, you know. A partnership—"

"Aristide?"

"With some house or other—later on. That is not so bad. A private bank, you know, is the needle's eye to influence in finance, in Paris."

"Yes, but does that satisfy you, Mr. Raccamond? You seem to have such a cultivated view," said Sophy, regretfully.

"Oh, yes. I was born for finance," Aristide said. What a curious look Marianne gave him!

"Give Mr. Raccamond a leetle more sausage with his tea," urged Sophy. At this moment Anna came triumphantly in, as if she knew Aristide's state—and who would not, seeing his complexion and bulging eyes and sweating chops?—and more tea was forced on him, as well as a splendid Doyenne de Comice pear, specially bought for him, "because he needed fresh fruit for his digestion." There was a hailstorm of protestations and inquiries, refusals and moral suasions. Sophy won. Suddenly, Georg said, two hours and forty minutes too late, "Sophy, you know it is not polite to press anything on people. They know what they want." She looked guilty and desisted.

When they got out into the quiet street and found it past midnight, they felt as if a battle had been lost and won. "Never again, Marianne," said Aristide choking. "I feel as if I will die. I can't do it again . . . . I am suffocating."

Marianne bit her lip. "When I asked you to go and get my handkerchief, didn't you understand I wanted to give you a chance to go out in the hall? Instead, you passed me yours."

"I didn't know, Marianne; please forgive me. It was kind of you."

"You should have refused."

"Oh, I tried . . . didn't you see that? But they are terrible; they are ogres. Marianne, we will never go there again. He comes to Bertillon's for quotations and places his order in Cleat, Placket, and Company, and I don't believe any amount of listening to his nonsense will make him realize that it's unethical."

"They must be fabulously rich, just the same," sighed Marianne.

"Yes, you are right, unfortunately. Well, it won't be until next month. They only ask us once a month."

"They are our friends, and true friends. Friends are true in the measure that they appreciate our money-making ability and financial staying power. Mme. Haller asked me to go shopping with her and I will. She will be useful to me."

Aristide looked at her curiously and after an inspection said, "How can she possibly be useful to you? You don't need anything, that I know of."

"I may," Marianne declared. "Aristide, I have been chasing a ghost light: physical goods are power. I am going in for moneymaking, flat. I've sold my play in London, but there's nothing in it. I'll go in for big money-making, naked business, and when I'm through I'll have enough material to write a real play, something in the Bernstein line."

Aristide looked at her with admiration. "Marianne, you have a man's brain. You never swerve. Whatever you want you will get. I wish I was as resolute as you."

"Why, so you are, my dear."

He shook his head faintly, then seeing her glance, smiled and nodded in acquiescence. "In my own way. We are well matched, Marianne. I will always be glad we married. Where should I have been without you?"

She was cheerful, resolute. "Still in the arms of Lucienne, I suppose."

"Ah, I don't know, I don't know. I had outgrown that."

She smiled to herself in the dark. "Do you feel better now, Aristide?"

"Yes."

"Our son, Aristide, is very like his mother; I see Lucienne in his eyes and brows; his mouth is like yours." There was a silence. "There is a sort of spiritual bloom over his face, which is like Lucienne's," she continued.

"I don't think so," he murmured half-heartedly.

"Ah, yes. She is very brave to let us educate him and have him come home to us."

Aristide said bitterly, "She is poor. She could not expect me to give her your money."

"A mother will do a lot for a son," Marianne said cheerfully.

Aristide looked at her in unconcealed surprise, "You are so strong, Marianne . . . you have an incredible strength of soul."

"Ah!" She smiled with intense secret gratification.

"Lucienne," he murmured, "never had your breadth of vision, Marianne. She was kind, she is good, she is a woman, but it is impossible for her to think with the moral vigor that you have. Nor have I," he ended with faint, instinctive malice, well hidden.

Marianne frowned, and they fell silent, until she changed the subject, to her advantage. "There's no subject so rich in ideas as Money." Aristide grunted. "I'm thinking," went on Marianne tenderly, with a richer tone than she usually used, "that money is a very pure thing in its way; that's why the Hallers have such curious habits. They have nothing more to do, they do not even need more money—they have enough for avarice. Now they are looking for the absolute. They caught that from their gold bars. It is an absolute. People have such a delicate love for money that if you speak jealously of it or of those who own it, all the dirt falls back on you: people take you for a miserable, poor-spirited person." She laughed richly. "I could almost love money, I should like to wash my hands in gold coins. I should feel like a princess. No, it is not sterile. No, water seems sterile, too." Aristide grunted. "I will, some day!" Marianne murmured with energy.

"Will what?"

"Will wash my hands in gold coin."

He laughed a little, looked sideways at her. A curl of her wiry black hair had escaped and softened her round, firm features. "I love you, Marianne."

Aristide observed that night, "I told you that two German merchants had got credits from the bank to set up a business: Rosenkrantz and Guildenstern? I thought it was in the air, but today I saw a letterhead from them. Look!"

The elegant letterhead printed by the bank's printers, read,

KAIMASTER-BLES, S.A.

Franz Rosenkrantz and Franz Guildenstern.

| *Agents for:* | 35, Boissy d'Anglas, |
| Banque Bertillon & Cie. | Paris |

"I'm astonished," Marianne said, in trepidation. "Then you knew nothing about this?"

"Don't worry: I went to see them today, told them who I was and they were most agreeable. In fact, I got the impression that they would prefer to collaborate with one man, myself, than with the chiefs who are anonymous."

"Then, why look so downcast, Aristide? It's very satisfactory. You might have struck a suspicious pair."

"Yes. They told me something. They signed their contract with Alphendéry!"

"Really! That's interesting."

"It's difficult to find out where anyone stands in the firm. Perhaps he is a partner."

"It looks like it, doesn't it?"

"I don't know what to think, Marianne. I don't understand the way it's run: everything in the dark."

"Probably that's their object—to keep everyone in the dark."

"Oh, of course; but how am I going to make my way when I don't know on which side of the hill to plant my orchard?"

"I have an idea, Aristide. Ask to visit the foreign branches, to pick up clients."

"And?—"

"And find out from the managers where things stand. In Paris we are in a stew of rumors; abroad the bank is seen in perspective. Some of the managers are close friends of Bertillon, some are aristocratic boys who simply regard him as one of themselves without any fal-lal, some are foreigners who won't be too enthusiastic: you are sure to be able to find out exactly how the bank is regarded. Also, my dear, you can introduce yourself to them."

"Marianne, perhaps I'm wasting my time. I dropped in at Cleat, Placket, and Company this afternoon and talked to a few of the boys."

"You're hedging your job?"

"It's not a bad idea, any time."

"No, but you're in Bertillon's. Make this trip, I say, and you'll come back with a very different view of the bank. You can snoop round in Amsterdam, for example, and find out their relation to Legris and Company. And you can find out who Alphendéry represents. *Mon Dieu,* surely your nose is good enough for that." She sounded impatient for a moment.

"My dear, I haven't been there very long, they might think it peculiar—"

"Eh, *mon Dieu,* you're timid, Aristide. You've got Carrière. You know Carrière. Carrière carries an account there and he carries a great whale of bonds abroad with their foreign branches. Isn't that enough? If they're obdurate, get Carrière to ask specially for you to go abroad and check up his accounts. Anything. You've no resource, Aristide. This clerk, Constant, travels for them. Bertillon doesn't stand on status."

"Yes, I'll do that. It's a good idea. Thank you, Marianne."

"I should think so!"

"You must find me a poor sketch sometimes, Marianne!"

"Oh, don't say that: you're my husband. I want you only to praise yourself to me. Whatever happens, I want to think well of you. How can I if you run yourself down, Aristide? Don't depreciate yourself to me or anyone else. That's a first rule of dignity."

"You're sharp."

"That's animal cunning: every dog knows it. You're too soft and human, you are too gentle. Hold your head up, Aristide. You don't know human nature. If you give way ever so little, the pack will swarm over you and tear you to pieces. You ought to know that. You must have suffered, Aristide!" She gave him a look of pity.

"Yes, I've suffered. I always thought it was temperamental weakness."

"Oh, no." She suffered herself and was angry. "This is folly. You are a brilliant man, Aristide."

"You're in love with me, Marianne."

"Oh, no, no . . . it's not that. Oh, how angry you make me! No. I have known lots of men in my life, Aristide: my father, my four brothers, my cousins in the Banque Czorvocky: my life has been nothing but men, and as you say, I have strong nerves myself. I have met bankers and brokers all my life. I know the temperaments that give promise. Yours is one. I saw it from the first. Now, listen to me a moment. There is some secret in the Banque Bertillon. We must work discreetly but continuously to find out who is behind Bertillon. There is certainly someone. There is this new rumor, for example, that the Société Générale Alsacienne owns part of it. And then you have the fact that Alphendéry has occult influence

302

there, and that he is an Alsatian. Can we run this rumor to earth? Now Cleat, Placket, and Company is just a little firm, struggling to appear thriving, like the rest. It seems to me that in Bertillon's, through the difference of your temperaments, you, Aristide, have the chance we have been waiting for. You were caught in a trap in Claude Brothers. We have botched things for the last ten years. Now we are starting fresh and with wind behind us. I feel it. I am full of confidence."

He was still moody, though brighter than before. "I found that sneak Parouart sitting in Rosenkrantz and Guildenstern's lobby, fresh as paint and very much at home. I am certain he is working with them."

"Working? He couldn't."

"Well, up to some of his games. Your people aren't in it?"

"I don't think so. I'll go and see Czorvocky though. He still works for my uncle sometimes, I know."

"Look here, Marianne, how the deuce can I get in with Rosenkrantz and his partner if your uncle is already tangling things with his toady Parouart? You know Czorvocky is not a friend of mine."

Marianne considered for a moment and then said equably, "I'll go and see him, dear, and find out what tricks he's up to. So, that is what you were worrying about?"

"Your uncle is a terrible thief, you know, Marianne. Let him keep his fingers off our bread and butter."

"Good, I'll see him. He'll do a lot for me."

Aristide trembled, and said excitedly, "I'll do for this Parouart if he interferes in my business. He's only a police rat. He has no brains."

"Listen, dear, you remember Claude Brothers? Don't forget there's a file in your name down at police headquarters. So much the worse. We must bear even with Parouart."

"I can't stand him, I can't stand this petty intriguing that goes on round your uncle."

"Calm yourself and don't go back over all that. We will make out and when the time comes I'll get uncle to dish Parouart. Let us get something on him. . . . . You say he's blackmailing Bertillon?"

"Yes, as I told you. He told me himself. There may be something in his complaint, of course."

"Oh, what's that? A man like that has no rights. Well,

tell Bertillon that Parouart is up at Rosenkrantz and Guildenstern trying to worm his way in. That will start the ball rolling."

"Good, a good idea. I'll do it tomorrow. You're very clear-headed, Marianne."

She looked at him deliberately. "No, never praise me, Aristide. All my ideas come from you. I would be nothing without you. This is not a world for women."

He walked beside her, his large head bent and livid, his full lips protruding, a gloomy expression still in his eyes, but she felt the mood had almost passed off. Presently he stood straighter and began talking cheerfully about the stock market, which was up. He always felt better when prices soared: he was a natural bull and he never felt honest when he had to tell clients to "bear" the market, even when he was convinced that this was the right advice. He was no good in a depression. She recalled something. "I found out something interesting about your precious bank today. The head teller, Henri Martin, you know?"

"Yes, a very nice fellow. Pleasant manners, very dignified."

"Yes, he inspires confidence."

"Oh, I believe he has real ability."

"Undoubtedly. He was an agent of the French Secret Service during the war, in Switzerland. He sent some twenty-five men to death."

"Good God."

"Yes; he could help us with Parouart if need be."

"What's he doing in the Banque Bertillon?"

"I don't know that."

"There is some mystery in the Banque Bertillon, Marianne."

"Perhaps Bertillon did some special work in the war, too. He has the military medal and citations, you know."

"Yes. Hm. We must watch our step, Marianne."

"Yes. But I don't think Parouart is so dangerous, you see, in the Banque Bertillon. Aristide, you must act. You are unhappy when you don't. That is how you get into messes. I want you to work with Bertillon because I don't think your temperament is suited to big banks. You would be swallowed up. You can't stand the idea of a sea of men above you; you stifle. We are money types. Bertillon wants a real lieutenant. If Alphendéry is acting for someone else, he is not an officer of the bank; if he is not, he is only one of these materializations of a vague desire or dream or need which a financier needs at times in his life. A financier is a strange animal: he needs props, grand viziers, and court jesters at times. If Alphendéry is only that he will go overboard one of these days. But you are not the court-jester type. You have a real function in the bank. You are afraid to investigate the bank from top to bottom systematically. One would say you are afraid to find out someone or something. Are you afraid to find Bertillon out? Or yourself? You hesitate with a weapon in your hands. This must be done piecemeal, Aristide. You have no psychological ingenuity, you rush into things—bull optimist, bull pessimist. What is the use of filling the ears of every evening with the mournful tale of your half-measures, your fears and frights? Our old age will come and you still in a state of indecision in an indecisive career. Perhaps, if you cannot push yourself to the top, you should go back into small business, Aristide? Give up all your ideas of making big money? . . .

"Listen, while you are wondering, other people are consolidating their positions, forming partnerships, learning what the books are about, getting positions abroad, like this Adam Constant, who was no one but a minor teller yesterday and today does secret commissions abroad for Bertillon and tomorrow will go to Shanghai. You are working alone. You must form partnerships, smile at the tellers, bribe the accountants, take the other customers' men out to lunch, flatter Alphendéry. You are too cold, you don't smile enough, you fall into a frenzy on the slightest accident, the rest of the time you go about sunk in the cold lard of your slight melancholy. You are, at bottom, quite a neurotic in business, Aristide, like a poet who has been forced into a countinghouse by his uncle. But no one forced you: this has been your lifelong desire, Aristide. You want to make big money, you like a life of ease: you would be miserable as a clerk or salesman. You must go ahead or renounce the whole career and go back to your father's business, waste the rest of your life in regrets and wish dreams.

"You see—you must take a different attitude. . . . It is very well to go out to dinner with Sournois, Carrière, the Carrière troop of chorus boys, and Oscar Rennel and his actresses and the people from the Théâtre Mogador and Mrs. Weyman, Fred Pharion, and Kensington Southe. It is

very good, I say. They have money and they are speculators, but you must not rest with them: you wanted to
be an actor yourself and when you are with them you
slacken up, you tend to dream. You must go in
more for politicians. When I got Czorvocky to introduce you to Carrière five years ago, I wanted you to
get in with the politicians. You must pursue that line.
Everything in France is politics and if you wipe your
feet when you leave them and wipe your hands when
you shake hands with them, you will get their leavings,
have their protection, and in due time, you will form
a lifelong alliance with one of them. Of course, it's
always possible that Carrière himself will become your pro-
tector. But you must hedge: and Carrière will respect you
more if he sees you have other alliances among the
deputies. . . ."

Aristide listened attentively and said nothing at the
end of this speech.

Marianne waited a few minutes. The sweet night air
blew round them and presently blew away the unpleasant
notes of Marianne's remarks, and then she said, gently,
"A character in a play, even a super, must at least elbow
the other players a bit to show he's alive."

"That's the convention of the stage and of women,"
Aristide remarked, "that there is some way of getting
things done and some way out. As if in a dizzy beehive
like the bank there was some way of getting anything
done. No, it is not a beehive, it is a merry-go-round. The
horses look splendid, their nostrils flash fire, their mouths
drip slaver, they rear, their eyes dart passion, their manes
float, and they even go round, but all is sculpted wood,
and a spinning platform. The bank is a stage, Marianne:
there is something in it I can't seize, for the life of me.
I don't know what gives it momentum."

Marianne did not pursue the subject: her thoughts had
turned to something else. "I saw about fifty apartments
free yesterday between Sèvres-Babylone and the Rue
Bonaparte. I may have to redecorate my apartment, after
all. . . . Raoul wrote for some more money: what are
we going to do with that ne'er-do-well, Aristide? With
both our apartments empty and Pierre's fees to pay, it is
really quite a squeeze. Thank goodness your commissions
are swelling."

"Money, money, Marianne: there is something else in life besides money," said Aristide suddenly.

"Not to pay the rent with: I shouldn't like to hear that from my house guests in Rue du Jardin Botanique. No. There is nothing else in life but money. Listen. The working people are not so foolish as we are. No sentiment with them. One reads nothing else in their papers but that—demands for more money, pensions, rents, price of bread, apprentices' wages. As a result of this single-mindedness on their part, we, the softening middle class, pay for it in taxes, insurance. We should have their hardheadedness. I really believe we will go under to them if we don't wake up. What do we want with the arts, for example, in a time like this? We should become more Spartan, Aristide: I tell you, we really deserve to lose the battle if we cannot throw overboard our fancy cargoes, pare our comfort down. Men like you, Aristide, my dear, are relics of a more comfortable age. Money, I don't despise it. It's a clean, honorable thing. Debts are paid in it. Tell me, aren't we uncomfortable, if someone starts doing us all sorts of vague favors, puts himself out for us: it is quite an annoyance! Everyone prefers to have services rendered to him in terms of pounds, shillings, and pence. Then you know what you owe. As for gratitude, it is only money teaches people gratitude. We despise the person who obliges us in things with no exchange value; we are grateful to those who lend us money; we are glad to know the exact price of everything that's given to us. . . . Doesn't everyone go sneaking round to the shops, after a birthday, to find out the price of the watch or lace jabot just given? Take a rich father: he neglects his children all his life, sends them to boarding schools, finds them the most inconvenient domestic animals. When they are twenty-one, he settles an estate on them and he suddenly begins to have an affection for them, he has evaluated them to himself. We live in an unsure shifting world: money gives us a sure set of values; everything else is mere opinion, but you and I and Mr. No-Name passing by can agree on the value of a louis d'or. . . ."

Aristide laughed. "You would have made a lawyer, Marianne."

She bent her looks on him. "My friend, you are passing through some crisis—what is it?"

"I don't know, Marianne. Always the same struggle; sometimes I wonder why I don't succeed."

"No one succeeds: there is only money to fight for. It has real gains and real losses."

He looked at her in amazement, nodded his head to himself.

Scene Forty-three: Polite Money

A FEW days later, Raccamond rushed into Jules's room. "Did you read the morning papers?"

"No."

"My client, Mrs. Wilson, was swindled at a stud-poker game by some American gangsters who were clients of the bank. All the papers have it. Everyone's laughing. What am I to say? How can I explain it?"

"Explain what?"

"What will I say to Mrs. Wilson? She met the gangsters in our board room."

"Yes," said Jules thoughtfully, "it's a pity. Dyson and McCahey, I suppose! Now those boys will have to leave town. Oh, you can tell her Eddie McCahey is a big shot. At one time, Eddie was washing shares through us at the rate of fifty thousand to two hundred thousand a week. She wouldn't expect us to turn down that sort of commission business! She's a sensible woman."

"But look at the air it gives us! What do we look like?"

"The backroom of a pub," said Jules, contemptuously. "And the Comtesse de Voigrand! She does a hundred shares a week. Could you pay your rent on that? Let me tell you, Dyson never squabbles over his account and always pays his margin calls promptly."

"But how can I explain to my high-class clients—"

Jules was bored. "You're a mystic, Raccamond, you're not a realist. Do you think clients are going to fill in a handful of questions when they come in as if they were asking to immigrate into our bank? Don't be such a pedant," he suddenly flung at him furiously. He got up and plunged his long white hands into his pockets. He looked sternly at Raccamond from the austere pinnacle of his wits.

"Raccamond, every woman is a whore, but the whores are the ones who never learned the game: every banker is a poker shark but the Eddie McCaheys are the poor fellows who don't get away with it. What is a whore? A poor girl who never had a chance to go into business with a man and set up a little home of her own. The same with the little swindlers. I'm sorry for them. Haven't you got a heart, Raccamond? Are you all for profit, dignity, reputation? Have you forgotten what sort of business you're in? You'll turn into a crank if you're not careful. And I don't have any cranks round me, Raccamond. Listen, there's only one rule in business. Anyone's money is good. That's my rule. When money walks in the door, takes off its hat and says, 'Here I am; I want to live with you,' the least of the polite things you can do, is to say, 'Good day; take a seat.' How else are we to get business? You're crazy if you're waiting for clean money. Did you ever hear of clean money?"

Aristide bumbled on. "Yes, but women are difficult. Women don't like gangsters, swindlers, and gamblers. What can I do? How will I explain? If it gets about—" He turned his great neurotic lamps of eyes on Jules. "I can't face her; I don't know what to say, Mr. Bertillon."

"You make me laugh, Aristide. You go and see Mrs. Wilson and see what she says to you. I know that type. If she's wronged send her up to me. But I bet she won't be. Apologize if you want to, but don't take arsenic. She'll get over it. She'll call herself a fool. She's one of the few women clients we ever had that I really liked. And if she draws out her account; I don't care. Women are tough but they're yellow. They squeal as soon as the shoe pinches. They squeeze the last penny out of you and when they're licked they expect a free loan. If I had my way I'd fill the bank with gangsters and sweep out the girls. They're not sporting. Run along, Raccamond. It's not as bad as you think. And don't go round pulling that long face and telling people about the tragedy that's happened in your life. Forget it. That's the secret of success: forget every morning the scandals and insults of the day before. That's the way to keep a pure heart and be happy though in business." He laughed Raccamond out the door, and went kicking his heels round the corridor to William's room. But when he pushed open the door there, he frowned at William and Alphendéry, whom he found there.

"I say, I've got a hunch. Why don't we fire Raccamond? I know all about his business; but he's a crank. They spend all their spare time developing manias. He's foaming at the mouth about how *he's* going to explain to Mrs. Wilson about Eddie McCahey and how *he's* going to build up the reputation of the bank. *He's* got to explain to all Paris how poor old Eddie got into our stock-exchange room." His carillon rang out. "D'ye hear. Fire him."

"You fire him," said William.

"Listen, I didn't take him on. You two said he had the biggest accounts in Paris."

"No. You said that Jean de Guipatin said he was the best man Claude Brothers ever had."

"I never said that. I'm superstitious about him . . . . I said I wouldn't have anything to do with him. That's what I said from the beginning. He must be a fool. He's a Flying Dutchman . . . always appears in storms, always scuds before a shipwreck! He's bad luck."

Alphendéry laughed hopelessly. "How can you be so primitive, Jules? You're no better than an Australian black with your superstitions."

"You're crazy," said William with disgust.

"What's the use of being rich if you can't be crazy?" flung out Jules. "I have ideas and I pay other people to carry them out. They may sound crazy but they're right because I pay for them. And then, I'm lucky. You may argue right and I may sound wrong, but I've got the wind with me and so I'm right even if I'm wrong."

"What a race of liars you all are!" sighed Alphendéry. "You work day and night at your schemes and then you love to pretend it's all pure luck; you just lie on your back with your mouth open and luck throws in *pâté de foie gras.*"

"Ptt!" said Jules. He darkened. "Listen, what's this nominees' game you thought up, Alphendéry? Why didn't you come round this morning when I asked you? Why doesn't anybody here do what I ask him?"

Alphendéry began, soothing, glinting, smiling, "I've been thinking about it, Jules. I wanted to get it pat before I put it to you. It sprang up from something

Henri Léon said. You know, he's got trusts for his whole family. But it's not that."

Jules melted at the sight of Alphendéry glittering, dewed with thought, melting with fertility, waxy with imagination, intent. Alphendéry seized this new love in a moment and began weaving a little figure of himself. "A Jew is like a spider because he sits and weaves; he is an alien because he can think; the Jews are not like the *Goyim*, no sitting round at polo matches, no ' 'oo won?' They think out schemes all the time, they have to think from babies . . . that's why they're not good leaders, too. Decision, giving commands, shouting at people, slitting Gordian knots, is often a way of expressing mental confusion." The telephone rang.

"What?" said Alphendéry: "What letters? FAQ? Yes, of course. FAQ."

"FAQ," said Jules, in a volatile state of mind: "I like that: sell five thousand: FAQ short for fakir."

"A businessman of genius," said Alphendéry, grinning wearily, "is no smarter than a pair of dice thrown up n times: the factors against his success are too numerous— hence his tragic belief in the coup that is to make him master of the situation. FAQ—'fair average quality.' Sell it short!"

"Well, sell FAP if there's a stock called that: I won't be satisfied until you sell something." Jules interrupted, "I'll tell you what, sell Allis-Chalmers."

"And why?"

"I have a hunch."

"What hunch?"

"Tony is leaving Aline for a girl called Alice Palmers."

Was Jules mocking? Alphendéry didn't know. He found that the bank was eighty-six thousand shares short on a nine per cent margin and he refused to sell any more. He had had two margin calls from Legris Brothers in the morning, and Jules had refused to put up any more margin. Was it charm, or was Jules partner to some secret undertaking with Legris Brothers?

"This isn't a life," murmured Alphendéry, disgusted, "it's an insane asylum and I'm the keeper, not knowing what's going on in their heads. I just have to take out the alarm clocks and alligators that they think they swallow, from time to time. And then they have the laugh

on me: they know what's what on the subject of alarm
clocks."

Scene Forty-four: City Whispers

E. RALPH STEWART took a pleasure in spitting out all
his irritable idiosyncrasy in company, but his letters
showed a brilliant and sometimes cool businessman, the
ideal type of his class, and a perfect indicator of what
the quickest (if not the most mellow) minds in the city
thought. Finding Bertillon elfish and enigmatic, the
straight-spoken Stewart communicated his ideas to Alphendéry. He looked upon Alphendéry as a man of his
own type and stature—a poor boy who had risen by
brains, personal attraction (for men), and lucky pertinac-
ity to an undue influence in a jealous profession.

Early in July, Alphendéry spoke to him on the telephone, cautiously indicating that the Bertillon Bank had
an interest in sterling and asking his opinion. Stewart
wrote back:

3rd July, 1931

DEAR ALPHENDÉRY,
I have been occupied and so unable to write to
you before this. I am so rushed that even now I can't
send a personal note, which excuse. I think we both
have the same ideas but local interests vary. Here is
my view in a few words. Governments' expenses
must continue and be increased in all countries. Inflation will follow government expenses whether these
are for unemployment payments or war expenditures,
or both. My impression is that there will be peace
long enough for every nation to be put on a war footing. In the meantime sporadic wars will be fostered
and encouraged to give an outlet and a try-out for
the war materials. In any case, this seems to spell
inflation. As to the mode and rhythm of inflation,
as you put it: inflation starts in commodities and
moves to currencies and stock markets. I see copper,
tin, rubber, and wheat up in the next few months.

The French and U.S. governments are one hundred per cent gold covered and so they can increase their credits and currencies to any amount.

In all countries the cost of living and wages must go up, or if not the latter, social insurance must increase. Of course, it is the *rentier* who will again be done in. Interest paying to the nonproductive class of *rentiers* must cease, for this is a type of social insurance we cannot now afford. It will be more economical in some little time from now for the nation to be divided scientifically into the two producing classes. I mean capital and labor. I have been divining this since 1929 and I think the events of the next six months to a year will bear me out.

Naturally there is much speculation; the Continent is busy. It has been my experience that August is one of the busiest months in general but there is no question that this year we will be snowed under.

The May report has caused a lot of discussion and some anxiety. Labor men are anxious about a rumored split and it is believed here that MacDonald will try to go to the country on a split, with a coalition following, to save sterling. But whatever the returns show, my belief is as I said above that some currency history will be written this year.

I hope all is well with you. You mentioned your health. The trip to Greece would be interesting. As for me, I would not be away from London until at least November.

Sincerely,
E. RALPH STEWART

Alphendéry showed this letter to Jules. "You see, he is sure of inflation. Let's send some more of our gold to London. We can make a fortune on the bars of gold we have lying idle here."

"Sure, send it," said Jules. "Ring up the gold brokers and ask them to take care of it."

When William saw the fatal letter, he strolled into Jules. "I say, you didn't sign any contract with Carrière, did you?"

"No," said Jules.

"It's just as well; the beggar seems to have all the clues."

313

"Ah, he's not smart," said Jules. "They all know, don't they? Didn't Léon come here months ago with his check technique? Why, the Swiss banks must turn down a dozen projects a day for selling sterling forward. Everyone knows it. But who can hold out? I'm not going to sell sterling that fool way. I've got my Securities Guarantee Corporation formed by Adam Constant and I've got my gold. I'll make plenty when sterling breaks and I can wait any length of time."

A few days later, E. Ralph Stewart was in Paris and so was Davigdor Schicklgrüber, Lord Zinovraud's man. The news of Bertillon's gold transfers had got round the city somehow, even though no one had broken the seal of professional secrecy. Paul Méline found himself in the bank, quite by accident, trying to place a large block of shares just being brought out by one of his concerns, the Interland Finance Corporation, and Lord Brookings-Plessis tumbled in, in a good humor, to tout and panhandle in his usual profitable way.

Ralph Stewart avoided the crowd and was upstairs on the second floor explaining to Alphendéry, "A few businessmen like myself in the Midlands have formed a secret sort of vigilant committee, to study the present crisis and to suggest and propel any measures that we think should be taken to save the country. The people can't be trusted and should not be trusted with the destinies of a nation like ours in a time like this."

"You don't have to worry," said Alphendéry, "your Labour Party is conservative and your trades-union officials once elected are in by divine right—they can't be kicked out."

Stewart, unlike his usual self, was cool and amused. "They don't suit the fishers in troubled waters, but they don't suit us either. They're in their own political game. You outsiders don't understand English politics. They've kept the country away from prosperity for two and a half years." He flushed and a faint irritation appeared. "If by any accident they remain in or they are returned, we'll use practical measures. We'll withhold credits from them; we'll destroy confidence in the country and send foreign holdings abroad. We'll break the Labour domination one way or another. It wasn't the Labour Party that made England and it hasn't the right to ruin its credit. . . ."

"Why, that may be the City view," said Alphendéry, "but what about the rest of the country? The West, the industrial North, Scotland? The mines?"

"The City is England," said Stewart obstinately.

Scene Forty-five: Christian Stockbroker

"I TOLD you the market would go up," said Ralph Stewart to Alphendéry. "Things couldn't keep at that level. It isn't natural. Was Bertillon still a bear when the market turned up?"

"Not so much," Alphendéry told him. "We cashed in before the turn." This was a lie.

"I'm expanding. I'd like you to come over and see our new premises in Austin Friars: finest in the city. Did that boy of yours—Constant—send you any information? Do you really think he can get anything worth-while like that? I doubt it, I tell you, going there without introductions. Now, if you'd let me take my time and introduce him properly. I hear he was seen down in Shorters' Court with Mulloney from Mulloney and Moonsteyn: showy fellow that Mulloney. Your man actually went round to the jobbers. My dear fellow, that's absolutely not done!" Stewart bridled and reddened at the idea.

"And the jobber told him in fact what we wanted to know about Royal Dutch and C.P.R.," laughed Alphendéry.

"Yes, but my dear fellow, you can't do it—you can't do things that way! No one can see the jobbers, my dear fellow, but ourselves. And we don't see their books!"

Stewart was quite ruffled. Alphendéry began to wonder if he had come to Paris especially to tell him this. But no, his business sense was too good for that. Stewart looked at a pretty woman passing and cleared his throat. "Mme. Bertillon is a handsome woman," he remarked. "I like the European woman—simply can't stand the English woman. They say, Mme. Bertillon has a lot of money in her own name."

315

"I believe she has. She was an heiress."

Stewart was calmer and said with a gleam of humor, "Financial types are divided into two: those who end by ossifying, preserving, and protecting their estate; those who create eternally and so disappear without leaving anything but crusts behind. In this business it is old age which appears to have the temperament suitable for money survival—mean, narrow, querulous, hard, and conserving. Unpleasant, isn't it? Now, Bertillon I don't take to be that type?"

His little trip, thought Alphendéry, is to test our solvency or see what good clients we may be: nothing else—and of course, everyone relishes an excuse for a trip to Paris. While he was pondering this and fishing for a reply—it was hot, the air was blossomy, ripe, Stewart went on pregnantly, "There are only two ways of getting on in life—have so much money that you can tell everyone to go to hell or owe so much that you can tell everyone to whistle for it."

"I am certain Jules is in one of those positions," laughed Alphendéry, slyly looking up at the tall choleric Englishman.

"I've got a smart young fellow in this week," pursued Stewart. "David Cohen, twenty-five. I have much more faith in Jews: they rarely let a Gentile down, always Jews, if anyone. But I've been in business all my life and never found them dishonest; quite the contrary. Of course, my opinion is not too popular. But I make my own. He was on the *Commercial and Financial Chronicle,* worked in some Yankee firm too, knows transatlantics backwards, and we'll have a big business in them later on, when things look bad in Europe and better in England and America. Now, I'll tell you frankly, Alphendéry, I don't believe in stealing the best men of other firms, but I always try to if I have a good excuse. Bertillon's-very-nice-fellow" (he suddenly said, apparently all in one syllable) "but-don't-know-if-h'm-his-position-neither-do-you, neither-does-anyone. The-point-is-that-if-you-want-to-change, that's-what-I-mean-and-want-to-throw-in-your-lot-with-us-and-can bring-some-of-those-accounts, when they're thinking of moving to London, you know. I'll be more than delighted to have you. Most extraordinary sympathy Englishmen have for you."

"Well, thanks very much." Alphendéry was touched.

"Of course, just now, I couldn't. Jules is a funny fellow and would take it as desertion. That's what makes it difficult. If it comes to that, I'll come in with you—on some serious basis, of course."

"Certainly, a junior partner, something like that. Naturally depends on the kind of accounts."

"A lot of people love me," said Alphendéry, "but between loving me and handing me their accounts is an Atlantic."

The little pink lip, the little scrub mustache over the rat teeth trembled irritably, but no, Stewart was smiling and his eyeglasses were dancing. "I have confidence in you, Michel. H'm, h'm, Bertillon reminds me of a firm I worked with before the war—Incarnat, Oliver, and Company. You must have heard of them, although you were a boy then. Still, they made quite a name for themselves. Had a capital of about three million pounds, some days more, some days less. Every day they put the whole kitty on the table, gambled the whole amount every day: arbitrages, Yankees. They sent more orders for Yankees through London than the whole of the New York market. They made the market in Union Pacific, U.S. Steel—few others." His glasses glittered and his pink sharp face became softer and boyish. "It was exciting, by Jove, despite the risks. I wouldn't mind going through it all again. There were some headaches—but isn't all business headaches?—and nowadays no one gets the thrill we got in those days. My first job. By Jove, we had fun. At one time they had a short position in Union Pacific which exceeded the floating supply in the market! Were they ruined? Not that time. They had to come to terms with them, my dear fellow! The fact that they had oversold alone saved them. They had to come to terms with them: otherwise a world panic would have resulted. They would have been alive yet, but the World War got them. They didn't believe a war was coming. It did. That was the end. They were left nursing a million quid of enemy bonds and stocks with all the markets in the world closed. Bertillon gives me the old familiar tingle when I come into his room. (It's just instinct and I may be wrong.) Only, he's not a partnership. He's one man. A sort of Quixote with a couple of Sancho Panzas and a donkey and it doesn't work. No Sancho Panza ever yet stopped a Quixote from getting his nose broken by a windmill. I sympathize with him. By Jove, yes. The Northwest Mounted, the Chicago gangsters, and a scrimmage in Mespot don't compare with a plunge in stocks. But there'll be another war one of these days and he'll guess wrong. I'm thinking of you, Alphendéry. London will then be the natural deposit bank for all these Continentals; one war scare and they'll fly to us. Why not forestall them? I am. Not now, of course. Even that fellow of yours, Aristide Raccamond, sees it. He wrote to me, you know, offering to throw me business. Not a dull fellow. I see he's one of your directors now."

"He told you so?"

Stewart said nothing without a purpose and now withdrew from his cardcase the card of Aristide Raccamond. He looked at Alphendéry sharply while he studied it.

"Nice card," said Alphendéry.

They reached the Avenue de l'Opéra and after a few minutes' walking came into the Rue d'Antin which runs into the Marché St. Honoré. There is Griffon's, a good restaurant. They entered.

"However," finished Stewart, "that's for you to decide. When the time comes. I suppose it pays you to risk it at present. (It always does.) You have no expenses. A Chateaubriand and peas for me. Shall we have a carafe of Beaujolais?"

Alphendéry took off his glasses, leaned on the table, and looked up, foreshortened, at Stewart, with his admirable large dusky eyes. "For myself, Stewart, no. But I have a wife. A very beautiful lady, elegant and 'aristocratic.' A Central European who feels Paris is outlandish, practically situated in the Atlantic Ocean. She prefers Vienna, Berlin, Brussels. It's not her fault. As a matter of fact," he continued, lower, making a queer face, "she spends most of her time in Brussels where she has two establishments to keep up, one house that she is furnishing and a *pied-à-terre* where she meets Theus, the minister. I presume her latest venture shows economy: she will use one of her own apartments for Theus. The whole of Brussels says that I am the only one who does not know that she is his mistress. And so, out of decency, I remain ignorant. The legend is that she and Theus are the most dashing malpractitioners of love in Brussels. Her library is absolutely stuffed with books on flagellation and sex life in ancient Greece, helped out with a little fortunetelling

318

—a modern lady's library. It's quite amusing. When I last went to see the Brussels office, Theus gave a brilliant dinner. University professors were there, some men of mark from Paris—Blériot the deputy, Tourcarré the physicist, Robert Menikian the financial journalist, a few ministers of the Belgian crown besides, Theus—Mme. Theus —she's a famous pervert, too—the Duchesse de Scheveningen, Estelle my wife, and I. Henri Léon was there too, a dolphin out of water, invited at the request of the reigning beauty, Mme. Cécile Ganse, mistress of a Continental royal personage, and also Léon's mistress. (He followed her all over Europe and finally ran her to earth at Bruges. The Bruges religious processions were on and when she saw them she got so emotional and mystic that she fell right into Léon's arms.) Léon was wretched; so was I. Every soul in the room except Léon was thinking about Theus, Mme. Theus, Estelle, and me. I thought, what the devil? What difference does it make to my reputation if my wife takes lovers? A wife is noble who lets her husband run around with girls and never complains. Why not a man? Ridiculous convention dating back to the harem. I'm not conventional, that's all." He said with regret and some pride, "I was brilliant that evening, Stewart. Even my wife turned her eyes on me a number of times with admiration. For once she saw ministers of the crown, scholars, diplomats, savants admiring me, chiming in; as our wits rose more varied and more harmonious, she began to concede a little respect for me. For naturally she despises me for the disgrace she herself brings me! Naturally, also, she has accepted the popular view of me that I am worthless, clever, but shallow, talented but aimless—that means, I don't care to make big money! A stomach of energy without head or tail or grasp. Women rarely love a man for himself. At least not women of the higher, refined society. They think it beneath them. I wish I had had the sense to marry a working girl."

Stewart was inexpressibly shocked; his fork stayed in the air. But he liked Alphendéry. "You can divorce your wife."

There was commiseration in Alphendéry's face: he smiled, "Poor thing! She's counting on Theus's marrying her. He likes his own wife too well. True, he doesn't sleep with her but he likes her. If I divorce her, where will she be? Poor, silly, vain, spendthrift, dishonest, shameful, beautiful Estelle! Where will she be then? She is not in love with anyone. Where would she be, divorced, adrift on the tides of society, trying to pick her living off men? Where do they all end up? I know a woman here—she has every natural advantage—the mistress of Achitophelous: what a charming, lovable, gracious, beautiful girl! And she is worn to a shadow calculating who's going to marry her next and what to do with her money to make it safe so that one or other of her quondam lovers won't take it back from her and what to do to grind a bit more out of her lovers and how to put up with the rest of her friends who hate her and whom she detests, and how to keep her beauty and late hours and what on earth she's going to do in exactly five years when she's forty! And her answer is—suicide! Of course, I don't think she will. There is still time for more prostitution in the grand manner, and selling herself to dressmakers and wearing new styles in jewelry for jewelers and going a bit to grand houses of rendezvous and scrounging her way on to yachts and in to banquets and wearing out the pity of her friends, and drugs and drink and sanatariums and the inexperience of a couple of young men, and then, perhaps, by the merest luck, some obscure hideous marriage, or mother, or some still loyal brother, and an old age full of lies. She sees it all. And in her I see Estelle. This delightful Mimi comes round to the bank now making a hell of a row if her stocks drop a point: she expects us to make it up to her—and Jules sometimes does, just to stop the noise. She is always sitting on the edge of her statement of account peering for mistakes in percentages, calling us up on the telephone, trying to gouge us, trying to jew us down from two and one-half to one and one-half per cent, trying to get it for nothing, squabbling about ten shares, wetting three handkerchiefs for half a share of stock dividend, outacting three Sarah Bernhardts for the sake of one hundred francs. And still she's a woman, and she once had a life fuller of promise than mine ever was, because of the ease of life for a beautiful woman! I'm sorry for her, I can't help it. I'm here and I forget Estelle. When she's old, I'll send her a little income if I've still got it and if not, she's got her brother and mother. She likes me in a way; she wishes me no harm."

Stewart, with knife and fork poised, said, "If it were

not for the immortality of the soul, life would not be worth living." Alphendéry raised his bespectacled eyes attentively and let them rest on the pink lead-pencil face. Stewart laid down his knife and fork. "I have been in the City since I was a boy of twelve. I like it. I'm a businessman. But if I didn't feel that Jesus Christ was leading me 'towards that distant Aidenn. The endless rough-and-tumble would be insupportable. Don't you agree with me, Michel?"

Alphendéry looked at Stewart's steak with anxiety. He half pointed at it, but desisted, "No, I'm an atheist, Stewart. My father and his father before him were atheists."

"Yes, but whatever you believe in, whatever the Principle is, gives you courage, I mean."

"Oh, yes, there are things I have faith in. Principles." He hesitated and pointed mildly, "Your steak, Ralph—don't let it get cold."

Obediently Stewart took a bite. Alphendéry cautiously, but with insistence, nodded at the glass of wine. Stewart drank some wine, obediently. He went on, "You know, Alphendéry—you know Austin Friars?—I look down from my window and just for a moment, I know there is a haven for me outside all those things. *The Lord is my shepherd, I shall not want. He maketh me to lie down in the green pastures. He leadeth me beside the still waters. He restoreth my soul.*" A rapt expression floated on the sharp, raffish features. Alphendéry looked round. *"He prepareth a banquet for me in the presence of mine enemies,"* went on Stewart, *"and I will dwell in the House of the Lord for ever.* I see it before me, there in Austin Friars, you know, the pastures, the still waters. That gives me comfort. That was why I took the places in Virginia Water and on Lake Windermere. I—"

Alphendéry slid in, *sotto voce,* "Your steak, Stewart."

He ate, chewing it thoughtfully, "This steak! Why is it so fine, Michel? Because the cow itself delights in green pastures. Poor beast. I suppose it spent a few happy months before it was led to the slaughterhouse. I never could hold with the vegetarians. I want you to come down to my place over the weekend, next time you come to London, Michel. I go to church twice on Sunday. The service is Anglican, but I go because it's the only church near and the singing is so good. But the Anglicans sing praises of their Redeemer through stiff collars."

Alphendéry, with an amazed look, as of a man who finds himself sleepwalking, motioned to the waiter.

"You'll like it," insisted Stewart. "Strawberries and cream for me, please. It's simply extraordinary how I like strawberries. They give some people a rash. By Jove, those are fine specimens, aren't they? Some have been gathered with white tips, of course. A thing that should never be done. A strawberry should be eaten straight off the soil: it loses its taste after a few hours. Good, these. It's because, I suppose, there are no fresh ones to compare them with. You'll like the Sunday-morning service, even though it's quite High Church, very snobbish in fact. I disapprove of anything High Church: Banners, Vestments. No, most amazing how Protestants can stomach it. These strawberries are really good. I had no idea the French had such strawberries. Well, what did Richard Ford say, 'We can't beat the Continent at two things—dancing and pastry'? Do you like strawberry jam, Michel? My housekeeper puts up very good strawberry jam. It's all a question of the amount of sugar put in and the sealing. The pots should be sealed with paraffin, dated, and used in sequence. I put in the sugar myself."

"I don't like sweets, Stewart; they're fattening."

"Yes." He took a sip of coffee, made a face, took another sip. He began to gobble. "Strange you're not a Christian, religious I mean, Alphendéry. A man and his philosophy are all of one piece, of course. No one has a right to know what passes between a man and his Maker. You always struck me as a man of principle—feeling, too. Very much so! At home in my garden, I like to ponder these things, in the weekend: questions of life and death, immortality, our destiny. There's a very good book, I must lend you—you'd like it. *Our Duty to God, Man, and Ourselves,* by Timothy Bletherall. A man is all alone in this world."

"Yes, he is alone unless he interests himself in man's fate." Alphendéry sat up straight.

"Quite so," said Stewart, not listening, "and it seems to me that the reason the English have their Empire is that they are true Christians."

"I beg pardon!" Alphendéry caught himself up. "You

...mean they believe firmly they're doing the right thing, no matter what."

"Exactly," agreed Stewart eagerly. "Look at the missionaries we send out to savages and heathens, Mohammedans, and Chinese; look at India. How else do we hold India? God in our work. Not only bearing a Bible but a plowshare. The most successful colonists in the world—in history, my dear fellow! We have been blessed with the fruits of the earth. *The earth is the Lord's and the fulness thereof. The world and they that dwell therein. For he hath founded it upon the Seas. This is the generation of them that seek him.* You see, amazingly apt. I take off my hat whenever I pass in front of the Royal Exchange and see that: *The earth is the Lord's and the fulness thereof.* There is always something amazingly inspiring about the crossing at the Bank of England. *He is the King of glory.* You see what we English feel is that the Empire is a dedication: the proof as well as offering of our service to Jesus Christ. You know the parable of the one talent and the ten talents. . . . Hey, boy, *garçon, un journal.* What's the name of the sheet?"

Alphendéry, slowly waking from a nightmare, said with a pale face, *"Paris-Midi."*

"Odd little rag. So unlike our English press. 'Farmer Finds a Corpse in Well.' Real French news, eh?"

Alphendéry, with the soft crumpling spring of a baby leopard, seized one sheet as it fell and devoured the noon stock prices. "Woe is me, Alhama!" Stewart looked severely at him. Alphendéry shook his head, "I'm afraid most of our bear customers have lost money. I'll have to call for margins. That Raccamond will be scuttling for cover. He nearly dies of fright when his customers lose. I always have to face the embattled comtesses and 'rectify' their accounts. They also always think that God is—or should be—always on their side. And if not God, their banker."

"Eh?" said Stewart.

"I mean, to get rich or powerful a man has to have God working for him," said Alphendéry cryptically. "I mean history."

"Ah," Stewart shook his head archly, "you call it history; I call it God. But we think the same, Michel; I rather thought so." He was pink with satisfaction.

Scene Forty-six: Friend of the King

THEY taxied back to the bank, through the hot, asphalted streets, crumby with people, cars, scaffoldings. "I met the King of Spain once," said Stewart. "He's a charming fellow really. Good businessman. Of course, the family has this disease, haemophilia. If he gets a scratch he bleeds profusely. Dreadful, isn't it? One would have to be careful. These overrefined old strains, you know. Comes from Louis XIV or someone like that, doesn't it? Probably a legend. You know their lives must be a mass of legend. I shouldn't like to be a king; most uncomfortable. Our royal family, of course, has always been so clean; no trace of any hereditary weakness, like these Continental families. Murthen met the King, our King, I mean, of course. In fact, he's quite a friend of the King, as much as one can be of a man like that whose entire life is public. In fact (you won't repeat this?), we've done a fair amount of business for the King on several occasions. Not for him directly, of course. And Murthen says he's really a delightful soul, virile, of course, absolutely practical, not at all unworldly as you might suppose, surrounded by chamberlains and not hearing the facts. But the King insists on reading the daily papers and acquaints himself with everything he comes in contact with, meets people, reads the stock-exchange prices; most creditable, isn't it? And so simple, Murthen says, not a bit of put-on. It's really rather wonderful. I think we English are to be congratulated on the way we manage the whole business. No frill and yet full dignity. Now, our King, Murthen says, if someone said to you, 'That's the KING OF ENGLAND,' you'd say, 'Not a bit of it: that's plain Jack Windsor!' It's all so simple, done without any fuss and frill."

"You've got to be careful with the King," mused Alphendéry. "He'll be a danger one of these days like all stale, rotten institutions. One party or another will use him and then one class or another will have to get rid of the whole family."

Stewart smiled pityingly. "The English don't think like that."

"No? Your name is funny."

Stewart flushed. "Yes, once, as a lesson, but never again. We originate: we don't repeat." He tittered as if at a very good joke.

"There's William just coming back from his beer and sausages," said Alphendéry delightedly looking out the taxi window as if he and William had been separated for a year. "Don't be misled by his manner, Stewart: he's a wonderful fellow, the soul of the bank—one of its souls. It has a soul, a ghost, a wraith, a spook, a double, a reflection, and a shadow, like an old Jew. He's the soul. Pretends to be thorny but that's all part of his game—his game in life, I suppose. He acts the crusty bachelor but his pockets are warm and wet with generosity. Really I never met such a foolishly, even nauseatingly generous man. After the first few months I got to love William."

They stood on the doorstep. "Silly notion to act like that all the same." Stewart was irritated. "You ought to speak to him, Alphendéry. It's all so simple. He-can-think-what he-likes, no-need-to-say-it. He was down there this morning saying a lot of darn silly things. Jules Bertillon, too." He turned, offended, away from the entrance hall and looked out into the cool street. The sun lay overhead; the leaves in the Rothschild garden hung like sunbathing philosophers, shone but made no sound, asleep.

As they entered Stewart said, "A cosmopolitan crowd." Alphendéry exclaimed, "Jules with his imaginative schemes, lavish spending, gay antics, disordered gilded postwar harlequinade, his playing bowls when the Armada is sailing down on him, appeals to these war boys, who have never settled down from flying, thieving, rampaging, giving orders, camping with the boys, raping the girls, spending their leave in cabarets and all the other sublunacies of the day, as it saw the sun fourteen short years ago. These rich young men had a grand spree then and they never want to grow up. Jules understands them. They flock to him. He will not grow up and accept his fate. He always reserves for himself in the future some great sunburst noon when he'll play truant. I don't think he could change. Out of his setting he would lose money. At present he doesn't seem able to. He's coining money."

"And also paving the streets with it," said Stewart.

Alphendéry started and laid his hand on Stewart's arm. "He has private orders with you?"

"Big ones," said Stewart. "Some days Bertillon makes the market in London and in New York in certain stocks." His voice dropped to a whisper.

"Good afternoon, Etienne," said Alphendéry. "Any letters for me?"

"Yes, sir. Here."

"Rosenkrantz and Guildenstern: their usual! This letter," Alphendéry showed a five-page, close-written spiderweb scrawl, "is from one of our lunatics. Do you get many?"

"Oh, dozens of them. He wants money. They're lunatics but they act like clockwork. They're so mad that they all want the one thing and it's the same thing that you and I want, but they want it with a decision and energy that I'd like to see in my clerks but not in my competitors. There's method in madness. I just throw them in the wastepaper basket. Never write to them. Never write to anyone. A mistake in business. No letters. It's all so simple then."

"Poor Légaré!—he was born with that name!—all he wants is five hundred thousand francs. Now a sane blackmailer, Stewart, asks for ten thousand and settles for two thousand." He looked at the letter. "He says that we really owe him a couple of millions, but knowing what sadistic ruffians we are, he'll settle for one hundred thousand."

"Or else he'll go to the Criminal Investigation Division," Stewart commented bitterly.

"Naturally."

"Whenever I see a man of mine getting discontented or moody, unless it's his wife, I send him to a doctor and if it isn't his liver or his lungs I sack him. Even then I usually do. I don't give him time to kill the goose that lays the golden eggs. Send him packing before he has a sense of injustice. It's really quite simple. Can't stand stupidity or animal resentment in man or beast, woman, dog, or horse. Sulks are the black flag of blackmail."

"Légaré seemed quite bright on the contrary," lamented Alphendéry. "I liked that man. Now he's turned against me, too."

"Be kinder if you could shut them up the minute they started getting poky."

"I'm not much of an authority on madness. Everyone has his lunacies. Suppose you told Breton fishermen that in Paris men sit all day watching figures jumping on a blackboard, some red, some white, and, some yellow, and that they throw away on red, yellow, and white chalk dust a fisherman's annual pay, enough to keep a miner and his family in comfort, enough to pay him an old-age pension from forty on and that they think heaven should reward them for their labor in watching the figures jump a thousand times as much as heaven rewards the fisherman for risking his life in storms at sea, wouldn't those fishermen think those Parisians quite mad?"

"If you put it that way, I suppose. You're quite a socialist, aren't you, Alphendéry?"

"I favor socialist organization," said Michel.

Stewart bit his lip. "You mean, Alphendéry, business should be organized. I quite agree. Fishermen—"

"Don't tell me what I mean, Ralph," cried Alphendéry. "I mean a revolution to wipe us all out, all of us who scrounge on others and ravage the wealth of the world—you and Jules Bertillon and me. We must all go."

"No," said Stewart, "of course not. I'm quite in sympathy with new methods myself. I think new brooms should sweep clean. I came into business without any backing myself, and got on through being with a new firm of young men. I quite agree that old firms should be broken up, like old models. And I suppose we are—even you and me—more or less old models, compared with, say, a Jules Bertillon." He looked dubious and became thoughtful. "But big interests use men like that to conceal their hand?" He searched Alphendéry's face. "Jules Bertillon is very mysterious."

While Alphendéry stayed down in the stock-exchange room, he went up to see Jules Bertillon, very much put out, rattled; ill at ease, and he scarcely knew why. He said to Jules, "Alphendéry was just talking of the Five-Year Plan and although I think state socialism is a monstrous mistake—machine planning, the draftsman, can never take into account the psychology of the market, the question of supply and demand—for if a man could foresee that, how would we make a living? Still, as I was saying, it is true that peasants have no idea of getting the most out of the land. Look at all the time they've been working the land, since the Middle Ages!" He looked round, feeling something cold at his back, and saw Alphendéry's shrewd expression and half-smile as he came through the door. Irritably, he added a codicil, "This childish idea of making the law for the rich and the poor the same: it's absurd, they haven't the same responsibilities! As well make the same door for a stable and a kennel."

Jules, who regarded Stewart as a serious bore, and always thought of everyone in his game as a grafter with grappling irons and nothing more, fixed a bright glance on him and let his thoughts wander.

Jules began to whistle softly, being in the fever of some new scheme. He wished Stewart would go. Trying to get him to buy back his position. Idiot. Did he think he ever sold them really? Did he think the world wasn't going to smash, British Empire or no? Did he think the Union Jack could keep the market up just by giving a sodden flap? Stupid Englishman. He imagined a Frenchman could never work out *his* schemes. Well, Stewart came to Paris for his own good. Let him rave. "I'll bet there's a good graft in pesetas in Gibraltar. Say, don't you think you ought to send Constant down to Gibraltar? He looks Spanish and speaks English. They say the hotel business is booming in London now, Stewart, expecting the barons of Spain to take refuge in their royal suites for a while. Gee, how those boys can rob! They don't have to pay anything back to their peons, practically. A lesson for our boys, with their social-insurance schemes. They keep on taking it out of the soil and they put nothing back, not so much as a sou of fertilizer. They're bright babies! Why don't we learn something? We've got to get the world down to a pauper economy: all the same-color pants, all the same paper hats, all the same rope shoes, like the Spaniards. Jesus, the Duke of Alva makes more every year than I make with all my tricks. Now, take the Duke. He has about one hundred thousand peons, Zurbaran told me. Say he gets two pesetas out of them a day, on the average all through the year. How much is that a year, Michel?" He started to write on his block. "I'm just working it out, Stewart. A second. Don't talk about the peasants," he laughed at Stewart. "We're the ones who are ninnies. I say, Stewart, I want to tell you something. A stone crop makes a lot of money for the landlord, don't worry. Michel, two pesetas surplus value a day."

"What sort of value, did you say?" queried Stewart, stiff but mystified.

"Oh, ask Alphendéry. That's a swell phrase of Alphendéry, meaning they squeeze two pesetas by taking a pint of their blood every day and rendering it down. When it boils right down there's two pesetas there." His wild, eerie laughter rang round the room. "Now, Michel, say they all work all the year. It's good land, isn't it? Christ above, that's seventy million pesetas a year, every year, not counting what they've got saved up from centuries of stealing—and they pass their own laws and that they're all in the army." He looked warmly desirous, with shining eyes. "What a game, Michel! I've been a fool all my life, working my brains out in dark rooms, trying to scoop the stock exchange. Upon my word, Michel, I'm beginning to think the original, stupid, caveman, Abraham-and-Isaac rackets are the best."

"The old Jews returned the land to the people every fifty years," Alphendéry murmured hastily. Jules took no notice.

"What are we wasting our time here for, Stewart, spending all our lives sweating in dark board rooms and dirty streets, with sad little chiselers setting private dicks on our tracks, with haughty girls that come screeching for profits straight from the latest title they've whored for? We could go out, sit in the sun, squat on a big bit of land, and set some poor dumb peasants to work and sit back and collect the rent out of the clods of sticky, wormy brown dirt. Isn't there some country left, Alphendéry, where you can go out and get the government to throw selections at you free if you introduce a few sheep? Do we make seventy million pesetas a year? No, we're pikers, Stewart, that's what we are. I don't say Alphendéry here, for he doesn't care for dough—he's mad—but you and I, Stewart, spend our whole lives dreaming about it, and getting indigestion for it. And where does the Duke of Godoy sit? Not here. No sir! He sits in Cannes, Hendaye, and Barcelona and lets the monkey men grub for him. They do it, too. Ask my boys downstairs to run the bank and send me the profits, and they'll all have worked out by tomorrow afternoon some scheme for stealing my money—but there's a mystery in the earth. No one wants to run away from it. And they think in terms of clods. They never think of robbing him of one little peseta."

"No?" said faraway the musing voice of Alphendéry, but Jules didn't hear it.

"Listen, Stewart. You think I'm a nitwit, don't you, because I have in my bank all this flossy crowd of young milkbellies. But they've got the easy, perennial, soft, regular, steep dough, Stewart. Because they all come from primitive lands where those peons grub for them in the sun. It doesn't depend on a turn of the market and they're not mean. They don't care whether your accountant, who has cancer, left out ten francs or not. That's the crowd to be with, Stewart. And if your sons go with the huntin' and fishin' and ridin' sets, you're lucky. That's the big money."

"Not in England: there's been a change," said Alphendéry, softly, unheeded.

"Listen, Michel, what do you say to hiring a fleet of wherries to pick up the Spanish refugees while the scare is still on and they're still running away?"

"Idiotic," said Michel. "What do you think there is, a reign of terror?"

Jules sighed. "Don't get peevish, Michel. If I didn't have crazy ideas, sometimes, I'd go crazy. You can tell how sane a man is by the number of crazy ideas he has. Be careful of a man who's always solemn. Either he's religious or he hates you. In either case he'll blackmail you. Like that Raccamond. Wish I could sell him to someone."

The conversation languished. Jules meditated. Stewart, nervous as a filly, sat upright in his pale gray suit and looked pink: his small blue eyes dilated and shifted with a hesitating intention. "I say," said Jules, having lost his spring, "Stewart, we've all got to think up some new dodges." He revived. "Tons of money changing hands: some of it ought to go on our weighbridge. I want to see some real money. That's it," Jules cried, his long hands, white collar, long money-sniffing nose with the gambler's drop of flesh pendent at the end, all coming together into a composition of sober acuity. "While it's on the wing, you whistle to it, see! That's not hard luck, that's good luck. Why, if all their money were safely tied up in government funds, Indian Railways, Shanghai tramcars, Argentine meat, thriving estates, safe percentages, sure crops, priest-ridden patient brutes of peasants, if there were no soviets, no Red propaganda, only Nicholas and Alfonso and God, only Alva and Medina-Sidonia still on their thrones drinking the dew off the mountains, all the water out of the rivers, where would a man like me be? I shouldn't have a bean. But as it is—the storm is good for wreckers, the river that changes its course over the sands lets prospectors go down and find the specks of gold in the shifting bed. I don't believe, Stewart, that there's any sense in spending one minute lamenting about the age of unrest. All ages have been ages of unrest. Haven't they, Michel? Michel knows: he told me all about it. Money was never safe. It's too valuable." He laughed. "Any more than a beautiful virgin is safe. Everyone wants it. You always had to protect money with mantraps, laws, and the militia. I wouldn't give a halfpenny to have the prewar world here again, Stewart. Surely, I don't object to the restoration of a monarchy or anything like that. Do you know why, Stewart? Because every time a king is put back he makes new nobles, and new chaps get the money. He doesn't put the old crowd back: no fear. He doesn't want that grudging jealous lot with boundary-fence complaint. He wants a new crowd, everyone of whom will be grateful to him. Well, what is that? Another transfer of funds. Another lot of sanguine money that can be easily brought into your paddock. I say, what's the matter with you fellows sitting round groaning it's not worth while making money? I wouldn't own a gold mine today. I don't have to mine my gold."

Alphendéry's low voice broke in, "A private banker has to watch his step though, Jules. When the Crédit Lyonnais goes broke, it's a patriotic duty to support it out of taxes. When we go kaput, it's a patriotic duty to see we take a taxi to the Santé. If you don't join up with the big boys, they'll scuttle you."

"I know, I know," said Jules irritably. "That's where you make a big mistake, Stewart, with your king business. They'll have to get rid of the king to have an exchange of dough; they won't want to afford a king and all his grandsons and nieces, soon. Too many unemployed to keep already."

"You don't know my people," Stewart remarked with a trace of pity.

"Of course, they'll lose their jobs." Jules flung out his hand. "Ptt! You don't think they're going to spend another hundred years working their bottoms off for a chap who doesn't even know their names, do you?" Stewart shrugged his shoulders and bit his lips. Jules smiled but in a moment, impatient, cried, "Big money! This isn't getting us anywhere. One-quarter per cent, one-half per cent, even two per cent! I want highflying cash, beautiful cash, in platoons, in platoons, zooming; I want it big, rich, and plentiful, and all mine. And I will get it, by heck." He got up restlessly, longing like a girl in love, looked at his half-empty bookcases. "I don't like these empty shelves, Michel. We've got to fill them. I want you to do that for me. Tomorrow! Send Adam Constant a couple of hundred pounds and tell him to scour the bookshops in London and get all the classics—banking, everything. I want it to look like a big-time show. Tomorrow you go down to the Rue Jacob and—you know best and get about—three hundred books. All good: only get the very best writers and the classics. I don't want any second-rate stuff. No simili-backs. That'll frighten them." He paced, took positions. "I'll arrange the light this way. Take that big Italian candlestick away, Michel. I look like the Pope. One is enough. I'll put the luster on full to see. This chair here. Like that. How do you think it looks, Stewart? And the shelves full of books. Yes. Do that, Michel. Don't forget."

"The ginks who come in here can't read," Michel said tartly.

"It would be quite effective," Stewart considered.

"That's the idea; fool them, impress them, flatter them, take away their money, eh, Stewart?" He was feverish.

Stewart's restless intention gushed out. He lifted his nose so that his eyes were out of Jules's line of vision, reconsidered, brought them back again. Boring into Jules's now impatient eyes, Stewart began to babble a word twenty syllables long: "When-Christ-cast-the-moneychangers-out-of-the-Temple, he-cast-no-imputations-on: the prohibition against usury was a tenet of the Old Testament. Usury, as Jeremy Bentham shows, only arises when it is prohibited. Christ said, 'Render unto Caesar that which is Caesar's'; he himself took money from a fish's belly. There is nothing unclean about money as such. In my own office I discourage light cynicism about finance. Take the custom of wearing top hats into the city, for bank clerks and stockbrokers' clerks! It gives finance dignity! There are too many outside the city, who ignore finance and commerce, their alpha and their omega, who talk about filthy lucre; but finance is the heart's blood of the national economy as London is the heart of a great commonwealth of peoples. The people see a bank clerk wearing a top hat and a morning coat in the tube in the morning. They know he's poor but he has the dignity of the power, experience, wealth of the men who rule the nation. They know they couldn't run the nation. And so respect on respect, you keep order in the country."

He was deadly serious; he looked at Jules, who smiled in his sleeve.

"Another thing . . . I don't like a loose discussion on general principles. If a clerk of mine says to me, 'I see the market is wobbly,' I make him show me the exact paragraph, the exact quotation. If he says, 'I see there's going to be investment in real estate,' the same thing. Loose discussion enervates in master or man; it takes the mind off the immediate job. What is the good of trying to take a ramble in the middle distance? Ramble on your own garden path."

He gobbled a little. "They get to think they can make money by easy, slick, even fraudulent," he said with immense distaste, "even fraudulent methods, by all sorts of chicane, and the human mind is too impregnated with that by nature. We have only ourselves to blame," he said in a lower tone and giving Jules an accusing look. "The worship of the ruling classes saves money. Things get done in our country without upheaval, without petition, without questions in Parliament. Our nation is a business nation. The ruling minds do not waste money on philanthropy or the arts or the theater, the way they do on the Continent. The people can see they are intent on their business. They respect them for it. England is the greatest taxmaster with the least frill and the fewest lackeys," he said with deeprooted patriotic pride. "We do not have to buy our servants. An Englishman is proud to serve. Here people certainly think that they have every right to chatter day and night about other people's affairs. Ignorant reformers and poor get-on-quick demagogues from the lower orders are too prone to that sort of thing by nature and it is the lack of tradition and classic principle in themselves, a sort of catchpenny, basic cynicism about themselves and other men, due to lack of education, which keeps them where they were born, poor and unsuccessful. They end up in jail for all their catch phrases and misleading the poor workers!

"Let them preach to each other in quod. No one likes his own medicine. England is the most orderly state in Europe, absolutely free; why, we haven't even got a constitution! No need for one, my dear fellow. They even allow atheists and radicals to sit in Parliament—godless men don't have to take their Bible oath. That is really the limit of toleration. It's amusing to see how intelligent men of the people learn as they get on in public life. For England welcomes talent. Yes, indeed, bastards, Jews, foreigners get on in England. Socialists even. Take Mac-Donald. He began by denouncing everything in sight—God, king, and country, for all I know, church, army, and state: they were lenient to him and he learned and because he had ability they allowed him to get to the highest seats, my dear fellow. It's very simple, if you'll look at it this way. Now, the more experience he had of public life, the less rabid he became, the less ridiculous." He flushed. "Until finally, by God, he's almost a gentleman. They say, he's a friend of the King. What can a coal miner down in the dark chipping at a lump of rock know about governing a mighty nation? What do you people expect your country to be like with a change of government every three days? England isn't some beggarly wild state, full of peasants and turnips like Russia: it's a society of nations, by Jove. Imagine a coal miner from Merthyr Tydfil trying to run the League of Nations!" He tittered.

Alphendéry said bitterly, "Don't be so sure, Stewart: you have seen your best days. Nothing that can happen now can benefit the British Empire. It can only disgorge."

"Your brother downstairs this morning said something that I would never allow in my place, not even if Murthen said it," Stewart discharged upon them, testily coming to his point.

"What was it?" Jules asked idly.

"He said, 'You can only make petty cash in the market now. No one runs a roulette wheel when it's losing. They'll close the stock exchange one of these days, when they find out there are too many wise to the fact that the end of the world's coming.' He was advising a client."

Jules laughed. "Who was it?"

"I don't know. A little man and a little woman in a fur coat."

The forelegs of Jules's chair came down: "The Hallers! Oh, don't worry about them. They think the same. Besides, my dear fellow, they've haunted our stock-exchange room for six years, got our information, and always placed their orders with Cleat, Placket, and Company."

"Just what I say," shrugged Stewart. "They lose, confidence."

Jules laughed, flirted the leaves of his gilt-edged diary. "No, we give no tips; on the other hand Cleat, Placket, and Company always give bullish information and it gives Haller a special pleasure to bet against them on the bear side. Do you want to know his maxim? A bull market is the quickest way to sell the public nothing at a high price, and then blame it on them." Jules looked at Stewart, balancing the paper knife; he was tempted and he fell.

"Ah! Ah? How are gold shares? I hear the Union Corporation is very secretive and making money. I don't believe in silver myself. But the silver talk is a bad sign. One hundred francs it's off before midnight, October thirty-first, this year, Stewart."

"All right, Bertillon."

"And cover those Phillips' Petroleum."

"I've telephoned that this morning."

"I'm still carrying Royal Dutch and Steaua Romana. I'll see next settlement. Telephone me every day."

"All right, Mr. Bertillon. Good-by. Good-by, Alphendéry." Stewart left.

"You have a big position in London," said Michel curiously.

"Uh-huh."

"Your bet on the pound. What about your bet with Carrière? You're betting both ways."

"Most people want to bet both ways all the time." Jules shouldered off any more questions. "Stewart! The English are not hypocritical—it's not true. They have a natural, ingrained double face from birth! They're the Western Chinese, Michel: old and smooth with deceit. They gabble along in their chop-suey language and you only get a word here and there. You have to think as if you're in a chess game. You've got to think: when an Englishman says, 'Ah-ha,' he really means part of the declension of 'te-he' and only that part that's out of date

335

and that really applies solely to Indian currency that's slightly chipped. God and Mr. Stewart run the Empire! Talk to an Englishman half a day and then go to a booby house to hear mother sense. But he's right, in his own way. If there were a God he'd be more like Rockefeller than Ramsay MacDonald."

And Stewart, when he got home, said to Murthen, "I enjoy a jaunt to Paris but the French are the most disorganized people in the world. Very bizarre people. You can never know what they'll bring out next. Perfect anarchists the way they think. Of course, there was no soap in the hotel, and I forgot to take any. I wish they'd get into the English system of bathrooms. There was a bathroom, of course, but the soap shows they're not used to them."

This was the latest cross-verdict from two peoples who have been facing each other for only a couple of thousand years.

"Listen, Jules," said William that night at home, "what's this I hear about Royal Dutch and the rest? If you run a bucket shop, never bet on the game yourself. The trouble is that you have a best seller, Jules, in your bank. The cover and the title alone sell the book. But when they open it, there's nothing inside. First you're a bear on the market, then you become too clever and become a bear on the whole world; next you're a bear on yourself, too. Where are you going, Jules? Don't speculate, Jules."

"Shut up, William: I know my business."

"Yes? What is your business?"

"I'm selling for Legris, too."

"Heaven above! They'll stick you for the whole raspberry bush, one day."

"I operate through them, without margin," smiled Jules.

"When did you start this cat's cradle?"

"A little while ago."

"Jules, you must tell me how you stand!"

"Yes? You think so? Leave me alone, William. After you and Alphendéry made me lose a fortune, not letting me skip the other day, I've decided to run things myself. This is my bank," he finished insolently, coldly.

William looked him over, smiled faintly and shrugged

his shoulders. "All right. I'll be here to pick up the pieces."

Jules mused, "When you come to think of it, a bank's creditors should be fined when the banker skips. Their credulity undermines financial security!"

"Why be smart?" complained William. "It's easy to make money. Take the client's money and let him die on you: that's all. You're like the rest: every financier is always waiting for the grand coup. The only grand coup that comes is his last act. . . . What's the use of making so much money? You can get more credit on a million-dollar debit than on having your place stuffed with gold from skirting to cornice."

"Credit has a home. It has an address. You can't fly with credit. That's the difference."

"Well, I'll see you tomorrow. I'm dead tired. Night-night."

"Goo' night. What makes you so sleepy?"

Jules got no answer. In fifteen minutes William was lying like a log in his gloomy, concierge-touched bachelor home. The street lamp through a crack in the drawn curtains fell on the night coverings of his sole companion—the sleeping Chinese nightingale.

Scene Forty-seven: Jules Dreams

MICHEL ALPHENDÉRY wore his good-luck red tie for two months, and Jules had good ideas every day. The morning after William's visit, Jules came into the bank bright and early after a brisk canter on his favorite chestnut mare and he went like an arrow to Alphendéry's room, where he produced a slip of typewritten paper, and seating himself, began to expound the ideas he had had the night before in bed. "At least one of them will be a gold mine." The slip of paper read—

sluggle tobacco navy
yahcht for getting lire out of Italy
snake CPR out of bank affiliates—write country laxyers
incorporare ho:ding company Deliaware

write Léon his scheme Dutch
Verger du côte-Vert
Sell Int. Nickel also United Cigar
Reno plan Monte-Carlo
consortum of richissimes

"I'm a type," Jules explained, "who succeeds with success. To make money I have to have confidence and to have confidence I have to make money. When I bear the market I am against the boobies and that gives me confidence. The stock market is like love! Most people begin by taking a flier and end by supporting it. That's why the bear is always right. Now, I want to get through this before William comes in with his wise saws: he nearly made me sick last night. He has absolute proofs that nothing whatever can pay. Listen, there's big money in smuggling tobacco into France."

"That's everyone's first get-rich scheme," Michel commented, "but go on."

"Don't form an opinion right away, Michel. I've got a grand idea. Get it smuggled in by the navy. They're always making trips to Smyrna and so on. Who suspects the navy? Who inspects it? All you do is pay some petty officer commission; he can get a trusty sailor, and there you are. And they come right in alongside, no customs. And I say, wouldn't it be better to get it brought in in a submarine? You know how sailors hate submarines. I'll bet they don't care what they do against the regulations to get a little dough. Every time they put to sea, every time they go through their exercises, they face death by drowning, suffocation, or collision. Sailors of the surface marine have a hundred chances to their one. A lieutenant would never be questioned."

"What are the risks? The lieutenant would be court-martialed and you'll get—five years, is it?—for smuggling."

"Is it smuggling? Smuggling is evading the customs. But there are no customs for a submarine. I'll pay a fine, that's all, and I won't get jail. I'll get a good lawyer, instead. No, I'm sure it's not smuggling. I'll get Pierrot to look it up."

"If you tell Pierrot, you're sunk, without any submarine. I want to make a little chart of Pierre's benefits to us, one day, just to look at when I feel downhearted.

There was the lease he made for us in the Rue de Châteaudun. Maître Friesz in Amsterdam collects rare legal documents: I've been thinking of selling him that lease—it must be unique in the history of French law. There was nothing too good for the landlord—a repeating nine-year lease for a one-room office and the rent fixed not in francs but in relation to gold. The lawyer on the other side must be the one who draws up the reorganizations of the Banque de France."

"Well, I'll tell him to consult with another lawyer," Jules conceded. "The next speaks for itself. There are plenty of fishing boats hanging about the coast that do a trade in rescuing refugees. You could do a double business: smuggle out lire for the refugees from their relatives; smuggle it in for commerce. Swimmers can go backwards and forwards with waterproof bags. I have a yacht I could use."

"Smuggle number two. However, go on, it's a fine morning."

Jules laughed and cast a glance at Michel: "The only reason I'm in business is to stop me from going crazy, Michel."

"You'd better work harder then."

"I'm serious, Michel. We've got to make money. We can't sit round listening to William's petty-cash fairy tales. What do you think now? He wants to go into cheap bazaars with Daniel Cambo. He'll be opening a haberdashery department downstairs soon. Ptt! That may entrance William but not two abstract money types like you and me."

"Go on, Jules: I'm listening."

"You know, last time I was in England I noticed that every bank has a sort of trust company affiliated with it and big wads of the best trust shares are held in its nominees department. If you could get them on deposit you could sell the market to a fare-thee-well and never be short. Then we might get some lawyer in England to get up a scheme for appealing to family solicitors—the sort that are always tempted to embezzle, those who manage small estates and trust funds or act as guardians, and invite them to deposit with us, say, C.P.R. and Royal Dutch shares. We could then sell the market and have a large supply. You simply give the lawyer a percentage. We could form a holding company and pay them a decent interest, say, one-half per cent—not too much—over bank rate. It would be a good investment for them and we would have a practically unlimited supply. England is clogged with widows and orphans living on embalmed shares."

"That has points," said Alphendéry. "Why not write to Adam Constant while he is still in England and ask him to see Ledger, Ledger, and Braves. We'll have to see what can be done. Perhaps nothing can be done. It's much like our guarantee scheme. That's bright! How about taking Stewart into your confidence: someone's got to sell for you, and he won't do it too far unless he knows you've got the supply. He could help you. You know the English private-interest octopus: you've got to have a façade."

"Oh, we'll buy up some old company through Ledger and Braves. Now, 'Incorporate holding company Delaware'—oh, I have to remind Pierre Olympe to get up the forms on that company I told you about and pay the tax. Listen, what was Stewart raving about—jobbers? How about forming our own company of jobbers and seesawing our own stock account. It's legal. And worth millions if it's properly run. That may be the great stroke we've been waiting for, Michel! Your red tie brings me luck."

"I need a new one."

Jules frowned. "It might change my luck: don't—to please me, Michel. Well—I want you to write to Léon. He just sent me a letter saying two Amsterdam merchants who want to start a private bank are willing to buy me out if I'll give them a private statement properly certified. I want Léon to come down and see me about it. I guess he's one of them? And tell him to put it all down clearly on paper. He's afraid to give the scheme away. 'Verger du Côte-Vert.' That's the little property the Princesse wants me to sell down in Provence. I don't know whether to take it or not. I asked Comte Lucé why he didn't go in for making peach brandy, instead of sitting up here miserably in the board room, waiting for his father to die. I'll stake him to it, poor chap. Tell that Raccamond to find out the price of orchards. He's got some land down there himself, I hear. I say, where did that fellow get his money? He began poor—his father's a tailor or something. His wife's got a cousin in the Banque Czorvocky. I suppose that's it. And see whether there's a market for a new peach brandy. The Princesse has a new formula but

340

she's willing to let it go with the orchard. All these people are so terrified of taxes now."

"Liqueurs—you're in enough pickles already," said the voice of William from the door. He was rosy from a good sleep and a hearty breakfast.

"Don't laugh: St. Raphaël is making a fortune," Alphendéry put in.

Jules went on, " 'Sell Int. Nickel'—um, um, um—yes. I've a hunch those two are both headed for the grave, or at least for a sanitarium. It might go from fifteen to five. Let's sell them."

"Hunches are only good in retrospect," William advised them.

Jules took no notice. " 'Monte Carlo.' Now I want you to listen to the best idea of the year. You know Monte Carlo's practically dead. No one goes there but two-penny deadbeats and stenographers on a holiday. But everyone's sick of Deauville and Le Touquet. How about making Monte Carlo popular again by making it a sort of European Reno? You know the Pope has a big interest in Monte Carlo. The Prince would never complain if the Pope agreed. Point out to the Pope that his profits will increase enormously if crowds start flowing back there and get him to make a special dispensation for Monte Carlo. He can issue a bull making divorce easy in Monte Carlo. And a special dispensation. Papal divorce business will have to be recognized by every state. He needs the money. They say Ireland is the only country he can still milk. Since the 1929 bust the Americans have stopped sending even moonshine liquor. We could also get the concession for a new hotel, absolutely up-to-date. Baron Koffer would pay us any·price to buy the site from us: his heart would be broken when he found out we were there ahead of him. Then we can float it and sell it as soon as the boom has started. Think of something else. Monte Carlo is a separate principality: all sorts of people not welcome elsewhere, ex-Russians and the like would go there. They'd really have to build an extension of Monte Carlo out into the sea. How about that? Extend it to the statutory limit? Well, it's good, isn't it? I propose that you should go and see the Pope. Popes only do business with Jews."

"That is a good way for the Pope to lose all his Irish income."

"Not a bit of it. All he has to do is to resign from Rome and go and live in Ireland and they'll be too happy."

"Yes, but would the Pope? You didn't sleep much last night, Jules. What would you offer the Pope? A share in the hotel, I suppose?"

"The last is the consortium of rich men I told you about. One rich man from each profession, each to contribute his own scoop, profits share and share alike. One journalist like some smart Hearst journalist, one English broker like Stewart, one man about town like Carrière, one deputy like Blériot (you know him, don't you, Alphendéry?), one man in high society like Theus (you know him, too), one French *agent de change*, and so on. Ourselves holding the strings. No shareholder in the Banque de France: they'd betray us. The bank a façade, the consortium behind it; maybe an insurance company, too, to make it look as if we were spreading into high finance. Make the papers talk about us. 'Who are the powers behind Bertillon?' Whispering campaign—'the Société Générale Alsacienne is behind Bertillon.' What will lend it color is your being here, Alphendéry. Your wife knows the richest people in Brussels. Why not?"

"And who will start the whispering campaign?"

"I will."

"Jules, it isn't true, is it?"

He laughed roguishly, "Ptt! Of course *not*. Why should it be? It's enough to whisper it is. Someone comes to me: 'Mr. Bertillon, I hear that the S.G.A. is behind you. Is it true?' 'Where did you hear that?' say I. 'On the Bourse,' says he. 'Run along,' say I, 'and don't ask questions like that.' Good. A confirmation. If I say, 'No, it isn't true,' it's still a confirmation. Does a secret influence admit itself? He goes to the S.G.A. 'I hear you are working secretly through the Banque Bertillon and Alphendéry is your agent.' 'Nonsense,' says the S.G.A. Good: a confirmation. Does a bank admit who is its secret agent? No. They deny it. People begin to follow Alphendéry in the street. The less he goes near the S.G.A. the more they are sure he is working for it. It will take fifty years to kill that one whisper. And what harm do I do them? (Not that that is in my mind!)" William's face was shining with admiration. He refused to encourage his brother but they could both see he thought this very clever.

342

"The only other idea I had was—sell short," continued Jules. "The American market is creaking upwards but it's only getting up to the springboard for a tumble. That's when I'm counting on the final cash-in. Oh, it may go on till October, November. Say the pound goes off by then. Confidence will droop."

"Indeed! Within two days of the pound going off, if it does, everyone will be patting England on the back and keeping up confidence, and the American market, as usual, will go a point higher, its usual reaction to news of earthquakes, floods, death-dealing, and economic crash. I'm always a fool, and I've taught you to be too straight-thinking, Jules. It should go down, but nowadays it gets a hypodermic every time it begins to wilt. That is the mistake we have made. I am too clever. I am right on policy but wrong on time."

"Jules told me last night how he first made any money," murmured William, when they had read the mail.

"Again?"

"Yes. He says he was in Berlin in 1921—he was, of course—and he peddled American telephone books—New York, Chicago, St. Paul, Lansing, Madison, and so on. He got them over for two dollars or less and they paid five dollars for them on the boulevards of Berlin. That was the time you paid a million marks for a piece of steak and a quarter of a million for a glass of beer, remember? Even for old ones he got four dollars."

"The mystery?"

"All the Schwarzes, all the Finkelsteins, all the Grumbachers, all the Schmidts, all the Epsteins, all the Müllers, wrote to their namesakes in America and begged them to send them a couple of dollars: it was nothing to them, and it meant millions of marks to the Berlin cousin-by-necessity. They did good business. America was rich then and the Americans thought it a hell of a joke to succor starving Europe for a couple of dollars. Others were really impressed. What Schmidt really has all his cousin Schmidts tabulated? Well, the telephone books with all those Schmidts in them were worth five dollars and more to Schmidt, and Jules was the first one to think up the racket and he soon controlled twenty peddlers who worked for him. He stood out on the street himself: he doesn't care."

"How much could he make out of that? A few hundred dollars?"

William looked carefully through some lists of bonds, "Oh, there were other schemes. He doesn't have to scratch his head."

Alphendéry smiled dryly, wearily. "Koffer insists on having a complete list of the numbers of these bonds. They're bearer bonds."

"He's a mind reader."

"He invited me down to his hotel in Cairo the other day."

"That's nothing: didn't Achitophelous give you two free tickets to his house of rendezvous? And tell you you'd get champagne free? These lavish gents will give you everything you don't want and couldn't ever use. It seems Raccamond thinks Baron Koffer is his client, because Fetterling knows his wife."

"Let him. What do we care?"

"The big mug," William was almost fond, "snooping, poking, struggling, persuading himself already that he's on the outside of the inside. Trying to oust you."

"I don't think so."

"Or enlist you in his great service," giggled William. "He's as secret as a Hollywood bathing beauty. His card, Raccamond attached to the direction. One of these days you'll find on your desk a little bundle of cards, Alphendéry attached to Raccamond."

"He's not a bad fellow. He got me a photograph of Yvonne Printemps for Henrietta."

"Charming. And boasted to Printemps, doubtless, that he knew Mr. and Mme. Theus of Brussels."

"You don't do him justice."

"I hope we won't have to."

Scene Forty-eight: A Ghostly Gathering

JULES and Claire-Josèphe went to the wedding, at St. Clothilde, of Toots Legris and Duc-Adam Lhermite, a handsome young fellow descended from a long line of cognac manufacturers, but of a junior branch and there-

fore very grateful for the million francs that he received
from Toots on his marriage to her. His family had a villa
in Alpes-Maritimes like anyone who is anybody, and a
hôtel at Paris in the Avenue Pierre de Serbie and, to even
things up a bit, after marrying he was to be allowed to use
the family château in Saône-et-Loire. A distant relative of
his connected the Franco-Argentine Mortgage Bank to
the Haute Banque and so he was, money apart, highly
satisfactory.

And Toots had enough money for the whole world.
The Legris family had only newly come to the ranks of
the multimillionaires, and this was the first alliance in
high society, so naturally there were very great rejoicings
on this occasion. Besides Jules and Claire-Josèphe, there
were present in the princely throng at the elegant Basilica,
from whose grand-inquisitor towers César Franck's
ghostly music had flowed into the sky, the following representatives of all that makes France great: four persons
representing the great insurance companies, the Paternal,
the Patrimony, the Phoenix, and the Providence; six persons connected in some more or less casual fashion with
the financial societies, Raoul de Lubersac and Company,
Mirabaud, De Neuflize and Company, De Rothschild
Brothers, Odier Bungener and Company, A. J. Stern and
Company; two directors of the Suez Company, three
members of the Bloodstock Association, one relative of a
director of the leading metallurgical company, forty persons representing diverse commercial companies, eight
exchange brokers of Paris, four governors or regents of
the Banque de France, eighty-nine individual shareholders
of the Banque de France, including leading board-room
princes and landed proprietors who represented the interests of the peasants in finance and saw that the proletariat of the cities did not get away with it, fifty-one
members of the Jockey Club, thirteen counts, three persons with the title of marquis, seventeen countesses, nineteen princes, foreign and domestic, fourteen American
millionairesses married to blue blood abroad, several ambassadors, three hundred and forty-one impoverished
nobles and younger sons, intimately known to their friends
as lunch detectives and sandwich snatchers, seven unlucky
suitors for the Legris millions, five priests, one archbishop, one ex-king, one hundred and two bankers, and
three pickpockets not of noble extraction. It was a gar-

land of youthful vanity and superannuated cunning, hoary rank and young money, famous beggars, notorious debtors, unsuccessful rakes, lordly borrowers, impenitent usurers, princely automobile salesmen and brokers' runners of Bourbon blood, shady viscounts, distinguished pillars of cafés, illustrious readers of the *Journal des Débats,* people who trusted to the Council of State in an emergency, people who trusted to the Republican Guard, to Mr. Chiappe, and to General Pétain. All of them were news items, and a certain number had money themselves.

After the solemn service the Archbishop in white and gold sent a priest round to the apartment of François Legris asking for the money for the service, and when he was not to be found there, the priest flew round in a taxi to the house of the Princesse Delisle-Delbe where the reception was being held. But François was not there, either.

François, Anthony Legris, Maîtres Vanderallee (for Toots Legris), Nanti, and Olympe, Jules, William, and Michel Alphendéry were in Jules's room at the bank quietly celebrating and avoiding the elegant crush at the Princesse's. The dear old friends were rather gay and found everything excessively funny. Maîtres Vanderallee and Nanti were most particularly gay and were even suspected of being drunk. Jules was in a delightfully intimate and trustful frame of mind. They all sat gossiping beside the three or four hundred books on economics from Adam Smith to Mr. Keynes, carefully selected by Michel Alphendéry, like lifelong comrades who after forty years of labor take a day off and resuscitate adolescent memories. What pleasant, carefree, ingenuous hours such old friends pass! How cheerful is the occasion of a wedding, for forgetting commerce, finance, mutual robbery, and for indulging in that frivolous chitchat which puts old friends and new at ease!

"Willem," said Jules to Vanderallee, "I can't understand you chaps playing such a dirty game. Listen, François, you know very well that when I went to Anthony and asked him to get the Scheldt en Dogger to advance me fifty thousand guilders to play the market, he did so on the understanding that it was never to be called, that, in fact, it was a sort of advance from yourselves and was only advanced from the Scheldt en Dogger (on your recommendation) so that it would look better on the books. Now I find Anthony has warned the Scheldt en Dogger Bank to call in the loan and I get a notice of it yesterday. What are you going to do about it? Didn't I arrange the marriage contract for you free of charge?"

"Yes, I know, Jules, old fellow, but suppose you go wild and go bankrupt? Where would we be, owing the Scheldt en Dogger fifty thousand guilders?" laughed François, all as a joke.

Willem Vanderallee, lawyer of the great gambling stock-exchange firm of which François and Anthony Legris were partners, lolled back in a deep chair, one leg tossed over the arm, blowing rings from a powerful cigar (donated by Richard Plowman), his white waistcoat, tie, shiny forehead, spectacles, and diamond ring flashing as he wallowed in his deep inebriation. He scarcely followed the conversation at all, laughed at everything that Jules and François said; his eyes closed from minute to minute. He now said thickly, "Jules, darling, I can't speak a word. Why is the world turning, round and round and round? I say, François, your daughter serves strong liquor: she forgets we haven't all had her experience. God bless her! May she be—ever—happy." His eyes closed. François giggled and proffered obscenities.

"I say," said Vanderallee, opening his eyes again, "she's a lovely-looking girl; she looked like one of those sixteenth-century paintings—absolutely cinquecento—not the same, doesn't matter—where the Madonna is a queen, on a throne, with a diamond—diadem, that is to say. She looks lovely in that tiara: how much they soak you for it, François? She's lovely woman, your daughter."

"Yes, she's an attractive bitch," bubbled François, "should think she would be—she's spent a million guilders a year on her looks since she was ten. She ought to look good. She doesn't give her old father much. She's kind-hearted though: very kindhearted. She always appeals for funds for the orphans. Every year. She's kindhearted. But she's not as soft as she looks. Not as—as hard as nails."

"I didn't say she looked soft," amended Willem.

François went in for even worse obscenities. Jules, never obscene, said, "Hey, François, she's your daughter: it's her wedding day—give her a break for once, as a wedding present."

François giggled, "Oh, the little devil understands me: we have nothing to thank each other for. You're right though, Jules, you've got nice instincts. Always had the right instincts. Perfect gentleman. Yes, it's my little girl's wedding day. When Duc-Adam asked me, I said, 'Take her, my boy, you been sleeping with her two years anyhow. The sooner she marries you the sooner she'll get tired of you.' He looked sick. She's not my daughter: what rot you talking Jules? She's the daughter of seventy million guilders. That's not the same thing at all as being the daughter of Mr. François Legris, perpetual soak, plain citizen. She hasn't got my tastes—she's got the tastes of seventy million guilders. She's too good for me. Not my daughter. I don't care what I say about her."

"I'm glad she hasn't got your tastes," murmured Nanti, from his armchair.

François winked, "She gave me her loose change; she'll give Duc-Adam her loose change. Let's have a drink."

"I say," Jules recollected suddenly, "you nearly did a lunatic thing, Willem. That marriage contract. You made a contract under Dutch law giving Duc-Adam a million guilders plus living expenses. You ought to know that in a French marriage a French contract for separation of estate has to be made. You nearly landed Lhermite with the whole fortune. Say, François, why don't you fire him? He's a freak lawyer. First, he lets the Scheldt en Dogger Bank know what I'm doing, and they call in my loan and —don't you realize I could sue you and Anthony for breach of contract?"

"Sue us, sue us," François waved his hand cheerfully.

About a quarter of an hour later, William Vanderallee, rolling, flushed, drunk, spoke boisterously, "We're going to put it across, William. Jules is going to give us a letter appointing us his agents."

The letter gave Messrs. Legris and Maîtres Nanti and Vanderallee power to act for Jules Bertillon in bringing to a satisfactory finality the claim of the Scheldt en Dogger Bank for fifty thousand guilders loaned to Jules Bertillon at the request of Messrs. Legris and Company, Amsterdam.

According to promise, Jules notified his Amsterdam lawyer, Michel's friend, Maître Friesz, to cease his counter-suit against the Scheldt en Dogger, because he had fixed

348

the affair in Paris himself with the help of Maître Olympe. The Amsterdam lawyer, in high dudgeon, sent Jules a stiff account at once. He had maneuvered and negotiated for six weeks and considered he had the Scheldt en Dogger in a deep hole and he had argument enough if necessary to sue Legris Brothers also. The next mail brought all the related papers flying back and an insulted and injured letter from the lawyer. This friend of Alphendéry had considered the brilliant double suit which he had prepared a good debut in the interesting and always actively litigating firm of Jules Bertillon. He was more than mortified to have to scrap it all for some chicane on the part of Vanderallee. He wrote a severe letter to Alphendéry saying that Vanderallee would certainly ditch the Bertillons, as he was hand-in-glove with the Legris firm. "He's just jealous," said Jules. "Trust a lawyer to prefer to fight a case to settling it."

Three days later they were notified, by the usual channels, in a brief style, that the Scheldt en Dogger Bank had drawn on Legris and Company, Amsterdam, for fifty thousand guilders for the account of Jules Bertillon, and had been paid; with a letter from Legris and Company, asking for a draft to pay fifty thousand guilders in Bertillon's Amsterdam account, to replace the money legitimately drawn by the Scheldt en Dogger in settlement of their claim settled by François Legris acting for Jules Bertillon. William Bertillon and Alphendéry were too polite to make any comment to Jules.

Scene Forty-nine: Various Matters

THE affair of the marriage contract being noised around, people began to consider that Jules was most intimately related to Legris Brothers of Amsterdam and Jules himself for the time being thrust far into the background his idea that business was a mistake and that he ought to fold up the bank before its bright picture was tarnished.

Jules, much entertained, in his empty, amoral life, by some speculations of Alphendéry, about Carrière's immorality, said, "Ah, Alphendéry, I'm glad to hear you say that about Carrière but I too will be out of the public eye in ten years: I don't care to stay in it as long and then if your argument applies to Carrière, it applies to me, too. I sleep with my own wife, true; but I sleep with other people's money. And raped money gets people much wilder than raped wives."

He felt much closer to Carrière than to Alphendéry; he admired his rascality while detesting his opposition: Alphendéry was a mystery to Jules. He knew that Michel knew that the business they were all in was (as he put it) "pure theft," and Michel had many a time proved to him that private banking of any sort was a "titanic pickpocketing." But Michel went on working for him at a mediocre salary and did not even filch a few thousand francs each month, which was what Jules fully expected him to do. If Jules had found out that Michel was putting away a little each month in a secret account in another bank, for himself and accounting for it somehow or other, or if Michel had even run up a sizable overdraft, or taken the money and put in I.O.U.'s, or even if Alphendéry had taken a big house and expected Jules to pay for it, or bought a car he couldn't afford and charged it to the bank, or if he had gone (as Jules had requested him to do) to Jules's princely tailors and got himself a wardrobe on Jules's account, or anything of that sort, Jules would have understood it, considered it his right, and thought the better of him. But Michel worked for the agreed stipend like any clerk and Jules quite openly thought it was something petty, limited, and clerkly in his nature which prevented him from providing for himself.

"Why," said Jules to William once, in private, "we've given him enough warning. He knows we're going to shut up shop one day. Why doesn't he take notice? For a bright man, he's subnormal."

"He's honest: there is such a thing," remarked William. "You and I don't know about it."

Jules mused, "The Comtesse said the other day, 'The day I found out there were men in France who couldn't be bought, I sent my gold abroad.' Smart girl. She's right. It makes me feel queer. It's a sort of fanaticism." He felt so queer that when he next saw Alphendéry, he said only half jocularly, "I say, Michel, why don't you put your

350

name to a few checks: it's your right. Your signature is good here!"

Michel said, "If you don't mind, I was thinking next month I'd ask you for twenty thousand francs overdraft to send to Estelle. I want to give her a hint that she may as well get another husband. I'm not much good to her, and the way to grease these things is with a present, to show there's no ill will. You can put it down on my account. I'll pay you back when I make some money in the market."

Jules laughed heartily. "You're never in the market, are you?"

"No. But I might take a flier. Just to cover some of my expenses."

"That's an old one," murmured Jules.

Alphendéry ruefully said, "I know: it's a sure road to ruin. I won't then. I'll pay you back."

Jules let out the most exasperated long laugh Michel had ever heard. He got up and walked up and down the room, looking at Michel glumly from time to time. Then he said angrily, "Michel, take it for a present. Good God, I don't want it back. Why don't you get yourself some suits, Michel? Why don't you provide for yourself? Who's going to know? I don't give a damn. One of these days, there'll be some sort of a smash, and no one will be better off for your modesty."

"It's not in my heart to take money I don't earn, Jules."

Jules was quite acid. "You're a fool, Michel."

"Jules, you know what is in my heart? When I leave you, when I've provided for Estelle and my mother, I want to join my friends—I couldn't do that if I'd been helping myself, even to your money."

Jules sat down and looked at him with interest, "I thought you belonged to the communists. I did, honestly. I thought you were working for them."

"You thought that and you left me to control your funds the way you do?"

Jules threw back his head. "Surely. I know you wouldn't give them dirty dough. I would, but you wouldn't. What do I care?" He looked at Alphendéry with a puzzled, half-derisive expression, "Michel, why are you in this game?"

"First," said Michel, rather desperately, "because I like comfort, I suppose, and because I haven't got the manhood, as Jean Frère has, to tell my wife and mother and child (if I ever had one) that they must live in poverty, because I couldn't wear my bones out for them. Second, because I have been in finance ever since I was a boy. My father was a small banker as well as lawyer, my grandfather a small steelmaster. When my father died, I became the secretary of Alphendéry, the Alsatian *rentier* millionaire who had retired and made a hobby of collecting proofs of Dreyfus's innocence. He was also a Marxist and while with him I became a fervent Marxist. You see, I have always been a revolutionary at ease, the shadow of a rich man. It would take a violent effort of will to wrench myself out of that setting, and I suppose I will some day. If I go round much longer with Jean Frère I certainly will. He is practically monosyllabic but when he expresses some vague feeling that I should go and see something or do something, about a month later, I find myself doing it. I have met my match."

Jules looked at him affectionately. "Oh, you are too kind, Michel! That is your only weakness. You have a heart of gold——the only gold you'll ever have."

The same afternoon Jules telephoned to Alphendéry in his office. "Come round to my office, Michel: I believe I've got something on old Legris." But when Alphendéry got to the office, Jules merely said carelessly, "You made a lot of money for me this year, Michel."

"Yes, I know."

Jules pointed to an envelope on the table. "You ought to take care of your mother: perhaps that will."

Michel opened the envelope and found one hundred thousand francs in Treasury bonds.

"Thanks very much, Jules."

"You earned it: you ought to hate me for it, on your theory. I get the lion's share and you made it all yourself!" He laughed kindly. He followed Michel back to his room, saw no one was there, and when Michel sat down, put some more bonds on the table. "What difference does it make? You may as well pay off that wife of yours too. And take some advice, Michel. Forget Estelle: join your friends and get used to drinking the two-cent wine of that friend of yours, Frère. When you come back from seeing him, you look ten years younger. . . . Why don't you bring him in? I'd like to see the fellow." He sauntered out.

352

Michel, with a heart strangely mute, looked at the other bonds—in all, one hundred seventy-five thousand francs in bonds. He looked at the money. He would assign it some other time. Meanwhile he felt unspeakably melancholy. Jules had recommended him to give up this mad and detested life and join his real friends. But Michel could not contemplate leaving Jules yet. Why? He went to a workers' meeting that evening and gave one hundred francs to the collection, immediately after felt extremely gay and lighthearted, and came back to the bank the next day without a thought of leaving and everything went on as before, except that he brought Jean Frère in to see Jules. Jean seemed to be struck dumb, Jules was in a bad temper, and everything went awry. Jules said angrily, after, "What the deuce do you see in that fellow? Don't get sentimental, Michel, or you'll be throwing over a comfortable life for a lot of fellows you don't know and you'll be intensely miserable. I know you, Michel. You couldn't stand it."

Mlle. Louise Bernard, confidential secretary of the Bertillons and Alphendéry, was called to the great directors' room where Daniel Cambo and Ephraïm Dreyer were installed. Aristide Raccamond, passing at the moment and peering in, saw Dreyer, Alphendéry, and, in a dark-green armchair, a great oxycephalic head but nothing more. All this secrecy annoyed him and gnawed at his tranquillity. William Bertillon passed him, tried the door, found it locked, shrugged, and came back again. Dreyer, though a man of fifty-five, sprang out of his chair and offered Mlle. Bernard a seat. Cambo put on his dancing-partner expression and came and stood at her elbow. After some little parley in Ladino, they agreed, and Dreyer dictated to the young lady in French:

July 15, 1930

Ephraïm Dreyer,
    Nieuwdoelenstraat, Amsterdam.

Dear Sir,

    We regret to inform you that your short sale of Docks du Havre is now undermargined, due to this stock having risen by forty-five points, as you will have seen. Will you kindly remit the necessary amount to us before tomorrow's closing?

Yours truly,

BERTILLON FRÈRES

July 30, 1930

(Same address)

DEAR SIR,

Will you kindly remit to us at once the amount necessary to cover margin requirements on your holding of Banque Franco-Japonaise which is now undermargined, due to the decline this week. We should appreciate your check in the sum of ("so much, we'll work that out after," put in Alphendéry).

(Same signature)

December 31, 1930

(Same address)

DEAR SIR,

In remitting your account as of December 31, 1930, we regret to observe that it is in debit 28,869–:75c. (twenty thousand, eight hundred and sixty-nine francs, seventy-five centimes). Will you kindly remit the amount mentioned in due course?

(Same signature)

"Get some old letterheads and type those letters," said Alphendéry, smiling sweetly. "Bring the typewriter in here. Wait, I'll tell Brossier to bring it."

When the letters were done, she gave them as instructed to William Bertillon. He signed them and Mlle. Bernard handed them to Ephraïm Dreyer, who bowed and thanked her with old-fashioned courtesy.

"I think," said Alphendéry, "that will establish your loss sufficiently." He followed Mlle. Bernard back to her room and said with false confidence, "That's a big service we've done Dreyer. They are after him for income tax."

Mlle. Bernard looked coolly at him. "The tax officials must have heard of antedated letters before this."

"Yes, but we're such a respectable institution," ex-

354

plained Alphendéry, "no one can doubt our word. And then the books agree."

"Do they?"

"I mean, they will."

Mlle. Bernard looked at him curiously. "What do you, the Bank, I mean, get out of this? He hasn't got an account worth mentioning, with us."

"We get nothing actually. Oh, this doesn't count: these little favors we do in the course of business. You don't get the Legion of Honor for a small thing like that."

Meanwhile Dreyer sent round one of the grooms to know what size gloves Mlle. Bernard wore, and in due course within a week she found herself possessed of one dozen pairs of very fine gloves. Dreyer was a glove maker. Alphendéry came smiling in the wake of the gloves. "Dreyer's very grateful to you: he sent his kindest wishes and thanks. It's very fortunate we have someone here," he flattered amiably, "who can be trusted with these private matters."

Alphendéry had a letter from Henri Léon, with whom he had been in correspondence for some months. Léon had laid his list of bonds before him and had promised him ten per cent of any profits he should make on Alphendéry's advice. Alphendéry had had this offer from other rich men in his time, but there was something personal and intimate in Léon's manner and in his letters which made him look upon Léon as his second line of battle, if anything should happen to the Bertillon Bank. Léon now wrote:

June 29, 1931

MY DEAR MICHEL,

I was very pleased to receive your letter for two reasons: firstly, because I was without news from you and I was relieved to have your letter; secondly, I was particularly pleased to learn that you would come to Amsterdam shortly, with my old friend Aristide Raccamond. . . . By the bye, I am enclosing a letter I had from a man who is trying to sell me an estate in the south of France. He is a friend of Mr. Rhys of Rotterdam, but his letter unsettles me: it is eccentric. You have more experience of men than me: would you look at it and write a suitable

355

answer? Do not show it to Raccamond or to anyone as I do not want commission agents for estates round me. . . . Since writing you, I have been investigating a chemicals factory in Germany: some friends have been trying to interest me in this business. . . . I am a little bit worried about your remarks about the U.S. Federal bonds. I have still got my parcel and am very much tempted to sell it, but frankly, I do not know what to do with the money and, what is much worse, I don't know what currency to plunge for. I am not at all impressed with sterling, the gold currencies are all risky; my impression is that the Belgian franc is at the moment the safest but I do not like to put all the eggs in one basket. The question is: When the pound? When the dollar? When the Belgian franc? When the Swiss franc? When the French franc? If you can put dates to any of those, you and I are millionaires. I see they say the pound market may be aided by a war-debt moratorium but I do not believe it. . . . I am looking to you for a Talmud interpretation. I must be more conservative than ever standing as I do alone and on my own resources. I do not want to lose the substance for the shadow. If I could only know what to buy. In the meantime, read the *New York Herald* of Paris and let me know what stocks to watch; that is, if you share my view that selective stocks and shares are worth buying. Business with me has been poor, though I am keeping my head above water. . . . If I was sure Russia would be a seller I would be very much tempted to go short. Could we make her a seller? There is going to be a great chance of some sort in this wheat market. I am watching it very closely and if the position still remains uncertain by the middle of July, I shall probably come down to Paris to see you. . . . If ever you want to come to Holland, let me know. We may be able to get together on some proposition.

Yours,
HENRI LÉON

Enclosed was a letter headed, "Jacques Terrien, Greffontaines, Vallée Heureuse." It began:

DEAR MR. ADALLO,

Your kind interest in the beautiful property above
has given me a new hope in life, where, I assure
you, everything before looked black and hopeless,
due to the crisis, in which I, no doubt, have not
suffered more than others "but I feel it more!" I have
not heard again from your agent who approve' of
the property but a few days later, Mme. Adallo
visited the place and expressed her great satisfaction
with it, suggesting one or two changes which I shall
be only too happy to put in hand. I know the people
of this section and can put you in touch with the
best workmen and also with two excellent share
farmers which is what you need to run the place,
and I assure you your taking them on will be a godsend to them both, as well as your taking the property an answer to prayer (so to speak) to me.
Forgive me speaking in this personal strain. . . .
Now sir, I should like to hear something definite
from you in order to have peace of mind myself,
not that I think you concern yourself with my peace
of mind, but only that, oh, sir, you cannot understand what miseries have reduced me to this state
of despair. My wife was in hospital and had two
operations for which I have not yet paid. She died.
My son tried to get work here and not finding any
ran away to Paris, but I believe is still unemployed. I have only a young girl, fifteen, who needs
medical care, suffering from tuberculosis, and I am
unable to look after her or pay a nurse for her.
So, my very dear sir, I am not trying to tell you my
troubles for any other reason than an honorable
one, that is, to pay my bills as quickly as possible
and to persuade you to come to a quick decision,
for I feel if it dangles about much longer I shall
surely go out of my mind; but if there is promise
of a quick sale and your letter or Mme. Adallo's
or your agent's is in my hands, I can get credit here.
I know you must have your own worries: I am
very conscious that mine mean little to you, my very
dear sir, and know that it must be so if the world
is to wag and I should not write this way if I were

not nearly distracted. Will you please answer quickly and in the affirmative?

Most sincere greetings,

J. TERRIEN

On the bottom Henri Léon had penciled: "New letters come from this man every mail, some to me, some to Madame Adallo (these are names assumed by me and a friend of mine in negotiations). There are now three on my desk, come today, which I have not answered. Please do something. I am not going to buy the property. I now have the idea that it would be better to buy a property in Spain, where the people are glowing with republican enthusiasm.

H. L."

Alphendéry sat down at once and wrote to Léon.

June 30, 1931

DEAR LÉON,

The market is up and I am a busy man. Your friend Raccamond having told his clients to sell is giddy with fright and has run off to hide himself at St.-Germain-en-Laye where his wife has a villa or something. I have to face everyone myself. Did you know him for a neurotic? My advice about the chap at Vallée Heureuse is—return his letters unopened if you get any more for Mme. Adallo and send him a brutal letter in answer to this one (it is the only way). Here is the letter: "Dear Terrien, I do not want your property; please do not write to me about it again. It does not suit my requirements in any way. Yours, etc." If you do not you are going to have a psychosis on your hands. In a few days he will be blaming you for all his troubles. So be curt. If he shoots himself his trouble will be over: if he shoots you, yours will. Choose. But he won't shoot himself. . . . It's awful, all the same. The world's going mad with the depression. Let me live long enough to see the world changed.

Yours,

ALPHENDÉRY

P.S. I am all for an estate in Spain and Alphendéry as your factor. About "wet and windy Amsterdam"

I have not yet made up my mind. But Raccamond and I will be up there soon. I have an idea of training him to take my place. I might go to London.

M. A.

He included a list of stocks in which Léon should invest.

By the same mail, Raccamond had received a letter from Léon, and it had been forwarded to him at Madame's old house on the heights of St.-Cloud (St.-Germain-en-Laye was a false scent).

June 29, 1931

DEAR ARISTIDE,

I am delighted to hear from you: I felt very uneasy to hear that you were under the weather. When you come to Amsterdam it will afford us an opportunity of meeting and discussing various personal matters, and investments, on which I particularly want your advice. I want you to run me out a list of selective stocks in the American stock market. I have got a curious impression that the stock market in America wants to go up and I think it will some day soon. The question is, will the dollar go off now, or in three years from now? In this you will be of valuable service, and you will get recognition from me: ten per cent from any profits you make for me, through your advice. I cannot afford to splash round though. I am poor, and things have not gone so well with me. I must make a big effort to get out of the marasmus in which I find myself, due to the depressed state of the world. The only risk is that the Americans may go wild, for they are not used to disaster: they are now trying to lock people up for saying banks are unsound. This is a pretty thing! We should all be on bread and water at that rate. If they don't hold their horses and do something pretty soon, we may have revolution in America and it is not time for it yet. . . . There is little business in Spain and little enterprise, but with the new republic people will begin to eye Spain as a new territory. You would be happy in that country, I think, and we could work together. We could coin money. The question to consider is where there is a future for business. I envisage two—cosmetics and drugs. Now they have very few drugs, and all they have come from Germany and Czechoslovakia. As to cosmetics, they have very poor stuff and poor scent, like you see in cheap Arab bazaars, yet the women are wild about beauty preparations and think of nothing else. There is a most important factory, situated in San Sebastian with a capital of about ten million pesetas; you might look round next time you are down on the Silver Coast and see what they are doing. Go to the banks and find out details of this firm, its prospects, its past and its future. I want you to find out if there are likely to be labor troubles and if they think the republic will hold. What a market it has opened up! I guess the future will find me there. Write to me, my boy, as soon as you have reconnoitered. . . . Do not let anyone in the bank know what you are doing. I am looking forward to the time when we can get together again.

Yours,

H. L.

Scene Fifty: *Honored Sir*

ALPHENDÉRY went up to Amsterdam for the week-end to see Léon and find out if Léon really wanted to employ him and what he would offer. Léon, pacing up and down his room in a hotel in Nieuwdoelenstraat, was struck by Alphendéry's prophecy of MacDonald's apostasy. He sat down and edged his chair close to Alphendéry with a confidential expression. "Boy, that's the clue!"

"You've got something?"

"A letter to the—a letter. Say, we'll write a letter that will get him. The Continent watching you with bated breath—flatter him—a letter from the Continent. 'My very dear sir.' No, 'Honored sir.' "

"He's the right honorable, by the way," Alphendéry said, with a little parade of learning. No one knew the designations of foreign statesmen but he.

360

"Is he smart?" Léon thrust at him. "A Scot, eh? They don't flatter. Would he suspect flattery? No, not used to it. Or perhaps. They call the English slimy. Coax. No, a virile letter."

"About what?" Alphendéry asked sharply. He foresaw another job, with the usual profit to himself. But, wearily or not, he was obliged to do it, for he very much needed to get away from the humdrum escapades of life in the bank.

"Why bank on Ramsay? You're not sure he'll get in. Suppose Winston Churchill has the *nous* to step forward?"

"Him? No. He misses fire. Do you think?—" he suddenly began to doubt himself. "Must be Labour Party," he said. He recovered himself. "Let's just get the scheme down first. Listen, Michel, if I get an honor there, will you work with me in England? Listen, I got a plan, get myself in good. Five-Year Plan for English finance. Listen, we write a letter: the pound dissolved, despite market flurries, shares in devalued pounds going up, *they* know it won't help England. We write a letter say to the Prime Minister, bring to the fore the serious situation. A merchant wishing to serve and showing the intense interest he has taken in English affairs—a sort of matriculation, eh? Good scheme. No American constitution, no language test. Give them a Five-Year Plan for finance. Listen, unemployment isn't going down. They're going to get it in the neck unless they do something. Lloyd George says the bankers are all wrong, maybe I'm all right. You see? Will you write the letter, Alphendéry? We go to the Prime Minister, we explain. You're my private secretary. I get my honor. Worthy merchant. Later on—anything. Maybe I stand for M.P. You go along with me. It's a career for you too, my boy. . . ."

"As your secretary?"

"No, no, no, no—not my secretary. A partnership. Spiritual partnership, eh? You write the letters. Will you write the letter, Michel?"

"I'll try. Will you tell me what it's about?"

"I told you. Listen, my boy. This is the plan—what is wrong with it? That is what we must ask ourselves: what are the alternatives? Lots of panaceas have been suggested and this is mine, the one I think best and now

361

propose because I have uprooted my inferiority complex—"

"Oh, you have?"

"I mean I read in *The Times* and the May report and Lloyd George and Snowden, and I'm good as they are, my boy. Maybe better. At any rate you write, you write—why don't you take some notes, now?" he coaxed. "Would you like some coffee?"

"Jesus, leave me alone, Léon! I'm absolutely all in."

"Rest, rest; sleep, and after we'll do the letter. Rest —you need it."

"All right." Crestfallen, he went off into the grandiose bathroom, done in marble with a black marble bath in the center of the room, the room big enough for a salon. He kept peeping at Alphendéry to see if he was sleeping. After a quarter of an hour, he tiptoed back and peeped at Alphendéry, standing beside him. Michel, hearing him breathing irregularly in his dubiety, opened his eyes and smiled rather palely.

"Forgive me, Henri. I've had such a week."

"I'm not bothering you, my boy." He looked so wistful that Alphendéry, always wax, got up slowly. "I'll do your notes for you, Léon. Then I'll do no more this weekend."

Léon rubbed his hands, beamed, flushed with joy. "That's right, my boy, just notes—then finished, eh? We go out, have a good time, make whoopee. I'll buy you wine, a good dinner, eh?"

"Go on," Alphendéry said, without gratitude.

"Well, at this time when it looks as if even the devaluation of the pound won't help England, I read their plans and speech, no cabals, no vigilant committee—won't help: that's not the English way."

He considered, then said briskly and loudly, "The *Plan*. Twenty-five per cent capital reconstruction lien—whether any exceptions or whether to be composed on a scale basis to be considered. Twenty per cent reduction on all salaries by law—and wages, with exceptions to be considered." He began to ripple with genial laughter. "That'll appeal to them at any rate. Everyone got to draw their belts in a hole, two holes. Ten per cent reduction on all postwar rentals, ten per cent reduction on all power, gas, electricity, that is, public utilities, ten per cent reduction on all road and rail rates, freight and passenger. Twenty per cent reduction on all rail, canal, and road freights where goods carried for export . . ."

"That would suit you," said Alphendéry.

"Surely, my boy, I look at it from the point of view of the small capitalist. What suits me, suits them. And it looks fair for all. Not worker but Englishman, not capitalist but Englishman. See? Write, 'And these to be enforced for five years.' Also a flat income tax or less. Twenty-five per cent reduction in death duties. Idea is, attract back money now held abroad, Switzerland, U.S.A., Oslo. *See?* What do you think of it? Have you got it, eh? These to be enforced for *five years*. English Five-Year Plan! Also flat income tax less the liens. It will appeal to all those with capital! Attractive! The people submit anyhow. They all pay their income tax in England—rush to do it, my boy, I've seen them. My duty to my country. The people are—no marrow in England! Drained country; people left are just bad Courlanders. Reduce rent and you can reduce wages. What is the Labour Party? Did they make the rich pay? No guts. Reduce wages, entice capital to England. I wouldn't mind putting mine—well, what do you think, Alphendéry?"

"They'll never even consider it. It's too good a gift to the rich. The English can't be fooled like that. They want a socialist or chauvinist or patriotic appeal to go to the country on."

Léon frowned. "Yes, my boy," he urged, "but they don't advertise it! They have it in hand ready to spring. You see! You and I go to wait on the Prime Minister and we say, 'Here is a present.' Friend of England. England has always welcomed foreigners. No prejudice. She has a right to their capital. She's honest. Doesn't steal money entrusted to her. Safe as the Bank of England, eh? Free country: make capital free. Give it the freedom of the City. Eh? Say to him, 'Give yourself five years. In five years you'll have a war, maybe. Anyhow, a war boom with the armaments race.' Give capital a chance to recuperate. And it will look almost socialistic for the people. The title: Five-Year Plan. Steal Stalin's thunder. Dress it up. You see? We go and say, *'The cancer in England is high cost of production and confiscatory taxation!'*" He proudly rolled his eye. "If he makes something, he has to give the government so much, a large proportion. If he loses—see? Besides, it permanently prevents enterprising foreign capitalists from coming there. You see, backward country. A Poland! It's a Poland. But you got to attract capitalists. And Majorca, Channel Islands, Blue Coast!" he finished triumphantly.

"Eh?" cried Alphendéry, staring.

"It drives *rentiers* from England who gladly would live there, their native heath and London, land of freedom, Karl Marx——"

"Whoa," cried Alphendéry, "throw a spanner in the works: I can't keep up with you."

Patiently, humanely, Léon explained, "it drives *rentiers* from London who gladly would live there because of its— word! *World!* Hum! niceties!—"

"Amenities," supplied Alphendéry.

"*Amenities,*" shouted Léon glaring. "Amenities, political, social, literary——" His voice faded; he came back on a gentle argumentative tone, "You see, we say, flatter them a bit—and it's true. We say, 'Window dressing for capitalists, enterprise.' Take me, I want to go into business in England. I employ labor, give food to the country. I already got money in England. Shows my good faith."

"In what?" asked Alphendéry. Léon seemed confused, but owned up, "In beet-sugar production: they offered—a bounty—bounty to anyone who went into beet-sugar production. I make money. That's enterprise." Alphendéry went into a long but amiable laugh. Léon eyed him askance, smiled shyly, came back brisk, "The *Plan*. One. Write, Alphen. 'By reconstruction levy we mean that the government has prior claim of twenty-five per cent on your capital equity. It doesn't mean that you have to sell twenty-five per cent of your holdings to give the government this twenty-five per cent. The government gives you a discount of five per cent to anybody who cares to liquidate this lien, so the question of forced sale either by merchants or *rentiers* would be compounded and there would be no disturbance in business either—it would be a question of bookkeeping and enormously assist the position of the state abroad as a solvent concern! See! *Hochem,* eh? Well, how does it read?"

"Good, so far," said Alphendéry. "It's all right."

Léon spread out his hand towards Alphendéry, leaned

forward, and bent the hand back as he straightened, *"Argument that this is confiscation:* 'Five shillings death duties is confiscation anyhow.' " He seemed grieved. "Now labor side of question. 'Under the present situation, since economy is not possible except by serious steps in retrogression—capital is faced with much more serious confiscation, due to rising social troubles and distress. As regards labor, even the U.S.A. and all European countries are reducing labor—they'll have to—' "

Alphendéry looked up. "Jules Bertillon says, and he's never wrong, 'It's getting harder and harder to buy the people off.' "

Léon cocked his head and considered this brightly. "Yes, h'm. But with what? Buy 'em off with formulas: that's the answer. They'll have to bring in new systems of reducing the wages of labor. Let's speak plainly: not as capitalists, as practical men, a merchant's point of view. You're kindest to labor when you keep them in jobs. See! And labor is *compelled to accept lower wages offered.* Englishman so proud of sitting on Indian coolie's neck, he will accept coolie wages and not look at them. We say to the Prime Minister: 'The best means of reduction are offered by this scheme'—my scheme. The Léon scheme. All right, they call it the Five-Year Plan. To build new state, every Englishman will do his duty. Say, they're better than them barefoot Russians, aren't they? That's the argument! Boy, it's a good selling line, eh?"

Léon rubbed his hands, beamed generously on Alphendéry's bowed head. "You say to them, 'Look here, boys, during the war, we took emergency measures: the circumstances do not now greatly differ. All pull together. Here we ask no one to die and leave his family, but to live and work for England. Work that England may live!' " He took a few excited steps. "That's a slogan that'll get them. They're patriots: no reasoning power, not like Frenchmen: 'If I die of hunger, I'm not a Frenchman but a corpse.' No, sir. You can count on their patriotism. That's what they teach 'em at Eton. Rules of the game. Then when you get in. That's your selling line to *them,* to Lloyd George, to MacDonald, or whoever it is."

"Too smart," said Alphendéry. "They won't like it."

"And," shouted Léon quickly, to show he was no fool, *"utilitarian,* let's remain utilitarians!"

"Eh?"

"Put it over," explained Léon, taking a long breath. He began to make a persuasive appeal to an imaginary public. " 'Let's remain utilitarians; it has always provided a sound basis for our public weal as against the hysterical humanitarianism of the Continent. . . .' Say, how am I doing, Alphendéry? Say, how's the Labour candidate? Here we ask no one to die for the country. John Stuart Mills. I'd do pretty good. With you," he remembered quickly. "And the beauty of it is," he confided largely, "is that it's true. My heart is with the people, Michel. Say, *This is not a party question*. Therefore this great scheme can be brought in by a National Government in which the Labour Party can take the lead. Few people realize what work the Labour Party is doing under difficult circumstances!' See the appeal. With the Five-Year Plan. See! Make statesmen out of the poor fooshers." His great noonday laugh filled the room with yellow sound. "We're going to see the world! What do you say now to being my political—h'm . . . my political secretary?"

"You mean, political ghost," said Alphendéry.

"Certainly, certainly, my boy—you're the brains, I'm the trumpet. I'm the brass band and the flags flying. H'm. We'll see the world together." He became absorbed again, "*Motto:* 'Who will *work* that England may live?' Good, that." He began dictating as to a secretary, " 'And delicate handling of the German crisis and salvation of our financial situation. The Bank of England has been our Rock of Gibraltar. Fortify the Mother Rock.' Eh? Eh? '*And* few people realize today the benefits of the Naval Conference. Which established our position today.' " He frowned ferociously. "No Vigilante Committee. Not English. Out in the open." He bit his lip and took a step, frowning. The thought of the merchants of England putting their heads together and getting up a privateering scheme to "save the country" without him irritated him. He rushed on, shaking a fist, " '*Therefore*'—letter to MacDonald, anyone, letter—'Therefore, a National Government including members of all other parties such as governed England in Napoleon's time—' "

"That reference will stink," Alphendéry remarked.

"Eh, stink, eh? No good? Throw it out. Gladstone, Grand Old Man's motto: Peace, Reconstruction, Reform.

Today: 'Coalition Government's version: Peace, Reconstruction, Progress.'" He breathed and sat down. "Boy," he said radiantly, "we're made! I give them this! I drop it in their laps! I became an English citizen. Left France for England. Is that a compliment! I say, 'Boys, you see I'm a patriot already, even before you take me in.' No mistakes! You bring me good luck. *Mahzel* No lion's share. I'm satisfied with little. I start in the cause of labor. Well, eh?"

He thirstily asked for flattery. Alphendéry, tired, emerged from his battle with the flood. "Why don't you devote your energies to French politics?"

He swung his great head. "No, no, no, *NO!* They're too smart. This hokum don't go. One day they won't be so smart, when they get an empire too, but I can't wait for that day. When a war comes, maybe England wins, maybe she's defeated. There's war! All right! I'm in. I'm doing a national duty supplying food. She wins. I helped the victory. She's defeated. They want food anyhow. England can't live six weeks without food. My relations on the Continent, America. What can be done without borrowing from America. See! Unofficial ambassador: Arcos in one man! he, he! A big straddle. I'm hedged for any eventuality. In France; no! They'll maybe go socialist. Out with the international crook, big capitalist. See! In England! To be levelheaded. Responsibilities of keeping the Northwest frontier."

Alphendéry seemed depressed. "I'll see what I can dope out, Henri. You can see the letter on Tuesday. I'll post it."

Henri was disappointed. "Tuesday?"

"Yes, Henri. I'm too tired. I came here for a rest."

"All right, my boy. Fine, swell. Tuesday. And then you'll come to England with me." But Alphendéry was not finished with the memorandum. Henri Léon took him out to dinner only to bounce up and down, answer telephone calls, send the waiters scuttling for telegraph boys, command writing blocks of the headwaiter, shout inspirations to Alphendéry in a Napoleonic style, and in every way behave like a lion in a fit, till Alphendéry's complexion was chalk-blue, and he threw down the block in a temper. Léon flushed, suddenly cooled off, and became extremely sweet. The waiters, like a band of dyspeptic gorillas, stood in a half-circle in the shadows of the nearly empty restaurant and looked at their tormentor.

"How can you behave like that, Léon?" asked Alphendéry when he had his coffee before him. His voice was acid-sweet and evidently Léon's roughhouse still rankled in his mind.

"What's that? Behave like?—"

"Léon, you know you only hustle these poor fellows and create a rumpus, because they know you're so much richer than they are. You dribble humility when you yourself are with somebody you can't buy out. Aren't you ashamed to be so grossly economic?"

Léon dropped his eyes and flushed; he grumbled gently, "No, Michel, no; you've got me wrong—I wouldn't do that. I didn't think. I was a poor boy. Michel, does it look like that? I didn't know. Pardon me, my boy." His immense murmur went on for a few minutes, and then Michel forgave him and the air was perfumed with the flowers of innocence for a while. But in a quarter of an hour Léon had become distrait and was blowing to himself, drumming on the table, looking at Alphendéry with cross eyes, silently humming and hawing. Presently he got up abruptly from the café table where they were sitting and said briskly, "Come on, let's walk, my boy—good for you."

After five minutes' walk, Léon as suddenly declared for bed. Alphendéry had been in his room one minute when he heard Léon's door softly open and, opening his, he observed Léon, in war paint, fresh and perfumed for the fray, rush out into the night and the streets, hot for women.

He sat down in his room and knotted his handkerchief. "Which is better, the quicksands or the—quicksands or the —quicksands, the quicksands or the volcano: the volcano? Jules is the quicksands, Léon the volcano. Can I stand —why don't I strike out for myself—Jean said. Jean said, 'It's time you cut the painter and—' cut the painter and —'cast off and—joined us. Too much wedded to luxury.' And what luxury? The luxury of being hounded to death by madmen. Mad egotists. His political secretary. Ghost! My life's a ghost's life. My tombstone. Here lies Heinrich Heine, poet and freeman. Here lies Michel Alphendéry, twenty-five per cent capital levy. R.I.P. Or, Michel Alphendéry: he sold short. R.I.P. Unwept, unhonored, and unsung. No. Professional lion tamer. No. 'Political, literary, social'—h'm, social amenities. Running electors in

368

Léon's car to the polls—to the polls—fat chance, chance. No." He took out of his pockets the notes Léon had shouted to him in the restaurant. " 'We are in a vicious circle: how can we cut the Gordian knot? Despite the fact that the—' " He murmured, " 'A vicious circle,' I should say, I should say—ha. No more. I must have peace before I die. . . ."

Scene Fifty-one: All About the Lord

WHEN Alphendéry got back from coffee, Jacques Manray hailed him. "Mr. Schicklgrüber's here and is looking for you. He's in Mr. Bertillon's office."

Alphendéry's face lightened. He became jovial and hurried upstairs.

But Jules had not seen Schicklgrüber. Alphendéry went round the doors and inside Comte Jean de Guipatin's room he heard a warm, callow drawl, "Well, it's all over London that Jules and Carrière have a big sterling contract and that's you're betting on sterling staying on the level. Do you know that's what I call crazy? I don't care, but he ought to. I heard it and the Lord heard it too."

The young comte answered dubiously, "Jules says no, but Carrière is bragging. It's his idea of a modern duel. The duel's old-fashioned and he's carrying it out with modern weapons—honorably and by subterfuge! That was the story he told me. Carrière's an old school friend of mine, as is Jules."

"Well—sterling's going off for sure: that's my guess," said Schicklgrüber airily.

Alphendéry opened the door, with a broad grin. "Hullo, Davidgor!" He began with a full throat, "What bloody reactions are you and the Lord promoting this week?"

Schicklgrüber didn't heed this remark which touched on universes far beyond his poor brain. He leapt up and towered grotesquely over Alphendéry. "By jing!" He grinned widely and said to Jean de Guipatin, "It sounds like the Bull of Bashan, it smells like Araby, it smiles like a Cheshire Cat, it can explain everything like a *Chedar* boy: it must be Alphendéry. Well, I hear you been inspecting the banks in Antwerp and Amsterdam with a view to taking over same. What's the result?"

"Marble is used for tombs and by a simple analogy for the places we keep our jack in," said Michel.

Davigdor lowered his voice, looked obscenely at them both, his way of expressing intimacy. "I hear there's a Dutch group wants to buy Jules out. Why don't he sell? He's only got to get a couple of first-class accountants in: I know a good firm."

They both laughed at his naïve and buffoon inquisitiveness. He leered joyously. "How's that new feller of yours getting on? That hard-luck feller that was in the Claude smash?"

"The market rose and Aristide ran, not even waiting to pick up his dignity," said Jean de Guipatin simply.

For a moment there was silence. Both the bank men looked at Davigdor with undisguised speculation. He smiled knowingly at them. Davigdor Schicklgrüber, a Rhineland Jew, in many respects resembled the ideal Aryan although he was not, as the saying goes, as blond as Hitler, as athletic as Goebbels, as manly as Roehm, or as refined as Goering. Instead, he was blond, blue-eyed, tall, muscular, and given to physical exercises. After picking up a living loafing in Rhineland towns, selling novelties, furs, and ladies' shirtwaists, he came, through an uncle in the Hebrew community, into stockbroking, thence into England and thus into a familiar's job and with Lord Zinovraud, the great Scottish peer and multimillionaire. As anti-Semitism was Lord Zinovraud's public policy, or rather one of the tricks he kept up his wide sleeve, for his private commissions he used the great lout Davigdor, who talked as if he had adenoids and so seemed stupid, and asserted that he had nothing on his mind but petticoats. Davigdor had a vocabulary of two or three hundred words at the most and a lot of those were primitive Anglo-Saxon, also common in low German. Davigdor's exclusive trick was professional Boeotianism: everyone loved him for a fool and no one suspected him. Everyone immediately said, "Now this great man, Lord Zinovraud, like all great men from time out of mind, keeps his jester, chuckle-headed Shicklgrüber," and they concluded, "No use trying to pry Schicklgrüber out of his job: I couldn't be as idiotic as Schicklgrüber if I tried—he was born for the job."

Thus the professional clod ran round Europe with the name of "the Lord" on his lips and the open secret of his connection with "the Lord" in everyone's heart: and yet no one suspected his missions or really asked why such a nitwit was forever taking de luxe expresses from Berlin to Paris and Paris to Lisbon and Lisbon to Rome. He did it for women, they said, taking their cue from Schicklgrüber himself. In fact, most businessmen had a sort of commiseration for Schicklgrüber who stood so close to the old childless millionaire and yet did not know how to make the best of such an opportunity.

Davigdor was, as usual, dressed in shabby clothes and had a seedy appearance, bloodshot eyes, and a jaundiced complexion. "I say, that was a wonderful tip you gave me, Michel," said Schicklgrüber. "I buy the *Inprecor* every week now, and I tell the Lord the news out of it: he thinks my political sense has gone up one thousand per cent. He dreams of the Reds at night. He thinks they have long ears and he doesn't know they can really put two sentences together. He's a pest . . . he's always ringing me up to find out what I know of the situation. You know me, Michel, I'm a fool: I don't know Mussolini from Hoover. But he's beginning to think I'm a politician. Can you beat it? He said to me, 'Go to Paris and nose out the situation.' What can I do? I tell you, it's not a blessing exactly. Day before yesterday, I'd been up with a girl all night. I only got to bed at six o'clock. I was lying on the couch, she on the bed: clothes—everywhere. Suddenly the phone rings. I take it in my sleep. 'Whazzat?' 'Jew, aren't you up yet?' he yells. He calls me 'Jew': a joke of his. 'Lemme lone,' I say, 'I just got to bed.' 'Whaddye think of Insull?' he says. 'Can't think, Lord,' says I, 'too tired.' 'Try sleeping alone,' he yells and jams down the telephone. In a quarter of an hour it rings again. 'Jew!' 'What?' 'Get down to my country place. Quick! My car'll be there in five minutes.' 'O.K., Lord.' I left the girl there. Maybe, she's still there. I haven't been home since. He's like that. What did he want me for? Ask me about this house painter Hitler. A nobody. Getting me out of bed for that."

"Where did you come from?"

"Oh, I don't know. I was all over the place last week. Germany, I think. The Lord had some message to send to Berlin. No idea what it was. He never trusts me: I'm too stupid. I met a wonderful blonde on the station and she started to flirt right away. I shied off her . . . you know how I am."

"Yes. I know."

"Sure. But she kept right after me. I slept with her in Berlin, two or three days: nice girl. Say! I hope I gave the feller the Lord's message. Did I? Gave me her address: Frau Florry Weiler, Poste Restante. I think I'll write. She said she'd come to London. I gave her my address. J. Davies, Poste Restante, Ipswich. Never had time to do anything else in Berlin. They say it's miserable now. Is it?"

"What are things like in Germany?"

"Oh, bad, good . . . do I know? Had no time to see. I was in bed all the time. Oh, I saw another girl, too. A Hungarian, too. Jing, what a girl! Blonde, too. She was married to an officer. Say! I couldn't get anywhere with the Lord if you hadn't told me about that paper: what's the name? Prinkor? I say; how you doing here? Bad, eh?"

"What makes you say that, Davigdor?"

"Oh, I hear in London. Don't know where I heard. Some ass journalist, someone in the office. Don't know. It's just instinct. But Bertillon is selling in London. Why? Only seems one thing. When the gold flies out of the coalscuttle, the bailiff is drinking a beer round the corner. Worth anything? Purely as sniffing, I mean, Michel."

"You interest me, Davigdor. Where are you lunching?"

"Oh, lessee! Ten o'clock seeing a blonde. Eleven o'clock. Don't know what I'm doing. Oh: eleven o'clock seeing a blonde. Twelve? Maybe some date with a girl. One I'll have lunch with you, Michel; You tell me all the dirt. He, he. Eh? 'Safternoon, can't see you—sleeping with some-one."

"Well, wait a minute."

Alphendéry went to Jules. "I say, Jules, the 'fool for the Lord's sake' is here. Do you want to see him? He says there are tales about you in London: selling gold and so on. See what you can get out of him."

"Certainly: where is he?"

Schicklgrüber, a boorish flibbertigibbet, was by now in the midst of a tale of his sexual prowess, to William. When Jules entered, Schicklgrüber sprang up, held out his hand with pleasure. His interest in rich men was so instinctive that it was robbed of servility: he had a manly style with them which came from the sympathy he felt for them.

"Bertillon! Why don't you send Carrière to a sanitarium for life."

"Why? Do they talk about it in London?"

"Sure, sure! They know everything in London. Why, everyone knows that brewery deal never went through and that he's just pulling your leg. Why, he had all the dope, Jules. He knew the pound was slipping. And he's tightening the noose round your neck every quarterday. What a *machaia* for him. Why don't you get him for grand larceny or whatever you Frenchmen have? You don't have that, do you?"

"Go to the devil," said Jules.

"Jules," Davidgor implored, "your credit is no good in London, no good at all. Because you haven't got the stomach to dish Carrière. You know he's going about saying he'll get you? Why don't you bump him off? Say, give the boys a show."

William intervened, "We don't owe him anything, Schicklgrüber; we don't have to pay him."

"No? And the billet-doux from Jules he's showing all over London and Amsterdam and everywhere. Say, you're dumb, Jules. Why don't you bump him off?"

William said, "What billet-doux? Then there is a contract."

"Oh, sure, just a little bit of a private letter: that's all."

"You lie, Jules," said Davidgor cheerfully. "It's a contract. I saw it. Everyone saw it. He says he's going to publish it in Sournois' paper if you don't come through."

"Does the Lord own newspapers?" inquired Alphendéry.

"The Lord? Oh, no, no, no. He wants to influence cabinets. He says, 'Look at Hearst, Rothermere, Beaverbrook, and Coty. They own newspapers and they're about as effectual as a dead leech.' "

Schicklgrüber, seeing Bertillon sit down, sat down again. "Jules, go the right way about it. For instance, you're going to have trouble with this louse Carrière. This self-decorated Christmas tree. Carrière has got the first infirmity of feeble minds. He's telling it round that he's going to buy a newspaper. Now, you keep away from all that and you'll win hands down. Never own a newspaper;

own journalists: never buy the news-services. Just pay a whisper: never involve a politican—he'll let you down or be let out. And compromise: don't fight."

"Too much to remember," said Jules curtly. "You've got to handle politicians, like live wires, with newspapers."

"But bait them, keep them swarming round, don't land them into your basket, or you'll find they're sting rays." The great horselaugh followed which made everything he said seem the gabblings of a born natural.

Bertillon cut this line off abruptly, with his teeth. He was darker than usual. "Does the Lord do all his share business through your firm, Ganz and Genug, Davigdor?"

"Not all—just a few dribbles. Don't know where he does most of his stuff. He doesn't trust me, you know. 'Imbecile,' he calls me. He rings up. 'Idiot,' he says."

"Well, Davigdor, couldn't you shuttle us a bit of it?"

"If we could get Zinovraud's business," said Alphendéry, "a hundred Carrières couldn't hurt us: it would be worth our while and we'd pay you a first-rate salary, Davigdor. Do you want the money?"

Schicklgrüber opened his eyes. "Really? It's not so very much, you know. I don't know where he does his business. Not with us. I have no influence with him. He does what he likes. No influence. No, course I got no dough. I could use money. But could I hand you the business? I don't know. He has no confidence in me."

Jules compressed his mouth satirically. "Go on, Davigdor, cut out the come-on!"

"No, no, really," protested Schicklgrüber. "I have to beg and pray him to give me a few hundred shares to keep me with Ganz and Genug. They wanted to fire me the other day."

Jules let a loud laugh blurt.

Schicklgrüber shambled out to get his shave; his blond-red hair had been sticking out of his graceless chin all the morning. He renewed the appointment to lunch with Alphendéry at one. When he had gone Alphendéry said, "Shave? No, blonde. He's probably picked up six since he got up this morning."

"If he ever went to bed."

William marveled for the tenth time. "How does he do it? He's the ugliest man in Europe."

Pettishly, Jules cried, "Go and wash the sleep out of your eyes: you're crazy if you think women like collar

374

ads. Anyone can see Davidgor can make good. I say, this is more important. What do you think Lord Zinovraud pays him?"

"Very little," said Michel. "Look how seedy he looks. That proves Schicklgrüber is honest. Another man would rob the Lord left and right. That's how he keeps his job."

Jules smiled quaintly. "He must make a pile in commissions. I hear Ganz and Genug have no other client: they don't seem to do any business."

Lazily, William, "Say, what other clients would *you* want?"

Jules was working away at the problem of Davidgor, like a hundred other men in Europe. "Do you think Davidgor is as stupid as he makes out? You can't tell me he's been with the Lord since fifteen years and got nothing out of it. It isn't human."

Alphendéry opined, "All rich men, especially in their old age, begin to long for someone who will hang round them, amuse them, apologize for them, be valet-and-son in one, new doormat and old dog. He'll probably provide for Davidgor in his will. But he's mean and crabby . . . I think it highly likely that Davidgor doesn't get anything out of it beyond his commissions on the stock-exchange business."

William clattered rudely, "He's the Lord's stalking-horse for women. He's his come-on man. He can't run all those girls himself. That's the secret."

"The Lord's seventy-eight if he's a day. Why he goes round in a Bath chair."

"You're crazy now: I saw Zinovraud in the paper this week. He believes in Hitler and he looks gilt-edged."

Bertillon stirred again. "He would put us on our feet, if he's Zinovraud's procurer. And this Carrière business. Zinovraud could crush Carrière if the brewery deal is a fraud."

"A pander is always nearest to a rich man's heart," said Alphendéry.

"His what?" William's lazy tones.

Jules waved his hand. "What should we offer him, Alphendéry? Have you any idea?"

Alphendéry said promptly, "Offer him two hundred thousand francs a year plus commissions, the fourth fifty thousand to be a permanent advance on commissions annually. That salary is for the Lord's Continental business and any tips Davigdor can give us."

William said, "That's a lot of money."

"If it gets to be known—and it would be known tomorrow—that we're operating for the Lord, money will flow into our pockets by itself. We can laugh at Carrière, the Comtesse de Voigrand, ex-kings, and functioning dictators."

"A multimillionaire as canny as Zinovraud doesn't trust his business to his decoy," objected William. "I don't believe he has Zinovraud in his pocket at all: that's his selling talk."

Jules insulted his bachelor brother. "Say, what do you know about it? Get a girl for a rich man and you're on his pay roll for life. And he'll trust you where he wouldn't trust his own mother."

At lunch Alphendéry made Schicklgrüber the proposition and Schicklgrüber turned it down.

"But Davigdor, do you get that much from Ganz and Genug? Surely not."

"Oh, sometimes no, sometimes yes—it depends on the market, you know. Sometimes the Lord gets big news and then he plunges heavily. I can never tell. I make pots, sometimes, but I'm such a fool about women, I spend it all. Then I send Louise, my girl, you know, to posh schools and then I send my old wife a lot. I'm having a good time; why shouldn't she? I never have a bean. But I don't want to give the Lord the idea I'm hawking his account about. You know. He might get sick of me and throw me out. After all, what string have I got him on? I'm not worth anything to him. When he wants to, he can enroll me in the unemployed. Nobody in the City of London or anywhere else would offer me ten francs then. That's the reason you boys want me. Everyone knows I'm the Lord's mongrel pup that he found pissing on his doormat one night. Don't I look like it? Haw, haw!"

His golden horselaugh, engaging, idiotic, rang out among the palms and mirrors of Philippe's. Alphendéry laughed. Other diners stopped for a moment and smiled, rare thing in Paris. He said lower, "I had a wonderful girl before lunch. By jings, Paris has wonderful women. Vienna, too. Berlin, too. I don't know how I manage to stay in London. I'm like a cat on hot bricks. I tell the Lord he's crazy but he cares only for money. That's his only weakness. He's a wonderful man," he went on earnestly, shaking his curly head over the plate, "he's a genius." A legato note of awe went trailing through his throat, "He's a genius, Michel! He's a wonderful man."

"He's not very wonderful to you, Davidgor. It isn't right. He ought to take care of you. He's got nobody to leave it to. He's got dozens of millions in sterling lying by. You're a fool, Davigdor. Doesn't he even offer you a small annuity?" The multiple millions of Zinovraud filled even Alphendéry with desire.

Davigdor shrugged his shoulders, threw out his clumsy hands, laughed, wobbled his head, "I know. But" (very low, with great simplicity), "what I'm telling you now must never be told, Michel: the Lord is very good to me. He treats me like a son—bastard son, haw, haw! The other day he called me over to his couch where he was lying. He says to me suddenly, like that, 'Jew, how much money have you in the bank?' 'Oh, about ten pounds, Lord, that's all. I spend it all.' 'Absurd,' he said, 'why don't you tell me to make you a transfer?' 'I don't want it, Lord. I'd only spend it on cuties. This way I have to work to get them for nothing.' He laughed: 'If you won't accept money, don't worry: I'll remember you. I'll see you don't want.' 'Thanks very much, Lord Zinovraud'—nothing more, he doesn't like it. Then he suddenly barks, 'Why the devil did you report to me those Modderfonteins? Buy some industrials and don't report them to me unless I ask. Worrying me with trifles!' 'Which industrials, Lord?' 'The ones you fancy.'

"Like that, put on, you know, to hide his generosity."

For an instant, something cracked: he turned a merry, enlivened eye towards the glass beside which he sat and through the slit of that eye, wicked Pan winked at the world. Alphendéry, his eyes trained on the piece of meat he was eating, and involved in his own calculations, saw nothing. Schicklgrüber had once more the same good-hearted, ugly, stupid expression as before. Was it an effect of the mirror, or of light falling high between the houses of the Rue Daunou? Schicklgrüber took a sip of water. He always refused alcoholic drinks. "It goes to my head and there's nothing to stop it running round and round. I begin to gossip. I have no control over myself."

"That's a very good salary we're offering you, Davigdor:

how can you afford to turn it down, even so? Even if you get that amount from Ganz and Genug, why not double it?"

"I'd rather not have money; I spend it all. It's better for me to be poor; I keep within bounds. Lord Zinovraud knows that; he doesn't give me much. I implore him not to."

"He's just mean to you, in other words. You're excusing him."

"Oh, no, no, don't say that." Schicklgrüber was really shocked, "The Lord—well, I'll tell you something, but you mustn't ever tell it to anyone else."

"Of course not, Davigdor."

"Oh, I can trust you, Michel. *Ai, yai, yai*, once I got into such a mess by talking too much. I'm always doing it. Seas of troubles. The Lord would throw me out if he knew I talked about his goodness. He doesn't like it. He has a wonderful nature. One day he says to me, 'I'm not too generous to you, Judas.' (Oh, he calls me 'Judas,' too—it's a sort of pet name, instead of 'Jew.' It's his idea of humor.)

"I said, 'I don't ask for anything more, Lord: you're decent to me. I live. I'm not rich but I drink, I whore. I haven't too much and so I keep respectable.' He says to me angrily. 'No, you have no one to provide for you; if I go, no one will bother his head two minutes about you. You've got to be provided for.'

" 'All right, Lord,' I said quietly, 'whatever you like.' You see, I don't insist . . . I don't ask him, 'What do you mean?' Nothing. And the funny thing is, he said no more for a few days; and he put the idea into my mind, I was just beginning to think, 'The old dog is mean to me.' A few days later he throws some papers rudely onto the table in front of me and says, 'Can you read? What's that? I found it among my papers. Some silly fool stuck it there.' So I read and find out it's a factory site he's got. I say to him, 'But, Lord, it's a factory site you've bought. It's only dated three weeks back.' 'That's it,' he says, 'I'm going to build a factory. See to it for me.' He talks like that, rough, quick. I say, 'Lord, you must tell me what you want to make. Is it knitted goods, is it guns, is it chocolates?' 'Novelties,' he says, sharp, as if I knew it all along. 'You know I wanted to make novelties. See to it for me. Toys. Modern, new toys.' 'All right, Lord.'

"And I go off and find out what it would cost. I tell him, he gives me the money, and when I ask him if he wants it this way or that, he says, 'You see to it, you do it the way you want it: you know as much about it as me.' So I build the factory and get in machinery and get supplies and employ labor, and I say to him, 'Lord, the factory's all ready and the men and girls are waiting for you to say the word.' He says, 'What factory, fool?' 'The novelties factory, Lord.' 'I don't want to make novelties any more. Shut it up.' So I shut it up and there it stays. Then one day, about six months later, he says to me, 'I've got a wonderful name for your novelties, Judas.' 'What is it, Lord?' *'Black Legion!'* 'Black Legion . . . no good. Not English.' 'Never mind. Go and see if anyone has it and if they have, buy it.' So I go and look and presently I find some poor little outfit upcountry actually has the name 'Black Legion' for shirts. I say to the Lord, 'What will I pay for it?' 'What you must. You know what I want.' So I say, 'Lord, you'll have to give me a few days off: I'll have to go and mosey around.' 'All right. Don't stay too long. Don't cut up.'

"I go to this place and I find two or three little Jewish fellers in one little room trying to make shirts. They're waiting for orders. So I think, 'How can I get the name away from them without putting the price up?' I think and think. My topknot isn't fast, you know. Then I get an idea. I get nicely dressed with a black hat with a broad brim, like a *Chedar* Jew not long from Poland and I go into them and I say, 'Boys, it ain't nice for Jewish fellers to be calling goods "Black Legion," a name that refers to that louse Mussolini, to fascists. The fascists are bad to little businessmen like you and then there's this Hitler in Germany saying he'll wipe out the Jews.' They say, 'Yid, what can we do? We have to make a living, don't we?' 'It seems to me, Yids,' I say, 'that you aren't making much of a living: it's the name that's the curse. Jewish fellers will never make money with a thin-luck name like that.' 'Business is business,' they say to me. 'Naturally we don't like that name so much, we don't like making black shirts neither, but what can we do—there is the wife, there is the children, there is Becky and Shorra to find a husband. Not nice, it isn't, but it's business. There you are.' 'Listen, Yids,' I say, 'would you sell the name? I think maybe I could get up a subscription amongst
379

religious Jews to take it out of circulation. You've got to think of the wives, the children, Becky, Shorra, good. So we'll buy it out of circulation, perhaps. How much do you want for it?' I see them looking at each other, I see them thinking, 'He's got something up his sleeve.' Naturally, they don't believe me any more than I expect them to believe me. So I say, 'All right, boys, think it over. I'll come back after lunch.'

"For lunch, where do I go? I know they'll follow me. I go to the poor kosher lunchroom. Sure enough, a few minutes later, I see them going past and looking in. They don't come in, they're too poor. But it's all right—it proves I have a bit of money, not too much. After lunch I go back and say, 'Well?' 'Well,' they say, 'mister, we would sell the name cheap for a good cause, but there is—and they start to tell me the seas of troubles they have. 'I know,' I say, 'I'm reasonable. How much?' 'Well,' they say (and I can see they're frightened to drop a sledge hammer on the eggshell), 'would one thousand pounds be about what you could pay? If you collected enough?' By jing, Michel, I had to admire them. There they are in a miserable room not good enough for an outhouse trying to sell a miserable couple black shirts to make a living and they ask one thousand pounds! So I let my face fall for a bit, and I can see they're terrified. But finally I say, 'Well, boys, I'll bring a lawyer and we'll draw up the sale and we'll talk about the price together, eh?'

"You can see they're nearly fainting for the money, now they've heard it mentioned. So I go and cable the Lord,

WILL YOU PAY UP TO THREE THOUSAND POUNDS? TOUGH BABIES.

NOT MORE, he telegraphs back.

"All right, the next day we draw up the contract but leave out the price. We go back to the little room where the two boys have their business, and I see they already have taken the little sign off the window BLACK LEGION SHIRTS and they have put up another: WHITE DOVE SHIRTS.

"'Poor boys,' I think, 'why should I rob them?' I can see they haven't slept all night and have been asking advice of their wives and second cousins. 'Well, Kone,' I say, 'I went to see a rich Jew yesterday and he's going to give me some money. He doesn't think Jews ought to make black shirts with all the trouble in Germany.' They watch me. Good. 'Now,' I say, 'I know you boys aren't doing any business. I know. I made inquiries.' They start up, but I quiet them. 'Now, boys, I've got some money and we'll put down the price.' 'What price do you mean?' says Kone in a little voice. 'Put it down, lawyer,' says I. 'One thousand pounds.'

"The boys nearly fell off their chairs. They never expected to get the half, I don't think. I could see them getting brain fever on the spot. '*Ai*, we've been robbed, it's worth a lot, our name, and we've sold it for one thousand pounds. Someone wants it . . . we should have held out.' Blah-blah. I couldn't resist getting a bit of fun out of it. I thought I'd torture them some more . . . I thought I'd give them something to think about on their deathbeds. When the Angel of Death comes they'll still have a second to think about me. So I said, 'Wait, lawyer: I've changed my mind. I've just thought of another rich Jew might help me out. Write down the price now: fifteen hundred pounds.'

"You should have seen those boys! But they signed it. They thought I might be mad, too. Yes, at that, they went white again; they thought I was mad and there was nothing to it. When I shook hands with them and no money, I thought their hearts would break. Then I get out my portfolio and give them three hundred five-pound notes. They thought I was a forger. They refused them unless I would promise to go to the bank and see them changed. They didn't dare ask me who I was acting for. I think they thought it was maybe someone in Germany. Poor little fellers!

"I came back to the Lord and said, 'I had an awful time getting that name. I beat them down to fifteen hundred pounds. They think it's going to be a wow, that name.' 'So do I,' said he. 'You've got to be a Jew to deal with Jews,' said I. 'I keep you for that,' says he. 'Open the factory now.'"

"But," objected Alphendéry, "there aren't any novelties
381

in England called 'Black Legion.' I happen to know because Léon's been investigating the novelties business in England."

"Oh, no: the Lord decided finally the time wasn't ripe for fascist names yet, so we changed the name for the time being. We've just got it on the hob. . . . . Then when it was all going about a month I bring Zinovraud the balance sheet and he looks at it and then throws it aside: 'Don't show me that, Judas: that's your department. You run it, if you can. If you lose money, tell me; if you make it, wait till I ask you.'

"See how nice he is to me? But say nothing, mind you. He would kick me out. He hates to be thought generous."

"He doesn't suffer much, on that account, then," laughed Alphendéry.

"Oh, he's all right. . . . Say, Michel, I tell the Lord about you: he thinks you're a wow. He told me to tell you you're mad to stay with Bertillon. That's the reason I wouldn't take your pay if you gave me twice as much. I can write fancy figures on paper myself."

"You think it's as bad as that? The Lord told you to say that? They exaggerate so much in that hothouse of the City of London. Listen, if it's from Carrière—"

"Oh, that's only one thing. The Lord says, 'Get a job in the City while the going's good.' You got a lot of clients, haven't you?"

"This fellow Carrière is criminal. Why, Jules is rolling in gold! I know what he's got."

"Do you know what he owes? I don't like to contradict a clever man like you, Michel, but you're wrong and you're goddamn wrong."

Michel, after some minutes of trifling conversation, said with some agitation, "Zinovraud really knows something?"

"Oh, rumors, rumors."

"I say, I'd like to meet the old rascal when I go to London. I might consider Stewart, Murthen, and Company. Stewart invited me to go in with him. Do you think you could arrange for me to meet the Lord?"

"Well, Michel, you know how I am. He's my bread and butter. I don't introduce my *donah* to a pal. If you do me some big favor, say like swinging some of your accounts to Ganz and Genug, I will. That's fair."

"Surely, surely."

382

"Well, what does Davigdor want?" Jules was unusually insistent.

"He said no—and double no."

"I'll pay him whatever he wants."

"Calm yourself. He wouldn't come at any price." Jules was hurt. Alphendéry soothed him, "I guess he does better than he says with G. and G. and the Lord."

William, watching his brother, drawled, "You bet. That guy doesn't lick the Lord's boots for nothing. Besides, every firm in Europe has offered him a job. We're not good enough for him, that's all. Did he give you any tips?"

"He says nothing doing in tips, unless we pass him some business. He's honest about it."

"Nonsense!" Jules cried, much irritated. "G. and G. don't make a cent on the Lord. It doesn't pay them to. Would we? What would Zinovraud's business be to us? Could we monkey with his account? Not likely. It would be good only as advertisement. Therefore Davigdor doesn't make many commissions on it; he can only get a salary; and how big a salary? What's the secret now?"

Alphendéry watched him with anxiety. "Jules, don't get excited: you can bet this is the three thousandth proposition Davigdor has turned down. He's dizzy . . . he doesn't know who's offering it, or what it is, by this. Davigdor, one of the great open secrets of Europe . . . Zinovraud's undercover man, travels incognito like a King-Emperor, preceded by stage whispers that can be heard from Balbriggan to Ekaterinoslav."

There was a silence. William finally put into words the thing weighing on them. "Michel, did he offer to introduce you to the Lord?"

"No. He said the Lord is his game." They laughed and were all relieved. Alphendéry prattled on, "He's going to Portugal. I'd like to know why he flits about Europe. He's going to buy estates for the Lord (he says) in Portugal. The Lord thinks Portugal with a bloody dictator, Carmona, with Reds in prison, workers dying on the streets and the rich enriching, by morning gray and evening red, is paradise for him. He's laying up treasure for himself near the Spanish frontier. One: he's afraid of the English workers. Two: he's afraid of the English finances. Three: he swears the republic won't last in Spain and when labor is cheaper he'll buy olive fields there."

"I'll bet Davigdor knows a lot he doesn't say," Jules sighed, longing.

William remarked, "Everyone tries to suck him."

The eddy of Davigdor's incursion died down, but left long afterripples; for weeks they were maneuvering to get Zinovraud's account or part of it from Davigdor and for weeks Davigdor was objecting, over the telephone, with pain and protest in his voice, that he was poor, they were trying to double-cross a poor plain dealer who couldn't defend himself, and that he wouldn't yield a single inch if they didn't transfer some of their giant accounts to Ganz and Genug. But neither would move. Ganz and Genug were convinced that the Bertillons would fail because no one knew their backers, and Bertillon heard, similarly, that Ganz and Genug would fail and were a scraggy crowd, beneath the notice of a society firm like Bertillon Brothers.

Scene Fifty-two: Rumor

THEY next attacked the morsel thrown them by Schicklgrüber: the "common knowledge" that Carrière had lied to Bertillon and that the brewery had never been sold and that the drafts that would be sent to Bertillon and the papers accompanying them were therefore a conspiracy, a concealed bet on the currency—the "common knowledge" that Jules had really signed a contract with Carrière and that Carrière would bleed him to death.

"I always knew it," Jules lied, to seem less the fool. "I was just waiting to get the goods on him."

Léon came in to find out Alphendéry's opinion of the market and heard jealously that Schicklgrüber had visited them. "That boy knows something . . . he must know something. Otherwise why did he drop in? Not for business."

"He knows nothing. That's his charm," said Michel.

"No, sir, don't you believe it. Why should Zinovraud employ a fool?"

"He's the only one who doesn't try to rob him," explained Michel. "Everyone else who comes within hail-

384

ing distance thinks he owes it to his own self-respect to try to promote Zinovraud."

"Yes, yes—and the Black Legion. How can a Jew put out Black Legion?—and—no, it doesn't *stimm*. Chuckle-headed—and the Black Legion story. No my boy. Let's put it he *was* stupid when Zinovraud met him. But no one could live with Zinovraud for fifteen years and remain stupid. Now it's just a good disguise. H'm? A fox. Foxy. . . . He sent me a prospectus, Parthis Goldfields. Do you? . . . I bought some. How did he . . . you told him you knew me?"

"Yes. Did he remember your address?"

"Oh-ho: my address . . ." The telephone rang; he grabbed it. "My call. Graetz? . . . Send me one copy more of every letter. . . . I know I had copies but I left them somewhere . . . I know I took them but I left them. Can't you send me some more, Graetz? I know the girls are busy . . . Graetz! That shipment: documents into bank with accompanying letter, copy to—got that? Safe custody, allowing for release to our order. Liverpool, Liverpool, if Liverpool up ⅜ to 2d. sell two-loads-March. March in Rotterdam very firm, ten cents and market not too—very firm looks like a—sell four hundred to six hundred Rotterdam—no gulden margins, get back guilder margins—Manitobas four loads Columbia, all grade, sell old, new: ALL; firm offer to have in hand so can sell Monday, take firm offers, give us firm offers. Graetz! Send me those letters like a good boy. I don't know where I lost them. Can't you do what I ask? . . . Danube—do not sell until sample. Graetz! Those girls got not too much to do. Now post them right away. What? Yes. If yes on Berlin yes, if yes, satisfied, happy. Sell in strong spots. Yes, and Graetz! The letters."

He rang off, dimpled to Alphendéry. "I lost a whole batch of important letters in the House of All Nations, or maybe—yes, the hotel. I wouldn't go back. Let him—those girls got nothing to do. He always wants me to explain. . . . When are you coming in with me, Alphendéry?"

"How can I help you, Henri? Short of a grandfatherly throwback, somewhere in Mannheim—and I guess he sold canary seed—I know zero of the grain trade."

"You could learn. And it's my bonds. I want someone for that. Now this—Schicklgrüber's—he offered to intro-

385

duce you to Zinovraud, eh? You ought to make money, Michel. You've got all the pipe lines." He whispered, "I got an answer from the Minister, from Honfleur."

Everywhere that Davigdor went he left insomnia and the gold dust of hope: nobody could sleep thinking of Zinovraud's uncounted millions which had passed them by, in the trail of the comet Davigdor; no one could stop wondering how this yellow-headed chump had ensnared the Lord: no one could stop calculating how much he had snared. And those who had brushed against him, found themselves, for the moment, the object of admiration and desire. No athletic beauty married to an invalid, no youth of sixteen, no debonair valetudinarian in a low vaudeville show, no dowager in pink organdie at Nice, ever felt the desires that rich men felt when Davigdor passed their way.

In his room, Jules, laughing for the world, frowned to himself, called William and Paul and Francis to him for a family council. "We've got to stop these rumors Carrière started."

William, in usual vein, "I'd rather spend my time getting accounts than stopping rumors."

"I had Adam Constant up here this morning," said Jules. "He's literary. I want to see if we can't start sending in pars and comic poems about Carrière to some of the dirt sheets. Also Jouhaud is putting in pars for me about Carrière in the *Agence Boursière*. De Ville-de-Ré is getting in touch with *Aux Ecoutes* this week. Those are the first rifleshots. I'll bring up my heavy artillery next week. . . . What he can do, I can."

"Put your money into United Gas Improvement, instead," recommended William.

Jules frowned. "I've been thinking over Schicklgrüber's visit. Why did he come? I guess he came out of curiosity. And I guess he's right. Either I get Carrière, or Carrière gets me. It's a straight play, now."

"Well, why plot? Take him out to dinner and drop a banana skin under his heel just as he gets out of the taxi."

"He's skidded over greasier patches than that and still alive to tell the tale. He's like Rasputin: arsenic wouldn't kill him. Can you kill a cobra with cobra venom?"

"Don't ask me: write and ask your kept man Bomba for details on his own family."

386

Exasperated, Jules cried, "What does Alphendéry think he is doing? I heard him asking Léon if he had heard any rumors about us in Amsterdam."

"Don't you want to know?"

"Not Léon! Hasn't he got any brains left? I don't trust Michel any more since he started going with the communists. His brain is wrong."

"You thought it was a joke before."

"Things were going well before. This Red talk is jinx talk. He's got to stop it."

Léon spent a long time over lunch asking questions about ugly Davigdor's fabulous success with women: he was jealous. Then he looked round, lowered his voice. "Graetz, my manager, tells me he heard from a lot of fellers on the Bourse that Bertillon is running a big long account not only with Stewart, but with other houses in London, with Paul Treviranus and other houses here and with Legris especially in Amsterdam . . . and that he's selling sterling."

"What's the explanation?" Michel asked, guardedly.

"There's only one, surely. He's plunging to offset the Carrière contract. Look here, my boy, why don't you get out of it?"

Michel looked melancholy. "I can't leave Jules until the Carrière affair is settled. That's got him in this jam."

Léon shook his head. "Michel, do you think he would sell the bank now? I'd make a settlement with this feller Carrière and pretty quick, too. Why be short and long? And we can work together. I need someone to give me advice—keep me cool."

"Give us a straight proposition and I'll try to talk Jules into it."

The twin brothers, Paul and Francis Bertillon, like Jules, but thinner and in dress, characterless fashion plates, Jules's chief *pensionnaires,* sat immaculately, but with depressed expressions in Jules's two green armchairs. Their cronies, in bars, restaurants, and clubs, had dinned into their heads the warning, "Carrière is the most dangerous man in Paris to cross and has threatened, in every night club and salon in town, to ruin Jules. Get him quickly: you owe it to your brother."

They saw their bread-and-butter, their clothes racks,

and their club fees in danger; they had come to ask Jules to make terms of peace with Carrière. In fretful elegant tones, Paul complained, "Life is not worth living, Jules, with all this talk buzzing about. It's not pleasant to hear one's brother talked about so frequently and in this strain."

Francis murmured, "Jules, the very waiter in Maxim's asked me about it this morning . . . it's so unpleasant."

"Now," ended Paul, "Jules, if you want any help, we'll help you. Tell us what to do."

Jules was marching up and down, a great strength, for their benefit. William, usually carping, today sat stern and quiet, upholding even the most fantastic things Jules said, supporting his authority against the parastic impertinences of the two boys.

"I'll crush him," said Jules, in a loud voice. "Leave him to me. I know him. He's soft. But it can't be done in a day."

"Don't leave it too long," urged Paul.

Francis brightened. "I know a couple of lads that would be glad to beat him up one night if you'll put up the dough."

"Pay some swordsman to provoke him to a duel: he's proud of his swordplay but he couldn't beat a professional, say, an Army man. And all Paris would be on your side." This was Paul's contribution.

"He's such a coward, he'll find a way out," Francis vetoed the last.

Their tired voices faded along the air, swooning with so much effort. At this moment, Alphendéry came in from lunch. The twins looked at him without too keen a glance of recognition. To them he was some emanation of the virile fiscality of their brother. They presently got up and drifted away, having some rendezvous for afternoon tea.

"They needn't worry, even if the bank goes bust," said William kindly. "All they have to do is to put an advertisement in the *Journal des Débats* to meet their case: 'Two retired gentlewomen, too dumb to beg, too drowsy to steal, are waiting for some kind person to give them a handout. Here is your chance to avoid the inheritance tax. Apply P. and F. Bertillon.'"

At this moment, Etienne Mirabaud, the doorkeeper, tapped at the door. "There are two gentlemen to see you alone, sir!"

"What—gunmen?"

Etienne looked horrified. "Gentlemen, sir."

"Go and look, William."

He came back. "The heavenly twins."

"Show them up, Etienne." Jules groaned, "What did I get in with those Teutons for? They're so fat and solemn I always think they've come to blackmail me. What do I want them for? I don't want anybody."

Scene Fifty-three: The Wheat Scheme

LÉON sprang into the bank in the morning, fresh, succulent, and fat, brimming over with intention. He said, "Good morning" from his vortex to Jacques Manray and went up the main stairs. At Jules's door he knocked. Jules was lounging over an airplane journal. He knew two of the entrants for the next Deutsch-de-la-Meurthe cup and at moments thought of inducing William to enter, as an advertisement for the bank. William was out of condition and flatly refused to leave the earth.

"I got an idea," said Léon. "This wheat scheme: do you want to listen to it?"

"Sure."

"Where's Alphendéry? Tell him to come in, will you? I like him round to get his angle."

"Sure." Alphendéry entered at this moment, having heard of Léon's arrival, by grapevine telegraph. "Hello, my boy. Listen, I want you to listen to this, get the points, so that we can put it over."

"I'm listening, Henri," said Alphendéry.

Léon straddled, pushed back his head, uttered an ultimatum. "America full of wheat because of, lack of— she's smothered in wheat, she's very depressed on account of the surplus. Can we put wheat into the Gulf of Mexico—can we find an outlet for it?"

"Can we?" Alphendéry was a tight ball of a thousand gummy layers of attention, springing along a parabola of intention.

"I mean, she says to herself, 'Can we throw the wheat into the Caribbean, twenty-one thousand feet, get rid of

389

it?' If we can find an outlet for it—wheat—in the U.S.A. —wheat would—the market's very poor—it would bolster up the stock market. Now, you see, the financial position is—"

"Shocking—" murmured Jules.

"Shocking but not, but not—shocking, but—"

"Not catastrophic," said Alphendéry.

Léon's great finger was wagging up and down like a baton, for the trio. "Shocking but not catastrophic—it might become—a rise in wheat would restore confidence. Am I right, Michel, am I right? Eh, eh?"

"You're right, Henri," they both said.

He shifted his giant Adam's apple quickly in his collar. "Here, in Europe, the situation is—the countries need wheat—"

"The consuming countries—" said Alphendéry.

"—the consuming countries have need of wheat. Watch me, Alphendéry, see if you get this. But there are reports of a big promising surplus in Russia. Russians are supposed to be ready to dump wheat at any price, first to dump, second to undermine the system." He laughed hugely. "The Russians are devilishly," he corrected himself, blushed, *very much* enjoying the low prices! Now *she* is around—"

"Russia is a seller of wheat," said Alphendéry.

"Yes, Russia's a seller of wheat (thank you, Michel) because, because she has bills to meet and her credit is— forty per cent, she's got—forty per cent—when she took cash—"

"Russia," explained Alphendéry to Jules who was listening idly (and not following, except that with a pencil he had written on a blank piece of paper, "How much?"), "Russia has very bad credit, no credit at all. She must get goods for the Five-Year Plan and in order to get goods for the Five-Year Plan she has to pay four per cent a month; that's the usurious interest she has to pay, because she has no money and no credit. She pays four per cent a month. Now this year she has got a wow of a crop, a bumper crop, the Black Sea's going to be jammed with wheat, she's never had a crop like it; neither has anyone else. That's what the reports are. So she doesn't care *what* price she sells it for, she can dump it for next to nothing, because for it she gets cash: she gets *cash*, pays no interest, get it?"

"Sure, sure," said Jules, "and what else?"

"Yes," said Léon, nodding thankfully to Alphendéry. "You see what they're all afraid of?"

"What chance has the U.S.A. to sell her wheat?" asked Alphendéry of Jules.

Léon said, "The question is," he shook his finger menacingly at Jules, "the question is: how can we find a buyer for wheat?"

"The Americans say to themselves, 'How can we find a buyer for our wheat,'" annotated Alphendéry. "Excuse me, Henri, with your elliptic style, I've got to make it clear."

"Elliptic style, what's that?" He brought himself up short.

"You think like a chess player, you're always two or three or four or eight jumps ahead," smiled Michel.

"A chess player," he said slowly and smiled, "a chess player, eh? Elliptic—that's like shorthand, then?"

"Yes. No one knows themselves, Henri: no one knows how they appear to others."

He spent a moment considering, then suddenly darkened again, plunged ahead. "Yes. How can they find a buyer for wheat, stop Russia selling and put the price up? Listen, don't interrupt, Alphendéry. You can tell him afterwards. Listen now, I want you to get it into your head and then you can explain it. That is the bright idea. Supposing we could arrange to take fifty to seventy-five million bushels of wheat on account of *Russia* and also have arrangements that contracts will be distributed pro rata to international grain markets. The question of sales must be—never a doubt. Do you see? And no jealousy. You see? Every firm would have a contract. The world would wake up . . . the telephones begin to ring early in the morning. 'Do you hear the news? I don't believe it!' Instead of Russia being a seller, she's a buyer! But how? Don't tell him yet, Alphendéry. This would cause a tremendous rise in the market—of course, we would unload on the option market on the way up to countries that really needed wheat—we'd give the proceeds to Russia. Now, it's got to be worked out, that's all. And I want someone to put it across. To put it to the governments. Michel can put it to the Russian government because he's sympathetic. I'll go to Berlin—chance to see a sweetie, eh? Anyhow, I'll—Berlin—then Jules can go to his friends

391

in the American embassy—we've got to keep it quiet, though . . . those boys would steal—Listen!"

"How are you going to do it?" asked Jules, who had not followed it at all.

Michel kept nodding at Jules as if to say, "I'll explain it all to you afterwards, get you out of the barbed-wire entanglements."

Léon rushed on, "You see, they would ask and find Russia was really buying." He pressed his palms together and gasped sunnily like a giant sunflower almost blown to shreds in a breeze. "The fact that Russia would not only buy, but *would not sell* her gigantic crop would justify us. Russia was only—she intended pressing wheat to get money—say forty per cent credit—and say forty per cent—yes, they are saving forty per cent if the market didn't go up they could afford to lose with forty per cent—"

"Sounds crazy," said Jules. Michel nodded to him. "I'll explain, just wait, later on."

"Wait till I get through and Michel will tell you, he explains it, elliptic," said Léon, quite unaware of the extraordinary manner he had of talking, himself, and putting Jules's incomprehension down to the fact that he was a Gentile, or fantastic, or unsound, or some other frailty, but with infinite kindness and calm, trying hard to hold in his horses, and going on, "The only problem is to get the U.S.A. government to accept Russian bills in payment."

"You are going to get Russian bills in payment? How?" asked Jules.

"No, no, no, no," shouted Léon, "there is no intention of taking the U.S.A. government into the secret; you mustn't let on, when you see your friends at the embassy. Not a word." He shook his head doubtfully and looked at Jules with alarmed speculation. "It's a practical scheme: that's how it's going to appeal to them. What's the good of all that wheat to them? They'd do better to throw it into the Atlantic. There's a Brazilian coffee situation in wheat. The wheat goes out of condition due to keeping. The Farm Board is losing hundreds of millions, the wheat market will be low for years. . . ."

"It's undermining the banking structure; if they're not careful there'll be irreparable trouble. It's led to a banking crash—if they don't want *Jacqueries*—" supplemented

Alphendéry, who had begun to see light through Léon's imbroglio. "The crash all over the West is due to it."

"Furthermore," shouted Léon impatiently, "furthermore, Michel, Michel! Furthermore," he reduced his voice and waved his short, muscular arm, "this is the point, this is—which will appeal to them: Russia meets all her bills on a gold basis, that's an additional gain to dollars. Don't let them know. The Farm Board will copy the idea. I don't want them to get my idea. It's brilliant, brilliant, well, what do you think of it?"

He looked expectantly at Jules. Jules looked blankly, with some reproach, at Léon. Léon turned to Michel, "Did you get it, Michel? If you didn't, tell me, and I'll go over it again. I don't care how often I go over it, you must get it, head and tail and—and—feathers, cockscomb—otherwise it's no good. It's no good botching a thing like this, bungling it would be—catastrophic; and they might get the idea all upside-down and even so—steal it—all wrong—"

"Explain it to me," Jules said petulantly to Michel. Michel stepped forward, with his hands in his pockets, his rounded torso and thighs potent in his much-worn suit. "I'll just go over it rapidly and explain it as I see it and Léon can correct me."

Léon said eagerly, "Yes, go on, go on, my boy."

"This is Léon's scheme. Russia is pressing her wheat on the market for sale at any price to get cash, so that she will not have to pay forty-eight per cent per annum, or four per cent per month for credit. Therefore, even if the market did not go up, they, nevertheless, by obtaining cash (from our consortium) for withholding their wheat, are obtaining cash with which they pay for machines and heavy manufactured goods which they need for the Five-Year Plan. Their bills would be unloaded on the U.S.A. indirectly, since the U.S.A. would accept bills from wheat-importing countries, which, in turn, are holding Russian bills. That's the concealed third play, you see. So that Russia would then receive the benefit from obtaining cash on her bills, she would save forty-eight per cent per annum in usury charges; whereas she can only expect to obtain a relatively small amount of cash by selling since she would have to dump her wheat and get low prices. Her object, in any case, is to get cash and save the losses due to this enormous payment of interest. Hence, four things would result:

"One: Russia could keep her wheat for her own people. This would raise her standard of living and make the Five-Year Plan safer.

"Two: by keeping her wheat off the market, it would *double the value* of wheat and thereby her prospects, since it doubles the potential value of her wheat production in another crop, next season.

"Three: it would make her credit-worthy by changing the rate of interest from forty-eight per cent per annum down to four per cent per annum, the normal rate, thus enabling her in the future to obtain credit far more easily. . . ."

Léon was walking up and down the room; beads of perspiration were standing out on his dome; he was congested, and yet listened with great passion to Alphendéry's exposition. Jules was still the pale prince, elegantly and indifferently reposing in his great chair but a very faintly discernible sneer had tightened his long nostrils.

"Fourth," said Alphendéry, taking in the indisposition of his audience and throwing his glances to entrap them both, "fourth," he repeated energetically, "it would enable the German government—if I understood Léon's idea —to turn Russian bills, which she now holds, into cash, or its equivalent in American wheat; instead of nursing bills she now holds for her machinery export to Russia. Old bills. This is advantageous to the economy of Germany and will save her from the necessity of taking up a thing like Hitlerism, whose shadow is now over Europe from her frontiers. For there would be no need for it: she would have the food and the cash."

"I don't care about saving Russia or Germany: where's the profit in it?" pouted Jules. "I like my own idea better. You make them the proposition, they hand you the wheat, you get the dough, you hide it, and you default."

Léon said hastily, "No, you've given me a few ideas, Michel, but that's not the way to put it. Save Russia paying the usury, that's good: I want to see Russia do good, well—h'm—but Germany—it's not that. Let's put it this way. You listen, Jules. I'm putting it this way for you."

"I'm listening," said Alphendéry patiently, humbly.

"What you say is right, right, but that's not it, Michel. It comes in, but—you see, lots of countries are anxious to buy wheat but can't buy. Russia would have been prepared to—given—poor countries American wheat instead of—exchange—of dollars—in exchange of goods which Russia was crying for, for which they give bills at forty per cent premium. Chicago wheat is now thirty-nine cents. Say it will be forty-one cents then and—say ten cents carrying charges. . . ."

Alphendéry advanced with his hand held up. "Wait, Léon, you haven't put it clearly. Your shorthand is all right for grain dealers. Let me—"

Léon laughed, in his beautiful husky voice. "My shorthand— Go ahead," he was subdued, holding himself in. "I want to get it straight. We must. We must work it all out."

"What Léon means is this," said Alphendéry, turning half-about and facing Jules, who fixed fatigued eyes upon him. "The market is dead, the financial crash has put most countries into a position where although they require wheat, they have no money to pay and mighty little credit. But if Russia could give to these poor countries American wheat (because the banks in these very countries which have accepted Russian bills would pledge their bills with the American authorities and obtain wheat), then, in effect, Russia would be giving wheat to these poor countries who would no longer need to acquire dollars with which to pay for the wheat, since they would be buying this wheat by *discounting Russian bills* with the American bankers. Is that clear?"

"Sure," said Jules, irritably.

"Russia will then be able to get from them the goods she is crying for, for her Five-Year Plan; since these poor countries could (if they did not have to part with foreign exchange to acquire American wheat), could be in a position to give her (I mean Russia) credit for the purchases from themselves; since the bills that Russia would give would be credit-worthy, that is, could be turned into cash by these poor countries by their rediscounting these very Russian bills at a nominal rate of interest with the American Federal Reserve Bank, through giving their endorsement to those Russian bills."

"What small countries?" asked Jules impertinently.

"Why—Czechoslovakia, Germany (poor countries, not small countries), Austria, Finland. . . ."

Léon blurted, with discomfiture, "What do you think

of it, Jules? You see, we need your façade; the consortium needs the bank's façade. . . . Tell me, really, what you think of it, Michel? Well?"

"Henri, it's brilliant, brilliant: you've grown even in my estimation," said Alphendéry with great enthusiasm. "You're a genius, but it needs to be worked out. We'll go over it."

Jules laughed good-naturedly, having observed that Léon was tired. "It reminds me of my first bank. I opened my first bank in the war zone during the war. Didn't charge the generals anything and gave the privates exchange. You know, Michel. What did I know about banking? Spent six months in a bank in my life and walked out on them, couldn't believe their humdrum—knew it wasn't like that! One day a lady I knew walked in and gave me a giro transfer. I'd never seen one before in my life. So I said to her, 'Just take a seat for a moment; I've got to make a verification, pardon me,' and I hurried with it into the lavatory. I've always found out since I was a kid that when you can't understand a thing if you take it into the lavatory and perch on the . . . er . . . sit down a while, you can always figure it out. I did that, and presently I said to myself, 'This must be a transfer from one bank to another by means of numbers in an account without a check'; and that's what it was, and that's what I did." He looked seriously at them. "You'll write it out for me, Michel, in notes, and I'll study it." He laughed delightfully, exquisitely, humanely. He got up to take a little exercise over his Persian carpet. "It sounds all right, Léon. Let's go over it again, after lunch. I'll do my best to think it over and stew in it. How much do you think you'll make for yourself, I don't mean Russia and the poor countries. I mean, what can we steal?"

Léon worriedly planted himself in front of Jules. "No, don't you see? The plan—we can make any amount of money, any we want to—two-three millions sterling, say ten million-twelve million dollars—that is, two hundred fifty million francs maybe, properly managed."

Jules opened his eyes, lost his fatigue, and went back to his chair. "How? How do you think you can do that, Léon?"

Léon laughed. "It's a temporary stave-off—the crisis—for them; for us, it would stave off the the crisis forever,

I think: we three will be in on it. On the third consortium. We'll make our fortune! Only don't let it out! No Bomba, that feller—or anyone who'll spill the beans." He took a turn across the room, smiled at Jules. "Listen, Jules, I think I've got it—the way you can understand it; I'm getting it in order. It's a concentric technique." He smiled at Alphendéry for a moment, murmured something like "technique of a *yiddisher Kopf*," went on to Jules.

"If I don't put it right, you'll get everything but the point. No one knows how he sounds to others. This is the plan. We buy fifty million bushels at a flat price. Contract with the American government. We get an option on another fifty million bushels on a scale-up, ten million at forty-two, ten million at forty-four cents, so on. That's an incentive to them to tighten their hands. If our plan is successful and the market goes up—it must, unless there's a leak—so much the better, we could exercise the option and sell it ourselves. It's a cinch . . . we don't have to exercise the option. To sell short—we'll always be able to buy it in." He looked at Jules confidently: this was A.B.C. to Léon.

Alphendéry rushed in, "You see, we have two choices: either we have confidence that we can resell large quantities at the market-price, that is, if, say, the market goes to fifty-three cents we can exercise our option to buy the wheat at fifty-two cents, or if we distrust the market, and it rises to seventy-five cents, we have then the privilege of selling short, knowing we will always have the supply (on option from the government) so that if the market goes down to sixty cents we make a profit of fifteen cents per bushel without using our option, and if, on the other hand, the market goes up to one dollar, we can be short sellers (knowing we have the supply), and if we are pressed for delivery, then we can exercise our option, which we had been afraid to exercise on the run-up, because we had no confidence. We could dispose of it when we were long of it, by having exercised our option to buy it at fifty-two cents. We tender this wheat in execution of our sale at seventy-five cents, even when it is at a dollar! Perfect! By no possibility can we lose!"

"Let me explain, let me explain," cried Léon irascibly.

"All right," said Alphendéry humbly. "I am only trying to make the process clear."

"Jules knows how to sell short," cried Léon, "a child could understand it," he continued violently. Then again, succinctly, waving his arm, he went on. "We could make ten cents a bushel on one hundred million bushels, or ten million dollars on the way up and the same amount on the way down. Easy. I could do it. This is the only proposition I ever had where I could talk in telephone numbers. It's possible. That's the beauty of it. It's honest. No finagling. The supply is there! On contract." He calmed himself. "Say, at fifty cents we sell two million bushels, at fifty-two cents, we sell two million, at fifty-four cents, we sell twenty-one million bushels, and so on every two-cent rise in the market. . . ." He peered at Jules, took a turn up and down the room, wrestling with his ideas. He came back to them and planted himself in their midst, most serious.

"The bugbear of Russian supplies hanging over the market has almost compelled the miller to hang off and to pursue a hand-to-mouth policy—Russia really oughtn't to sell wheat, despite her bumper crop, but she needs goods for the infant Five-Year Plan. Then her bills are trickled through at forty per cent. She's got to get the goods. You see the beauty of this is—everyone's boycotting Russia. You can't boycott a tiger, even if you're not an animal trainer—don't like it. We've got the brains to see that Russia exists, she is living, hitting round. She has to eat, she has to consume. No good shutting your eyes to her: use her, use her, she's the new possibility. Use her to make money. The munitions makers never hesitated a moment. Let us be as smart. And we're selling wheat. Things people need to keep alive. It's more decent, too. That's where our bright idea comes in. We don't groan about Russia—we take Russia into account! You see, Europe needs wheat—she's crying for it, starving for it, but you've got to have something in exchange. The American tariffs pull their punches. There's no question of credit at all. *Valuta is cracking!* That's it, Jules! You see, valuta is cracking, credit is dead. The Credit-Anstalt failed a month ago. Europe is dead. Now, I'll put it to you, this way. My *schematism* is this. There's a genuine home for wheat, no need for American silos to be stuffed to cracking and mice to eat it up. Russia is to be a *buyer, not a seller.* That'll give everybody confidence that nobody has now. Then Russia will buy *in the trade,* through the trade, that looks genuine and it gives the trade confidence. 'Things are looking better!' We only want them to accept her bills till her gold production goes up. It won't be so long. . . ."

Jules, whose face had hardened by now, through this constant dinning in and rehashing of the various elements of the first plan, had absorbed some of the facts of the situation. The idea of profit, profit, ached in his jaw. He now said rapidly, "You mean, you and I form a consortium and buy one hundred million bushels from the U.S.A.?"

"Yes," said Léon. "Now, we've got to get the details clear. Yes, that is the first. Then there is the second consortium. A consortium of international grain merchants to sell wheat to the Russians. We also have to be a third consortium to resell the Russian purchases of wheat to Germany etcetera, for goods that Russia needs. But this is secret: this is just between us and mustn't go down on paper."

Jules's face livened: his eyes became almost black. "It's a good idea. I'm with you."

"It's not complete yet, Jules. I want Michel to work on it. We've got something there, eh? What do you say, Jules? It looks like a winner, eh?"

"Let's have lunch," said Michel. "I think you've got a wonderful thing there, Henri: a real stroke of genius."

"The greatest thing of my career," half whispered Léon with awe. "I don't know—myself how it came to me. But it's good. Now we've got to make no mistakes. It mustn't slip. We'll come out of this—rich, my boy, you and Jules and me, rich! And in a depression. And doing no harm."

He continued talking about the plan as they went along the corridor, as they put on their coats, as they walked to lunch at a cheap Armenian place discovered by Michel. "You go to the Farm Board in the U.S.A. and you tell them, 'You're looking for a market for your wheat. This is a genuine proposition. There is demand in Europe where there is a very poor crop.' There's another thing: the rise in the market price will compensate the U.S.A. on the remainder of its stocks of wheat, for any possible loss on Russian paper. . . . It's perfect." The gaiety ran over the dam in short, lolloping, easy boyish laughs, "Perfect. No one has ever had a scheme like it. The more I think of it, the more I see it is watertight." But he became worried. "Do you think Bertillon understands it?"

"How do you like the goulash? You haven't noticed it at all," said Alphendéry, "you one-track brain."

"One-track brain? Is that what I am? He-he-he." Woodwinds laughing over the dam. "Will he understand it, though, eh?"

"He will," said Alphendéry, "when I get through explaining it to him."

"It would be a tragedy if it slipped up," said Léon, wagging his head.

"Why didn't you go to Strindl's?" asked Michel, mentioning the second largest grain firm and one with which Léon was intimately connected.

Léon said, "No can do. They'd steal it from me. They've got the organization all ready. They don't need to pay me a salary, a participation. They only need to hear the idea and they'll whip into it. I want to make this my grand coup. Michel, you're along with me. You're lucky." Once more, as always, his eyes earnestly searched, as for a jewel, in Alphendéry's forehead. "You've got the lucky touch, Michel. You're a messenger." He became grave with sentiment and superstition.

Michel said, "You mean, I have the Hebrew letter Shin in the middle of my forehead. I know. If I ever come and work for you, Henri, it will be on the strength of that Shin. I know your superstition."

Léon did not laugh but was both anxious and abashed. He did not speak of these things aloud. At last, he said, rather timorously, "There is something—a *shilee'ach*** you might be." He trembled.

Alphendéry laughed but was troubled. "My wife, when she was my wife, told me I should have been an alienist . . . I was able to cure mental disease, disorder by my physical presence. Why was that? Nothing magical. I do not think I am any better than they are. That's all."

Léon was much embarrassed. After a moment he looked up and said with false, loud briskness, "Do you think Bertillon understands it, eh? Do you think he knows men? Can we trust his judgment?"

"No," said Michel, "Jules has not much sense of men, but if we prime him, brief him, see that he gets away with the right entourage, tell him whom to go and see,

---

* Inspired messenger, he means.

give him a schedule and a map, he can't go wrong and he's well regarded in Washington. One of his ancestors went over on the *Mayflower* or died at Bunker's Hill or got the Congressional Medal, something like that. The Americans are always soft with Lafayette cases. If he ties up properly with the American embassy, it's all right. Of course, he's hot stuff here because he is the flower of society, with his aviation cup and his Auteuil cup, his plane, his stable and his yacht and the rest. There's no harm in having him with you on the first consortium—it makes it look grand, kosher, and Parisian. But he'll have to act rather as a figurehead. Why don't you go to America yourself?"

"No," said Léon, "no, I can't go. I'm a foreigner. No *Mayflower*—a European, they'll think I'm a jumping jack; you know how they look on Roumanians, Spaniards, bohunks, dagos, there, all those over there. There's Russian paper mixed in it. Those yellow press. Better not give them the idea it's entirely Central-European and Slav. They wouldn't like it: bad publicity and they've had enough publicity, God knows."

"You ought to go along in Jules's suite," said Alphendéry. "I can't see why you don't, as his secretary or something? You'd be miserable if the plan fell through and you'd blame yourself. It's your plan. I don't see why you don't guard it like the apple of your eye."

Léon shook his head and would say no more. Léon had once been in New York, and neither Alphendéry nor anyone else had been able to find out why he would not go back to a place for which his great trading talents eminently suited him. Achitophelous had something to do with it, Guinédor had something to do with it: perhaps they knew. Little Kratz knew, and the venomous threats he spat at Léon when he left him for good and all referred to it. Perhaps it was nothing more serious than income tax. There were many strange embroiled histories between these men: they had concocted many a bizarre plan between them, in the days of their friendship.

To cover the silence, Alphendéry coaxed, "Tell me, Henri, how did you make your money? One day you were eating rye-bread sandwiches and wondering where you were going to get the three dollars to pay the rent in the old house in Twenty-first Street in New York, full of cockroaches and lice, over a leather and upholstery base-

401

ment; and in a couple of months, Méline tells me, you were swaggering down in the best tailoring in New York, with a gold-headed cane. How did you do it? Now, don't tell me your usual lies. Who am I to bother you? You know I'm no crook."

Léon gurgled good-naturedly, glad to be let off the New York question. "I'll tell you, my boy, but you needn't tell anyone, although there's no harm in it. I was with Strindl's New York office, see. I should have gone to Valparaiso, but when I see the name of the boat, *Morea,* that's Roumanian for death, I renege. And I go to New York instead. It's after the war. Russia isn't paying anything. A complete moratorium: you can only get payment by seizing Russian property abroad. Strindl's had a cargo of spelter landed at Archangel for Russia. Don't turn up your ears—lots of grain firms delivered funny grains those days. Strindl's made their fortune during the war. You can imagine in what grain. The Russians wouldn't pay. There wasn't a chance of getting a ruble out of them. Strindl's stood to lose the entire value at the then prices, about one hundred fifty thousand dollars. So I heard something from a Jewish feller who knew a Tammany judge who was fixing up the claims against Russian property in New York. I cabled them to Amsterdam, 'Will you settle for sixty thousand dollars if I can get it? Ask no questions.' And they cabled back, 'If you can get sixty thousand dollars for us, good on you,' or words to that effect. So I made a good split, don't worry: I gave something to the Jewish feller, five thousand dollars to the Tammany judge, I sent them sixty thousand dollars, and I got sixty thousand dollars myself. He gave me a judgment of one hundred thirty thousand dollars—not bad, eh? Nearly the whole value. That's how I got my start. That's why I'm superstitious about Russia. Good luck for me." He finished glibly and smiled at Alphendéry, refreshed.

"Well, I suppose I'll know some day," said Alphendéry patiently.

Léon flushed faintly. "I'm telling you the honest truth: I wouldn't lie to you, Michel," he gabbled. "Ah, you can only make a fortune in a war!"

He studied Alphendéry for a while and then floundered briskly into the wheat scheme. Alphendéry, whose busy brain, full of little elves, had worked over all that had been presented to him of the plan by now and who saw further perspectives, mused aloud, "What about the reaction of the Washington officials, to Russia being in the plan?"

Léon said at once, "At forty-eight per cent premium, Russia could afford to be honest: even a murderer would be honest if he was saving forty-eight per cent per annum. They can tell that to the people who object. She's bound to keep to her contract." He burbled his recapitulation: "Europe needing wheat but faced with a coffee situation in wheat in America—there sits Europe waiting for the wheat to be made a present of . . . or America can dump it in the ocean. And there are the Russians who must ship wheat to get the cash. You see Europe unable to buy because valuta is beginning to be shaky in Europe and so is credit, because of U.S.A. tariffs, too. The U.S.A. couldn't accept goods to pay for the wheat and ship it overseas in exchange for goods. Therefore," Léon said with marked emphasis, "the problem to a Gemera feller* is, first, see a way to stop Russia selling. Now, what are you to offer Russia to stop her selling? *NEXT*, to find a buyer for the wheat. Next, what to do with the goods that the wheat buyer wants to exchange. Next, a revolutionary stroke to change the whole market psychology— You see, Michel, the European buyers sabotaged, too. And the European buyers sat down and pursued a hand-to-mouth policy which threatened the world structure—" Light broke on the tossed planes of his great face, "I've got it, my boy. I've got it now." He rumbled on.

Alphendéry's fresh voice broke in, "I congratulate you, Henri: it's a stroke all right. To turn the Russians into buyers instead of sellers is sensational, completely sensational . . . it revolutionizes the whole market situation— and it's dialectic, it's along the right line, that's why it's perfect: don't you realize that?"

"Dialectic—what's—h'm?"

"The logic of world history, in the line of evolution."

"History? No. No history. This is new: it takes account of the situation." But he was not thinking about Alphendéry any more. He mused, "To take goods that Europeans wanted to export to America, instead of to Russia—to give them Russian wheat—to make them buyer of one hundred fifty million bushels, maybe, instead of them com-

---

* "Student of commentaries on the Talmud," he means.

403

ing out with one hundred million bushels—it'll double the price of wheat, say from fifty cents to a dollar in Winnipeg-Chicago. I'm not dreaming, Michel. We could sell right away—fifty million bushels and probably make —" his voice fell—"particularly in exchange for goods that Russia wants."

Alphendéry, seated opposite to him in the restaurant, looked at his face, broad as the wheatlands of Roumania he was born in, at his eyes which, though the openings of the lids were relatively small, flashed, rolled, and looked enormous under their great lids and high brows, the jutting nose, a very promontory of passion and willfulness. He had at this moment the kindliest, most brotherly feeling for Léon, although he knew that in any business deal he would only get scrapings from the plate. Léon did not notice the glance. He noticed nobody. He did not know what he was eating either, except that when they brought him rose jelly, he laughed up into his eyes and said boyishly, "My poor mother, God rest her soul! made this jelly always. I never had it since." Léon always ate sparingly, and took no alcohol, except on fete days, fete days decided by his own secret, internal calendar. Then he would suddenly drink two bottles himself and begin to talk about his star, begin to dream of his fate, his power, begin to feel the dark, quick blood smoke in his veins. But now he drank water, intoxicated enough by the view of this gigantic citadel he saw the invisible but strong hands of his genius building up in front of him for him to inhabit. He smiled, darkled, glinting at Michel, his confidant; in every aspect the Oriental potentate, the Turk, talking to his favorite, supine counselor, quite sure that his own favorite topic—himself—was also the theme that Alphendéry's ears yawned to hear.

"We would come in one morning and we would say, 'We have sold fifty million bushels to the Russians on a basis options'—to be fixed—and the merchants—each in what each—proportion—to make contracts out for certain quantities—brokers getting commissions from the selling consortium. The whole trade satisfied; no depression any more, revival in all the markets! Not only wheat! And we know it is coming! Two-three fortunes. The idea is to leave no doubt in the world trade that there has been a real contract—encourage the world markets—oh, there's no end to the profits—they would hasten to buy hedges in ahead of the Russians while we were unloading on the way up, but between the U.S.A. and Russia there would be a fixed price—and we're holding the fifty million. Michel, we've got it, we've found it. It's genius!" He gave a great crunching chuckle, the crushing of sunflower seeds in saliva. "What do you think of it, Michel? It's good, isn't it? What do you think of the Gemera feller?"

"Good," said Alphendéry with the first far note of impatience.

Léon reached across the table, his face creased with smiles as a happy peasant boy's. "Boy, we're made. Michel, stick with me and you're a made man. You can keep that beautiful wife of yours in silk and satin and pay her such a whooping big alimony she'll—what do you think of it? Good, tell me, do you think it's good. Do you think you can sell it to that Gentile, in there? We need someone to approach the Gentiles on the other side." He swallowed a glass of water and clapped his hands: "Waiter!"

Alphendéry spoke, nastily, for him, "Gentiles! Morgan is a Gentile, so is Rockefeller. You're medieval, Henri. I don't go about thinking I'm a Jew."

"You're an Alsatian Jew . . . that's not a Jew. No, sir, I'm the Chasidim." He cried sharply, "Waiter, bill, bill!" He turned to Michel seriously, softly, "Imagine all them fellers in the morning coming on the telephone and saying, 'What's this I hear?' and I'd be saying, 'Listen, Meyer Benz—' "

"The beauty is," said Alphendéry, "that everything goes through normal banking and trading channels, so that business gets a real fillip, not like usual government business which goes through without intermediaries, excludes the trade and does no good to the trade. Our scheme takes care of the intermediaries. Everyone plucks from the trees—more than that, *it has to be.*"

"How's that, how's that? It has to be."

"Why, the reason the American government couldn't be party to a three-dimension is because they couldn't admit they are dumping: there has to be a legitimate demand."

"Excellent." Léon rubbed his hands. "It gets better every minute. Listen, you and I must go over this, work out all the points. Then you write them down, Michel, and give them to—Bertillon to read. He must learn it by heart. He'll get it anyhow, won't he? I'll go over and over and over—he must get it."

"Oh, of course, good heavens!" expostulated Michel, now at the end of his patience. "Jules will understand it perfectly. How do you think he made his money? He can't be a complete goof."

"I don't know, I don't know—"

"You sprang it on him like a thunderbolt this morning; you've been working it out for days—he only just heard of it."

"Listen," urged Léon, himself not listening, "the reason we're not frightened to go with this plum to a government is because they can't steal the scheme because, say they sold a certain big amount to a consumer country on credit, it would do more harm than good: they wouldn't be so stupid. It would ruin them electorally."

Alphendéry was cheerful. "They wouldn't be so stupid as to only see the smart-aleck trick of going past us and making the direct sale on credit, because that would undermine the structure, while our spectacular project would revolutionize values—"

"Of course, them government fellers are pretty stupid. You've got to point out to them the danger of selling direct. They don't care about the state of the European market. A danger—"

He came back to Alphendéry's office still talking it over, still recurring to the points of his scheme, which stood in his head without words and to which words fitted badly. Léon saw these moves, as perhaps an engineer sees a bridge in his mind, or a musician an overture. He did not see it in words and, therefore, people not forewarned thought him stupid or confused, but his mind was never confused on the wheat market or on the mechanism of his own schemes; although, true enough, many of his schemes were cut straight out of the broadcloth of fantasy, because he was too impatient to study.

On the way to the bank Léon suddenly cooled off, however, and Michel, who knew the man by now, divined that he had a rendezvous somewhere about four o'clock. As he pressed his hand in good-by, Léon roused himself from his urgent amorous preoccupations enough to murmur, "Impress it on him. Russia must get through the Five-Year Plan. There's a limited outlet for bills at forty-eight per cent discount; her gold production's still small.

She's compelled to ship wheat, she needs—got to get valuta to pay for the Five-Year Plan goods. Wheat in America the same as coffee in Brazil."

He left. He was half across the pavement when he turned dubiously and came back to Alphendéry still standing hatless between the two staves of Mercury in the door. He said urgently, as if it had just occurred to him, "At present European buyers are sitting down, doing nothing, pursuing a hand-to-mouth policy. Make a revolutionary stroke—change the whole psychology—" He nodded and went off again.

Alphendéry, aflame with the scheme, turned into the bank and hastened upstairs to find Jules. Jules was figuring on a piece of paper and looked up when Alphendéry entered.

"I say, Michel, I've just been figuring out this scheme of Léon's. We can make plenty of dough out of it, can't we? What did he tell you at lunch? Do you think we can trust him or will he try to steal the swag? Perhaps I can make private arrangements with the Washington bunch."

"I went over that with Henri," said Alphendéry with circumspection, avoiding the question of pure booty. "The commission to the Bertillon-Léon consortium from the U.S.A. would be one-half per cent plus carrying, freight, perquisites, say up to two per cent, not more, and the U.S.A. could afford to do this, on account of the increased value given their supplies. You see they know what's coming, or at least part of it. They would ship wheat as the contract with Russia called for it, and store it in silos in parts of Europe (this is not an essential part of the scheme, this is just mechanical). But the big money is made through us holding the wheat at our disposal and putting it on the market when and how we like when the news gets about and the demand comes in."

Jules seemed grieved. "Isn't all this merchandising a lot of bunk? Why can't we make a straight steal? I don't know all this wheat game; Léon will do me in. I'd rather get the money myself and never pay the government bunch. How do I know Léon won't try to get away with it all?"

Alphendéry laughed. "If you don't, you mean. Now you two boys will have to have a letter of agreement, a public one and a private one, too; something special so that you two bright babies will be held to the straight line. But do me a favor, Jules, and give Léon's scheme a tryout. Don't start pulling off any bright ideas of the second degree."

Jules laughed vainly. "Oh, I've got some ideas of my own. I'll put it into the hands of Bomba and get him to organize a little publicity. It'll help the thing along, give us a big start-off; the Washington crowd will be waiting to eat out of our hands, public opinion will make them—everyone will be pleased. The market will go up. The lambs will come in, it can only be a temporary boom, and we'll sell them till the cows come home."

Alphendéry saw Jules travestying himself, with mortification. "For God's sake, don't do that, Jules. You don't want rumors about before we've so much as got hold of the wheat. This is secret business. You only have to tell the U.S.A. about consortium one, too, don't forget: consortia two and three you keep in your vest pocket and buttoned up. If I see Bomba getting wind of this, I assure you I'll have him shanghaied. William is only too anxious to do it now. He's all that's needed to ruin the finest scheme that Léon ever thought up, with all his genius."

"Genius, ptt!" Jules was willful.

Alphendéry had borne the brunt of the whole conversation, and in the scheme he thought he saw a real chance of making money for himself; enough to "get out"—his favorite dream. He said in a high despotic voice to Jules, "Jules, if you put Bomba, that tinhorn brass band, into this, I'll resign. Tell me you're going to do it, and I'll hand in my resignation right now."

Jules raised his face with the disingenuous soft surprise of a spoiled child; he stopped his everlasting tracing on the writing block and smiled affectionately. "Michel, you surprise me! If it is so important to you, I won't tell Bomba."

"You mustn't, Jules—it would ruin the whole scheme."

Jules began to trace again and laughed offhandedly. "Well, you write it all down from your angle and we'll go over it." They began writing it down. William entered.

"My original idea is the best," flung out Jules, irritated by ten minutes' application and by some compliment of Alphendéry to Léon. "A consortium with myself—giant capital, form a society on the books, transfer funds from the bank on the books—any amount, offer the wheat to the French government at any price. Get it from the U.S.A. government, telling them we're the agents for the French government, get the money from the French government, sell the wheat secretly, and then skip. It's the simplest and you get double the money without all this finicking with scale-ups and short selling."

Alphendéry looked pained. William said, "Well, let's try to understand Léon's scheme, at any rate."

Alphendéry pleaded, "If you want to make money. Of course, if you want to cool your heels in the Santé for a few years, that's another story." He felt a shiver of despair.

"Why doesn't Léon go along and do the dirty work?" asked Jules next, angrily. Fifteen minutes' work and he was willing to throw the whole thing into the wastepaper basket.

Alphendéry laughed. "No one knows why he won't go to America. It's one of the mysteries of life. His Old Man of the Sea, Achitophelous, has something to do with it, so has a lady and a gun, and a gangster and a gun, and a stock exchange head-on collision and a gun, and a corner in chicken feed and a gun; but whose was the decisive gun I've never been able to find out. At any rate, there's a gun somewhere and look what a target Léon is. But he'll never tell. Why doesn't anyone in the world ever come clean?" He sighed. "This is a stroke of genius, Jules. There's no question of thieving. Get that right out of your head. You've got to work in with politics and you've got to work soon, for war and crisis are coming, and you've got to be prepared to make money. Ninety per cent of prewar money doesn't exist any more. You've got to be there when the cat jumps. Léon is right: Russia is the cue. You don't see the beauty of it yet. Germany now has no more credit. Dr. Luther is going from door to door with his hat in his hand. The Credit-Anstalt has just failed. There's no credit to be had. Valuta is cracking. The French are withdrawing funds from London. Why? What a mess! And Léon's taking all this into account! The man's superb! I've never understood why he's not the head of a great concern. He can wipe the floor with any of them."

"He doesn't know enough . . . he remains a peasant," said Jules carelessly. They speculated for some time on

Léon's characteristics. Jules said, "He could have been the head of Strindl's but he doesn't know how to blackmail them; he believes in making money through grabbing and cooking the books; now you can only get in with the big fellows by blackmail. He's a mug and he'll remain in the middle millions."

He let them gabble about Léon under his nose, but his mind was made up and he found a good excuse for despising Léon by saying that he was a mug. He was really jealous of his talents; Jules went on to say that his own smash-and-grab scheme for the wheat was the only one that interested him.

Alphendéry affirmed impatiently, "We don't want to be like the rest of the two-penny *Luftmenschen** who snatch brilliant schemes out of people's brains and tear them to pieces in their madness for an unearned profit."

Jules said, "Ptt!"

"Jules, it's not the idea that counts, although Léon's idea is superb, it's the use it's put to. All the little suckers and blackmailers round our bank are lousy with ideas, but they don't want to work, they don't want to put others to work; they want to suck unearned livings out of the air. In other words, stealing is the easiest thing and every sneak thief is our equal, if that's all we can do. You don't need a façade for that."

Jules was nettled. "There's more to my scheme than that."

"Perhaps . . . but Léon drops a master scheme right into our lap."

"I wonder why."

Alphendéry said bitterly, "Here we sit bandying about the people's bread. The eccentric thing is that to restore confidence we have to put up the price of bread, which is the chief food of the French people."

"How are you going to make money?" asked Jules, in astonishment.

"You've got to sell the people what they want," said William soberly. "No good selling them what they don't want."

"Oh, no one makes a fortune out of commodities . . . no great fortunes have been made that way," charged Jules.

* Fantastics.

Léon came back to it, in the morning, before he left for Rotterdam. He was charming, persuasive, his thunder mitigated. "It's not easy to make money out of a rock field; but that's where you get nuggets. A cactus patch looks bad, but them big globes' leaves are full of milk. We have to learn to lick honey from thorns. . . . We'll get it from *A* to *Z*. I'll be back on Saturday morning. We'll make a fortune between us, you'll see, Jules." He clapped on Jules's table.

Ironically Jules measured him. "We'll make some money, I suppose, but not a fortune. No great swag was ever made out of commodities. To make a fortune, you've got to steal it, with nothing honest at the back of it. All great fortunes are financial . . . came out of the air. Anything that has hard work in it doesn't spell dough to me. They don't go together. The poor work hard and see what they get! Rosenkrantz and Guildenstern are trying to pay their rent out of 'honest' commodity business. Not for me! There's got to be a superstructure of graft, otherwise there's no sense in going into it."

He shrugged his shoulders and looked at them both coldly. Alphendéry sprang up. "You're all wet, Jules, in saying that great fortunes have been financial. None has been. How many people have made money out of air? Perhaps Morgan—and then not air but steel, high explosives—but ninety-five per cent of the wealth of great financial oligarchs comes from industry and nothing else. The market ramps, the consolidations, the thefts, the flotations, came later. The money was made out of goods—it has to be."

"But Morgan was different, and he's my ideal man," said Jules, clinging to his theme.

"Money comes from exploited resources and manufactured goods," said Alphendéry, incisively. "Pardon me for instructing two great men. Where do you think surplus value comes from? You can't extract surplus value out of a desk and swivel chair, whether you get them secondhand, or get a new Louis XVI set."

Léon shouted, storming, but not angry. "No surplus value! Nothing about surplus value! It's the productive urge; you have it or you don't, that's all. I get the idea: the excess wheat. Are they going to drop it in the Gulf of Mexico? We can pass the buck."

Alphendéry laughed. "They want to drop it in the

411

Gulf of Mexico—don't you see?—because—it is surplus—
Something that's over, and that they can't consume.
Would they give it to the people free?"

The two looked at him, dubiously, with ant-busy eyes,
seeing darkly his intention. They recognized the catch-
word and, though completely ignorant of its meaning,
hated it. Alphendéry laughed at them. "They would not
give it free; they want it to be a form of surplus value.
They're hoping that one day someone will come along
who will show them how to use their surplus with a profit."

Léon shook his head free of all such irrelevant discussion. "Michel, can you come round to your office? There's
very little chartering being done. I'll make a private arrangement—cheap freights, the freights is easy. Ask your
telephone girl to get my Amsterdam office, will you?"
Outside in the corridor, he whispered, "Does *he* lack
confidence in me? What is it? He doesn't see it!"

"Yes, yes, give Jules time. He's obstinate. Leave me to
handle him."

Léon said, "He likes to do things alone. A sort of vanity, eh?"

Alphendéry soothed him, standing between one and the
other with his diplomacy and fighting for the big deal
which would put him on easy street and let him get out.
Léon had no idea of this dream: he shook his head.
"Lone-wolf ideas don't go. If I have something good I go
to another man and I say—cement big friendships—I take
another in—" he rattled out something confused about
"Van Rhys, Rotterdam, he'll lend me five thousand tons
wheat, guilders—lend gold forward wheat and I got wheat
forward; I buy wheat, I hedge it—instead of paying five to
twenty per cent I pay—friendships you've got to—I pay
next to nothing—you cement friendships; something good
comes of it. His son now—Henrietta Achitophelous met
him at St. Moritz, nice Jewish girl, pretty girl—nice
Jewish lad, good business—the question is, has he got the
constructive urge? Everything is there."

"Oh, Jules is a genius, a pure genius along his own
Monte-Carlo lines . . . don't underrate him. You've been
in grain since you were twelve—born in it, indeed."

Léon studied him while he made this statement, laughed
his morning laugh, considered, and then said, "How he
makes his money—I don't know but—no commissions—
no bank loans; but— You buy calls when you are—

412

contre-partie—don't you see? The man thinks you know something and he goes and buys options. You see?"

"Let's get the wheat scheme down first, Léon. That's the most important."

"Yes, yes, yes, yes. Now—remind me, after, my boy, reciprocal business, Jules does hundreds of thousands of shares, he ought to get half-commission or else—'Listen, Legris, you pay my telephone bill'—don't understand—remind me. I've got a scheme. I don't like to see him—I'll tell you after: an offer for the bank—we'll make a study of it. When he told me Rosenkrantz and Guildenstern, I had an idea—what are you writing there? The wheat *schematism?* That's right!" The telephone rang. Léon grabbed it, began shouting, "Hello, who's there, who's there? That you, Graetz? Listen—documents by—get your pad, Graetz—documents by S.S. *Vega*, get it out even overtime: we have sold, underline 'sold,' Jonathan the two cargoes. Saturday. Quote the selling letter in confirming, confirm we quote cif. Leith, cif. Dumfries. If Bang telephones from Edinburgh offer maize, offer . . . make terms clean, London contract—some at time of shipment. Pay against documents, discharging charges, cif. alongside. Barley, barley, get a broker to keep posted. Have you got it, Graetz? Listen, get the Roumanian wheat out of clearing. You may sell to May if market's strong. Tell Purley you will sell basis 127/-, basis 7/- and 2/- a quarter under U.K. price, sell Jeanson sixpence a quarter less, or ninepence. Two! If market very firm say seven and a half cents over cost, underline that! On Saturday sell July especially, several tons, *sell only what you have.* Take care of the spread, Graetz. Three! *Re* Hans—give him a *talking-to,* not to go short on freight, on position and on price at the same time. You can sell freight and position if you are assured of delivery at the price. No firm bids to other people unless we are advised as co—We know Ganz bids Ente before he accepts—same for us! Three! Graetz! Write! View America on Europe, view England on Europe,* essential we cover our short near maize† as quickly possible in Antwerp or Rotterdam. In

* In Léon's "shorthand" this means, "in view of the fact that American maize is at a premium over all European markets and that England is at a premium on the Continent."

† Similarly, this means, "our short positions in early delivery maize."

Antwerp save banking expenses. *Three!* What's that? Well, make it four, or five, whatever it is. *Five!* Preferably buy maize few days earlier, and pay a premium than risk arbitration by Ganz if boat is late. Charter freight the moment bought and risk demurrage. Now, Graetz, if the market is quiet you can buy cash maize and—running long—September—if strong liquidate both." For understanding this elliptic hurricane, keeping his temper, running the business, and making a neat profit, Graetz earned one thousand guilders a month plus a percentage. When the receipts were added up at the end of the year, before the attributions were made, Léon's living, traveling, personal, and whoopee expenses were deducted as well as repairs on his house, his daughter's schooling, and his wife's permanent waves. But the same deductions were not made in Graetz's favor. Graetz saved his money with the hope that some year they would make a giant profit and even with his small slice he could "get out." Léon was not aware of this desire of Graetz's.

Léon turned from the telephone and watched with approval Alphendéry figuring and ciphering in the corner of a sheet of paper. Cambo and Dreyer came in. Dreyer went, but Cambo tried to install himself there to see what they were doing. Alphendéry laughed up at him and said, "Scram, Danny, my boy: we're making millions."

Daniel Cambo left with a good grace and the remark, "Well, I better leave you multimillionaires and go back to selling braces."

"Who's he, who's he, what's his game?" Léon demanded, panting into Alphendéry's ear.

"Making peanuts into gold bars, making shoestrings into liens: he's in the French Woolworth-type business, trying to make a go of it. The department stores here get away with it, no competition at all. They don't give value."

Léon showed intense regret that he hadn't thought of it himself. "Do you think it'll go? Do you think the French'll buy that junk turned out in a row?"

"Most people say no; I say, what man does, even the French will do. Cambo is sure. He's a genius in his own line."

Léon peered hard at Alphendéry. "Yes? Yes? I'd like to meet him!" He looked alert for a moment and then went back to his wearisome song of the wheat.

He took the evening train to Amsterdam. He and Alphendéry walked up and down the platform waiting for the train to leave and Léon said, "When you want to leave Bertillon, my boy, you come with me. You're good luck. We'll work together. From the first—" But at this moment his eyes fell on a particularly artificial beauty with a particularly good figure, and murmuring, "Goodby, write to me," he jumped aboard the train to make sure that from his seat he could stare the traveling Venus into a quick bargain. The train moved out with Léon's immense head, hat, stick, and yellow gloves suddenly thrust from some window, in a gorgeous bouquet of gesticulation.

Meanwhile each day Jules was shut in close conclave, and there were goings and comings. Jules had decided to send Stevie Pentous, a young gilded friend who had some relations with the U.S. embassy in Paris, to Washington to broach the wheat scheme. Stevie knew some Republican vote thrower in Kansas and was at home in Park Avenue penthouses. Jules had also telegraphed Theodor Bomba at Nice, telling him to sail immediately for Washington, against the advice of Alphendéry, Richard Plowman, and William. In fact, he asserted that he had not telegraphed to Bomba; but Alphendéry heard Léon's diminished, startled voice on the telephone from Amsterdam: "Michel, Bertillon has told the whole scheme to Bomba, and Bomba hasn't got it at all!"

"Oh, no, I don't think so; Jules swore to me he would not."

"Listen to the telegram I got then:—'SIEGFRIED SPILLED WOTAN'S SCHEME FOR RHEINGOLD. FINE OPENING BUT NEED TO GET DETAILS FROM YOU. WILL I JOURNEY AMSTERDAM. BOMBA."

"I can't understand it, Henri . . . Jules told me—"

"He hoaxed you then, my boy. We'll have to make the best of it. Bomba—has he got any brains?"

"He understands Kabbala," said Alphendéry dolefully, "but the rest we'll have to see."

Léon's potent chuckle came over the telephone, "Kabbala? Then we're all right, my boy." Alphendéry went on writing down the names of bonds and their maturities, but a shadow had fallen across his hopes and presently he stopped and began pacing up and down the green carpet.

He tried to conceal from himself until the last moment the notion that the great wheat scheme which was to liberate him, was taking on strangely quixotic contours in this hall of Bertillon's dreams. The only thing that gave him happiness in this dreary time when neither the markets, nor politics nor the people were stirring, was the certainty now that the French would sign a trade treaty with the Russians, and the Five-Year Plan, which he had studied with such eagerness, had more chance of coming through.

Scene Fifty-four: The Affair of Henri Parouart

JULY, 1931.

The mail and the morning were full of lunacies.

There was a four-page letter from Légaré, on the Côte d'Azur, threatening to shoot himself if he did not receive by return mail two thousand francs immediately and to make a complaint to the Parquet* if a monthly stipend was not promised to him.

A medical client, who dropped in to the bank on his way to his surgery, found in his mail the latest version of the Spanish Prisoner confidence trick, written on café paper:

DEAR SIR,

I am imprisoned here for bankruptcy and I am writing to ask you if you will help me to save a sum of 1,800,000 francs that I possess in bank notes in the false-bottom of a trunk which is, actually, owing to circumstances which will be revealed to you, in the luggage room of a station in France. It would be necessary for you to come here to pay the Clerk of the Tribunal the costs of my judgment so that they will lift the lien on my baggages, so that you can thus get hold of a valise with a secret bottom in which I have hidden the receipt of the railway, in-

* Financial frauds division of the Central Police.

dispensable to get the trunk out of the station. In recompense, I will give up to you one-third of the sum. I cannot receive your reply directly in prison, but if you accept, you will send quickly a telegram to a friend who will give it to me safely. As soon as I have your response, I will let you know my name and I will confide all the details of my secret. Awaiting your reply, I sign with my initial—

S.

The most absolute discretion. For reasons outside my control, do not write, telegraph exactly as hereunder—Luis Marin, Lista Correos, 2233. F. Sitges (Spain). Possible.

This letter, which was showed round to everybody, put the bank in a cheerful mood for an hour or so.

Michel Alphendéry had a truculent letter from the Gemini—Rosenkrantz and Guildenstern, complaining that the subalterns at the bank, customers' men, office manager, cable boys, telegraph girls, accountants, were not sufficiently attentive to them.

We have gone to great expense and spared no trouble to make the name of the bank known. We have printed it on all our stationery. We should like absolute assurances from you that the personnel of the bank will be given instructions about our important relation to yourselves. If we cannot have this assurance, we do not understand the basis on which you expect us to conduct business. Let us point out that when we came we found the bank's name in very bad odor and despite the rumors we heard, we decided to come in with you, but you are doing nothing to assist us. We do not wish to have to complain about a breach of contract. Distinguished greetings!

FRANZ ROSENKRANTZ AND FRANZ GUILDENSTERN

"Those damned Teutons," cried Jules. "Why did we take them in? Charity will be the death of us." Alphendéry, who felt himself accused, because he had pleaded for them, murmured, "That's their way, Jules. I must admit, I'm sorry I let my Alsatian origin get the better of me, though."

William Bertillon had a letter from Mr. and Mrs. Wade threatening to seize the funds of the bank in one of its depositing banks, if they were not paid the sum demanded immediately.

In putting this in the file, to get it out of sight, Jules found another blue paper, reminding him of the decorating contractors' suit, claiming fifty thousand francs on the decoration of his Champs de Mars apartment; he had already paid three hundred and fifty thousand for redecoration and now refused to pay more.

A bad day. Jules rang up his wife and asked, "Are you all right? Everything's crazy here." A few minutes later she telephoned saying, "I just found out that there's a strange black cat in the house."

"Did you kick it out?"

"Yes."

"That's good."

"And it's the twenty-third—my unlucky day and yours, too."

"You don't have to tell me!"

The last event was petty enough. Henri Parouart, who lived by petty blackmail and was already on the hush-money list of a number of financial institutions, had been maneuvering for nearly two years to get on to the Bertillon blackmail-pension list. He did not know that, although Bertillon supported various and vagarious peanut enterprises, restaurants, boulevard sheets, powder-puff inventors, attic industrialists, rich ragamuffins, and superannuated gangsters (out of lavishness), he had no blackmail list. Bertillon enjoyed the thrill of facing out and double-daring the little multitudinous creeping pest of sneaks, go-betweens, crooks, and drain fishers that regarded the bank, as every other bank in Paris, as their natural prey. In one respect, this minor rascality was exactly like Jules Bertillon himself: they were not impressed by the great golden wall of high finance—they brought along their chisels and knives to snick off flakes for themselves.

When Parouart reviewed the dubious collection of reformed and active ruffians, fools, and commercial pigmy brains that Jules kept, he assumed that all these people had "something on" Bertillon. His tongue had been hanging out for a long time now and it was dusty. His knowledge of men gained in shady occupations, in doss houses, suspicious quaysides, and police courts in various countries told him that Bertillon was lucky rather than careful, and too overweening to be safe.

Henri Parouart was modest. His feet were always on slippery ground. He knew that if he asked too much, it would pay his victims to shoot him, or to send a modest check to the police and ask them to shove him over some frontier. Now by this date there were almost no frontiers left over which he could have been shoved, with safety to himself; and the complaisance of the French police, based on a little mean sleuthing that he did for them, a little stool-pigeoning, was dear to him. He had calculated that Bertillon could be stung for about four thousand francs a year—"very little to Bertillon but the rent to me," he said to himself.

The chief rumor spread about stock-exchange houses is that they bucket the orders, and this whisper is current about every house in existence that deals in stocks.* Parouart had been a small client of the bank for some seven or eight years, being a gambler in all varieties, pathetically hoping to earn his bread and butter on the turn of fancy of the great "pools" (or gambling syndicates). He now suddenly demanded proof of the actual buying and selling in some transactions done five or six years before, and as such proof was not immediately forthcoming, on account of the time that had elapsed, he immediately threatened to go to the Parquet with a charge of "abuse of confidence." He further pretended that a sale had been made at a bad price and that thus while he had lost an original amount of, say, twenty-five hundred francs, what with interest mounted up in these five or six years and with accumulated moral and other damage and the loss of capital, his real loss now amounted to about ten times that. He further pretended that the price quoted to him on another distant day was a bad one and he had been cheated, so that he had lost a further, say six hundred fifty francs, which, of course, in five or six years, also mounted up.

Naturally, Parouart, as well as Jules Bertillon, knew perfectly well that a claim of some forty thousand francs, which was what he now put in, was entirely absurd. It was simply a way Parouart had of saying, "Let us pretend

---

* In "bucketing" (American usage) the broker instead of passing the orders to buy and sell to the stock exchange, acts in the same way as a race-course tout. If you lose he wins.

I have a capital of forty thousand francs and that it yields ten per cent per annum. You pay this ten per cent, Mr. Bertillon, and you will hear no more scandal from me; but if you don't, I can make things sticky for you, for I know, as well as you do, that no banker can afford to have his books looked into."

Parouart had for his lawyer a man of intelligence who had got into some foul affair with a politician who had dropped him. He still clung on in politics and was vaguely connected with Dr. Jacques Carrière. Jules, when he found this out, hoped that Carrière would kick Parouart into the gutter for him. But Carrière said "it could not be arranged: Parouart had some secret power, someone behind him." Jules laughed. One day he got a blue paper from Maître Lallant, Carrière's lawyer. On the heels of this blue paper, today, came Henri Parouart, mean, hungry, crafty, neurotic, dirty, and foul-smelling, with a ragged pallor and holes in his shoes. Petty blackmail does not feed her man. He walked straight upstairs without being announced and went into Jules's office, where he sat with an uneasy but hardened impertinence.

"Did you get my letter?"

"My secretary attends to letters, Mr. Alphendéry, you've met him . . ." said Jules sweetly, knowing Parouart feared the cleverness of Alphendéry.

"I have influence, Mr. Bertillon: unless you agree to cover my entire loss, I will show up your business for what it is. Look at my rags! Can I see this Persian carpet without grinding my teeth? You can't blame me!"

"Oh, ptt!—you don't mean to say you're still talking about that fantasy of yours you were gagging about a month ago? You're crazy, Parouart . . . no court in France or anywhere else would listen to you."

"The American Stock Exchange would listen to my complaint, even if no court here would. And as to the latter—don't worry; I have taken advice. Your correspondents in the New York Stock Exchange would get into a nice mess if this charge were made and proved. I can prove it. This republic favors the poor. I can make the charge. You have to prove you are innocent. The onus is on you. In France, the poor victim is protected against the rich victimizer: I will bleed you to death in lawyers' fees."

Jules looked at him shrewdly, "And who is paying

420

yours? In this republic—since you are making ham speeches—no lawyer is allowed to take up cases on speculation!"

"Never mind about that, never mind about that. I have backing. Enemies of yours who would like to see you K.O.-ed." He sneered and looked so rotten with poverty and craft that Jules found a ghost of pity in his heart. Or was it superstition?

"How much do you—think you've lost, Parouart?"

Oh the thin and bitter eagerness in his face! Jules had decided, at this moment, to give him some money, not being able to bring himself to fight against a man with torn collar. There was superstition in this, too. Jules noticed the unusually pale face, the trembling hands, and crouching stand. Drugs. "This poor rat hasn't a chance if I really go out to get him," thought Jules. And Parouart said harshly, "At least forty thousand francs."

"Wha-at! It's impossible, Parouart. Be sensible, Parouart. I know you're running a tiny blackmail business. And I'm not trying to put you out of business. You don't seem to be doing very well at it, I can see. I don't mind being on your list of keepers, if you're reasonable. But yours is a repeat business. You want to be reasonable. You don't want to kill the goose, you know. You're after all just a common blackmailer, Parouart. A blackmailer ends by tying a knot in his tongue and hanging himself." He looked straight at Parouart. He suddenly got into a pet. "You're a police rat, Parouart. The police have been cleaning out the lowlives and fourflushers from the Paris cafés ever since the depression started. And a bundle of bones like you still haunts the Café de la Paix with a bunch of swarthy Venezuelan crooks and Greek conspirators that would frighten the gargoyles off Notre Dame. Now, if you're still there, with the company you keep, then you're a police rat. It's plain. You can skip. Let the Prefecture keep you." But common sense showed itself the next instant; Jules softened, smiled, as if he had just been playing with a paper knife, the moment before. He drooped his lids, rolled up his glance, and pronounced in plain tones, "I'll give you five thousand francs for a complete written release on everything prior to this date and the opportunity to sue you in court if I catch you whispering your fairy tales round Paris." He ended in a tone of lordly contempt, leaning back in his chair, his fine, fair face looking over Parouart's head.

Parouart flushed. He made as if to stamp his foot. The veins stood out on his temples. "No. The total loss. I have influence with a chain of newspapers. I'll ruin you. I'll see your finish."

"You haven't even influence with the sewer rats you belong to: don't make me laugh. I'm making you a fair offer—because I don't owe you a sou. But I'd rather pay you, you poor croaking raven, and tell you to get to hell out of here, than see you drag out of here with your melodrama and your miserable threats. Don't make me laugh."

Jules looked at him, as he played with his pencil and wondered if Parouart had been born with or had manufactured that scurrilous mask that covered his face. It could not represent the mind of any creature that he could conceive. To Jules's mind this face showed the futility of all mere scheming. Parouart's face was evidence that Parouart had spent all his life plotting, undermining, blackmailing, selling himself and others to get money. And at present he stood there in a frayed collar and a belligerent cowardice, his thin quarters feeling in prospect the boot, his thin elbows the pavement. More was needed than brass and cunning, more than crookedness, more than "knowing what the game was about," Jules's intuition told him. Jules was not accustomed to study his fellows. It must have been the sudden revelation of a spearhead of evil pointed against himself, and his very existence that made him rub his eyes. Jules had the honesty to recognize Parouart, even at this moment, as a dissolute, worthless brother of his, in the confraternity of thieves. He was in many ways a democrat and never, never a Pharisee. He thought of his business as a crooked roulette wheel, a confidence trick, and of himself as a clever pirate, and no more. In the same way, like a gangster, he regarded morality as a poor trick of mean brains to excuse their failure. He despised good-humoredly the people who allowed him to pick their pockets, but he thought it was right, proper, natural, he should do so. This system was what he favored with the term, "human nature."

Jules added now somnolently, "I know what your game is, Parouart! You want to make a little chicken feed out of me so that you can eat and buy whatever dope you take. I don't object to that. Why don't you come to me straight, like a white man, and make me a straight proposition? Why do you put on these Grand-Guignol airs? You chaps from the Eastern Mediterranean must always be sirupy. I'm willing to let you welch me of a trifle: that's one of the axioms of my business. Only, be reasonable. If you petty gangsters start to give me headaches, I don't have to work for you, you know. I can go out of business. I can live at Nice. You don't frighten me with the Parquet. Who's to stop me closing tomorrow morning? Five thousand francs for complete written release. Take it or leave it."

Parouart was furious at not getting a couple of bank notes without strings tied to them. He was aching, furious for his drug. His face creased painfully with an angry smile. "I'll never give you a release. When I present the check you will give me for payment covering the whole amount of my loss, that will be your release. You are guilty! You want a release."

"Then you won't get a centime. Get out."

Parouart realized he had behaved ridiculously. "I'll put the bailiffs in yet: you'll hear from my lawyer this afternoon."

"If any bailiff comes I'll throw him into the gutter he came from," yelled Jules.

Parouart backed out, sneering and spitting hate. He was ill. Jules watched him to the stairhead. At the bottom of the stairs near the stock-exchange room, fatal, desperate room for all his kind of petty speculator, Parouart saw Aristide Raccamond by himself, looking through papers he was taking out of a satchel. Parouart was pale with excitement, the bank whirled round him. Alone in the world the face of Raccamond, last seen in Carrière's house, stood in living colors. Parouart had a flash of inspiration.

"Mr. Raccamond! I have something very urgent to tell you. Can you leave the bank for a few minutes?"

"Of course. What is it? From Carrière's?"

"No, no. And not here—of all places."

Raccamond pricked up his ears and examined his interlocutor carefully. He was under the influence of some excitement—or drugged again, he supposed. He was afraid he was going to be touched. Nothing doing. However, like many of his class, Raccamond occasionally took drugs and often handled them for rich clients. Raccamond believed Parouart was some sort of miserable police spy. Moreover, Raccamond at one time had been attracted by a band of young white slavers for the South American trade —this was in Aleppo just after the war ended. Raccamond afterwards knew all of the low theaters of the boulevards of Paris and the provinces and the prostitute cafés. He had an unholy respect for even the Cinderellas of the law. He gravely looked at Parouart for a minute, with a kind of authoritative gobble, went to get rid of his papers and joined him, his face covered by an extremely dignified and occupied expression. Jules had gone back to his room and had not seen this collusion at the bottom of the stairs. He called his brother William, shut the door, and entered into a long talk with him.

"The little louse Parouart was in here blackmailing. Did Alphendéry write to Henri Léon in Amsterdam to try and get Parouart's Dutch police file? I lost my temper and told him to beat it. I don't believe he'll go to the police. It's too flimsy. I look like too rich a *pot-au-feu:* he'll try fishing here again. He'll try to frighten us first with a few more of his little blue billets-doux. Who do you think's backing him?"

"Pay him off," said William. "What's the use of playing with a drug fiend? Pay him enough to buy his drugs and let him doss down and be happy. It would pay you to see he had pocket money to sniff himself to sleep. What do you care?"

"He's got delusions of grandeur now. They go mad, don't they? He may go to the Parquet; as crazy as that. No, he couldn't. What do you bet he's back here tomorrow? Come on, one hundred francs he's here before three tomorrow."

"You're on," said William indifferently.

"Before twelve tomorrow."

"O.K."

Alphendéry knocked at the door and peered, brightly placating, in the crack, "What's biting you fellows?"

"Come in, Michel: it's only Henri Parouart. Wants a pension."

Alphendéry said, "Don't buy him off. Get something on him. Listen, my advice is simple. That little scab is forty-five or forty-seven years old. He has never done an honest day's work in his life. He's mysterious. He's not French but he's got a French name. He's been in Germany, all the Balkan states, in Russia, in the Far East. He's been seen from Edinburgh to Salonika. A chap like that must have left a trail of police photographs which if placed end to end would look like the trail of the viper out of Ireland. It's obvious. Then the boys tell me he's always meeting people in out-of-the-way corners and shaking hands with them, or pressing their hands and scuttling off. Drugs. And he's seen, loathsome little Constantinople dog that he is, talking to fine-looking young women round the Faubourg Montmartre at night. White slaving. The police tolerate him but they can't actually be in love with him. A good protest and out he'd go. Why don't you have him trailed? You boys never think of the simplest things. His record must have a whiff—eh? I'd like to see a few pages. It would be a M.A. degree in European roguery."

Jules lifted the receiver. "Alphendéry, you're right. (Hullo, get me Maître Olympe!) He's cockroach-poor. (Pierre? Say, which is a good detective agency. No, not divorce. There's a chap bothering me I want to get after. You'll find out? What? Wait till I get that down—Green Ray—silly sort of name. Sounds imbecile, doesn't it? All right. Send one of their men round, will you? Wait—I don't want them to start blackmailing me, too. You come round right away, will you, Pierre? I'll give you the dope.) That's a good idea, Michel."

Michel laughed with innocent vanity, "You didn't ask what they charged."

"It won't cost what it would cost to buy him off."

"I don't trust Olympe's judgment. He'll let out who you are."

"I say, you don't know Olympe. You're against him because he's a divorce lawyer for the high-steppers . . . By the way—you never went to Lemaître about your own divorce?"

"I took a taxi to the door: then I thought, why force Estelle to divorce me? I have no false pride. I have no other girl I want to marry."

"You ought to get one, Alphendéry, you're lonely. That's why you run to the Reds. It would organize your life for you." They began to talk of business again. Not once in a blue moon did Jules mention the private affairs of his associates.

"A terrible crash of the pound sterling: you'll have to renege on those Carrière contracts. His next draft is due in a week."

"I won't go back on him yet," said Jules. "The pound will go up again. It's just a flurry. Why with the sterling bloc they can't let it go off. That's how I figure."

"Do you think they'll jail Oustric?" asked Alphendéry.

"No. He got everyone into his net. They'll jail nobody but some little twopenny clerk. They'll throw a big hunk of Senate-Committee shorthand notes at the raging lion and then they'll fold up the books and sneak off in silence. Gives too much argument to the radical press. I bet you one thousand francs, Michel, Oustric will not stay a day in jail. He's too cocky. He must have the whole cabinet in his pocket."

"Do you remember the first day I told you about him. I marked him down long before anyone else as a coming man," murmured Alphendéry.

"He's done now: they use them up fast in France," said Jules regretfully.

"The government is a gang you have to watch," William interjected: "they are gangsters. They play along with you for a while and then suddenly they smack you in the head and make a colander out of you, with Senate inquiries, to suit their own game. I don't believe in getting in with the government gang, the way it's the fashion in France. That's why I'm against your having anything to do with Carrière, Jules. They're all so rotten that they infect everyone they touch. They've got all the dope and you've only got a bit of it. How can you win against them? Oustric was a bright baby and now they've done with him. They won't let him go to jail but they've spiked his game, now that he's filled their pockets with gold. . . . If I were you, I'd ditch Carrière and quicker than that."

"Oh, shut up, William."

"Did you sign anything with Carrière?" insisted William.

"No, I told you."

"And if the pound goes off you're not bound to pay him any losses?"

"No, I told you," yelled Jules. He continued in a normal but irritated tone, "Do stop harping on Carrière, William."

Alphendéry was studying Jules minutely, and he put in,

"It's just as well you didn't give Carrière a written guarantee on his sterling contracts, Jules, the way things look. I don't see how the pound can stay on gold. I'm certain there's nothing more in the vaults of the Bank of England but a few sheets of blotting paper and a *mont-de-piété* ticket."

"Who knows that?"

"Why, some of us can read balance sheets and make calculations."

Jules, without replying, turned down the sheet with the market quotations and began to discuss their market policy for the day. Alphendéry let it pass, therefore, but said to William later, "I have a most uneasy feeling about this Carrière thing. He swears he signed nothing and yet you can never trust Jules. He certainly acts as if he signed a contract with Carrière."

"Well, I've stayed back at the bank a few nights and I've looked everywhere." William smiled. "I've got skeleton keys to every desk in the place, you know. And I don't see any agreement with Carrière, so I think it's all right. Besides he wouldn't be so wild."

"Did you hear the rumor about Carrière—that a boy was killed at one of his parties?"

"Oh, if they don't kill themselves with drink and boys, they smash their neck at bobsleigh or in speedboats. That's the way we make money." His gray, even tones ceased and Alphendéry only heard the jingling of the money he was lifting and silting back into his pocket. He laughed, "We don't even have to send them wreaths like the gangsters in Chicago."

In a few days the detective agency, The Green Ray, turned in its report on Henri Parouart. A fragment follows—

AFFAIR OF HENRI PAROUART

July, 1931*

The watch was taken up at eight o'clock in the morning in the Passage de l'Opéra, where Mr. Parouart has a small room, as stated above.

* The date, of course, is made to fit in with the calendar of events in the tale. No real events are referred to.

At 8h.45, Mr. P. comes out bareheaded, goes towards the Galérie Feydeau, then brusquely makes a half-turn and by the Rue Vivienne gains the Great Boulevards, in the direction of the Rue Montmartre, stands a few seconds in front of the Maison du Café, looks into the interior, seems to make a gesture, goes, after this, to the Grand Comptoir, drinks, and goes to get his traditional cigar, not without stopping frequently at the windows he passes. He comes back, thereafter, by the boulevard and reaches his domicile by the Passage de l'Opéra. It is 9h.14.

At 10 h. he comes out again, crosses the street, goes to the Banque Czorvocky, mixes with the groups there, exchanges a few words with several persons, and once more goes home.

At 12h. we see him direct himself by the Rue Vivienne towards the Stock Exchange, which he enters at 12h.05, always by the same door, whence he comes to his habitual place, near the *corbeille* of the *agents-de-change*. The inspector stationed in the interior sees him talk with the same personage of middle height, dressed in gray, that we have already mentioned, and he quits the Stock Exchange at 14h.-17, after having come out of it, for a short moment for his needs. He comes back to the Rue Vivienne, where he shakes for a long time the hand of a person of Semitic aspect, dressed in a beige suit, whom he met leaving the Bourse. Having reached the Rue St. Marc, he starts to run and penetrates down the Galérie Feydeau at a rapid pace. He passes the Galérie des Variétés, arrives on the Great Boulevards, goes to a newspaper kiosk situated in the neighborhood, where he buys the *Intransigeant* which he puts in his pocket without unfolding it. He looks around him, saunters a few steps as if he was waiting for someone, then enters the Rue Le Peletier, re-enters the Banque Czorvocky and comes out almost immediately and goes up to his room. It is 14h.45.

At 15h.01 he comes out again with his hat on his head and goes towards the Bourse, of which he mounts the steps, rapidly disappearing from us. After having looked for him, some instants at his usual place, where he does not appear, we go back to the Rue Le Peletier to watch there.

At 16h.40 he reappears by the Rue Rossini, accompanied by an individual tall, brown-complexioned, and dressed in blue, apparently about forty years old. Mr. P. appears very worried and goes up to his room with the *quidam* described.

At 17h.50 the latter comes out alone, by the Rue Le Peletier and disappears along the Great Boulevards.

At 19h.30 Mr. P. has not reappeared. The watch is maintained until 8h. without anyone having seen him.

July 25, 1931

The watch is taken up at 8h. A.M. At 8h.30 Mr. P. comes out by Rue Le Peletier, goes at a pace not usual with him at such an hour, towards Rue St. Marc, rapidly crosses the Place de la Bourse and goes to the Café du Vaudeville, stays there ten minutes, comes back as rapidly as before towards the Great Boulevards, and enters this time the Maison du Café where he drinks coffee. He appears disquieted, comes out of the Maison du Café, and goes home at the same rapid rate. It is 9h.

At 9h.10 we see enter very rapidly the person dressed in blue and holding an umbrella, the one we mentioned yesterday. This person goes upstairs, without any doubt to Mr. P.'s room and we are confirmed in this surmise by seeing him come down about ten minutes later, after making a sign of adieu to a person that we do not yet see and who stays behind him in the staircase. This person is none other than Mr. P., who, moreover, by the Boulevard des Italiens goes to the newspaper kiosk which is on the corner, whence he goes back home.

We then take up a position near the florist's shop at the entry to the Passage. It is 9h.30. At 9h.40 we perceive that a person is approaching us with muffled footsteps, from behind, and is spying upon us: a rapid glance behind permits us to recognize the personage in blue, of which there is mention above: after having stared us over from head to foot, he goes to Mr. P.'s place. At 11h.50 he comes out in company with the latter and we can hear the following words, ". . . it's a filthy thing to do . . ." Mr. P.

and this person say good-by to each other at the subway station Opéra. Mr. P. comes back alone and immediately goes to the Bourse, which he enters at 12h.05.

We have observed, during this period of surveillance, several persons pass and repass on several occasions each, looking us over with insistence, notably a man carrying a net bag containing some merchandise which we were not able to make out. This person came out of number 6 Rue Taitbout. Trailing him, we find ourselves in front of 9 Boulevard Montmartre.

At 12h.40, Mr. P. is still at the Bourse.

At 15h.30 we take up our stand at the angle of the Rue Le Peletier whence we watch the door by which Mr. P. is obliged to enter his house and we are warned by one of our "indicators" that Mr. P., whom we have lost in the crowd at the Bourse, has just passed the Rue Vivienne, whence he is going rapidly towards the Great Boulevards. We immediately start on his trail, but it is in vain that, at the crossing of the Great Boulevards, we attempt to find Mr. P. We come back to Rue Le Peletier, but wait vainly, until 8h.30 the return of Mr. P. whose window is not even lighted up. We leave our watch, since we have no instructions to maintain it.

July 28, 1931

Mr. P. comes out at 9h.15. He has his hat and seems more and more wary. He goes by the Boulevard des Italiens to the Maison du Café where we see him talk and laugh with a lady in black who is drinking beside him. He comes out at 9h.30 and by the Rue Louis-Le-Grand goes to his barber in this street where he is shaved.

At 10h. he goes to the Crédit Sennonais to look at the stock-exchange sheets, and then goes home. Some minutes afterwards we see the brown-complexioned person in blue, already mentioned, go up to his room. At 11h. this person comes down alone, while our "indicator" perceives the landlady of Mr. P., Mme. Calcaldo, at the window of Mr. P.'s room, looking attentively up and down the street, then turn

430

round, at which moment, one sees the head of Mr. P. scarcely visible behind her, and disappearing rapidly.

At 12h.30 Mr. P. comes out at a rapid pace, walks several meters, stops brusquely, coming towards us with a hostile air. He is pale and seems very angry. He continues his way, then, almost running up to the crossing Richelieu-Drouot and ourselves going along at a smart pace to keep him in view. There, he stops and turns round again. We hide behind a kiosk, but being alone in the watch, we lose sight of Mr. P. during the few seconds in which we hid behind the kiosk. We take our watch up again to the Rue Le Peletier and at 5h.30 of this afternoon, we see Mr. P. appear, his hat in his hand. He seems exhausted, and we see that his feet are covered with dust, like someone who has walked a long way. He goes straight home. At 8h. of the evening he has not come out again.

The results of inquiries made by us in "special circles" show Mr. P. as being an accountant at the Banque Czorvocky, Rue Le Peletier, where he is perfectly intimate with one of the directors, Dr. Marcuzo, Bulgarian Israelite, living Rue du Docteur-Blanche, at La Muette.

The Banque Czorvocky is reputed to discount Russian drafts. An inquiry is being made on this subject. We are probably not wrong in supposing that Mr. P., who seems absolutely determined to break the trail, went to a correspondent where he receives orders and it is possible that this correspondent is Dr. Marcuzo. It is for his account, apparently, that Mr. P. gives Bourse orders to the mysterious personages that he meets almost everywhere. It would be wise then, in our opinion, to reinforce the watchers, particularly on Saturday afternoon and to take the chance of a surveillance after 8h.30 in the evening.

NOTE. We recommend that the watch be doubled and kept up after 8h.30 P.M.

GREEN RAY

Jules and William and Alphendéry howled with laughter. Even the clients down in the stock-exchange room began to look upwards and titter.

"At any rate, he gave Parouart a terrible scare," Jules

remarked, "I suppose it was worth it. Olympe tells me that if I pay them a higher fee they will tell me the name of the person in blue."

"Olympe is very useful," William said with calm. "Get him to pick out anyone for you, lawyer, indicator, agent, and then take someone else, for you can be sure Olympe will have picked for himself the stupidest in the whole city. It's instinct. It's uncanny. To have such a sure touch!"

Jules was speaking lazily over the telephone, "Pierre, what on earth's the idea of sending me this? My messenger boy downstairs knows ten times as much as this about Parouart. No, of course, don't continue the watch and don't pay a higher fee. Good God! No, don't get another detective agency. Let it slide. He hasn't been near us since your beautiful agency advertised all over Paris that he was being watched. He's been scared out of his wits: he does nothing but run to the Bourse and run home. . . . We'll never get anything on him now. . . . Oh—" He put down the telephone. "If it wasn't that Claire-Josèphe adores Pierre. I knew him when I was flying. What can you do?"

"I knew him too, when I was flying," said William grimly.

"Oh, you—you're the flat-footedest airman I ever saw."

Alphendéry put in, "Maes in Antwerp says he was thrown out by the Belgian police. I asked him to try and get his record. It's not easy."

"Ah, I'd rather pay him than go to all that trouble for Parouart," cried Jules. "Next time he comes make out a check, William. Let him have the pleasure of blackmailing us. We can afford it and he can have the fun."

"Nothing doing," said William.

"I looked up this chap with the unpronounceable name, Czorvocky. Marcuzo is the nominal chief but he doesn't seem to have any money in it. He's doing a nice little business in discounting German bonds. I wanted to do that: I could have made a fortune if you hadn't put me off, Michel," said Jules, with annoyance. He resumed loftily, "He makes them loans, and they hand over the bonds and sign a paper. On the back of the paper, printed in nonpareil type, are at least a dozen excuses for him to sell the bonds the next day. They pay interest, too. Seems a smart fellow. . . . Do you think Rosenkrantz and

432

Guildenstern could get us that business, Michel? All grain merchants are plastered up in bonds."

Michel and Alphendéry started. "You went to see him?"

"Sure. I went to see him as soon as I got the confidential report. I thought I might smell out how he did it and if I could steal some of the business. He's got a nice little office, some grilles, some clerks, no business that I could see. I asked him about Parouart, saying he was placing orders with me. He looked queer at that. I suppose he's paying him to make a stink round my place. He told me Parouart is connected with the police. If he tells me, it's hard to believe; if he says it! He belongs to the special milieu they're talking about. . . . Forget it . . ." his lip curled. "All these Balkan geniuses have got Russia on the brain, anyhow. Perhaps he is in with the Soviets. It made me suspect Léon's scheme, too. I see it's just a geographical obsession of theirs, not a great scheme at all. I thought it was original with Léon. They're not Western European. *Weltpolitik,* heu! Want a finger in every pie. Want to make the whole world one big pie! They've got el-e-phant-i-asis," he pronounced with care.

Alphendéry shot up to the defense of Léon. "He has his foolish hours, when he thinks he's a field marshal of industry and then he makes his worst mistakes: 'Don't stop me, Alphendéry, don't interrupt me!' He's Napoleonic and has a star: 'My instinct tells me to do such-and-such and do it now. Even if you're right, and I'm wrong, I'm right. The creative impulse can't go wrong!' He is a giant, he makes giant mistakes. He never stops to know whether he is ridiculous or sublime. Why should one? You can use such a man. To make profit out of a man who is such a natural 'bull,' you have only got to notice his good points. He is very simple at heart, good, generous, and a superb moneymaker. Now this scheme. . . ."

"I don't trust any Roumanian, or any Bulgarian, either," said Jules with petulance.

"He doesn't trust you, either, don't worry," William consoled him. Jules turned his back on his elder brother.

"Bomba has got all his publicity ready and Stevie Pentous is sailing for America tomorrow," he threw out at Alphendéry imperially.

"Does Léon know?"

433

"Where is Bomba now?" asked William.

"Bomba is in New York. Got there yesterday." Jules's tone forbade exclamation and inquiry.

"That's fine," said William.

"Does Stevie know anything about the scheme?" Alphendéry was appalled.

"Sure, I told him all about it and I gave him your notes. Besides, Dan Waters, who just came from official business in Germany, is going over on that boat and Stevie can explain it all to him on the way over."

"That might save the day; Waters is a brilliant fellow." Jules refused to answer any more.

There was a knock at the door. A boy in uniform came in.

"From Van Cleef and Arpels, sir."

"Here, give it to this gentleman." He pointed to Alphendéry. He signed for it, thrust his hand in his pocket, and, without looking, gave the boy a fifty-franc note. The boy said, "Sir?"

"It's yours. Go on, scamper," said Jules.

Alphendéry was clumsily trying to undo a knot. He slipped off the string. In a purple velvet case, on purple satin, lay a long thick gold pencil. Alphendéry picked it up and let it roll back into his palm in surprise.

"It's your birthday, isn't it?" asked Jules.

"Yes, but Jules—it weighs ounces. It must be pure gold."

"I shouldn't be surprised—or nearly," said Jules carelessly. He took out his hat and coat and wrapped himself elegantly in them. He always had the curious appearance of being less material than the rest of mankind, part of him seemed always to belong to the chiaroscuro of a room, to the dark substance of lampposts in a street. When he moved amongst the pillars downstairs, it was almost impossible to see him clearly. He passed through crowds of his clients and they never saw him unless they ran into him, face to face, when, if they were intimate, he gave them a steel handgrip. His hands were long, beautiful, sculptured, firm, as the hands of one whose family has been in high commerce for long generations. His handshake showed a most uncommon strength in that frail form.

Scene Fifty-five: Bomba

JULY-AUGUST, 1931

Stevie Pentous played the grand seigneur all the way, trailed by enchanted telegraph boys and reporters. The first intimation of Stevie's state of mind received by Alphendéry was a telegram from the luxury-liner *Ile de France*.

DAN WATERS ABOARD STOP ARRANGING PARALLEL COTTON RACKET STOP MODIFYING YOUR SCHEME NO ATTRACTION AMERICAN PSYCHOLOGY ELIMINATING RUSSIAN BILLS STOP ARRANGING STRAIGHT CREDITS SCHEME STOP HAVE TELEGRAPHED DEMOCRITUS HERMES

"Hermes" meant Pentous; "Democritus" meant Bomba.

"But Russia is essential," cried Alphendéry. "Oh, I hope at least, Bomba understands the plan: he spent a weekend in Amsterdam with Léon." This doubt was not settled by the telegram received from "Democritus" in New York the next day.

THALES, ANAXIMANDRE ASSURE INTERVIEW EMPEDOCLES AND LEUCIPPE IF ARRIVAL WITHIN MONTH STOP SUCCESS BEST OMENS STOP NEED TO WATER THE TIGRIS ONE THOUSAND THANKS DEMOCRITUS

The translation of the code was penciled above. Thales= Waters, Anaximandre = Delvin-Smith (a Washington official who blew hot and cold in one breath according to Bomba), Empedocles = Jules himself (apparently Bomba, in traditional style, was sabotaging Stevie Pentous), Leucippe = the President of the U.S.A. himself (who being an engineer preferred material values). The "best omens" was in keeping. "Need to water the Tigris" Jules, without the help of classical learning, understood well enough

435

meant "more money." Democritus = Theodor Bomba (a self-flattery; he likened himself to Democritus born in a colony where Asiatic culture entered into contact with Greek culture, the reference being to Berlin).

No one commented on the code. Theodor Bomba knew men's weaknesses. The code was sufficiently uncanny to impress unlettered businessmen as a sort of incantation, when proposed in Bomba's inimitable medicine-man style.

Bomba had once, for example, organized a "financial service" in Europe, on the strength of such a code, using the names of the characters in the *Nibelungenlied,* and half a dozen bright financial journalists with himself had gone abroad in the service of several of the leading American banks to gather "secret" information. Each one was to cable each Monday from the leading European capitals.

On the first Monday morning the opening salvo was from Bomba himself (well-planted in Berlin, his favorite city):

DUE DE FACTO RECOVERY RING ALBERICH KRIEMHILDE RENOUNCES POLITICAL DESTRUCTION SIEGLINDE WILL SEEK RHEINGOLD WOTAN STOP MIME CONVALESCENT 1927 BALMUNG UPSWEEP TARNHELM REPORTS HAGEN IS SEEKING ECONOMIC PLAN

The solemn conclave of the werewolves of Wall Street which had assembled at twelve noon to receive the "secret" message from beyond the Atlantic read this telegram and were greatly impressed. But they had entirely forgotten the code except that Rheingold meant the U.S.A. dollar and Wotan meant the U.S.A. However, it took them several weeks to get over their gratification at their private European service and, of course, in due course, with the mails, arrived Bomba's confirmation with the translation,

"Due de facto stabilization of the franc by Poincaré, Germany (Kriemhilde) renounces (the idea of the) political destruction of France and will seek loans from the U.S.A. England expects recovery in 1927. Belgium (Balmung, the sword, pointed at the heart of England) bull market.

Secret agents (Tarnhelm) report Russia is seeking an economic plan."

It had been months before Bomba had ceased to draw a salary on the basis of telegrams so conceived, telegrams which grew and grew in an undeciphered pile in the desk of a secretary: and he had never failed to draw on his "ring of the Nibelungs" trick in later employment. He knew men very well. He knew that financial giants have two skins, "one to face the world with and one to show a crony when they love him." The first is the *Financial and Commercial Chronicle* face and the second is their true face, their face of superstition, mental chaos, and childish absurdity. He was ashamed of nothing.

To Léon he spoke of "Kabbala" and *"Chedar* techniques," to Jules of "hunches" and "lucky touches," to Alphendéry, when he met him, of "the materialist interpretation," and "we undercover auxilaries of the Third International" and the "fascist-liberal Keynes," while he laughed uproariously at William's jokes, keenly aware that William's detestation of him was measured by the number of francs in his salary check. He even discussed cribbage with "Old" Berthellot. Once, the Comtesse de Voigrand being in the bank, while he was dancing round Jules's coattails, Bomba spoke so eloquently about Jesuit culture that the Comtesse very nearly sacked her professor on the spot and employed Bomba.

Such a man, unquestionably, deserves whatever living he can get. Even Jules thought so. Thus he found more amusement in Bomba's telegrams than Alphendéry, William, or Léon did, and so he paid Bomba's calls for money and went pacifically on his way, convinced that if anyone could put across the wheat deal, Bomba, his private magician, could.

Bomba had exactly his idea of moneymaking, that it was a great swindle and that the greatest swindler got the biggest prizes and that the greater the "superstructure of graft" the greater the "surplus-value" (a phrase which Jules had oddly adapted to mean booty).

Bomba and Jules understood each other very ill: each, in his vanity, saw himself in the other, thought of the other as a complex intellect and bowed to him, secretly impressed by the most frivolous decisions. Besides, when Jules got home each evening, he found a new telegram from his court jester, couched in this style,

437

NLT FOR YOUR PRIVATE EAR: LÉON'S SUPER-
STRUCTURE OVERREFINED, OVERORNAMENTED
ALPHENDÉRY'S INTELLECTUALIST GLOSS;
YOUR KEEN LINES PREFERRED. AM FOLLOW-
ING YOUR SCHEMA, JETTISONING REST: GREAT
GOOD WILL RESULT. REASON DELAY: LEUCIP-
PE COULD NOT SEE WOOD FOR TREES. LITTLE
DANAË SHOWER NEEDED: SEND REQUISITE.
AVE. DEMOCRITUS

Jules was getting a classical education, losing a fair sum
of money and amusing himself rarely. He concealed his
domestic telegrams from his family, from Michel and
Léon, and in secret delight saw the whole fortune promised by Léon pouring into his own white hands. Meanwhile Bomba had little to do but compose his macaroni
messages. He had sent sixty reporters to meet Stevie
Pentous on his arrival in New York by the *Ile de France*,
and headlines went flashing across the Continent,

PENTOUS PARK AVENUE PLAYBOY HEADS
FRENCH CONSORTIUM TO BUY COTTON
EXCESS

and elsewhere,

FRENCH GOVERNMENT BEHIND PENTOUS SYN-
DICATE IN SIXTY MILLION DOLLAR SCHEME

and again,

BOMBA, FINANCIERS' AGENT HERE: SCHEME
SEEN AS PEACE MOVE

with the addition,

PENTOUS HAILED AS UNOFFICIAL
AMBASSADOR

and a helping hand for Bomba,

BOMBA FRENCH FINANCIER SCORES FARM
BOARD

Bomba and Pentous had by now persuaded themselves
that everything was going great guns and were sweeping
through expensive hotels and luxury trains in magnificent
style, dropping ten-dollar notes and King's Ransom whis-
ky in the style of a maharajah who has just won the
Derby and the Spanish Lottery.

Pentous was duly escorted to Washington, heaven of glittering walls and flowery speech, by Bomba. Bomba, a subtly swaggering subaltern, was trying to give the impression that he was the spirit of the thing and was sent by the European consortium to keep a watch on the playboy. He had Pentous throned in the Mayflower Hotel—and sent their cards to the "Thales" and "Anaximandre" whom (he alleged) he had "lined up." When Stevie Pentous got stage-fright and suddenly admitted that he had very little idea indeed what he was to say, or what to propose, Bomba walked in on some high officials and being overexcited by the publicity he had got up himself and by the millions of dollars he seemed to see rolling like hailstones at his feet, he allowed himself to use the ridiculously cynical, thieves' jargon that he had heard Jules, William, Léon, and Alphendéry joking in, in their sanctum in Paris.

"It's a brilliant racket," he informed the officials, persuaded that he was speaking American. "It will make us all rich, you, me, and the other guy. It will astonish the natives from Tokyo to Painted Post: it's the great steal of the century, boys."

The astonished officials, very polite, were sure that they had to do with a lunatic; and so he came away with equal grandeur, but hollow grandeur, for he had to admit even to himself that he had come away with empty hands. He had so fooled himself that he had expected to carry it all off with pure bluff and blarney: he was living in a mushroom dream of monstrous unreality.

Bomba came home to Paris, preceded by long explanations, sneering telegrams about Thales, Anaximandre, and Leucippe, with dark but evasive insinuations as to the character, ability, and double-crossing capacities of "Hermes" (Pentous). Jules got these telegrams in the office and at home, and William, the twins, Alphendéry, Léon, and even Claire-Josèphe received others; not to mention the Comtesse de Voigrand, who was handed the following by a mystified secretary,

GOLD COAST FIASCO: NEITHER SLAVE NOR FAKIR: CAN WE KNIT RELATIONS ON ECONOMIC BASIS.

DEVOTED,
THEODOR BOMBA

The Comtesse turned it in her hands, finally tore it up. "I remember: the poor man must have gone mad; he did look a little odd."

Léon came down to Paris full of woe and exclamation marks. "But Jules, before Pentous so much as landed in America, Strindl's rang me up one morning from Mannheim and said, 'What's this I hear about Bertillon arranging U.S.A. wheat on credit?' I was thunderstruck."

"Ah," groaned Jules, "what can you expect: Pentous did his best. He put the scheme before Dan Waters on the boat but Waters didn't grasp the importance of the Russian technique, or the effect on the market: he only saw the smart-aleck trick of going past me and you and selling direct, not realizing that this direct sale on credit would undermine the structure."

Alphendéry looked at him with penetration: Jules glibly used Léon's vocabulary, a half-unconscious means of averting Léon's protests. "Yes," said Jules, "our spectacular project would have revolutionized values."

"The fact is," Léon said sadly, "Pentous didn't grasp the scheme fully enough to point out to Waters the dangers—I had a telegram from Bomba in Chicago. He recapitulated what he had said. My dear Jules! He put it upside-down. Instead of putting the situation as it is, he gave the Farm Board the impression that Bertillon's consortium would sell to two or three countries on credit; but the officials said, 'What do we need you for? We can do that.' My dear Jules! Your Bomba simply invited the double-cross: he marked the place with a double-cross. It wasn't a question of finding a credit buyer. It was to get a dramatic catalyst for the world wheat market. He gave the Farm Board the impression that the poor countries wanted the wheat on credit. So what do they do? They invite the poor countries to buy on credit themselves. Why not? They agree to sell twenty-five million bushels on a few years' credit. Thus they made it look as if wheat is valueless. Russia, Canada, and the Argentine hear of it —they fall over each other to sell to the few cash traders left. My dear Jules! Oh, dear! A basic commodity going round the world on credit. Tropical storms of wheat! Krakatoa dust storms of wheat. It ruined the trade! Instead of saving the sick man it finished him. Normally such a sale of wheat would stiffen the market: this was the executioner's ax. My dear Jules!"

Léon was pathetic, he was mourning deeply: he scarcely protested. He saw his glittering tower of fortune in little fragments of powdered glass. His voice was mild and gentle, his heart was bruised. And no one attempted to console him, for everyone, for the first half-hour of that meeting between the two men, Jules and Léon, knew that thing that stops the blood, irreparable failure; the chance of a lifetime lost.

Léon, the builder, feebly tried to raise his drooping crest: in broken phrases he brought out of his memory the plan that had looked like the Million-Dollar Stroke, only a few weeks before. "A secret arrangement," he mourned. "Three years' Russian notes. To sell ostensibly to Russia. We were to slip up, execute the contract option of further fifty millions on the way up. . . . They threw away a twenty-five-million bushel secret. . . . We, also—to be the third consortium to sell the Russian wheat purchases to Germany for the goods that Russia wanted. Not, like now, straight to Germany on credit. . . . What a mistake, Michel! What a mistake! Why the feller didn't understand a word of it; didn't you write it all down for him, Michel? How could he? How could he misunderstand, Michel? Explain it to me." He shook his head. "Also to exchange these new Russian notes for older Russians—notes—how could he misunderstand?—other Russian notes already endorsed in the Reichsbank. Give the impression to the U.S.A. public that U.S.A. not accepting Russian paper. . . . Them political self-seekers . . . Waters saw a chance to get kudos relieving wheat situation, giving wheat abroad to poor countries. . . . He let it slip. The chance of a lifetime. I never had such a brilliant idea, Michel . . . Jules, didn't you *drill* him?"

Léon, as low as Alphendéry had ever seen him, went to lunch, quietly howling, his tail between his legs. "Michel, listen to the truth: my heart is broken. Bomba saw a chance to get an advertisement for himself and Bertillon. You know? He wrote and asked Bertillon to open a branch of Bertillon Frères in New York. Himself a bank manager: that was what he saw in it all. I tell you, my boy, that boy is no good . . . Pentous saw a chance to have a royal progress and the only thing in Bertillon's head was his original mug one-dimension plan . . . If the scheme had gone through, the market would have gone up and everything improved—at least for six months a year."

But by now, Bomba had alertly guessed that the larger part of the scheme and, perhaps, of the money was Léon's. At the same time he believed that the written scheme was Alphendéry's and he had depended on Jules to pull him through at the crucial moment.

His conceit, even now, prevented him from seeing the real enormity of their act, the colossal hoax he had foisted on everyone. In a few days, besides, in America, land of great deeds as well as great hoaxes, the publicity had died down and he had privacy in which to meditate his excuses. As soon as he reached home, he telegraphed Léon who, as we said, rushed to Paris to see him. Léon could draw nothing from him and came to Alphendéry in despair. "The man is a charlatan; he's a prewar wow; he's never advanced, since he began shocking the café philosophers in 1908."

Alphendéry now said, "I told you to go yourself, Henri. It's your own fault. Why didn't you?"

Léon, most troubled, rushed out something about, "Murdered Barnett Baff, poultry merchant—they come up to me, they say—*You remember Barnett Baff?* I was making a lot money—I hogged the business. No one did as well as me. I had the lion's share. My name too. They don't say, 'Léon's making a fortune': they say, 'We'll see that son of a gun don't get away with it.' One day a feller comes up to me coolly on the floor of the Produce Exchange and says to me, 'I see you're making a lot of money, Léon! Yes! Well, good day, Léon,' he says, and he walks off smiling coldly. Then he turns, about six-seven paces off, and says over his shoulder, 'Ever hear of Barnett Baff, Léon?' I packed that night and I came to Europe."

Alphendéry shuddered slightly but said pertinently, "But now they're not gunning for you. Your business is all here in Europe."

Léon looked anxious, studied Alphendéry with knit brows, then suddenly became extremely rosy and confiding. "You know—I've never been chaste! Not exactly—chaste. I can't help it! I usually avoid married women: just a policy. But in America—and in America husbands shoot, too."

"And this husband is still after you after fifteen years? I don't believe it. Even if he took a memory course."

Léon was silent. He had not heard the last and Alphendéry saw the sorry expression on his face. "Always wrong," said Léon and went on communing with himself. He recollected that Alphendéry had heard this defeatish remark and looked up engagingly. "You know, Michel, you've always got to learn. Now take—the first thing I learned was the time factor of speculation. Now —information always comes too early. People don't believe." He laughed with minor husky gaiety. "For instance, they never believe the crop is ruined till it is ruined. No good buying six months before when *you* surmise— They don't believe and so they don't buy (or sell) and you're too early. You can be too smart in life, Michel. I had no margin to wait—when I was a little feller: so I always got fried, always cleaned out. *They* had a big turnover. Dreyfus, I mean: I was with— I figured: Drefus has a big overhead. They took me in you know. I don't know how it was: in a few months they gave me the letters to file. I couldn't help looking. You know, my eyes just ran over the letters when I was filing. I see *'Drought all over the Middle West sure.'* I was working at seventeen and six as a filing clerk for Louis Dreyfus. I was always behind in my month's pay because I went in with the boys for fifty to one hundred tons wheat: I had the finest information from the private letters. I put them away every day: I couldn't help looking. And, he, he! oh, he, he! knowing I had the *finest information* I began to doubt the firm's stability. I figured, you see. Knowing I never made money on the Dreyfus information, I thought: Jesus Christ, they must have lost a thousand times as much as me. I was frightened for my seventeen and six. How could they keep on paying me? That was my first lesson, Michel; I learn all the time. This is another. You see, don't you, Michel? You see: they could revolve! If they sold twenty thousand bushels and were wrong, they could sell another twenty thousand and the difference of prices would compensate them, or reduce loss. Say, sixpence a quarter. They could carry it or revolve it, so the grain don't go out of condition; replace it by fresh wheat. Or, they were important capitalists; I was a peanut, no, mustard seed (that's pretty small, eh, smaller than that) capitalist. He, he! Or—concentrated

443

capital always wins. Oh, boy! To think I laid awake nights wondering if Dreyfus would go broke. Say, I figured, Dreyfus had a big overhead and I had no overhead, so they must go broke. Oh, boy! Then, with information. Because I had no capital I learned my first lesson. Don't sell right away. Don't sell when you have the information; sell when people believe it will be bad; and when they are convinced, it will be bad, bad, black, black: sell! So, I learn again: bad luck. All right, I should have known."

Alphendéry listened with the most flattering attention. He was delighted that Léon was getting back his spirits. "I should have gone," said Léon suddenly, getting back his healthy bluff, and pretending he had mentioned nothing about the murdered poultry merchant. "You're right, Michel, my boy: I should have gone. Yes." He began to meditate unhealthily: "Michel, tell me, tell me: how did *he* make his money?" His voice was very low. "Michel, how, *how*, how! I've asked myself a hundred times? How did he make his money?"

"Bomba has no money."

"Not Bomba! Him!"

"Jules?"

"Am I standing on my head or my heels? I feel as if I'm asleep and dreaming an insane dream and I know it's insane though I'm asleep. How did he make his money? It isn't true, Michel. He couldn't misunderstand the scheme. It's so clear. A two-year-old baby— Michel, you wrote it down for him? You're sure you wrote it down right?"

"You saw it."

"Yes, I saw it . . . I should have gone. I'm to blame. No one else . . . Millions, Michel! No one would have lost. Everyone—we would have made— The golden opportunity." He sat shaking his head. He came back to his astonished fortification again and again.

Presently Alphendéry said sharply and with bitterness, "Why are you so astonished, Henri? Have you ever known a businessman, yourself included, who wasn't mad with conceit, superstition, disorder, and egotism? Who didn't think himself a combination of Machiavelli, Napoleon, Rockefeller, a vulture, and an imperial eagle? Would you have asked any questions of how Jules or Bomba did it, if they'd put it over? What surprises you is that Jules is a sort of madman, to you; he isn't as keen at your schemes as he is on his own. You could have picked up any clerk in our office downstairs, Adam Constant, the poet (whom Jules employs, by the way) and done a thousand times better than Jules, with his Stevie and Theodor: you say. But would you have picked better people? Look at the people you pick for your own deals! Little Kratz, who denounced you to all the authorities in the world, a sneak and a fantast; Achitophelous, who spent his time between dumping daybooks in the Seine and trying to seduce your mistress and faking telephone accounts; Aristide Raccamond, a fat louse, who looked giddy and sucked, and squeaked and sucked, and ran round in circles and sucked, and who, when you tried to crush him, still sucked. Is it such a beautiful circle of friends you have yourself, to call upon, to use? What people are in our game, Léon? Thieves and streetwalkers: you and me, too. Who is there to pick on but leeches, double-crossers, and vain fools like Bomba. You won't go to America—on account of Barnett Baff. Jules won't go to America on account of— do I know why? You all make me tired, Henri. I can't listen to your lamentations. You all sell, not grain and stocks, but flesh, human hope, blood, and desire, children and the future of the human race. And then you're all alike, you and Jules and Achitophelous and William and Daniel Cambo, the Comtesse de Voigrand and Madame de Sluysforêt, you all come round me and expect me to get out a black-rimmed handkerchief and weep because you didn't make a million francs through a stroke of the pen."

Léon looked miserable, hung his head, said very low, "You're right, Michel: we're no good to the human race. Michel, if I didn't think I was going to do something brilliant, I wouldn't take any interest in life. I've got to do something, Michel. Now, Michel, I don't want you to look on me as a parasite. I'm not like that. In New York, when I was a young man, I was always the quickest— dearest buyer, cheapest seller, made a fortune, only on commissions; I never went past the brokers, even when I could, and they all came to me. They made my market. I went wrong! I thought there was a big market; but no, it was only that they all came to me. After a few weeks I find I'm doing all the business and I'm losing money. What's wrong? I find out. I'm making the market my-self. Quick in, quick out, never holding the bag and yet never making a profit. How come? I find out. Another lesson. You see, I learn, Michel. I like to be progressive. I like to construct. Destructive—doesn't appeal to me. I don't want to go down and leave nothing, Michel. Now Jules," he became sad, "he's not like me." Alphendéry brought up short, swallowed his wine, and said nothing. "Jules," said Léon, with immense regret, "Jules is unable to realize a first-class business scheme through remaining in a fantasy world. I started without a cent, without a cent."

"Jules made plenty," said Alphendéry, in the dumps. "He's full of irresistible charm."

"Really? I don't see it, Michel. Not so much."

"No? Others do. I know twenty people who, if Jules robbed them of every cent in the world, would go before a judge and swear he never harmed them, that he was innocent and had been tricked by someone else."

Léon's eyes opened wide, "Really? Say—can he do that? He just gets people's dough—eh?"

Alphendéry said in a curt tone, "Despite the lying and bragging of self-made men, there is usually some honest little incident of real business on which their money is really founded—plus a few windfalls—but they never tell about it: they're ashamed of honesty. They consider it dull."

Léon looked self-conscious and changed the subject, saying with a brave gaiety, "Go on, go on: I've never been able to make out how he made his money."

Alphendéry told him as much as he could of the career of Jules, without injuring his repute: that is, in the eyes of a businessman. Léon listened with divining eyes, shaking his head. In the career of others, as in his own, he believed firmly in the "grand coup," in the sudden blazing of the star of fortune, the star foretold, from cradle days. He refused to accept the pedestrian fact of fortunes built up from day to day, by hard work and unwinking devotion to money, by good salesmanship, some superlative quality of inspiring confidence, hustling buyers or serving others to their vanities. For if magic exists, obviously endless fortunes can be gained by "lucky" men, even into their forties, fifties, and sixties. There must be no iron law of fortunes, or where would we poor millionaires be? In the same category as other men? Subject to old age, disintegration, empty old age, the shelf? A thousand times no. No, there is magic in it, and the key, though invisible, is in our luck-shaped hands.

"Jules," said Léon, after the story, evidently disbelieving all that had been told him, evidently still searching for the secret of his success, "Jules should get—a man gets things back from reciprocal business. Is he living off capital? Jules does hundreds of thousands of shares—everywhere! If Jules gets back half-commissions he does not need to bucket. Now, Michel, do you know whether he does or not?"

"No, he doesn't get half-commissions."

"You don't know, Michel," Léon shook his head paternally. "You think you know; you don't. No feller tells you his game. Now, say he was doing the legitimate business you began, Michel; taking care of the house, when the clients go wild speculatively, say he gets sick of being legitimate, 'What do I want to be in this peanut business for?' He goes in, in big licks for himself, he becomes a sucker himself then. You see? You don't know that, Michel. No, I got to find out. . . . If he made money —of course, we don't know. There's a rule: if you are bullish, buy; if you are too bullish, sell. Call the turns. Who can do it?" He meditated. "Participations. He could say. 'I'll send you my telephone bill every month. Legris, and you pay it.' Supposing Legris agrees to take one hundred thousand shares General Foods for Bertillon and guarantee him against loss. Expenses would be paid. . . . If not. Michel, Michel! He has a best seller there. Will he go in with me? I have a proposition. Only. He lacks confidence in others."

Alphendéry had become attentive. "Jules goes into propositions with lots of people."

Léon shook his head, "His own class: playboys. They won't let him down. His right. He plays the class game. Now with me . . . Lonewolf ideas. No. They don't go. . . ." He murmured something like, "The government allows him to lend gold on forward wheat and I got wheat forward: I buy wheat, I hedge it, I—instead of paying five to twenty per cent—"

Alphendéry put his hand to his head. "Funny," he said to Léon, "my head's going round: I had the impression I heard you say that before."

Léon said, "You need coffee. Waiter! Coffee! Because he lacks confidence. He wants to be the only one. It's

447

vanity. A man doesn't go in with you either because he doesn't like you or because he's dishonest. He lacks confidence in—himself or you. If I have something good I go to another man. . . . No, no. We got to find out, Michel, my boy, which is it? . . . I got some boys there: they would buy the Bertillon Bank. Only, he's got to go in with them or show them a balance sheet. Lacks confidence."

Alphendéry laughed, "You've got to convince him you're not just trying to get him to show his books for nothing."

Léon was troubled. "No, no, my boy. You know I wouldn't. . . . You see, put and call. You got the bank. You begin by selling calls; the man pays commissions; then *he* got to buying puts and that was where he went wrong. He sold short twice: once on the client's judgment, then on the market; you can't take a position against yourself. That's where maybe he went wrong. . . ."

Alphendéry laughed. "Don't you sell *him* short, just because he didn't fit in with your wheat deal! How do you know all this about selling short?"

Léon worried, "Why won't he show me his books?"

Alphendéry laughed. "He hasn't got any books perhaps. What would you say if I told you I was his books? I've got a God-awful long memory: Huet D'Avranches and Lord Acton are just about my rivals. Say we don't keep any books and I'm all the bookkeeping there is."

"No, no, my boy. You don't know the whole story. There are books. No one tells anyone the whole story. William doesn't know it; the twins don't know it. Claire-Josèphe doesn't know it. Only Jules knows it."

"How do you know that, Henri?"

"It is always so. Trust me: I know."

"You may be right, Henri."

"Why doesn't he take a partner, otherwise? He's had offers. I've just brought him an offer, Michel. A real one. No hoax."

Alphendéry opened his eyes and looked in surprise at Léon. "Henri, I suppose, after all, I don't know everything."

"Nothing, Michel. Consolidate your position, Michel. The boys don't owe you anything. Look out for yourself, Michel."

"Well, didn't you offer me a job as your secretary?

. . . And Ralph Stewart offered me a job. I figure on being out of the whole game in five years."

"What are you going to do?"

"Join the workers' movement."

Léon was in a panic. "And your wife? What will she do? She's a lovely girl, Michel: you know, a wife's a wife. After all. She wants a home, Michel. Is she going to marry, eh? We have responsibilities, Michel."

"You keep her, then, Henri: you seem so excited about her fate."

Léon shook his head slowly but said no more.

Scene Fifty-six: Interregnum

JULES, anxious to avoid giving Léon a direct answer about selling the bank, and also, sick in his pride, because of the failure of the wheat deal and the folly of his toady, Theodor Bomba, went away silently to the Blue Coast. In such voluntary types especially, the will works persistently, unconsciously, day and night, and when the body is fatigued, it works as much towards death as life. When the body is tired, it bends to disease and suicide to have rest. Jules remained sick for some weeks. During this time Carrière called in for a payment: the drafts had come through, the pound was exactly at 122 at the time, and William paid him out without more ado.

Jules rented a magnificent suite in the Hotel Magnolius and now rang William, Alphendéry, or Raccamond or Manray, every day, not asking about business, but delivering bizarre, operetta ideas on the market, ordering quantities of shares to be bought or sold, predicting political turns in a style which betrayed his invisible audience; full of whims and commands. Sometimes he masqueraded for the lounge lizards as "the great banker"; sometimes, in the restaurant, he was "the Great Man" running his business from afar, commanding his humble servants, pulling invisible wires; sometimes, they could tell, it was only for himself, to keep his courage up.

Every time he telephoned, William and Alphendéry looked at each other with amusement, with impatience, smarting in under his impertinence as much as laughing at his sallies and absurdities, thinking that he would come back soon, get a sense of reality, and get into harness again. William, who loved a jog trot, remarked, "Let him stay away: he does no work anyhow. When he's away he only gives us a pain once a day." He refused to write to his brother, opened all his letters, boycotted him completely. He was a little annoyed, both over the American expenses of his aversion, Theodor Bomba, and over the refusal of Jules to sell the bank.

Bomba meanwhile had installed himself as Jules's pet, sick nurse, and state flatterer in the Hotel Magnolius and his cash drawings, being confused with Jules's own, escaped William's retributive eye. This annoyed William even more. But Jules was on the upgrade: tired of showing himself everywhere as the rose crown of young bankerdom, his sense of theater warned him that he must soon return to Paris. He had been away two months. The bank was running itself. The last fact was becoming evident and was no compliment to the chief. During that time no great strokes had been made, but neither had any money been lost. There was no champagne in it.

"What's the use of running a bank like that?" clamored Jules again and again. Sometimes, true, for two days he would go to sleep and forget that he was a great man, a financial wizard and all the rest of it, till one of the innumerable Peggies, Tonies, Fifis, Pippies, Nonos, and Dédés who deposited money with him (or had overdrafts of him), would run into him on some yachting expedition and say, "Julesy darling, aren't you going to be a banker any more?"

Then Jules would get on to the telephone in a rage with himself and them, full of worthless suggestions and recriminations. For it is a rule of creative ability, that it does nothing of any value, while it is possessed by this afflatus of vanity.

Curiously, as time wore on, the "boys" became convinced that Jules would open a branch of the bank in Nice to please himself: they spoke of "pensioning" him there and of taking over the bank themselves. They had, between the twins, William and Alphendéry, enough powers to do this. An arrangement with Jules, and they could work the bank rationally, cutting off all the rank wild flowers of fantasy which drank up the hard-won profits; drilling this brilliant musical comedy into the functions of an ordinary exchange and bourse office "without any strings," as William said.

Raccamond, now on the Blue Coast, was lying low, working hard, conversing respectfully with William and Alphendéry over the telephone about twice a week, sending in clients and orders, looking for a site for a Nice office, proposing personnel, and altogether behaving so rationally modestly that William and Alphendéry began to cherish his good qualities and look upon him as a third mate.

One afternoon, William came in to Michel with the cheerful expression of a constitutional pessimist vindicated. He stuck a double sheet of notepaper under Alphendéry's nose. It said,

> Hotel Magnolius,
> Promenade des Etats-Unis,
> Nice.

DEAR DICK,

Thanks for your letter. I hope you get down here soon. I think your're right about William and Alphendéry, I especially have no confidence in Michel's judgment: he's a pessimist and subversive by nature and we don't want that. It ruins business. William is a muddleheaded donkey: I've known him since the nursery and even there while he was hiding his penies the twins were stealing his toys. I must come back and take charge of things. Of course, things are slipping. But I'll soon put that right. In the meantime, try to get down. Best love to Anita and Johnny.

> JULES

P.S. Thanks for keeping an eye on the boys for me.

William smiled as he retrieved it. "I got it out of Richard Plowman's desk. Wait till I put it back." When he came back he found Alphendéry walking up and down the room, twisting his handkerchief, his brows twisted, the hollows that would be in his cheeks twenty years from now, painfully apparent, his large brown eyes very sad. He said swiftly, painfully, "How can Dick Plowman betray us? I know he's always thought Jules was too good for any one of us."

451

"What can you do?" William, smiling, as if he had just had the best news in the world, his hands in his pockets, easily promenaded about the room. It amused his slow, sardonic nature to discover stupidity or treason: he preferred a person to lie to him; he found it more amusing and a sign of weakness in that person. Even treason against himself seemed to him a particular comic sort of boomerang. He had nothing to lose. Or, thought Michel, watching him covertly, he was too canny to appear to resent it.

William laughed, a mellow, youthful tone in his voice. "It's typical of someone you're keeping: it's like a woman. You sweat to give her all the comforts and she criticizes you to her friends. Open a wife's correspondence and discover what love is. We're both working to keep one wife: Jules." He smiled at Michel, soothed him. "Why do you get upset at that idiot Jules? I've known him since he was a baby. He's always been the same. Thinks the sun couldn't get up if he didn't. He thinks he works. He says Ouf! and that's the wind that starts the mills going. Daniel Cambo was passing through there the other day with his woman, Raquel Gerson. He told me Jules is holding a regular court there every day, with Bomba, Raccamond, and Raccamond's nephew, a gilded wastrel. Bomba boasts about his trips to the United States. Raccamond calls himself a 'director.' Jules is getting the idea that the bank made a great hit in the United States and that they will all be rolling over here with their gold. He forgets the money Bomba and Pentous spent: he thinks he's a friend of the President, I don't doubt."

Alphendéry took the medicine. "Well, it's his show: it's his to run or ruin. But why don't we get out and let him have his sanctum in the Hotel Magnolius? He doesn't want us."

"You get a good salary, Michel."

"Aristide Raccamond is now drawing more than me and nearly as much as you. A splendid salary doesn't compensate me for the loss of my youth. I stay here like a fool because I'm loyal to Jules, whom I love dearly—"

"Who asks you to be loyal? To love? Jules isn't loyal to you. Jules loves you yesterday, Bomba today, and Raccamond tomorrow. You're dizzy if you're loyal. It's money. I'm loyal to Jules and I'm his brother: does that make any difference to our Prince when he's discovered that he's

452

another Rothschild? He's not human. I know him. He's keeping a retinue of yes men now and they're bathed in glory, but in a couple of months he'll be tired of them, too, and their more-than-loyalty, their bootlicking, their voluntary flunkying, their dribbling admiration, their whipped-cream flattery won't do them any more good than your loyalty."

"You don't quite understand, William. It's just because he's so unprincipled, because he has no knowledge of the principles on which his business is running that I love Jules and I fear for him. I think he has a right to a sweet fate. He is as beautiful as light. There is something not entirely human about Jules. I fear, I fear to see him go down in some all-too-human crash. He runs on so wildly and impetuously. He seems unconscious that there is any-one above him or below him. He does not seem to know there are lawcourts, people who hate, who pursue—dis-aster, death. Perhaps I'm deceiving myself: perhaps he would do better if I left him without all my philosophy: it isn't his. He doesn't want it."

They had one victory. They had handed Parouart's af-fair to Maître Lemaître and presently, to their great surprise, Parouart was nonsuited in the courts. With the announcement of this nonsuit, they witnessed a slight in-crease in deposits. They mentioned it to Plowman but they both refused to write to Jules.

Henri Léon, always in correspondence with Alphendéry, wrote,

> I am coming to Paris.
> P.S. Be careful vis-à-vis Theodor Bomba.
>
> H. L.

On top of this, they had another flying visit from Daniel Cambo, in Paris again to look over trash goods for his shops, and Daniel informed them that Jules was unhappy now in his court on the Blue Coast. Theodor Bomba and Aristide Raccamond were at daggers drawn. Mme. Raccamond had turned sour because she got no in-vitations from Claire-Josèphe and, woman of action, had made a scene about it to Jules. Meanwhile, Aristide, always with his melancholy expression, had got very close to Jules's skin, and Jules introduced him everywhere as "my new general manager." Alphendéry and William

453

looked at each other: the bank (for them) visibly trembled. There was silence for a full minute in the company until Paul piped up. "I think Francis and I ought to go down: Jules always listened to us."

William got up and went to the door, grimly satirical, "If we've reached that stage, Michel, it's time for you and me to take a holiday and forget to come back."

When Léon got to Paris he immediately engaged Alphendéry in a long discussion about his stocks and shares, forgetting even to ask after Jules's health and it was not till long after midnight that Michel was able to ask about Bomba. Léon went to his bag and got out a letter. "He sent that to me. I didn't answer it. He came and saw me in Antwerp. Jules paid his fare. I sent him packing. He's your enemy, Alphendéry: I have that instinctive feeling and on that I'm never wrong. He's bad luck."

Alphendéry read the epistle from the would-be jackal.

DEAR LÉON,

Forgive me for being a faithful jackal once more. I continue to wish that it had been possible to unite our economic destinies in the *wheat deal* (but despite earnest Kabbala on my part, your hobgoblin friend undid at once everything I built up). Nevertheless, continual cohabiting with the sibyl (I wrote fourteen sibylline books once, burned them myself and so reached the quintessence of sibylline wisdom), forewarns me that we will one day soon find the Midas touch together, you and I. . . . In the meantime, I am Mercury to your interests and purely in an interested fashion for present mead is like to turn bitter, vile Sir Sycophant Pickthank and blockhead Mr. Merryandrew Messmate I.R. (idle rich) turning the silly head of our poor Fortunatus. I desire nothing so much as to join you and work economic miracles on your behalf. Self-interest is the best alchemy: I say naught of "mankind" and the "Russian El Dorado of hope" indulged in by sentimental vassal exquisites of the intellect. . . . I know you were badly disappointed over Bertillon's failure with the wheat deal. I had consistent talks with him on this and emergent economic problems and found him like a colander full of soup: you smell something but when you try to lick it up, it has run away, God knows where. . . . Now it is being bruited around the best financial circles (Tarnhelm tells me) that Jules's whole establishment is a hollow sham and that the money he is lavishing on all and sundry at present on the Blue Coast is the last anyone will ever see from him. This is for your private ear: if you have money with the bank *protect yourself!* I require no recognition for this: this is but in the course of nature. It is even said that the money he is spending at present is got from a soft young nobleman (as noble as *our sons* will be if they descend to that last infamy of merchanting and buy a title)! Do not let William Bertillon or Alphendéry know that I have written to you: envious both. Their object: to get control of the shell of the bank as it stands. They are trying to thrust the Chief out entirely. The one thing you must realize about both of them, Alphendéry with his Mongol-risen face, his social-fascist line, is that they are both smooth-faced liars. Jules, constitutionally a liar, rather beautifully so, so that he doesn't know himself whether he is one or not and likewise it is impossible for anyone to unravel his lies: William, a consistent, voluntary stubborn liar; Alphendéry, weak, intemperate, sensual, a jocund, Rabelaisian, and very poor liar. One can see through anything he says. This unholy Trinity, which I thought holy and holy-ghosted for, are jogging in uneasy harness to a short and unhappy end: the everlasting penal bonfire. They will have neither remorse nor comprehension when they drag down with them those of their friends who remain faithful to them . . . More of this when I see you.

In secrecy, and devotedly,

BOMBA-MERCURY

Alphendéry laughed.

"You laugh," said Léon with great round eyes.

"Oh, he is out on the flat of his back: he is greener than totties in the dark of the moon."

The next morning Jules, in an acid, dictatorial mood, telephoned that he was coming back to work. The brothers and Michel were torn between relief and anxiety. When a Great Man comes back from two months' vacation he arrives in a dust storm of trouble of which the heart is self-conceit.

But the next morning when Alphendéry came to work he found a telegram,

JULES BERTILLON INJURED IN PLANE ACCIDENT IN HOSPITAL NICE ADVISE PLOWMAN
BOMBA

Jules had concussion, a broken ankle and two broken ribs.

"That's perfect," groaned William, "though how he got concussion puzzles me. He had it."

He refused to appear upset by anything Jules did. "I hope he'll come to his senses after this: instead of spending his life with idiotic playboys. So there they are: Prince Jules in a private suite, Claire-Josèphe engaging nurses and bringing surgeons from Paris, Bomba blowing his own kazoo on a platform of gold, Raccamond that great jelly and his Diana-wife hunting in open season on our preserves."

Meanwhile, as he said, the parasites and gilded friends in Jules's court knew their Maytime. Jules had nothing to do and his jack-in-the-box temperament made it hard for him to lie still, still harder for him to follow a regime for concussion. He fretted and had a thousand bees in his bonnet in a day. It was some time before they allowed him on to his precious telephone and when he did it was only to exchange snarls with William who called him every name in the cap-and-bells catalogue.

Curiously enough, the brothers, who had seen each other through storms for years, did not forgive each other this concussion. William had been looking forward to a holiday of his heart, driving fast but prudently up and down all the roads of Europe; Alphendéry had been planning a trip to Italy to see the fascist system at first hand. Jules, though he would never admit it, was greatly hurt that William had not written to him condoling with him. But although, out of that pathological obstinacy that often arises between members of the same family, William had never written and scarcely inquired about Jules, ashamed, no doubt, to seem one of the flock of self-seeking inquirers, he theorized every day with Michel about Jules's crash and his recovery and even made extensive inquiries of everyone who had been near Jules. But, except with Michel, he did it with a bantering, sarcastic air, with a show of indifference, a jovial style, a set of adjectives and names for Jules, that completely misled people; and, such people, either shocked or vicious, reported William's words to Jules.

Scene Fifty-seven: Exorcism

ALPHENDÉRY refreshed his philosophy every day by reading the leading communist dailies and weeklies, in several languages. Although he told everyone he got his information from them, people chose to regard this as a freak of his, for few people at the bank could believe such a thing. They thought him gifted by nature and were constitutionally unable to believe that the workers, robots between eight and six, suckers between six and ten, raw-labor producers between ten and six, pulp readers between six and eight, who had no brilliant schemes but for turning the hat trick and scooping the football pools, that these dull stone-choppers and animated machine minders could say anything of any value whatever on economic problems and on moneymaking. They knew quite well that if they asked the first workman in the first cabmen's bar the price of St.-Gobain he would probably look blank: how could he possibly have anything to say on the world at large? Whereas they knew the price of St.-Gobain and also of U.S. Steel and were therefore entitled to run the world at large. This was, in a nutshell, the simplehearted philosophy of the bank's clients. No, they concluded, Alphendéry made up his ideas himself or got them from a "secret" source and, out of a perverted vanity and a queer sense of humor, liked to pretend he got them from rags like *L'Humanité*.

When Alphendéry came in one morning, full of sap, Dick Plowman came out of the stock-exchange room to hear his discourse on the gold-letting of the Bank of England, the first serious suspicions of the pound sterling, which was now resulting in a run and the overthrow of the Labour Government, with the formation of a National

Government "to save the pound." This, of course, affected Dick Plowman very deeply. If the pound went off gold and a serious inflation set in, the prices of bonds on a gold basis would fall, the prices of stocks would rise; a small boom would set in, prices of commodities would rise, due to heavy buying to escape from a wobbly currency. It meant a great loss to anyone who owned property, mortgages, or lived on rent of land and buildings, as well as any with deposits in banks: and Richard was in this class, although the greater part of his fortune was held abroad, in France and America. Nevertheless, he was not opposed to inflation, on the ground that it would "bring back prosperity."

"It is, in the first place," said Alphendéry, "not a patriotic move. It is an expropriation of the workers— because wages never rise as fast as prices, and of the poor middle classes, who have invested seriously in savings banks and insurance accounts. Moreover, the operation is not complete. They must expropriate some more, before they have finished. In my opinion, Britain must expropriate to keep alive. And although it is a clever trick to get in a Tory Government, the National Government cannot 'save the pound' and must inflate. That can be done in England. How is it to be done? I don't know that. But they have some trick up their sleeve and the stampede election of the Tories is to cover it." And much more in this strain.

Richard Plowman followed Michel upstairs, thoughtfully. Since Jules had lain in bed, Plowman had been accepted, without protest, by the brothers and Michel, as unofficial censor: they knew that, with the deepest devotion to Jules, he ran a paternal check system on their acts and comments. Naturally, they treated him more playfully than ever, told him nothing, and amused themselves with digging up scandals about past associates of his and making sad deductions about the deviltry of "the most respectable bankers." He had entirely forgotten how money was made and was much saddened not only by the proofs of roguery but by the "boys'" cynicism. He pinned Alphendéry down this morning, as he sat over the morning mail.

"Michel! I admire your intelligence but I think you look at the world upside-down."

He hesitated and Alphendéry went on, laughing, "What

458

I say, Dick, most economists in the world today, say. Do you want Jules to go on living in a dream world made from the debris of 1919–1920? He's in most markets: he's got to know what moves them."

Plowman had recovered. "The beauty of his character, Michel, is in its fine intuitions."

"Imagination—and experience."

Earnestly, Plowman went on, "It is a great mistake of yours, Alphendéry. Besides, it is not true. Your saying that nothing that can happen now can help the British Empire. That was said before the war. I have seen many a panic and depression in my time, my boy. And the war increased Britain's colonies. . . . I was down with Jules the other day, however, and what does he do but talk about 'selling the British Empire short' in a restaurant full of people. He got that from you. Alphendéry: you are a Frenchman, the traditional antagonist . . . well, friendly enemy, shall we say. Not only the French, but the rest of the world has had the same hallucination for years."

He shook his head, his clean, blond head-clerk face, his blue eyes full of integrity, seeking to convince Alphendéry by his honest expression. "No one wants to do business with a bank that thinks the capitalist system is not going to last. Men with your type of mind don't make money, Michel. You are Quixotes: the wind blows and the world whizzes round—whoolloo-moolloo! Oh, they're reaching out to catch me, those giant arms, think you! And in you run, bravely, full tilt. But the world's not trying to catch you . . . or Jules. It's just going round and round. The wind bloweth where it listeth. Neither you nor I, Michel, are going to make any difference. All our theories are feathers in the wind. You see, you don't believe in money. You believe the financial world is nothing but a carcass—"

"A bluebottle," said Alphendéry grinning.

"You have no sense of history."

"The sense of history is that the British Empire will last for ever by divine right? And the rest goes spinning brainlessly till London organizes it. Oh, worthy race, admirable illusion!"

Plowman frowned and came down to the downstairs manager, Jacques Manray, who happened to quote back at him one of Alphendéry's remarks. "The history of Europe since the war has simply been that of a South American republic—dictators, repudiation, paper money, civil war."

Plowman said smartly, "Mr. Alphendéry does not think like a banker; he thinks like a radical and is from our point of view irresponsible. He is injuring the credit of the Bertillon brothers, Mr. Manray. Please do not repeat his remarks."

He was angry. When William hove in sight, he buttonholed him also. "When a boom comes Jules will have sold everything short: his phrase to me last week. The world is not going down and down. It's against common sense. Why, if booms don't come naturally, they'll ease things up by spring booms and market booms, even inflation. It's so absurd to think bankers will allow values to disappear completely. They aren't there for that. If Alphendéry were to leave the bank, Jules would begin to see with his own eyes again. It's absolutely essential that Alphendéry should stop being a bear or go: otherwise, you boys will be ruined."

William jovially went to caricature all this to Alphendéry but to his surprise found him very depressed. "I know." He looked at William with great, distressed eyes: "Plowman is right. I mean I subtilize overmuch. I am too eager. I belong to those who want to see the great change in their lifetimes and so I overlook the truth that our overlords will not give up the ghost without trying to strangle us to death first. My philosophy is only casuistry, as far as you boys are concerned. Plowman, the old fool, is right. They have a hundred tricks up their sleeves before they'll lose and then, the last trick, machine guns." He put his head on his hand. "I am too clever by half."

William roused him, cheered him, "Dick is doddering; while we work, Jules and Dick have been patting themselves on the back down there. How to explain why they're not rolling in profits? The old trick: make the Jew the scapegoat."

"No, no, William: although he doesn't know why he is right, Plowman is right."

Scene Fifty-eight: Return

MEANWHILE a client arrived from the south with a note scribbled on the card of Aristide Raccamond, "Director of Bertillon Frères." William smiled. "Every day someone sends us roses."

A letter from Jules commanded them to pay Aristide Raccamond henceforth twenty thousand francs monthly, ten thousand as salary and ten thousand in commissions, any balance to be settled on December 31.

"Listen," said William more seriously than usual, "you and I have power of attorney. We will be doing Jules a service if we transfer his money to some other place and maybe some other person. Shall we pay off the big clients and close the shop?"

But Alphendéry had lost his verve: he was trying to thing in another vein, for Jules's sake, and to draw out his telescoped wishful view of disaster. He would not take any step, even with William behind him, yet.

And now Jules, accompanied by Raccamond, arrived suddenly from the Blue Coast by train. Jules was mad as a centipede self-stung by months of pain, idleness, and insane flattery. He did not speak either to William or to Michel, when they came into his room, ordered them to go about their business, and tried to set up his court once more in his own office. He received many calls of solicitude. The charm began to wear off in three days and it was hard for him to reconcile his grandeur and the wild pretensions of his toadies with the everyday work of the bank, the docile application of the cashiers and accountants, the questions which began to crop up every hour and which William plentifully showered him with, about accounts, shares, and taxes of clients. People began to drop in, as before, with propositions. At first Jules spoke of making a million dollars in a week, whereas those two blockheads had done nothing but had turned the place into a café during his absence and made no money at all; but presently he began to see that Michel and William, though hurt and

461

silent, were working persistently, giving exchange, settling disputes, even paying off Carrière without any reference to himself, and perhaps one morning in the cool hours, he suddenly came to himself. At any rate, at this moment of near disenchantment, who should arrive, in full bloom, but Theodor Bomba! He had left himself behind on the Blue Coast, first, not to compete with Raccamond on the journey up and second, to fix up some small affairs hanging over for Jules, and third, to see what could be seen round the new office which Jules had just opened in the Hotel Magnolius.

Bomba blocked out a lot of air with base, blond fat. He was gaily dressed in a Homburg hat. He had a well-molded face with square forehead and long, fine amethyst eyes: the attentive, rapidly changing expression was part of his dress. His hands were longish, loose, with tapering fingers, but they jarred with the face. He usually compressed his canoe-shaped red mouth and his eyes with a certain expression of pensiveness, dignity, or excruciatingly flattering attention, but when he smiled a horrible change took place: he leered as if he knew degrading ludicrous secrets about his vis-à-vis, as if he had the whiphand of him in a peculiarly humiliating illegal affair, and he almost imperceptibly hunched his shoulders, as if hugging his own cunning to his breast. He could not conceal his malice at the undoing of others, or at their degradation by his hands or his tongue. He used his hands in an outward stirring motion, as if he was fishing round in a cesspool to find some delectable bits of garbage. Both William and Alphendéry found it very hard to take his flabby hand and when he smiled, this first time of his return, Michel fell back two steps as if from infection.

They were thunderstruck. How could Jules, that delicate, fragrant creature, even sit in the same room as Bomba? He had changed: on Jules's money he had got fatter and more noticeably unpleasant. William said agreeably, to Jules, "Claire wrote to me that you swallowed something that gave you gripes down in the Hotel Magnolius. I don't blame you."

Jules frowned. Bomba, refusing to understand anything but a commencement of hostilities, smiled once more his revolting smile: he seemed to use it as a weapon. Alphendéry stopped Jules in the corridor, despite Jules's bad temper: he was still in a fit of astonishment and fear as if he had just discovered something in Jules's nature that he had never known.

"What has happened to you, Jules? Bomba is a leper so evident that he seems to carry a bell round his neck: I'm sure mangy dogs lick his ankles in the street. Overdressed, he is Vice naked. He's rather a miracle. What are you doing with such a fellow round you? I don't wonder things went queer in the U.S.A."

"Bomba knows the whole of the Internal Revenue Department. He's in touch with gangsters who have been revenue detectives for years. He can do anything for me in the States. He's no theoretician." Jules was furious. "I still expect to get the wheat and cotton deals through, through Bomba. I've been working ten times as much, on the Côte d'Azur. Don't criticize the men I have round me. I want new ability. I want someone who believes in making money and can help me do it. I don't want wisecracks."

Alphendéry's face fell. In a very sad voice, he acquiesced, "All right, Jules: if you feel that way—but we all have an instinctive aversion to Bomba. Believe me, it's nothing personal."

"I don't judge by men's faces: I judge by their advice. I need a person with ideas in my place. I don't say I like him. That's not the point." He flung into his room.

Alphendéry faded into misery so far that he almost became a ghost. He went down into his room, took up *L'Information* and sat for a long time without being able to fix his mind on a single sentence. He was frightened by Bomba. He resolved to fight it out with Jules anyhow, even if he lost his job. Plowman came in cackling with glee.

"Did you see Bomba? Smart fellow, eh? You should hear what he's got to say about markets. He says in Wall Street, everyone's expecting a gigantic rise. We've definitely turned the corner, I believe. There's nothing for it but to buy, buy! The world," he smiled paternally at Alphendéry, "can't go on negatively. You've been making that mistake, Alphendéry. When you're my age, you will have seen so many depressions that you won't get depressed. Ha, ha! But thank goodness, Jules is always right. He sometimes makes mistakes but he can always retrieve himself in time. My money is on Jules!"

"Do you like Bomba, Richard?"

Plowman was less confident but did his best, "I like his positive way of thinking. I like his connections. He is well-known in all the capitals."

Alphendéry followed up his advantage. "I suppose he tells Jules what he wants to hear?"

"I approve of that. Jules is naturally a straightforward simple architect: his instincts are right when he's in that mood and he should then be simply approved."

"You've worked with hundreds of men in your career, Richard. Would you employ a Bomba?"

"If he had good references and his act was good."

"And the American act was good, in your opinion?"

Plowman flashed indignation, "Jules was sabotaged from the beginning by Léon."

"I see! I see everything! And Bomba says that Léon is responsible for the fiasco?"

"Obviously he was. And sabotage in the bank itself. You, in particular, I'm not accusing of that, Michel."

Alphendéry smiled.

Bomba, unable to keep the triumph out of his face, was spreading himself in Jules's presence. Jules, like a madman, stung by a crowd of impulses that blotted out the sun, angers, frets, remorses, doubts, found it more and more difficult to listen to his new virtue. Bomba had a whole bestiary of smiles for himself as he developed his theme. So fat was he with the prospect he saw here of a rich pasture, that he neglected to watch Jules whose character was changing every hour, as he became impregnated with the habits of the past and the familiar air of the bank, his home for twenty years.

"Jules," Bomba said familiarly, "I am no philosopher, but a sorcerer. I live by turning imponderables into gold. A proposition in real goods, like the wheat deal, good enough for the thick sinews of Atlas-Léon, baffles me. Besides, there was something queer in the memorandum they gave me. I said to myself, 'There is something awry here: it's tail is missing. Nothing to hold it by.' I set myself to it like a child learning a lesson. It sounded fine but I missed the milk in the coconut. It was a nut all milk rather, no meat. White, wishy-washy. Nothing to it. That's what Léon landed you with. No mistakes without malice aforethought is my rule of thumb. Now I am forced to believe there was no nut but Léon's self-conceit. These petty Napoleons—he builds up schemes which sound glorious and you keep tearing them apart to find the stone on which they are built. He assures you, the philosopher's stone. I assure you, not even anything so solid as ambergris. The reason is a—biological necessity. Self-glorification."

Jules paid great attention to the last part of the speech. "You're right, Theodor. He just wanted glory. When it came to putting it across, he quailed. Didn't want to show himself up. What was the idea of sending you across with a hollow offering like that? . . . Only I have an idea —I think we can work it ourselves."

"I had a letter from Dan Waters only yesterday." He felt round in his pockets: "Funny, I left it at home. I can repeat it textually, though."

"Why didn't you tell me before? This is important."

"I know, I know!" He patted the air down with his hand. "Only this has to be worked tenderly, with psychological tricks, with attention to crotchets, with Kabbala." He had caught the phrase from Léon, and Jules recognized it. Bomba waved his hand. Jules was struck by the ugly strangeness of this hand. He himself had a very beautiful hand and he was shocked by physical disharmony, unless it had some bizarre key signature of its own. Bomba spoke grandly.

"Let your grand vizier think. You know what you are? You're a prima donna and you want a manager. You are full of miracles but you don't know how to give them a local habitation and a name. That's why you're so restless. Now your brother is a good sort, but he is absolutely without genius, and he can't understand you. And Alphendéry, a defeatist. He has no class, no caste, no country, no occupation: he's an intellectual *déclassé:* and what's moving him are the mild, open-minded liberal sanguine impulses of the old-fashioned professional bourgeoisie. When I see an open mind I want to put a padlock on it. To account for his having no money left in his family, he says the whole world is going to blazes. A very logical attitude, Jules. But why should you participate in it? For you the whole world is not going to blazes. On the contrary, there are fortunes to be made this very year and you are one of those going to make one of them. You're what is wanted in these times, a brilliant mind, a genius. What you have lacked, hitherto, is an executive who un-

465

derstands you without participating in your genius. Now, well, you have one. I am devoted to you, Jules. Self-interest! Why not? Self-interest is an engine in perpetual motion. You had one once in your old associate Dannevig that I ran into in your suite in the Hotel Magnolius. Poor old Dannevig! he's nothing but a scarred warhorse now. Poor old crab! I'm afraid he's been giving a very bad impression in your Oslo office, of not understanding banking at all, but of having a purely totemistic view of finance. Shocking, his unconscious sabotage of your inspirations, Jules. The unconscious hate of the old for the young. He tried to keep me away from you."

"You say?" Jules was impatiently counting on his fingers.

"Well—that doesn't interest you. You're right. You're interested in making money. . . ."

Jules had half-forgotten the violent interest he had taken in him down on the Côte d'Azur. His impulses were veering. He dismissed Bomba, who sulked cautiously for half an hour and then disappeared.

Jules pressed a button and called William. William appeared, pale skin, pale shirt, gray eyes, gray-shadowed eyes, gray suiting, immaculate, unmoved, satiric.

"Go on: don't tell me you want to hear something about your business!"

"Stop fooling, William. What's been going on here while I've been away. Have you made any money?"

"All the goings-on have been elsewhere. What's the idea of the janissaries? Are you going to run for king in the Vendée in the next elections? Why don't you come to earth and realize you're a ham like the rest of us and that you've got to work. Daddy goes to work and bacon grows in the pantry. Kid notions. Forget to be a genius, will you? You made your money giving fair exchange rates when everyone else only dreamed of gypping. Did that teach you anything? No! Alphendéry and I slave here—we never leave the bank, we meet everybody, get everybody's troubles. And you spend your time with the choicest bouquet of hand-picked hallelujah men I ever saw in my born days. I'm sorry if you're sick, Jules, but no one else is. These fellows are only using the crutch you just threw away to climb into your pocket. Jules, have I ever deserted you? I felt miserable when you were lying there on the Côte d'Azur. But how could I get away? And my gorge rose at the idea of elbowing my way in past your handout men to say, 'How d'ye do.' Now will you come to your senses? Sack them and let's start with a clean sheet."

Jules listened with downcast eyes, tapping slowly on the blotter. "You can't blame me. I can't make any money when I'm with psychological *saboteurs* like you and Michel. Besides, you didn't write to me once while I was in bed. You let a type like Raccamond look out nurses for me. Why, even Daniel Cambo came to see me."

"Yes, and you let Daniel Cambo deposit a postdated check in sterling for his balance in the hope that the pound will go off and we'll only get eighty per cent of the money he owes us, maybe less. And this with talk of a frantic loan from Paris, going on. I say, out of what fairy-tale book did you get the idea that people are *in love* with you? Let them be in love with you, but you sing them to sleep."

The two brothers faced each other with a certain repose now. Jules wanted to keep up a pretense of anger but had no heart for it. William's apology had healed the rankling hurt. William saw it and pressed home. "Another thing. Alphendéry. What's the idea of writing to everyone that he was no good. You're so clever that you can't get your bus off the grass without smashing yourself up and yet you know what's going on up here, by second sight. You know Michel is loyal and you damn well know how hard he works. We all do. Now, he wants to resign."

"Let him resign. He nearly ruined me, with his despair philosophy."

"Said Mr. Richard Plowman. What's the use of talking to you?"

"I want to see the position of the clients."

"O.K. Come and see them. Michel's in there making up margin calls. You've scarcely seen him since you came back."

"Shut up! Leave me alone. You give me a headache." The brothers were silent for a minute. Jules said in a lower tone, "Who's talking about either of you leaving me? They pestered me down there. You don't know what a hole I was in. I suffered too. Don't tell anyone that. If you or Michel had come down they wouldn't have been so thick around me. Blame yourselves."

During the next few days Jules was cold to Bomba, who slavered round till he found out that William was asking for his dismissal. Then he got up a mental card index on William. He came round one day, in a humble way to "borrow" 12,500 francs. Jules gave it to him gloomily and suddenly told him to go to Oslo and help old Dannevig in that branch.

Scene Fifty-nine: Time Forward, Time Abolished

JEAN FRÈRE had a stew on the fire in his workshop-flat and they walked that way. It was in an old house looking on the Rue des Grands-Augustins, at the corner of the Rue du Pont de Lodi, near the Pont Neuf. It was twilight and they, like the macadam and the buildings, were coated with that faint lucent ghostly gelatine light that makes Paris-real so like Paris-graved and Paris-memoried. There was a great atelier with one or two bench rooms leading off it, that Jean lived in at night when he stayed in town. It was used by young art students and their teacher in the daytime. The stew greeted them in the slimy bricked courtyard. Jean took a key of medieval proportions from the rack, and a letter, and showed them the way up the worn wooden staircase. They sat down in the angles of the workshop, angles made by walls, tables, cupboard, a bookpress, a stove, chairs, and sat on all sorts of things the natures of which were concealed in the thickening night.

The violet luminosity, like a distant glow from some giant blueprinter's hole, stole in through the upper panes of five windows, one on the courtyard, three on the Rue des Grands-Augustins, one in a bench room with no door and the only other light came from a few embers in the stove. Jean got out four soup plates, talking about his stew, meanwhile, and served out the stew to Adam Constant, Michel Alphendéry, and Charles Lorée, a physicist, issued from one of the "grand families."

Charles Lorée was already known all over the Latin world. He was a giant, "six feet four," he explained carefully, "but only six feet three when I take my shoes off," and weighed "two hundred and eighty-nine pounds and five ounces, on the average." He wore a cloth cap usually over his bald pate and its size was seven and three-quarters, he told them confidentially. He was a great physical phenomenon: his brain box was immense, completely overshadowed his eyes, so that no one ever saw them, unless they looked very close, through his eye-brows: his nose was great, his chin great and powerful, his biceps were great, he was powerfully ventripotent, he walked with a slight stoop, like most tall men: when he sat down with his legs outstretched like pine logs the whole company was in danger of somersaults and broken crowns.

The stew was remarkably good. Charles Lorée himself ate four soup-plates full and then stopped with a foxy glance at the rest of them, as if he had calculated their stomach capacity. He took a whole bottle of Jean's light wine to himself and kept taking a pull at the bottle mouth. He said little. The night fell completely and the street lamps shone yellowly in across the benches under the windows, showing all the paraphernalia of the studio, pencils, chisels, hammers, a gluepot, drawing paper.

Alphendéry made one or two attempts to bring in a political discussion, but after some ragged, distrait responses, they died in his throat, and he settled with the others, into the blood-warm silence of the evening. Some-one moved—it was Jean. He opened a cupboard and got out something. He came back and sat down. The lamp-light laid a golden thread down the outline of his wild curls, short neck, and bowed shoulders in a blue work-shirt. They heard the first reedy sounds of his accordion, and he began a recital for them—for himself—in the dark, and presently broke into song. They heard the clink of Charles Lorée's bottle on the floor and then he broke into a vast, sweet baritone humming. Jean's selection was simple—street songs, family songs, movie theme songs, famous national ditties—*Auprés de ma blonde, Ma Normandie, Les Filles de la Rochelle, Ma Femme est morte, Sous les Toits de Paris, Annie Laurie, Black Eyes, Old Man River, The Varsovienne, Di provenza il mar, il suol, Ecco ridente, The Internationale, Marching through Georgia*—people's tuneful songs.

Alphendéry spent the time falling deeper in love with Jean Frère and conscientiously picking out grains of pedantry in himself, for he had been brought up to sing (in his flawed and untrained voice) themes from Bee-

469

thoven, Brahms, Bach, and Mozart. In fact, he never allowed himself to hum, even to himself, any popular tunes —strange results of having Dutch uncles! But Jean and Charles Lorée went on singing away in their two beautiful and blended voices and Jean urged softly once or twice, as he drew breath, "Sing, sing." Alphendéry sat there, turning large, soft, defenseless, black eyes on the outlines of things in the dark. He was not used to sitting in the dark: he always sat in the brightest lights possible and thought and talked in the most brilliant manner possible. It unnerved him to sit with the "great people's leader" Jean Frère and the "famous physicist" Charles Lorée in the dark and hear them singing *Old Man River*. His world swiftly dissolved and slowly rose up again from cells.

At home, they had sing-songs, when he was a boy, but they were the great themes from "the great masters," trumpeted, droned, double-bassed, celloed in his uncles' great Rhineland pipes; there were orchestration, a conductor, and the devil to pay it you went out of tune or forgot the score. It was not really singing: it was a concert under an iron conductor, with the regulation jokes at certain passages, and three or four or even a crowd of passers-by listening intently outside the window. And bright lights, Heine, Goethe, Racine, Corneille, Molière, Shakespeare, Pushkin on the library shelves, works of philosophy and medicine and endless coffee and apple cake. If Michel had at that time ever forgotten himself and fallen into *Ecco ridente* he would have had a lecture on culture beginning with Alaric (at the latest) and ending with barbarians yet unconceived even of fascist poets. . . . So there he sat and thought of the great lover of culture he was and the great oddity he appeared in the company of Jean and Charles and Adam, and he sweated. "But happily, happily," his lips moved, "I know now—oh, thank God, they never got me to take a professor's job. Happily—" Shades of his uncles Guillaume and Robert arose and he saw their heads together with his mother's over the long waxed table.

"He is a born lawyer: that's it."

"Yes, Michel will become a judge, no doubt whatever."

But now there he sat, the brilliant polemic orator of the past and felt mellow; his anxiety was dissolving, and he had no right, he felt, to expound anything whatever, out of all he knew and had stored up in all these years.

He studied the golden thread on the back of Jean Frère with ardent, silent attention. Adam Constant broke the enchantment by saying, "By the way, Michel, a friend of yours is coming in a little while—Henrietta Achitophelous."

"Oh, is there any stew left?" cried Alphendéry. "Old Achitophelous, moved by some mysterious superstition, wants Henrietta to learn cooking and scrubbing—when Henrietta gets her portion she'll only be able to hire twenty servants!—I must introduce Achitophelous to you, Jean. He'll certainly try to find someone with a million francs for you to marry, on your culinary accomplishments. . . ."

"In the country," said Jean, "my mother fed us entirely off the soil, meat, poultry, herbs, and she cured our sicknesses, too, out of the fields and woods. My mother was a wonderful woman: I am not half like her. I was lazy. I regret it now. One day—no, this is really funny—a schoolteacher saw me dawdling round the village and gave me a book, saying, 'You ought to read this book, Jean: you're a boy who could do something for France.' After that I got to like reading. If not for her—I would be soling shoes now, I suppose." Jean shook his head. The room was invaded with the smell of paddocks, and sunlight on distant wild banks and rutty roads, on copses shading milch cows, boundary stones, straggling apple trees and madly obstinate little bull calves straddle-legged and loud-voiced, on their way to market. "My father makes his own furrow still," pronounced Charles Lorée, with the idiosyncratic warm rush in his voice, as if he defied the world to say the opposite. The telephone rang. "Yes?" said Jean in his warm, lingering voice in which was always an enchanting touch of self-deprecation, "Yes, Suzanne: I have seen him. In fact, he is here now, Suzanne. A moment. Adam—" he whispered, "your wife!" Jean turned on the light. Adam got up with a set, sober, little face.

"Yes, Suzanne," in that dead tone of the man haunted by the wailing ghost of a love affair. He listened for a few moments and answered, "Why don't you come over here to Jean's? No, I have no other engagement, Suzanne. Come over, do please, yes, do please." He put the phone down and came back to them. "She's coming over: she's just through a meeting." There was the silence accorded to a man's troubles by his intimate friends. Adam explained, "Sometimes the impulse gets too strong for Suzanne and she has to come and look at me across a room, or in the company of some woman I like. A sort of need for the convulsions of love. She's not getting so many naturally, as I live with her again." He turned his head aside, to indicate that the conversation was at an end.

But Jean said, "She's a great worker, excellent comrade. Gets violent at times, that's the only thing but—she'd —h'm—make a good commissar. A woman of destiny— unhappy destiny."

Adam shook his head. "She wants to let me go but she can't: poor Suzanne!"

"Strange in a communist woman . . . relics of the property sense," sighed Alphendéry.

Jean shook his head slowly. "No, no," he laughed broadly but with a faint embarrassment, he shook himself in his overlarge clothes, laughed again: "Poor girls! They have been after me with a knife too." He sheepishly held out his white muscular arm with two great crisscross scars on it and pointed to a scar on his forehead. After a moment, he said, "Wonder where Judith is? I'd better get out the cups: we'll make coffee." He got up and wandered to a broken-down, chiseled-off, rat-bitten, much-painted closet door. On the shelves inside were assorted bits of china, a man's emporium, and on the three others, brushes, little bottles of oils and acids, dirty plates, a glue boiler. Jean threw a cloth over the deeply incised bench and put five assorted cups and saucers on it, and a plate of honey cakes. He went and smelled the steaming copper saucepan. "Judith and I put it on this morning and I tested it this afternoon and just put in anything I could think of," he said with shy vanity. "My mother—I like going out getting the herbs. Some they haven't heard of round here. If Judith wants anything she says, 'You go and get it: you shop better than I do.' I like housekeeping, do you, Michel?"

Alphendéry hastened to deny it. "No, I can't even shampoo a cup. I suppose I *could*. I can dry cups and— saucers—and things, but there's a technique about washing-up, it's not so easy: there's the question of getting the right amount of soap in the water, you mustn't get too much. Then there's the splashing. . . ." he was going on seriously but they all exploded with laughter.

"You will like Judith," said Alphendéry to Charles Lorée.

"Judith is time-forward," said Adam, became conscious he had said it before, and added, "and Suzanne is time-abolished: she crumbles conventions, abolishes distances, and pierces matter for the construction of her own primeval psychic world."

Jean murmured, "Judith is a good girl—yes, she has her faults, we all have our faults: I have mine, I know." He made an effort. "Judith has brains—too—doesn't always know how to—that is, temperament I suppose. Geinus—a word I never use. Judith—oh, well, she's my wife, what—" He stuck. This was the workers' writer, known for his simple direct language, his rousing analysis, his fearless swordplay, his splendid diction, one of the few new writers in the grand tradition. Alphendéry smiled to himself, thinking unconsciously of the supple, perpetual, illuminated eloquence which was his to command. Jean said suddenly, "You're wasting your time, Michel: you should join us. You have responsibilities—there are greater ones, too." He blushed. "Would your mother understand?"

"No, but she'd stick by me grumbling," laughed Alphendéry.

Adam moved, strange masses shifting slightly in the slanting lamplight by the bench: his deliberate, pure but lonely tones said, "My mother was a grand and splendid character, chief among ten thousand: a general, who made her sons her lieutenants. I always hated her. She quenched every revolt in fire and ashes. She utterly destroyed the spirits, brains, and souls of my three sisters. I am not lucky in my women!"

"You are too pure, Adam," said Michel. "Women like twined fire and smoke: they fear the pure man."

"There's Judith," grumbled Jean good-humoredly. "Did we eat all the stew? We did, you know, how did that happen?"

"I—er—h'm—it's this way, I had no lunch—" explained Charles Lorée, "—just a spoonfu', there wasn't any more."

"There are only two eggs," said Jean. "Never mind—"

The door opened and Alphendéry, straightening up, smothered a word and looked keenly at Judith. She had come from some small group meeting and looked excited. She was very dark, with an oval face, a proud arched nose, large dark-gray eyes, ovals set somewhat wide apart with dark long lashes under crescent brows; the low rectangular forehead, swelling at the temples, bore a falcon cap of separately set black hairs. The mouth was firm and rather long, the chin jutted forward and was round, white, and knobby, producing a firm oval jaw: the face of a tempestuous being, a firm will, a firm destiny but ignorant of it; meditation was stormy and fruitful in this head, but the first unconscious gesture of the chin, the faint shades flying over the face showed a restless mind, not well buttressed against the affronts of life. She had a short columnar neck and was robust but not large, of medium height, with long hands. She carried a dozen yellow rosebuds. Her glance rested first on Alphendéry with surprise. Evidently the stew had been for Jean and herself! It moved in a moment from his short square form to the others. Her face lightened, became a beam and a tumult, "Hello, darling," she said to Jean, and to Adam, "Hello, Adam," in a lower tone. She went off into one of the bench rooms; she rustled various things making the noise that women do, of animals rustling softly through woods, and a little radiance came through the doorless opening. She called, "I'll have a plate of ragout, darling: I'm starved. Such a crush to get home. Someone stood on my foot. A little wretch kept tickling my leg."

Adam got up and slowly picked up the roses which Judith had spilled over one of the benches where they lay beautifully astray among tools, pieces of leather, and paints. He smiled over them at the room, "Like an unrealized passion!"

Judith came out like a ball of night wind, "All the poems about love are about unfulfilled love: why is it impossible for me to write poems to Jean? When I was a girl I wrote poems to everyone—trash, of course—but passionate! Look at Jean! He's a whole forest, sunrise, birds, but can I write it? Never." She laughed.

"Poetry," said Jean, "is desire painted on the eyeballs, a calendar ideal pasted on the dark inside of the skull, legends painted on the colorless wind, spotlights changing spider-gray silk through the spectrum, a stereoscopic view of dreams, lunacies starched and boned; but family love is flour and honey made into a cake. Even so, I don't see why you can't sing about cakes!"

"Yes, love is an illusion," said Judith. "Look how flat

and impersonal the name of your sweetheart sounds when you are in love! It doesn't correspond to the thing in your heart at all."

"I only love pretty girls," said Charles Lorée. "That shows there's no illus' about it." He looked round at them pugilistically. "No illusion—point-to-poi' aff'. After that, you take what you can get. I'm speak' of unions where money cannot enter. In marriage though—always, no, great percen'—would say—mater' interes' enter'. . . ." His characteristic was to speak on an intake of the breath so that most of the final syllables were lost.

Alphendéry looked at him, face creased in comic veneration, "I don't know much about love, Professor Lorée. Would you say there were affinities as among the atoms, for example?"

"H'm. Ah. Varyi'—er—degree'—proper condit'—biolog' plane depen' communit' origin'—spiritu' plane—nev' experimen'—ah—possible, ah—have to try people who never saw themselves in water, in a looking glass," he said suddenly speaking on an outgoing breath. "Question of—charm fel' by a' or onl' one—ques' fertilit' probab' akin—ah—*QUESTION OF FERTILIZATION ENTIRELY NEGLECTED*"—he said loudly and clearly: "race-perpetua'—neglec' race-extinc' has attent'—due to small number of women in biology and the sciences," he ended belligerently. "One man, one empha'—anoth' man, anoth' probl'—preoccupa' of women entirel' differ'n'—need them for balan' of scientif' pursui'—I ask to be permitted to speak," he suddenly said, with the voice and air of a boy in school. "Female organiza' round love put into slide rule not shotgun. . . . Love an eddy current ah—yes." He took a deep breath and brought himself up roundly, "Affinities—we are often the victims of the panderism of our friends. . . ." He seemed to decide to say nothing more and took a swig at the bottle.

"You're quite right," clamored Jean Frère. "We won't know anything about vital statistics until Negroes, untouchables, Aruntas, women, and children start drawing them up: I've seen a lot of prejudice in a figure of eight. Ciphers have no conscience." Judith was lying back, her hands behind her head. "Do you know what I dreamed last night?—now don't interrupt me, Jean (Jean gets so bored with my dreams)—" Adam watched and waited:

he had become silent since Judith entered. "Listen," said
Judith:

*In dream, a cavern bore, a dusty lamp above the flicker
  of war;*
*As paled the shut-in fire, the ragged groundling flame
  sprang higher.*

It's not very poetical and it has no sense, has it? It's
terrible, some days I think all day in bad poetry and I can
never write good poetry."

"Do you often dream it?" asked Adam quietly.

"No, but when I do, I can be sure the next day everything is going to be blank verse—not always blank, that
is. Today, all day, rhyming couplets, for example."

"Queer tricks," said Adam: "I have no memory for
music at all to speak of and one night I could not go to
sleep I was forced to go right through the overture of the
Marriage of Figaro three times—forced, I say. The next
day—only a bar or two. One night, I dreamed—yes, it
was soon after I met you, Jean—and you Judith—for the
first time: I noted it down. I dreamed there was a
brilliant procession in ancient Rome in its prime. Judith
rode at the head of the procession on a white horse, with
Jean in her train: everything was jeweled leather and
gilded trappings and they were singing a symphonic song
—I don't know how long it went on, it was quite original
and indescribably noble and splendid. I can see the
cortege flashing in my eyes to this day! But the song! It
was a wonderful song. I could not remember a note.
What a wonderful song it was!"

"I had a dream once," said Lorée, daring them all to go
on (for everyone suddenly felt a dervish whispering in his
ears to go on and tell them, tell them all about his
dreams). He felt in all his pockets, keeping them waiting,
and produced a laundry bill on the back of which he
wrote something and then passed it to Judith.

"Well," said Judith.

Lorée smiled guilelessly. "It is all wrong but it resembles a trisection of an angle. I dreamed once I was in
the trench' and ever' time we popped up we took off our
heads. Usefu'—he, he, he. . . ."

Alphendéry was most impatient with all this talk and
was struggling through the sea of dreams with breast

476

strokes, gasping towards the safe rocky shore of important discussion. "Professor Lorée, I last heard you at the meeting in the Salle des Sociétés Savantes, on the platform with Lacour, Cohen, and Amillé—pity Amillé takes drugs—"

But Lorée had decided obstinately to talk about himself. "I take drugs!" They all stared at him. He peeped at them all through his bushy eyebrows—they saw a few live gleams under the pink bluff. "I spent a fortnight with Amillé in Libya, he gave me the maxium dose every day for a fortnight," he boasted. He took another swig at the bottle, wiped his mouth, and suddenly heaved himself off the floor and went blunderingly to look for the door.

"Upstairs, outside," called Jean Frère. At the same time, they heard someone running upstairs and the exclamations of collision. It was Henrietta Achitophelous. Adam started and recomposed himself. Henrietta bounced into the room, her eyes black diamonds, her hair all curls, beautiful as always: they perceived Lorée filling the doorway, stooping, looking after her in surprise. Then he faded away, and they heard his steps on the stairs.

"Oh," cried Henrietta, "we had the most frightful row at the cell meeting! Everyone has always given the right advice in retrospect. It was about expelling—*you know who*." She blushed and added, "Pierre. Of course, everyone said they had their *suspicions*. Oh, Jean, isn't it terrible! My father is sending me to *Scotland!* Scotland is simply terrible." Her voice trailed off, warmer. "Of course, if you like that sort of—grayness and cragginess—it's all right—if you like golf. I suppose I could get in touch with the Scotch party. The Scotch are all for the French, aren't they? Oh, Judith, who was that man, it *wasn't* Professor Lorée, was it? It he *really* coming over to us? Isn't it marvelous," she breathed in ecstasy. "What a marvelous man, why it's the *leviathan!* I do—oh, I do worship that sort of cosmic biology, don't you? What were you talking about?"

"Dreams," answered Alphendéry.

She was disappointed. *"Freudianism,* you mean?"

"No, just plain boloney dreams," said Alphendéry.

"Oh, you don't suppose he'd let me write up his conversation—I mean a sort of interview at large, you know —for our quarter journal, for Young France, do you?"

"Ask him," advised Adam.

477

"Don't make him nervous," said Jean. "Let him alone, Henrietta. . . ."

"He is—wonderful," she sighed in her deepest whisper: "Sh! Here he comes." The professor came back to his seat with his eyes glued on Henrietta's lovely, glowing face.

"Henrietta Achitophelous, Lorée," said Judith.

"Oh, I am so—" breathed Henrietta. "I *do* think you're the best stylist we have alive in France today. What do you think, Professor Lorée?—"

Alphendéry broke in, "Do you see any evidence for the theory of secular movement of cyclical returns of depression and prosperity, Professor Lorée?"

Lorée turned pointedly to Henrietta, and asked, "What were you saying?"

Alphendéry, baffled, fell back in his chair.

Henrietta babbled at once, "Oh, you don't think Marxism is boring, do you? My father says it's so boring I'll become absolutely ugly reading it. I think it's terribly—turribly exciting," she finished in her low voice. "I just bought the whole of Lenin—two hundred francs."

Lorée laughed delightedly. "Boring—no one can say it's boring; false perhaps, but boring, never!" He was speaking quite clearly. He turned to Alphendéry. "No, I think it's dialectical—you see—"

"You *are*," said Judith, "a good scholar, you *are* a neophyte!"

Lorée turned to her, on the defense, said at once, "Please, may I say something? I didn't mean any harm: I was just—funning: Pardon me, just a joke. . . . There is no evidence that I can see for theor' of secul' return'." He stopped suddenly and relaxed in the low chair. His boots stretched out across the room. He appeared to be contemplating his folded hands, but everyone in the room became aware that he had no other interest at the moment but Henrietta. The conversation languished, mental life was difficult in that atmosphere; they had all been disintegrated and everything had been dislocated since the mammoth sat amongst them.

There was a ring at the door. Judith started and hurried to open it. "Who can it be now?"

At the door stood a woman of stone, with a face dug up from the grave. "Suzanne!" exclaimed Adam.

"Mme. Constant," said Judith. "Why, come in." Suzanne walked past Judith without a word, took off her hat, gloves, and coat and threw them on a bench. She walked to the middle of the chamber, threw herself into a reclining chair opposite Adam Constant and beside the stove, and said dryly, "Hello, Jean. I see you've got the usual female phalanx."

Lorée, aghast, shrank into the back of his chair and surveyed them all as if they were wild animals.

"Don't you want some coffee, Suzanne?" asked Judith. "You must be all in."

"Yes, I do, thank you. Yes, with milk and sugar." Judith put it in front of Suzanne who took it, tasted it, and after gulping it down set the cup on the stove. She darkled and said with lowered face, looking upwards, to Alphendéry, "What do you think, Monsieur, of a man who torments his wife like that? What do you think of a man who leaves his wife? Or do you think anything?"

"I don't know," laughed Alphendéry, trying to keep things going. "Tell me the man and I'll tell you what kind of a scoundrel he is: every man is a separate kind of scoundrel when it comes to girls. . . . We spend our lives figuring out only that!"

Suzanne laughed loudly at this, lifting her white teeth and the whites of her eyes into the light. "Ah, Monsieur, I see you are of my opinion! You must stick by me. All these others are against me. . . ."

"Don't say that, Suzanne," pleaded Jean. "I'm not, Adam's not. Nobody is, in fact."

Suzanne savagely got up, went to the cupboard, and cut herself a piece of bread. "No one serves me: I serve myself. I take the pieces, don't worry: I don't say thank you for tag ends." She looked with a ferocious grin at Adam. "No tag ends." She looked at Henrietta. Henrietta paled, composed herself. Suzanne laughed. "Imagine, 'The little gilded bitch.'" She said to Lorée, "You're Lorée, aren't you? Aren't you famous for your women-chasing? If they have a good time, I will too. Don't worry, I'm not a novice." She came up next to him and grinned down at him with her frightful, greasy face, about which hung her long black hair in locks. "You like pretty girls, don't you, Lorée? Look at all the wine he drank! Jean, give Lorée some more wine. I want to have a good time: I feel wild, wild tonight. Adam—a cigarette. Don't stir your stumps: I'll light it at the stove. . . . Ha, ha," she put the cigarette in her mouth, clapped her hands, and walked in front of Lorée. Lorée was still watching her, on the *qui vive*, taking in the attitudes of the other people there. She burst into a long shriek of laughter. "Look at him, look at the professor looking at me to see if I'm crazy. I am! Take me, professor: see how I feel. Give the ugly girls a chance. Tell me, have you ever raped an ugly girl? Let's have a good time. Look how frightened he is."

"Not frighten'," said the professor, giving her a hearty push.

"Lorée," she said harshly, "just a filthy gourmet like the rest of the whoremasters: wants his chicken done up fancy. I don't give a damn for you and your breed of alley lovers. I've got lovers enough. Ask Adam! Ha, ha. Haven't I, Adam? Haven't I slept with dozens of comrades, I get undressed with them in the room, don't I? And you say nothing: because I'm mad. Don't I? Tell them, Adam: how I torture you." She laughed low and long. "Why? Aren't I right to live my own love, Messieurs? No one loves me. Don't you think I'm right?"

"If you're happy, Madame," said Alphendéry; "but how can you upset Adam this way?"

"It's because he plays such rotten tricks on me, goes out with women, tells them all about me. Tells them he won't marry me, tells them I'm hideous, that he hates me. Shrieks it out aloud in bars, till you can hear it over the street. Tells them about me: how I ruined his life. . . . What about the time I fed you, fed you? Do you hear that, Lorée? He was out of work: I slaved for him day and night. I tramped the streets with him, going up and downstairs, begging, humiliating myself with him to get him work. I know all the insults, looks, rebukes, silences, moralities an ugly woman gets. I did it all for him. . . . Ask him about the time he was sick: he had ptomaine poisoning. I looked after him; I sat up all night. How do you think I got this complexion? Not with a life of milk and roses. . . . Roses! Not a single rose. It's been a dog's life. I'm not a woman but an old pack mule he's sorry for: society for kindness to animals and he's to be a saint for that! Not I. I'm not the one to stand all that! I'll drink, slobber, caterwaul, and muck up and bawl him out as often as I want to. If he doesn't like it, he can go and hang himself. I've slaved for him for ten years. He can go and talk grandly with his fine friends, his fine words, politics, economics: how sick I am of them!" She laughed and said in a deeper voice, "I'm a woman. I want something out of life, too. I didn't know I was well off when I was a virgin: I had to get myself tangled up with a sort of martyr-saint. . . ."

"You didn't do so badly," said Adam calmly. "Don't make such a noise, Suzanne."

"This is intolerab'," suddenly breathed Charles Lorée. He heaved himself round and up. "Mlle. Achitoph', will you come with me? This wom' is intolerab'. Why don't you shut her up or shut her up?" he asked Adam.

Suzanne got up and flung her arms as far around Lorée as they would go: "You are gigantic, Lorée." She placed her hands on his shoulders and sprang up to his face to give him a resounding kiss.

"Going," said the professor. "Sorr', Jean."

"Oh, sit down, Lorée," cried Jean bouncing up and taking him by the sleeve. "Please stay. Suzanne will go off the *rampage*, won't you Suzanne?"

"Can't bear to see a wom' raggin' her husban'," breathed Lorée: "detestab' upset me completel'. Why in publi', why not wai' till you get home?" he asked Suzanne sternly.

"Thanks for the prospect," said Adam. "She does, Lorée: she does both."

Suzanne flung herself down in the chair. "All right! I'm sitting down. Sit down everyone and enjoy yourself. I'm sure I am." She smoked like a chimney with a furious sarcastic expression.

"I'll get you people some sandwiches," said Judith.

"You go and help her, Adam," Jean murmured.

Adam rose with a smile. Suzanne flung her cigarette down. "Alphendéry! you see that? This is a conspiracy: Judith is in love with Adam and Jean like a fool wants to give them a minute alone. I see through you all. Your piecrust conspiracies. I know what's boiling in all your pots! So do we all: but everyone's too much a fool to say it. Sit down, Adam."

"Why, Suzanne," Judith was dignified, "don't talk like that. It isn't true: I don't see why Adam can't help me. There are six people here."

Suzanne became more energetic, throwing wild anxious glances at them all. "Lorée, I'm abandoned. Help me: stop him from going out. She's pregnant, look at her, and

481

she wants my husband. What are they going to the kitchen for? What do you think? I know. Don't let them go, Jean."

Adam, probably without thinking, moved off the bench and took a step towards the kitchen where Judith was juggling crockery. Suzanne made a bound and let out a cry, her cigarette falling to the floor. "Don't you go out to her!"

"Oh, Suzanne," said Jean ashamed. She turned on him. "You leave me alone: you've fooled round with enough girls in your time. I won't stand for anything like that in Adam!"

Lorée rolled himself out of the chair again, "Can' stay, Jean," he said. "Got lectu' prepa' tomorro'. You wan' go, too, Mlle. Achitophel'?"

"What are you so anxious to drag her out for, Lorée?" Suzanne heckled. "I can't imagine: none of us can imagine what you'll do as soon as you get her on the stairs. The courtyard's dark, too. Nobody much lives in the Rue du Pont de Lodi. Nice district for gallant professors and the strumpet daughters of the bourgeoisie. Where did your father get his money, Mademoiselle? Tell me that! Out of sending white women out to Buenos Aires. I know, out of selling working women on the quays in Antwerp. He knows it pretty well, eh. Out of buying up run-down property and letting it out for sweatshops till an entrepreneur comes along to put up a new building for factory girls to sweat in or a new cinema for young lovesick kittens to fondle their boys in. Out of buying and selling little girls in China, out of the silk crop, eh, Yes, yes. I know. Your pretty manners, your little red nails, your big almond eyes, your little fern-smelling curls: I know. Go away, get out of my sight, you, you, get out with your sheep's-eyes professor, you with a diploma: do your picking-up somewhere else than round my husband. Lorée wants to go on a necking party. . . ."

"Shut up, Suzanne," cried Adam.

She smiled broadly and relapsed into silence. "Intolerab'," murmured the professor. "Come, come, Henriett'. Take you home."

"In a taxi," screeched the possessed woman, "in a taxi! Do." She watched them both hungrily as they shook hands all round: Henrietta even held out her hand to Suzanne and Suzanne took it and shook it and then pushed it away with a sound of disgust. "Bread and butter," she jeered, "bread and butter." The professor turned his back on her. "Good night," she called after him: but he refused to say a word and blundered out the door with Jean, Adam and Alphendéry after him in a contrite, sorrowing bundle. She smoked and smiled to herself.

"Well, he got a fright," she announced, when they returned.

"You are a tartar, Suzanne," said Adam. "You have no right to behave like that in Jean's house especially. Why insult Henrietta?"

"To throw her into the arms of Lorée and get her out of your way," she said, between laughs. "I saw he had his eyes glued on her and she was frothing at the mouth with baby veneration for 'the great man.' Suzanne the matchmaker. Eh, it's not the first. I've put more than one couple to bed. . . . Thanks, Judith. I need this tea. I'm dry, I'm sick. God, what a thing life is! You just begin to know what passion really is when your body's too sick and old to be able to stand it any more. You'll all be the same as me in ten-fifteen years' time, youngsters. Adam's going to commit suicide some way or another, either get chucked out of the party, or go and fight and get his chump head blown off and all my troubles will be over. Judith's going to be the mother of bouncing children, a real hen and chickens, keeping Jean in her apron strings, destroying all his work until she's got him stuck at the other end of a corncob pipe and humanity's forgotten; Jean's going to slow down, turn out good-fellow trash that he'll be praised for and that'll be thrown into the dustbin by even his own children. Alphendéry, you sweetbread, Alphendéry," she shrugged her shoulders, laughed, her head thrown back, blowing smoke into the air. "Oh, God, what a joke when I think what life will be for all of you! Such jelly fish. I frighten you all with my tantrums. You really believe I'm mad. No. I'm just strong. I break him and myself because I'm too strong. I'm a female gorilla amongst chimpanzees. Look," she crouched forward on the chair, let her arms hang, "look, it's striking isn't it? A gorilla-ess." She clenched her teeth. "I make the bars of my cage dance, all right." She began her infernal smoking again. . . . After they had eaten and drunk again, she subsided and sat there musing savagely, throned on her squat hips while the others talked in fragments, softly and without confidence, politely, as if they had just met. They all feared the insane goddess of darkness squatting there and dreaming of inchoate things. When it was time to go, she took a fancy to stay there, but Adam roughly hustled her out with the others: they heard her ringing insults over the courtyard, and Alphendéry's good-humored answers. Jean and Judith looked at each other, speechless, smiling in a dazzled way.

"Chronic jealousy," said Judith at last.

"Curious brute," commented Jean. "Yes, I *did* think she was jealous. When she walked in, I thought it was some archaic corpse resurrected, maybe a woman of the Parisii from far under the Arènes de Lutèce: I shuddered."

"We all shuddered: my heart stopped."

"Adam's gorgon."

The next day Adam murmured to Alphendéry about Suzanne, "I venerate her courage in loving: most women are such beaten dogs. They have such immense passion and they give vent to such poor, sniveling words. Nothing in the world seems to me so beautiful as woman's love for man, nothing is so deformed. You understand."

"When will your poems be out, Adam?"

"In the autumn, just before I go to Shanghai."

"I'm going to miss you, Adam."

"And I you, Michel: what a good fellow you are! You have the courage to be kind and unassuming. Few have it."

Scene Sixty: Marianne

THE Raccamonds came to the Hallers' apartment, invited to dinner. No one was at home. Marianne looked at the letter. "How did we make the mistake? How did we get the letter so late?" Marianne fretted over this problem the whole evening: she had had a bad fright. "Show me the letter. . . . But Aristide, it's a month old. It must have come while I was in London."

"I was so preoccupied, I left letters in my pockets, I remember, for days."

"It's unheard of! Why? What took up your time so much?"

"You know, while you were away, I began to hear things about Bertillon—the clients said he plunged on the pound and had an arrangement with Carrière: so I went to Carrière. Yes, it's true. If the pound slides any more, goodness knows what he will have to pay; now it comes to several millions, I guess. . . . Can he pay? . . . I did not sleep at night. At my age, I could not stand another fiasco, you see. So I visited Carrière. At the same time, Carrière—he's a dirty beast, too: I hear it is true that a boy was killed at one of his orgies. Is that the sort of man to be mixed up with? No. But needs must when the devil drives. They are all brutes."

A gross mocking line formed round her mouth. "And what are we? Anyone looking at us from the outside—your history with Claude Brothers, our marriage a marriage of arrangement, because of my connection with Czorvocky and Marcuzo, your mistress Lucienne's child given over to us because she couldn't support him in style, her second child born after our marriage, brought up a slum child with heavy skull and starting eyes and anemia—I shed my illusions when I—well, after my son was born. I don't understand how you can still deceive yourself. Why believe in anything? I don't have to. Why pretend there is a world of men different from the ones you call brutes, in finance. You really think that, say, painters or actors are finer and more generous? There are people who go through life with their hands over their eyes: they are sure to blunder into dung quicker than the others. Life is only sordid if you're looking for something else. I see what there is to do and I'm going to do it."

"At our age? You think one can start again at our age? I call that an illusion."

"Age? I'm getting stronger every year. I'm going into finance. It's a splendid profession: hard work, insecurity, plunges, great chances, success, if you've got the right mind for it."

He looked guilty. "My dear, while you were away a letter came from a journalist. I put it somewhere. I don't know."

She looked at him suspiciously and with contempt. "You were certainly in a state."

He took a resolve. "Marianne, really, I don't want you

to do this: it isn't fit for a woman. You think you're made of tough material. You don't know: you would be miserable. And think of me. No home. Stock market, overdrafts at the office, bourse in the streets, tips in the cafés, spying out personalities in the restaurants, political scandal in the Bois on Sundays, and at home—more finance. . . . No. It's a fantasy."

She looked at him with a lift of the head and a faint smile: she thought (so intensely that she forgot to answer), "No, but you don't think I have to depend on you, do you? I have passed the time when I asked myself with astonishment why you left Lucienne (perfectly charming, after all), for me. I can get men. I like you, but looking forward to fifty empty years to please you is another thing. . . ." She felt impatient and bit her lip, "God in Heaven," she thought, "I understand a pure happy-go-lucky wastrel: he understands life and won't play the game; but I have no patience with a gloomy sentimental fanatic, like *him!*"

Aristide, surprised that she did not answer him, half seized the expression on her face: he sat up. "Marianne, you must not do this. I don't want it. If you do, I'll take you away from the city: we'll go back to Picardy."

For a fraction of a minute, she shivered and recalled the morning twilight of her life with Aristide. Odd, she thought: and softened. He was a good husband: and easy. Or had it always been so easy as it was now? She did not remember any more. Now Aristide was an old overcoat, good for the storms, good for warmth, but bulky, frayed, soiled, broken-backed. "Still, I'll go by easy stages," she thought. "I'll drop the pilot when I'm sure I know the channel."

He tried to keep up his authority. "Two in the family is too much."

She smiled. "You will see, Aristide: it will not be so bad as you think. And then, think, we need more money. A small example: I only mention it to show you. I have no good fur coat. Oh, don't think that what other women think bothers me. But still. Raoul—that lummox will always be in hot water. Until they settle down and we have grandchildren, we must have a full life. I won't be the old mother who has to be fed pap. . . . But only if we have enough money. You don't think of that?" (Raoul, he thought: she doesn't call that an illusion then; of all the misbegotten pickpockets—however: a woman's son, that's an illusion so solid I suppose you must call it a reality.)

"No," he said, "oh, go ahead, Marianne. I'm not stopping you. What do you want to do?"

"Listen: I've thought it all out. I have interviewed a lot of people. Marcuzo will help me at the beginning. You must too. I'm going to start a financial tip sheet in opposition to Marthe Hanau: I won't sail so close to the wind to begin with. There are plenty of people who think women are lucky in finance."

He sulked. "Who is going to put up the money?"

"Marcuzo, perhaps others: I don't know yet. I intend to run it alone. When it is going, you can say, 'That is my wife's sheet.' That's all. And it will—" she stopped: she was going to say, "Give you prestige: people will think you're behind me; that will start up rumor as to the powers behind me," but she just shook her head slightly and let the sentence die.

"It will—what?"

"It's fortunate, I made a point of meeting everyone," she said. "We met the new American ambassador last month. Connections are everything."

"I admire you, Marianne."

She was pleased, nevertheless. "Why? It's nothing. You see, I fool them: they will all say, 'Who is behind her?' Men never believe a woman can do anything: they let her through, unsuspecting. An immense opportunity for a career." She regretted saying that but it gradually disappeared into the waters of the ensuing silence.

"About Raoul, we will not have to worry so much," murmured Aristide. "I have managed to get him into the Biarritz office. Bertillon seems quite pleased to have him in. That gives him three thousand a month of which I told him he must pay one thousand a month to me, to make up the. . . ."

"I know, I know."

A dismal affair of a check passed without provision: the casino, the bathing heiresses, a young man's head is turned—and that was not the only escapade. There was a Voisin stolen for a joy ride, from the automobile showroom, where he had been salesman. Aristide had settled that. Where did Raoul get this gallant streak?

"I think," said Aristide, "I may be able to get Bertillon's

permission for a car when I'm running through the resorts on the Argent Coast. It looks better considering the class of client: purely a business car."

Marianne's eyes brightened. "Well, that's really an idea. Then you can leave me the Ford to run about in."

"Good."

She hesitated, then, "And as to the bank, dear—I have only one motto in all these things: sound the Jew and you reach the bottom of the mystery."

"The Jew."

"This Jew, Alphendéry, is at the bottom of all that's hazy and bizarre in the bank. I had a conversation with Bertillon's old friend, the banker Plowman. He was head of the Timor and Arafura Banking Corporation. He's well known in London. He told me that before they took on Alphendéry it was all plain sailing but Alphendéry brought in an intellectual diablerie, too cunning for Bertillon and yet so glittering that Bertillon was induced to take it up. . . ."

"What on earth does that mean?"

"I only conjecture. On his advice, contracts are not paid, checks held up: transfers of funds delayed, bearer bonds sold out and bought in again when called for, and so on, and so on. You know better than I do. He's never shown any positive profits except for his great foreign clients—evidently, since he still manages their accounts: as far as the Bertillons go, merely guile and negative suggestions. If you had only come into the bank an hour before he did. I hear Bertillon picked him out of the street, literally."

"It's not possible, that."

"Indeed, it is. I know lots of things about the history of the bank. I did not waste time in London. . . . And you, my dear, have underrated Alphendéry. Don't let yourself be set up on strings: the other puppets dance for him. Be advised. Find out something about him? He's brilliant. He was formerly with a house in Nancy. Find out why he left them; why a man like that was wandering in the streets of Paris; why he appears to be poor even now, lives in a cheap flat; find out the scandal about his wife. Arm yourself, Aristide. A moment will come, and if it is not far off now, I judge, when you will need ammunition against Alphendéry, both for yourself and for the good of the bank. Bertillon will thank you. Plowman will aid you. You can move into the bank on proper terms—perhaps a partnership. You know as much about the market as Alphendéry; you are better situated, you have even visited the U.S.A. . . . You had nothing but the one letter from your man in Amsterdam?"

"No: I had another today. There are at least two secret journals A and B respectively which the head accountant keeps himself and will not let him see."

"Good. . . . We must get at them."

"He says he has a plan."

"That's a good type of fellow. Should you send him something?"

Aristide was scandalized. "Wait till he's found out something. Don't let him think money is easy to come by."

She let the question drop. "I think I'll write a note to Mme. Haller, explaining." She wrote and also slipped in a story of the strange visit they had paid to the Hallers' flat. Mme. Haller wrote back at once and explained that they always left Anna in charge of the flat; she never let anyone in, she was a perfectly good watchdog: she regarded it as her flat till they came back and she was very angry indeed if the Hallers came back before the appointed day. This two months was her reward for the whole year: she queened it over the empty apartment and the goods in it; it rang with her voice and her songs. She went out once a day to do her shopping but spoke to no one and after an hour or two trailing the streets, looking in shopwindows and making to herself strictures on the behavior and clothes of the women, came back to "her apartment" a free personage, for once. She was not mad by any means, said Mme. Haller; she worked for very little and she really did not need money: she sent it all to a brother much younger than herself and sick, in Transylvania.

She had been with the Hallers twenty years, and was well content, for Mme. Haller always saw that she had good shoes and hats. Naturally, she had been too ugly, poor thing, ever to have a man and Mme. Haller had tried to make it up to her by giving her a new dress on her birthday every year. "Thus, my dear Mme. Raccamond, our house is the only home she knows. She loves Mr. Haller better than me, for he is a man and he has a big voice, but I manage. One day I heard her laughing to herself in the pantry and talking and singing in rather a strange way over the washing-up and I went straight in and said, 'Anna, you must stop that, or you must leave me. You know you need not do that. You must control yourself.' And this is all I have to say to her when she gets queer. She is odd. I often have to laugh at her. When she does talk, she talks about her troubles. We have known her for twenty years as I say, and she was brought up in my mother's house. She was there from the time she was twelve, so you see there is nothing in her life we are ignorant of. And she has never had any troubles. She has always been protected, in a way: no husband, perhaps a drinker or a man who would have beaten her, no children, no slavery in a cottage! Always getting better food than peasants eat, too. But she so often talks about her 'troubles' that I really do think at times that she is getting a little queer. What do you recommend, dear Mme. Raccamond? I am sure you are perfect in your management of servants! But no, don't answer me this in a letter. Mr. Haller would be very angry. I am not to tell about Anna, he says. But you understand, you are a woman, dear Mme. Raccamond. We will talk of this again, one day and perhaps you can think of something Anna would like. Naturally, I think about her. Why not? She is, after all, a human being. Do you think it is so wrong, dear Madame? No, I am sure you don't. I know your kind and rational nature. . . . We are doing splendidly and the food is so good. Of course, Swiss food is very, very good, almost as good as our own. . . ."

"You see, Aristide, it pays to write letters, my dear: she is a real friend now; and only because I have written her a letter or two. So few people know this secret!"

"Yes, and yet it is such a farce: people tell such lies in letters!"

"Oh, you have no sense of comedy; you are not grateful. You do not see that a letter is a work of fiction written specially for one person. It must give excessive pleasure."

Scene Sixty-one: A Sanitary Measure

SEPTEMBER, 1931.
London was wild in those weeks. The torpid English-

man could be heard, in the underground, the buses, in Leadenhall Street, in Maiden Lane and in Oxford Street, coming out of warehouses, pubs, and offices, walking to lunch, waiting for the tram and standing in the gutter, discussing not only politics, but the currency. This had even been going on in the months of July and August and one felt that this race of century plants was waking from one of its cyclical sleeps. Meanwhile, in the cafés round the Baltic, the Royal Exchange, and in the dives off Throgmorton Street and its associated alleys, many schemes both rich and wild were heard for keeping the pound on gold, many speculations were made about the amount of gold in the great Bastille in London's heart, the Bank of England.

On September eighteenth (this was the last act, not the first), it was announced that the stabilization of the pound was threatened because of naval unrest and the report that a general election was imminent. The conversion of British funds into foreign exchange was attacked by the press. People talked of a foreign conspiracy and "attacks from abroad" on the pound, Englishmen always having the strange illusion that (far from their living coming from abroad), harpy nations and bandit races are always trying to rifle the boundless treasure of the little island. On the twentieth the pound was pegged, the possibility of its going off gold everywhere announced: the pound was then below gold shipping point. On the twenty-first the Bank of England suspended the gold standard and immediately the congratulations started and the suspension was "seen by bankers as a first step towards the solution of our economic problems." Nevertheless, there was a violent reaction in Berlin, Vienna, Copenhagen, Tokyo. The stock exchanges closed in many parts of the world till values were readjusted. The congratulations went on, to cover this and stop a panic. "The attempt to stabilize at prewar parity led to the European economic situation. Now prosperity would come on." J. P. Morgan called the suspension a "hopeful event," a "second step towards financial recovery." Hoover spoke of the "good" to come.

Commodity prices in the U.S.A. had fallen and Léon, forewarned, had not only made considerable money selling short, but his expected advices had come through from Copenhagen and Swiss informants and his "check

technique" had worked. . . . Jules, in so far as he owned
gold in his branches abroad, found his position worse on
the books. Towards the end, just before the steel trap
closed, he had sold the pound short in a small quantity,
and the gold he owned aboard (a virtual short sale on
the pound) resulted in another profit. But he sat and
mourned the "lost opportunity."

"Down on the Côte d'Azur I said I was going to sell the
pound till Kingdom Come and that fellow Bomba talked
me out of it; and Stewart with his 'everything's splendid,'
and Plowman, with his patriotism!" He laughed helplessly.
Hardly had he said it than Carrière appeared in their midst,
very jolly.

"Well, Jules, I had you that time! Eighteen months to
go on my brewery contract! What do you say to that? I
called the turns nicely. Ah-ha, I bet that'll just about clean
you out, my boy."

"Don't stay awake at night congratulating yourself,"
jeered Jules. "I can always pay your drafts out of my
petty-cash drawer."

"Indeed? I hope to see it. Well, I'm celebrating on the
strength of it. I'll be seeing you."

"Can't you keep bad news to yourself?" Jules joked.
"Don't spend too much: Snowden's going to limit the
pound."

When Carrière had gone and William had cleared out
Plowman, Cambo, and the great crowd of lively folk who
had come in to discuss the pound, he inquired, "Carrière seems to think you're still going to pay him on those
drafts?"

"He thinks so. I'll see. If I have the petty cash, I'll pay
him. If not, not."

Scene Sixty-two: Sealed Orders

"First," said Jules, "let's send Constant to England
again to find out about the Carrière brewery transaction:
I know there's something very fishy about it. The Comtesse de Voigrand told me his mother, Madame de Bene-

zech, was very persuasive about it and begged Voigrand to put me into the bet with Carrière."

William said their English solicitors, Ledger, Ledger, and Braves, could find out more than a lost Frenchman like Constant. But no, Jules had to send his own envoy. He haggled and heckled for Constant. William was cantankerous and asserted that he only wanted to attach a good honest hard-working boy to his team of necromancers. Alphendéry, out of friendship for Constant, exclaimed, "Why no: Constant is ideal. No one will suspect him; no one but Ledger knows him. He can represent himself as a student, say of finance, at the London School of Economics: that explains his inquiries, his accent."

They called in Adam.

"Adam, I want you to go to London. Can you leave this afternoon?"

"Yes. What am I to do?"

"Never mind that. We'll tell you before you leave. You must have lunch with Mr. Alphendéry. You can leave by the 4.40 this afternoon?"

"Yes. . . . When will I get my instructions?"

"At lunch. Run home and get your bag now, and meet Alphendéry for lunch. Tell Mr. Husson to arrange for a first-class return ticket for you, for this evening's train."

Alphendéry said hastily, officiously, "If you'll kindly have lunch with me at one at the Brasserie Universelle, downstairs first: I'll tell you over the *apéritif*. . . ."

When Constant had gone, dazed, Alphendéry said, "Now what do you want Constant to do, Jules? I don't know more than he does."

Jules was surprised at the rapidity of events himself, but he passed it off. "Oh you just leave it to Constant: he'll find it all out. He's smart. We don't have to give him instructions. Let him work it out his own way. Just sketch it: you know how. We want to find out about Carrière's alleged sale of a brewery. Tell him to go to Ledger and Braves, in High Holborn. They'll go over it with him. He'll probably suggest something to them."

"Good gracious! they don't know anything about it themselves. And they don't need his help."

"Well, let Adam tell them what we want and let them put their heads together. Let him find a way. Say, he's maybe smarter than all of us."

"But it's not necessary."

"I want him to go to London for me."

"You ought to have an ambassador permanently in London," said William.

"That's an idea too," Jules smiled back, impudently. "I'll consider it. You're coming along nicely."

At lunch Adam brought out a notebook and pencil. "Will you let me itemize everything I have to do? I want to use my time economically, and I had the curious feeling last time that I hadn't got the gist of the thing at all: I mean, I felt ridiculous, I didn't understand my mission, or its importance."

Alphendéry said, "To tell the truth, Mr. Bertillon and I had little time to go over it this afternoon. I can give you an outline. I'm going to go to his home this evening and go over things with him quietly. The best thing is for you to take this afternoon's train—he's very keen on that, and I don't want to disappoint him—and then I'll telegraph you at your hotel first thing tomorrow if there are extra instructions. . . . You may as well get straight away; the sooner, the better." Adam looked puzzled. Alphendéry laughed. "In the meantime, another St.-Raphaël? My favorite."

"Yes, thanks, but the? . . ." Constant was baffled: he wondered, if by some trick of strained attention, he had missed out a whole sentence of Alphendéry, explaining the purpose of his visit. Alphendéry suddenly spilled the whole affair, though.

"Dr. Jacques Carrière signed an exchange contract with Mr. Jules Bertillon some six months ago, whereby Mr. Bertillon was to receive drafts in pounds sterling and to change these into the equivalent in francs and to pay to Dr. Carrière the stipulated amount in francs. You see, it is a long-term exchange operation. The pound sterling was always to be paid out at a rate of 122 francs in the pound. In other terms, Mr. Bertillon bet that the pound would not fall and that when the draft came in, the pound would be either at 122 francs or even above that figure. And Dr. Carrière bet that the pound would fall to below 122 francs, and arranged that even if the pound fell to say, one hundred francs, Mr. Bertillon would be obliged to pay him at the rate of 122 francs and therefore would be twenty-two francs out of pocket for every pound in the draft. These drafts are still coming in: therefore Mr. Bertillon is still losing money, the pound having dropped considerably. Clear, so far?"

Adam made a grimace. "Yes, I've heard about it and the brewery at Burton-upon-Trent. . . ."

"Now, although I have not seen the contract, I believe it is in order and that Mr. Bertillon is obliged to pay out this loss unless it is proved that the alleged sale of the brewery did not take place. In which case, Dr. Carrière is guilty of misrepresentation and the contract (which I am pretty sure exists, although I have not seen it) can be contested. . . ."

"Hasn't Mr. Bertillon a copy of the contract?"

"If he has, he won't show it to us." Alphendéry grinned, looked round, then softly: "A secret: he *says* there isn't one; but we are pretty sure—never tell this to anyone, not even Ledger, Ledger, and Braves. Just act as if the contract existed. It does, I'd stake my last franc— However, you see how it stands. If no sale of the brewery ever took place, then Carrière is just having his agent present drafts in sterling at pleasure. His theory, you see, was that he was to be paid for the brewery by two-monthly drafts of two thousand pounds each. He did not want to lose on the two thousand pounds in terms of francs, if the pound were to fall. Therefore he got his guarantee of 122 francs per pound from Mr. Bertillon. The pound is now at 96. . . . But if the brewery was not sold, then he is simply presenting drafts of two thousand pounds each two months, through a dummy agent, the two thousand pounds (devalued) coming out of his own pocket. Do you see? In other words, he is paying Jules two thousand pounds at 96 francs to the pound and receiving at the rate of 122 francs to the pound; or he is giving Jules 192,000 francs and receiving from him in exchange 244,000 francs, a profit of fifty-two thousand francs every two months, for nothing! You understand! Now, if Jules had made the contract outright, there would be no help for it. But as the contract was made theoretically for payments on a brewery, we could charge misrepresentation. . . . Do you think you could by any means discover whether that brewery was sold or not?"

"Nothing should be easier," remarked Adam coolly. "This is very simple. Why don't you write to the solicitors and let them do it? . . ."

"Well," Alphendéry was embarrassed, "Jules is very anxious to have someone on the spot. It is his mania . . . don't cross him!"

Adam laughed.

Alphendéry argued his case (his nature, he did it unconsciously in every dilemma): "You get a trip to England, you improve the tongue, you get to know our solicitors, you get the opportunity of presenting a case, and of ferreting around; you have full authority—and no doubt while you're there, we'll find other work for you. And you'll get a holiday from Suzanne: she'll like you better when you come back. . . ."

"Oh, I don't mind. Would it be necessary to go to Burton-upon-Trent?"

"If it's necessary, you've only got to telegraph me and you'll get the funds or you can draw on our London brokers or on Ledger's: I'll advise them."

Adam asked, "Good! But don't you think you could find out whether there really is a contract or not?"

Alphendéry said controversially, "There must be! A man like Jules doesn't pay out debts of honor: the idea is ridiculous. To Carrière? No. You pay a debt of honor to avoid being expelled from a club, but for no other reason. However, as you say, if we had our hand on it—I'll try again!" He sighed. "You don't know Jules."

Adam smiled. "I'm beginning to. He's fascinating! 'Tis pity he's a banker. He's only made to be a flier, a dancer —a messenger of the gods."

"Well, is it all right now? You know what you're going for? We want you to trace this alleged sale of a brewery, go to Burton-upon-Trent, take advice with Ledger, Ledger, and if you don't want to go, instruct someone to go up there for our account. I don't need to say that this is entirely confidential. . . . Also, you can pop in on Dacre-Derek Caudal, the chap you employed for Mr. Bertillon on the last occasion, for the loan company and see how he is getting along. He's probably doing nothing. Cheer him up. Tell him we'll make money one of these days."

When Alphendéry got back to the bank he found Jules delighted that Adam had gone and almost believing that his troubles were all dispelled.

"Telegraph him when he gets there and tell him—tell him to see your friend Buck Fellowes, the secretary of Lord Reddermere. Mme. de Benezech had an English mother who belonged to the Chemicals gang, and Mme. de Benezech was brought up in England, knows Reddermere intimately. . . . Then tell Constant to go to the communists. He is one: he'll be *persona grata*. They're always muckraking; tell him to tell them we'll pay them—how much would they work for?—they'd be glad of twenty pounds, wouldn't they?—see how much they want to trail Carrière's operations and show him up." Alphendéry laughed. Jules said in a spirited tone, "Sure, they'll do it: it's a pleasure and they're paid for it. . . . Then tell him to go to the *Investors' Critic* and see that little fellow who came here once or twice: Smethers—he's a good sleuth and always needs dough, like all the journalists. Get a dozen people on his trail: you're sure to get something on him. . . ."

"Did you ever think that the papers here (not suffering from the English libel law) are full of the true oil and triple-bottom lowdown on Carrière and *that* doesn't do you any good. . . . You don't need such an enlistment, to find out if the sale really took place."

"You don't know the Carrière gang: they'd even close their ranks and stop squabbling for a month to get my head under water. . . . You see, you can't tell Ledger, Ledger, and Braves all that; they're righteous Englishmen probably; they haven't got the worldly style of our own lawyers; they'd probably be offended and hypocritical if I told them the truth. . . ."

"You're fantastic, Jules: lawyers are never offended. The higher you go, the better the name, the less offended they are. The poor lawyer is offended because he's raising his price; the expensive lawyer knows that if you walk into the office, you'll pay the price."

Jules persisted, childishly, "Then if he's good at this, we can use him for other secret missions."

"What secret missions have we got?"

"Besides," Jules ignored him. "Besides, he has the instinct of an amateur, not hidebound in presuppositions, you see. He's like a woman: he'll put his finger on the spot."

"There is something in that," conceded Alphendéry. "All right, Jules. Good night. Then you don't want to see me tonight?"

"No, no. Tomorrow is time enough. Just write him to see the communists and Buck Fellowes and so on."

Alphendéry laughed and rolled himself out of the room. He was confused: he felt as if Jules had yet some other scheme in mind and had not yet the courage to put it forward. He was puzzled and did not know how to tie Jules down to the main issue: that of getting the goods on Carrière and breaking the (apparent) contract.

Two days later though Ledger, Ledger, and Braves had yet received no letter from Bertillon's confirming Adam's mission, Adam himself received the following letter from Alphendéry explaining a further discussion that he was to have with the lawyers. It was as follows,

DEAR ADAM,

Please ask James Ledger the following questions. 1. In time of war would the English government confiscate the gold of aliens and if so, 2. Would it recompense at the statutory rate? 3. Would the British government ever violate the integrity of a safe-deposit vault for the sake of confiscation in war-time or similar panic? 4. Would an English bank visit its own vaults and report gold holdings to the government; could it be forced to do so? 5. If the deposit of gold became known and the declaration of gold holdings had become obligatory, would the government confiscate and pay the holder off (with penalty or not), or would it permit him to exchange the gold for partnerships, estates, or other property, etc., in England?

"Why," said Mr. James Ledger, with dignity and with a sunbeam of respect in his eye, nay even love, for the gentleman who asked these welcome gold-bearing questions, "the British Government has never confiscated the gold of aliens or violated the sanctity of the safe-deposit box. Britain is, after all, still the leading financial nation, London the leading financial city, her vaults the greatest strongbox, except, of course, Switzerland (and is that safe with *her* frontiers?) in the world: and as the crisis deepens in Europe, we expect gold to pour in here. We have solved our problem. The French will certainly have to go off gold soon and with their turbulent politics no one has any confidence in them. . . . You may tell Mr. Bertillon that any gold deposited in that fashion—may I ask whether the gold mentioned in the hypothetical case is thought of as gold coins or gold bars? It is not necessary to answer" (he interposed desirously) "—is perfectly safe. . . . But I doubt that the question will arise: the City will certainly have some inkling of it, and your relations in the City are not of the very worst." He laughed. A legal joke. He recalled himself and permitted himself a question of more than curiosity, on account of the youth of Constant.

"Might one assume that the value of the gold would be fairly high?"

"Yes." Constant realized suddenly that Ledger belonged to a club and that Ledger's reputation would in no way be damaged if the members of this club learned or inferred or deduced or dreamed that Bertillon was worth round about so-and-so. He therefore went on. "It would be—large. We might hazard a figure like—half a million sterling."

"By James," said James Ledger, admiringly, "that is quite a figure."

Ledger resolved immediately to redouble his efforts to uncover the traces of Carrière's crookery: nothing was too bad for a man so base and immoral as to attack half a million sterling in gold bars.

Reaching his hotel, Constant found yet another note from Alphendéry:

Make further inquiries on the point brought up before. This is very important and relevant to future profits. Be circumspect: do not let him know our projects (J. Ledger, I mean); 1. What are the prospects for a trustee shareholding company: could it be formed along the lines of the "Nominee" departments of the Big Five? 2. Who manages the present trustee shareholding cos. if there are any? Who manages the "Nominee" departments? 3. What type of shares do they hold? What quantities? What restrictions? Is C.P.R. one? 4. Can we get hold of these shares on any consideration? Could we lend money on such shares ourselves, holding them as equity? 5. What right to sell them out and/or replace? Also go to the C.P.R., Dominion of Canada offices, etc. and get what information you can about the C.P.R. Go round to the Big Five, represent yourself as a young fellow coming into an estate, and ask for information on C.P.R. as an investment, and inquire about "Nominee" departments.

James Ledger looked bewildered when Constant came in on a third day with a third line of inquiry but he settled himself to the job of finding out what he could about the formation of an investment trust.

On the fourth day Constant reappeared with a further inquiry.

"Could a bank-deposits-insurance company be formed, for German depositors in German banks, business office in London, on account of the prestige of London, but head office (secretly) in Paris: the object being to avoid income tax and if possible responsibility?" Due to the failure of banks all over the U.S.A. the failure of the Darm-städter and other banks in Germany in July, 1931, no one had any confidence in banks and Bertillon reckoned that he would easily get people all over the world to pay insurance premiums. If one bank caved in and the depositors came to him (by mail) clamoring for money, there would always be a saving clause that would either be an argument against paying the claim at all, or would delay the payment of claim for years. This scheme arose from Jules's conviction that the *whole system* would eventually go under and that he could put off the payment of any particular claim, until there was a general banking disaster and a moratorium. Until then the accumulated premiums would be his, he could use the money for stock-speculation and for supporting his own bank. . . . Adam was desired to form a new insurance company to make it possible for them to send out letters to German and Scandinavian banks, offering insurance.

When he got home on the fourth day Adam found a letter saying that Jules was very irate that Ledger, Ledger, and Braves had discovered nothing yet about Carrière, and that Constant must go at once to another lawyer, the brilliant but theatrical firm of Quidd, Soleck, and Company.

Quidd was thirty-five, had thick black shiny hair and considered himself a diamond. In fact, he wore a diamond with a peculiar air of intimacy on his little finger.

"What firm has handled these heretofore?" he asked Constant, with excessive politeness, after having given him the softest seat, set at an angle, and offered him a cigarette (which Constant refused).

Constant hesitated.

"I understand your prudence," smiled Quidd with much good humor and *savoir-faire* and a smile that made Constant feel like a schoolboy again. Constant murmured, "I see no harm—really: it was our ordinary solicitors, Ledger, Ledger, and Braves."

A smile of greedy triumph appeared ill-masked on Quidd's face.

"A very good old firm: routine, of course, but for routine matters— However, as far as the present matter goes—I think I can promise you" (a savant emphasis on the *you*, a personal favor, undoubtedly to Constant, whom he had just met), "that we will unearth something." He smiled widely, "I think I can say that here we have—*pipe lines,* direct wires, to persons of importance, in the affair."

Constant was astonished, but kept a modest face. Quidd considered him and appeared to take a great liking to him. He inquired in a honey tone, "Did you ever chance to look through *this?*" It was a thick volume of letters of Ambassador Page which had just come out and made a "sensation" in the right-thinking papers. "Personally inscribed to me and sent by a friend of mine, one who was in short a secretary," said Quidd, with an air of discounting such greatness, and being given over entirely to the anxieties of his profession.

"No, no," said Constant. Such things were really a pest. Quidd apparently took his denial for modesty, timidity even, and became splendidly friendly.

"Take it, take it as a personal gift: you must read it. He was a great friend of England," he said with index finger slightly lifted from the desk.

Constant was astonished again and perhaps too apathetic. "I don't want to rob you of it; really, you are too kind." Quidd only needed this to become compelling: he turned his magnetic eye on Constant. "Yes, you must take it: you really should read, if you have not read already: we owe it to ourselves—a peacemaker."

Constant took it grudgingly, feeling he was being made ridiculous, quite apart from the appearance Quidd gave of doing him a solemn, an intimate favor. . . . Suddenly Quidd relieved the air by smiling graciously and saying almost whimsically, "Tell Mr. Bertillon I am his to command. I will give this my very best attention. It shall be in the forefront of all our business. And we are busy. But nevertheless—! And Mr. Alphendéry. Mr. Alphendéry is well known to me. He is a remarkable man: don't you think so?"

Constant was so weak as to say with a tone of enthusiasm, "Yes, I think he is remarkable."

Quidd became compellingly patronizing. "Yes, indeed, take it from me: a man almost of genius. I have had some long talks with him. My French is doubtless not absolutely native, but it will serve; and then Mr. Alphendéry knows a little English. . . ." A pause intervened. Constant unconsciously left the book on the table as he rose. Roguishly Quidd pressed it on him. "Oh, but you must not forget Page's letters: they are very important as documentation—for an understanding of our own time. Yes, indeed! Please read them as a personal favor to me. And remember me especially to Mr. Alphendéry."

Constant was quite angry: he had an impulse to leave the book in the corridor, outside the door. And with this book under his arm he had to go straight back to Ledger, Ledger, and Braves and get some papers which had escaped—perhaps had been taken, for this very purpose, from the folder. Ledger smiled, when he reappeared. (He had been admitted at once, which was unusual with Ledger's: Ledger's usually made clients wait exactly five minutes, for the good of their souls.) Constant thought, "Why keep up one absurd unreal play to support another absurd unreal and criminally misplaced drama?" He said soberly to Ledger, "I am very sorry to give these papers to another lawyer: I am only acting under orders. I think they are mistaken. Mr. Bertillon, I hope you understand, is—he's a charming person, charming, I am very happy to —but he acts on impulse, he is a voluntary type; he is impatient if things are not done like a streak of lightning. You surely must meet clients like that. The other firm is Quidd, Soleck, and Company."

Ledger smiled at the discomfiture of the young men, his point gained. "Yes. And besides, I am glad you told me: it makes things straightforward between us. . . . Here are the papers. And thank you. . . . By the way, purely a personal curiosity, this has nothing to do with business:

what do you think of Quidd? You saw Quidd, didn't you?"

These lawyers are shamelessly inquisitive, thought Constant. He teased Ledger, wondering what was the phrase he so clearly wanted to get out.

"I only saw him today for the first time. Henri Léon, a Dutch merchant, knew him long ago, it seems. Through Léon to Alphendéry, that's the connection. As to his character: he struck me as—h'm as—well, the career of a football, well sewn-up, well blown-up, but only to be dashed about from pillar to post, and the goals he makes of no consequence to himself—"

Eagerly, Ledger rushed in, his lips trembling with gratification, "Exactly, exactly: a bounder. Isn't that the word?"

Constant blushed and said, cowardly, "Yes." It gave Ledger so much ease that one could not really say, "No."

Ledger beamed on him. "I understand: you can't help this. And if there is anything else *I* can do, I will. No personal feeling whatever . . . none whatever."

When he got back to the hotel, another letter again, from Alphendéry, transmitting wishes of Bertillon: he was to make the round of the brokers and get their ideas on the oil situation: there followed a list of the brokers he was to visit—a dozen of the most imposing in the City of London. Three brokers gave him no information whatever, that Adam could not have got better from the *Oil News*. One broker, an immense, earnest, fat fellow of sixty, in a Germanic accent spoke to him with lugubrious eloquence of the flag, the dear King, the dear Queen, the admirable Royal Family and the friendship with all countries, and the forgiveness even of Germany. "They will pay us yet, you will see." He even showed him a picture of the King, with a Union Jack pinned in the office. The offices were a wandering little dusty honeycomb of cells, divided by glass-and-wood partitions. Thin young heads of clerks popped up curiously as he followed the earnest fat broker about, mild grins.

In the fifth, by pure innocence, he reached one of the directors of a bank that had suffered greatly through the German default. The young man knew little of oil but cordially explained to Adam a possible technique for German repayments.

"Unless I get back to Paris soon," thought Adam in

despair, "I will look upon myself as a ninny and have to get another job at once or take ship to Shanghai: this is no longer endurable."

He therefore telegraphed Alphendéry that he was returning and was surprised to receive his telegram in reply:

RETURN WHENEVER YOU FEEL YOUR MISSION IS ACCOMPLISHED. LETTER FOLLOWS.

The letter said he was to find out how the Bank of England was regarded and for that he was to visit such and such financial journalists, brokers, and bankers, again, if necessary representing himself as a student at the London School of Economics. Likewise he was to ask what bonds were particularly recommended by bankers, for long-term investment; and he was to go to the *Financial News* and *Financial Times* and discover what a quarter-page advertisement of a new company (he supposed the investment trust) would cost and whether any guarantees were required.

He bit his lip and set out once more on the weary lope, upstairs and downstairs, into all sorts of little offices, and grand upper stories of banks, to face surprised kindly little men, who treated him with a coddling air as if he were a rather advanced five-year-old and they had to amuse him till the policeman arrived to take him home.

If they invented nothing else, he would get home the day after tomorrow. He sent a firmer telegram to Alphendéry, received no further instructions, and, with a sigh of relief, felt the Channel airs on his face. The sea was blue, the crossing smooth and sweet: a raft on a duck-pond. The shores of England faded away in their usual ambiguities of haze. Behind the haze was the mire, thickness, and filthiness of London, the trodden, thin, tall dark ways, the old buildings, himself wandering anxiously about seeking he hardly knew what; behind there was a miserable evening in a cinema, where he sat with burning heart and saw nothing of the film, sick with the vacuity of his job. On the boat again he felt his head swiveling round and round: what a useless week; he felt the City must be holding its sides laughing, getting together whispering, "Bertillon, ha, ha, his clerk-envoy, ha, ha: they're both cracked, ha, ha; but you've got to humor their

504

moneybags: he, he." Disheartening. He would ask for the post at Singapore or Shanghai—they hadn't decided yet—as soon as he got back.

France: he hardly looked out of the windows, so glad was he to snuggle back into the contentment of being at home. When he came home and spoke of making a report to Mr. Bertillon, Alphendéry held him back: "Not yet, in a day or two: he isn't interested in that now." The days went on: he made no report. The Ledgers had been writing letters all along, though, and had kept Alphendéry *au courant,* and now Quidd, Soleck, and Company sent in a grand, suave letter.

Jules met Adam in the corridor, the day after he came back: he shook hands with him gladly and said, "You must go to London again for us soon!" How strange! As if going to London was a profitable business in itself.

Adam Constant had lunch with Alphendéry for several days in succession and started to tell him all that had happened in London, but Alphendéry was displeased: he wanted to talk philosophy, Marxism, poetry; he wanted to hear Adam's poems and ask about their publication, but he did not really want to know what conversations Adam had had with the bankers—at least, any more than Adam had already incorporated in his daily letters. Once he even said, with a paternal air, "These things are not so serious as they seem. It was just a trial balloon we were sending up. But Jules was delighted, delighted: he wants you to go again soon. We learned a lot from your surface impressions: they were so original; it is even much better that you know nothing about the business and are a stranger in London; your impressions are the truer and believe me, we were greatly guided by your ingenuous remarks." He laughed kindly.

Well, even so, thought Adam, no more of that. And he began to ask about the Shanghai office.

"That's coming along. Are you so anxious to leave us?"

"No, no: but if someone must go, why not me?"

William came in one day when they were having a long tête-à-tête. "Glad to see you back," said William. "Hope you didn't get too bored with all that phony business. . . ." He explained to Alphendéry, apparently ignoring Constant, "You see, the fact that he has a bank agitates him; he sends Constant to London because he has a bank.

What can Constant do in London that you can't do over the telephone? But no. He has a bank and he has to justify it. Good. The bank has paid for a first-class return ticket to London. It's justified. Now he'll go to sleep again until next time he wants to dream he's an international banker. . . . Who would believe we were so cockeyed? No one. Thank God!"

Scene Sixty-three: Trouble Brews

THE time for paying Carrière's fourth draft approached. After long conferences and much jibbing on the part of Jules, they decided to send him a message, by Guipatin, a friend of both parties, and ask him to compound the debt, which might run into Heaven knew how much, and make a reasonable settlement. De Ville de-Ré, Jules's secret go-between, Raccamond, and William came in every day with the news that Carrière, although a multi-millionaire, was strapped, and needed money badly and that doubtless he would be glad to have a cash settlement. On alternate days, William agreed to a lump sum and to nothing at all: it was either "settle it outright" or "don't give the bastard a cent, let him sue for it," with him. And as he had not yet seen any document of any legality referring to the debt, he had concluded that the reported letter between Jules and Carrière referring to the "debt of honor" did not exist and that Carrière had no claim, or only a shadow of a claim, on Jules. Guipatin, an old intimate of Carrière, found Carrière not at home. Carrière demeaned himself stagily, threatened, clamored magnificently that he would "bring down Bertillon." Raccamond was present when this was recounted, for Bertillon was a strange fellow who sometimes dared publicity and open scandal; and Raccamond's cloudy eyes lighted with understanding and ardor when he heard the challenge. The next day, bowed with the weight of his body, gloomy, he brought into Jules a paragraph which had appeared in one of the papers owned by Sournois, the deputy.

Certain small independent private banks, badly hit by the fall of the pound, are obliged to pay off exchange contracts in installments and are even disputing these payments; these are for the most part concerned with payments on commercial drafts on sales of long standing and not, as was said by an interested press abroad, with rank speculative deals. Such arrangements, of course, occur daily and are essential safeguards to the buyer and seller in international deals. Let us take, for example, a hat factory or a brewery which would have been sold in England by a French citizen some months before the English gold embargo. . . .

Carrière had sent it to Raccamond, marked with a blue pencil.

"Bad publicity," said Raccamond, and trembled in a blue fit of fear.

"He won't get anywhere with that," drawled Jules.

"He's threatening a suit," said Alphendéry. "You'd better settle with him quick!"

"Let him sue me—on what?" said Jules. "He's a baby, he pulls faces."

"Bluff," said William.

"The Comtesse de Voigrand is his closest friend," murmured Raccamond.

Everyone saw the paragraph and it got about like wildfire that it referred to Jules and Jacques Carrière: Willem-Cornelis Brouwer wrote in from Brussels; their chiefs and customers' men wrote in from each of their branches, and this came with the mail:

DEAR JULES,

Please forgive the intimate line—the reason is that I am in distress and have two major enemies in your bank, *A* and *W*. But it is not my purpose to disturb your equanimity. Since your happy return in August last, when I found that antipathy ousted convalescent sympathy, and I came to Oslo, pride impelled a patient canvassing of the job market and this to the point of exhaustion. The outlook, now, is hopeless, at least for the next sixty days and my first northern Christmas looks black: my days are spent in weariness, my nights in disquiet. Likewise since that time my earnings—due to the antagonism, I would not say sabotage of Tramp-Dannevig, as well as mental conflict and my economic inferiority complex since being sent from the center of things—my earnings have been next to zero and obligations accumulating to a point where I am numb. In this situation, friend (I say instinctively, though I have how little right!), I turn to you. It is no dilemma when I want aid—there is but one place and but one man. Every so-called friend (perhaps self-deluding so-called friends) and every possible refuge out of the past exists no more: the world marasmus has seen to that: broke, or concealing the fact, and if still rich, timid and with timidity, callous. Dannevig sees my distress and although he owns a row of houses (as I find, despite denials and complaints of poverty), he denies my application. . . . Whether or no, friend Jules, you can stretch out a helping hand—and speed, here, is soul and body—I am persuaded you will enclose this matter in your breast. Always be in no doubt that any money sent from you to me is my first care and that any advances will be *made good*. If I am to do work for it, why, be assured I prefer that. I am not sitting here giving way to the wretchedness which is now part of my life: while waiting for the postman who is (humble Mercury) to bring me salvation, I am unceasingly conscious of your hopes in me and of my duties as a man and pursue other work here with a smiling front (and, as we all know at our age, men take that for the *heart:* it's better that way). Perhaps you wish it: *you have had blows*. Deepest, sincerest friendship, whatever your attitude,

> *Believe me,*
> > *Ever at your service, private and public,*
> > > THEODOR BOMBA

"That's good," said Jules throwing the letter to Claire-Josèphe, "then Dannevig wasn't ruined: he still has some property. Write him a letter, Claire, and ask him to come and stay with us for Christmas. I always liked that egg. He doesn't work but he knows everyone up there: friend of the King, the Wallenbergs, all that. . . . Obstinate, old-fashioned duck: lost a mint of money, though, when he wouldn't go into the Swedish Match concern. . . . However, if what Alphendéry says is true, he did better to stick to his houses. . . . What does Bomba want? Some cash? How much shall we send him?"

"A couple of thousand francs, for Christmas, I suppose; of course, it's throwing money away: as soon as he gets it, he gives a big dinner and blows it. What does he mean 'pride impelled' him to look for a job? . . ."

Jules said easily, "Oh, that's just a howl about his salary: he doesn't think he's getting enough. He can't live on it. He's a nice fellow though, means no harm. Those boys, William and Michel, are against him, call him so much dead weight. I'll send him five thousand francs off my private account so that he'll be able to give his girl a Christmas present. . . . Then," he darkened, "he's got to show results"

" 'You have had blows,' " quoted Claire-Josèphe. "Then he too has heard of the Carrière debt?"

"I'll shoot that fellow: it's the only thing."

As soon as he got to the bank in the morning, he drew out five thousand francs and posted them to Bomba, with the note:

Herewith five thousand. You're mistaken: I have had no blows. Look up Swedish Match and find out if we can sell it short. If we can report here.
                                      J. BERTILLON

He went upstairs and, half coy, threw Bomba's letter on Alphendéry's table. "How do you like that?" He was amused when he saw the contempt and annoyance in Michel's and William's faces. William said, "I hope you're not going to send him anything?"

"Oh, no, not a cent: he's got to do some work first; he just sleeps in the office all day when he's not out drinking akvavit, Danny tells me. I'm going to have Danny down for Christmas. Say, do you think Bomba would be any good running Carrière to earth?"

William flushed. "I won't have him, Jules: I warn you."

"He loves spite and vengeance," suggested Jules. "He's just the fellow."

"If you want to be sold out," said Michel, with a shrug.

"I wash my hands of it, Jules: you're arch, you're frolicsome, when Carrière is threatening your life. He has sworn, in all the salons of Paris, to ruin you and you can only think of watching Bomba at his tricks. You behave like a demigod watching men's pettiness, not like a man likely to be crushed by fate. It's insanity."

Jules laughed, "What if I am a demigod and never told you boys!"

"Fool," said William and flung out of the room.

From Bomba the next day Jules had a note:

DEAR JULES,

The storm has been beating into my poor shelter these sixty days and many, many thanks for the *stopgap*: it will not be forgotten and I am bending every effort to retrace my steps and even go forward. Your instructions religiously followed and I will shortly bear you full details to Paris on the Kreuger business. Will be more happy than I can say to re-integrate our circle again: your optimistic genius requires not only a curb, but an aspiration and what you have but chafes. I know your dislike of correspondence but write me soon even if on the back of an 'order to self'! . . . The foul oil emitted by Jacques Carrière around the bank spreads and spreads with every tide. Be advised: he is a nuisance and should be drowned now. To be aide-drowner would be my only pleasure. Give Claire-Joséphe my best and sincerest and take the residue for yourself.

As ever,
THEODOR

P.S. Tramp-Dannevig says Kreuger must go under but I see rainbow horizons, the pot of gold having been found in the U.S.A. But whether to invest—another question!

To tease his brother, Jules left this note on his desk, too. But the same afternoon, retribution visited him in the shape of a telegram from the irrepressible Bomba:

ARRIVING PARIS IMMEDIATELY WITH DETAILS REQUIRED AND A FOLLOWING TELEGRAM: SOME HELICAL THINKING REQUIRED HERE.
BOMBA

Jules did not show this telegram to his brother and was himself rather disturbed, for William had threatened to resign if Bomba showed his nose in the bank again. Jules decided to make Bomba visit him only at his home. When he had a further telegram from Bomba telling the date and hour of his arrival at the North Station, Jules instructed his chauffeur to call for Bomba (whom he knew very well by sight) and lodge him in some middle-class hotel in the Place Malesherbes, out of the way of the bank's superior employees and its clients.

Scene Sixty-four: Definitely Not Cricket

ACCORDING to his plans of some months before, Jules, Alphendéry, and Adam had set up in London a small business, the London Reinvestment Guarantee Banking Corporation, with one bank clerk who called himself "manager," Manrose Thew, Esq., one stenographer, with nothing to do and one office boy. Mr. Thew had spent the first two weeks of his employment (the first after two years of misery and hunger) having himself measured and fitted for six suits and two overcoats, the bill for which he immediately sent in to Jules Bertillon, on the ground that it was a "business investment." Jules paid for three suits and one overcoat and Mr. Thew therefore found that the bank had started off with the left foot, as regards himself at any rate, and showed evidences of a cheeseparing spirit. He next suggested that Mr. Bertillon, being a multimillionaire, as was generally known, should stand him at least a good secondhand car and running expenses as this would save taking the railway, changing to buses and indulging in other irksome and unnecessary expenses. Mr. Bertillon, however, refused this small request and Mr. Thew, in no good humor, set out by train (but first class, of course, to make a good impression) to sundry "large centers" where he visited, according to his report, sundry family solicitors, heads of firms, small bankers, local managers of great banks, and other persons likely to put him on the track of small *rentiers* needing immediate cash or solicitors willing to "advise" their clients to discount or

511

deposit their stocks and shares with the London Reinvestment (etc.) Corporation, an affiliate of the distinguished Paris bank, Bertillon Frères, which was (it was commonly said) backed by "high finance," possibly a great Alsatian bank. But this happy confidence, invented by Mr. Thew, had a dismal effect on the Midlands and the North which have little if any faith in Continental or American banking, although an unlimited belief in their own. . . . After about five months of this, Mr. Thew explained to Adam that it was little use his soliciting this business, that there was a defect in the set-up which was that when people drew commercial reports on the London (etc.) Corporation, they found out that he, Thew, only drew six hundred pounds a year, a petty salary, and that therefore it appeared either that the London . . . Corporation was merely a booth, a stall, a pushcart, or that Thew was of no importance. The remedy he suggested was the raising of his salary to one thousand pounds a year. Commercial reports would then paint him as someone of consequence, and immense prestige would surround a bank which could pay one thousand pounds to a man from its very inception.

Thew now wrote a very irate letter to Jules. He had found out about the proposed Bank Insurance Company. He had found out that though Adam Constant visited him, when in London, Adam had not confided in him the secret of the Bank Insurance Company; and that this was an indignity as he regarded himself "justly" as the earliest and most important supervisor of the bank's activities in London. He did not know of Caudal's company or its connection with the Bertillons. "How," he asked Jules, "could he get business if he was ignorant of the bank's activities? Persons asked him about the Bank Insurance Company just being formed, and he was completely in the dark: it made him look small, trivial; it made people look askance at his own institution. Did Bertillon (people asked) now intend to devote his energies to the Bank Insurance Company and not to the London Reinvestment Guarantee (etc.). This is the question that has to be faced. Not to mention," went on Thew, "that he was not told of the true position of Mr. Constant. In short," went on Mr. Thew, "let me explain myself this way: we English have a term taken from the realm of sport—cricket. It means, being sporting, fair play: this, Mr. Bertillon, was definitely *not* cricket. I understand that Mr. Constant advertised for and engaged a manager for the new (and even now inchoate) Bank Insurance Company. Surely I, with my knowledge of the city, would have been fitted to assist Mr. Constant in this task of selecting a trustworthy man from the numerous and possibly unknown English types which presented themselves."

Adam found himself called up from his window to Jules's office. Jules handed him the letter. "What do you think of Thew?"

"Vain, self-indulgent and lazy and he will eventually make trouble," said Constant.

"Fire him, close the offices of the London Reinvestment Guarantee Banking Corporation, tell Ledger to take the books, the safe, and the key, and to put the name on his notice-board. We'll just keep the name by us for future use," commanded Jules.

Adam got up. "I will."

"And," said Jules irritably, "I don't want you down at that window any more; I want you in an office. Tell William to give you an office. I want you to run the London businesses."

Adam countered humbly, "But I don't know anything about these businesses, Mr. Bertillon: neither investments, banking, nor insurance."

"Neither do I," laughed Jules, in surprise, "at least not much: you don't make money by *knowing* anything. You make money by having a game and employing smart dumbbells to work at it for you. I'm setting you up, Adam! You run the Insurance Company, but you employ an old insurance manager to do it for you. Isn't that sufficient? Go on: if you want to know anything, ask Alphendéry. That's what I keep *him* for!"

Adam retreated and in a speechless daze found himself shortly installed in the room with the strongbox, where the gold was kept, with a beautiful glass-topped carved desk, ten drawers, two bookcases, and a map of the Mediterranean. Alphendéry was delighted at the innovation and every time business palled nipped round to Adam's room for a whiff of conversation. Adam, after waiting honestly for some work to put in an appearance, for three days, set himself out to finish his book of poems, and he presently made such progress that he was able to

513

approach a publisher and promise the book for early spring. Alphendéry almost danced with pleasure at this and said, "Wouldn't it be too funny if your book of poems proved to be the only constructive thing this bank ever produced?"

"It's also keeping forty Paris homes going," grinned Adam. "Isn't that something?"

Thew got the sack, with three months' salary, a good reference, and a heavy trouncing from James Ledger, who was delighted to find himself so deep in the bank's affairs and who also took a private pleasure in censuring people who didn't "toe the mark" in his estimation.

Thew wrote two letters to Jules Bertillon, one insolent and complaining and (after the trouncing from Ledger) one pitiful and pathetic, "Am I to go back into the helpless misery I came from? What chance have I of ever getting a job again. I admit I was foolish, vain and unreasonable. Take me back. I will work as a clerk in your new insurance company: I will not complain, even if I only get three pounds a week. I have a wife with cancer and an old mother."

He wrote the same to Adam Constant. Jules came into Constant the same day and murmured, "Write to the poor wretch and tell him I'll accept his offer: he's to work in the London Bank Deposits Insurance Company as a clerk—no gadding about—for four pounds a week, and a raise to six pounds when we start to get premiums."

Adam, though, had moments of amazement: the "London businesses" only had entries on one side of the ledger, the debit side—advertisements, leases, solicitors' fees, incorporation fees, paid-up capital, taxes, salaries, trips to London. And this Mississippi of cash flowed out without a murmur from Jules, without a sign of fluster, embarrassment or worry, without a demand for a return: idle employees were kept on the books for months and if thrown out, were only thrown out for outrageous impertinence and were usually re-engaged if their case was pathetic. The only conclusion that Adam came to was that Jules was indeed wonderfully rich and that there was indeed some high financial interest behind him. And on this point Alphendéry, frank usually, was hazy and of two minds.

Adam had to leave off his poems and make another trip to London before Christmas and this was to engage a manager for the Bank Insurance Company. The first man had been unsatisfactory. Constant therefore chose this time an Australian who had had long experience with a big insurance company in the United States, a large, slow-going, genial, confiding fellow, ruddy, with a thick white-blond thatch and sea-going bright blue eyes: his name, Noel Dinkum. Everything he was given to do made Dinkum happy: he undertook to confer with Ledger, send out circulars, keep a stamp book, train a stenographer, organize the "service": he was to receive further instructions, and to learn how many men he was to employ, from Paris "next week."

And thus for weeks he was left posting circulars: Jules slept, Adam wrote poems, Ledger wrote letters cheerfully covering every stage in the business, Dinkum sent in his checks for salary and anxiously inquired of Adam whether he should pay three pounds or three pounds five shillings to the stenographer, and another distinguished name appeared in the commercial directory.

Scene Sixty-five: The Gemini Angry

THE telephone rang and Jules said, "Yes, Jacques? *What? What* did you do that for? O.K. I'll see you later. O.K." He looked at William and Michel, "That's Manray. He says he refused to give service to Rosenkrantz and Guildenstern this morning. How did that come about, Alphendéry? Didn't you tell Manray and all those boys downstairs to give Rosenkrantz and Guildenstern every help?"

"I did. But don't forget they get it free and as soon as you do a German a favor, he gets a sense of injustice, if he's the wrong sort of German; which they probably are, I'm thinking."

"Go and ask Jacques what the row is about. I'll see the Gemini alone first."

In the corridor Alphendéry crossed Rosenkrantz and Guildenstern who looked at him superciliously and barely greeted him. "They look pompous: storms brewing."

William touched him on the shoulder. "They kicked me out. That idiot brother of mine: he would do anything for

515

a stranger, as long as he was sure he could insult his real friends. Let's get Jacques up and get the lowdown."

Jacques Manray came up with an honest busy face of injustice. They called him up twenty times in a morning demanding quotations and asking questions, so that he had made three mistakes of various degrees of loss to the firm.

"They treat me like a corporal in the German Army. They're only parasites. You don't see it and Mr. Bertillon doesn't see it, but I face them all day long and have to listen. They care for nobody. Reciprocal business? Not the shadow of it. Nevertheless, we've thrown them many thousands in commodity business."

Alphendéry then tapped on Jules's door. The conversation was heated inside. Alphendéry, at Jules's cross "Come in," plunged in, and without his usual tact began to berate the heavenly twins for their discourtesy to employees, their irritation technique, and their bad faith in the matter of reciprocity.

Impudently and proudly, Rosenkrantz replied, "It's impossible to get a client for you gentlemen: you have the worst reputation in Paris."

"True," Jules said. "I've had the worst reputation in Paris for twenty years and more; so has every other small bank. But we all survive. . . . You don't know how to do business, Rosenkrantz. Reputation! I flout reputation! Our business doesn't require reputation: it requires execution."

"Manray cuts me off in the middle of a conversation," cried Rosenkrantz. "He resents my nationality. I distinctly heard him mutter, 'Plaguy Huns!' "

"Why, he has a German wife!" cried Alphendéry.

"No matter, do not contradict me!" Guildenstern cut in. "I say what I say: there is an organized sabotage in the downstairs office against us. I do not go into causes. I insist on an investigation and sanctions being applied against the guilty party. I could lay my finger on him at once. If you demand the name. . . ."

"Our relations have not been happy," said Alphendéry. "Who is to share out the blame?"

"Speaking for ourselves, our conduct has been blameless. We put in an installation, we spent money on advertising: we employed runners. We have been all over Paris dining, visiting, putting your name about, with our own. And what is the answer we get? That your house is unreliable, speculative, that no one knows its funds, that its funds are abroad, that it has enemies in the government, that yours is the most unreliable house in Paris, that it has no big backing as we were led to suppose: by what insinuations, we, of course, disdain to recall. If we had known this, beforehand——I must say it, I must underline it——poor as we were, without resources, we should not have gone into business with you, thus blemishing a long and honorable business career. It is more than a loss in present prestige: it is a mortgage on our future here."

"For the rest," threatened Rosenkrantz, "we know very well what prompted you: you had no intention of really giving us assistance, and you counted on the complaisance of the French courts towards Frenchmen. There's an answer to that. The sinews of justice in this country are well known! Ha, ha!"

How can anyone be so unpleasant? thought Alphendéry. Of course, it is nothing but a Chinese mask to frighten us; where did they get that Oriental stuff? He held out some papers, given to him by Jacques Manray: "These accounts: you charged our clients for cables, and we did the cabling ourselves; therefore you pocket the cable charge. There are other items; I intended to leave them till we came to the end of the six-months' contract and to our accounting."

"There may have been some error made by our accountant; but your sabotage of us had some other reason. We must have a sufficient reason, and some compensation! This is mere accounting!"

Alphendéry said bitterly, "I like your generosity: you come here, miserable exiles, wretched expatriates, the future glowering at you over native land, and here, nowhere to turn. Mr. Bertillon and I take you in, give you a home and a business, and at the first contretemps you rob our clients, upset our workers, and ask for a compensation into the bargain. . . . Don't you think you're scandalous?"

"We did not come here for recriminations," Guildenstern declared, tapping his foot. "We came here to demand that you reprimand Manray, the employee concerned, and discharge him if he remains insubordinate. Or at least transfer him to another department. If the sabotage continues we will be obliged to have recourse to measures which we had hoped not to use. That is all.

Good morning, gentlemen!" They started to march gravely out of the office. Alphendéry went after them.

"Mr. Rosenkrantz!"

Guildenstern turned in the doorway. "We came to
speak to the head of this institution. We did not come to
suffer interpellation by anyone whatsoever. We have
spoken to him; we have made ourselves clear. There is
nothing to discuss. Good morning."

"The prigs," Jules said, cheerful on account of the last
acknowledgment of himself. "They seem to be business
getters, though, don't they? Call Jacques and tell him to
pipe down: he ought to forget his wartime hates now."

"Oh, Jules, you don't realize what those junkers are
like," protested Alphendéry, pallid since the defiance
thrown at him by the two. He was brave for others, but
for himself he couldn't stand insult.

The next morning, Jacques Manray came up to Alphendéry in a sweat of fury. "They insult me over the
phone, they demand to talk to someone else; they threaten
to report me to Mr. Bertillon. And when I said I'd pass
them to you, for you can talk German to them, they refused, saying that they only deal with the Chief of the
House. I won't do a thing for them. And the boys are all
up in arms."

Alphendéry went to see William who said laxly, "Oh,
get rid of them; we've got enough on them, haven't we?
We can always say they sabotaged us, didn't pass us any
orders, charged our clients for expenses, fraudulently.
Isn't that enough? Write them a letter telling them no
more money. They signed with you, didn't they? They
found out they made a mistake and they're trying to
smoodge round Jules, but they're sunk. He's half inclined
to stick up for them and let them ride roughshod over
faithful old employees, because they always call for him
as if he were a king and visit him as if they were ambassadors from Germany."

"Will you authorize me to write this letter?"

"Sure! Why, they're getting you, too, with their official-
dom! Don't take it to heart, Michel. They are not the first
pickpockets we have thrown out—nor the last."

They therefore concocted a letter between them and
sent it after getting Jules's lazy consent. He was sick of
them; although, if they appeared, he thought they were

fair game and then willingly played the part they handed him.

The very next morning the ambassadors from Germany to the Bertillon Bank hove in sight.

"We insist on having Mr. Alphendéry brought in."

"Talk to me," said Jules hotly. "I'm the head here: no one else has anything to say."

"If we are not readmitted at once, our demands satisfied, Jacques Manray at least transferred, and Mr. Alphendéry's real position in the firm revealed to us, we have no other course but to sue."

Jules tried to pacify them, both because he had nothing else to do at the moment and because the Parouart, Wade and Carrière cases had for the first time made him tired of suits. Alphendéry arrived on wings, armed for them, having tossed and turned the affair over since the day before.

"Gentlemen, I am obliged to tell you you are wrong on twenty-two counts and that if you go to law you will get nothing but a bill of costs!" He laughed, his white teeth danced, he positively caressed them with a glance.

"We'll see to that."

"Moreover, don't forget that you are aliens in this country. I don't say that because it means anything to us: as you know I personally have always been your deepest friend; but law courts habitually treat a foreigner worse than a native."

Guildenstern thrust back, "Don't forget that you yourselves can't very well stand another lawsuit. We know that you have two million francs tied up in the Bank of France already, more in the Crédit, more in the Bank of Paris. We have nothing to lose but a desk. You are ready to crumble. We can bring you down. You have no alternative but to compromise with us."

"You still have something to learn—" began Alphendéry, but Jules broke in, "What would be your demands?"

Alphendéry signaled to Jules to let him continue, but Jules rudely turned sideways so that he would not see him. This was perceived by both the complainants, who likewise turned their backs on him.

"First," said Guildenstern, "who is the last authority in this institution: and to whom have we the pleasure of talking when we talk to Mr. Alphendéry?"

"Talk to me. I am the bank," said Jules, in a high tone. "Mr. Alphendéry is my employee like any other."

"Has Mr. Alphendéry any say in the bank's policies?"

"None whatever: he is a mere salaried employee. He has nothing whatever to do with the policy of the bank."

"Then we are to ignore him? We are to ignore the letter sent by him to us yesterday?"

"Certainly. The letter was sent without my knowledge. I didn't want it. I was not consulted."

Alphendéry had gone very pale and said nothing.

"Then" (triumphantly) "if that is his position, how is it that we have an agreement signed by him?"

Jules stirred, looked at his long white fingers tapping on the table. "You insisted on signing with Alphendéry. Who am I to stop you? Alphendéry is of no importance. He has not even power of attorney. Your funeral! If you look at the paper you see it has no seal, no counter-signature. Your haste!"

Guildenstern said impatiently, "It's a trick."

Alphendéry rushed in, in a hard voice, "You have only yourselves to blame. You came here and hoped to get the wedge in through me. You began by dividing the bank against itself. German politics! You thought you'd get Jew against Gentile, subordinate authority against senior, me against Mr. Bertillon. You worked the Jewish-brotherhood racket with me, trying to wheedle the secrets of the bank out of me, and then you tried to sap behind my back in conference with Mr. Jules. You have the hate of both instead of the confidence of all. You expect Frenchmen to work under the whip like your countrymen?"

Rosenkrantz flushed and turned to him, but Guildenstern turned quick as a snake to Jules: "Since this man has no authority here, why does he insult us? Will you ask him to leave the room!"

Jules, irritated beyond endurance by the whole thing, which he had started as a tragicomedy, said, "Leave us alone, Alphendéry."

"I have only worked for your interest, Jules. Why do you allow these two men to flatter you at my expense?"

"Leave the room, I tell you."

A despicable triumph showed on the faces of Rosenkrantz and Guildenstern.

Rushing blindly out, Michel ran into William.

William looked, swung to the door. "What's he done now?"

"Ask him. He threw me out at the request of our faithful friends, the Heavenly Twins."

"He's out of his mind."

"I don't know and I don't care. I'm never coming back again."

Madder than before, Alphendéry rushed into the corridor, his eyes starting from his head. William showed a rare alacrity and tenderness. "Come into Plowman's room."

"No, I've got to get out of here."

"Wait till I get my hat. . . . I'll tell him that if he insults you, I leave too."

"And leave him at their mercy?"

"Why not? If he wants to commit suicide, let him. I'm through. Mlle. Dalbi! I'll be out fifteen minutes at least. If anyone calls from Brussels, you talk to them."

But no sooner were Jules, Rosenkrantz, and Guildenstern together than his fury turned on them and theirs on him, and they parted the worst of friends.

Alphendéry returned with William to his work, soon after his hurried exit, but he did not speak to Jules, nor Jules to him, for three days. Jules, in fact, went about the bank with a stormy and martyred air and comforted himself for his behavior to Alphendéry by telling Plowman several times that Alphendéry was responsible for the misfortunes of the bank; and he found it easy to justify himself. As did Alphendéry.

However, Rosenkrantz and Guildenstern had their own hobbies, and three days later Alphendéry found himself served with a blue paper, in their name, emanating from the bailiff who served one of Dr. Carrière's lawyers, the notorious Maître Lallant. He ran into William.

"Here's the clue! They have gone to Carrière's lawyer. The plot thickens."

"I don't like it," William said calmly. "It was a bad move to take them in, a worse to throw them out. Those boys are hard luck. You're too heady, Michel. We can't afford any more lawsuits. Especially as the lawsuit king is too grand to speak to us and too expensive to put his hand to the plow himself. It only means a dozen more headaches for you and me."

"Don't worry: I'll fight it all myself," said Alphendéry.

And Jules said to Claire-Josèphe, "Those boys are ruining me. It would be cheaper for me to turn William and Michel out to pasture and keep them as I keep Paul and Francis."

"Do it, then, Jules darling," she urged, with some anxiety. "Jules, we have four sons. We have to think of them first. We've had our chance."

"Yes. I'll run the bank my own way."

"Yes, do it, Jules darling. They're always giving you the wrong advice and you listen to them. . . . Jules, does it pay us?"

"I don't know."

"Let's take the money, darling, and go away with it. We owe our children so much. If you keep on, you'll keep paying out money to all sorts of people who have enough. I'd never forgive myself if I thought I'd not given the children their future. They've got to have a start."

He waved his hand carelessly, "Claire, their great-grandmother is still living and rolling in cash. They have nothing to fear."

"Well, at any rate, I want you to segregate the money for them right away, Jules. We must do it tomorrow."

"All right."

Scene Sixty-six: Façade

THE more Michel looked at these façades, fine furnishings, crystal panes, brass rods, chased mirrors, carved frames, and soft carpets, the more depressed he became, the more was he convinced that he had to leave the bank and find another job. This came not only from his natural penchant for simplicity but also from a constant guilty picture in his mind's eye: a ganger sweating on the permanent way and the subtitle "these stones, grilles, mahoganies came that way." It was too much: it was too good.

Raccamond, on the other hand, coming from a sturdy artisan family, which handed down its carved peasant wardrobes and beds from generation to generation, and where lace curtains and linen were still given as part of the marriage portion, was admirably affected by all this, thinking that the grilles in Bertillon's bank, the gilt letters in the Place du Palais de Justice in Brussels and all the rest, with the marquis customers' men and the Rothschild glorified office boys, were all the result of generations of accumulation and saving and only the just reward of a good hard-working breed. For the first time, Aristide, with a new conspectus of the bank and its affiliates, in his mind's eye, looked upon Bertillon's as one of the rising houses. With the hoarding instinct of his blood, he saw Bertillon going from one to the other of his relations by marriage and birth, weaving them into a pattern of his own, or as building a pyramid of influence, stone on stone.

Alphendéry had begun by teasing him but was soon anxious to convince him that the bank was the Canaan of his dreams. "If Raccamond is there," thought Michel, with a sudden access of weariness, "he will fight off the Bomba, out of self-interest, and he will help William, for William will not desert his brother, for all he says. Raccamond will marry himself spiritually to the family Bertillon and a good union it will be. And I shall be free: free to starve, but free, and I won't starve."

Like a lion Aristide now leaped on all the morsels that Alphendéry threw him: he walked among the cities of Europe absorbed in himself and the possible grandeur of the house of Bertillon, Raccamond and Company. He haunted by day and by night the fine white walls and arched entries of the bank and its foreign depots, already talking to the clerks in a haughty tone, with that breath of inner confidence which a feudal master uses in talking to old servants. His head was feverish at night; his dreams were thick and threaded with anxieties—he saw himself bald, gone white in a night, suddenly old and nerveless; he feared that all this would take place before he had the position he had worked and lied and betrayed for all these years in Paris. When he got up in the morning, he had himself well groomed, well perfumed, and then rushed off, passionate, strung up, to the office he was visiting, or to someone who could give him information about persons in the service of the bank. He was always there before Alphendéry, listened silently to everything Alphendéry said in the careless largesse of rhetoric, kept a diary and noted everything down in it, all the connections, all the scandals, all the pipe lines.

Raccamond found that an accountant was lacking in the Brussels office, and he installed there Posset, a man who had worked with him in Léon's office ten years before and who became entirely his creature, being fabulously grateful for the job. Inspired by Raccamond's rich dress, fine eating, dignified air, and the solemnity with which he spoke of himself and the house and moved to a real distrust of and disgust with Alphendéry, whom he pictured as a sort of shifty, horned beast, Posset promised to serve Director Raccamond in all things. Raccamond unfolded his plans to this unfortunate fellow in a *brasserie* in the St. Hubert Gallery in Brussels one midday, the day after he entered the Brussels downtown office in the Place de la Gare.

"You are now getting three thousand francs monthly?"

"Yes, Director. Really, I don't know what I would have done. I'd given up believing in Santa Claus and you turned up. I had thought of doing away with myself. You may be sure I'll be as loyal to you as your own brother."

"Good. I told you my plan for reorganization: a strictly methodical business organization parallel with the splendid organism of social relations set up by the Bertillons."

"It's a very fine system, Director."

"You have to go carefully, not arouse jealousy or suspicion, not annoy old employees: that would not help me at all. But these older employees are embedded in the more or less feudal old business habits of the firm. I want to introduce New World efficiency. I will consult with you. Forward me copies of any books or documents which seem strange to you: we will unravel all the knots. You know these branches are never visited. There has been no check-up. It is a scandal. You understand!"

"Perfectly, Director." And only a shadow round his eyes showed where a smile and even a leer would have stood in more prosperous days.

"If anything unusual comes your way you can send me a memorandum, send it by registered post to my home address. Some of the secretaries at the bank have a habit of opening mail. Telegraph me if you find cause. Take it out of office expenses, naturally. And you have my home address?"

"Yes. I'll do everything you want, Director. I will never forget what I owe you!"

There is something disconcerting in proclamations of indebtedness: the next creditor is entitled to the same fidelity! A crumbling rock on which to build a career; but Raccamond had been in quagmires. Moreover, Raccamond was building a dike and had determined to stop up all possible leaks with the fingers of accountants and others owing him a debt of gratitude. According to the system, he had also installed, within the last few weeks, his former clerk, Perrier, in the Amsterdam office. He was curious about the way the bank made money, about the accounts held abroad, the amounts paid out, the brokers, salaries. Perrier had been reporting, he was none too lucid. He had a jealous suspicion still of Alphendéry: rumor said he had been well paid through participations with the Bertillons in the past. Aristide had cultivated Alphendéry's company during the last few weeks, listened with great attention to everything he said, sifted and weighed, trying to find out his net worth, and his position in the bank. But Alphendéry, with all his fire, his aphorisms and inconstancies, his continual generalizations and philosophies, was constant in one thing: he represented himself as a poor man interested in the poor, and he ridiculed and ran down the rich all day long. This was a jigsaw that Aristide had to put together. Alphendéry, far from reflecting Aristide's jealousy, was far too open for comfort.

"You are right to organize the routine, Aristide. Mr. Jules Bertillon belongs to the species of which Buffon remarked that 'servile imitation costs more than a new design.'"

Did Buffon say it? Alphendéry was such a mountebank that a man had to doubt the authenticity of his authors and citations. He disliked this intense mental life of Alphendéry apropos of anything, nothing; he found it impractical and repeated the well-worn saw of striving dullards, "A brilliant man cannot be sound."

Scene Sixty-seven: The Cholera

SPLENDID Zucchero Zurbaran, with dark skin, bulbous forehead, and deep-set eyes was the very pinnacle of South American society. He entertained the Prince of Wales, married the most beautiful young European actress in Hollywood. When in Paris he negligently deposited his check with, and drew on Jules, along with the other extrarich gallants of his race and type. He never asked for an account and Jules never gave one. In this, Zucchero and Pedrillo were alike. The other South Americans were more businesslike and some of them, though rich, played Jules for a goldfish: but there is give and take in banking as elsewhere. All these dashing young fellows moved in a restricted international, which takes its orders from Paris and New York. They spent money like water and tried to keep down their mortality, manslaughter, and murder account, in order to stay in Paris. These young men are the *ne plus ultra* of today, handsome, rich, lawless, powerful. They are aviators, sports champions, riders. When they die young, at bobsleigh, hunting, or flying, one cannot regret it; they have flown over the Andes, thrown away gold on the roof gardens of New York, been feted at fashionable crushes with sixteenth-century music in London, talked with Hitler, flown with Mussolini's son-in-law, for a prank run out to some new ruins dug up by archeologists in the Sahara, outyachted, outflown, outridden each other; they have had all the toys in creation, from superspeedboats to new drugs; they are the wonderful race, the supermen of a weary, middle-aged European society, these young broncobusters, the carnivorous orchids of South America.

When Zucchero went home to Brazil, so that his two young sons, aged two and four, could be brought up on the paternal acres, Jules was sorry, Mayfair remembered, Paris forgot him; there were others.

William, strolling in one morning, pointed out to Jules that the time had come to send Zucchero a letter ("if he could read," he nastily added). Zucchero's account was overdrawn some twenty-five thousand American dollars. Jules replied, "Oh, leave it; he's good for the money. Zucchero can't stay away from Paris. He'll be back in the spring."

But Zurbaran went up into the sky one blue morning, zoomed over the flashing walls and avenues of Rio de Janeiro, and suddenly came down into the bay. Small Rodolfo Zurbaran became the owner of the several million acres; and William gnashed his teeth.

"Don't worry," said Alphendéry: "Pedro will go home leaving us—what? Eighty-nine hundred dollars. The Zurbaran estate owes us twenty-five thousand dollars. They'll pay. We're in nearly thirty-five thousand dollars. Not much but a mouthful. As long as Jules doesn't conceive the idea of letting it run on till Rodolfo grows up."

"We won't be here then," said William, with more than customary spleen.

Arturito MacMahon, son of richissimes of the Argentine, originally of Scottish stock and devilishly proud of his name, was twenty-eight, blue, handsome, long, cold, and amiable as an English hunting rifle. Even in the bank and among the forgiving and understanding South American society, gloomy tales were told of him. Arturito spoke Jockey-Club French and Eton English, with a cutting snobbery, but if he carried on any conversation any length of time he produced a strange imbroglio of accents of all classes, for in London he ranged from Mayfair to the East India Docks in the raging pursuit of fashion and vice, and in France from the apartments of the Avenue Foch to the bars of the "milieu" behind the Boulevard Barbés and the Mayas of Marseille.

Arturito MacMahon was therefore to an Englishman or a Frenchman an anatomical section of his national dialects. Elegant, smooth, and cold, avid and detached as a black leopard, Arturito in the bank relished its green corridors and shady corridors, spoke to no one except Jules and the richest members of the South American colony. With his somber eyes, he seemed to see visions of hate and ferocity and to ignore all that passed in front of him. As instinctively as they loved Pedrillo, the women hated Arturito, who was nevertheless, possibly the most handsome of them all. Nevertheless, on account of his immense wealth, his unlimited vice, his beauty and elegance, and his savage temper, MacMahon was courted in South American society and it was for this reason that Jules paid him the "small" salary of about twenty thousand dollars yearly. Arturito for this only had to say that he had his bank account with Jules Bertillon and that Jules was a good fellow. This was practically the only work that Arturito had done in his life. His family had made a great fortune out of lumber in the Argentine, and Arturito was the sole heir. He had a superlative head for business and, even at his age, was grasping. He turned in accounts to Jules, who rode, flew, raced, gambled, and dined with him, but so far the profit on those accounts had only equaled about $15,000 yearly. William chafed and Jules laughed elfishly.

No one knew exactly how sophisticated Jules was. Nightly to Claire-Josèphe, rarely to William and Alphendéry, Jules went over his game, spoke of them all as his pawns, gave his reasons, hung up the cloak of irresponsibility and intuition which was one of his great masquerades and charms.

The South American colony was Jules's stay. They liked him, were not penurious or querulous, gambled and spent with a large gesture, paid whenever they were asked: they did not care whether their accounts were right to the centime; they preferred to live as magnificoes and have no questions asked.

But when they were out of pocket they expected Jules to help them out, and he gave them overdrafts for large sums, out of his own pocket and the bank. Every two or three years a fresh river of South American money would flow into Paris, with a new boom, in coffee, lumber, tea, or phosphates, and when a depression came and some Arturito or some Pedrillo had to go home, they sent young men of their caste and more fortunate in some new boom to take their place. Like all children of booms they spent freely and to the last penny, they spent with hope, and returned home broke with hope and often returned again to Paris in a space of time between three and twenty years.

Jules, a Walloon by origin, during the war, founded a friendship with a young French liaison officer, Edmond, who had a beautiful young French southerner for mistress. After the war, when Jules married Claire, Claire and Simone, Edmond's mistress, were great friends and bought their clothes and were seen having tea together. José MacMahon came to Paris, exiled for the assassination of a man of his own class, met Simone and married her. Edmond's second mistress, Aza, married another Argentine living in Paris. Paris belonged to the South Americans during the war, and Jules had known them in their glorious time: they clung to him. He was also both generous, immoral, and fantastic, much in their own line, although quieter. "Soft," Pedro told him he was. "We'd send you to a convent in the Argentine: you can't ride a morning in the Bois but you complain of a raw seat: I've spent three weeks in the saddle, sleeping, eating, drinking, raping, and never grown a corn."

"What were you doing three weeks in the saddle?"

"Whipping the peons when they were troublesome."

The colony Jules called "the silvertails," his English clients and brokers "the umbrellabirds." Arturito had been gone nine months and was receiving regularly a check from the bank for "invisible returns." William was smoldering into revolt, when José MacMahon penetrated the shades of the bank one morning to give an item of news: Arturito was dead, assassinated one afternoon in a street in Buenos Aires. Accident, thief, hired assassin, plundered peon, mistress, feud? No one knew. "And who cares?" asked William coarsely. "Tigers are hard to catch: thank God the world has one less!"

Aristide Raccamond hove busily in sight at this moment, elephantine in a new suit draped rather than cut, to hide his fatness. William called, "Aristide, you'll need an armband to that suit: one of your friends was taken for a ride in Buenos Aires."

Raccamond paled excessively, looked at José MacMahon; William pointed to José. "Arturito MacMahon."

"Do you believe it?" asked Raccamond of José.

"Why not?" José looked at him with dislike.

"You have three brothers."

William handed him a newspaper clipping. "I don't often get pleasure out of reading the paper—excuse me, José; but you know your brother."

José gave his flashing smile. "Unflinching and ferocious —he was rare, even with us: he was the flower of our family, a true chief. The cowards see to it that such men die quickly and by stealth, of course."

William observed that Aristide was ill at ease, even

trembling; he turned his back and was walking towards Alphendéry's door, humped, in his usual curious style of distress, wandering a little from the straight line. William nodded to José, did not smile, said softly, "*He* had so much experience in the Eastern Mediterranean after the war—Constantinople, Smyrna, Aleppo, Port Saïd, Morocco—Marseille! How do such types escape assassination: his back is broader than Arturito's."

William smiled creamily at José. It gave him a real pleasure to gloat over Arturito's death and the other's discomfiture in the presence of Arturito's brother. He detested all the silvertails, except Pedrillo; he detested Raccamond, their customers' man, a curious jack-of-all-trades of rascality.

José took his leave and William went straight to Alphendéry's room.

"I regretted Zucchero," said Alphendéry. "He was a good scout, a lovely boy; but I can't regret Arturito. I felt a tooth in my spine every time that adder glided in." William slumped into a chair opposite Alphendéry and contented himself for a minute with chuckling and flushing; then, "A coincidence! I was out playing tennis with young Mouradzian last night. He told me Arturito was a white slaver in the grand style and Raccamond did jobs for him as well as others. That's the reason he spends so much time down South—it isn't funk at all. As soon as the market collapses and his clients won't put money in the market, he takes time off to look after the white-slaving and drug end. Easy. Madame, that moral dame, covers his tracks and receives his mail at their villa."

"Aristide seemed down in the mouth; he didn't say it was Arturito."

"I never believe in psychology," jeered William. "When a fellow like Aristide walks round with an old man of the sea on his back, it's real trouble, not melancholy. He isn't a poet and he's got enough bread: a man doesn't worry like that over a son forging checks—that's all washed out, anyhow—"

"Why not?" asked Alphendéry, who would have liked to have had a son.

William flapped away the idea, the eternal blond spring of his round face looking forward to no son.

"Hippo Raccamond is in a mess. He's got a bunch of

girls going out, and Arturito's not there to carry out his end: that's about it."

"I wish," said Alphendéry philanthropically, bitterly, "that the people of all the Americas would rise and just wipe our precious clients clean off the slate. I could stand the loss financially. It would be a pleasure to see the Mac-Mahons and their breed stood up against a wall. But Aristide couldn't be such a fool as to be white-slaving. He's terrified of the police as it is, since his two *faux pas* in banking. He's not too bad a fellow."

William bit his lip, smirked. "Forget it!" He flapped his hand downwards. "Forget it, will you? The police! He tricks his income tax, doesn't he? What about his company formed in England, to pay him half his salary, so that only half is paid in France? What about his goings and comings with Carrière? A southerner who behaves like an archdeacon is someone to watch. Young Mourad-zian knows an earful and he hasn't got his knife into Raccamond—quite the contrary: he says he's a fool, who doesn't know how to keep his shoes clean. He says everyone in the white-slaving cafés knows Raccamond. And Raccamond meets Parouart in his famous alley. What for? For canoodling, for friendship? Vultures would turn pale at the sight of either. I've only got one principle in business, Michel, and that is—when a fellow is high in the collar and down in the nose, he's worse than the rest, he's not only crooked, but a lardy fool. Listen, we're all crooks, aren't we? What's the use of putting on the face of a gravedigger? It can only be that he has something in his record which stinks even to crooks." William shifted and went to look in the card index. "I'm going to send in a claim to the MacMahons straight away. We don't have to get rid of Aristide, it's true: the police will be round with a butterfly net, one of these days. Carrière's his friend, but who's Carrière? A thirty-million-franc cheese."

"Jean told me that Laval called him in and said, 'If you want to stand for Parliament in January, you've got to call off the Bertillon affair: it's too unpopular.' At the same time, we've got chiefly foreign clients, we've got the largest slice of the South Americans, Belgians, and Dutch, the floating population, that is: the other banks would like to see us close our doors. We don't want it given out that our bank is a rendezvous of white slavers."

William did not answer for a time, busy over Arturito's

card, then, "Oh, don't worry: you worry too much, Michel. Every bank has its pigsty customers' man, someone who procures, runs drugs, knows the addresses of whores, is a herring catcher for usurers, has an abortionist, a photographer, and a clap doctor on a string—and he can't be a little blenny like Parouart, he's got to look honorable so that the best people can be seen round with him and if the wife drops in, 'This is Monsieur Wetfoot': his presence explains itself, is in fact, honorific. That's why Parouart goes round in tatters. He has not fat on his bones: ergo, he isn't respectable. Respectability is a matter of fat. Raccamond's moral look and his moral feelings are an asset in his business."

Alphendéry leaned back. "He really is moral, that's the funny part of it. But to him there's one giant, shining virtue, white and all-quashing, as a virgin beauty on the Cours Belsunce, and that's big money. And what big money wants he does, he gets, and he gets it with an instinctive glow of self-fulfillment." Carried away by this personification of the psyche of the man he had just been defending, Alphendéry expanded in a rollicking laugh. "Hey-hey! What a mountain of sneak rolls in with Aristide every morning! Oh, William, you and I have a good time looking at the wild animals that bounce in and out of our poor little shop. What would we do if we retired?" But, more seriously, "Don't think I mean it; their company isn't healthy for longer than a few years. After that you see that what you took for a rash is really syphilis. It's time to take a rest cure."

"I'm in that stage now," said William, gloomily, turning round on his swivel chair. "These boys dying down in the Argentine and in Brazil—it's queer. I'm not superstitious; but I think for once Jules is right. Shut up shop! Go while the going's good. Jules and Claire have the same feeling."

Michel looked at him with anxious penetration: was this a warning, the prelude to a dismissal of a sort? He and William knew each other as well as a husband and wife, long, but not too long, married. They talked much of the day in glances, apart from pure news. William turned back to his cards.

"Aristide's always fooling round the card index. He doesn't collect from clients. What does he do? Snooping I guess, to find out our game. 'Old' Berthellot says he prods him day after day for information. 'Old' Berthellot pretended to doze one day, and Aristide goes in and tells Jules 'Old' Berthellot is superannuated."

"He's ambitious, poor flea," said Alphendéry, easily. "I really can't believe Mouradzian's tale: you know what *Grand-Guignol* minds these Mediterraneans have! He's a young man, too, got women on the brain."

Jules lounged in shortly after. William looked up.

"Can't we sell out a few accounts? Fifty per cent of the piker accounts are undermargined."

Jules, white-gilled, white-toothed, white-fronted, waved his hand with a graceful adaptation of William's own gesture.

"Leave them be: I don't waste my time thinking about the small fry. Say, boys, guess who passed out yesterday? Poor old John Tanker, Sr."

Alphendéry did not draw his hands out of his pockets, laughed faunishly. "Say, Universal Cholera is getting the boys."

"Three in a string," said William.

"You can't count John Tanker, Sr.," hastened to interpolate Michel. "He's been dead for years, only he didn't know it: a nicely embalmed corpse. I wonder what he left?"

"That's the titbit," said Jules. "His children have nothing coming to them: he made settlements on them long ago and thought he paid them off. The old man passed out just after lunch yesterday. Two sons and a daughter arrived in Paris by midnight. This morning, his sons came in to find out what balance he has in the bank and to ask for an affidavit from the bank: they're going to fight the will. He just had it in a drawer at home and his sister had it waiting for them. Everything to charity. They haven't much chance of fighting it but they want us to help."

William turned up John Tanker's card: "One thousand Anaconda, 575 U.S. Steel, um, um . . . he didn't get rid of those Eastman Kodak, after all. What do they want us to say?"

"That the old man was dippy."

"Sure, we'll do it," said Alphendéry. "Why not? Everyone's dippy. It's not hard to make out the evidence. Help the boys along; they won't win, anyhow."

"They'll refuse to pay this month's hotel bill," said William. "The hotel will be trying to seize his account."

"I was calculating this morning," mused Jules. "Michel, do you know how much we'd have if Dick Plowman were carried off, say, by his liver?"

"Certainly: old Dick himself has a dollars account with us of almost two hundred thousand dollars. His son, Richard, forty thousand dollars; his daughter-in-law, Mrs. Richard, twenty-five thousand dollars; his daughter, Pearl, fifteen hundred pounds; his son-in-law, he's not much, a few thousand francs; his daughter, Estelle, lives in Ireland, four thousand pounds, half her current account; his son-in-law, Tom, two thousand pounds. Dick has outdone himself lately bolstering you up, Jules, ever since Carrière started to bother you. In all—"

"About three hundred thousand dollars—not bad, eh?" He sang to himself, tapped with his fingers on the blotter, "Not good enough to skip with, but sweet. With the rest—"

"Do you think he's got everything in the world with you?" asked Michel.

Jules answered, "No, these rich men always keep half a million out: they don't trust their last reserves even with their alter ego." His mouth twisted. "None of them. Plowman is certainly protected. I don't have to worry about him."

"Still, as he has stood by you since the beginning, Jules, you'd do better to pay him off," protested Alphendéry.

Jules smiled with scorn and disillusionment. "He's always putting it to me that I should dismiss you, Alphendéry."

When Alphendéry went out, Jules came in to William and said in a businesslike way, with no trace of the guying gibing tone which they adopted before all outsiders, even Plowman and even Alphendéry, "Come over to the house tonight, Will. You and I and Claire-Josèphe will go over everything together. I don't like our position." Lower, "After the English money, the French money will slip. Let's go while the going's good. Trouble is coming. My luck has changed. I lost twenty-five thousand francs at Deauville this weekend. I don't feel like betting on the franc. That's what we've got to discuss. You sound Alphendéry on the franc, see what he knows; but say nothing about our going futt. He'll get nervous and land us in a new mess. He's only a Raccamond with a good heart."

"Sure, sure."

In the afternoon Alphendéry was in Jules's room, at the top of his form.

"The *scandals* of our society appear to be the romances of individuals; in reality they are indices: Hatry preceded the British crash, Oustric-Tardieu indicates a crash in our own country; reverberations will be heard in Europe. In France, the general index of production from July, 1930, to July, 1931, has only gone down eighteen points, which is inconsiderable compared with the U.S.A., Germany, and England, but this figure doesn't give the real story. Our country is going through an agrarian crisis: the prices of wheat, despite the bad crop, are low. An intense crisis has struck the vineyards, although the 1930 crop was exceptionally bad. The quantity of materials used in manufactures has decreased by almost a third. The economist of the *Journal des Débats* estimates that the foreign trade deficit will exceed thirteen milliards of francs. . . . Likewise for the first time we have a state budget in deficit; we have also the difference between the sums which Germany will not pay us, in accordance with the moratorium, and the sums which we owe the U.S.A. The French stock exchange is beginning to feel the effects of the decline of sterling. First, because twenty-six per cent of all French exports went to England and the fall of the pound decreases the cost of English production. Second, the Banque de France holds in its vaults stocks and paper worth fifteen to twenty milliards of francs, payable in sterling; sterling has gone down twenty-three per cent, so that the Banque de France must suffer an enormous loss. A certain number of French banks and industrial enterprises, also, had and have considerable sums in English banks and enterprises. You will remember several failures and several institutions seriously shaken. The B.C.N., controlling the greater part of the heavy industry of the East of France, and installed in the handsomest building on the boulevards, failed: the Comptoir Lyon Allemand and the Bank Chapuis at Reims, both connected with English exportation, failed. The Banque de L'Union Parisienne, one of the big six which finance the Schneider-Creusot interests and a part of French heavy industry, was badly bunged. This bank has extended its interests to the whole of Central Europe and even in South America. She has a large interest in the Skoda factories in Czechoslovakia, controls a certain number of war industries in Poland,

Belgium, and Roumania. Its shares fell within a year to less than one-quarter of their value. . . . And don't think that it's all over, Jules, because there have been these earth tremors. Worse is yet to come. It's sure. It's therefore a question of whether you want to weather the tempest, betting on the bear side throughout, with a possible exception in England, by contrast, or whether you want to shut up shop and wait till the worst is over. . . . Bank shares decreasing in value, stocks ceasing to be quoted on the exchanges, currencies inflating—this is sure to be followed by annoyances of private bankers, by restrictions, the grip tightening and monopoly growing. Will you stay and face it?"

"No, no," said Jules, "no, no. You are right."

"Loucheur said recently, 'The franc is solid: but take care, no imprudence lest we find the franc imprisoned between countries with depreciated currencies; in consequence of the fall of the pound, British industry will be favored: let us watch our own.' French and American capitalists cried so loud and rallied round the British bourgeoisie; it is not a question of saving Europe but of saving ourselves! We have to save our own bourgeoisie and how? By an attack on the standard of living of the working class of our own country: Britain began by an attack on her own. A fine example. We will see accentuated in France, as in all capitalist countries an increased exploitation and the screw turned on the colonies."

Very far from resenting Alphendéry's reference to the class system, Jules found it delightful, sought pointers from his discourse, as to how to direct his own course, picked up ideas from one who liked them, about the temper of the "working class," how they might be exploited, fooled. He regarded Alphendéry as particularly valuable because Alphendéry "had their lingo," "knew what they wanted": through Alphendéry he thought he could spy the course of the next few years. He hoped for no more. He was no coward, he was not playing for survival: the attraction lay not in the money he was building up, but in what he could "get away with," in the game.

Of his future he never thought; he never thought of his age, although he was just on the edge of forty, surrounded by young spendthrifts and men attached to him since the ageless and casteless generation of the war; he scarcely knew the passage of time; he never had a presentiment of the failing of his own forces. This was due not only to his gaiety and imagination but to the fact that William himself did all the heavy routine work and arranged the books at the end of the year. . . .

Jules interrupted Michel. "What good does that do me?"

"If the reaction wins in France, there will be a general decrease in the standard of living, of commerce, followed by restrictions and the crushing of the small enterprise, that is you, Jules; if socialism eventually wins, we may look forward to some prosperity a few years from now. In between you will have to go through a difficult period. Foreigners are not so frequent in Paris now: you will have to act as a coupon-clipping establishment abroad for your clients, as an agency for gold deposits, a stock-exchange agent for bears . . . and there is no money in that for you, unless you risk your own funds, since you are a bear yourself. You can bet on the franc if you wish, but the French are used to banks trying to make a fortune on the franc and they may catch you. The question in currencies is—the franc, the Belgian franc, the Swiss franc, the guilder—when? If you can solve that, you're a Rockefeller; if not, don't stay in business."

Jules slowly opened his eyes. "What will I sell short?"

Alphendéry laughed. "You haven't the guts to sell Kreuger and Toll."

"Why not?" But Jules got up languidly, exhausted by the lecture, as he had always been at school. "I'm tired of selling short: I'll see. I've got to get a haircut. Maybe the Belgian franc? What does Léon think? See about the Tanker memorandum, get eye witnesses, you know——"

He took his hat and coat. When he had gone, William said, "He's going to the movies. No sight or sign of the magnifico till tomorrow: that's something to be thankful for. . . ."

"Kreuger and Toll," began Alphendéry——

"Forget it: we're short two hundred thousand shares already—it's enough. If Kreuger crashes, it'll be months off with their etching the thing out, and the market will crash, anyhow, and we'll be in the money; we're up to the safety valve now. I've a theory we're going to make a fortune."

Alphendéry's phrase. Alphendéry turned chagrined eyes on William: William was concealing something.

The next day Alphendéry went round smiling and murmuring to certain of the employees in the bank best known to the customers and most experienced in their accounts. He said to Jacques Manray, "You remember old John Tanker? He died about a week ago. He left about six million dollars odd, his estate, to charity, not a penny to the family on the pretext that they were all provided for. They're trying to break the will. They haven't got a chance, I believe, and so there's no harm in our trying to help them out. Would you say that old John Tanker was gaga before he died? That is, about the time when he made his last will? Now, do you remember him at all?"

"Of course: many's the time the old fellow sat in that very chair all the morning talking to me. A nice old chap. He was always thinking about his shopping. He didn't eat enough. I used to tell him to take a taxi to the bank, poor old chap—"

When the letter was sent off to John Tanker, Jr., it read,

DEAR SIR,

In reply to your letter of the 30th October, we wish to relate that during the last twelve months of his life, your father, Mr. John Tanker, Sr., visited this bank every business day, both morning and afternoon, to inquire about his position in the stock-exchange department, about the possibilities of the transfer of his specie, and to watch the stock prices. He was well known to all our employees. We regret to have to say that during the last twelve months your father showed numerous signs that his mental faculties were failing; this was the impression given to various members of our staff, by his behavior. He constantly entered private rooms in the bank, without knocking, even the directors' rooms and Mr. Bertillon's private room, asking for persons who were not there, or who had never been in the bank. Having begun a conversation he would suddenly get up from his chair and walk out; he would ask questions, walk out before the response was given, return in a quarter of an hour, ask the question again, and often walk out again. He interrupted important private

538

conferences of our directors to relate some trivial incident. He occupied the time of our employees with relations of quarrels between a member of his family and himself and consulted our clerks about the price of porridge. . . . He was very concerned about his financial affairs although these were in excellent condition, as you will have observed, and was haunted by the idea of ruin, although this was effectively impossible in view of the nature of his investments and gold holdings. He also several times mentioned that he ought to commit suicide because his children no longer loved him, and that his only friend in his old age was a clerk in the bank. . . . Despite his fortune and the state of his health he refused to spend any money on food beyond coffee and porridge or on transport and walked to and from the bank on every trip, so that he often arrived here exhausted and would sit speechless for half an hour in one of the armchairs. . . . When one of of our clerks, the one referred to above, called a taxi for him occasionally on summer days, when he seemed too feeble to get home, Mr. Tanker, Sr., invariably dismissed the taxi with the explanation that he was too poor to afford taxis. . . . When the clerk reproached him he uttered these words, "Men eat the face of the old before death, rats after: I'll have no money-relations with any man I see. Did you notice how his eyes ran over my face calculating how much tip he would get? I never give tips: and they call me, 'Old madman, sordid beast.' " This certainly points to a species of persecution mania.

Your very truly,

MICHEL ALPHENDÉRY

There were tears in Jacques Manray's eyes: "Poor old beggar; the children of the rich are all savages. Why do you do these things for them, Michel?"

Alphendéry was embarrassed; his glasses glinted; he ducked and said with a childish smile, "Oh, at the last moment, Jules and I could not resist sticking the last paragraph in; they're not giving us anything for this. It's not convincing and they'll hate us, anyhow, so we thought we might as well put a little sting in the tail. Why not?

What difference does it make? He's dead and they're bastards. And I'm a whore, Jacques."

His soft bluish pallor arranged itself into masses and shades: he became a mask in the bad light, the mask of tragicomedy, a sort of pathetic minotaur.

Old Richard Plowman came in quite shaken. He had chatted every day with John Tanker, Sr. "Did you see the suit of his children to break his will and stop the bequests to charity on the ground that he was insane?" He sat down. He looked older: they both saw that Dick Plowman, who had been so chipper till yesterday, till seventy-two, would lose hold and age suddenly. At seventy-five he would be senile.

Jules roved up and put his hand on his shoulder. "Don't think about it, Dick: your children are not that sort."

"I've done the same thing," said Plowman. "I've bought them off!"

Alphendéry said, "They're Americans: they have a more brutal way of behaving, they waste no time in foot scrapings—that's why it shocks our European sense, that's all. Why, Dick, your head's not going to start turning at human venality at your age! Tanker would not have been in the least surprised; the proof is, that his will is unbreakable—he foresaw some such procedure! He laughs at them from his funeral urn."

But Plowman was suffering from a revulsion and fear they were twenty or thirty years too young to understand, the fear of the dishonored sepulcher, the unloved grave; as well as a respectable horror at the snatching of a property and charitable piety from a dead hand and soul. He raised his head with a strange look, his lips moved and they heard:

> *How sharper than the serpent's tooth,*
> *It is to have a thankless child. . . .*

A look of astonishment grew: "Why, they are trying to prove their father mad."

"Only make your will so well, Richard, and you'll have nothing to fear," advised Alphendéry.

But Richard was broken by another idea. "Jules, I don't say it's true, it must be a rumor, but they say you sent a letter saying Tanker was insane and appeared bizarre in the bank."

Jules said indifferently, "Not I, I didn't; did you think I would?"

He was troubled. "No."

Jules said coolly, and with cheerful perfidy, to Alphendéry, "You did no such thing, did you, Michel?"

Michel could not lie any more, he suddenly found. "Yes, I did, Jules."

Jules had reddened: a low and cowardly trick of Alphendéry to let him down; he knew Alphendéry's coward conscience. Alphendéry looked grave: he was irritated with Jules finally. Jules said in a harsh loud voice, exasperated, "Michel, why the deuce do you do these things without consulting me? I have no idea of what's done in my own bank! You compromise me without so much as letting me know that you've written a letter. Where is the letter? I want to see the Tanker letter. Get it at once!"

Alphendéry knew the letter was in Jules's desk, under his hand. "I tore it up, Jules! I threw away both the letter and my answer; it was just a fantasy, it will have no weight."

Jules snarled, "What the deuce do you waste your time for then, sending letters with no weight?" He looked to Plowman for comfort. "You see, Richard, how things are run round here. How can I make money? The two of them lost fifteen thousand francs last week." Fifteen thousand francs was a sum paid to Carrière the week before. Jules threw in, "Your advice, Richard, is better than theirs: I don't know why I don't always follow it." In a calmer tone: "With their fantasies I'd be ruined, if it were not for my exceptional luck. I make back at Deauville in a night what they lose in a month!"

Plowman hung piteously round the bank all day getting under the feet of them all. In Alphendéry's office he returned to the attack. He continued, sermonizing Alphendéry's drooping face. Alphendéry had taken off his glasses and his large dark eyes opened rebelliously or melancholy on Plowman from moment to moment like two limpets.

"You're probably laughing at me. You're a great mystery to me: you are half an angel and half a devil, half dishonest and half honest. Pardon me: that's what I say to myself. I'm not a psychologist: I'm a simple man, that's the only way I can express it. I'm sure you're not like that. At first, I thought you were Jules's friend, simply devoted to him; then I thought you were a vaudevillist, a Rabelaisian sort; then I got worried: I thought you were two-faced; now, I know you're not that, but I'm puzzled. . . . At any rate, you must forgive an old man. I've been so upset by this letter, this affair of Tanker. . . . Banks aren't asked for services like that! What sort of a reputation have you? . . . That isn't banking."

A smile was beginning on Alphendéry's crushed face. "Richard, this is a telescoped bank, a private luxury bank: here we do things on the first floor that they do on the fiftieth story in a fine New York bank, that's all. This is a bank between friends."

Plowman frowned. "No honest man could think the way you do, and yet you do nothing dishonest, small things like this letter, squibs they would be if it weren't so macabre, so horrible. . . . Alphendéry, I'm certain that Jules would make more money if you left him. Please leave the bank. I'll help you with some of my friends. I can recommend you: I know you're a good man. But you need someone who can stand up to you. Other men, men of another type, would take what you say, sift the grain out of the chaff, but these boys can't. I'm making no imputations on your honor. It's strange, but you're honorable, straightforward. You're extremely subtle. It's the question of Jules especially. These boys are more to me than my own children, or rather, Jules is and dear Claire. It's selfish of me to talk this way." He wiped his eyes. "You have your life, I have mine. I'm an old man. I'll be going the way of John Tanker."

Alphendéry looked at Plowman with pity. "I don't see them so much, Richard." Rarely, he told himself that Jules was a snob: Alphendéry would not wear dress clothes and further had not dress opinions. Jules, who flew all the color of rebellion in business, at home with his "Babs" and his "Camillas," his "Tonies" and "Alines," kowtowed to their fluff universe, and Claire, a sensible woman of character, babbled incessantly in a baby accent simply because it was the fashion.

Richard murmured, "I'm not jealous, Michel. It's another thing. You make them think too much about their place: that gives them a sense of futility, so that they don't construct—they only think of bearing the market, destroying, getting in on 'rackets,' as they say. Then, you spoonfeed them, you dramatize the bank for them; they see too far. They talk things over together like two boys playing back in the nursery."

Plowman looked at Alphendéry calmly, with his dignity of old bank manager. "Without Jules this bank is nothing, empty stones; your talk is clever, but it leads nowhere. Without Jules you could shut up shop tomorrow. Why do you hobble him? Jules is not only brilliant, but solid: a rare combination. Akin to genius. And modest, so he thinks you have more brains than he, and he listens. I know you've a good heart. If you'll consent to work elsewhere, Alphendéry, I'll give you what introductions I can."

Alphendéry's eyes were moist, he looked at Plowman with a curious mixture of resentment and self-deprecation: by moments, his eyes scintillated too, with amusement, with anger—it was hard to say.

"I can't see myself in that light, Plowman."

Plowman hardened. "I'm not fanciful, I'm not theatrical, I don't pretend you're an agent of Moscow." His simple staid face, with its lines of married ecclesiastic, comfort-loving, full of unresisting, blue-eyed compromise, tried to place a penetrative suggestive look in Alphendéry's candid and now rollicking brown ones.

"My word," murmured Alphendéry, restored to calm and watching the old man with circumspection, for, after all, his job was in question, "you give me credit for a lot of spiritual cross-purposes and moral power, Richard. Are you sure you're not taking me for a Jew; you know, the hornèd Jew?"

Plowman flushed. He had always been a sensitive liberal. After a silence Plowman said, "Jules's idea was to make a fortune; now, what is his idea?"

"To make a fortune," said Alphendéry, laughing all over again, tumbling into the well of his own fun and glistening.

"No," said Plowman. "I don't see the same thing now. Now, he wants to win at all costs, when others are losing; he wants to be brilliant when the rest of the world is going bankrupt."

Alphendéry said with gravity, "We get in clients with the idea that they will destroy themselves, that what they do is wrong, fated to ruin them, that whatever they do can only bring them nearer to the day when they will be begging their bread or living on their children. Tanker escaped it by dying too soon: nevertheless, his fortune declined by three million dollars while he was with us, and that entirely without any aid by us. But apart from this natural mortality in business and private fortunes, we have now reached a stage of the world where all rich men of mediocre fortune, that is, all but the very highest, who have already banded themselves into iron companies, are going under; the poor have been bled since all eternity; the middle-class doesn't count any more—its blood has been sucked: now is the turn of the medium rich and they are our clients. Whom have we on our books? Only one or two shareholders of the Banque de France, for example, and then they have given us the parings of their business. Our clients belong to the parvenu and accidentally rich, who are rapidly being shorn of all they have. Every year or two, storms come: the plums fall, some into our lap. We wait. Is that criminal? Is that 'destructive.' We are small prospectors, Richard: we must be satisfied with washings. We're trimmers. Consider Jules's nature, too. No, my function with Jules is most serious. I know his function, I know his chances. I instruct him carefully in them: he makes no mistake as to his role. He is a raider. Don't forget he and I have made some twenty-five million francs since 1929 on my policy."

Plowman regretfully nodded. "I don't deny it; but I deny it was made on your policy: it was made on his."

"You don't understand the postwar world, Richard, if you'll forgive me saying so. You walked into a neat subaltern position in a banking system already past its golden age. Look how astonished, even wounded you were when Insull weakened: you knew Insull, you could not believe that such a 'fine fellow' would be involved or would be the fantastic he suddenly appeared to be. And Lord Kylsant, a noble lord: dear me! Ah, worse is to come, Plowman—your green old age will be full of surprises. Kreuger will crash, bigger fellows than that will crash before you're through." He laughed, "You have a definite impression that I'm responsible, at least partly for the crashes of Loewenstein, Hatry, Royal Mail, Besnard, Gualino, Oustric, and company."

"You're making a joke of it as usual, Michel."

"If you examine your heart, Plowman, you'll find you have that impression: you blame me."

Plowman was silent for a moment, then said with an evident lack of determination, "No, no, that would be simply an antipathy. I only mean—there are incompatibles, as they say. You should be working with brilliant men of the world, with an old banking family, with—with men like yourself, of—of—with—"

"With Jews?" hazarded Alphendéry cruelly.

"No, you know, Michel, that I am—and have always been almost fatuously philosemite. No, I mean with men of a profounder European type. European? The fact is in the East I've met Chinese of your type. The same fatalism, the same cynicism, the same disbelief in everything."

"How you misunderstand me, Richard!" said Alphendéry affectionately, flattered. "I am neither fatalist nor cynic; I am a young-hearted optimist; only I have hope in things not yet born." Alphendéry looked at him with glittering eyes.

Plowman suddenly felt immensely fatigued. The emotion of the morning, the fear of death, disputation. He hardly knew how he had taken this bold step with Alphendéry. He had dreamed for over a year of evicting Alphendéry, kindly, respectfully, if possible and with no financial loss to Alphendéry. He had lain awake at night, reasoning with the docile shadow of Alphendéry.

Plowman smiled a little: "Well, good luck, Alphendéry, but I want you to seriously consider my proposition. You don't perhaps recognize your own—hem—"

His old friend Frank Durban had entered the room and was standing round and solid between them.

"Hello, Frank!"

"Hello. Take his advice, Alphendéry," said Durban. "You've had the good fortune to get a reputation of wizard and mystery man from the nitwits. Get yourself a good job while you can. Anyone will take you at the moment in Amsterdam or London, even farther afield. The cholera is going about, and I'm cholera-wise: I smell it here!"

Plowman murmured, "Frank! A joke is—"

"A joke! Priests tuck up their skirts and run when it rains, even though they believe in God; this place looks all wet to me. You're a fool if you stay, Alphendéry—but you have your reasons for what you do. This old cobber of mine is a double-fool, fool-born and fool-matured: his boys, his Jules, his William. I don't have to wonder what his boys are thinking about in secret: I know. Take your money out and buy a lot in the cemetery, Richard: it's better than burying it in Jules's vaults."

"Hey, hey," cried Jules, coming in at this moment, "do I hear anyone talking sense round here? What are you doing, Durban, forming a bank yourself? Do you call that British fair play, whistling away the flowering staff of my old age. Without Richard where would I be? He's my fount of wisdom, the only man who doesn't believe me when I say I'm a crook; a sort of combined father and mother to me: I never get on with my own and I've adopted Richard. Frank, I'll sue you for alienation of affections."

He smiled ineffably on Richard. Richard, steadied, smiled fondly at him. "Just Durban's way."

"The hell it's my way," cried Durban. "I mean what I say and Jules knows which one of us still has his wits about him. It's all right, Jules: this old fool will stick to you till the last. I'm giving him good advice, but he'll frown at me and reproach me. I suppose if you took the shirt off his back, he'd forgive you."

"Eh, eh, eh," Jules cried seriously, "Frank, what have I ever stolen from anyone? Hey, hey, where's the evidence? Instinct is all very well! You John Bulls have your privileges, but if I lost Richard I'd be a boat without a rudder. If Richard wants his money, he gets it at once, instanter and over the counter, he knows that."

Plowman got up. "Frank! Jules, it was only a joke, his idea of a joke; I've known him fifty-two years, he never had a bit more sense. He got away with it out there in the wilds."

Durban shrugged his shoulders, looked bluntly at his old friend. "You were always a mooch, Plowman: I don't give a damn, except that I've been jogging along by your side all our lives, before you were married, during, after. We went to the same school, we belong to the same clubs, we're real imperialists. And now our partnership's going to break up—I won't be able to give you the dressing-downs you still need."

Jules let the legs of his chair come gently to rest on the carpet.

"Where are you going now?" asked Plowman.

"I have a warning," said "Rhodes" Durban. "I've always been in good health: I'm a good standard clock. I heard a whirr this morning, let's put it! It's my belief that in two days I won't be here. I don't know how I know, but I know." He smiled at them, passed his hand over his face. "Making a scene, what?"

"Sit down," said Alphendéry, pulling at his sleeve. Durban laughed without amusement, said to Jules, "I leave Plowman to your mercy: I'll leave him something in my will, not to be touched till he comes of age, you know."

When they had gone out together, Alphendéry brightened. "The death of other people usually cheers the old: they chalk up each one they bury and it gives them an extra kick. It wasn't old Tanker's going under, it was the dispute over the will. Even the dead hate to have their pockets picked."

William said nothing. Then, brusquely, "Jules is becoming more like Clément every day."

"Clément? I thought he was a sort of café philosopher with run-down heels!"

"That's another of *his* tales, probably invented to please you! Clément's another of our burdens. He pays five thousand francs a suit, you know, and his clothes don't fit him because there's nothing inside them. When Clément comes into the room, you think, 'How his clothes creak!' To tell you how brainless he is, he goes home to change his clothes six times a day, takes a taxi. This is Clément getting dressed." William heaved up his slow blondness, deftly took a light pose on the carpet between Alphendéry and the door, forward on the ball of the foot, one foot advanced. His face had an expression which made him resemble the thinner Bertillons, Jules and the others, quaint, mercurial, anxious. William unbuttoned his waistcoat and eased his tailored, semistiff cambric shirt round the waist of his trousers, darting glances into an imaginary pier glass. "That way: no, no," he murmured, worriedly resetting a gather. He stuck two fingers into his waistband, giving a delicate hitch to the trouser leg. He consulted Alphendéry, "Look, William, look here a moment, now is that right? Or do you think the crease falls too near to the inner line of the leg? No, I think it's better eased—look, how do you think that looks? A little tighter. A little fullness is necessary but not too much. I'm slender. It's a question of being as close to the ideal as possible and yet remaining individual. It

547

seems to me this height is right. Look, William! Should I tighten the braces? The trouble is that when this leg is right and this leg is right, the catches on the braces are at unequal heights. Now, what do you say to this? So, so! Yes."

William slumped and fell into a chair. "For two hours together," he said gloomily. "And always smiling, always watching his walk, trying to catch the look of his hat in glasses on shopwindows as he walks along Piccadilly, Fifth Avenue, or the Boulevard de la Madeleine. Always a pair of new gloves, worn once, always the same ties and cuff links as Jules, the same shirts, socks, suits as Jules—because the monkey has the sense to see that Jules looks better-dressed than he does. It's like a photomaton picture trying to look as dandy as its original; it's like these raw dancers in vaudevilles in the suburbs who imitate Fred Astaire: everything there but the man and his elegance! That's my brother Clément. Oh, Jules likes him, Jules keeps him—and to date he hasn't cost much more than his tailor's and shirtmaker's and boot-maker's bills. He's had two wives to keep him. Now he's on the loose, that's the bad part. Jules let him go to Germany in the skirts of some society girl who was stuck on him; now she's got sick of him. Clément can always get a rich society girl to take him out for three months; he proposes marriage to all of them. He'd marry them, too. But his charm wears off as soon as they have been through his wardrobe once." William gave a smile of complicity. "Not too strong in *that* line, either, believe me: and you know that sort of girl—she doesn't buy blind."

Alphendéry had finished laughing over William's comedy. "But does Clément gamble?"

"No, I only said that in a general way. Oh, no, Clément is very mean, very niggardly. He'd rather go without a girl for a year than buy a coffee for one. If he does by accident find himself in the uncomfortable position of being forced by circumstances to buy a girl a coffee, she has to listen to his life history and innermost thoughts and personal tragedy as well. And the continuous silence is more than any girl can bear: the result is what? He always loses the girl. No, as to the gambling, I only meant, Jules was going to seed."

Alphendéry got up, made a move to get his hat. William proposed that the two of them should go out together and "leave the bank to that sap" (his brother Jules, its owner). In the men's room, they found Pedrillo cavorting and exclaiming at the top of his voice, "Oh, Jules, just now on the Boulevard de la Madeleine. Jules, oh, oh, oh, I nearly fainted, oh, ouch, ee, ee, what a girl! Oh, what girls this morning. And this one, I assure you, Jules, the finest, the—*ai, ai!* what a neck, what breas', *ai, ai!* I couldn't control myself, I started after her! Oh, oh, what a world, what a stupid world where such women, who ought to be—oh, just the mere thought—ouch, Jules, hold me up!" he fanned himself with his hat, which he had before folded into a desperado shape for some previous comedy. "Fan me, Jules, feel my head, feel my wrists—ee, ee, when I think of how I might have loved her. I can't stand it, I foam at the mouth. William, like this, I held her"; suiting the action to the words, he grasped William's arm and shook it frantically, rolling his sexy glance into William's annoyed face. "I could hardly stand. Oh, darling, darling, darling!"

William shook him off: "Say, try your stuff out on Alphendéry, he's got more charm."

Pedrillo stood up and put his hat on his head. "And she said she would call a policeman! And what eyes, what a glance with the words! Could see she loved me, worshiped me, I could see she was turning to fire! *Ai, ai*—someone in a pair of pants comes up, 'Monsieur!' 'What did he say?' 'I don't know!' 'I love her,' I shouted to him. Oh, oh, they pulled me off! What a scene, what a world! I love her, I can't bear it, Jules; what shall I do?" The whole accompanied by frantic gestures, mimicries, the most serious accents and desperate gestures in the world. Jules, after laughing gently, prepared to leave the large white-tiled room, one of the really intimate corners of the bank.

"All that doesn't make me a sou, Pedrillo," he said cheerfully, "you and your adventures. Why don't you be decent and go home and see your dying father?"

Pedro frowned. "I hate a pants civilization: I won't go home."

Jules turned back in the doorway. "They'll filch the estate from under your nose then, Pedro."

Pedro looked vaguely about, as if he thought Jules was referring to Michel or William; then his glance returned

549

to Jules. He brightened. "You mean, money? Oh, the peons bring us money."

"Your brothers!"

"My mother," said Pedro vaguely interested, "and my cousin, the one they want me to marry, always stand up for me. I have nothing to worry about, absolutely nothing." He frowned. "It's true my mother says the Jesuits are intriguing to get money for a new church. *He's* built forty-seven chapels for them. They threaten him with years in purgatory." He appealed to Jules with a glance.

"Go home," said Jules promptly; "the old buffers wander at the last: he may get mad with you, Pedro!"

"It's a choice between harem women and cabaret women at home," said Pedro. "You see?" He appealed to Michel: "I look at the plains, I see steers grazing: I look at the women we have to marry, the same cow foreheads, cow locks, cow eyes, cow hoofs, cow gait, cow shivers, cow bellows. If you think that interests me! Here, I see grand passions twenty times a day: what women!"

Jules said dryly, "Now don't fall into a trance, Pedro. Go home, see the last of your old man, and then come back. Marry your cousin and leave her to manage your business. Do it for me, Pedro: I want you to."

Pedro suddenly made a diabolic grimace, showed his teeth, lifted his head like an Aztec image high up, in the sun, pretended to whip out a revolver and shoot it off, while yelping and howling like a dog, shake it, curled his lips in an intense grin of vengeful vanity. Pedro relaxed. "My dear brother Julio!" He bowed low, as if presenting a number in a variety show. "A brute, a savage," he said coolly. "They are all complete savages down there: I don't want to be near them—I wish I had been born in Paris. What a shame to have to go back to those barbarians, for a miserable inheritance! How they bore me!" He yawned, took on an expression of hopeless ennui. "Pranks of bloody squires, mixed up with illiterate superstition. The women are the same, savages under their rolls of fat and their cowish pale wide foreheads and cowish jowls. Do you think love can be interesting with such primitive brutes? They have no elegance: their idea of fun, for example—nothing but jokes about buttocks, beds, and—members." He made a grimace. "If a woman is indelicate, I can't love her: it makes her a combination of the mother, the slops woman, and the cow: taboo, in other words. And you want me to go back to that, Jules, you a Frenchman, a Parisian! Puh!"

"Then stay off them, for a month or two; you can do that surely, until your father passes out."

They walked out and Michel and William after them. William was cross, having been interrupted in his confidential mood. At lunch he was sulky, but towards the end, he said with difficulty, like a young girl admitting that she has felt the pangs of love, after all, "I was going to tell you, that is, about Jules. Never say a word to anyone! No one speaks about it and I am not supposed to know even—I would only tell it to you: my father and uncle were both lawyers. My uncle gambled away all he had, embezzled, converted, shot himself. My father worked himself to death to repay—died of a cancer; that's the story! He died just before the twins were born. You see what the family is? I'm slow, Clément and the twins are—minus. Jules has all there is, except sanity!" It was the last of diverse family histories.

Michel gave him a good smile. "There's not much to the idea of family heredity, William; I wouldn't worry. The theory that genius, or whatever Jules has in that line, is akin to madness, is also a moldy old one: don't let that eat into your night's sleep."

William shook his smooth shoulders. "Nothing does that, nothing. Cannon fired under my window wouldn't wake me." They ate. "Nevertheless," said William irritated again, "Jules is gambling—more than he's telling us. I sniff, I trace, I snoop, I find out things here and there. He asks me for money to transfer to private accounts, to buy gold. Where does it go? I don't know. He won't tell me. 'It's safe,' he says." He lifted porcelain, strange eyes on Michel. Michel thought, again, as always, "If any of them go mad, this one will: it's always these slow, unbending, ingenuous natures that break." A romantic idea of his perhaps? And the way William's idea buzzed round and round, like a mechanical leaden hornet that could not get off the ground through having no vital spark? Round and round, maddeningly repeating the same maxims, the same fears, the same assurances, until Michel was ready to scream, like an hysterical wife. He saw William, the broad dull rainy plain of Holland, and beyond that a curtain of cloud and beyond that some sort of shapeless terror. Imagination again! He knew that his febrile imagination inspired not only the Bertillons but others with unease, discontent, and dislike, at certain times. Jules regularly said about him, "One grain planted differently in your brain, Michel, and you would be a lunatic!" That was the misery of working each for a private ambition; the hopes of the others were mysterious, hateful, and insane. He sighed.

It went on like this day after day. "If I don't take a ticket to Alsace," said Michel to himself, with a lowering expression, "I'll go clean crazy. It isn't the speculation, it isn't the clients all going mad with notions of the millions they might make, it isn't Jules with his hunches and cries, it isn't Estelle, it isn't my mother scolding me for not being a schoolteacher or a government official, it isn't my weakness in not joining the communists: no, it's William. I can't stand his drone; I'll take French leave some fine morning and that will be the last they see of me."

"You should have seen Aristide's face when I told him Arturito was bumped off," cackled William. "You bet he was in on the white-slaving racket with him. Young Mouradzian had the dope."

Michel snapped his fingers. "Waiter, another black coffee." Would it continue?

"And this afternoon," said William, "first thing, he wants to get me to find a buyer for his house down in Biarritz: what does that look like, I ask you?"

Scene Sixty-eight: No Money in Philosophy

JULES sat at his desk, and William leaned against the bookcase full of the classics of political economy and statistics.

"Can't you stop your pal from going mad? He's been ticking off Michel and telling him he's ruining you, that he ought to be singing happy days are here again. Tell him to pipe down, won't you? We don't want Alphendéry running out on us in disgust, just when we're going to need him most. You know that the entire reserves of the bank have been withdrawn twice; we're getting them back again, probably only for a third withdrawal. This wolf Carrière means to sink you. How are you going to arrange to fly with a flea in the flue, if Michel isn't here to hold the fort?"

"You haven't told him yet—you fool!"

"Keep your shirt on: I haven't."

"Anyhow," said Jules cantankerously, "if it weren't for listening to Michel's bolshevik boloney, I'd be worth a hundred millions today. It's fatal to know too much: a hunch is worth a hundred items out of *Die Welt im Zahlen*. If statistics made a man rich, every Poincaré-emulate would become a Rockefeller. Statistics are a heavy meat, indigestible, they send a man to sleep. What does a pirate like me want with philosophy? Did Jean Bart want any philosophy? Did Prester John? Philosophy is by the timid for the timid. The men who have made billions have hardly been able to write their own name. Let's fire Alphendéry. I thought it was a lark. Now, what do I know? I believe he is really a communist. He's one of their agents, for all I know; probably the police follow him."

Jules scowled. "This is my bank: I don't want anyone's name on it but mine. Alphendéry is too much of a circus, anyhow. I don't want smart men: I can do the thinking. I don't want a salon here with philosophers giving out epigrams or whatever you call them—anagrams, for all I know. What do I care if the system's wrong? I know it is. But I'm wrong. Look at Plowman! No need to say, 'What an ass he is!' But look at the money he made by simply believing in 'the system.' Of course, 'the system's' wrong for those who aren't on top. Do you want Plowman to get angry with me? You want him to draw it out before we make the grand getaway? Let him think we're fighting Alphendéry. Send Alphendéry away and let Plowman and this ox Raccamond think we've put things to right. They'll both be pleased as punch. I can manage my getaway without Alphendéry. And think of Carrière! Carrière will think I've lost 'the brains of the firm.' It doesn't suit me to have everyone saying, 'The power behind the throne is Alphendéry.' I want my name to be the name; I want my name on all the accounts; I want all my accounts to be in my name; I want myself to be the directors of my holding companies; I want my holding companies to be called not the Holding Company, but Bertillon Deposit Co.: I want the Zurich trust, to be called, not Claire-Josèphe Trust, but Jules Bertillon and Sons, Incorporated: what am I in business for? You're married to Alphendéry. If that boy ever gets on the witness stand in our case, and if the *Humanité* starts to say he's a dirty capitalist we're done for. He'll do anything to prove he's their friend." He ended on a high note, almost a scream.

William looked at him medically. "I want to tell you one thing. After all Alphendéry has been to you, and the way he's worked for you, while you were away, you can't insult him. If you're going to insult and annoy men like Alphendéry who've paid for all your fantasies by their hard work, you've got to do the same for me. I've done the same for you. If you think it good policy to send him away to calm Plowman's nerves, ask him to investigate Brussels, Geneva, Antwerp, anything. Ask him to set up a new London office, a new London or New York or Oslo office. It's cheaper."

"Another thing," said Jules with intense preoccupation, "Raccamond hates Alphendéry. Raccamond is asking too many questions. He's acting funny. I think if I sent Alphendéry away, Raccamond would calm down: he'd see no one between himself and the throne."

"When are you and Claire going to Geneva to release the gold?" asked William in a low tone.

"Next weekend . . . I'll tell you tonight. You'll get the tickets. I'll tell Jean de Guipatin to say I've gone to Deauville for a couple of days."

"I don't like that cake-eater the way you do."

The old porter came in and William departed.

Meanwhile Alphendéry had been extremely restless and unquiet and had nervous crises every day, sometimes fainting in the evening when he came from work. At the end of this week, the morning before Jules left for Geneva, Alphendéry, with crayon blues in all his hollows and lines, came in to say, "Jules, I think I'll have to ask you either for a holiday or a release. The air of Paris is getting me down. Another thing is, I can't go about openly to meetings and the like here, out of respect for the bank; and then anyone from Upper Rhine, Lower Rhine, and Moselle is suspect, especially watched by the police. My father and mother were German . . . that is, Alsatians under German rule! I think perhaps I'd better take leave

554

of absence and then look for another berth. It's only a
question of political loves, not human loves. There's no
one I love more than you, Jules. But I feel I have no
future in Banking."

Jules said soothingly, "Yes, I know, Michel. Anything
you like. You can take a three months' holiday and then
leave. I'm sorry to see you go, but I know how you feel.
A man at your—our age—has a right to change his
destiny. I'm going to Deauville tomorrow; think over what
you want to do, and we'll talk it over when I come
back."

"Thanks, Jules."

"Nothing to thank me for: on the contrary—"

He said to William, "There's something about old
Michel: he's positively psychic."

William said, "His mother! he worships her. He complains about her but he's crazy about her! He told me
there was no one who could tell character from faces
the way she could. She was famous for it."

Jules, who hated his mother, laughed elfishly. "She
didn't know his too well."

"You expect a mother to know her son? Well, for
Michel, perhaps it's better this way."

"As long as he gets out in time, or stays with us to
the end: that's what's essential with his nature. He needs
a coward's excuse, or else to be pushed to the wall."

Scene Sixty-nine: Léon's Letter

ALPHENDÉRY went up to Amsterdam, Léon, after hanging round the bank for a day or two, had not made
his offer, and Alphendéry wanted to find out why. On
the Saturday afternoon Léon had nothing to do. He bought
a dozen newspapers, ordered some coffee, and imprisoned
Alphendéry in his hotel suite while he talked to him,
boasted, romanced, grew loud and tender by turns, all
about himself. Alphendéry, worn out by a week of wran-
gling, stretched out on one of the beds and listened to
Léon, going and coming, going through his lengthy toi-

555

lette and spinning out the web of things seen and hoped-for.

"Why do Bertillon's schemes fail? He has solid ones," asked Léon, and hurried on, for fear Alphendéry would answer. "I'll tell you, I'll tell you, my boy. Listen to me. I've studied him. . . . Although he has very large ideas, he is a very mean man: he is frightened to go into partnership with people who have ideas, with people with more energy than he has; he's frightened to see me, to school me in his business, to grant me participations. He lacks a sense of loyalty," said Léon triumphantly, lifting his head nobly and looking all round the room and out into the street, as if he could call on anything, the picture frame, on anyone, the streetcar conductor, for example, to say how loyal Léon was.

"Yes, sir, he has no loyalty, and he thinks others won't be loyal to him either. Now, I say to myself, if that boy's going to work for me, I've got to give him a square deal. . . . Then," he frowned, "Michel, it don't matter how harebrained his schemes are, they'd go up if they were built up. He lacks the constructive urge, Michel. A creative urge and a wholesome urge. He has to go down to build it up even if it's a house of cards, like one of these toys you blow up, one of these. . . ." He went round flipping his fingers.

"A balloon?" queried Alphendéry, with shut eyes.

"No, one of these toys—"

"A Mickey Mouse?"

"Not a Mickey Mouse, anything. You got to blow it hard while you blow it, while it stands it's got to have air in it, while it stands up—like a model of a ship, it's not a ship, it's not for freight, but it's got to be built just the same."

"No," said Michel, "he's an actor—a great actor. He would have been a superb actor. Sensitive, reflecting—"

"An actor. But he couldn't put on a show. An actor is an actor, a show is a show, but he couldn't put on a show, you have to arrange it. . . . You know me: I'm very persistent. I'm a pest but I know how to put on show. . . ." In a lower tone, he continued rapidly, "I kept on going over it: he left me with the impression that he had the wheat deal from A to Z, every delicate point, the light and shade. But somehow he gave me a very curious impression, that he had it superficially—"

"As an actor learns a part," said Alphendéry.

"No actor. Like a feller whistling a tune: you think he knows it, he goes down to play it on the piano, and you see he doesn't know the notes."

"He always believes in lying to his own side," said Alphendéry, almost defending Jules.

"He's got trackless, trackless—" Léon's voice trailed off.

"Trackless?"

"Trackless: it proves his bank account's shrinking, *I* think. You know what he is? He is one of these half-baked *Goyim* with a bit of a *Yiddischer Kopf* and it drove him mad. . . . I said, 'Are they going to drop it in the Gulf of Mexico? . . .' It was a stroke of genius, Michel. Genius, my boy! I said to myself, 'How to put the market up, revolutionize values?' The millers were buying hand to mouth. It was the golden opportunity, my boy. . . . And I thought, 'It suits him, because he can only make money when the rest of the world is fut.' "

"He can shake down the plums but he can't get them to his mouth."

"That's it . . . I'll never understand it. . . . Those Bomba! . . . It was a calamity," he suddenly said, very loud and cheerful, standing right above Alphendéry. "It was disastrous." His voice trailed away into the wardrobe. "My girl's . . . h'm."

"He never recovered from his plane accident."

"He thinks his star cracked. He's a man of one star. I chose the Milky Way. Ho, ho, ho! . . . Listen, Michel, if I become an English O.B.E., will you work with me in England?"

Léon revived his project for a letter to the cabinet.

"Why not," asked Alphendéry, "write straight to the President of the Board of Trade? Let's get down to the scheme and write the covering letter afterwards."

"All right, all right." Then he smiled wisely. "No one can say I don't work for my golden crown. Mind you, I don't say if I get an English honor. I put my capital there. The rest to follow if all is satisfactory. If not, I'll try to become a Belgian baron first. One or the other. What do I care? It's a business proposition."

Alphendéry spent the weekend getting out Léon's letter to the British cabinet and scheme for Government Control of the Wheat Supplies of England. When it was finished, they both regarded it as a masterpiece, and put it at once in the post. Meantime, Léon offered Alphendéry a job and his everlasting ten per cent of all earnings on stock-market speculation advised by Alphendéry. Alphendéry was to take six weeks off, go to Greece, and then join Léon in Amsterdam.

Scene Seventy: Love Letter

DAVIGDOR SCHICKLGRÜBER came to see Alphendéry on his way to Berlin, "to nose things out for the Lord: of course, one of these days he'll wake up to me and find out I simply sleep and eat, but in the meantime, I don't mind taking a holiday from the dear old man, at times. . . . Say, Alphendéry," he continued calfishly, wagging his long head at Michel, "I forgot all about that interview for you with the Lord: next time you come to London don't forget. . . ." Alphendéry realized that this unexpected and dishonest offer was a preamble to asking him for the famous letter to the Berlin blonde. He therefore got out pencil and paper and after some difficulties (for his German forgotten since his childhood was not very solid), he vamped out:

LIEBES GNÄDIGE FRÄULEIN,
Entschuldigen Sie, bitte, mein Deutsch, warum, ich, als Ausländer, schreibe es wenig. Ich glaube dass es war eine grosse Freude fur Ihre Bruder ihnen zu besuchen in Berlin! Es war leid dass in Bahnhof wir hatten so wenig zeit sich zu unterhalten: und besser sich zu kennen. Aber macht dies nicht schöner mein Hoffnung ihnen wieder zu sehen in Berlin. Ich habe ihre Gesicht nur ein paar minuten gesehen aber ich bin sicher dass es voll reizend war . . . Hier ist meine Adresse in Paris. Ich erwarte ihre liebeswürdige Briefe . . . Welche Schade dass ich so schnell nach London müss wiederfahren! Vielleicht eine andere Zeit, also, können Sie nach Brussel oder nach Paris fahren uns nur zu unterhalten. Dann wollte ich viele täge in kleines liebeskämmerlein mit ihnen

leben. Ein Leben ohne Liebe ist kein Leben: und Sie
sind meine Ideal. Schreiben Sie mir, bitte. Höffent-
lich—WILHELM MEISTER. . . .

(Wilhelm Meister was the name used by Davigdor in
his German love affairs. The young lady's address was
Frau Florenz, Poste Restante, in a Berlin postal section.)

After Alphendéry and William and Davigdor had
grubbed around for some fifteen minutes they produced
between them the above linguistic and amorous masterpiece and Alphendéry set to work to copy it out in a
fair hand, Davigdor never wrote to any girl in his own
handwriting . . . In return for this favor, Davigdor gave
them a few pointers, while protesting that he was practically a born idiot and could never understand anything:
that there would be a prolongation of the accord on
German frozen credits and that the politics of Social
Democracy in Germany was all the capitalists of the
world were hanging by, until they had determined on a
policy for themselves. They could only now depend on
the errors of a Bruning, the coat-turning of a MacDonald,
and the ultimate though not now apparent wealth of the
U.S.A. to save them till they tried out some expedient—
possibly an extension of fascism. . . . Davigdor laughed at
those who still pinned their hopes of Germany's paying
her debts and returning to "sanity." "She's between the
devil and the deep sea, between a moratorium and an
inflation: bet on which you will. . . ."

"And the Lord?"

"Ah, ah, the Lord is getting old but he's not so weak-
minded yet as to tell me his business."

"What about Deterding: he is really cuckoo? Is he going bankrupt? Is he going to ruin himself in silver?"

The speculations followed. Davigdor let fall some of
his idiocies, to amuse them: "They say in London that
you're working for Ivar Kreuger now."

"Don't joke, Davigdor: what do they say about
Kreuger?"

Davigdor wouldn't be drawn: "Oh, Kreuger's got a couple of old communists working for him, I thought maybe
he'd bought you in too. I hear you went to the Rothschilds,
Alphendéry, with a scheme for selling Royal Dutch short."

"Yes."

"More fool you," said Davigdor rudely. "A peasant

559

takes his daughter to the landlord to taste and then expects him to marry her . . . no, no . . . oh, oh. No one knows the boys but me; no one but me has seen them skin a flint . . . you boys," he said cavorting, "will all be ruined, all. . . . Hey, Alphendéry, I hear you're sleeping out."

For it was a fact that nothing went on in Paris, Amsterdam, Brussels, or Berlin in their circles, which was not immediately communicated to the other centers; and Alphendéry, "Bertillon's mystery man," was one of the minor beasts in their fables.

"Well," said Schicklgrüber, preparing to go, "excuse me: promised to sleep with a sweetie this afternoon. . . . What currency are you boys going to make a fortune on next? . . ."

Alphendéry threw out his hands. "Sound money's no good, bad money's no good, high interest is no good, cheap money is no good: it requires the leaven of the U.S.A.'s dough before they do any good here, and when will that come? The only thing that would save Europe is socialism, higher wages, higher productivity . . . tell that to the capitalists. . . . I predict a crash in all European markets within three months: there's no hope anywhere. . . ."

"Thanks," said Davigdor, "I'll write that to the Lord."

When he had gone, William smirked, "What's he up to in Berlin?"

Alphendéry pondered, "I've a hunch that the Lord is thinking of punting on Hitler. He's making a mistake, Hitler will never convince them; they've had too much socialist training since the war . . . what has he got to sell?"

William ripped out his usual cranky speech. "You can sell anything to the Boches: they're regimented . . . goose-step heroes with tin medals, like kids. Say, you don't know them, you're too sentimental; you can't change a Heinie overnight with a few speeches about sharing the wealth or whatever it is. For all they know, this Hitler can really change things, turn the big ones into little ones for their sake: they invented fairy tales, didn't they? They still believe them."

Alphendéry was irritated beyond endurance by William's crabbed stupidity. "I know them better than you, I'm an Alsatian."

William laughed bitterly: "You're too open-minded,

Michel: intern your mind, shut it up; don't be so fair-minded. This isn't a fair world; this is a lousy world since the war, and it's going to get worse. You can start a society for the prevention of cruelty to tigers but that doesn't stop even the kitchen cat from chewing your leg off, if it's hungry and you can't shoo it. . . . Say, Michel, if you hadn't been living off rich men all your life, selling yourself with your sweet line, would you be so soft? You would have had to bring down a few birds yourself before this if you hadn't struck it lucky. It's too late now: you mark my words. And if your bunch of Red friends don't get tough too, they'll go down before even a Tardieu or a real ironsides, another Poincaré."

Instead of answering, Alphendéry got up and moved through the door; he walked up and down outside in the corridor. William was getting beyond endurance. Inside William shrugged his shoulders to himself and sulkily went to look through the card index. Thirty-five clients under-margined: he was going to call them for margins this very day. Alphendéry being kind to the clients and he, William, had to face a half-empty cashbox! For this secret, the inroads made by Carrière's campaign, on their reserves, William had never revealed even to the observant and experienced Alphendéry. No one but Jules's eldest brother would ever know Jules's danger.

The telephone rang; William called, "Michel, Davigdor on the wire for you."

Davigdor said, "Michel, there are rumors all over London that you're looking for a job elsewhere," and laughing with a certain emphasis, Davigdor put down the telephone. A girl was laughing beside him. Michel knew that this was a warning.

"What do you want to see the Lord for?" queried William suspiciously, leadenly. "Are you trying to land a job with him?"

"Not at all; but I don't see what harm there is in getting to know one of the richest thieves in the world. It will be a great help to me later on, if I write."

William's voice held a bitter note: "You wouldn't use your own name when writing for them?"

"No, perhaps not . . ." said Michel dubiously.

William cried with one of Jules's pets, "I think you're getting us into a lot of trouble: Plowman says everyone says the bank has Reds in it; you know what these mugs are where their money's concerned. How do I know that that isn't behind these . . ." He nearly said "with-drawals." He changed it to, "cases that are being hurried through the courts against us at breakneck speed. . . ." He laughed, somewhat ashamed.

While Jules was away and Alphendéry absorbed, Aristide Raccamond was taking the subordinate chiefs of the staff into his confidence: Henri Martin, one of the chief cashiers, a brilliant, close-keeping fellow, well knit, solid, giving an impression of manliness, was one to watch out for. Aristide had it on good authority that Martin was a retired war spy and had sent seventeen men to their death in Alsace. Why was he in Bertillon's bank? A friend of Bertillon, it was said, picked up during the war. But why? Was he set to watch Bertillon? Was he watching Alphendéry? Was he simply doing nothing, earning his living? Did ex-war spies ever simply earn their living? At any rate, Mme. Raccamond, consulted, warned Aristide to have nothing whatever to do with Henri Martin.

Jean de Guipatin, really Aristide's friend, was loyal to Jules before all others. This left Urbain Voulou and the customers' men upon whom he would not call, and Jacques Manray, manager of the ground floor, a loyal and ready fellow, sensible, experienced, and cheerful, who had confidence in everyone. . . . Raccamond, concurring with Marianne, his wife, had therefore cultivated Jacques Manray's acquaintance, and the two had begun to visit each other's homes. But Jacques was cautious. Nevertheless, in his honesty, he talked over some of the troubles of the bank with Aristide. Marianne, after their second visit, smiled to Aristide, "He is a man for you. Count on him."

Carrière found that Aristide was not bringing him enough information now: he expected Aristide, he told him, during Jules's absence, to get on the inside of the bank, learn its secrets, and take the opportunity to make his grip felt, to announce himself as director pretty generally, make Alphendéry take a back seat. He invited Aristide to his home to a private lunch with his secretary and then, confidentially, showed not only that Jules had cheated him on a plain exchange contract but that Jules was bankrupt: if he had the money, why didn't he pay and get rid of the counterpublicity?

Scene Seventy-one: Aristide in a Stew

CARRIÈRE attacked Jules and the bank every day in the widespread press of his friend, the Deputy Sournois, and the more he attacked, the more Jules absented himself from the bank and filled in his time swimming, yachting, riding, gaming on the Mediterranean and Channel coasts. The mess of lawsuits, clients' demands, rumors, and blackmail petitions became the daily meat of William Bertillon, Michel Alphendéry, Adam Constant, and Jacques Manray. All of these four were haggard and harassed. The customers' men as well as the cashiers began to lose confidence in the bank. William tried to be even more thick-skinned, Michel even merrier, to make the place more lively. Clients clustered downstairs but there was an unhealthy plaguy atmosphere in the bank: the Carrière-Bertillon duel was the subject of all conversations. The clients became suspicious and touchy; the workers in the bank foresaw the ruin of the bank and their unemployment. The luster was turned on every day in Jules's room, and William and Michel entertained visitors there to warm the place up, but Jules was not to be seen and the spirit of the bank was missing: the bank seemed to have gone soggy like a house of cardboard left out in the rain.

Michel and William had now taken counsel and secretly sent several emissaries to Carrière suggesting settlements, variously of seventy-five thousand dollars and eighty-five thousand dollars, but Carrière had refused even to parley. His close friend, Comte Jean de Guipatin, found it impossible to influence him. He was honestly out for Bertillon's blood.

Raccamond saw not only ruin but conspiracy ahead of him. He got to the bank early in the morning and as soon as Mouradzian arrived took him aside trembling and said to him, "Have you heard all the rumors about the bank?"

Parisians, women, South Americans, who came into the bank and saw little Mouradzian, a desiccated man with crafty face and brilliant eyes, in the gangways, immediately thought him a crook and white slaver, a blackmailer, a danger to the house, perhaps a sell-out too; clever and dishonest. But it was not so. He was a great admirer of Bertillon, in his moments of genius, and of Alphendéry. And as for the "rumors": an Armenian after two thousand years of buffetings, would he bend before a storm in a teacup such as this quarrel between two rich young upstarts? Whenever the bank and its troubles were mentioned on the Bourse or else round the cafés, Mouradzian listened, picking up all the information he could for his own sake; but he gravely declined to take any part in the discussion or to give any opinion. He was an Easterner, a deep one; not a monkey or a parrot like most of his compeers.

"I'm fifty years old and I've heard a wash of rumors in that time. . . ."

"What are we to do? We can't get accounts now! Everyone throws the Carrière quarrel in our teeth."

"People must put their money somewhere," murmured Mouradzian.

Aristide became more and more restless. "Do you think it is not your duty as a respectable customers' man, to withdraw your accounts from a bank with this reputation? Do you think it right to risk them? I am terribly worried; I have so many fine names." He bent closer to Mouradzian. "Besides, I have firsthand information Carrière is really being swindled; he has a contract with Bertillon. Dr. Carrière told me himself."

"Of course," said Mouradzian. "Otherwise, why would Bertillon pay a sou?"

"I thought it was a question of honor between two *gentlemen*, two *clubmen*." Aristide used the English words, to give his idea more distinction. Mouradzian watched him with dark, unspeaking eyes. Aristide hastened to say what he had come to say, "Mouradzian, I regard you as an important figure in the bank. You have excellent clients. I confide in you this information which I have directly from Dr. Carrière. Dr. Carrière is sure to win his suit on the exchange contract and he intends to ruin Bertillon. If you and I consort, withdraw our clients together, we can make a very impressive entry into some other bank. We can control the situation so to speak! If you wish to team up with me—"

"Thank you, *confrère*. I will think of it. You have begun relations with another bank?"

"I have always done a little business with the Crédit. I always keep a door open. We all do——"

Mouradzian nodded his head. "Good: I will think of it." Aristide was taken aback. "You are leaving your clients in danger!"

Mouradzian rose politely. "Pardon me, *confrère;* I have my reasons."

"Wait, wait! What do you make of the rumors proceeding from the Parouart case and others, that the bank takes a position against its stock-exchange clients?"

Mouradzian sat down. "I hope it is true."

Aristide paled. "Why?"

"The client is always wrong," said Mouradzian. "The bank is sure to be liquid if it has taken a position against its clients." Aristide began to tremble. His chops fell, his eyes started. "But Mouradzian, they are betting on our clients' ruin; where is our living to come from?"

Mouradzian's eyes darkened, but he said amiably, *"Confrère,* I go to a big capitalist and I say, *'This Bertillon Bank is a famous contre-partie* (offset) *house.'* I do not know if it is true. That is my selling talk! I say to the personage, *'This bank cannot fail.'* "

Aristide slumped in his chair. "But it is abuse of confidence; illegal!"

Mouradzian continued without paying attention to this objection, "And I do my best to protect my own clients; that's all." Aristide looked at Mouradzian with dislike. "But if anyone got their books he could ruin Bertillon!"

Mouradzian took out an immense silk handkerchief and wiped his little, bald head, "What good are books, what good is ruination? Profitable accounts are what we make a living from. Bertillon is rich. Why shouldn't he try to welch on Carrière's contract? Why shouldn't he save the money? A scandal! People who don't like scandals should not be in finance! Scandals should be limited by influence, that is all. Bertillon is rich. Bertillon likes good society. That is all that should interest us as customers' men." He got up again and toddled off.

Aristide thought, "Yes, indeed, but he has no position to think of! I have wedded my luck to this bank—immoral little Easterner! And what clients he has!"

When he reached the bank he learned that Mouradzian had just brought in as a client, Paleologos, a Roumanian statesman famous for thirty years, a democrat who had lined his pockets and his safe deposits with gold, who had squeezed streams of gold from exchanges, shipping, contraband, ministerial power, taxes, perquisites, a Midas with a reputation for liberalism and learning.

"These foreigners come here and place our accounts, take our place," thought Aristide; for he could not get rid of the idea that Paleologos should "by right" be his.

Sunk in the great armchair in the entrance, Aristide waited and watched for the clients. Alphendéry's voice was borne down from the gallery. "Mouradzian's family has served the Paleologoses for nearly a hundred years; Machuca's family were treasurers to the kings of Spain and Greece; Achitophelous has had the great families in Greece for a hundred and fifty years; what a team, boy!"

Mouradzian came back to the bank while Aristide was still sitting there. He gave him a rapid indecipherable glance and moved quickly upstairs. He wished to have no collision with this fellow of peasant dramas and storms. Mouradzian had the lofty contempt of a race which counts backwards. He well imagined the reflections of Raccamond. Forty years in business of all kinds had left him no illusions, much astuteness, elasticity, and resource. He had never gone into business on his own account because he had taken his own measure from the first: a man to spin silk off cocoons, not to make silk cloth by the yard.

Aristide, like a sick dog, crept out of the passageway. He heaved his great body out of the chair and into another in the board room, waiting, watching for a crisis. It was yet early and no one was about that he knew. The telephone rang and Jacques Manray spoke into it, "Yes, Mme. la Princesse. . . ."

Aristide bounded. He had to himself nearly all the princesses that there were in the place.

"I will verify it, Mme. la Princesse! Will you wait an instant?"

Jacques came back and said, "Yes, Madame, this afternoon, whenever you like."

"Why didn't you tell me? What does she want?"

Jacques, although angry, looked at Raccamond, drooping and sweating. He thought, "He's got something wrong; syphilis maybe, a persecution idea or something. . . ." He said amiably, "The Princesse Delisle-Delbe, as you heard, wants an appointment with Mr. Jules, or Mr. Alphendéry. I arranged it with Alphendéry. It's about her account. . . ."

Aristide bounded. "And you didn't try to talk to her! She's complaining that she's been overcharged for New York state tax on her American shares. What if she withdraws her account! How do you expect to eat if she withdraws her account? Why don't you calculate the taxes correctly? Every week I am hauled over the coals over some mistake in the accounts."

"In their favor," said Jacques patiently.

"Mr. Bertillon always adjusts."

"Mr. Raccamond," responded Jacques, "you know as well as I do that most of the time the clients are wrong and we pretend they are right in order to soothe them. You can gamble on it, that they know how to count and that they know as well as we do that they're cheating us. I've been in this business since I left off being a captain in the war" (he had to get this in), "and I've never seen an honest client yet, comtesse or king. The ones that behave the best are the gamblers and professional crooks, they'll take a loss, but your comtesses don't impress me, they're petty thieves. Don't worry yourself so much about them, Raccamond," he said with some pity.

"You take orders from me," Raccamond cried, getting excited. "Here I am a director; I know nothing about Alphendéry. This is my client."

"Why, yes," said Manray, surprised.

"It is not right; it is irregular; he has been allowed to— Mr. Bertillon is too—" there was a faint line of saliva on his lips, "too—kindly," he bit the word and threw it from him like a dirty piece of fat. "Mr. Bertillon allows himself to be guided: a man without a position here, without any recognized office, works secretly—how do I, or any of us know what is going on here? We work, I work —I bring all the big accounts into the place (those that are not taken from me), I have all the connections, and Alphendéry—is the only—director you know—and the others! The others are the same! This is all incoherent. Who is the chief of the customers' men?" he asked Manray, with tragic satire. "You don't know? There is none! No one knows anything here. I don't understand it. Can a man work for an anarchy? We are throwing our work away, Manray; you and I, too—it's hopeless; what's the good of our struggling?"

Jacques Manray's color had receded; he looked at Raccamond like a doctor.

"Sit down, Mr. Raccamond, you are not well."

"I am well. Manray, I want you to tell me as soon as the Princesse comes this afternoon; I must see her first. I am going to telephone." He disappeared, leaving a swirling silence behind him. Jacques sat down. He began mechanically to classify some order slips. "All prima donnas," he reflected.

Alphendéry came in cheerily. "Hullo, Jacques; how's the old general this morning? Still commanding the front trenches from the rear? What's the matter, Jacques? Have the police been bothering you again about Parouart?"

"They were here, trying to get information but I told them they now know all I know. I can't tell you any more unless I make it up, I told them. And there was testimony in the Rosenkrantz and Guildenstern case. I can't get my work done; it's all behind," he seemed about to cry. "No, Michel, it wasn't that; I'm not afraid of the police. It was Raccamond! He acted like a prima donna because the," he lowered his voice and looked round, "the Princesse Delisle-Delbe, one of his princesses, wants to talk about her account, and she sounded all on edge."

Alphendéry looked worried. "She wants to take it out? They have no gratitude; you work for them for years and at the first rumor of trouble, they start a run."

"Don't worry," said Jacques fraternally. "Mouradzian turned up trumps; he brought in the Paleologos account this morning. He's the only one of the lot that's worth his salt. He's upstairs waiting for you."

"Good, good." He started up the back stairs. Jacques cleared his throat.

"Michel!"

"What is it, Jacques?"

"Aristide is in a jam of some sort, acting frantic: look out for him. He's ready to blow. . . . He made a scene here just now; said everything should go through him; said he was a director and you were his subordinate. He's nothing but a scrambled egg of grades, laws, regulations, and authority; never got over the Army—he wants to have the orders of the day put up on a slate every morning. He's going to telephone Mr. Jules."

"About what? Have we all done him wrong?"

"I guess he's upset about the Princesse. Michel! Do you notice anything funny about him? You don't think he's sickening for something? The way he walks? Do you think he's been to the doctor and found out he's got clap? Some men have a nervous breakdown over that. He's that type."

Alphendéry laughed. "Perhaps; why speculate?"

As Michel turned to go upstairs again, Jacques came close and said in his warm, low voice, "Michel, I know Aristide; I've been at his house twice. He's lunatic jealous of you. The whole thing seems to be that Mme. Jules did not invite that wife of his. I think if Mme. Jules would invite her to tea, say, at the Marquise de Sévigné, Raccamond would not be so angry. It's that," he dropped his voice very low, "excuse me, bastard wife of his that sets him on. She's a vixen; and she's got a mother with a face to stop a clock, lives near them, comes and visits them whenever there's a party. Between the two, poor Aristide —I'm sorry for him—hasn't got a will of his own. You mark my words; it's *she* that sets him on. . . ."

"I've always been nice to them both," said Alphendéry, hurt by this. "I've done everything; I pleaded for him to be taken in here."

"Jealousy knows no gratitude; jealousy resents favors."

Alphendéry laughed roundly. "Who can be jealous of me? Am I a director? Do I put a brass plate, COMTE ALPHENDÉRY, on my desk? Do I spend a lot of money? Have I got a car? Do I wear golden raiment? Do I ask the boss to put out a red carpet when I come in in the morning? Do I file my nails? Do I even have my shoes shined? No, you must be wrong, Jacques; no one can be jealous of me. . . . I live—do you know where I live? In a miserable apartment, with one good room, and one room made by running a partition through the corridor. And before I lived in a hotel room in a students' hotel."

On the way up the back stairs, Alphendéry talked to himself and forgot his sudden pet. Upstairs he found William doing nothing but smoking his tenth cigarette of the morning.

"Hullo, Jacques says Raccamond is busting up the furniture because he's a director and doesn't get enough respect. He says he's got a vest-pocketful of new director cards."

"Surely," said William easily. "He visits the branches, appoints a new man here and there, lords it round on a two-sou basis. He's happy and we lose nothing. What do

569

you and I care? After all, you sign nothing; he signs all he can to impress his wife. Who will be in the soup when the soup is made?" He laughed cynically. "Fat pig! Let him chortle; he treats me like dirt. First sign of trouble, and he squeals like his brothers at the abattoirs."

With a sort of gray-flannel malice, he saw things taking a course that would complete the financial and mental ruin of Raccamond. He was capable of much patient fatalist plotting. He continued in the same tone, unpacking his philosophy, "Let the fools struggle to trample on each other's head; what do we care? We're the cabal; they're on the inside-outside. You and Jules and I, Michel, one day will just close up our bags and take a fast train somewhere else, and where will be their vanity then? Let's forget them. You imitate me, Michel. I take no notice of them. I close my eyes to their insults, for I know who is boss. And that is all that's worth knowing. They tussle and snoop and eventually find out everything but the one thing that counts. Fools. . . ."

Michel paled. "We're not making any money?"

"Not a sou: everything we have is going out to lawyers, or is under lien in the banks to fight our cases, or is tied up in numbered gold bars and certificates to clients. This account of Paleologos is a stroke of luck but I don't know whether to give thanks for it or swear at it. I heard this morning from a friend of Toots Legris, who is a friend of Carrière, that Carrière is sure to win his case and then we must pay up or—what? Bankruptcy. At present no one knows whether there isn't something funny in the contract—and you and I know there is! But as far as the law goes, Carrière is in the right. And I was fool enough to believe my brother, who's never told the truth in his life, when he said he never signed a contract with Carrière." He said grimly to Michel, "Don't think you know anything about this bank, Michel! Every day even I find out new lies of Jules's and as for you—you're not much better off than Aristide."

He caught up on his bitterness. "Oh, don't worry, you're one of us; what I know, you know. Jules promised me six months ago not to gamble in the Paris market without telling me, and I find I've got to pay out 120,000 francs in losses since he went away. Cristopoulos, Sweet, the crowd—imagine a man knowing what Jules knows about the game, and yet falling for it! Of course, Jules doesn't know how to tell the truth; he doesn't know what it is. I don't think he knows his own name. He lies about it to himself at night. My name's Evarist Zugger, or let's say, Peter Mugger or better Timothy Hugger: I have twenty million francs, or 150,000,000 francs; I've sold short eighty-five thousand shares yesterday and two million today, that makes a handful of fireworks! What a spendid firebug I am! I'm a genius and my name is Aristide Scarface, I'm a *nervi* from Marseille, I'm Pop-off the anarchist, I'm getting the White Russians on Tardieu's payroll, what a smart fellow I am! That's Jules's conversation with himself at night. An eagle of finance who only lays duck eggs, and who doesn't know whether he's a mocking bird or a vulture."

"We've got to make some arrangements with Carrière."

"How? When he's got a chance to get his knife into Jules? He'd take it for the signal to gore us to death. We've made enough advances to the animal already. He'd think we were afraid. He'd be right."

"He's lost thousands of dollars in the American market. And Mamma won't pay for his losses. He might be glad of the ready money."

"Don't kid yourself. No, we've got to fight this through if we get some more accounts; or scram, and quickly. I don't often pity the lambs, but I hate to see a good account like Paleologos going into Carrière's maw."

Scene Seventy-two: Marianne's Philosophy

MARIANNE RACCAMOND took the letter from Brussels out of the morning mail and read:

DEAR MR. RACCAMOND,

Following your instructions (H'm, she thought, he's cunning: that's blackmail for Aristide in case our specimen gets caught!), I have gone through the books available to me. I must here add that certain books, called, as far as I can see, "books of the Amstel Corporation" are kept in a special safe and I am not allowed access to them, although I have represented to the chief accountant that it is impossible for me to check through unless all the papers are available to me. I have gained the impression that the chief accountant does not wish me to see the key books. "Who is employing you?" he said to me. "If it is Mr. Bertillon, I am your superior; if it is not Mr. Bertillon you have no right here, for you are then falsely on the Bertillon wages account." This man is, as far as you are concerned, quite antipathetic and even makes things difficult for me. Of this, later. In the books that I have been allowed to peruse and check, that is the books of the Brussels office, for Brussels clients, I find everything in order and every order sent through to the Bourses required and filled automatically. I have watched carefully for any sign of trickery or double bookkeeping, but to date I have not been able to trace anything . . . I will not go into my feelings, or suspicions . . . The foregoing is contrary to our expectations and I fear you will be disappointed in me. However, please consider what follows. With regard to the books I am not allowed to see: Mr. Perrier, chief accountant and, it seems to me, the agent of Mr. Alphendéry, at any rate, obliging to him, as well as intimate with Mr. Bertillon, and occasionally his guest, when he comes to Brussels, informs me that these (secret) books represent "special and private" accounts and the records of operations of private corporations run for private clients of large fortune, known only to one or two members of the firm. He informs me that not only is he forbidden to show them, but that he does not himself know what persons or corporations are represented here.

Although I accepted this explanation with a good grace, as I am bound to, I observed that whenever orders came through for our ordinary clients, orders come through, not balancing orders, but companion orders, for these private clients. . . . It therefore, seemed to me that these "private clients" of large fortune are kept informed of the orders of the general clients and that their agent acts for them, following a general line of policy predetermined, an irregular state of affairs, but still not an offense. . . .

To satisfy myself, I resorted to a stratagem, in

order to have a chance to look at these private books. I gave every appearance of having no interest in them and of being satisfied with Perrier's explanations. One day when the safe was open, I suddenly asked the clerk, Perrier's confidential man, for some documents corresponding to entries in the ordinary books, for some cables to wit, and my stratagem succeeded, for he left the safe open and went to fetch them. Thus I had a moment to see the name of the books: they are labeled, the Amstel Corporation, The Alpha Trading Corporation, and Accounts Nos. IA and IB. This is all I have to report at the moment, except that entries are made daily in these books and the orders to which they refer invariably come through from Paris, while at the end of the month, a statement for the first comes from Amsterdam, for the second from London, and for the other two from Zurich. There are therefore four clerks in the know. At the Paris end, my impression is that the person to question is Mr. Alphendéry himself. (Refer to the name of the second corporation.) Possibly, of course, J. is trading for himself under these names (J. was Jules Bertillon). . . . I only wish to add that in the event of any complaint being made by the accounting department here about my activities, you will protect me and make it clear that everything I do is done under your orders. . . . I am proceeding with my work.

Yours faithfully,

Marianne walked in to Aristide with the letter in her hand. "You have a nice case of blackmail developing here, he forgot to sign."

He shook his head. "No, no, he's all right. Poor blighter, he needs the job too badly! He's been out of work for three years: he'd lick my hand. Besides he's got a police record at Brussels. He forged some entries for Paul Méline, when Méline was with Léon. I found it out and threatened to give him up to the police; he begged me to let him off because of his sick wife and children, or some such tale and since I've kept him in mind. . . ." He smiled fatuously. "The little card index is in here," he said pointing to his forehead and looking at Marianne for approval. "He was working for me for a while just before Claude Brothers went down, don't you remember?"

"Your bird of ill omen," she said sarcastically. "I remember. . . . However, in that case, he could write your biography, too."

"Don't worry, he thinks a lot of me, I fancy: he's so grateful for the job. It was quite pathetic. Such changes in a man in three years! . . ."

She hemmed and hawed: "Don't write to him, at any rate, for a week; don't rush him! Let him simmer. Spies are two-edged sharpers. . . ." There were a few moments of rumination. She said anxiously, "You're getting much plumper, Aristide."

"Yes, it's bad fat, too; but I have to eat. You can't follow a diet when you're having dinner with businessmen."

While he read the letter, she looked his clothes over to see that there were no untidy creases. When he laid it down, she handed them to him and inquired, "When and if you have the information, what will you do?"

"Get the books and demand an explanation in the interests of my clients."

She nodded. "And then?"

"See what he offers."

She shook her head vigorously. "No, you must have your demands on paper; so as not to lose your head."

"I never lose my head, Marianne," he began impatiently.

"No, I know; but he's a queer customer: with his head-over-heels temperament you can be caught unawares. Show him the books, have your plan ready, stand firm, yield nothing, and you're safe. You did well enough in the Claude Brothers affair."

"Oh, I'm an old hand at business now."

She meditated. "Listen, Aristide: why keep Carrière au *courant*? A Midas is a dangerous friend. He has no feminine society, besides: that means one door of access is closed. Bertillon is flighty but he's taking to you; you will, in time, oust Alphendéry, I've no doubt of that. Play on Bertillon. My feeling is that you need a straight line of action: playing two men is difficult and it torments you. I believe the crisis will strike France; if so, a straight game is the best: the rotten plums will be shaken off the tree. Perhaps there won't be so much room for the Carrières, with all their money."

"Fantasy," murmured Aristide. "Money is king, especially in a republic."

"Evidently," she continued, "Bertillon is on a smaller scale than Carrière; but my idea is this: drop relations with Parouart and as far as is possible, give up lackeying for Carrière; my uncles will stand behind you—although the Czorvocky Bank mustn't appear to be behind you, or Bertillon will be jealous and suspicious. You must appear as an enterprising lone hand: be servile and modest with Bertillon. He's lackadaisical, vain, and imaginative; his health is poor; he has good relations, among the best, but he has no idea of building a name for himself: he is not full-blooded. You get control of Bertillon and when you have your grip on him, Carrière will have to do business through you, not direct with Bertillon. Two good results: it blunts Carrière's revenge psyche, so that he won't try to destroy the bank entirely, for he will think he can control it through you; second, you will get the backing of the South American colony and the rest of the clients. Jean de Guipatin will support you: thus you are on your way yourself. In the end, who knows, you can retire Bertillon and his brother; bring Alphendéry back under your aegis, if he is willing; if not, get in one of my cousins —we'll see to that. I don't want to introduce my family too quickly, don't think that: on the contrary, I want to keep them under my wing, in my portfolio, so to speak. Therefore the immediate move is, be assiduous with your own clients, cultivate the others, drop the—" she dropped her voice, "—the traffickers of all sorts, and bring in a comtesse or two, whenever you can: he is a snob, for all his easy manners. In fact, this weakness is developing in him: he gambles, goes out more, dines more with comtesses and elegants. . . ." She smiled with rapture. "What a lucky day the day you took on Jean de Guipatin for your fifth wheel! I'll say this for you, Aristide, you give a feeling of weight, people believe in you."

He smiled at her also weightily, murmured, "Yes, people seem to have confidence in me."

She made a grimace. "The trouble is, if the Argentine money situation gets worse our fine gentlemen will be bloating it home: they're an undependable element; the theater is in a wretched way; as to the movies, perhaps the barring of American films will help our actors and actresses but they will never get the salaries of the Americans, and if our actors go to Hollywood, we lose their accounts, they speculate straight through New York firms. Consider the possibilities of a brokerage office in Hollywood! I wish we had the money to shift our headquarters, Aristide! I don't like Europe. There is no confidence. Why do they have to shake out the Oustrics, the Erlichs, the France Mutualiste concerns? Public sanitation? In my opinion, a free society has room for them all and plenty; if they are locked up, their locking-up should be attended by a feeling of relief, not of anxiety and neurosis, such as there is now. . . . Your clients at the bank are not investing in France: they are putting their money in gold and sending it abroad. They're selling their vineyards, their houses, their orchards, their farms—putting it into gold. Even America has no promise any more. America is putting up people who say a bank is bad or unsafe! That's American hysteria; but it's driving our people's money out of America. Where can they put it next? In South America, with Chile going back on bonds, Chile that never repudiated; with the exchanges suspended in Argentina, elsewhere. All the bourses of the world are lower, whether you count in gold or paper. Our government itself has no confidence, it does not want to loan money abroad. What a situation! How are we to make money out of all that? That's the question we have to ask ourselves. Answer: Get a position, whether by easing yourself in, or by blackmail, or by getting your partner in a bad posture, or by any means. Own nothing, have debts, and get control of the board: the only way. When you have by the mere fact of being a male, and of having a string of clients with high-sounding names, got yourself into a commanding position at the bank, then you can talk business, salary, participations. The easiest way is blackmail and with Bertillon you certainly have an opportunity. Our inquiries seem to show that contrary to rumor he has no one supporting him, he is acting on his own, with possibly some large accounts in other countries brought in by the local managers, all men with connections. They are ignorant of Bertillon's business; they are infinitely subordinate. The man who would hold the key to Bertillon's position and business would control the whole network. It can only be done by finding the key and pressing an advantage. Blackmail, in some vocabularies; just plain business, just ordinary virility, however, as we know. I have no fear for the future, although it's difficult and we've got to think every step of the path."

She meditated. "Ask the Hallers to dinner if you see them: when the day comes that they begin to fear gold, and all their ridiculous reserves of jewels and furniture begin to turn to water, they'll do business with us."

Aristide preceded her into the coffeeroom, biting his lip, silent, furious with her for her speculations, although common sense told him that he must listen to her: he picked up valuable points from her—she had the head of a Marcuzo and no mistake. He sat down heavily.

"Did you change the coffee?"

"Yes, but all the brands are bad nowadays; they shovel coffee into the sea and meanwhile the grades get lower and lower. I have ideas, Aristide: I should go into finance myself if I had any money. I don't want to be beholden to my family. I know their stock in trade."

"Women in finance have no chance, even if they're geniuses; there's the jealousy of men—and then they inevitably fail at the critical moment." She smiled at this childish saw.

"Ah?" he smiled cunningly. "Finally, at the sign of Mme. Hanau?"

She smiled wisely back. "I have my fingers on a couple of journalists, one in debt, one a soak, both inspired, to begin with. You know, your Alphendéry—if he would write an article a week, there's a source, too."

His eyes and mouth flew open. "You're drifting now, surely."

She shook her head. "He has no money, he has left his flat and lives now in a little hotel near the Panthéon, the Hôtel des Grands Hommes—think of it!"

"Impossible: he has a mistress there perhaps."

"No. He lives there. They say he keeps an army of dependents and himself cares absolutely nothing for ordinary comfort. He likes to eat well, and he buys a lot of books."

"But he goes to dinner with the Comtesse de Voigrand!"

Marianne laughed. "Gilded slumming, my dear Aristide: a comtesse and a whore who want to make a solid reputation, keep a cheap philosopher at their table. But he is not invited when there is company. I am right, you see!

"Mme. Haller—imagine it—the Hallers have taken to going home by tram, and they invited the tram conductor to lunch! Ridiculous! I have no patience with it, but it has its comic side. A bookbinder tells me that *rentiers* and government functionaries are learning 'a manual art' in case of revolution: they won't get guillotined, see! They belong to 'the workers!' " She became dark red with anger. "All the same, what crawlers! What a yellow streak!"

"All the same," said Aristide, "Alphendéry is neither a bolshevik nor unemployed."

"A little of both," she said in a contralto voice, ashamed of her anger, at the breakfast table.

Scene Seventy-three: Sell the World

"You'LL have to call in Carrière and buy him off," said William soberly.

"He won't even talk to us now: haven't we been sending De Ville-de-Ré, and Guipatin and Dumans and God knows who for months? He's sworn to get me. Lallant, who is his stooge, has collected round him every crook in Paris who gets his living off blackmail."

In between attending to his usual business and writing speeches, at Jean Frère's instigation, Alphendéry now had to run down to the courts two or three times a week to give evidence or argue in several cases. The Wades looked likely to win the case, in which Jules would have to pay the wife one hundred thousand francs. The landlords in the Rue Tronchet looked likely to win. Parouart, Rosenkrantz, Carrière—it had come to the point where William said with truth, "We live only to give evidence against our clients."

They had been confidently assured by not only Olympe, who was farcical, but by Lemaître, who was all that was finest in Parisian jurists, that it would be possible, taking advantage of the natural delays of the courts, to postpone a final decision in Carrière's suit, for two, three, or four years, the same with the suits of the decorators, the landlords, the Wades, Parouart and the Gemini. Parouart's suit had been rushed through at unprecedented speed, and the decision, unexpectedly in their favor, given in record time. But now this case rose again from the dead in the form of a John Doe proceeding. Although they had nearly five millions in caution money tied up while these cases were in progress, they were all gambling on the chance that their "big chance" would come before any of the decisions were given, expecting to weary out their opponents—all except Carrière perhaps—or to seize the one chance in a million before the Carrière decision was given, and place the sum total of their funds abroad. Their daily conversation had now for the most part become a discussion of the chances of their own and their enemies' survival; every rumor to their enemies' disadvantage and discredit was marked up, every piece of bourse gossip favoring them was discounted.

As it was then possible to comment publicly on affairs in the courts, Carrière lost no opportunity of calumniating Bertillon, holding him up to ridicule and innuendo, and even mentioning in small paragraphs the cases of Parouart who recently sued the Banque Bertillon "against X" and the other plaintiffs.

"Carrière is making the mistake of his career, attacking a secret alliance of the Banque du Littoral du Nord. Débuts" (the head of the Banque du Littoral) "won't like that. I'm surprised too, because Débuts is a liberal radical, the same as Carrière." Thus Jules to journalists.

He told William later on, "And what have I to lose?" sitting back comfortably in his cardinal's chair and looking as cool as a cucumber, although all the troubles in the world were buzzing about his ears. "If Débuts asks me, I deny it: a newspaperman's canard."

They comforted themselves that Carrière's newspaper campaign would presently be its own antidote: in the capital of smart-alecks the readers would say. "This Carrière has his knife in Bertillon and that's all." They comforted themselves that Carrière was sinking a fortune in his campaign, in bribing underministers of finance and commerce to arrange quotas his way (in fruits and wines); that he dropped so much money in the market and in gambling that he would soon be pockets inside-out; that he was at loggerheads with his wife, who was sure to shoot him; that Caro, his chorus boy, had left him; that Carrière would shoot himself out of chagrin; that he was in the Oustric mudhole up to his ears: that he was bankrupt and his uncle and mother, who administered the estate, would give him no more money till he came of age "officially" at thirty-five, a matter of three years; and so on.

The employees of the bank were also much harassed and embarrassed by the questions of their friends and families on the Carrière scandal. "If Bertillon had really a contract with Carrière why didn't he pay it? Wasn't it a shame for a man of Bertillon's distinction? What was the *inside story?* Was it true that it was a duel to the death between the two? Why? Weren't they old school friends? Was Bertillon bankrupt? Of bad faith? How did it come about that Bertillon made such a contract, that is, with little consideration, with Carrière, knowing his influence? There must have been an unwritten consideration, probably disgraceful—these bankers, after all, everyone knew — If Bertillon really had the goods on Carrière, and could prove that he was an income-tax evader, why didn't he push him to the wall?"

The employees, according to their lights, answered these questions with different kinds of cynicism and despair. They liked Bertillon, according to their salaries. They had no use for Carrière simply because he was "the enemy." Without doubt, with his campaign against Bertillon he was threatening their existence. Fifty members of French working-class families on the unemployment lists—was that likely to increase the popularity of the government, of the finance minister? Especially at a time like this when the working class needed to be hoodwinked, appeased, when times were getting worse.

In defense of Jules Bertillon his own employees used these arguments. . . .

Michel said, "Carrière's in with the high banking crowd; they'll drop you, Jules, and they'll back him to the finish: don't fool yourself."

Jules frowned: "The Comtesse de Chamfort is for me, Voigrand is for me, Jean de Guipatin is for me: they're high bank, I think."

Michel laughed with self-mockery. "Those two girls are for me, too, as a side line; even Bomba got as far as a rose-garden interview with the Comtesse de Chamfort: she's rich enough to keep her own menagerie." He hastened to add, "You're a lovely, lovely fellow, Jules: you could charm away the consciences and the prejudices of judge and grand jury, even if you'd committed matricide and they'd been paid for a decision against you . . . but softhearted as gold is, it is impervious to the smiles of the poor; and, no use fooling yourself, Jules: in their terms, you are poor. Furthermore, you don't know how to build up a fortune."

"Now you tell me," jeered Jules gently.

"Why not? You think you're a critic of painting, but you've never even drawn a face on your blotter!"

"Ah, ah," grinned Jules, and after a few strokes, he held up his blotter: a very passable face of Carrière, "for example!"

"Hatred, not art," said Michel.

"Ah?" Jules spent a few minutes sketching faces of other persons round the bank. In fact, he had a little talent.

"And what then? Can't I make money? Haven't I made some twenty million francs for you, purely by speculating in the market, these last two years."

"You can't make it for yourself; you can only make it on someone else's risk."

"Defect of temperament."

After a few minutes they both abruptly came back to the center of discussion: Michel said, "Let's work out our old scheme. It will dispel the cloud of blackmailers in a minute. Sell the bank, take a small luxurious secret room or suite of rooms, near the Opéra, say, and do business for a few rich men. It will increase your prestige and make you nothing but money. You can't beat Carrière at the publicity game: all the cards are in his hands. You can beat him at the prestige game, simply by retiring: unheard of move! He'll be furious." Jules smiled slyly at the vision, tapped affectionately on the desk. "Become a mystery man." Jules laughed softly. "Only I like glitter, brilliance, you know . . . old fogies can maneuver behind the beyond. Not me. I'd do it for six months and then I'd be unable to resist the splendor of the façade."

"At any rate, try it."

"I might"; but his expression showed plainly that he would never be intoxicated with the idea.

"Nevertheless, it was your own idea: you suggested it as far back as ten years ago. You were more modest then, Jules—you had a sure footing."

Suddenly Jules cried, "Let me be damned in my own way!" He came down on the four legs of his chair, twisted his face, his blue eyes flashed. "Who told you I wanted to build a bank? I don't! I want to play around and go up in smoke perhaps! Why not! It's my bank, it's my fun. You people are crazy wanting me to make something! What for? To keep you all going! I don't give that much" (a flip of the fingers) "for anyone, understand! I don't want to be pensioning forty or fifty people for life. A mystery man!" He got up and impatiently took two or three steps up and down. "Children build houses with blocks; I don't build. I'm a bear, you hear that." His passion fell off him, like tatters falling off a Prince Charming, his sun came out again. "Michel, I'm a borer eating the leg of the pier!" He laughed, placed his two hands on Michel's broad thick shoulders, shook him: it seemed as if all his vigor was in his hands. He said affectionately, *"Capitalism is spitting blood:* ha, ha! You teach me that, Michel, and then, like a grandmother, you want to see me make a career!" He took a few steps in the room again. "But how did I make my first money? In a *krach!* In the war! And after? During the mad inflation of the mark! And after? In 1929! And now? I lost a golden opportunity when the pound went off: you see? You two are urging me to build, and I'm losing my grip."

"No," said Michel, "believe me, Jules, it's the Fragonards you have at home; their baleful influence."

"I have a hunch," cried Jules laughing, his skin luminous, his eyes jellies of vivacity, "in the next two or three months, there are fortunes to be made—on the bear side; let us bear the world! Michel, we'll become Rockefellers: all we need is the daring! Let's stake everything on a crazy hunch I have! Something tells me."

"Yes?" said Michel very dryly, disgusted. "Is a picture on the wall upside down? Did you run your tire into a horseshoe this morning? Call in the fortunetellers: I'm leaving."

Joyously but with determination, Jules caught his arm. "Michel, you're my fortuneteller, I need no other. The sign I go by is this: when Michel, *ursus major,* as they say, tries to make me a great figure in the community, a real catastrophe is coming: why? When *they* have converted you there's no one else to convert! Your own reasoning!" Michel smiled sheepishly: "All right; perhaps you're right. And what will we sell?"

"Everything," said Jules whirling his arms with the gestures and smile of a dancer. "You say Kreuger? O.K.! K. and T.? You say Insull? O.K. Insull! Let's sell the American market, the French market, the Swedish market."

"Henri Léon says wheat," remarked Michel.

"No, no," Jules wagged his finger vigorously, "nothing real. I don't speculate in commodities; that's bad luck. Speculating in rust on wheat is bad luck. Speculating in heart failure among the mandarins of the Bourse, that's good luck."

"What a Red Indian you are, Jules, the original Voodoo Kid!"

Jules snickered in his engaging vanity. "My dear boy, do I need fortunetellers? I'm the topnotcher of fortunetellers. *They* buy their curtains at the Samar Pont-Neuf, and I buy mine," he made a large gesture, bringing in the cardinal's chair, the pillar lamps, the lusters, the tables, "I buy mine at Alavoine, Place Vendôme, and Jansen, Rue Royale: a fortuneteller, I!"

Michel got up, half convinced, in spite of all his knowledge, by Jules's fire. "You really want me to sell?"

"Sure, sure!" Jules collapsed, sank into his chair, became sardonic to mask his fatigue.

"What, Jules?"

"What I said!"

"K. and T.?"

"Whatever you like"; a burst of energy: "but sell, only sell, sell only; sell the world!"

"Our experience."

"Sell it!"

"Jules, a hunch is a hunch, but—"

Jules smiled wearily and pityingly at Michel. "Michel, there is nothing to life but a hunch. Cause and effect? Philosophy? Economics?" His hand cut an elliptic in the air. "Like the charts nuts make of throws of the dice. Nobody who ever made any *money,* ever had any *brains*—a proof—"

Michel laughed. "Men sell highest ex brains," finished Jules, with fatigue, "unless brains is their racket! No money in ability! Look at Mahmoud! Did you see the wonderful little telephone board he figured out? An Arab; a savage! Starves himself into a swoon at Ramadan and all that; does what they tell him at the mosque. I could do it too, but if I did, if I learned to do a single useful thing in life, Michel, only one thing, I would not be able to make money: utility and moneymaking are incompatible. My Fragonards are useless, my evening jacket is useless."

"It makes you beautiful."

"My beauty is useless: so, I'm a howling success." He smiled, radiant in his folly, full of sorcery, "And you are useless, Michel; that's why I intend to keep you with me forever: the Reds will never get you!"

Michel laughed and went to the door. "You're babbling. I'm going to put through the orders."

"Sell, sell, sell," said Jules mocking. As he went down the corridor, Michel heard the airy voice, "Sell, sell." And in fact, Jules, a successful fakir, had the upper hand of his good sense: and Michel sold fifty thousand shares of Swedish Match. A few months later, everyone was to ask himself where Alphendéry, "the mystery man of the bank," and Jules, "the young banker of great promise," got their information.

Scene Seventy-four: Worldling versus Mercury

CARRIÈRE, with his idea of vengeance, irritable and melodramatic, swollen by vanity and drugs as well as by a very competent knowledge of his own superiority in position and wealth, required a speedy end to the short duel. He had boasted of his intention all round Paris and the resorts of the Upper Ten Thousand to which they both belonged, and he was anxious to see the leers, fears, congratulations, and swarming of parasites and petty ambitions which would follow Jules's complete crushing, as well as the new polarization of his society. He dreamed of it at night, unhappily, sometimes groaned, sometimes woke dreaming it was all over and he had his hand on Bertillon's slender, long, and muscular throat. A dream he had one night reminded him of a day in vacation time during his schooldays, when he had gone bathing with Jules Bertillon for the first time. Sensitive to beauty and endless sonneteer at that time, he was seduced out of indifference by Jules's youthful delicacy: for a season he had tried to make friends with Jules. His dream had always been the "ideal friendship." But Jules always chose for friends rich idle healthy mediocre boys and discussed with them countless schemes for getting on in the world.

Jules thought Carrière something of an ass, and in a short time, bored to death with the school ritual and his failure at it, left for a commercial career. Jacques went to medical school, published poems in reviews, made an art collection, learned fencing and elegance, bought a yacht, and in the yacht club met again Jules Bertillon, grown into one of the most elegant, lackadaisical, and charming youths of Paris, newly married to Claire-Josèphe, with a Spanish fortune, of irreproachable life and simple manners. Jules, with a fortune of his own, picked up in the war, in Poland it was said, or Russia, Jules, a newly fledged banker and feted companion, always accompanied by blueblood youth: Comte Jean de Guipatin, of Bourbon blood, Prince de Monteverde, bobsleigh champion, Roger Flowers, South African millionaire, amiable chief rowdy of Blue-Coast bars, Robert Legris, wartime friend and now his inseparable, son of a banking and stock-exchange house of Amsterdam. Carrière tried to complete the sketched friendship of years before—but Jules always wafted himself away and the result was no contact. But Carrière this time wasted few days on Bertillon: he had developed a tropical thicket of sensuality, and the "crowd he hung round with" were wilder and certainly not irreproachable.

One day he heard in the club, "Carrière's always under full sail; Bertillon knows how to trim his sheets to the wind: he'll get there. He's got the lucky streak!"

At that time Bertillon seemed to be shooting into the higher and more gilded skies of finance; he was said to be intimate with Débuts, influential liberal head of the Banque du Littoral du Nord. Carrière never for a moment believed that anyone in his world could take *his* place, and he thought he would soon prove it, but in pleasures he let years slip by. He lost money in 1929, for he had large investments everywhere, and about the beginning of 1930 he had reckoned up his books of accounts—he was thirty and Bertillon had eclipsed him as far as personal prestige went: Carrière, for all his family wealth, was horribly smirched, and it almost seemed lost, by the well-known scandal of his life. He suddenly bent his wasted powers and not yet wasted health to overtaking

Bertillon, the only other young man of personal fame in his entourage.

Ambition was Carrière's core as the love of turning a trick was Jules's. Jules, not out of cynicism, but out of the clarity of his nature, believed nothing that was told him, sought the person's interest behind each sentence, lied perpetually for the pleasure of tricking even the credulous, tried to recast every situation, for the pleasure of changing it; he cared not so much for money as for moneymaking, and, when he had got the hang of money-making, not so much the making of money as the endless field for speculation and fantasy it yielded him. He hated to think, he liked to depend entirely "on inspiration," and his inspiration was fertile enough not only on the principle of hit-and-miss but because through endlessly studying in one field and experimenting in it, with his original and single-minded talent, he was bound to make some good strikes. Jules had some gifts of nature, also: an unusual generosity, a visible harmony that tamed even critics, cynics, the unquiet, the suspicious, and the blackmailing, at least for the moment of their conversation.

Jacques Carrière finally admitted that nature, not Jules's intelligence, had given him a worthy pacemaker. He began to make political relations, to advance himself as a possible candidate for deputy, to figure the cost of launching himself, by means of press and social pressure, to calculate how long it would be before he could start his own private bank. It would be a moderate task for one of his ability, not too hard. Jules was a gambler in life, basically, he told himself and his friends, and he was ig-norant of ambition, that is, in the sense that he neither maligned nor aligned, nor campaigned. "An innocent!" Carrière said, sneering. But an actor from the Théâtre de l'Oeuvre, who cultivated good society and heard Ber-tillon's bank called the "Banque Mercure," exclaimed, "Now I understand: an allusion has been rankling. . . . Bertillon is altogether the personage of the old-world Mer-cury!" The name stuck to him and Carrière had the dis-pleasure of hearing his rival referred to by the caressing and satiric name . . .

William and Michel Alphendéry knew some moments of panic now: William was all for settling with Carrière, when Michel was for fighting, and when Michel's courage failed, William had become obstinate. Jules was swayed by one, the other, Claire-Josèphe, and the moods of the day. Each hour of the day, they were hagridden by Carrière and his threats, and they perpetually thought out new schemes either for denouncing him, showing him up, bringing him "to reason," and circumventing his design.

Alphendéry thought that the following representation should be made to him: that, if he continued to demand the gigantic profit that Jules insisted on paying him on the "gentleman's agreement," a profit that was beyond all honor, equity, or reason, he would either force Bertillon to his own ruin or they would be forced to fix up a bankruptcy to save the funds of the bank and the clients' deposits. . . .

Scene Seventy-five: A Family Brawl

ALPHENDÉRY was summoned before the judge on the Rosenkrantz and Guildenstern complaint.

"I'm going to make a human speech," he said to William before leaving. "Let's try and mop everything up before Jules comes back. By doing something they don't expect with their smart official manners and 'literal interpretations,' I'll try to terminate the case today." William smiled.

The judge, prejudiced against the Bertillon bank by the host of little cases which had been filling the courts, and also by things whispered in the corridors of the courts, turned severely to Alphendéry. "Mr. Rosenkrantz claims that you have not fulfilled a single one of your engagements towards Kaimaster Blés, S.A., that he has been a victim of what he calls sabotage, and that you yourself, acting by yourself, and conscious that he thought you were mandatory in the bank, not only first tricked him and his partner in the first place, pretending to engage the bank when you only engaged yourself, but that further, this is a part of the bank's system of avoiding its contracts, that you are not responsible, have no seizable assets in France, and, in the last place, broke the contract with them, before the agreed time was out, with the intention of annoying them and damaging their credit."

Alphendéry, who had taken in the insolent assurance of Rosenkrantz and Guildenstern on the other side of the judge's desk, the almost smiling ease of Maître Lallant who was handling their case, as the cases of other enemies of the bank, came forward with a debater's supple resolute alacrity.

"*Monsieur le Juge,* may I present my story to you in its entirety?"

"I should like to hear it."

"Good! These men came to us from Hamburg, unknown, unannounced, without any letter of introduction. They walked in from the street."

"We already had an establishment in Boissy d'Anglas," interrupted Guildenstern promptly.

"They were negotiating for half a shopfront precisely," continued Alphendéry. Their argument before you, *Monsieur le Juge,* is that on us they built up a business and when we broke the contract it crumbled. Therefore, they had little or no business before."

"Proceed."

"Their own books will show that ninety-five per cent of their customers came from our bank. Now, sir, they have therefore made money through us since the beginning of their contract. As an aside, I mention that we have never made a penny out of them. Their statement was that they would transmit to us stock-exchange business and solicit their clients for stock-exchange business for us. They never did this, but as we did not, really did not, desire to *make* any money out of them, we pass this by."

The judge said, with low cunning, "You didn't want to make money out of them?"

"No. In the first place, we are, primarily, a bank. In the second place, although we signed on a basis of *quid pro quo,* for the sake of commercial routine, since we were not in competition with Kaimaster Blés, S.A., and we handed them business that was of little use to us, we regarded the whole thing as a minor courtesy, and not as a profitable undertaking. . . ."

"But you lent them your name on their letterhead."

"Publicity. We even designed the letterhead for them, so that the name of the bank, though in small letters, would be presented with elegance. One thinks of those things, as a routine. Thus the contract was made, in the first place, to enable them to use our name, to help them only, and not with an idea of profit to ourselves."

"But you say you also agreed to hand them your commodity-exchange business. Why, if with no hope of return?"

"Commodities have never been a branch of our business. Occasionally, to oblige board-room clients, or bank clients, we have passed through an order for wheat, cotton, barely, etcetera, but it is an expensive nuisance and we never encouraged it. We quote commodity exchanges on our boards, because they are an index to the trend of stock markets. Our books will show that commodity business has not been one, not one-half per cent of our business."

"Then you deny that you asked these gentlemen to act for you in developing the commodities business, with yourselves?"

"We gave them that business as one gives away a new pair of shoes that don't fit. They got no business for us; they occupied themselves only with their own business."

The sneering suavity of Maître Lallant broke in: "My clients found it impossible to get any business for you on account of the bad reputation of your bank, and the publicity round the broken contract with Dr. Jacques Carrière." The *maître* smiled knowingly at the judge.

Alphendéry, with passion, turned to Maître Lallant. "There is too much of Jacques Carrière in your activity against us! Strange, that all of our enemies, poor and rich, find their advocate in you! I say nothing more. I wish to proceed without interruption from parties whose interest in this invites examination."

"Gently," said the judge, with enthusiasm. Debates, personal enmities, especially when conducted with vileness and venality, were the sauce of life to him. "Proceed, Mr. Alphendéry. *Maître*, you may speak later."

The lawyer folded his robes round with ease; what did he care?

The judge rolled his lips outwards and leaned forward: would he hear anything of the inside story of the quarrel of these two rich youths, anything of the seamy side of the Haute Banque? He hoped so. He was a poor man, completely stupid, immoral: getting secrets and making relations with the financially great were his only hope. He almost smiled at Alphendéry.

"Mr. Alphendéry?"

Alphendéry threw himself into the debate again with the gesture of a surf-club hero in a relay race. "All we did was out of pure generosity, out of pure humanity, to help two exiles, two Germans who might not find it so easy to make a footing here. The financial world is jealous."

The judge took out a toothpick. "Ah?" A little smile, the unspoken sneer of the lawyer's drudge who "knows his world," broke on his face. Maître Lallant turned his head, nodded to his two clients. "Is that usual—such generosity—Mr. Alphendéry?"

Alphendéry had paled. *"Monsieur le Juge,* these two gentlemen, these *three* gentlemen are Jews!" The three looked at him somewhat startled. "I myself am a Jew! Messieurs Rosenkrantz and Guildenstern came along, and when Mr. Jules Bertillon had refused to see them two or three times, he deputed me to see them, because, coming from Alsace, I speak German with ease, and he thought I could find out their business more easily. As it happens, the gentlemen speak French. I came to them and said, 'I represent Mr. Bertillon, I am his deputy: what do you want?'

"As soon as they saw me they recognized that I was of Jewish blood. They said to me, 'We come to you as a Jew, we appeal to you as Jews. There is an anti-Semitic wave rising in Germany, and we believe it will sweep the country. We believe our race will again be dyed in its own blood. Our property, our lives, are not safe. Therefore, we come to France, where there is still liberty of thought. Nevertheless, as well as Jews, we are Germans. We are not as acceptable to Frenchmen as might be Englishmen or Americans: there is the race-hatred!' (A phrase and a concept," said Alphendéry aside, "which I regard as stuff and nonsense, but let that pass.) Mr. Rosenkrantz here was a lieutenant, Mr. Guildenstern was a liaison officer, I believe" (Alphendéry smiled sweetly at them; Maître Lallant frowned), "and 'although' (said they) 'we have sent our children to a German school in Switzerland, on account of the superiority of German thought and education, and we hope to return to the fatherland when the trouble is over—we are obliged now to seek the hospitality of French soil and French tolerance. We know no one here and we are foreigners. We hope that you, Alphendéry, as a brother in the Jewish faith' (which I am not, *Monsieur le Juge,* being an atheist), 'and that Mr. Jules Bertillon, that gallant onetime enemy, that hero decorated with the Legion of Honor and the Military Medal, will unite your sympathies and lend us a helping hand.' I said to them, 'I am not a synagogue Jew; but of Jewish stock, that I am. I will do my best to help you, though, not as a Jew, but as a Frenchman who detests intolerance, loves liberty, and sympathizes with your difficulties.' Messieurs Rosenkrantz and Guildenstern then told me a long tale of their miseries and the difficulties which begin to appear in the path of business in Germany, explained that their business was commodities, and asked me to help them build up their business. I explained to them that we did no commodities business but that the few orders that accidentally came our way, we would send through them. I went to Mr. Bertillon and took it upon myself to plead for them, because they had moved me with the story of their business troubles and also, undoubtedly, with the story of their persecution. I said, 'Here are two men of high character and good business ability who are practically thrown out of their country for no fault of their own.' Mr. Bertillon is a kindhearted man who detests all kind of fanaticism and he said, after some discussion, that there was no reason why we shouldn't throw them any commodities business that came along. In return they made many protestations, urged that they would endeavor to get clients for us among the North Americans and others they proposed to canvass. That was the origin, the whole background of the contract."

The judge had finished picking his teeth and the lines of his face had firmed. "Do you agree with this story?" asked he, of the plaintiffs.

"Mr. Alphendéry has related facts," said Maître Lallant. "The coloring is his own."

"That's all right," said the judge, turning to Alphendéry with more warmth than before. "Mr. Alphendéry, what happened atfer that?"

Maître Lallant was about to protest, bit his lip, and said nothing. Alphendéry went on, "The contract was drawn up by Mr. Bertillon and these gentlemen and me, presented to them by me, and signed by them and me."

"This was where the misrepresentation occurred," said Guildenstern.

"What misrepresentation?" asked Alphendéry angrily. "Are these gentlemen children in arms? They signed with me. The paper has the bank's letterhead: I work in the bank. They had service from the bank. No rubber stamp or typewritten indication of status followed my name nor theirs. They appealed to me as an individual. I used my power to get them the bank's help: they got it. What was the misrepresentation? They have a paper . . . it is before you. I am given no designation; they are able to read."

"You have no property in France," cried Guildenstern, suddenly outraged. "We made commercial inquiries about Bertillon and the bank, which were none too good but we decided to risk it, but about you none—only later, when it was too late. I assure you if we had known what we knew later, we would have signed nothing."

The judge had now taken sides; he waved his hand with negligence towards Guildenstern. "Calm yourself, Monsieur. You will speak later. Meanwhile, it seems to me, as an observer, that you had made inquiries about the bank and had decided to take a *risk*."

Guildenstern was furious at the false step. He cried, "This man has no property in France that can be seized. Does that look like a responsible personage, a personage who intends to pay his debts and constitute a proper commercial responsibility?"

Alphendéry looked at the plaintiffs. "You made inquiries as to whether the Bertillons and the bank had property that could be seized?"

"Certainly: we found that there were bank deposits—and so forth—"

"Does that look like good faith?" inquired Alphendéry of the judge.

"An ordinary commercial proceeding," said Lallant. "My clients simply do not express themselves in routine language."

"Exceptional language expresses exceptional intention," said Alphendéry hotly. "I contend that Messieurs Rosenkrantz and Guildenstern came into this business, *because* they had picked up rumors about us, heard of the scandal being made by a person that need not be named, a person who uses his influence unduly to persecute Mr. Bertillon.

I contend that these men approached us with the insistence that characterizes all their relations with us, because they thought they could utilize the reputed idiosyncrasies of the bank and its owner for their own purposes, that they designed us as a victim, they conceived a plot and they intended to hold the bank up, cut its purse, take its clients and by holding it up, I mean they intended to hold it up by legal means, in the first legal trap they could catch it in. Their admission that they first found out what the bank had that could be seized is a very fair testimony on my side."

"This is not pleading, this is abracadabra," said Lallant hastily, for he saw his clients, Rosenkrantz especially, were raging.

"Ah, ah," said the judge, tapping happily on his desk. "There is much that is curious in this case, *Maître*. I am not prejudiced; I wish to hear the full story of this witness."

"Detective story—" said the *maître* with composure.

"Repeat what you said, *Maître*," said the judge.

"I said, invective has no force." The *maître* was sober again: he continued, "This witness has no evidence whatever for what he says. It is pure fantasy. He is a very imaginative man." He smiled at Alphendéry, like an appreciative opponent in a simulacrum-boxing contest, though. Alphendéry ignored this marking of the thrust. He nodded his head, appealing to the judge.

"*Monsieur le Juge*, Maître Lallant represents also Monsieur Parouart, a sinister person without visible means of support, who sued the bank for fraud and whose case was thrown out of court for want of evidence," he said in a louder voice, throwing his defiance into Maître Lallant's face. "Maître Lallant represents Messieurs Rosenkrantz and Guildenstern, suing the bank on a dubious contract; he appears in court on other cases for Dr. Jacques Carrière, who, incidentally, is conducting a campaign against the bank and Mr. Bertillon in particular. I only suggest that it is unlikely that Maître Lallant's imagination would go so far as to take our side, if we had all the proofs and the purity of newborn babes."

"I work for who pays me," said Lallant, unruffled.

"As to *their* good faith," said Alphendéry, "if they had not been accumulating complaints against us from the first, what is the explanation of one aspect of their behavior, which I am about to relate? Every time we had a private conversation in a café, at dinner, over the telephone, or informally at the bank, these German exiles 'confirmed' (as they said) the conversation, by a précis or summary report of all that was said, in their own terms of course, by *pneumatique* or registered letter. Even the first conversation I reported to you, and in which they made an appeal to me on the basis of brotherhood and common faith, was 'confirmed' to me by registered letter! Why were they laying a foundation for injury for themselves, why trying to trip us from the beginning?"

"Have you these confirmations?" asked the judge.

"Yes."

"Let me see them."

The bank lawyer, Maître Lemaître, who was in attendance, passed them over.

"We naturally took no such measures with them. We laughed at these registered letters and regarded them as freaks. In the second place, *Monsieur le Juge,* as soon as we had begun business with them, they made friends with me, Rosenkrantz especially, and plied me with questions, asking me, as a Jew, to communicate to them as Jews, private information about the status of the bank, its financial position, its balance sheet, and the rest, blithely supposing that I had a stronger fidelity to them than to the man who gave me my living and paid my salary. When I avoided or sidetracked their questions, they went to Mr. Bertillon and to subordinates in the bank, to find out my position in the bank, tried to confirm all that I had said by the mouths of others, asked Mr. Bertillon the same questions, and put their questions in such a way that he would think I had been babbling; they pried into my private affairs, gossiped about me to the other employees, complained about me to the two brothers Bertillon and to the twins Bertillon, in the hope of getting some advantage to themselves. I know all this, because, as we are a most united society at the bank, these things were immediately told back to me. But my private annoyances do not count.

"Our contract was for nine months. As the seventh month passed and the eighth month was entered, they became more exigent, irritating our employees, till the whole business downstairs seemed upside down: it began to seem as if we were living for them. I need not say, that we had other things to occupy our minds and that the bond with these two brokers galled very much. Finally, in the middle of the eighth month, our manager, Mr. Manray, who has to see to the execution of clients' orders and keep their daily accounts straight, became so angry with them that he came to Mr. Bertillon and said he would rather resign than answer them again on the telephone.

"We received a blue paper from them within thirty-six hours: they did not attempt mediation, compromise, or a parley. Like a man who at last sees that he holds the winning number in a lottery, they threw themselves on what they considered their prize—damages.

"Shall I proceed to further points?"

"What is all this?" asked Guildenstern rudely. "We have a contract which was not fulfilled; we have been damaged and we want reparations: the rest is beside the point. You could have sued us; you did not. We are the plaintiffs."

"We do not sue for a living," said Alphendéry sharply. Rosenkrantz grinned derisively. "I should like to know what you do for a living. Eh? You are known."

"If you thought that our business, you'd try to imitate it," said Alphendéry. "You might make some money; you wouldn't be forced to chicane."

When they left, Maître Lemaître, who had not intervened at all during the hearing, said with some feeling, "You made an appeal I could not have. Before you began he was our enemy: he thought of you as swindlers, and after you finished he thought of our gentlemen as conspirators. You will see: I know my judges. You will hear no more of this. You cleverly reduced it to the size of a family quarrel—and the nationalist line—"

"Oh, it was a low brawl," said Alphendéry with discouragement. "Those fellows put things on such a plane."

"It's all right," laughed Lemaître. "I am satisfied. Technically, of course, they can still claim damages; but I know my men: they will actually never get them. I think we can count—three down for the count."

"Three! Parouart? The landlords?"

"Yes," the lawyer turned to him smiling. "Perhaps luck is favoring the most careless man in the universe, Mr. Jules Bertillon! If it were not so, Mr. Bertillon would be even now selling his wife's ring to pay his blackmailers. What a man, what an erratic genius! Frankly I still can't believe that such a bank exists. I know it does; I have the papers. I plead for it. But— Tell me frankly, why doesn't he take at least one lawyer into his service and let him advise him?"

"Jules would rather go to jail than tell the whole truth to anyone on earth: that's his foible."

"Ah, in that case," said Lemaître, displeased.

"Don't desert him, *Maître;* he is a splendid fellow; he is worth your defenses: it is a question of temperament! He has never been any different since he was born."

"Nevertheless, it is for your sake that I take the trouble," said the lawyer, not entirely appeased: "I regard you as a friend, although our views on life and politics are at opposite poles. As a friend, if I might be allowed to say a word as a friend, I would advise you to leave Bertillon. He will wreck himself and you, too."

"I want to leave him but I can't when he is ill and harassed. . . ."

"In that case, I can only hope to help you by giving you legal advice," said the lawyer, with a gallant smile. "No man can be dissuaded from his—" he softened the rest with an affectionate glance, "—his mistaken loyalties. Being a conformist, and having passed the age of vanity, my meaning is that there is no loyalty but to yourself in the world we live in. I count no other."

They parted. By the next morning's mail, Michel Alphendéry received a booklet: *Modifications in the Assumptions of International Law since 1914:* by Marcel Lemaître, Doctor of Jurisprudence, Professor at the Sorbonne. He took it in, showed it to William. "Our bigwig is a learned fellow."

"Ah," shrugged William: "I always knew he was some sort of a pedagogue: no wonder we get nowhere with our cases."

They heard no more of the Rosenkrantz affair. It was their first piece of good luck, and the whole thing had been managed honestly.

Scene Seventy-six: Markets Down

ARISTIDE RACCAMOND was much torn between two ideas
—the idea of worming himself into Jules's confidence and
making a career for himself through the bank, backed by
his wife's family; and the idea of supporting Carrière on
his new-shining path to a ministry.

In France, once a minister, always a minister; and if
Carrière reached power at an early age, and Aristide was
his sucker-on, Aristide could count on the support of him
and his party from then on: Aristide's fortune would be
made, and he would have to worry no more. Aristide's life
was not a happy one. Not only that once again, as at
every other turning point in his career, he could not make
up his mind between two tempting paths (or two chutes of
disgrace), but he was worried by the very campaign of
Carrière, which made it difficult for him to get clients for
the bank, and to answer the complaints, doubts, and questions of the clients he had.

The markets all over the world were poor, and Aristide
was forced to advise his clients not to buy—advice contrary to his ambitious nature. The future of markets was
uncertain and Aristide, himself a heavy gambler, fretted
all his waking hours over his own future. Apart from
family troubles, he had others of his own. He was an
officer of reserve, he was within the age limit, healthy,
with no claims on him, and the news from Germany was
depressing. Some people clamored for France to declare
war on Germany straightaway before the latter threaded
her way out of the present impasse, before she had time to
restore Wilhelm II or acclaim his son or a dictator, before an *Anschluss*. Others declared that the German people were too socialist and too commonsensical to put up
with any dictator of fake socialism of the Nazi variety;
others said the Red movement would rise in Germany
and there would be another union of soviets over the
Rhine. In this case, too, France would be obliged to fight
her to prevent the virus spreading: others urged her to
fight *before* it got to that stage.

"Germany is unprepared," said some, "fight her now; march into Berlin and let her give up all hope of revenge: that is the only way to treat the Boches." Whatever happened, these hopes, threats, and plans tugged poor Aristide this way and that by the ear.

Aristide had just induced Madame de Sluys-Forêt to sell all her shares, in the belief that the market was ready for another dive, when markets rose all over the world, and Madame de Sluys-Forêt, along with other dames of consequence, began to din their complaints in Aristide's ears all day long.

He said desperately to Marianne, "I shall blow my brains out if this continues; it is the finishing touch. They tell me to get my clients to sell out and then they expect me to face the music: nothing doing," and took a train for Biarritz.

At Biarritz, too, he had something to attend to. His foolish son had got in with a band of young Spaniards who intended to foment a "Carlist" rising in favor of old Don Jaime. Young Raccamond was negotiating the sale of old ships out of Marseille for gun running: a nice business. Young Raccamond was "sick of the French" (who had arrested him for signing checks without provision) and had become a royalist; there would only be purity, he opined, under a king.

Raccamond was a center conservative-liberal: he had no illusions about "the forty kings who in a thousand years made France"; and although he knew the nobility that he courted were tender to pale youths who went in for royalism and general rightist rebellion, he wanted no political involvements. He had his own and they were with Carrière and Jules Bertillon, Bertillon being an intimate friend, as he believed, of Débuts of the Banque du Littoral du Nord.

When he was safely in Biarritz, he telegraphed Marianne Raccamond, who put on her best tailored suit and went in in tears to see Mr. Bertillon.

"My husband has had a nervous breakdown: Mr. Alphendéry advised him to tell his clients to sell out—they did so, and now they are threatening to withdraw their accounts. Mr. Raccamond fears that he will lose them all. Of course, I have assured him that there is nothing to worry about, as the loss was sustained on the advice of the bank. *Doubtless,* you will make some arrangement with them."

"Tell him to take a rest if he feels bad and come back as soon as he's well. We need him. In the meantime, we'll fix up everything with his clients. Tell him not to worry."

"He has always been on good terms with his clients, and he has worked so hard to build up a position that naturally he feels as if all his work is rooted out: his is an absolute nature."

But Madame de Sluys-Forêt stage-managed a creditable scene of hysterics both over the telephone and in the front office, and as a result Marianne was able to tell Aristide that his clients, Madame de Sluys-Forêt and the Princesse Delisle-Delbe, were "reinstated," their losses made good by the house. Aristide came out of his hiding place.

Scene Seventy-seven: A Changed Man

MICHEL ALPHENDÈRY, speaking to a Sunday congregation of socialist workers at Juvisy, was very different from the baffled, romantic, encyclopedic but neurotic Alphendéry of weekdays. His serried, dry, and humorous lectures, delivered in an even voice at great speed, gave him a following of young disputatious student-workers and old socialist wiseSbeards, union secretaries, former orators, former admirers of Blanqui, Ferry, Garibaldi, Jean Jaurès and others whose names are multiplied in the avenues, boulevards, streets, and squares of southern France, especially.

Alphendéry commented on Mussolini's dictum: "Without fascism bolshevism might engulf Europe."

"Fascism, something that Engels foresaw but that the capitalist class happened on, as they happen on any expedient, irrational but resolute, a sort of introvert imperialism, bringing back into Europe the methods used in South America, the dictators of South America, the prison and bloodshed of South America, and India, and Indo-China and the Congo—fascism has not been presented in one of its simplest aspects: it is the savior of capitalism (they say); but what saves fascism? The money of free peoples. Just as no South American dictator was able to exist without financing by free and therefore rich commonwealths, nations with liberal forms of government and free trade, as France, the U.S.A., and England, so no European 'Supremos' can or will be able to exist without financing by freer forms of government, without the financial aid of England, France, the U.S.A. . . . if they exhaust the sympathy of these peoples, or if a socialist revolution, such as that which has taken place in the U.S.S.R. should deprive them of financing they must fall: they cannot produce, they can only imbibe from outside; they live on the juices of more vigorous states. Now capitalism is only vigorous as it knows freedom. The decay of the host brings the decay of the parasite. Far from saving capitalism, fascism exhausts it. But capitalism is not an abstract idea, it is not a dying tree, it is a form of organization of peoples, and fascism exhausts those peoples: it oppresses its own and robs others. If one remembers that fascism has, so to speak, no normal internal financing and lives on repudiated loans, that is, on gifts, we perceive that it is an ugly temporary expedient."

Alphendéry's emphasis and pauses were as expressive as his sentiments. Jean Frère was ravished. "I always knew you had the stuff, Michel; but by jingo, I didn't know you were a socialist orator of the grand school. You're a changed man. I don't recognize in you the fatalist Alphendéry of the bank."

"I am not the same."

"How you have wasted your time, Michel! What a pity you went in for banking! What made you do it?"

"My father died. My mother wanted me to take up a liberal profession. An old inventor who had made himself rich, a real inventor, adopted me and put me to work at fourteen, saying I should have nothing to do with the schools. He put me into finance. He intended to make me his heir. There was a rupture, I never cared to court him since—he's still alive, anyhow, at eighty-eight: money is a great embalmer. And I've been in his finance ever since. In a nutshell . . ."

"Yes, but since you became a Marxist, why—?"

"Defect of temperament, dear Jean."

"What a pity! You must change, Michel; you must not be lost."

"I know this is my real métier."

Jean clapped him on the back. "Of course."

A broken-down, middle-aged worker approached him, began mumbling to him. Jean, with embarrassed looks around, gradually edged away from the crowd and from Michel. He pulled his broken hat farther over his eyes, peered anxiously through the fallen lock of hair. The man talked on, argued. Jean's face dropped, his eyes became woeful. After some seven or eight minutes, he excused himself abruptly and reached Alphendéry's side.

"A loan?" said Alphendéry.

The man stood gloomily against the platform. "You see," said Jean, hopelessly, "you see why I hate to come to these things? If I don't get him a job, or get him local relief, all he can do will be to commit suicide. If I don't help him out at once, he'll be found floating in the Seine tonight, or tomorrow at the latest. He doesn't want money. His wife doesn't know he hasn't a job. He goes out every day at six-thirty in the morning to fool her and comes home at five-thirty. He's been doing it for nineteen months, giving her money each week out of his savings! Now, they're all gone. It's horrible, isn't it! What can I do? You see what they expect me to do. Why me?" he suddenly said with an explosion of wrathful misery. "A folk hero! I am to work miracles! I'm sick of it. Every time I come to one of these affairs it's the same. I'm afraid to show my head." He pulled Michel by the sleeve, "Let's get out of here!"

Michel dragged himself away with regret. Jean went up to the miserable man, smiled, patted his shoulder, then rejoined Michel. "I told him to come and see me tomorrow at the paper. What can I do for him? At any rate, to prevent him from throwing himself under the subway tonight. A day gained. Ah, Michel, Michel; it's no life. I must get away from Paris for a while. I can't stand their miseries. To forget politics for a while, to forget the unemployed, the fellows with their miseries, the scandals, the alarums, the war that's coming. You see, I'm not a political type, Michel. They don't understand that. Even with a Lenin, even Lenin, they had to wait twelve, twenty years, before they had any hope—and now, the first Five-Year Plan not through and Europe waiting to fasten its fangs in Russia's throat. It's no life, Michel; or I'm tired. Michel, come down with me to my garden; don't talk politics. I'll go down with Judith tonight and you come tomorrow or the day after. Get a day off. Come down and don't chew the rag; just sit and let me be quiet and breed ideas."

Alphendéry was speechless at the mention of the garden, shuddered. Jean's heavy muscular hand fell on his shoulder. "Michel?" His caressing voice entreated him: "Michel, you can do it."

"I have a heavy position," Michel said nervously. "I can't leave it. Jean, I'll tell you because it's no interest to you. We're short 83,700 shares of stocks of all values, a position worth, at the moment, in the neighborhood of eighty million francs. I alone, outside the Bertillon family, know the position. I alone, excluding the Bertillon family, am managing the account. You see that I can't leave."

Jean had turned pale. "Michel! If the market goes up?" He took his arm.

Michel laughed. "Oh, don't worry. If it goes down, we make a real fortune, Jean; if it goes up—we skip! Our money is abroad. Now, hush, not a word."

Jean looked entirely addled. "Oh, heavens, not a word, no! But Michel, if you skipped, what a scandal! Michel, you could not work for us. Oh, what danger you are in! Michel, get out of it. Don't be in that danger! How do you manage it? I wouldn't sleep a wink any night."

"I stay up till three or four o'clock," said Michel with a sad smile. "I work things out, I read Marxism, consoling myself, and then I fall into bed, dead. That's how I sleep. I get up late in the morning. The hotel boy wakes me and brings me my shoes. I go down the street, have coffee at a cabmen's bar, standing up at the zinc. I talk to the bus conductor. That's how I keep sane. When I get to the office, I am ready for their lunatic world. In between times, I used to go and talk to Adam. Then I have to wait for you boys after work. That's how I keep sane."

Jean's lips were trembling, "You oughtn't to be in that business, Michel. How do you think the market will act?"

"Down," said Michel grimly. "Otherwise—"

"I'm as dumb as an ox in finance, but those eighty million francs, er, are they Bertillon's? I don't understand."

"I'll explain it all to you, Jean. But not tonight, if you don't mind. I'm more tired than I thought, and the mere thought of our position," he laughed gaily. "No, don't worry about me: it's too monstrous, you see. One can worry about five thousand francs. If they're lost, it's a tragedy. But about eighty million—if they're lost, the world's come to an end—who could worry?"

Alphendéry in his Rue Volney coat and Jean in his rough campaign coat went out, leaving the secretary to trim up. The book peddler made a few sales, the meeting organizer took up a collection, the few friendly groups shivered together for a few minutes, prefatory to returning to their cold cheap hotel rooms and pallets and holes and close family bedrooms. The secretary, in his greasy dilapidated trench coat, his healthy thin blond face eager and battling, rubbed his hands, asked members what they thought of the new lecturer, took notes of their criticisms, bloomed with content at his new acquisition. "Did you notice how I advertised it?" he asked them, genial. "I got in first, under the *A's, After the demonstration*—it's very important what is read first." He had a piece of paper in his hand with notes on it. He had yet little but open-air and strike experience, so he had taken a few notes on Alphendéry's manner of presentation and delivery, Alphendéry being above all a class-amphitheater and hall speaker.

The members of the audience now pressing out, either pretended not to see Alphendéry out of courtesy, or dropped him a timid smile. One or two engrossed in union affairs bustled along by themselves. A thin small fellow with faded blond hair and caved-in chest, without an overcoat, his poor boots covered with slush, from the dirty miles he had walked in the "demonstration" that day, scuttled out, giving Alphendéry and Frère an angelic little smile. This night the air was biting and the temperature of the lecture-room, frigid.

"Oh, my God," cried Alphendéry as if he had a shooting pain, "look at them! Look at him; in this weather!"

The secretary came up, flushed with success.

"You need a stove," said Alphendéry suggestively.

The secretary looked annoyed. "Yes, I've asked the man who runs this hall—a dozen times: he could put in an oil stove. I must remember to ask again."

"The way they come," said Alphendéry. "The courage of these men."

"Eh, eh?" said the secretary looking round.

"Coming here in this weather, without proper clothing after marching all day. . . . And then they pay voluntarily for learning, for hearing about the finances of Europe,

603

for hearing about the Rothschilds, the De Wendels, the Schneiders, the Du Ponts. And they're grateful to me." He put his hand to his face for a moment, laughed in an embarrassed fashion. "Oh, oh, and to think I used to despise people who went to night schools as piddlers, dreamers."

Jean Frère looked round vaguely, rosy; he smiled. "You've got to know the background."

The secretary, who had often gone to lectures in the same conditions, but was a healthy vigorous animal, strong and ambitious, and with enough of the honest careerist in him to enable him to cut his way to the top, only listened to this with half an ear. "They're mostly regulars," he explained; "I'm disappointed that there was such a small attendance tonight, but the demo always takes my people away. Another time you'll get more. You'll get known, you see," he explained encouragingly to Alphendéry. "They wanted to talk to you tonight, but another time is better: we ended late. You talk to them, Michel, and you'll learn what they most want to know. They're very eager; you can say that those who came tonight are the most loyal. I missed a few." He frowned. "Excuse me while I see that the lights are all out." He came back, took Alphendéry's hands in his, shook them hard. "Thanks ever so much," and hurried back.

Jules was mildly interested in Alphendéry's account of his lecture. When Alphendéry described the poverty and perseverance of the worker-students, Jules showed a frank and innocent satisfaction. He spread himself in his chair and tilted it tenderly backwards. "Poor coves! they haven't got a chance against us, have they?"

William, hanging there in the background, put in cantankerously, "They don't know what they need. Instead of sitting in a refrigerator listening to a guy who earns in a month what they earn in a year, they ought to be at home by the fire. They give their money for lectures and books when they ought to put it by and give themselves a holiday on the Côte d'Azur and cure their chests. Does it put any butter in their fry to know whether it's De Wendel or Schneider who's got the most dough? Dreamers: that's why they get nowhere."

Alphendéry had bitten his forefinger once or twice, a

sign that he was exasperated, "The Côte d'Azur," he said, tapping his foot. "The Côte d'Azur, ah!"

"Don't be silly, William," said Jules contemptuously. "They'd rather get the lowdown on us than go to the Côte d'Azur. Only they don't know one thing: it isn't what you know, it's what you have. They've got nothing. Say, wouldn't I rather get the goods on Carrière than go to the Côte d'Azur? Surely, I *understand* them: they want my fur coat and I've got it." He shone at this, looked his softest and most tender, laughed humanly. "No, but they don't; they don't want my fur coat, they don't want my chauffeur. They only want a second suit for Sunday! They don't want enough! That's their mistake! Say, I know them. The communists don't even hand them out a free overcoat and yet *they* give fifty centimes a lecture. It's a racket, a little racket. Now a person like Mussolini or Hitler who'd hand them out a free suit, a uniform, he gets ever so much more out of them. It's a cheap racket, but what can you get out of broken-backed nags? It's a stupid racket," he suddenly threw out, coming down on the four chair legs with violence. "What can you sell them? That's why we've got to get out . . . we must get out of this game for a few years."

"A revolution is built up patiently this way, while everyone jeers at it," said Alphendéry bitterly.

"Oh, to hell with the revolution," cried Jules, laughing. "Say, Michel, I'd rather take you to Deauville every Sunday than have you waste valuable time with the ragtag and bobtail at Belleville. You're not doing them any good: you're just robbing them of fifty centimes and keeping them shivering in the filthy little hole when they ought to be at home keeping warm by the radiator, with the eiderdown round their feet and a good liqueur." (Jules's usual picture of the worker's home.) "Another of your illusions, Michel! Besides, I don't like it. The police will be on your trail."

"What would we do if you got locked up?" said William.

"If you're really for Moscow, it's bad for business," Jules snapped.

"You two boys make me sick," said Michel, getting up and looking at them. "Go to blazes. To preserve your miserable few million francs, you'd have them unable to read and write."

Jules chuckled endlessly at the vision. "Why not? Ha, ha, ha. Oh, Michel, oh, Michel. You do take yourself seriously. All right, what the deuce do I care? Amuse yourself, have a good time. I know what's behind all this. It's not Moscow, it's this Jean Frère you're crazy about."

They all began to laugh and Jules remembered he had a letter from Adam Constant. Constant had found a location for their office in Shanghai and asked that the man who was to replace him be named.

"Who is it?" asked Alphendéry. "Jacques Manray?"

"Rubbish," laughed Jules. "Etienne Klotz!"

"Who is that?"

"Wait and see, wait and see! Etienne Klotz is just the man."

Alphendéry looked at Jules suspiciously, used to his fantasies, but he said nothing more.

"Etienne Klotz is no Red," Jules cried after him, as he went out—and laughed. He followed Michel. "Wire Constant as follows: 'Etienne Klotz, your successor, sails when fully instructed. Hold the fort. Greetings!' Sign it." He had an unpleasant air that forbade questions.

Scene Seventy-eight: The Grand Coup

KREUGER'S secretary rang Alphendéry from mid-ocean, on their sad return from New York where they were refused a loan, said that the correspondent of Legris of Amsterdam had put it round New York that Bertillon's thought Kreuger was bankrupt. "We will sue you," said the secretary.

"Sue," said Alphendéry. "Two months from now you will have to choose between Loewenstein and Hatry."

"You had guts," said Jules admiringly, when Alphendéry put down the phone.

"Why not? When Kreuger the colossus rings up a flea like me, what am I to deduce? That he has shrunk to the flea-state? I don't care, anyhow. Let him sue me. Do you care, Jules?"

"Of course not."

But a few days later, not two months, Kreuger was

dead except to legend, and even legend fades fast these days.

On the Kreuger crash in Sweden and on all markets and the Insull crash in the U.S.A. and on all markets, Jules in 1932 won the great prize in the lottery! Rumor flew, putting his profits at tens of millions; money rolled back into the bank, the employees smiled, the customers' men forgot to envy, and society gave Jules a laurel wreath: the white-headed boy of finance, this time headed for the "high bank." Demain, leader of the schism in the Banque du Littoral du Nord, tried to woo Jules away from his old friend Débuts. Many interesting affairs were proposed to him, and the actor of the Théâtre de l'Oeuvre smiled in society; "Well, now you have all the required proofs! Jules Bertillon is really Mercury. Who else would have sold Insull and Kreuger?"

Alphendéry was again whispered about as the power behind the throne, and Ralph Stewart, as well as a firm of gold brokers in Paris, made him offers, supposing him to be really rich this time. But Alphendéry had not sold short either Insull or Kreuger for his own account! "I am small time and I remain it," he said. Jules, floating on a cloud of glory, made Alphendéry a present of half a million francs; Alphendéry sagely put them in a safety deposit and went on living in the Place du Panthéon. The Hallers, enchanted that Alphendéry was both socialist and rich, invited him, sure that he would understand them. Aristide was unable to support the idea that Alphendéry had told him to sell short in Kreuger and that he had not done it. Nevertheless, all the men of the bank profited by the Bertillon glory, and customers were easy to obtain. Carrière was laughed at, and Jules's maxim was justified: "They don't care how crooked you are if you make money!"

Impossible to find out what Jules had won: he let the rumors speak for him.

Léon, at the bank, like Schicklgrüber and others, to congratulate the king of good fortune, ran across the famous Pedro de Silva-Vizcaíno, once again over the frontier, no one knew how.

"How does he do it?" inquired Léon, jealous and admiring.

"You've never seen that silky dark eye boring into a

girl's defenses; I say, the battering-ram method isn't the only one!"

"No, no, you're right, Michel, you're right: I've got something to learn. And Schicklgrüber! He's not handsome, is he!"

"No, he looks like a dirty bellwether. But he worships women, that's the secret; that's something the girls know in the second."

"Yes, yes, that's right." He half closed his eyes and rolled over Michel a cunning look. "For one," his sweetly tolling laugh rang out, "for one, Michel, my boy, who isn't a woman-chaser, you know a lot about the *technique*. Well, I've got something to learn. Never thought I'd learn anything about women at my age. He, he, he: women." A radiant smile washed out all the cunning and all the age; he said mysteriously, "And Jules—a charmer but doesn't care for women, does he?"

"No, only to get their accounts. . . ."

"Of course, he's made millions." Lower, with exquisite suggestiveness, Léon said, "How much, do you think, just roughly, I'm not prying, how much did he make, Michel? He was pyramiding all the time, eh? How much?"

"About fifteen million francs! Perhaps a bit more: I don't know his private position."

"*Ayayayaya!* Fairy money! Together we could have cleaned up the world. He won't work in anyone else's show."

"Jules is fantastic almost all the time. Once in a year he's hard, clear-sighted, and cuts right down to bedrock; then you see the man that built the bank. Don't forget he built it all himself. Richissimes leave their family fortunes here. Paleologos, our lucky star, for he turned the tide for us, has plumped for us. Campoverde has just put all his mother's money with us. We are at the top, Léon."

"Luck," said Léon superstitiously. "He didn't deserve it, Michel, but he's born lucky. Another man, with the risks he took. . . . Cash in, Michel. And if you want a job, you can come to me any time. I trust you: money follows you but it doesn't stick to your fingers." He became a meridional sun of gaiety. "Michel, Michel, since I'm not paying, I can give you good advice. He's good-tempered now: cash in, my boy; get what's coming to you." He became severe, gave Michel the once-over. "Think it over, Michel."

Scene Seventy-nine: Dividers

MLLE. ARMELLE and Monsieur Etienne had richer hauls in the mail again. Mr. Philippe Légaré wrote:

When you were only a struggling exchange booth in the Rue Notre-Dame-des-Victoires, my inventions in the way of codes, systematization of indexes, my arrangements with houses at that time most lethargic about doing business with you, my letters advising clients, my indefatigable liaison work was your chief support. As soon as you saw your foot on the road to success, you got rid of me in case I should claim my profits. . . . Now you are rich . . . rumor says you are the richest stock-exchange banking house in Paris: where do I come in? Nowhere? I am forgotten, outcast: a charge of insanity has been trumped up against me; I write letters demanding my rights and people are not ashamed to show them around as a proof that I am insane. It is men like you, Jules Bertillon, that make atheists and revolutionists: what proof that God or government exists? L.E.F.! What a comedy! If I did not hope that one day conscience would smite you and make you give me my rights, I would denounce you to the police; but I am a good man. I have never hurt a fly in my life. It is beneath me to denounce even one who has stolen from me everything that I possessed. We are poor men: our inventions, our instruments, our labor, our salaries, our bread, is snatched from us by men like yourself, men who appear angels and are devils. Why does God allow this? Is there a God? There is a God! There is retribution! Think of this, Jules Bertillon! . . . Never think I have forgotten our past contacts: you were very kind to me (I thought, poor fool), you took me in out of the street—not to be kind to me, no, because you were sharp enough to see I had something to give you! Like all your kind! What a sucker I have been! Weakness is its own reward, say you! Say on! Revel in your highway robbery! Retribution is around the corner! You have prospered on ill doing long enough! This high reward you have reaped is the last you will see! You will end your days in sorrow and desolation, despised of all; beggars will not ask you for a penny, so low will be your estate! Men will point and say that *was* Jules Bertillon! There is a God. He watches! He watches the weak and foolish like me, I admit it; he watches those who were victims; he will repay.

Take warning. If I do not receive 5,000 francs by Friday evening (the last post is delivered here at 6 P.M.) I deposit a plaint at the Commissariat and simultaneously post a letter already prepared directed to the (head of the) Parquet. The Minister of Finance will hear; there will be no passport for you when you want it at the Ministry of the Interior. Enjoy your money while you may but unless you divide with me, in the small, poor, pitiful percentage that my cowardice makes me ask for, you will regret it, once and for all. . . . Mr. Bertillon! You were kind to me once. Forgive my *vituperations!* I am poor, I will soon be starving! My wife has some disease no one can cure: a visitation of God. . . . I have annoyed people; I have blackmailed: I am now blackmailing you. Have pity on one so much weaker than you, Mr. Bertillon. Send me enough for *bread:* all I ask. You have your Hispano-Suizas, you eat at Larue's: send me enough for bread and to pay my apartment rent: All I ask! Send it to me and little as it is, I will bless you for it and not annoy you any more. Want is my master!

May God bless your enterprise!

P. LÉGARÉ

P.S. If the 5,000 francs is not in my hands on the due date and in due time, I will be obliged to act as indicated above.

Nice, March 30, 1932

Before he had read two sentences of this Jules had thrown it to Alphendéry:

"Oh, for goodness' sakes send the fellow a couple of thousand francs and burn the letter."

"Don't answer it."

"And tell Campoverde when he's down there to call in and see what the doctor says. I'll send him to Aix or wherever he wants; I don't want Légaré's curses even though he's crazy. It's bad luck."

Jules was irritable, but the next letter made him laugh. He threw it across to Alphendéry, "A friend of yours." It was from Theodor Bomba. As usual he was angling for big money, and ended: "With the best wishes and heartfelt greetings of the unhappy, Theodor Bomba!" Hospitals and charitable institutions wrote, of course; relatives, odd acquaintances who hadn't been heard of for months and were down on their luck: jealousy, poverty, and blackmail raised their voices. Jules received most of these, but other members of the bank also found the pathetic cry of the empty purse in their mail. Alphendéry opened the usual weekly letter from his mother,

Strasbourg, March 31, 1932

MY DEAR SON,

Thank you for your letter. Look after your health. My own health is bad and I fear I am not long for this earth. But do not worry about me: what can't be cured must be endured. Here is a letter from Estelle's sister-in-law, Betty, the Dutch girl, you remember. I think she is very fresh, but I send it on since she asks me to. I am glad your nice Mr. Bertillon has had good luck; everyone knows about it. What a surprise for you! I am so tired that I need a little fresh air: I asked the old coachman to come every day at three and take me out; it costs so very little, but if you do not wish it, I will tell him not to come any more. The fresh air gives me a little interest in the world . . . I have so little now. Estelle writes me nice letters. Write to her, Michel: I have few friends; she is not a bad girl, giddy, that is all. May you ever be happy, and wiser than you are!

Your old sweetheart,
MOTHER

And the sister-in-law's letter sang a sweet, but opportune tune,

611

Amsterdam, March 28, 1932

DEAR MOTHER ALPHENDÉRY,

Thank you so much for your sweet letter and it was so *sweet* of you to answer my little card so promptly. I had your address from dear Estelle and of course Amsterdam is ringing with the success of the bank Michel is in, so I thought I would write and congratulate you, and him; but I know that is one and the same: I am so glad that you are feeling much better and think you are *quite right* to engage a little carriage for the afternoons, especially with the good weather. The weather here is the usual, but warmish. Amsterdam is so charming and you would adore it—it certainly is a wonderful city and I am happy here with my dear husband and our little ones. . . . It is strange, but we spoke of you all this very afternoon, you and Michel and Estelle and other dear ones. My Willem and Jan remember you and ask, "Will dear Mother Alphendéry come to Ams'a-am?" We have a nice five-room apartment on the top floor near the Kayser gracht and I pay 100 guilders but I will rent out two rooms and help with *our rent*. Jan was very ill and we thought he was going to die—he got a streptococcus germ in his throat and ran 40 for nearly three weeks, I had to take him for X-ray treatments. Think of the expense for such poor people. But the children are everything to us. Now we are strapped. I asked Estelle if she thought Michel could help us, and we will repay. What do you think, dear Mother? I would not ask unless I asked you first. . . . And now, good-by; let me hear a yes or no—I shall write to you again soon. All my dear love to you and kiss from Jan and Willem who love you.

Lovingly,
BETTY

P.S. Remember me to Estelle and Dear Michel when you write.

William suggested an exhibition of begging letters: all members of the staff to contribute. Jules was rueful. He was for paying them all something to hear no more of it; he felt that these were mildew on his good luck and he wanted no ill wishers. At his request, therefore, Michel sent off small checks to everyone: to Légaré, two thousand francs; to Bomba (unknown to William), five thousand francs; to Betty, twenty guilders; and Jules told him to send his mother two thousand francs extra to pay for her carriage. "Spoil the old thing," said Jules. "There's this difference between her and the others, that she really loves you." Armand Brossier came up genteelly but with a certain assurance, and said that he was marrying and would like an advance; he received an advance of five hundred francs a month. Jacques Manray asked for a holiday and got it. Jules paid out these propitiatory offerings to his gambling god. This done Jules shrugged with a faint contempt, put on his hat, and vanished from the crystal towers of his dreams, into the daytime street.

The news of his gift to Alphendéry became common talk in the city; even the cashiers and tellers felt some envy. Aristide Raccamond's heart turned upside down: for days and nights he raged at the injustice of it. He trembled looking back at the danger the bank had been in! If the scale had tipped the other way—where would they all have been? Between envy and fear, he came to the edge of a nervous breakdown, quarreled with his clients and every day hysterically brought their troubles on to Jules's carpet. They had lost where Jules had won and they were bitter: Jules must pay them off, repay their losses, divide something of his enormous winnings with them. . . .

"Why?" asked Jules calmly of Aristide, but unable to bear the neurotic pressure of Aristide and of Marianne, who came to see him when Aristide was taking headache powders at home, he paid off the cinema star Freddie Pharion, twenty-five thousand francs, and to Dr. Froude, Raccamond's largest and best-paying client, thirty-five thousand francs. No sooner were these acts of grace performed than Aristide conceived that real injustice had been done his clients, and he began gloomily to read past records and find out other losses that his clients had sustained, and to clamor that they now were dissatisfied. Jules, although he detested him, and had a fear of him tainted with superstition, took him out to lunch at Fouquet's and promised him a participation in all future operations. Aristide was relieved at this and immediately proposed a "paper to that effect" to be drawn up by his lawyer.

"No paper," said Jules with sudden wrath, bringing down his firm hand on the table. "No one has to complain of me."

Aristide paled and pondered. When he reported the affair to Marianne, she proclaimed, "There is trickery there and it will have a bad denouement, unless you are careful."

He was silent for several minutes, then: "The thing that terrifies me, Marianne is—the policy. All that short position!" He stared at Marianne, his great cheeks drooping: impossible to say what his physiognomy was like because of all the timid fat that covered him. Marianne knew. When he came out of the war he was still thin, lank, great-eyed, blue-chinned, with the look of an Italian peasant. The fat, as his bourgeois dress and his city manners, were acquired since. He had intelligence; the war had given him *savoir-faire* amongst men and necessary vices.

"Nevertheless, they made money," said she, not quite understanding.

"But it's not natural: it's against nature, to be always betting on the wrong side," exclaimed Aristide honestly. "It seems almost—crooked. And suppose they always do it! Suppose they have, even now, some such position in another stock. It can't happen all the time! This was just luck. When it turns the other way—where will we all be? I won't sleep at night, Marianne, you know me."

She considered, "That's true: too bad you didn't get him to divide on this cleanup. Well, we will think of a way. Now, another thing, I went to Carrière today and he's agreed to put up twenty thousand francs towards my sheet. I told him I had a friend in Hollywood, in the Hearst interests who would give me original dope. He was impressed. I rather think the French cinema attracts him."

"We could do something along that line, one day. If I got an organization—"

"We will make out together. Léon won't part up, Bertillon is not interested in enterprises, but Carrière is the man with vision, the man of the future."

Jules's spring suddenly dried up. The last one to drink was Cancre, an artist picked by Alphendéry. He came from a miserable town, Troyes, had come to Paris to pick up a living as a tailor. He went to Montparnasse by accident, was dazzled by the *Vie de Bohème,* and discovered a talent for drawing. Some famous artist praised him and Cancre saw a brilliant future opening for him. He borrowed money for his hotel bill, for paints, brushes, canvases, left work, had no money for lessons, starved, and occasionally, to put a bite between his teeth, cadged from the flush and the drunk at Montparnasse, or painted uncouth, brilliant washes ("after Cézanne and Van Gogh") which he sold to the unsuspecting and round the Montparnasse station. There Alphendéry found him, encourage him, and bought his works at "any price you like to give." For a while Alphendéry was convinced that the "early sketches of Cancre" would be worth their weight in gold. Cancre had now exhausted all his resources, all his friends. His wife, a young pretty tubercular girl whose father was a railway ganger at Aubervilliers, and whose dream of romance seemed fulfilled when she fell in love with an artist, had fallen into a frightening decline. The letter told this. Would Jules lend Cancre the railway fare to take his wife to a sanatorium, and to take him back to Troyes to work as a tailor with his brother? Cancre was an honest man. He sent Jules by Aristide a "portrait of Jules the banker, by hearsay": a hard, crude thing in oils, together with a copy of his "manifesto."

"Vous êtes poèt? Alors, vous n'est pas un homme! Vous n'est pas simple! Vous avez compliquez votre jeoi et votre douler. Tout la nature se réveille, tout la nature s'éffleuris, se réjeouis, et le pas de poèt devient gràve et loud comme si c'été le dernier jour de la terre. J'ai pitié de vous mon poét, et pourtant c'est à moi que je parle comme a vous. Ne cherchez jamais rien. Selon les mérites, vous aurez tout ou rien. Apprenez de poèt qui cherche toujours et trouve jamais, ou qu'il le cherche, le paradis, il en trouve l'enfer. Son printemps n'est pas un printemps, son printemps est un calvair. Faut-il être misérable, pour être un poèt! Bref, oui! Ou faire tomber son oéuvre de bateau ivre? Dans un village ou il n'y a pus que des poètes. Paris!"

Jules, to whom the illiterate complaint of the miserable and starving *poèt* meant nothing at all, paid for the portrait another two thousand francs and told Alphendéry in a hard voice "to give it to him and tell them both to get back to Troyes and forget the Bohemian boloney." If he had no influence he'd get nowhere: Fragonard, Boucher,

Derain? A question of getting the right people to support one!

"I don't say he's bad," said Jules, squinting at the portrait. "I even think he's pretty good, but he's poor and it shows in his drawing; no one wants it." Alphendéry went with profuse thanks and Jules became sulky. Like all openhanded people who go in for an orgy of spending, he suddenly knew satiety. He would spend no more; he would have the pleasure of saving, for a salutary change. He suddenly regretted the stream of cash that had flowed from his open hands: he shut them. He determined to make up the loss; and Mouradzian, Cristopoulos, and Thomas Sweet began to find him a source of commission-income again. While others cried, "The purification of the system," he smiled sardonically, "Where one Kreuger, one Oustric, one Hatry is found—there sprout a hundred; and for each one ruined, there are a hundred making money hand over fist. Why not—they're all like me," he explained to his intimates, ". . . crazy, expensive, flighty, daring—birdmen of finance!"

Scene Eighty: Measure of Brains

"RACCAMOND has just appointed another accountant in London to replace the one we sacked. And what has he done, the other accountant? Found work! Astonishing! No one will sit idle! Mad world. Worse than that, the more he steams and puffs, the more he's convinced he has ability. It's fatal: a man employs one clerk, he has a minimum of ability; he writes one letter, he's a zero. He employs one hundred clerks and he's earning his stripes. He says, 'Dupont, write this identical letter to five thousand people in the telephone book,' and he's almost a captain of industry. Of course, that makes 'work.' And poor Dupont thinks he's important: he begins to fret because he's not getting on, he wants to be as vacuous, as viciously useless as his boss."

Jean Frère said curiously, "But it is a bank like the others, after all!"

"Of course. The terror of it! Don't forget there is this

bank, which is Jules's, and that of the employees, to whom it represents not only the old order, a stable financial system, the basis of the center-left, republican, catholic or socialist politics they go in for. It also represents their home, hopes of marriage, children, summer holidays, life insurance, old father's kitchen garden, medical expenses, everything in life. They take it very seriously. They must. They read the newspapers, particularly any news affecting banks and banking, and imagine that they have penetrated it more easily, due to their experience in Bertillon Frères. They are getting on in life. They are 'well-placed.' And this bank is nonexistent: it is nothing! It has no purpose. It is a privateer's fantasy: here today and gone tomorrow. Oh, God, it frightens me! Look at Raccamond struggling the way he does, trying to oust William and me, jealous of Mouradzian, treading on the corns of the lesser employees, flattering the clients, running himself to death, being egged on by his ambitious shrew-wife, hoping to cover up all the muddy steps of his early career. Look at Betty, my cousin; at this poor Cancre, at Légaré—the lot of them, believing in an illusion, spending their lives round it. A fantasy in the brain of an ignorant, a flighty, self-centered freak. How unreal, Jean, is this whole world I struggle in and get my gray hairs in!"

"The employees at the bank, and their idea of the bank, are real, too," said Jean.

"No," said Michel, not able to bear a good word on the bank, "no, because they're secretly in league with Jules and the rich people they serve. . . . They believe Jules's dictum implicitly."

"That is?" queried Jean Frère.

"A man's salary is a rough measure of his ability."

At times Michel resisted the influence of Jean Frère, as now, and feared him. Richer by five hundred thousand francs, he felt less like casting himself adrift.

Scene Eighty-one: Shadows

RACCAMOND came in one morning in a delirium of fear, and went straight upstairs to see Jules.

"Mr. Bertillon, what do you think of the threatened publication by the fisc of a list of all the private banks which defraud the tax collector through holding in their branches abroad, the taxable bonds of clients? What will we do?"

"Nothing," said Jules.

"But if they publish we will be on the list."

"Oh, Aristide! Let them publish, Aristide: I'd be only too glad. It'll bring business."

"But it's illegal," cried Aristide.

"Oh, Aristide!" He was irritated this time, then laughed, "Illegal! Oh, Aristide. Don't tell me you didn't know we had our clients' interest coupons cashed abroad! Where have you been?"

"Yes, I knew, of course; it's the regular thing. But if they *publish* it! We might be ruined, Mr. Bertillon. They might shut the bank up."

"They won't shut me up! I'll buy off the inspector."

"But it will be flagrant; they'll say our foreign branches are only to collect interest abroad and avoid the taxes."

"So they are. Listen, Aristide! It isn't the government worrying about the eighteen per cent deducted at the source that our honorable clients are all evading; it's the pressure from the overrich, trying to shut up little banks like me, because I've got the Salon trade . . . we're getting too much of the private business. Look at the accounts I've got! A lot of people like little banks: secrecy they think, privacy. No clerks to blackmail, no postal clerks to see what's going abroad. Just big bear eat little bear, that's all, Aristide, and no 'legality,' at all. They can't shut me up," he said with bravado.

"Some clerk here could blackmail us," worried Aristide.

"Nobody blackmails me!"

"They could," worried Raccamond.

"Listen, Raccamond, I want to tell you one thing. The

618

lists are kept abroad; foreign clerks don't care twopence for the French fisc or French newspapers. They won't blackmail. I pay them too good a salary. They won't blackmail. When clients prefer to keep their bonds themselves, or here in the bank, the coupons presented for dividends are *taken abroad by a clerk*. That clerk does not come to this bank. He meets the clients in a room rented in a hotel."

"An Englishman?" asked Aristide, involuntarily.

Jules did not hear. "I'd threaten to publish the lists myself of all the clients keeping bonds abroad and accounts abroad through my branches and thus defrauding the fisc themselves. If I'm guilty, aren't they?"

"You couldn't . . . you'd lose every account, overnight! We'd be ruined."

"You are simple, Raccamond," said Jules with dislike. "Would Carrière and his like *allow* such lists to be published? They'd back down at once. Let them. You'll see nothing will come of it."

Aristide, with a sullen and sidelong look, walked out. Aristide did willingly what the law or its silences allowed, but to dare, to affront was not his line: he suspected it. What were the secret thoughts of a man like Jules so venturesome, so contemptuous of threats? Aristide had seen others in difficulties or faced with disgrace. Léon was cunning but ran; Claude fought and broke down. Marianne's relatives were evil and supple. But the rash Jules when desperate? In a moment of clairvoyance, Aristide saw that the clients, the bank itself meant nothing to Jules: Jules was a lone hand. He went in and tried to alarm Alphendéry about the proposed revelation.

"If they do it," said Alphendéry, "they'll make an Aunt Sally of one or two small banks that they're trying to abolish from the horizon, and that's all. But they wouldn't dare do more: are they going to bring mobs into the rich quarters? Is there any one of them who keeps his accounts at home and pays taxes? A patriot, Aristide, is one who takes interest in other countries."

He laughed. That was all? Surrounded by such recklessness and such incomprehension, Aristide suddenly found his stature: either he was the only real "banker" amongst them, or else the world he had been struggling to get into was chaos, or else he had once more landed on one of

619

those rotten houses whose bottom would fall out overnight. Poor Aristide, sailing to prosperity on a death ship.

The following Saturday afternoon William stayed behind and fossicked in all the files and private drawers of the establishment. He had skeleton keys made long ago. In the evening he met Alphendéry and after some unusually slow and satiric remarks, he planted a fold of papers under Michel's nose, saying, "There's something to give you pleasant dreams."

Alphendéry read the copy of the agreement that Jules had sent to Carrière long ago, promising to pay the drafts at a fixed sum in francs, and a copy of further letters covering various payments, one of which, the last, said, "Here's the money coming to you on the sterling drafts, according to our contract: stop court proceedings, for now you are paid up to date."

Alphendéry said, "He admits that the contract has force, after denying it all along. The result of his win on K. & T. Well, now we are sunk. It certainly is hard to have to work for a Carrière."

"I thought Jules learned nothing at school," mused William, "but I see he learned too much: how to write."

"A fatal gift!"

He also showed Alphendéry the list of Jules's losses in the past six months, and finally let him know that the bank had lost all its money *three times* during the Carrière press campaign, and only been replenished by fortunate accidents like the Paleologos account.

"We had nothing, we owed Carrière, and also showed two millions loss in the stock-exchange account when the Kreuger windfall came! Let's take the hint and close up."

The only political shadows were the first great Japanese attack on Manchuria and the terrifying rise of Hitlerism in the May, 1932, elections. All those who had been depending on German Social-Democracy, and on a return to liberalism or monarchy financed by Germany's creditor states, were bitterly disappointed; at this moment the wing of terror spread its shadow over Europe, and the governing classes, in despair since 1929, began to see that Fascism was not simply an expedient to be used on a lackadaisical southern people, but a real salvation for their

620

property. At this time the socialist friends of Alphendéry began to tremble; the wisest predicted ten years of black reaction; the conservatives predicted a hundred years of domination. Jules even became captious and cruel and couldn't bear Alphendéry to mention socialism or to wish the comfort of all. . . .

"If the stock exchange is abolished," said Jules, "men like me will always set up a black bourse: it will come back. What you dream of are opium-den dreams, and besides you're wasting time . . . You can make money . . . That's what I want you to do . . . none of your communist friends has ever made money, and so what brains have they? Forget them. You're working for me!"

Alphendéry laughed with contempt. "Jules, don't worry. You've got time. There are plenty of tricks they can and will pull yet: every measure designed not for economic recovery but to put up the market, as if that were the first reality of economics, not merely the mercury of the middle classes. . . . This is the period of effrontery of capitalism and you think right, Jules, you've got the general line!"

"Yes," said Jules, cooling. "I know it won't last long, and I won't last long; my three sons will be engineers, don't fret! This is the day of the short-play heroes. No more Rhodeses and houses of Rothschild!"

Scene Eighty-two: The Factor X

THE panic deepened in France despite all efforts, and by June, 1932, all values, however expressed, whether in paper or gold, were at the lowest point of the century. Recovery attempts had begun on a grand scale.

In the U.S.A. the fall of the Dawes Bank in Chicago foreshadowed the moratorium of March, 1933, but the panic was staved off in order to produce an election boom for Hoover: a campaign was worked up even before the Kreuger suicide and crash.

In England the government reversed the price of gilt-edged by conversion, and the English, in the hope of profit in the Empire, accepted the conversion, and paid their taxes as they were requested.

The world was really crumbling: all speculators hoped to make money out of the death and decrepitude of something or other.

Jules had a proposition from a poor author, for the constitution of a library of rare and antique books, bought from the libraries of financially decrepit nobles and landed proprietors, in order to "raise prices and sell high to foreign speculators."

Carrière bought up mortgages on old houses in the new building quarters, hoping for a market rise; and Achitophelous at this moment announced that he had bought and was renovating the finest hotel on the Promenade des Etats-Unis at Nice. The hotel had gone bankrupt the previous winter.

Everyone had a last glimmer of hope and thought that with exceptional cunning they could get in before the rise in prices. Only Daniel Cambo, Dreyer, William Bertillon, and their partners went on steadily with their cheap-bazaar projects, convinced that today's money was in rubbish goods. "There are only two businesses today," said William, in excuse to Jules. "Yours—selling to those who believe in substitute money; and mine, selling to those who believe in substitute goods."

This was a world which Raccamond did not understand and in which he floundered. It was not a world to build a career in but a world in which crust, derring-do, luck, and lawlessness had the upper hand. Raccamond felt that someone had cheated him.

And at this time he received from his secret man, entered as accountant in the Brussels office, the following note,

Dear Mr. Raccamond,
   I have made very serious, but none the less, expected discoveries. Come at once. For your own interest and for your clients', lose no time. You will be in a key position.

                                   Yours,
                                   P (Posset)

Raccamond admired the calm with which he received this intimation; but a few hours afterwards, seeing himself in a restaurant mirror, he found that he was pale as dough. He divined quite well what he was to learn. He put through a call to Brussels at lunchtime, from the Brasserie Universelle in the Avenue de l'Opéra, where he would not be likely to meet any of the bank's men, and there he got the guarded information from Posset,

"I have found some private ledgers which will explain a great deal. A. manages very large accounts." (A. was Alphendéry.)

Aristide went to the bank and for a few hours hung about the board room, a pallid bloated brooding thing, without saying a word to anyone. The word went round that he was neurotic because he had just discovered that he had syphilis. This was natural, for almost every man in the board room, from time to time, was suspected or known, or reported by his best friends, to have just contracted syphilis or gonorrhea. Now, some more imaginative and more learned declared that they had always suspected it, and that he was certainly now in the early dementia stage of general paresis; some thought he should take insulin and some thought milk should be injected; some inclined for salvarsan, and others thought a wound in one of the feet or hands would draw off the madness from his head.

Aristide sat in a chair near Jacques Manray's desk, unaware of these whispers, wretchedly intent on finding out what Manray was doing, whether he was marking orders in a special way, whether he really sent orders through to the telegraph room, through the pneumatic tube, and whether these orders were sent in complete, just as the client gave them. But Manray sent every order through the pneumatic tube. It suddenly occurred to Raccamond then that it was Alphendéry, sitting within, who was the secret agent; and he figured him sitting in the telegraph room, marking the order slips malevolently, pretending to execute the orders, never telegraphing them to the stock exchanges of the world, but making up the prices himself and presently sending down confirmations to trusting clients. The clients were now sitting at ease in Jules's fat green armchairs, in peaceful rows, in a contented daze, staring at the figures marked up by the board boys. Some few thin, fretful clients, habitual gamblers with small incomes or wasted patrimonies, walked up and down, starting every time the pneumatic tube whirred.

These were the ones that bought and sold their tens and fifties of International Nickel, I.T.T., Mexican Eagle, and American Radiator, dealt in stop-loss orders, and spent their nights figuring out schemes of incredible complexity in which, by the manipulation of ten or twenty shares of a cheap stock, they would secure a handsome profit. Abernethy Gairdner, the most insensate of them all, now handed in a slip to Manray. Manray noted down the amounts, but before he sent it down the pneumatic tube, Aristide suddenly observed that the slip was covered with notations. He snatched it out of Manray's hand, thinking he had a clue, and read:

> BUY 10 shares of Int. Nickel at 15: put in an order good this month to sell 20 shs. Int. Nickel at 20. Put in a stop-loss order to sell 10 shs. at 13; and if this is obtained, cancel the order to sell at 20.
> *Signature of client:*
> ABERNATHY GAIRDNER

Aristide stood up and rushed to Gairdner with the sheet in his hand, "Is this your order?"

Gairdner looked at him, outraged (he thought some question of margins had come up), looked at it, "Yes! Why, hasn't it gone up yet! It ought to be on the floor of the New York Stock Exchange by now!" Crestfallen, Aristide thrust the slip back at Manray, "Send it through, marked *Hurry!*" Manray looked at him insolently but said nothing, and sent the order through. Aristide was ill at ease. The solution was inside, in the telegraph room, where Alphendéry sat deviling the orders. He pushed open the door behind Manray and penetrated the inside corridor. The door to the cable room was locked: inside he heard the voices of Jules Bertillon and Alphendéry. Alphendéry could usually be heard all through the corridor: just now he was talking in a very low voice. Everything seemed to hang together, though, to confirm Aristide's suspicions.

He went to his own room, restlessly came out again, patrolled the inside corridors of the bank, and when Jules at last came out of the cable room, Aristide approached him and said nervously that he must have leave of absence at once, to go to Brussels. His son, he muttered, his son was in trouble: he had tried to obtain money by hocking radios obtained on time payment.

The next afternoon the phone girl gave Alphendéry the ritual warning, "Call from Brussels for Mr. Bertillon. Mr. Bertillon is out . . . will you take it?"

"Hello, hello! Why, is that you, Cornelis? . . . About Raccamond? . . . What do you say, I don't hear . . . He's taken the books; what books? . . . Are you sure they were *the* books? . . . How did he get them? . . . Fire that man at once. Where is Raccamond? . . . Now, look, now look, Cornelis, don't worry, calm down, and tell me what happened: he's rather a neurotic you know, blows off . . . he'll cool down. It's blackmail obviously: he'll come to terms, and we'll meet him if we can't get them back in the meantime . . . Don't worry, Cornelis: his police record isn't so hot—you know he was on the wrong side in the Claude Brothers—What? . . . Did he? Yes, come if you want to; but no, wait till we telephone you again—at your house tonight. Don't worry, Cornelis: we've had these gangsters before. . . . Thanks very, very much, Cornelis. I'll telephone. Thanks, very, very much. Don't worry. . ."

Alphendéry, pale but collected, gathered himself together and bounded out of the room. He bumped into Jules who, with negligent elegance, and too lazy to work, was taking an airing up and down his corridors, gently whistling.

"They told me there was a Brussels call: I expect it was Raccamond. You took it? Say, you look as if there were a moratorium."

"It was Cornelis: Raccamond has stolen the books of the Brussels office."

"What books?"

"The books of the anonymous numbered accounts and the *contre-partie* books . . ."

"He can't get away with that: that's a crime. I'll jail him."

"Listen, Jules: Raccamond has been to Legris, to the gold brokers, to Vanderallee, to the Scheldt en Dogger Bank, to our own lawyers, and to one of Cornelis's family friends and has told them that we are crooks, that we cheat the fisc, bucket the clients' holdings, and are on the verge of bankruptcy! How's that for a bunch of news for an innocent client? He told Cornelis's friend that we've been making a fortune out of the ruin of our clients, as with the K. & T. position."

"He's crazy. Do you think we can get him shut up?"

"Let's get the books first. The *contre-partie* position. Cornelis says he's like a madman: he expected him to fall down in a fit on the floor."

"We should have thrown him out the first time he ratted on us. Tell Cornelis to arrest him."

"Cornelis says give him the word, and he'll do it; give him forty-eight hours in jail to think things over. The police scare him blue. But there are the books. The police will get them! Think of that! The best is to let him come here and show his hand."

"Why didn't Cornelis get the books from him?"

"He had them under his coat; he stood there, shouting and denouncing with the books under his coat. While he was in Byng and Company's office, young Byng rang up Cornelis and asked him if he should arrest him. Cornelis said yes. Only it might drive him battier. You can't tell. Suppose he has got syphilis! Everyone says he has. He's the factor X."

"What the deuce did you let him go up there for? You're supposed to be looking after him," raved Jules.

"I tell him? He said you told him."

"He lied. I told Brouwer to keep that safe locked if he had to sleep there all night."

Alphendéry nodded in a melancholy style. "Yes, but this fellow he introduced there, Posset the accountant, well he knew him in Léon and Méline's business."

Jules's eyes flashed, "Léon! that guy is nothing but hard luck. Is he in this?"

"Jules, Jules! Let's stick to realities. Our meek and hard-working friend Raccamond, whom we took out of the gutter, has been paying Posset a bonus out of his own perquisites and Posset got the books on a ruse. He nearly got them two months ago but Brouwer thought it was impudent curiosity. The only thing is to let him come here as if we were unwarned, and steal the books from him. Brouwer says that Raccamond has been laying for us for months, that he's not just a victim of moral indignation as he pretends."

"I'll get him if I have to shoot him myself," said Jules.

They had gone into Jules's room and shut the door. "Where is he now, Michel?"

"Disappeared: perhaps on the train. Cornelis says he's amok at present; he doesn't even know his own mind. He nearly went out of his mind; he rushed in with the book open in his hand and screamed, 'You've been eighty thousand shares short, pyramiding all the time. I've been swindled. My clients might have been ruined: you're a bunch of thieves.' "

"I hope he drops dead," said Jules. "Go and get William."

Jules, after some hours of conference, remarked easily, "You may think I'm crazy, but I'm going to call in Jean de Guipatin and tell him our troubles. He got us into this: he recommended Aristide."

"Don't do it," pleaded Alphendéry. "I don't trust aristocrats."

"We're sunk as it is, aren't we, with Aristide broadcasting his news," said Jules, taking up the telephone. "Mademoiselle! Get me the Comte de Guipatin."

Guipatin was in his office with the works of Vicki Baum. He came in at once and smiled to see them all looking so iron-browed. "What's the trouble? Markets are down."

Jules was cheerful at once. "Sit down, Jean, and we'll tell you a bedtime story. It's not secret. All Brussels and Amsterdam know it already. Etienne's just carted out a wastepaper basketful of telegrams of congratulation." He picked up some telegrams and passed them to Jean; "Your bright baby, Aristide Raccamond: heard of him? He's stolen the books from our Brussels accounting office. Aristide's amok. They control the English accounts there —divided sovereignty. He's on the train now, coming to Paris, either to blackmail us, or report us to the Criminal Division. What's your bet?"

They were watching Guipatin carefully.

"Heads for blackmail," said Jean suavely.

They spun a coin. It came down heads. "Blackmail," said Jules.

Jean looked at them and asked, "What can he blackmail you on?"

"Selling out the clients," Jules acknowledged frankly. "He's got two of the *contre-partie* books. And fiscal fraud. He's got the Brussels and Brussels-A. (that is, really, London and Zurich) anonymous accounts."

"My clients! My brother Paul-Pierre is Brussels-A8, the Comtesse de Voigrand, Brussels 1."

Alphendéry laughed. "Brussels 2 is Dr. Jacques Carrière, his own client. And Reformer Raccamond has stolen his own account, Brussels-A23."

"Twenty-three," cried Jules. "My unlucky number!"

"What can he do with the anonymous accounts?" asked Guipatin, mystified.

"Oh, that shows he's crazy," Jules said testily. "But he's already shown the two books of our short and long position to Legris and Company! Naturally, they do the same thing: they sell out their clients—they bet against us!—but I'd like to break his neck."

Helpfully, Jean de Guipatin considered. "But blackmailing you on income-tax frauds is really blackmailing Carrière, Voigrand, and the other big clients you have. Has he got a scheme for wholesale blackmail?"

"He doesn't know what he's doing," Alphendéry suggested. "He just took what he could and fled."

Guipatin reflected, "The selling-out, the *contre-partie*—how many clients does it affect? I mean, of course," he put in, hastily, "in the books he's stolen. *How* can he annoy you?"

"He can't hurt us at all," said Jules. Alphendéry gave him a reproachful look and said, "A good many clients and large quantities of shares are involved; but the account is operated properly. We have a defense *in law*. The point is simply that the clients would be annoyed if they found out."

"It's operated as a bloc account," deduced Guipatin. "Don't worry. As to your working *contre-partie*—I knew it, or guessed it long ago. Who didn't? The Comtesse de Voigrand said, 'Jules *must* do *contre-partie*': she said that months ago. Raccamond is still in the kindergarten if he didn't get that long ago. How do you make money otherwise? Why, Jules, everyone has always said that you bet against your clients—ever since I heard of the house. There isn't a client who hasn't said it one time or another. Even Abernethy Gairdner."

William laughed, "And so he sends up those jigsaw orders."

"Aristide's a submerged volcano: he has to keep blowing up to a boil," said Alphendéry uneasily.

Guipatin murmured to Jules, "This doesn't upset me at all, Jules: not in the least. It's not criminal; it's not illegal. We'll show him he has no case."

"We've got to get him here," said William.

Alphendéry anxiously said, "What a pity he's crossed the frontier! He didn't steal the books in France: you can't arrest him for larceny here."

Jules said, "I'll send Manray to the station to wait for all the trains coming from Brussels—"

"From Feignies, at the frontier," said Alphendéry, "he may have changed trains."

"All right. Manray will follow Raccamond and try to get the books from him. You'll have to tell Jacques some story—that Raccamond has stolen books showing clients' positions: Manray will be horrified," said Jules.

They dispatched Manray to the Gare de Nord. Waiting for his telephone call—and they knew they might wait a long time—they discussed in detail Raccamond's career. Jules kept saying, "Ptttt!" and, "I told you not to employ that fellow," and "I had a hunch against him from the beginning." Alphendéry kept saying, "I say, if I'd known all this dirt, I would never have—" and, "All the time I was helping him, pushing him, I didn't know his record." William contented himself with gloomy wisecracking. "When they've all learned to blackmail, Jules and you boys can go to work without further interruption by clients," and, "Well, now we can all take a holiday." Jean de Guipatin lamented his own shortsightedness.

"He's just a cunning, dopey peasant," opined William, "like one who terrorizes the village with a gun, to get back the cow he's just sold and keep the profit, too. That's Aristide. Don't get so refined."

"He ruined Claude Brothers in just this way," said Guipatin. "They told me, but I thought it was their excuse."

"To think," exploded Alphendéry, "that he snoops on Jules's money!"

Guipatin shook his head. "If you treat him any differently from the common-or-garden blackmailer, you'll get into trouble. Be short and quick with him. Aristide is a dervish: he works himself into a frenzy of self-justification and hate."

The telephone rang and they heard Manray's voice telling them that Raccamond had just got off the Brussels express and carried numerous baggages with him, including a new valise. A porter took the bags and he the valise. He had taken a taxi and given his home address. Manray wanted to know what he should do now. Should he follow him home and trust to some accident to get the valise in Aristide's own lobby?

"No, come back here: we may need you."

Alphendéry was nervous, "Suppose he goes straight to the Parquet!"

"No: he's got to make out a formal complaint," said Guipatin. "Besides, are those books by themselves enough evidence?"

"No, he can't do a thing with them. I don't suppose he really knows what they mean himself."

"But Posset, his man, has been working on them!"

"Yes," said Jules, "he's a lunatic. I've an idea he'll try to get us. The only thing to do is to watch his house tonight, hustle him into a taxi, and take him for a ride through the Bois de Boulogne, out into the country for a few days until he coughs up."

"He's a coward, coward," said Alphendéry.

"His house is in the Rue du Docteur-Blanche," said William. "How are you going to hustle him into a taxi there? It's full of families and there's a street lamp right outside. And if you think Madame wouldn't inform the police right away! She's more than his lieutenant: she's the field marshal. Perhaps he just wants to give us a fright. He was always gumshoeing around. He could never work out our system. Now he's got the secret, he thinks. Michel ran the bloc account for the house! Michel was on the inside-inside and he's only a poor outfielder! Hence the mental crash and the mixture of honest and fake indignation."

They digested this sensible analysis of William. William had been studying his antipathy for months and was surprised by nothing. All that happened only seemed to him natural—fate gradually squeezing the pomp and life out of one who had despised him.

Jean de Guipatin said solemnly, "Suppose Aristide goes to Cleat, Placket, and Company with the books! He's done odd business with them the last few months."

"No!" cried Michel, turning indignant eyes on Guipatin.

"I knew, I knew," cried Jules impatiently. "He got Smith, his man in London, to copy the lists of our clients, and he sent these lists to Cleat, Placket, and Company. What good did it to him? In the meantime, Smith took Aristide's bribe, and because it wasn't big enough, Smith wrote to me, asking me what to do! I told Smith to give Raccamond the lists of clients, always omitting important names and to take his money. Why not? Smith's got the soul of a double-agent. He works devotedly when he has two bosses. And Raccamond has been slowly tying himself in knots. You see! Luck is with us. Now, if Smith had been faithful to Raccamond we would have been in real trouble: the key books are in London. As it is, he has only books written in what is almost a code."

"When we've finished letting the cat out of the bag," murmured Michel, "we'll be left with a fine stink."

Guipatin laughed, "The old sultans used to punish a faithless wife by tying her in a sack with two wildcats and sinking her in the Bosporus. Imagine the scene inside the sack in the last few moments! Inventive, the Turks! Jules's idea is to sink Aristide with two double-agents—" William was the only one who did not give a nervous laugh: he said, "Double-agents can double again. Aristide won't care what domestic charges you have against him: he's got more on us. He may know the whole story. Get the books or keep him dangling, and in the meantime turn him over to the police."

"On what charge?"

"Income-tax fraud by private denunciation," said William calmly. "I forced his desk and got his private accounts. I also found some letters from the Argentine he would find hard to explain. And he has a bank account in Marseille. I should have had him shadowed all this time."

William had not forced his desk. William had skeleton keys for all locks in the bank. But he was not going to admit this to his brother Jules.

Jacques Manray entered breathless. Into their spiderweb of anxiety he brought a drop of hope, perhaps only his bright-colored face and clear blue eyes. He told his story again. He added, "He's been acting funny for a week."

Jules brusqued his confidence, "The Comte de Guipatin has discovered that Raccamond bribed Smith, the new London clerk, to get the lists of clients holding bonds abroad in our branches."

"Really, sir?" Jacques did not seem overcome by surprise.

They gave him some standing instructions. Manray was to occupy himself normally in the board room; he was to ring on the interphone twice if Raccamond arrived, four times if the police inspectors came in, but without saying a word either through the phone or downstairs.

As they sat there, the telephone rang again and Jules took it up, "Who? Ah, wait a minute." He covered the mouthpiece and murmured, "Here's our man. Michel, take the other earpiece: I want you to get his state of mind. Hallo. Is that you, Raccamond? You were away a devil of a time. How is your son's malfeasance, or whatever? . . . What? You have my books! Who gave them to you? What are you doing with them? . . . Bring those books here at once. Those books are mine, *mine*, my private books! . . . You had better come straight over to the office and bring those books with you. . . . And bring the books or I don't talk business with you. . . . Well, send them to me at once; or better I'll send for them: those are stolen goods. . . . You'll what? . . . Don't make me laugh. They'll— *What!*" Jules puffed with laughter. "Don't be a fool, Aristide," he said, suddenly kind. "Come over here tomorrow morning and talk to me privately, or if you like I'll come and see you tonight. No, tomorrow is better. Let's see what sort of a cock-and-bull story someone's been handing you. . . . You're crazy, Aristide! You come over here and bring the books—if you've got them!" He jammed down the telephone and at once his face blackened with anger.

Alphendéry looked nervous; "Bad!" he said to them all.

"He says he's in bed, he can't come over," said Jules. "I'll bet he's having a conference with his lawyer."

"Who is his lawyer?" asked William.

"Let's see: he had a fight with a tenant of his and—" Alphendéry started up. "Yes, I remember: his lawyer— Maître Lallant! Carrière's lawyer."

"He used to be Carrière's man," Guipatin said dubiously.

"The weasel!" Jules cried, with contempt.

"I don't think he's a real blackmailer," Alphendéry explained. "I think he's terribly startled at what he's found out: he thinks we have never put through a single share to any bourse in the world. He says the telegrams of

632

confirmation we have from Legris and Company in Amsterdam and Stewart in London are a put-up job. He's sure of that, because Legris kicked him out yesterday."

"Not a real blackmailer? And how to explain the accountant pushed into our Brussels office?" Jules sneered.

"He couldn't put in an accountant to look at books of whose existence he was ignorant," objected Alphendéry, unconsciously pleading for Raccamond.

"Let me go and see him tonight, not you," Jean de Guipatin suggested in the end, and this was agreed upon.

Jules asked for Manray on the interphone again, cried, "What!" and put the earpiece down. "Jacques has gone out: what does that mean?"

Scene Eighty-three: Manray's Dilemma

ARISTIDE lay on the couch in the living room, in a dressing gown. Marianne sat in an armchair beside him.

"Don't come near, Mr. Manray: it's influenza. I don't know how he managed to get here. He collapsed as soon as he got into the house: forty of fever."

But the business could not wait. They had telephoned Manray at once to come quickly to the house in the Rue du Docteur-Blanche, because they regarded him as an intimate friend.

"Bertillon is nothing but a swindler, a little Kreuger!"

"You can't say that without proof, Mme. Raccamond!"

They showed him the books, bringing them out from under the covers on Aristide's couch: Aristide would not have them away from his sight. "Complete *contre-partie* accounts, showing that the clients were regularly sold out and had no positions at all when they thought they owned shares."

Manray, who had seen some such maneuvers, was embarrassed. "It is within their rights, Mr. Raccamond, to protect themselves if the market looks bad."

Marianne said firmly, "In most, in almost all cases, the orders to buy and sell shares were never sent through. They were done *on the books* at prices fixed by the bank for the clients."

Marianne did all the talking and Aristide weakly agreed from time to time. Aristide moaned and breathed heavily, "It is terrible, terrible."

"These books show that the clients have been swindled for years."

"Well?" said Jacques.

"What are you going to do about it?"

"How do I know it is true, Mme. Raccamond?"

"We have the proofs, Mr. Manray."

"How do I know you have if you won't let me look in the books? You show me the covers. Brussels A1, B1 . . . that tells me nothing. I know there are bloc accounts called Brussels A1, B1: we execute orders for them."

"And this book?" She held up a large book labeled LONDON FINANCE CORPORATION.

"We have a large client with that name. We do many orders for it."

"What is that client?"

"I don't know."

"It is the Banque Bertillon *contre-partie* account."

"How do I know?"

Marianne Raccamond leaned forward. "Mr. Manray, why should we deceive you? Why should we bring you here?"

"You say Bertillon is a swindler, but you show me no proofs: I think it strange."

Marianne was irritated. "That's not your affair, Mr. Manray. We have those proofs. Let it suffice that we can and will go to the Procurator of the Republic tomorrow if nothing happens!"

"What can happen?" Jacques was confused.

Bertillon had told him Raccamond had stolen clients' books but Raccamond pretended that he had taken the bank's own books. Manray imagined that Raccamond would demand an explanation: it had not yet occurred to him that Raccamond would blackmail Bertillon.

Marianne murmured something, but she had not got her point, and she pressed the dubious Manray again. "Mr. Manray, what would you do if you found out this were true?"

"If it is true, I'm going to Jules Bertillon and I'll say, 'Keep your salary. Mr. Raccamond has told me about the *contre-partie* and the fixing of prices for clients, that you

634

never bought or sold at all. It's no business of mine, but I must resign.' That's all." Jacques was angry for various reasons. He had not sorted out his reasons.

Marianne started. "No, Manray, not a word to Jules Bertillon. You can't do that, don't you see!"

"Why not? Why can't I?"

"No, no, I forbid you absolutely to do that, Mr. Manray."

"You forbid me? Look, Mme. Raccamond, I don't understand at all what you're getting at. What business is it of yours? Why won't you tell Mr. Bertillon? It's bizarre."

Marianne explained energetically, "Don't you see, if he knows, he can make some move? Those rich men are determined. He'd do anything to get the books back. He'd give anything—"

Jacques flushed. "If it's blackmail you mean," he said rising and taking his hat, "I'd better get out of here." He left without saying good-by.

Scene Eighty-four: The Honorable Nations

ORDINARILY they all stayed until the cables from the American market ceased at 8 P.M. or a little later, if the ticker was behind time. This evening they put Urbain Voulou and the telegraph girls in charge and went off to Jules's house to dine together. As they were leaving, at about 6:45 P.M., Mouradzian the Armenian came to the door and asked for an interview with Jules. The other two, glad of the interruption, went out to confabulate and dash water in their faces. Mouradzian sat down gingerly, in one of the armchairs. He was small, dark, and evil-looking.

"Mr. Bertillon, I speak to you as man to man. I have been a long time in business. There is a man in your employ who is damaging your credit."

"Go on," said Jules. "Who is it?"

Mouradzian moved uneasily. "I wish to name no names: it would be wrong of me to inculpate a colleague. But take measures to protect yourself, Mr. Bertillon. For some months, a colleague of mine has come up to me and insinuated that this was a *contre-partie* house. He has doubtless gone to others with the same speech. Only two days ago this colleague came to me, seeming very much tormented or angry, and said that he would shortly have the proofs that this is a *contre-partie* house and that he would tell the interested parties that they were being cheated. He asked me to withdraw my clients from this house and to take them, with his, to another house. Mr. Bertillon, I have been a long time in this business. Please listen to my advice. Do not employ Frenchmen in stock-exchange business."

Jules was surprised at this. "Why not, Mouradzian?" He was as serious as the Armenian.

"Excuse me, Mr. Bertillon, because men of that type and of that class are untrustworthy in stock-exchange business. They are ambitious, jealous, and they think of nothing but sapping and blackmail. They are rotten with love of money and ambition. They will destroy anyone who stands in their way. If they can't do it one way they will do it another way. I know. I am very old in this business. Mr. Bertillon, I have been loyal here. Please, please, take only Levantines in this business. Levantines are honorable: Turks, Syrians, Cypriotes, Greeks, Phanariotes, my own nation, even Georgians, Jews, Arabs, Roumanians, Persians are better than Frenchmen. We cannot betray you: we are honorable nations. We have been trusted for centuries! We have fulfilled all the duties of honorable financial posts for centuries. I do not wish to speak of myself; but, incidentally, my own family for five centuries has been respected in finance. And what were the punishments if we failed! I speak from a base, because a disputative point of view. There was no mercy if we failed. Employ only Easterners, Mr. Bertillon. They are not jealous of you. They understand your business. They are not frittering away their time trying to pry into your secrets. They do not care what are your secrets, as long as you do business yourself. In this venal democracy of money-changers and tip-beggars, your compatriots are your foes, those who want to see you trodden underfoot. Success breeds hatred. I say this because I have lived in the East and seen different things. We try to do our own business. Weed out your compatriots, Mr. Bertillon: they are treacherous and hypocritical."

"Thanks, Mouradzian," said Jules, cautiously and without affection. "I don't see how I can get rid of my Frenchmen. This is a French bank."

"I understand very well. But I say—a man here is trying to ruin you. You have a blackmailer here. I cannot name him: I can only say, he is here."

"Mouradzian," Jules said pleasantly to the old man, "do you think we bucket the orders? I know people say it."

Mouradzian shrugged his shoulders. "That is not my business, Monsieur. That is your business. For myself, I don't spread rumors."

Jules tapped with the paper knife on the table. "We do *contre-partie,* you know."

Mouradzian lifted his intelligent crafty eyes to Jules. "I always thought so, Monsieur. Otherwise, how would you have kept afloat and stayed solvent in this crisis? You have done your clients a favor. I find myself well placed here. *Contre-partie* in times like this is nothing but an insurance policy—and one that will be paid. But some, sons of artisans, are too thick to understand that!" He looked at the carpet with contempt. "And such say that one is bankrupt, although he pays all claims!"

"Stick with me, Mouradzian, and we'll do well together," Jules finished jocularly, leaning back in his chair, elegant and distant. Mouradzian bowed and retired. Jules got up sleekly, called the others: "Let's go."

"What did the little fellow want?"

"To warn me against Raccamond: he did it nicely. Raccamond asked him to withdraw his accounts; says we are going bankrupt and we do *contre-partie.* That fellow has to be wiped out."

Scene Eighty-five: Jacques Returns

WILLIAM expostulated, "He's been living in a fairy world: every time the market went up or down against his clients, I paid out and paid out, making up losses, and all to prevent his having a nervous breakdown."

Jean de Guipatin looked worn now. "You shouldn't have done it, William; it's an option on trouble. The man calculates that there's something wrong, if you can afford to do that; for he reasons, 'Then how do they make

637

their money?' Follows a stretch of spying and blackmailing. Or the fellow is so stupid that he thinks money grows in banks and when he's undeceived and he finds it has to be made, and that he's been living in Cockaigne, he goes mad. There's probably a bit of both in Raccamond."

"Where is he? Where is Manray?" cried Jules restlessly, unable to bear the anxiety any more. The telephone rang. Manray was downstairs and asked to see Mr. Bertillon alone.

"Come up!" He said to them, "Manray knows something."

Manray looked round at the company when he came in. "I must see you alone: it's urgent," he said low and earnestly. His round face looked tired, too.

"If it's about Raccamond, you can tell everything: we know all about it."

Manray was embarrassed but he said manfully, "Mr. Bertillon, I just went over to Raccamond's house, and," his voice fell, "he looked wretched. I know everything that he has to tell. He has a lot of books there, the London Finance Corporation, and all, and he says they're blinds, for the bank to sell out the investments of its own clients. He says no shares were done in the markets, only written on our books."

Jules cried, "What the hell did you go down there for, anyway? I told you to wait in the board room."

"Mr. Bertillon, what else could I do? As soon as I got downstairs, he was on the phone. I rang off, telling him I was busy. He rang up again, then she spoke and they kept insisting, 'Come right away, most important, secret, for the bank; otherwise it would mean ruin.' They said not to tell you: I was scared."

"You had no right going down there without telling me. What did he say to you?"

"It was the woman who kept talking all the time. He hardly said a word, and when he began to speak she shut him up and turned to me and said, 'No, this is the situation.' She's the real Raccamond, Mr. Bertillon."

He told them the conversation he had had with them. Bertillon said, "And are you going to resign, Jacques."

Jacques hesitated, "No, Mr. Bertillon. I didn't know what to do. It was all news to me; I was confused, and I was trying to make out why they wanted me over there to tell me all that. I couldn't make out why the woman was doing all the talking. I said that to gain time. And I didn't know what I was going to do. But I didn't want to play whatever game they had." He hesitated, looking round the circle, said in a lower but firm tone, "Raccamond's sick but that wife of his is determined: either they want to ruin the bank, or they want blackmail. I can't make out. Maybe Carrière is behind him. He used to be Carrière's man."

"I don't think so," said Jules. "No, no: Carrière wants us to pay him, doesn't he? Listen, Jacques, are you going to stick by me?"

"Yes, Mr. Bertillon," said Jacques in a low tone. "I don't see what else I can do." He realized that Alphendéry and Comte de Guipatin were standing by Jules. Jacques was worried, though; he got up the courage to say, "Only, I'd just like to know—if what he says is true."

"You've given us prices yourself, Jacques," said Alphendéry.

"I know, I know," worried Jacques, "only" (almost to himself) "I didn't know it was so ba—so much. But the rest—that you never bought or sold at all?"

"No," Jules reassured him, "in that he's just gone clean off his head. Don't bother about that."

Jacques thought of something else. "They're going to ring me again tomorrow and make another appointment with me: they say they'll show me the books, they think. I don't know what they want me for. I told them I couldn't stay long this afternoon, because there was work to do. They kept saying, 'you're working for nothing: it's all a swindle.' What shall I do?"

"Put him off."

Jacques worried, "He might go to others."

"Listen, Jacques: he's been to about a dozen people already. He spoke to Mouradzian two months ago, and since. Mouradzian came here and warned me in his own way. If he wants you so badly, he must have something in mind. Be nice to him but coax him along till we find out his game."

"It's a time equation," said William.

"He must have something in mind for you," said the Comte. "Let me do something for you, Jules? I'll go and see the Raccamonds this evening myself."

"Say," Jules exclaimed, "while you're there, see if he's

in cahoots with this rat Parouart. There's some tangle there."

Scene Eight-six: Samson Redivivus

ARISTIDE strode into the Paris office on the morning of the next day with a portentous air. He frowned at the appointments of the bank. "Handsome as a share pusher's bank," he muttered. He said nothing to any of the personnel, simply went in and said to Urbain Voulou, "Everything all right while I was away? I caught flu: I've still got a fever, but urgent business arising from the Brussels visit—I hope Mme. de Sluys-Forêt got her *restitutions!*"

"Yes," said Voulou meekly. The market being down, he was ready to flatter the proud. "Alphendéry saw to that. She was very nice when she left."

Aristide waved this aside. "Is Bertillon in yet? I think I saw his Hispano outside."

"Yes," Voulou admitted in mild surprise, "but I think he's got someone with him."

"He will see me," Aristide said.

Aristide Raccamond burst into the room, haggard, swept them all with a "terrible" avenging grimace, and threw three large books on to the carpet in front of them. Then he placed his right foot on top of them, balancing his great body with an elephantine dignity, and thrusting his head forward, glared under bent eyebrows at Jules.

Jules surveyed this with calm. "Well, Aristide!"

"Answer," said Aristide, pointing at the books with an accusing finger.

Alphendéry had a flash of illumination: he cried, "Harry Baur!"

Jean de Guipatin gave a clap of laughter. "That's it!"

"What?" asked Jules, turning his head with the slow dignity of a stick insect.

"Aristide's imitating Harry Baur in a Bernstein play," explained Jean de Guipatin.

But they did not laugh. Jules turned his head with the same motion, back to Aristide. Aristide looked suddenly at them, bent and picked up the books. At the same moment, they all had the same regret: why hadn't Jean given Aristide a blow and got the books? Had Aristide this idea, too? He looked at Jean de Guipatin and moved away from him, replacing the books cannily under his coat.

"Answer," he said to Jules. "You have no answer."

"Don't act the fool, Aristide," said the Comte de Guipatin.

Aristide swung round to him. "You," he said weightily, "you, Comte de Guipatin, do not know what they have done? You do not know that your friend Jules Bertillon is a blackguard?"

"What Bertillon has done is his own affair: I don't steal books," said the Comte roughly. "You are acting like a blackmailer, Aristide, and you deserve to be treated like one."

"Monsieur le Comte, you stand by your friends—but if you knew what I know, you would consider it an affair of honor: you have been swindled by this—" he turned round and gave Jules a glance of contempt—"this skipjack."

Before the Comte could answer, Jules said sharply, "Cut the act, Raccamond: give me the books and tell me what you want. You want something."

"Gangster," said Raccamond forcibly.

"I'll knock you down if you insult my brother," remarked William, rising and eying him. Guipatin motioned William back; William took no notice of this, for Aristide was a coward and had taken a step towards the door. In his warm, pleasant voice, Guipatin begged Raccamond to be reasonable, give up the books which he had no right to, and which concerned private accounts. He was surprised, he said, to see Raccamond, of whose ability he had the highest opinion, behave so irresponsibly. Someone had lied to him, some miserable clerk, perhaps, with the idea of plundering Raccamond. What a position Raccamond was in! He could be blackmailed by this clerk forever. And Raccamond was lucky if Jules Bertillon did not dismiss him immediately without handing over his clients, for, Guipatin assured him, "People of my acquaintance do not deal with blackmailers. A blackmailer is welcome nowhere. You do not realize, Aristide, that your present behavior will only be called blackmail by persons of position.

You do not see yourself this way, Aristide, because you are a dramatic type and you see yourself as a personage in a financial drama. You are excited by the Kreuger history. You think you have walked into a robbers' lair; you have only walked into a mare's-nest. My poor, my good friend, collect yourself; think where you stand. If you think you've been robbed, let's go over the accounts, all together. No one here wants to rob you. You're not a subordinate—you're a person very much valued by Mr. Bertillon and by myself. I myself asked Mr. Bertillon to accept your clients." A pause. The Comte de Guipatin was every inch a comte!

Raccamond looked at them all dubiously, with a certain cunning. He looked strange enough, in his lamentable heavy fat, with the books bulging his coat. After a moment he said, addressing himself only to Guipatin, "Monsieur le Comte, I must respect what you say: you are an honest man. I must see you alone. Will you come outside with me?"

Jules nodded faintly. "What have you to tell me that you cannot say here before my friends, Raccamond?"

"You don't understand, Monsieur le Comte!"

"I can't speak to you while you have some books stolen from the offices of my friend. You don't seem to understand, Aristide, that it is—simply and plainly impossible for me."

"I will take these books home and come and meet you," said Aristide. "Monsieur le Comte, I cannot give the books back, I cannot: they are my only defense! They have ruined us all," he cried suddenly, looking at them all, in misery. "We are all ruined, Monsieur le Comte."

"You had better leave the books here, Aristide: whatever you think, it is not your business," said Guipatin.

"No, never!" cried Aristide, starting back. "No, my whole future is bound up with them!"

"Where shall we meet?" asked the Comte.

Aristide moved impulsively nearer to him; the Comte, carefully indulgent, watched him come. "Come with me, Monsieur le Comte!"

"Go," said Jules coldly.

They waited. In half an hour they had a phone call from the Comte, telling them that Aristide, who was very decided, had agreed to come to a parley at Jules's house at eight-thirty that evening.

"Why my house?" argued Jules. "I don't want him there: let him come to the bank."

Jean de Guipatin's persuasive voice over the phone detailed their conversation. "He's always been anxious to see your interior, Jules: if he can achieve this great visit, with his books, perhaps we'll have him calmer. Raccamond is a holdup man with weaknesses: his chief foible is luxury and period furniture. Be as grand as you like, Jules: put on evening dress . . . pretend you've just come from dinner. I told him you were dining with Débuts of the Banque du Littoral du Nord. He's impressed. I'll be in dinner jacket myself. Tell your butler to be theatrical. That is what Aristide understands. I can't say I've succeeded. He's gone home to talk with his wife. But this is the first step gained, at any rate. He's not going to the police tonight. By the way, he insists on seeing you alone, without your aides-de-camp, in his language. At the same time, have someone there—William, Michel perhaps. Do you mind my coming? I'm supposed to meet him this evening and act as his second. I thought it the most likely way to get hold of the books!"

"Yes: meet him at my house."

"Let it be grand, Jules: put the lusters on . . . act the grandee!"

"Trust me!"

Scene Eighty-seven: An Interview

AFTER dinner Jules took a book and seated himself in a divided reception room. The others went behind the double-doors and took coffee with Claire-Josèphe. She was one of the prettiest women in Paris. She was now in a sober dinner dress from Molyneux, without ornaments, but with her hair curled and piled in a ravishing design, calculated to impose respect even on a blackmailer.

When Aristide rang at the door, the footman, in evening dress, opened it and greeted Aristide with the air attributed by the goodhearted to grand dukes. Aristide did not reply, but walked in heavily, burdened with the three books.

"Mr. Raccamond?" said the footman.

"Yes."

"Mr. Raccamond," announced the footman, in half-tones.

Aristide looked up, saw another splendid domestic at the head of the staircase, and bit his lip. He thrust his hat at the footman and began to climb the stairs, his eyes wild, sorrowful, and rimmed with fatigue. He now stared with spite and hate at the white stone stairs, the tapestries, the carved chest, the metal plates.

"Mr. Raccamond," announced the butler loudly at the entrance to the salon. Raccamond lingered behind him for a moment to adjust the sliding books and his eye fell on a beautiful lacquer vase. He trembled. He pushed aside the half-draped curtain, pushed back the butler, and, rushing towards Jules, cried with trembling finger, "You're a thief, you've stolen all you've got. I know you!" He looked back at the butler to see if he had heard and cried again, "You're a shark, a low thief, a pickpocket: you're not the grandee you pretend to be. I know you."

The butler hesitated, waiting for a sign from Jules to pinion Raccamond.

"That is all, Meadows," said Jules.

The butler went off to tell Claire-Josèphe and the coffee drinkers that their visitor had arrived. But they were already silent, listening to the raised voice. Guipatin frowned. He had left Raccamond in a reasonable state of mind: where had he drunk up this fury?

"From that woman," said Claire-Josèphe. "I just know she twists him round her finger. She's like these men that climb telegraph poles: he's the bit of rope she pushes up, knots up, and puts her foot in."

William was listening at the door.

Aristide, bowed, bullish, his loose lapels hanging largely out from his tortoise belly, stood in the archway looking at Jules.

Jules got up and came forward. "Aristide, sit down. Put the books down. What are you afraid of?"

Aristide came slowly forward until he stood in the middle of the room: his grip on the books tightened. Then he suddenly said in a loud stormy tone, "I brought you clients worth millions of francs and I don't know what's going on in the bank. They might all have been ruined! I would have had to commit suicide. These books conceal gigantic—" he took a step forward as if he staggered slightly—"incredible operations of fraud."

"Say that word again," said Jules in a low menacing tone.

"I say, of fraud," cried Aristide. "The bank is no bank but a miserable bucket shop: it exists for no other purpose. I have been robbed, the clients have been robbed, systematically, over years. I know, besides, where to lay my finger, to put it on the instigator." His face darkened; he looked round at the empty room. In two panels in the wall two splendid Greuzes hung.

"Have a drink?" said Jules.

"No, no, nothing. I will not drink in this house, till I get some explanation, some satisfaction—"

"Wait a minute, Aristide," said Jules in his brittle high voice. "You haven't told me what you were doing in Brussels the days you were supposed to be looking after your son and the clients. Why don't you sit down, put down your books, behave normally? You're a most abnormal man; never the smallest thing happens but you're instantly at boiling point. I think you must be ill. If you are, say so and we'll give you leave of absence."

"My clients!" said Raccamond wildly, as if he were going to sob.

"Your clients have never suffered with our house. Your clients have often had money restituted to them when they have lost. Your clients! Find another house in the city to treat them the way we do."

"You have good reason," said Raccamond viciously, looking straight at Jules. "You have good reason—you should restitute all. I'm going round to see them—to tell them—to blazon your name, to make your name a byword. I'll let them know what you have been doing with that Jew."

Jules had a forced laugh. "You'll make yourself ridiculous, Aristide."

"Yes? And these books? They talk, I think."

Jules said decidedly, "You're going to leave them here: they're my property."

"Never!" He paled frightfully, looked behind him. "Never! These are to bring you and your accomplices to justice."

"Aristide, what is it you want? Tell me: I'll make some arrangement with you."

"How can I believe a word you say? Liars, liars, swindlers. One moment after I leave here it will be new combinations, new plots, new conspiracies, and my clients are to suffer. I will be ruined! My God, what did I let myself in for? You never kept a straight account! Every time they put in an order to buy, you sold; every time to sell, you bought. Those orders never reached the stock exchange. My God, when I think what's been going on! Mr. Bertillon, I always thought of you as an honorable man . . . how could you have done it? I can't believe my own ears and eyes. But I have the books," he suddenly ended cunningly. "They convince me."

"Sit down," urged Jules.

"No, no, I can't sit down here. I don't trust any of you. You have all told me lies; you have never told me a thing. I asked for a statement, I got jokes. I asked for special attention for my clients, when all the time behind my back you and your brother, and I don't know who else, were fleecing them. How can I believe a single word you say? Away from me, away from me!"

"It's hard to get away from you in my own house," commented Jules irritably. "Although it would be a pleasure," he said to himself. "If you can't talk like a human being in business and not a prima donna, there's no doing anything for you. Now what do you want?"

Meanwhile he was walking round the room, apparently carelessly, with his face towards Raccamond and his eyes on the books. "I don't know what you're talking about," Jules decided to say. "Aristide, show me these books! I have certain connections, certain arrangements which I am not obliged to reveal to you nor to anyone. Mr. Alphendéry conducts the whole Brussels side of the business. Perhaps he has done things without consulting me; that is possible: he has the power."

"If he has, if he has—he'll pay for it: I'll denounce him to the police," cried Aristide.

"I'll ask him myself," said Jules. "If either of us has been swindled, if your clients have lost a sou, even a sou, I'll discharge him."

A faint color mounted into Aristide's cheeks, but he said painfully, "It isn't a question of loss—not in financial terms. It is the security of our house!" He suddenly cried out, as if in the greatest trouble, "The security of the house is at stake! You must call him to account. If you don't I'll know that you and your brother are in league with him. Think of my position vis-à-vis my clients! Suppose the house fails tomorrow morning with this—frightful, frightful position! What am I to say? They'll blame me; they'll bring in the police! Where am I to go for my bread and butter? Who will believe I didn't know myself?"

"You mean," said Jules equably, "because of the immense salary you get?"

Aristide stared at him and became furious. "You're threatening me now? I knew you weren't sincere. You're all conspiring to ruin me and my clients. I always knew it!"

"You're a fool," returned Jules with irritation. "Your clients haven't lost anything. What damage has been done them, eh? Eh?"

"I'm charging *abuse of confidence*," said Aristide, looking terrible. "You know there are laws against that? You and your gangsters haven't spent years poaching on the law, for nothing: you know the law . . . you know where the shoe pinches. You'll come to terms with me, or I'll call in the police."

"What do the books prove?" asked Jules. "Can you read them?"

"I know what they prove; I know what I have."

"The fact is," said Jules, "your clients have never lost a penny: their losses have sometimes been paid back to them, and you're this minute wondering what you came here for? I'll tell you what—for blackmail. But you have nothing to blackmail on; you have a few innocent, but strictly private books in code."

"I can read these books," said Aristide, with cunning, "because I have in my hands the records of orders passed through—confirmations of orders received from various brokers, plus transactions in these books, tally with orders sent in by clients."

"You couldn't have found that out in a week," said Jules.

"No. I have a right to safeguard my clients' interests."

"Listen, Aristide. Your clients put their money in the market; they lose it to the market. If a broker simply sits on his heels and doesn't give a word of advice, his clients will ruin themselves, simply on the turn of the wheel. All their money is gone: it goes into the market. Supposing, for the sake of argument, the broker does not execute the orders given to him. A client wants 100 International Nickel at 15. The broker gives it to him at 15. That is, he writes down in his account books: Mr. Smith, Jones, or Robinson, owns 100 shares of International Nickel at 15. Where is the loss? A month later the client comes and says, 'Give me my 100 Nickel at 15,' and he gets his 100 Nickel at 15. Where is the loss?"

"It's abuse of confidence," said Aristide. "And if the market goes up, you have to pay him 100 Nickel at 17, perhaps. You are ruined."

Jules smiled caustically. "Aristide, the market goes down. The market always goes down for the wise."

Raccamond was baffled. "It's abuse of confidence."

Jules continued, "But we have not done transactions on the books for your clients. For the rest, as I was saying, if we like to assume that the client is always wrong, and we bet against him, what business is that of yours? We don't stop you from putting in your own orders."

"You never executed my orders," exclaimed Aristide.

"I can show you thousands of confirmations, thousands of telegrams to and from our brokers," said Jules coolly, "yours among them."

Aristide said stubbornly, "What is there to tell me that one single order has ever been put through in this house, for the clients? But I see you charge for state and local and federal taxes in various countries, and for telegraph charges! That is robbery. I can bring in the police for that."

"You can look at my files, Aristide," said Jules, wearily, "because I hate to see you in this state. I liked you. You were a good customers' man."

"I can believe," sneered Raccamond, "that a man who has jeopardized the entire fortunes of valuable and loyal clients for years will do something especially for me because he worries about my health. And Alphendéry! Explain his role! Don't soft-soap me. I've been in business before. I know rogues are smooth-tongued when their backs are to the wall."

"And what would you do with your back to the wall, Raccamond?"

"Confess and make my terms with a man," said Aristide.

Jules laughed. After a moment he said, "Then you don't

648

want to see the confirmations, the duplicate orders, and the rest? That's curious, for a man who makes such a point of nicety, who is so scrupulous about the execution of clients' orders! You have something else in mind, Aristide. Confess and make terms with me!"

He turned as if stung, irritated by the constant perambulating of Jules, whose design, he suspected, was to get hold suddenly of the books. "Suppose you show me the duplicates! How do I know they weren't made this afternoon to your order?"

Jules did not trouble to appease Aristide. "You know something about running clerks yourself. Your record would look nice, you paying a clerk in my Brussels office to steal my books and the private papers of clients and bringing them yourself to another country to blackmail me."

"Blackmail! No one can say that of me," cried Aristide, looking at Jules with revulsion. "You are trying to frighten me. I won't be put off. I know your resources, men of your type. Bluff is your only weapon."

"You can talk to Berthellot in the morning," said Jules. He took no pleasure in this caterwauling, and his delicate head was beginning to ache. "In the meantime, leave the books here, and I assure you you'll have the satisfaction you want."

"How do I know that Berthellot isn't your agent, too? How do I know that all the employees in your Paris office are not bought and trained to conceal your special methods? Berthellot! I never liked him; I suspected him. And Mlle. Gentil! She never co-operated. She refused to let the accounting departments give me information. I *had* to bribe to get information I expected to get freely. I didn't want to. As for your accounts, I can imagine how reliable they are! These lawsuits haven't been collecting round the bank for nothing. When you are brought down, Bertillon, do you think it will be any satisfaction to me? I must do it, to clean the city of a swindler; but what is there in it for me? No one will trust me any more." He was silent. After a moment's thought, he said mournfully, "Alphendéry was working in the background for you, against me. I was nothing."

"Yes. Alphendéry was against you. I listened to him too much. You are right. But you don't treat me humanly, Aristide. Don't look so tragic, Raccamond. You're the

649

only one in the bank who could take the whole business in this way. Anyone else would spend some time confirming and running to earth before he made this sort of riot. You have almost made me sick of the whole thing: I can close the bank when I want to, you know."

Aristide, moved at first, was shocked by Jules's conclusion. Unfortunate expression of lassitude! It was intended to frighten Aristide; and did so. "Without paying them—the clients!—then it is all over! I—my moneys—" He saw William Bertillon, with a flushed face, coming through the doorway. "I know you: there's nothing you can say to me that would interest me."

"Calm yourself, Raccamond." William smiled balefully at his enemy. "If it's assets you want to see, you'll see them. Assets aren't what we lack round here; all we want is a little common sense and less drama."

"Don't try to be clever with me. Unless you can show that you have sufficient assets to cover all the equities of all the clients, I am going to call the police."

"We'll show you," said William.

"I'm damned if I'll show you my private business," cried Jules suddenly out of his calm. "Who are you to call me to account? Go to blazes! I'll run my own bank in my own way. I'll run you out of town if you try to threaten me. You miserable bourse runner! Where did you get all the poppycock that you're full of! You aren't a customers' man, you're an actor. You run round all day thinking of nothing but your own importance. Pipe down, man! The world will be easier for you. I've got assets; bonds, stocks, gold, silver, what you want. . . . But why the dickens should I show it to you? How are you better than the rest of the customers' men? You forget yourself. You've been well treated. You'll never get the treatment anywhere else you got with me. Your accounts are nothing, especially now—they're mostly in the red. You'd have a lot of difficulty transferring debit balances to other houses. But we've been more than merciful to your clients in particular, because of your peculiar temperament, Raccamond. Their margins have often gone down to two per cent or less, and we've neither called them nor wiped them out. Where else would they get such treatment? Some of them haven't even got equities."

This unwise catalogue of his commercial impotence only angered him. He took a step nearer to Jules, who was leaning languidly on a table. He suddenly took a chair and sat down on it, leaning his head still nearer, "Ah, yes, why? Yes, I asked myself that question several times, without knowing the answer. I thought you were unusually nice to me, as you say. Now, I know why. It meant nothing to you. The accounts on margin did not exist. The clients kept a margin for shares which were not in your account. You had already sold them out. Or never bought them. It did not matter to you if you never called them at all. Yes, I understand such charity. Admit it. I know the whole truth."

Alphendéry, who was standing at the door, advanced joyfully, like a man liberated, straight upon Raccamond, who recognized his tread and bounded out of his seat.

"Aristide, so you know the whole truth? What is the whole truth? Let us hear it! We should be glad to know it ourselves!"

"Don't you talk to me," cried Aristide, "don't say a word to me: I won't listen to you." He made the gesture of covering his ears, impeded by the books. "You lie, you do nothing but lie; I don't think even Mr. Bertillon, even his brother, your crony, knows all your lies. You're too clever. Don't come here. Go away." He thrust his thick arms towards Alphendéry. Jules said nothing.

"Don't be medieval," said Alphendéry agreeably. "What books have you got? What do they prove? What does anything prove until you have all the books? And how do you know what you have? Do you imagine we keep all our private books at Brussels? Not likely. Mr. Bertillon has an apartment; all the brothers Bertillon have apartments. I have one. Our loyal employees have homes. We keep nothing there? There are no safety-deposit boxes in the world? Everything is in Brussels for a spying clerk to get at? Don't go to the Parquet with your ridiculous story, Raccamond. 'What, two books! You indict a house with seven branches and dozens of types of operations on two books in semicode! You're absurd, my good sir, Good day!' That, my dear Raccamond, will be your reception at the Criminal Division. Calm down, my friend, and see where you stand. Besides, your fury is big and the offense you suppose, abuse of confidence, is small. There's some other reason why you're angry. Tell us! We can't believe your moral story, Raccamond. It doesn't ring true. You were in the war, you were in the tailoring business, you were in one grain and one financial house before you came here. You're a suckling babe, I suppose! Why, I remember a certain incident: the actor Pharion wanted to buy five hundred Rio Tinto and I had recommended him against it. You came in and whispered to me, 'Don't buy it all: tell him you've bought it all and we'll see later. I'm afraid.' That rings true. That won't be doubted by anyone, for it's just like you. You're just as cowardly as you are treacherous, Raccamond. You're a moral man, now! And you buy our accountants! Another trait: I remember it very well. Jean de Guipatin will bear me out. Before you came in, but after he came in to the bank, you paid one of our customers' men and got our list of customers and you tried to take away our clients. When Claude Brothers went down you came over to us, very humble and complimentary, and showed us a list full of our own clients! We know you, Aristide! Don't think we've been taken in by your mouthing and blustering all these months. In the name of morality! That's delightful! And what do you tell clients, to get them to come to us, despite the negative rumors about us round the town? You tell them that we have an organization abroad whereby their bonds and shares will appear to be in Switzerland or England, and so escape French taxes. And now you steal their records! What an imbroglio of sentiment is here! Patriots and moralists of your breed, Aristide, are sufficiently well known, especially to the police. You'd have to queue up, my dear friend, to place your complaint. They keep a special window down there, for clerks who steal something or other from their employer's office and run to the police! A special hole for rats: and a special filing cabinet." He mimed a stout policeman tearing a sheet in two and putting it in the wastepaper basket. "Why don't you be an honest man, but really, for once, and say what you have up your sleeve, what you crave: for you certainly desire something very much or you wouldn't bring this hornets' nest about our ears."

"I won't listen to you," said Raccamond, frowning. "I don't want to hear your clever talk. You are all nothing but swindlers as far as I can see. You are a swindler, Mr. Bertillon; you are a swindler, Mr. William; but he is more than a swindler—he is the motivator, he is the secret spring of everything. I know! I have observed. I see the secret threads which have been pulled. Unless that man

652

leaves the room and never re-enters it when I am here, I am going straight to the police."

Alphendéry laughed persuasively. "For everything you run to the police! If we come in, if we stay out, if the books are right, if the books are wrong. I assure you that those books you have stolen, in your moral anxiety, are by no means the whole story, and the whole story, my dear Aristide, is only here!" He touched his forehead. "You will be a laughingstock at the Parquet. You will come there, slap down your books: 'A scandal, a crime!' The policeman at the desk will open them, his eyes, his hands —they fall to the desk, his mouth opens, and he begins to laugh: 'Oh, ha, ha, ha! Oh, look here: just another of them! Another bird telling on the boss!' They nudge each other: 'A moral man, a righteous man; look at him—that stout middle-aged man down there, that's he!' 'Let me see the chief of the division,' say you. You burst in! 'What?' says he. 'Another of your sort! Wait your turn.' When *you* and *the books* finally come together at the chief's desk, he keeps you waiting (that's their only amusement, you know) while he thumbs the pages: 'And what does this all mean?' You try to explain, 'It means abuse of confidence.' 'And the evidence, fellow?' says he. 'Your theories don't interest us. But you have no evidence. Good': then he keeps the books, but he kicks you out. 'Come back with more,' says he, 'or mind your own business.' And there you are again, trying to make terms with Mr. Bertillon, but on how much worse ground are you! You will get nothing from us, nothing at all; you will be dismissed, Raccamond, and we will take care to let everyone know what you did. You will get nowhere."

"You seem very anxious to get them back," said Raccamond.

"They are the accounts of a giant concern I represent," said Alphendéry.

"What is its name?"

"The London Finance Corporation."

"That name is there," admitted Aristide, "but its position tallies with the clients' position, plus about eighty thousand shares sold short and that, I have calculated, is the bank's own position."

"You calculated?"

"Posset told me," Aristide said, in a hard tone: he knew Posset would be dismissed anyhow.

"You have a nice team," said William.

"We are trying to avoid a scandal, for our clients, but if you force us we will let the owners of our anonymous accounts know what has happened and you will be ruined. No one will ever take you in again," said Jules.

"Ah, no! I should be sorry to disappoint you," Aristide cried in triumph.

"You have even looked for another place while buying clerks with our money," commented Michel; "so you forgot nothing. In the great wave of pious rage which took you unawares, you first made time to run off and look for another job, leaving your clients to sink or swim in the bank's horrid whirlpool."

Jules impatiently pressed a bell. But Raccamond did not see it. He was speaking to Alphendéry. "The time has come for plain speaking. Then, you may as well know something yourself. Everyone in town is saying that you are running the bank onto shoals. Without you, nothing of this would have been done. You are a pessimist; you believe in selling short; you believe business is rotten: all this is done on your advice, or without the knowledge of Mr. Bertillon. He says himself that everything in Brussels is done by you. He knows nothing. Then—" he said turning dramatically, to Jules, "this man has swindled, cheated, and lied, Mr. Bertillon. He has tried to bring you down: he must have put hundreds of thousands in his own pocket."

"What are you talking about?" Alphendéry was puzzled.

"Isn't it true," Raccamond pointed at him, "that you ran a gigantic short-position in Brussels without Mr. Bertillon's knowing?"

Alphendéry laughed and looked at Bertillon; but seeing Jules's expression, he remained silent.

"Well, what have you to say?" said Raccamond tragically. "Answer! Answer us all!"

Alphendéry was still silent. A suspicion dawned in Aristide's eyes.

Jules had half closed his eyes and was listening without a word.

"If Mr. Bertillon assures me that he knew nothing about it, I will believe it; if Mr. Bertillon speaks to me, I will know he is telling the truth, but I do not believe a word that comes from you, Alphendéry, or you." He swung round with a gesture to William, who smiled like a stupid doll of flesh.

"Or me?" said a voice. Raccamond lowered his head in characteristic gesture and turned round slowly. "You have all come to scare me?" he queried. "Why are you here, Monsieur le Comte? You do not know what is in those books."

"I do."

"Did you know what they were doing when you came into the bank?"

"No, and no one told me, but I guessed as everyone else has guessed but you, Aristide."

"It is impossible that everyone has guessed that the bank is nothing but a *contre-partie* shop."

"It is the pet name the bank goes by, on the Bourse, my dear fellow, surely you know that."

"I didn't think so," said Aristide Raccamond firmly, "and I never heard it said."

"What is your salary?" said Jean de Guipatin seriously.

"Monsieur le Comte——"

"It is twenty thousand francs a month, is it not? And last year you drew nearly two hundred thousand francs. Is that the salary of a customers' man? Is there any other house attached to the Bourse giving that? Where did that come from? There is no judge in France but would believe in complicity."

Raccamond said, "No, no, I am innocent——"

"Judges get five thousand francs a month," finished Jean de Guipatin. "You can make a big outcry if you like but in France the social aspect of a scandal is the most important. Suppose you drag the bank and its clients into court: what will you show? That there is not one poor person amongst its clients; that every one of them is rich, or is married to, or is one of a family of, richissimes; that the only poor persons in the bank are its employees whom you are depriving of a job in bad times; that you are depriving the French state of enormous taxes, paid by the banker; that yours is one of the six large salaries in the bank, starting with Mr. Bertillon's, and that Mr. Alphendéry, that occult influence, receives considerably less than you."

The fervor of Raccamond had fallen: he looked doggedly but more calmly at the Comte de Guipatin.

"A discussion of the books in open court will show that

the majority of your clients are engaged in petty larceny of the fisc; naturally, for they are rich people. I am afraid, Aristide, that if you air the private affairs of your clients, no one will be grateful to you, neither the press, nor the judge, nor the masses on whose indignation you count, nor your clients, who will not only desert you, my poor friend, but will do their very best to sew up your mouth."

At this logic and vague menace, Raccamond felt all his force go from him. In Guipatin he recognized another member of the Bernstein drama cycle, the suave intelligence of the gilded young manhood of the seventh *arrondisement*, and he could not flaunt his formulas at him. Jules saw that the wind was out of his sails and came forward supply. "Well, Raccamond, we're all tired: let's get some sleep. We'll talk this over in the morning. Come to my office, bring your books along, and we'll come to some arrangement that will satisfy you."

"Monsieur le Comte de Guipatin is the only one I trust amongst you," declared Aristide, coming back to a more rugged state of mind. "Will he be there?"

"Yes, I'll be there, Aristide."

When Raccamond was escorted out the four men looked at each other, and smiled.

"Well," declared Alphendéry, "the hat goes to Jean. One drop of blue blood makes the world go round— think what Jean can do!"

Guipatin said seriously, "No: that's only the first round. Aristide will think it over and that fury, his wife, will have him full of hop by the morning. We're a long way from the finish. Another means would be to segregate him from his wife, but that can't be done. What can we do, to give her a soothing sirup? She's the secret arsenal, there, you know. I'll think up something."

"Yes," said Jules impatiently, "that woman! He's so transparent: you could see her discourses shining behind his eyes where he was reading them off from his memory."

"What did you think of his insults to me?" said Alphendéry. "Should I come tomorrow or would that only infuriate him? Where does he get it from? I've always been almost a brother to him."

"Don't worry about that, Michel," said Jules, "we want you to keep your nerve for the trouble I see coming: I don't want you to get depressed."

William smiled his slow smile, difficult to break through

the Chinese calm. "Aristide has two months' start on us or more; he's nearer the finish. His nerves will never outlast ours. We've only got to finagle him along for a week or two, and he'll go mad or to a sanatarium, Marianne aiding, and we can cook his goose for him. The police haven't finished with him on the Claude bankruptcy yet."

This sedative consideration sent them home with a certain amount of cheer. At the same time, all except William, to whom this reasoning was flawless, slept ill that night and the bank was running a high fever by the morning.

Marianne received Aristide with a smile and a questioning look. He put the books down on their dining-room table with discouragement. "Have you got any coffee? I'm so tired I could drop."

Marianne let him droop on the couch for some minutes while she was making the coffee: this was a simple stratagem to make him talk immediately after she came in. He drank the coffee, however, and said nothing. A slight anxiety filled her. "Well, Aristide, what did they agree to do?"

"Nothing . . . we did not have time to go over it all tonight. Comte Jean de Guipatin was there and we went over the thing together. I am to see the Bertillons and the Comte in the morning."

A deep and old knowledge of her husband filled her with suspicion and anxiety. She had regarded the filching of the books of the bank as a godsend, a sure lever for Aristide into the higher heavens of the bank: she saw him marching side by side with Jules Bertillon, the only man in the bank of Aristide's caliber. But such a thing was not to be obtained by merit; she herself often said it to him, "In the world in which we move, my poor friend, merit does not count; pressure, relations, and moral blackmail alone count. It is sad but it is true, and we must accommodate ourselves to this world."

She said with that firm high note which he knew was a note of alarm and decision, "My friend, you will not go to that bank tomorrow without a form of compromise, a series of capitulations drawn up by Maître Olonsky."

He looked at her with startled, almost fawnish eyes, "Why; do you see something wrong?"

"They fooled you, Aristide, with Guipatin. He is an

657

aristocrat. If you listen to him, he'll deliver you to the
Bertillons tied hand and foot. He doesn't care for you: he
does care for the Bertillon millions. Open your eyes.
Money is an exact measure of the friendship of all our
sucking-doves of the Faubourg St.-Germain."

Aristide opened his eyes a little and surveyed her closer
than he had done for months. "Marianne! You said to me
that he was the only wholesome character in the bank."

She brushed this aside. "No. Your first interview was
check to your king. Let your queen act. Henceforth,
Aristide, listen to me. This is the most important period of
our lives. You have taken an irretraceable step. You must
go through with your plan. You must force them to the
wall and show a firm will. If they beat you, Aristide,
they will pretend to be nice to you for a month or so
and then they'll throw you out. Keep those books, value
them as your life—or my life, at any rate, and insist on
your conditions."

"All women are good in moments of decision; they do
not face the issue themselves—they see it as a bystander."

"That is true, but I could fight too. I am always resolved, always," she continued flushing a little and exciting
herself. The end of it was that she could not stop talking
and felt herself obliged to torment Aristide with questions
and exclamations long after he should have been asleep,
and even after the light was out her healthy mind kept
them threshing the thing over till both their minds were
dancing like chaff.

Scene Eighty-eight: Dodges

AT HOME that night, Alphendéry took paper and pen
and wrote to Thargelion asking the price of a winter
cruise for six weeks round the Mediterranean and the Isles
of Greece. For some reason, he was angry with everyone,
and he had fully decided at last to leave the brothers Bertillon after this holiday. He wrote to his mother, sending
her some money and telling her to prepare to have him as
a boarder after two or three months' time. They were to
live on a narrow margin, because he was going back into

scholarship. He had written a book on grain for Léon and turned it over to him, but had received from Léon only two thousand, five hundred francs, and nothing at all for the advice he had given him on stocks and shares.

"Why should I wear away my life grubbing for rich men?" he wrote bitterly to his mother, although he knew she thought his acquaintance with rich men the one glory of his life.

He sent these letters off and went to sleep assuaged, as if by this simple act the bogeys of Raccamond, Carrière, and the rest were conjured away.

The next day, following Marianne's advice, Aristide rang up to say that he would not be in to see the brothers Bertillon and the Comte de Guipatin that day, or not until the afternoon, whereupon Guipatin with hauteur mentioned that he was playing a match that afternoon at the Stadium Roland Garros in the Parc des Princes, and the whole thing would have to be put off to the following day. Everyone was relieved; even Marianne. She spent the whole day with Aristide couched beside her, stuffing him with arguments, every half-hour seeing new difficulties, new grandeurs.

Meanwhile, Maître Olympe called Jules on the telephone, announcing that he had for him a very fine, very profitable business, and that if Jules was agreeable Olympe would arrive in the afternoon flanked by representatives of a foreign power.

"They're friends of mine," said Jean de Guipatin apologetically. "I'll try to put off that match this afternoon."

William and Michel Alphendéry were forbidden the chief's room all the afternoon. Their discontent grew. William was irritable. "What the deuce is he doing in there now? Signing some more I.O.U.'s, no doubt. He's got two Spaniards, picked out by Olympe—you can imagine. One looks just like Gil Robles; one's got a face like a bad Walloon. As far as I can make out, it's about oil monopolies. Do you know what's going on in that line?"

"This is a great oil year," remarked Alphendéry, "but why come to us?"

"Since the Kreuger money we've got a rep for being too smart."

They pumped the doorkeeper Etienne and found out the names of the persons with Jules—Señor Rodriguez Damora and Señor Fadrique Palmones, one of whom represented himself as vaguely attached to the Spanish embassy and a friend of the chamberlain of Alfonso XIII. They represented themselves as participating in a group willing to form under the financial leadership of Jules Bertillon and using his bank as part of their window dressing.

The room was hot with dandyism, mystery, international secrets, fantasy, millions. Jules was glad to fly to this to forget the Raccamond terror, and a conscious as well as an unconscious motive made him exclude Michel and William, his judges in the Carrière affair and fellow tremblers in the Raccamond affair. Even Claire-Josèphe, formerly gay and irresponsible and charming in a savant way, was now anxious and practical. Claire-Josèphe the delicately proud, the rashly independent, had offered to invite Marianne Raccamond to tea and call on her womanly feelings! What a descent in the world was that for the Bertillons!

The Spanish economic plan under the Azaña government provided for a state monopoly of oil of all grades, said the pair of Spaniards; and they had come to Jules to suggest that he could get an unlimited supply of oil through an American company whose representatives were then in Paris for the oil conference, and could sell it through the state monopoly organism at a reasonable profit to himself. The two Spaniards assured Jules that the Spanish government would accept his tender, if he provided the requisite quantity of "palm oil," which they would place themselves. They were in touch with the right officials: and as for the other tenderers, they would be found either too dear, or blinds for Russian oil. At the moment there was a peculiarly strong campaign of publicity against Russia. It was asserted that Russia was supplying arms by all the frontiers of Spain and preparing "the revolution." Therefore, the cry of "Red oil" would be sufficient for public opinion. Jules, to make the affair look proper, was to form an Oil Supply Company with these two liaison men, with Comte de Guipatin on the name plate, Maître Olympe and others at the moment remaining in the background. Jules would make such a fortune selling to the oil monopoly that nothing else need worry him: the bank would become a mere toy, a necessary screen, that is all.

Jules finally revealed the scheme to Alphendéry. Alphendéry made the natural objections—why would real potentates come to Jules?

"My reputation since the Kreuger fortune," said Jules.

Possibly. How was Jules to know that these fortuitous Spaniards would really spend the "palm oil" as indicated? They asked for fifty thousand pesetas to begin with.

"Jean de Guipatin knows them, and Comte Lucé vouches for them," answered Jules.

Alphendéry objected that if only comtes and marquises answered for them, it was a poor guarantee.

"You're the sort that wouldn't accept a thousand-franc note handed out free on the Pont-Neuf," jeered Jules. "Listen, I have friends. I'm going into this with you and, if you don't want to help me, without you. . . ."

"Well, don't sign anything without asking us, or asking Maître Lemaître," begged Alphendéry. "Your scheme is too simple: it just looks like plain graft and asks for a Government Commission of Inquiry. You must mask it."

And he worked out a scheme.

"I've got to make some money," Jules clamored. "You two only sit about and wait for Raccamond, your protégé, to pull another fit of hysterics. Every time I get a good proposition, you two either wet-blanket it or you try to make it look respectable. I want to tell you one thing: money isn't respectable. Money is a steal."

This was Jules in his worst mood. William and Michel cautiously kept out of his way all day; and William began to talk about a fine little run-down hotel he had seen last time he was in Aix-les-Bains. It only needed good management.

Scene Eighty-nine: A Solution

ARISTIDE came into the bank carrying a satchel. He went to the door of the board room and said with dignity, "Manray! If the Princesse comes in, telephone to Mr. Bertillon's office. I will be there. Don't keep her waiting. I have an appointment with her."

Manray murmured, "All right, Mr. Raccamond," and

came to the door to see Raccamond plunge into the lift. His pallid face loomed through the open lift.

"What's eating him?" asked the genial Voulou rather sadly of Jacques Manray. Manray had already given the preconcerted signal on the interphone.

"I don't know what's eating him, but I wish he'd never come in here. If he asks you any questions, Urbain, don't say anything. Be dumb!"

They both looked up to the chief's room which hung over them, between the two galleries, on the outside wall. All the lusters were on, and the decorated panes of the inner doors sparkled. Someone was now always talking privately with the chiefs and their lawyers. They turned back to the clients with sober expressions.

Upstairs, Richard Plowman (taken in by the advice of Claire-Josèphe, his "sweetheart"), William, the Comte de Guipatin, and Maîtres Olympe, Lemaître, and Beaubien made a full session. Alphendéry was missing, a concession to Aristide's invidious temper. Aristide, full of fever, entered with brio, advanced into the center of the circle, and sat down in the hard chair they had kept for him.

"Well, Aristide," said Jules, "what is it? You have given me enough trouble."

"I didn't come to talk about trouble," said Aristide. "Trouble is the only weapon with men of your kind! . . . I am glad to see that your brother *William* is here. I know his signature is necessary. I know he has power of attorney."

"What have you in mind?" said Maître Lemaître.

"Never mind about me!" Aristide rudely turned to Bertillon. "You are in a corner, Bertillon. Don't try any tricks. You can't outplay me. I have the books!" He said this with a strange air of triumph. "Let Alphendéry be present! I want him too to sign the agreement."

"What agreement?" asked Maître Lemaître. "Let's have some sequence."

Jules looked quizzically at Aristide, unhooked the telephone. "Where is Mr. Alphendéry? Alphendéry, come here to the office: I want you. No, Raccamond wants you!" He laughed, put down the phone and smiled at Raccamond. "Take it easy, Aristide; don't look so tragic! If anyone looks tragic, let it be me or William!"

Raccamond carefully drew from an inner pocket a

662

long, thick folded sheet which he put down on the desk. "I have a duplicate."

Jules cast an eye on it, tossed it across to Maître Beaubien. The lawyer read:

MEMORANDUM of agreement between Jules Bertillon, William Bertillon, partners of Bertillon and Company, known as the Banque Mercure, on the one hand, and Aristide Raccamond, director of the same bank, on the other hand.

An Agreement can be arrived at between the above Parties, only if based upon the following principles:

1. A complete certified statement must be submitted to Mr. Raccamond, showing the entire financial position of the bank, credit and debit balances; gold, stocks, and bonds held for the bank, and held in safekeeping for clients; the equities and share positions of clients; the equity and share position of the bank operating for its own account, must be shown separately.

2. A list of the personnel must be drawn up showing the status of each person.

3. A list of directors must be established; there are not to be more than three directors: of these Mr. Jules Bertillon and Mr. Aristide Raccamond will be two.

4. A list of customers, with accounts in Paris and in the other branches, must be drawn up and the person specially charged with the care of the account of each must be named.

5. *Contre-partie* account: it must be recognized *in writing* that the bank has conducted a *contre-partie* account. Further conduct of the account: Mr. Raccamond, realizing that it is not possible to reduce the *short position* of the account at once without causing disturbance in the markets, is agreeable that the position should be reduced *slowly*, month by month and according to the course of the markets. Nevertheless, to safeguard the interests of the clients, Messrs. Jules and William Bertillon must institute a guarantee fund of two million francs to equalize losses possible in the liquidation of the *contre-partie* account, and this fund is to be administered equally by Jules Bertillon and Aristide Raccamond—no other person to

know how it stands. In the operation of the account, for withdrawals or deposits, each signature requires the countersignature before it is valid. Mr. Bertillon will pay into this fund the two million francs necessary, and thereafter Mr. Bertillon is to be considered as participating in it to the extent of 50% and Mr. Raccamond to the extent of 50%. If Mr. Bertillon is shown, at a later date, not to have shown full accounts to Mr. Raccamond, or to have shown bad faith, or to have contravened the principles of agreement set out in the clauses of the agreement, Mr. Raccamond may withdraw from the guarantee fund his 50% participation, that is, one million francs, and not be obliged to give an accounting to anyone for this million francs.

6. The *equalizing* account of the bank must never involve more than 50% of the shares bought or sold by clients, unless Messrs. Jules and William Bertillon and Mr. Raccamond agree to act to the contrary and sign a paper to that effect.

7. Mr. Raccamond is to receive a monthly statement of the financial situation of the bank and to be allowed to withdraw his clients' accounts if he deems it necessary and to have priority over the customers' men in this instance; he is to be allowed to act according to his lights and in full secrecy. To guarantee this and to guarantee Mr. Raccamond against bad faith and error, Mr. Raccamond is to be considered the owner of 50% of the two million francs of the guarantee fund, but if his clients are not paid out immediately on his demand, he can withdraw the one million francs, and for this withdrawal alone, the signature of Mr. Raccamond is to suffice, without the countersignature of Mr. Bertillon.

Everyone was laughing quietly. Alphendéry, behind, said, "Why so timid, Aristide?" Maître Lemaître said nothing, but calmly took the document from Maître Beaubien. Maître Beaubien, however, frowned and in his most elegant accent pronounced, "You're a rogue, Mr. Raccamond." Jules laughed. William said with bonhomie to Raccamond, "The carpet's nailed down, Aristide, but we can always get a man in with a tack hammer to take it off for you."

Aristide bent forward, lost his temper. "It's merely a safeguard for the clients. There has been so much imprudence here—and undue influence, not to say worse—"

"It's impossible, Raccamond," said Jules sharply. "Don't run away with the idea that we're going to turn the business over to you. I offered you a limited partnership one time. You've drawn up an agreement which—why go into it? It's ludicrous. You could browbeat us and blackmail us forever. Every time it pleased you, you could blackmail me into signatures, whatever you wanted. Are you crazy?"

"Blackmail," said Aristide with indignation, "how dare you say that? I have the books. I'm basing everything on the books I have in my possession. I have a real right to safeguard myself."

Maître Lemaître said quietly, "You're a vulgar blackmailer, Mr. Raccamond, and that's the whole story."

"Do you know where we keep our gold and our bonds?" asked Alphendéry.

"Yes," cried Aristide. "In London."

"You see, Aristide," Jules remonstrated, "if you're reasonable, it's worth our while to stay in business. If not, you can have the dust and ashes. You understand?"

"You only pay half your income tax," said William pleasantly. "You remember: Brussels account number 23!"

Aristide went paler and twined his fingers together; his eyes looked like two black poached eggs. "You won't sign the agreement you promised?" he said in a low voice.

They saw that he was serious: he had expected them to sign it. "No, Aristide," said Jules: "you're too much of a crook, you see. You run about stealing books: how can I sign with you?"

William laughed, "Naturally we'd like to hand you two million francs but your character forbids."

Aristide turned on him. "You're at the bottom of this, you're against me, you and your crony Alphendéry. You've always been against me. Bobchinski and Dobchinski," he said slowly, "against Mr. Bertillon and me. He doesn't understand you."

"Pttt!" said Jules.

"I'm my brother's partner," William answered dryly. "I see you trying to railroad him. I advise him, no. I'm against you because you're a crook. You're a failure because you're a hypocritical crook, and you're a crook be-

665

cause you're a failure. But if my brother wants you to go in with us, you go in like any other junior partner who is contributing no funds and no decent clients and who has no guts and is not a money-maker."

This unwise gibe was frowned on by Jules, who broke in, "Give me a real proposition, Aristide, and I'll consider it. Only you must return the books. That's the first item on the program. What you give here—is fantasy, just plain fantasy. You're feverish, or you'd see it. Naturally," he flipped the document aside, "it's impossible for me to give you a two-million-franc guarantee fund."

"Simply ludicrous," said Maître Beaubien.

"And I won't have a partner," said Jules getting irritable. "This is my bank. I run it. No busybodies. I'd rather shut it up. Ask something reasonable or I close the bank. You don't mean a thing to me! Your blackmailing doesn't touch me because I don't give a damn. Who says I have to keep in business? When I close the bank tonight I can pay off the boys and say, Don't come back tomorrow. Who can stop me?"

Aristide sagged. "You can't do that."

"Can't I? You don't think I see all my clients holding their assets abroad and that I keep mine here!"

Then Aristide said, "I see what it is: you gentlemen have decided to cheat me out of my prospects, my clients, and my money, and you came here this morning to fool me out of the agreement you promised me. You said you'd make me a partner and now you won't do anything. You force me to go to the police. You're all rogues."

"You already sign checks and letters as director," said William sweetly, "so if the police, your friends, corral us, they will take you along: all in one Black Maria. No one will believe that a director getting two hundred thousand francs a year *didn't know* how that vast sum was made! You're caught in your greed, Aristide."

"You don't frighten me: I have friends."

"Carrière!" said Jean de Guipatin. "Carrière is furious with you, if you want to know, Aristide. He thought you were working for him, and he finds you're trying to gouge Bertillon for your own benefit. He knows quite well Jules can close the bank and he doesn't want that: he wants Jules to pay him on the sterling contract. I rang him after I saw you and told him you were playing the fool. He says if you go to the police, he'll drop you."

Aristide changed ground. "What do you offer me then?"

"You must return the books," said Maître Beaubien. "As an evidence of good faith. We will give you a promise in writing that you won't be dismissed, that your clients will be paid off, and that your clients' positions will be held here intact, as they are recorded on their monthly accounts. That is what is worrying you and that is what we will guarantee. We do not admit any truth in any of the statements you make. You have taken one set of books: the bookkeeping of this bank is done in several countries, and the full position is not known to anyone employed. You have not been treated differently from all the others. In fact, you have received better treatment."

Jules said suddenly, "What's your opinion of the London branch, Aristide? Do you think you could run that end? If you want to work in with me there, I'll agree." Aristide loved London: he was one of the Frenchmen who much preferred it. Besides, they had said that the "other books" were in London.

"Yes, I could work in London. I'd like to. If full authority is given to me and my position is assured. All my clients have their assets in London."

Aristide was fatigued and this seemed to be to him a good ground for temporizing. He said, with relief, to Jules, "Mr. Bertillon, I have always had confidence in you: I never believed that you were really crooked. If you treat with me on this basis, we can come to some agreement. I would still require a complete statement of all the clients' positions, not only my own but Mouradzian's and others', and I would be willing to supervise a slow replacement of any shares that had been sold out. I realize that the bank must sometimes protect itself, when clients are trading on margin."

"We're getting somewhere at last," said Jules, smiling exquisitely at Aristide. "You're not a bad fellow, Aristide, but you get yourself all mixed up."

"But I will only treat with you; I will have nothing to say to the others," Aristide emphasized. "And Mr. Alphendéry must have no authority over the London branch."

"That's right, we'll talk it over. Now, Aristide, go home and get into bed: you're not well. When you're better, we'll have everything ready for you, and you'll have nothing to worry about."

Jules was smiling, gently tapping his green blotting pad and occasionally looking at Maître Beaubien under his lids. William looked up once, winked at Jules, and studied Aristide's bull crouch, his pale wattled face thrust forward, the starting eyes, the veins pulsating in the head. In their stillness, Aristide started to speak, and then lost himself. They were a threatening audience; yet, even in that way, he liked to have them for audience. "I will take an interim statement for the London and Brussels branches only. If Mr. Bertillon certifies it, I will accept it as a basis. But I will only deal with Mr. Bertillon."

"I will show you everything that isn't mine," said Jules peaceably, "when you come back, Aristide. Only, you must go away for a few days. You are worked up now. You don't do yourself justice or me either."

"But while I am away," began Aristide, glancing round at William and Alphendéry.

"Mr. William is my junior partner," said Jules insolently, "and Mr. Alphendéry will not be here. He is going to Zurich this evening for a fortnight."

"If that is so," said Aristide. "I—"

"It is so, Aristide. Now you go down to Biarritz and set yourself up. You're rash to be out as it is, but I understand you. Keep in touch with me by telephone. When you come back, you will find that I will have an arrangement for you, a compromise that will take in your interests and mine. No one else will be considered. Then I will show you part of the assets. And when you are satisfied you can go to London and take over the London branch. As second in command, if you like him, I'll give you Theodor Bomba. You can have him for private secretary. How is that?"

"Can I think it over?"

"Of course. But I really think you should go to the Côte d'Argent as soon as you can travel. Mr. Vallat downstairs will get tickets for you and your wife, if you like. Shall I tell him? How do you travel? First-class sleeper? I will send you away at my own expense, Aristide: it won't cost you anything, and in the meantime everything will be prepared for you to sign by Maître Beaubien."

Both William and Alphendéry looked anxious. Aristide noted this and said, "You are leaving this evening, Alphendéry?"

"Yes," said Alphendéry promptly, "for Zurich to see

668

my doctor. He has told me to go on a three-months' vacation, and I must see him: it's so long and I can't afford so much."

"Oh, you stay away three months, Michel," said Jules. "You're run down. You're not to run this account any more. When you come back you must get on to quieter work. Your nerves won't stand it."

Alphendéry bit his lips but murmured, "Thanks, Jules."

"My man will take you home, Aristide," said Jules. "Do you want those tickets?"

Aristide could not resist the offer. "All right, if you wish," he said ungraciously.

Jules took up the telephone. "Let's take our hats," whispered William. They did so. As they walked out the front door, they saw Aristide in a gloomy corner of the foyer watching. All the cashiers' grilles were now closed and they had the bank to themselves.

"Quick, in," said William. They ran in through the great doorway two doors away. On the staircase was a blinded door which led to another dark descending staircase and this second staircase led through another door back into the bank, by the tellers' offices. Through the tellers' offices they ascended by a spiral staircase hidden in the wall. There was a small landing on which was another hidden door leading to a cupboard in Jules's room; and by this series of doors and by this cupboard William and Michel found themselves back in Jules's room. They came in silently, looked around at Jules and the lawyers.

"He's gone; my chauffeur took him. Sit down," said Jules.

"Do you think he'll go to Biarritz?"

"I hope so."

"And the agreement?" asked Alphendéry heartily.

"Bull," said Jules quietly. "Michel, you've got to get to the station tonight and take that train. He's sure to be spying after you. Get out at the first stop. Hard luck I know. But you've got to help me out. As soon as the chauffeur comes back we'll go to the Rue de Grenelle post office and telegraph to Newchurch in London to go straight back to the bank and remove to his home every book connected with the accounts. Parouart is after them, too. I'll bet you anything you like this cockroach Raccamond thought he'd get to London in time to discover the books while Parouart was making trouble there. And

I'm going to see he goes with his wife. Don't go back to your apartment after you leave it tonight with your valise. Put in your valise all you need for London. I want you to go to London as soon as Raccamond leaves for Biarritz. I'll telegraph the fellow in Biarritz, also, to expect him and treat him nicely. Of course, that fellow's in his pay. He got his son in there, too. Now, Michel, when you get to London you must stay there and not come back. When Raccamond comes back he'll ask if you've been round (because he's crazy jealous of you), and I want everyone to answer, 'No, he's been away for weeks.' You stay in London as long as you like and don't go near the office. Do what you like. Get the books from Newchurch and then go and hide your head. You can do our business with Stewart."

"And what agreement are you going to get out for the imbecile?" William asked sardonically.

"Do you think I'm crazy?" asked Jules. "None. I'm just going to give myself a chance to get him. I'll tell my chauffeur to try to steal the books tomorrow evening. Paul is to look after the luggage for the Raccamonds and I'll tell him to make a mistake, send it to Bordeaux. I'm going to have them followed all day tomorrow, to see if he or she goes to a bank vault."

He rose and they all rose, fatigued. When the two lawyers had gone off, Jean de Guipatin said, "Aristide's not so soft as he looks: he's just tired tonight. I'd feel happier if we had the books. Jules, I can get you a couple of strong-arm burglars in a shake, if you say the word; you'd also better burgle his home in the Rue du Docteur-Blanche while he's away. Aristide's got a house there to himself and no doubt some faithful retainer with a strong-box."

"Yeh, we'll do that, too," said Jules negligently. "That guy doesn't frighten me; he's pitiable. He makes me laugh. Wait till I get those books. I'll show him what sort of an agreement he'll get. Just itching to get at my cashbox, like the rest of them. I won't finish with him till I see him sold-up and begging for a five-franc bit outside my door. Imagine it, the cheap Shakespeare! 'I'll ruin you; I'll drag you in the gutter!' I say, how do fellows get that way? Come and eat with me, Jean. Do you want to come, William?"

"Gladly," said Jean; and "No, thanks, I've had enough,"

scolded William. Michel, hovering round, rather sadly, said, "Well, I suppose I'd better jump if I have to catch that damn Zurich train."

"Yeh," said Jules. "Have you got any cash? Here take some!" He opened his billfold and handed Michel nine or ten one-thousand-franc notes. "Do you want more, Michel! Fifteen, twenty thousand? I don't care. Put it down on the account."

Michel smiled palely and took five thousand, "Thanks: I've got to pay for it, after all."

"Why? This is my picnic, I pay for it," Jules said with amiable insolence. "Now, get home, get your valise and scram to the station. That's your role." His laughter rang out. "Well we're getting some fun out of it, after all."

At dinner that night Jules declaimed, "I went into banking because I had a streak of luck. I wanted some fun, people were always wanting to stake me, and I thought folks were more or less happy-go—they'd give me a break if the wheel went round too far, one time. Luck's with me: but they won't wait! I'm tired: I'm lazy: I don't want to work any more and I've got a hunch that now is the time to stop. There's something *fatal* about Raccamond. I've seen him making a whirlpool round my ship and I want to fly. I don't make agreements with bogeys."

He lay back in his chair languidly, looked cross and tired. "It's—Carrière! Parouart! Raccamond! And Alphendéry wants to leave me. He's my luck. He's afraid of me. He wants to go and work in London with Stewart." He pouted, hung his lower lip, "It's not kind," he cried. "I treated him well. They think I'm speculating, they think I'll blow up one of these days, and not one of them will stay! It's ridiculous. I don't want to stay in business. I'm tired of it. You see."

Claire-Josèphe murmured, "I hear Michel gave you money back."

William laughd affectionately, "Oh, Jules pulled out a handful, some fell on the floor, and Michel didn't see it, or wouldn't. Michel took five thousand francs and refused the rest."

All went well. The man in Biarritz telegraphed that Mr. Raccamond had arrived. Those left behind went to sleep, after their few harassing days. Rumors, of course, flew round Amsterdam and Antwerp. Numerous curious

671

persons telephoned Jules, Alphendéry, and William, and Carrière even sent a message to Jules Bertillon by Jean de Guipatin to assure him that although he wanted to do him in, he hadn't told Raccamond to get the books, as they seemed to think. Raccamond was his man for some business, not for this. He assured Jules that he was very anxious to keep the bank open.

Henri Léon, Méline, and Stewart all came to Paris to see what they could see. They saw the bank functioning as before; they called in amiably on Jules, and were told by him various fairy stories, all glib, all satisfying, and all making fine table talk. Each one had his own method for getting rid of Raccamond, and almost everyone thought that the easiest way would be—first, to murder him; second, to send in a burglar to steal the books; third, to denounce him to the police for something or other—blackmail, say, or income-tax fraud.

"Fire him," said Stewart. "Let him run with his books. You get up new books and say he bought your clerk to get up a blackmail case."

Léon had the best scheme. Jean de Guipatin was to let the police know that an ex-agent of the bank was about to come and put in a complaint, with books. The police were to demand the books. Friends of Brouwer would then set the Belgian police in action. The Belgian police would notify the French embassy that a Frenchman had stolen books from a Belgian banking concern and would say that they had private information that these books had been turned in at the Criminal Division in Paris. Friends of Léon, Brouwer, and Bertillon in the Belgian Ministry to France would ask for the return of the books, "for verification," to their own offices. The books would be seized at the frontier as stolen property, by the Belgian police who would "mislay" them with Brouwer, and so complete the return. When Raccamond tried to push his plaint the police would then reply, in Paris, that the books had been returned to Belgium "for verification." And Raccamond would be out of a job and would "come crying for mercy."

Méline's idea was to "go over Aristide's head and apply to the woman": he charged himself with that.

"You couldn't dally with that battle-ax," said Jules. Méline was sure he would succeed.

"What's your method, Paul?" asked Jules.

"I flatter them," said Méline. "I flatter their beauty, their brains, and their temperament; I lay it on. I do it delicately, I do it grossly—oh, why go into it? I'll do it for you."

Léon looked nervous. "Won't do, my boy: not Mme. Raccamond," he said with distaste.

"Send Marianne poisoned chocolates anonymously," Claire-Josèphe suggested helpfully. "He would be simply a dishrag without her. Or a basket of *glacé* fruits, say."

Méline suggested, "Send José MacMahon to him with a revolver and tell him he'll denounce him as a white slaver and the accomplice in the murder of Arturito, if he doesn't give up the books. . . ."

"Not José," Jules objected dubiously.

"Aristide has a gun himself," said William. "I've seen it. His service revolver, I think. I guess he's expecting burglars."

They had an amusing time and began to let the urgency of the case slip; only Henri Léon and Brouwer were really anxious. Henri Léon said to Jules privately, "My Dutch merchants will still buy, as you stand, if you'll give a private statement. They won't care how your accounts are, my boy. Your reputation is all right since the Kreuger money; lots of people think you're a hell of a smart fellow. If you let me bring in my friends and give them serious consideration, we can fix it up so that I'm their agent, and we can tell Aristide that he's breaking up a business deal. Leave me to deal with him. He's ambitious and he shilly-shallies. I can get on the right side of Marianne, I *think*: she's more ambitious than he is. I'll pretend to go into this Hollywood magazine she's got on the brain. I'll tell my girl Margaret Weyman to go into it with her: that'll keep them off until the deal is done, or until we see where we stand. See! You don't have to complete the deal, although, frankly, Jules, between one luck-child and another, I think you ought to get out of here. Your name, your bank—listen, Jules, if it's only a shell—if you *have* stowed away the cash—you can still sell it. What do you say, eh? Will you consider it, Jules?"

"Thanks, Henri," Jules said, very offhand. "Thanks, I'll think it over. Yes, that's right: you tell Mrs. Weyman you'll go in with her and Marianne on the paper and tell Marianne to come right up to Brussels. You can give her a talking-to, and I can send someone down to hold up Aristide in a dark street, while they go through the apartment. . . ."

Jules became more and more fantastic in his replies, until he had confused them all and driven them away, to leave him to his own musings.

Scene Ninety: Aristide's Friends

ALPHENDÉRY, in London, found that Newchurch had received no instructions from the Bertillons and would not give up the books, secreted in his home, no doubt. Alphendéry wrote to Bertillon: "Tell Newchurch you want me to have the books." But Jules, still irritated, veered round and telegraphed, "Don't want you to have books. Don't do any business. Amuse yourself. Keep in touch."

Alphendéry was humiliated. He visited the branch every day, to show that he was not lazy, he looked through the London orders, interviewed Stewart, sent to the Paris branch his day's gleanings. This irritated Jules, too, who telegraphed him, "Keep away from London branch. Do nothing. Amuse yourself." Alphendéry presently discovered that Theodor Bomba, who had secretly been on Jules's charity list for months, was now re-employed by Jules and was in a big chair at the London office. Theodor Bomba greeted Alphendéry the next time the latter went in, therefore, with a regal smirk, "What are you doing these days?"

"What is happening?" wrote Michel to Jules. "I find Bomba in London. Are you actually sending Aristide there?"

"It's my bank," Jules wrote back.

Alphendéry had no more but a note from William, asking him to come back soon. But Alphendéry, dismayed by these contrary orders, stayed in London and moped. The bank, the last few weeks, had been swarming with new individuals he had never met, with all sorts of queer businesses he had never been told of—the oil business, the negotiations for which were carried out without him; an "aviation" business. He had to leave.

Jules and William were now closeted together daily. Even Richard Plowman rarely saw them and complained of it good-humoredly. "I told you I'd stick by you till the finish but let me know when the finish is." He whiled away the time by visiting Claire-Josèphe and the four sons of Jules Bertillon; convinced, no doubt, that he was so far in the family affections that they would do nothing serious without consulting him. He hated to appear importunate to "the boys."

Two days after he arrived at Biarritz, Aristide telephoned Jacques Manray at his home at night. "Jacques, I saw the Bertillons and asked them to reinstate the clients' accounts. They agreed to do so but would put nothing in writing. I am afraid of double-crossing. Keep your eyes open. Let me know if there is difficulty in paying out any account. Let me know if the clients make any complaint. Tell Mouradzian to write to me. Mouradzian is with us, Jacques."

This put Jacques in a panic. He and his wife sat up till two in the morning wondering what this could mean! Bertillon had *refused* to buy back shares for clients that had been sold out. If, for example, there was a big rise in the market and suddenly Bertillon was forced to deliver out eight thousand or ten thousand shares, what sort of a loss would he have? Suppose there was a panic, war, markets, rebellion—and the clients began to ask to transfer their accounts out, to other countries? Suppose Raccamond got hysterical and started a run? Could Bertillon meet it? These were bad moments for Jacques.

"Raccamond himself is our worst danger," said Jacques to his wife.

"So you must humor him, keep him in a good temper, work in with him," said the small dark-eyed woman that shared his troubles. "Always say, 'Yes.' That way, too, you will see what his scheme is and whether he really has a scheme. What are you going to do about Mouradzian?"

"I'll sound him."

Jacques went out to lunch with Mouradzian in an Armenian restaurant near the Rue Chauchat.

"Mr. Raccamond has gone away to the Côte d'Argent for his health."

"It's a good thing," said Mouradzian. "There are some men who can't stand our business. They should be in— selling pictures or rugs. Raccamond and his wife have a

675

certain understanding of—esthetics, perhaps—they should be in that business. They only make trouble for themselves and others here."

"You know he made some trouble just now for Mr. Bertillon?"

"I know."

"He told me you were working in with him."

"On what business?" asked Mouradzian hotly.

"On this business; getting the positions of the clients reinstated."

"Certainly not, most certainly not. He is ridiculous," Mouradzian said angrily. "He wants that? Where will we be? Bertillon would lose money hand over fist. Now he makes money. Listen to me, Mr. Manray: I have been in business forty years and my family five hundred years. Do schoolteachers, do young girls, go into business? No, only men, and only cunning men. The laws are made by men to trap some: others are more cunning. The point is: don't give your adversary a chance to catch you. The law is your adversary. Not because law is wrong, but because law is only made by your adversaries to catch you. Law is not for the people; law is not for right, or purity or charity: law is made by cunning fellows to trap cunning fellows, and it's a game, therefore, to know and to get the better of. The law is made by Mr. de Wendel and Mr. Rothschild so that they won't have any competition and we've got to get the better of them.

"He howls about law! What a hyena; what a dingo! Your Frenchmen of that breed are such hypocrites! He is a radical, too. Of course, they talk liberty, equality, and they tread on as many as they can, oust as many as they can, sell, kill, outsell, betray, rob, and cheat. And what is the result? When they have an *adversary*, Mr. Manray, instead of fighting back like a cat or a snake, they are caught in their own ritual. They don't say, 'I'm beaten because I'm a fool,' but, 'I'm beaten because the other side is ungodly.' That's cowardly, Mr. Manray. In the East, we don't think like that. We think straight. We are honorable men. I would not even eat with this Raccamond again. Do you know what he would do? He would take the bread and butter out of everyone's mouth, Mr. Bertillon's and Mr. Manray's and everyone's and put it all in his own. That is what he is. No, I am not with him. I will never make a scandal or such an outcry. He should be ashamed.

676

Everyone ought to laugh at him. He tried to rob a client from me. I have no illusions about Mr. Raccamond. Ah! Ah!"

The next night it was Marianne that telephoned Jacques Manray. "Try them out, see how they feel: get my husband's team together, Campoverde, even Voulou, although he's soft. Find out if they'd move with my husband, but say nothing definite, you know."

"I don't know what I'm to do, Mrs. Raccamond. What is your husband going to do when he comes back?"

"Confidentially" (she uttered it like a battle cry though), "he will become general manager; he is taking over control of the London office and all the foreign accounts. He is making a thorough examination of the bank's files and accounts and if he is satisfied, he will stay there and reorganize, and if he is not satisfied, he will withdraw his accounts and those who go with him will have his protection in the Crédit. Or he may organize a bank of his own through Carrière: Carrière is proposing to found a private bank. You know what Carrière is worth." Jacques was dumb. "You are working with us, Mr. Manray?"

"But—Mr. Bertillon, Mr. William—"

"We have them, Manray: they must work in with us, or without us; but we have the power. . . ."

Jacques let her ring off without saying another word. He was dumbfounded. Who was deceiving him? He had allowed himself to promise his co-operation to both sides and in his timidity he was glad of it. There was "something rotten" in Raccamond, yet sick and hysterical, he had been able to gain this power at a single interview.

The Raccamonds rang him for four evenings and in the end he was obliged to take Campoverde and others to the counter of some near coffee bar and ask, "Has Raccamond been talking to you lately? What do you think of him? Do you think he's sound?" Farther than this he would not go, and his results were negative. By the fifth day Marianne was suspicious and discontented. Thereafter, he heard nothing. He worried for a day and then went on with his work in the old way.

The brothers Bertillon were almost invisible—they spent hours with Jean de Guipatin and with strange persons not seen before. This looked like new business, indeed. At the same time, several large new accounts had been opened in the bank by persons of financial or social consequence, and the employees who had suffered some moments of anguish in the past year began to look cheerful again and think that the trouble was over. Business ran more smoothly. The "boys," the commission men and the clients, got their information from the usual financial journals, but markets were "looking better," shares were going up in price, and some of them were only too glad to think that even inflation might help the country and even a fascist *Putsch* in Germany might help the Germans out of their marasmus. Alphendéry, with his perpetual song of ruin and the "decay of the system," was not there. Even Jacques began to think the bank was more wholesome without this theorem!

Richard Plowman walked round the bank a good deal alone, but he courageously tried to keep everyone in a jolly mood by inquiring after their rheumatisms and children and by saying gaily, "Cheer up, the worst is yet to come, as Alphendéry would say"—sure sign that the old man thought all trouble was over. Jacques knew that old Plowman had a considerable part of his fortune in the bank and that he had never made a move to withdraw it. He had been sixty years in banking. He had seen the world. Was it likely that he would go about so peaceably if things were wrong up above?

Suddenly Jacques received a letter from London, in Raccamond's handwriting:

DEAR JACQUES,

I am vindicated and everything is now in my hands. I have got the London books which dovetail into the Brussels books I showed you. I am completely master of the situation. Be ready for me on Friday. I am completing the survey here and will return immediately. My subordinate here, Mr. Bomba, is with me up to the hilt, and I am sure we can count on general loyalty, especially when the facts are revealed. I am now able to reveal all, and you will have my confidence. In the meantime, line the rest of the men up, separately and sound them on the Bertillons. Tell them nothing! Say nothing to the Bertillons! If they knew what I had they might close the bank overnight. This is most important. I have terrible news, but through it I see a way to save the bank, take it out of the wrong hands, and make our own fortunes. Say nothing, but keep your eyes open and have a report ready for me when I come on Friday.

ARISTIDE RACCAMOND

P.S. Have confidence: London is with us to a man and I find that Alphendéry, who was in a very real manner the inspirer of evil, has gone home to visit his mother. I see in this a dismissal.

Jacques became miserable with doubt. After a morning of wrestling with himself, he walked upstairs to Jules's room and without a word put the letter open on his desk. Jules started up. "Newchurch lied to me! Jacques, I want you to manage things here for me for a few days: I must go to London."

Jacques smiled. "I'm so glad: I think that's the best, Mr. Bertillon. Calm him down, Mr. Bertillon. He's a funny sort of fellow."

"I may not see Raccamond," Jules said quietly. "If he comes here while I'm away, play him, see these books, and get them if you can. If I can I'll have Raccamond arrested before he leaves England, for theft. It's possible I'll miss him. Ask my brother William to come in." He looked at Jacques, smiled ravishingly. "Thanks, Jacques. Hold the fort for me."

"Has he got anything serious?" asked Jacques.

"No, no; but he's a fool and he can do us a lot of damage with his bawling. Get my brother, will you?"

William and Jules Bertillon left for London by the afternoon plane. Richard Plowman, still smiling and constant, perambulated round the bank during their absence. Daniel Cambo came in bronzed from his trip to Morocco, with tales of the *ouled-naïl* and of complaisant officials. Mouradzian uneasily trotted round the bank, asking about Alphendéry and Bertillon, and young Prince Campoverde, tall, quiet, slow, and ambitious, went about his business. . . . He had heard some rumors of further trouble for the bank, and he hoped to get a partnership out of Jules. A bank of this nature was just what he wanted to start out in life. Born during the war, he had never known anything but political excitement, trouble, and wild changes of state forms. He tranquilly perceived his chance in a shaky bank and his proper partner in Jules, another postwar pirate. Campoverde was a daredevil flier, and he and Jules had had an equal number of serious accidents on the roads. Campoverde was already forming his "team" for the partnership, with Jean de Guipatin, the Marquis de Chabot-Alpargatos, the son of Mouradzian, and other brilliant young fellows round the bank, full of postwar elegance, political freakery, ingrained cynicism, and derring-do. He was the one who had introduced the "aviation plan" to Jules just now. It was being whispered about the bank.

Scene Ninety-one: The Faithful

JULES and William Bertillon returned from London by plane on Thursday afternoon. While they were away, Claire-Josèphe had taken a trip to Lausanne to see her boys and had brought the four children home with her "because they were homesick." The brothers went straight to the bank when they arrived and found Richard Plowman there, in a new panama hat and a light gray suit, telling Jacques Manray about different kinds of sea anemones he had cultivated at home. Richard flushed with pleasure to see the brothers, ran to meet them with outstretched hands like an uncle, gave news of Claire-Josèphe and the boys, asked after Jules's latest motor injury, informed them that Jean de Guipatin had broken a collar bone again at polo, and asked William if he had seen the doctor about his low blood pressure. The children and Claire were expecting Plowman for lunch. "I'm going to look for a school near Paris for the children, Claire doesn't like them so far away and—" he smiled apologetically, "it'll be something for me to do in the weekends: take them out."

He was following the boys up for a cozy chat, when Jules said, "Oh, please excuse us, Richard, we have to count in some gold that was just deposited with us by the Comtesse Campo-Formio this morning. Manray didn't want to send it to the safe deposit till we counted it. You don't mind?"

"No, no, Jules, of course not." He was very disappointed, wanted to know the latest news from London, whether Mrs. Fairfax still remembered him, whether Frank Durban had been to the Mayfair yet, whether they had got his herbal treatment for the liver. "I never see you boys now: business is booming, what!" He smiled cheerily, covering his disappointment, not to rebuke them. "An old man like me has nothing to do but sit round in an armchair and wonder why the brisk young fellows are too busy for him. I remember when old fellows used to sit round my outer office, smoking cigars and chatting, nice old johnnies who couldn't tear themselves away from India, couldn't go home to Cheltenham and vote for the latest tory candidate. I thought they were taking it pretty easy, too! I've had my day. I'm not grumbling. I'll just run along and see the next generation."

"Hope I die before I'm fifty at the most," said Jules. "I can't stand the aged. Never had a minute's sympathy with them in my whole life. The first day I catch myself thinking about easy chairs, I'm going to take a first-class Fokker and loop the loop: end of a first-class Fokker. . . ."

"Don't worry about that yet," murmured William. "Just what's this idea of showing your gold to Raccamond?"

"I'm going to show him what we've got in Amsterdam, and what we've got in Paris, and then I'll take it out the very next day. We've taken the gold out of London where the big ass thinks he's going to sit in grandeur. They'll never think it's in Oslo because I told Bomba that Dannevig was incompetent and also broke, and I'm liquidating the Oslo office. They're so anxious to fleece me they believe anything I say if it suits their game."

"Jules, we're finished, I feel it in my bones."

"So do I; so does Claire. That was smart of her to get the children. Effie wants to divorce Paul! Effie has the best nose for money in the world. That shows she thinks we're going down. Let her go!"

They laughed. "Where is Michel?"

"Gone to see his mother in Alsace, I think: I don't care."

"Don't be silly," said William. "We could use him still. Send him a nice letter, saying we want him back as soon as his health's better. Tell him we'll pay him his salary as soon as he comes back."

"Do what you like! What good is he? He didn't get the books from Newchurch."

"You're wandering: you told him to keep out of it."

"What difference does it make! He should have had the gumption to go against me."

William looked through his brother, seeing a thing to come, perhaps. He did not reply to this last, but said, "We're in a good position if the market goes down again. We'll have enough to leave the bank about seventy-five per cent solvent. Alphendéry can explain away a lot with that much dough."

"Don't worry about Michel," Jules cried, in a scot. "Worry about me."

"What do you bet Michel won't come back?" William asked, jingling his coins.

"He'll come back if I ask him."

Aristide came back, not in triumph, but in another paroxysm. His calculations had shown him that if there was a run on the bank, the clients demanding a transfer of their positions, and the market being against Jules, there was not enough money in the bank to buy back and pay out even his own clients. Aristide saw no gold accounts; the partially informed accountants in London made him think that every share which arrived in the bank was immediately sold out, that even bonds were sold out, and even bonds on deposit and lottery bonds had been sold. On the train back, Aristide, figuring with Marianne, had seen the figures of indebtedness mounting and mounting. The bank was also a debtor of Claire-Josèphe for two million francs, to Claire's mother for half a million, to big preferred clients like Plowman and Campoverde's family for several millions. The Comtesse de Voigrand, Jean de Guipatin's client, the richest woman in France, it was said, would be paid out before Aristide's Napoleonic princesses, Chicago comtesses, and stage queens. He could not get back quickly enough. Yet he was too timid to take the airplane.

Scene Ninety-two: Carrière

HE WENT first to Carrière and saw him with his secretary
and his mother in his home in the Avenue Montaigne. He
showed both his sets of books and showed his calculations.

"The best thing, Dr. Carrière, is to close the bank at
once, arrest Mr. Bertillon, by making a general complaint,
in the hope of preserving what assets he has. How do
we know he won't fly the country?"

Carrière said, "Where would your clients be, Aristide?
You wouldn't get preference over the other men. Better
to draw your clients out carefully first. If they pay them
out, you'll be able to bring down Bertillon afterwards. If
they don't pay them out, you can complain to the police
on that ground. Don't be rash. You've given Bertillon a
scare. He may have moved his movable assets in case you
make a scandal. Go quietly."

"I haven't the strength, Dr. Carrière."

"Then you should never have started this, Raccamond.
You can't get out of it now. Don't forget that I have an
account in the bank. You're not thinking of me, are you?
You know I have a foreign account with them. With the
books in the disorganization they are now, and everyone
upset, an incursion by the police might only reveal what
we are anxious to conceal. Think of my own situation: a
man about to run as Mayor, who defies the Poincaré law
and avoids taxes by keeping his bonds abroad? I know
everyone does it and you've got to do it to protect yourself, but the *little people* will always make a fearful stink
about that sort of thing. Now, Aristide, if you're looking
to me for help, you've got to consider me, too. We've
got to pussyfoot for a few days. Go home. I'll call upon
you this evening, if I may."

When he had got rid of Aristide, Dr. Carrière said
to his secretary, "Now's my chance! Jules has refused to
pay me the last sterling drafts, despite the court decision.
This fool Raccamond will burst out one of these days
and bring down the house—I've got to get in first, for
Jules is my kill. I'm going to plaster the bank for every-

thing that's owed to me—how much is that?—a million and a quarter in all? I'm going to bring Jules down. See the lawyer—and get him to send in the bailiffs when the bank opens tomorrow morning. I'll be there too: I'll see Jules ruined." He laughed healthily. Nothing was going right but his affair with Jules. "And after," he said, "give Aristide chicken feed but never let him in here again. I don't want that amateur sleuth round here."

"Why close the bank, Jacques?" asked his mother Inès. "Why not get your money? You know that while Jules's bank is open he can still get in accounts. Why shouldn't he work for you for a bit? Frighten him, make him sign something, but give him a chance to pay you. You need the money, Jacques: I'm not going to keep you."

The mother prevailed. Thus, when Aristide came to the bank early in the morning, without his books, but with a long memorandum of requirements, Jacques told him, trembling, that Dr. Carrière was already upstairs. Dr. Carrière came in early in the morning, made a great scene, waved his arms, and threatened to close up the bank.

"What is to become of us?" said poor Jacques. The tellers were talking in the booths; one or two clerks and secretaries were going about their businesses with mousy tread and earthy faces. A noise of shouting could be heard from upstairs. Aristide rushed out of the room and upstairs. He listened in the corridor for a moment and heard Carrière's voice: "Unless you pay me the lot over counter now, I'm going to close you up, Bertillon!"

"Go to blazes," said Jules. "You won't get a cent."

"Then you won't be here this evening," cried Carrière. "My lawyers have the seizure papers ready."

Raccamond rushed in, breathless, thinking that Carrière had been seized with fear. "Dr. Carrière, don't do that! Remember what you said. Don't ruin Mr. Bertillon. Think of my clients, think of our clients! Mr. Bertillon will make an agreement with us: he will pay us. He has accounts, he has some money somewhere. He'll pay us. We'll make a settlement; you'll get your money and I'll get my money. Why should we rush things like this! Let's look at it all ways and get the best we can out of it."

Carrière smiled unpleasantly. "But I want the money, Raccamond. You got two hundred thousand francs out of this place last year: what do you want?"

"My clients," stammered Raccamond in terror. "I won't

have a client in Paris. You can't ruin me, Dr. Carrière.
I've always been loyal to you."

Jules watched them playing this scene, with a grimace.
Aristide seized the telephone, in so much of a panic that
he was no longer playing a part, and asked for the lawyers,
Maître Beaubien's friend, Maître Metz, and Maître Beaubien.

"We can settle it all in a friendly manner," said
Aristide. "These two meet socially: there need be no un-
pleasantness. You'll get your money, Dr. Carrière. I'll see
to that myself. And then I'll get out my clients. The bank
must close up then. That is the only way."

Carrière, curious and faintly amused at the change in
Raccamond, sank into a chair. The lawyers would be there
in fifteen minutes.

Jean de Guipatin hurried in from downstairs, visibly
upset. He heard the story from Jacques and Jacques had no
doubt been listening in the corridor.

"What are you doing, Jacques?" he turned to Carrière.
"Why do you want to shut Jules up?"

"For money," said Carrière. "He's a simple fourflusher,
although you've covered him with romance."

"Jacques, you know Jules will pay if you give him time.
He naturally feels a little piqued at the arrangement. It's
a question of pique: Jules felt humiliated at the publicity
in your friends' newspapers. You could have gone about
it in a decent fashion, Jacques."

But Jean had no charm today: he was too anxious.
He was ready for Raccamond: he was not prepared for
a plot between Raccamond and Carrière. Carrière was of
his own world and would not be impressed by his title
of comte or his rich relations. Jules seemed to be wilting
now. Raccamond busily got a hard chair, drew it up to
Jules's desk. "How much is owed to you, Dr. Carrière?
Three hundred thousand francs before the court decision?" He wrote it down. "If we pay that off straightway,
will you accept payment of the rest of the money, the
two drafts owing, at à rate of 20,000 francs a month? . . ."

"No," said Carrière. "I want the three hundred thousand
francs now, spot cash, and the two drafts owing in a
check to be sent to my home tonight. . . . I don't want
to upset your cash balances," he explained to Raccamond,
ignoring Jules. He took a pleasure in humiliating the head
of the bank and treating the vain employee as the real

chief. "If I'm not paid the three hundred thousand francs before I move out of this chair, I'll close the bank." He looked stern, for he really needed the cash for current debts.

Aristide said, "Sit there, Dr. Carrière, you'll get the money. I'll go and get the manager, Mr. William: he'll pay you immediately. Everything will be in order. I'll take it on myself to see that you are paid." Jules sat there as if he had fallen asleep or fainted. Only a faint chagrin showed on his thin face. Aristide ran out to fetch William. The three sat there, without looking at each other, waiting. Jules felt as if the slightest move would bring him disaster. Carrière savored the bizarre moment.

William came in hurriedly. "What are you doing, Jules?"

"I am taking care of this, Mr. William," said Aristide. "I am trying to do the best for both, but Dr. Carrière must be paid. Otherwise he will close the bank."

William looked grimly, but hopelessly at them all. Jules's voice was heard clear and faint, "Pay him, William."

"Three hundred thousand francs?" William said angrily.

"Whatever he wants."

"I'll let you pay me off the total amount at today's rate," offered Carrière with an unpleasant smile.

William bit his lip. If their struggles of months were to come to this—that Carrière was to be paid the moment he walked in. . . . He took Jules's telephone. "Mr. Martin? Send Vallat up here immediately with three hundred thousand francs in thousand-franc notes. I'll give you the order. Mlle. Dalbi, bring your notebook to my brother's office! Mr. Manray! Have Maîtres Beaubien and Metz arrived yet? Ask them to go straight up. Tell Etienne to send them straight up."

"That's better," said Carrière. "I don't want to do you harm, Jules."

Jules stretched out his long hand, picked up a paper knife, and began to tap with a real, a morbid indifference.

"My brother is relieved," William explained. "He has been thinking all along that you did want to do him harm. How could he have made such a mistake? You have such a sweet reputation, Jacques."

Carrière smiled wryly. "Yes, I know. I do my best to justify it."

When the lawyers arrived, Aristide, with Carrière, had

formulated an agreement to pay, by Jules and William, giving Carrière the right to close the bank for debt, if his drafts were not paid on the dot.

Maître Beaubien frowned when he saw it. "Absurd! Would you support your client in this, Maître Metz? If this is what they want to impose on you," he said to Jules, who had recovered his voice and sweet manners, "you would do better to close the bank."

"Carrière, Raccamond, Jules, and the lawyers all want to close the bank and each one is holding off the others," commented William. "Thus we can all get together if we close the bank. Why not do it?"

"Nothing doing," said Carrière. He signed the receipt for the three hundred bills which he had received and pushed the memorandum towards Jules. Jules scarcely looked at it.

"I'll sign it."

William said, "I'm damned if I will."

Carrière got up in a fury. "I'll get the bailiff in, damn you."

Aristide jumped to his feet, his eyes wide open. "Dr. Carrière, I beg you. Mr. Bertillon, this is for the best. Why should there be a tragedy? Why should any of us go without our money? It can be arranged." He was reassured since the three hundred bills had come up, and he began to regret that Dr. Carrière had got in before him.

Jean shrugged his shoulders sadly. "It's true, Jacques: do be reasonable. You may want to get Jules, but what about us? What harm have we done you? You have been paid at once this morning. Jules is sending you a check to-night. I will take it upon myself to persuade William and Jules to the rest. So will Aristide. Would you rather see Jules in court, or your drafts fully paid up? If it's the first, you're not what I thought you were. . . ."

Carrière abruptly terminated the scene. He disliked it himself and Raccamond who was anxiously watching his face. "Oh, get your man to sign and it'll be all right," he flung at Jean de Guipatin. "It's the same to me either way. But no caviling and no further refusals to pay. If our positions had been reversed, he would expect me to pay. Jules is a cheat. He's smooth and languid. He says I'm a bounder, but he's a cheat. That's what it all comes down to."

Raccamond accompanied him to the front door with many grand gestures.

When he had gone with his lawyer, Maître Beaubien said, looking at the agreement, "You have signed it, Mr. Bertillon! How do you stand with this Raccamond? If you keep making treaties of this type with these two men, you are lost. You would do better to close the bank and fly: I say it as a friend, not as a lawyer. These men are voracious, unstable, bitter, and they keep sharpening each other's appetite. They're dividing your bank between them: on that they're both agreed. Why fight? I tell you frankly, I wouldn't. It's hopeless, as far as I can see."

"I am not ready to go yet," Jules said quietly. "I'll sign to give myself a breathing space, and I'll ditch them all. Let them wait."

"I don't see how you can do it!"

The *maître* heard Raccamond returning and gathered his papers. Raccamond entered, "I think you can thank me for saving you from a nasty moment. Carrière was determined to shut the bank. He's a dangerous enemy."

"Enemies and friends act the same nowadays," said William. "They all want to close the bank. It's a serious mania that half the population of Paris is suffering from. Collective bank-closing mania. Anyone would think it was the U.S.A. Say, they've got a dandy law over there that would settle a few hashes over here: they jail fellows who go round spreading rumors about a bank. You couldn't make a living over there, Aristide!"

"You owe about eighty million francs. I presume this debit is covered by your holdings of bonds, gold, and fully paid-up stocks. I wish to see those holdings . . . first of all."

"We have not made a statement," Jules said starkly, "but I am willing to go round the safety deposits with you and show you our gold and bonds. That is all. That must satisfy you. No statement. No statement. You can't drag one out of me, so don't harp on it."

Aristide suddenly gave in. "Well, it's not satisfactory; but I will see your assets. I have a plan here for buying in the sold-out shares; a pro-rata scheme which I propose to work through myself. I want control of the stock-exchange department while doing so."

"Well, Alphendéry isn't here. I've dismissed him."

Raccamond was so pleased that he did not insist.

688

"One can always do business with a man as thoughtful as you, Aristide."

'The point is that I am thinking of the house and the clients, whereas a man like Carrière is only thinking of personal vengeance, or some single motive; the multiple motive takes care of everyone's interest."

"We'll write that all down in the agreement," said Jules. "I don't see why not: I see you've got the hang of things."

Scene Ninety-three: Restitution

AFTER lunch, William's door opened, and Raccamond's hulk filled the doorway; he stood there, tragically holding open the swing-leaf, with well-marked misgiving, then said gloomily, "Mr. Bertillon wishes to see you in his office." Aristide looked ill.

They got up simultaneously and went in, in slow time. Jules, leaning back in his chair, highhanded and sour, said, "Raccamond has another agreement for us to sign, a six-months' schedule for restitution."

Raccamond waved his hand. "I have worked it out—a question of insuring the clients, while making the Carrière payments; I think it better to make separate agreements for each part of our compromise, so as not to seem to make one article contingent on another. It gives better guarantees. It is better for Mr. Bertillon as it does not give away the whole basis of the agreement."

"Raccamond is right," murmured Jules.

They read:

We, Jules Bertillon, founder of and chief partner in the Banque Bertillon Frères, and William Bertillon, junior partner in and having power of attorney for Bertillon Frères and Paul and Francis Bertillon, junior partners, agree hereby to restore, in the amounts and quantities and values and to the numbers showing in each account, the share positions of the clients of this bank, within a period of from three to six months from this date, without loss to the bank if possible.

689

Aristide Raccamond is hereby designated head of the entire stock-exchange department, and all books, papers, files, and relevant records are to be open to his inspection at any time, in Paris or in the branches abroad. All steps towards safeguarding the accounts of clients and aligning the real share position with that shown on the books are to be taken privately by the persons named above, so that no surprise or discontent will be caused among the employees or clients of the bank.

A weighty and wordy document which pleased Aristide entirely and gave him control of their business. For their profits arose, not, evidently, from the relatively small amount of exchange business, or the small charge for keeping accounts abroad, but from the manipulation of stock-exchange accounts. He had now, by slowly munching over the situation with his wife, and by a comparison of the books, been convinced of this himself. He had decided slowly to profit by this knowledge on a later occasion, when he had withdrawn his accounts from Bertillon. Either he would take his clients to a small bank and insist on control of their accounts, or he would set up a bank himself, with the backing of Carrière. A study of the Bertillon accounts, which had first shocked him, had later enlightened him.

Aristide commented quietly. "Now, Mr. Bertillon, we must have a further guarantee to cover operations at the end of the six-months' limit. You must write me a letter from you and your brother, that will suffice, saying that you are giving up your stock-exchange department at the end of six months, and do not intend to go into this business in France or England at any future time: and that you will allow me to transfer out my clients' accounts when I please, whether they are completely restored or not, and that, further, if I find another position, or set up a stock-exchange business myself, you will give me preference over any other house for orders that your bank clients may require; and that I have conducted your stock-exchange business here and you recommend me as highly competent and that I have been your 'confidential man.'"

Jules laughed. Jean de Guipatin looked helplessly at the two brothers who were soft as butter and made no move; then said to Aristide, "Raccamond, you have the whip hand, but you are too greedy. Let go half the nuts, you know the story? You can't come to any good if you seize and plunder in this way. It would really pay people to put you out of the way. Don't you understand that?"

"I know," said Aristide grandly.

William waved his hand. "We've told you a hundred times. We got books and books and we can get up books and books when we want to."

"Bluff," said Aristide. "I know your style. You are all bluff. It doesn't work with me. I will write out what I want." He made alterations on a paper from his pocket and handed them the following draft letter:

The brothers Bertillon (four names), sole partners in the Banque Bertillon Frères, confirm by this letter that as it will take time to *align and liquidate* and otherwise arrange the clients' accounts now in the house, and the clients must be allowed time to make their own arrangements, the brothers Bertillon will only give up this business gradually and progressively and within the same period of from three to six months, and pay Mr. Aristide Raccamond, director of the Bank a chief customers' man and comptroller of the stock-exchange accounts, a person in whom they have absolute confidence, six months' advance salary.

Maître Lemaître refused to give his consent to the agreement or this letter. Jules seemed on the verge of hysteria and showed it by wisecracking, cynicism, compliance with Raccamond's most insolent demands, slackness, and a refusal to admit that he had hung himself by these papers.

"What are you going to do with such a paper?" asked Guipatin.

"I am going to show it round to get new business for myself, in due course. It is a guarantee that Mr. Bertillon will restore the positions, and that he will execute all the terms of our agreements."

"You have feathered your nest—" said William (Aristide turned his rounded fat back contemptuously), "—with porcupine feathers," finished William. "You are too smart, my hearty."

"You are contemptible," said Maître Lemaître. "I say it to your face."

Raccamond smiled palely. "You are a great lawyer, I know. Tell me one thing: what explains the terms of these contracts, what explains *their* weakness before me, if not their guilt and their fear that I will show them up! You are not here to insult me: you are here to save them; but you cannot, although you are one of the greatest lawyers in France: because your clients are guilty men. They are thieves and swindlers. There is not an ounce of honor in them or in any member of their staff. They have corrupted everyone. And you are paid, my dear *maître*, to look out for the interests of thieves and crooks. You have nothing to say to me. You don't like this agreement: it means their ruin. But you don't dare advise them not to sign it."

"I do advise them!"

"You don't dare force them not to sign it, though. I am going to force them back into plain business where they will barely make their livings, for they'll have to make them honestly and—it suffices! If they go out of business, what does it matter to me or to France? They are the scourge of business: they should be driven out." He picked up the papers, read the signatures, folded them into his pocket. "Don't try any hold-ups at night, any Chicago stuff. Your books are not with me: I have given them into safekeeping, and if anything happens to me, they will go straight to the Public Prosecutor."

"So you have us sewed up," jeered William. "Well, if he isn't the smart little negotiator!"

Aristide looked at William with soft solemnity, nodded. "At the first hint of bad faith or trouble, the books go to the Criminal Division. That is my last word. I am protected. And now I will see your gold."

Jules leapt up. "What, you want to see the gold after gouging those letters out of me! Get to hell out of here."

Aristide flamed. "You were lying to me again? Perhaps you have no gold. Unless I see it, I will send in my books this afternoon."

Jules began to laugh weakly. "The books, the books, the books. Raccamond's raven cry: 'The books, books, books, books, books.' Listen, Aristide, do me a favor. Come back this afternoon. I'm going to have lunch. We'll talk about the gold. We've got to arrange an itinerary: it's in different countries. . . ."

"I'll see the biggest deposit first," said Aristide. "I'll be back this afternoon at three. In the meantime, I am putting these agreements into safe hands." He went out full of importance.

"Mr. Bertillon," said Lemaître, "only ruin can come out of this. I advise you once and for all, shut the bank and take a holiday. This fellow is the worst kind of blackmailer. He is capricious, unstable, and inflated; he has some sort of megalomania. His demands will never be satisfied. Personally, I think you would do better to refuse to recognize all your agreements with him, say that he forced you to sign them when you were ill, or delirious, or at the point of a revolver, whatever you like, and refuse to hold to them. Let him send in the books. What do they prove, after all? That you have kept bloc accounts abroad, which more or less correspond with and nullify the positions held by your clients. These bloc accounts are in the names of corporations, legally constituted. It might be a breach of trust, but it is not criminal. Why don't you fight him?"

"I can't fight," said Jules. "I'm too tired. None of them is going to get a cent."

The *maître* hopelessly said good-by to them and went, only asking after Alphendéry whose advice he thought of as invaluable at this moment. Jules, seizing on every straw, feebly and superstitiously, cried, "That's it. Why didn't we send for him before? What's he doing away? Tell him to come back immediately. Let him fight for me: I gave him lots of money. I gave him all the money he has; tell him I want him. He'll come."

"He mightn't," said William who didn't want to complicate things again. "You were pretty crude with him."

Jules began laughing foolishly, almost crying. "He'll come back for me. He loves me. He told me he'd do anything for me. He's well off through me. Send for him; he's my friend. He's my only friend. He wouldn't have made any bargains with Raccamond. He wouldn't have sent Bomba to London the way you people did."

Willam shrugged silently. Jules continued, "He is the only one that cares for me. What's he doing away? Tell him we'll give him six months' pay at once. Tell him I'm

693

terribly sick and I can't do anything: I need him. Well!"
he cried angrily to William, "why don't you do it?"

William wrote.

Alphendéry did not return.

Scene Ninety-four: The World Against One

IN AN empty, gilded resturant, in a whorehouse street
off the Boulevard de la Madeleine, they were eating a good,
cheap lunch. Jean de Guipatin called the manager, sent
back a wine-glass smirched with lipstick. He looked at the
plush seats, and at William.

Jean said frankly, "You act like a man with either no
money or a lot of money hidden away."

William uttered another of his blanket remarks. "I have
taken my precautions. Wait till Noseybob sees our gold: he
won't rest till he's thought of a way of doing Carrière out
of it and till he's got his own fingers glued on to it."

Jean was somewhat cheered. "You're really going to
show him the gold?"

"Sure! What's he going to do? He can't run to the
police and report us for that."

"I hope he'll be satisfied then."

"We're good for eighteen months—two years yet, and
Aristide can go to hell," said William with unparalleled
calm. "We'll all live to see him in jail even if we only
live another six months; and that day we'll have enough
dough to celebrate the event. I'll go and see him behind
bars. I didn't know there was still a pleasure in life." He
smirked. "Don't you worry, Jean: even Jules doesn't know
everything I've been doing." He toyed with his spoon. "And
I don't know what he's been up to: that's the weakness
of our strength."

No sooner were they back than the telephonist rang
through and told them that Raccamond had been trying to
speak to them for three-quarters of an hour. In five minutes he was on the wire again. Jules was out; William
said irritably, "What do you want now? You've gouged
our eyes out, slit our ears, bit our noses, sold our tripes

694

for cat's meat: what else? We've only got our underwear."

Raccamond said, "We have forgotten the guarantee fund. We must have an agreement on that!"

"Go to hell," repeated William and rang off.

"I never saw a man with such epiloguing wits," remarked Jean de Guipatin. "Every time he leaves us he's calm and satisfied, and in half an hour he's boiling again."

"His wife, or else Carrière: he runs like an office boy to them to report his messages of the morning."

When Jules came in they wearily went over the old ground and Jules said, "Thank God someone has told him to go to hell."

At this moment young Campoverde strolled in and said, "I say, that man of yours, Raccamond, is running all over Paris showing your books, you know. He's saying you're going out of business in his favor. He said he had a letter. He said he'd stolen your books. Shall I get someone to lock him up?"

"The rat," cried Jules. "We've signed everything away and he doesn't keep his word a minute."

"All the honors go to Raccamond," William said agreeably.

"Is it true then?" insisted young Campoverde, startled.

"On the understanding, expressly stated, that we were to have three to six months to clean up, you know, and in that time naturally we intended to get rid of him. We couldn't at the moment. He had us in a jam. How did you get to hear of it?"

"Why, he came to me at lunch hour all out of breath, begged me for a minute, told me a garbled tale I couldn't make out, except I thought he wanted me to go in with him in some move against the bank—he showed me the books he's taken, finally: he had them wrapped up in his overcoat. He said he had two agreements but wouldn't show them—said it was a question of honor—" Jules laughed. Campoverde said to him sadly, "What made you give in to him, Jules? It's so damaging. Before, anybody would have had to have had an accountant to find out what it's all about; now it's a perfect admission."

Jean de Guipatin looked at the young aristocrat intently. "You think the charges he makes, then, are true, Campoverde?"

"Yes," he said simply. They studied him. He sat on

the corner of Jules's desk. "Of course, Jules, I was surprised in a way. I know, why everyone in Paris has known for years, that you were a big speculator and everyone thought you ran a bucket shop." He laughed his candid boy's laugh. "I didn't know of course that you were in so deep; but I didn't come here to say that. It's not my business. . . . I, and everyone like me who came here, first heard all the rumors about you and we all figured the same: he's safe because he's lucky and he's got some system. We left our money here because we trusted your star, Jules. You're a big man. You're a financial genius. No, no, I wasn't knocked over, not a little bit, by his books. I take my gruel. So do we all. And you've protected me with that agreement on my mother's estate. But what I'm here to say is—you've got a bad case on your hands. I would have given him a horsewhipping or knocked him down if you'd called me in and told me to, Jules, and that would have gone miles farther than all these thug agreements he's got out of you. . . . He's an outsider, a cad, and a coward. A touch of the stick and he would have cried with terror. He worships titles and he worships cash: I say, you've got a regular hedge of janissaries round you, Jules: anyone of us would have given him a beating for you. . . . Why didn't you tell me? You can trust me, you know that?"

They all looked at Campoverde with surprise and admiration. Jules and William distrusted aristocrats as a matter of course and regarded their friend Jean de Guipatin as something of a freak.

"How did he get the books?" inquired Campoverde. "I thought you didn't have any books, anyhow: you told me Michel remembered it all or something, or I thought you did."

"No: a memory like Michel's might be dangerous if it turned wrong," Jules said caustically.

Campoverde who knew nothing of the rift said, "Jules, how?"

"Oh, suppose he went nutty. He's a neurotic as it is. I suppose a freak memory and freak learning like Michel's make a man a bit unbalanced. Like a cousin of my mother's. She had hair six feet long. I've seen photographs of it trailing on the ground. Horrible, bughouse. She died of continual headache and tuberculosis. Couldn't make a living for the hair. Supposing Michel's memory got a bit longer: he might get moral tuberculosis like Raccamond has. Michel's unhealthy. I don't want unhealthy types round me. I want to clean them out. I want barbarians who can just sign their names, that's all." They all shivered at this freakish treachery on Jules's part. Everyone became aware at the same time that Jules was on the edge of a nervous breakdown.

Jean de Guipatin said slowly, "What we have to do now is to put the gag on Raccamond somehow. The damage is done and I'm afraid to look forward. He seems fated to do this. He ruined Claudes', he's practically done it here: we've allowed him to get away with it. Here we are, all sane and sound, and yet he's got away with everything. There's a positive fatality in it. He acts like a madman, but he's reasonable: he takes us in our worst moments." He fell silent. They all looked at him appraisingly. In this interval, Aristide appeared in the door. Jean de Guipatin looked up and said, "Ah, Aristide! We were just talking about you."

He was pallid and suspicious; he came forward with his lagging tread. He looked at Campoverde and walked to him. "Has Bertillon been getting you into his toils again? Why do you go near this place? I warned you, Prince. *He* has the ability to charm anyone out of their last franc. If he has tried to explain things, it is only because he is going to run away with your money. Why did you come here? Listen, Prince, I know what he's done. . . . I've got his books, and yet he is able to charm me, too: I go away from here forgetting what I came to do. Don't listen to him: he is sick, he is insane, he's an insane liar and swindler."

His voice had risen: there was a suppressed scream in it. "He wants to be a Kreuger; he'll never get that high; I'll never let him swindle thousands of poor people who believed in him . . . he'll get everything out of you." He stopped, breathing hard and let his round eyes sink into Jules's face and figure.

Jules laughed harshly. "I wish it was true. Sit down, Aristide. Is it true you want another agreement? I don't mind. I'm born to sign agreements. You are the charmer round here. Bring them along. I'll sign anything." He rollicked, hysteria still not far off.

William's rattling throat went into operation. "Raccamond is getting more reasonable: he only wants us to put

697

up a two-million-franc guarantee. He knows that we have to pay Carrière, that three hundred thousand is tied up with the Rosenkrantz and Guildenstern suit, one hundred thousand with the Parouart suit, one hundred thousand more with the Wades, and he doesn't see why he shouldn't have his couple of million. Our whole operating capital got up in red ribbons like a Christmas tree. Perhaps Aristide will take over the bank, or rather give us a short lecture on how we can run it in these circumstances?"

Aristide was ill with thinking of the money already tied up and lost to his clients. How could he have been so lax, so credulous, so kindly, so that everyone with a less claim had got in before him? He was too good, as Marianne said, too soft. They said, "Take us on our word," and by heaven he did. Others were not so childish. He saw the Bertillons escaping, being gazetted as embezzlers or bankrupts, everyone running in for their cut and himself involved with them, probably sued by the clients along with them. By what frauds had they involved him with themselves?

"You can take over the bank, Aristide," Jules offered freakishly with a hint of anger.

Just so! They would leave him the wreck.

"You've got to pay me off: what's the use of your gold in Amsterdam! You won't bring it here to pay my clients, will you?"

"No fear. Do you think we're crazy, with everyone trying to get our money?"

"I'll ruin you. You're trying to defraud me. You won't get away with it: I'll ruin you. I don't care for anyone. I'll bring down the house, to show you you can't treat me like this. You're in my power. I'll show the books to everyone. I'll go to every client. I'll brand you as swindlers everywhere . . . you'll never dare to show your face here again. You'll say all your lives, 'Raccamond ruined us: curse Raccamond. Raccamond was our end. We tried to fool Raccamond but Raccamond wasn't a fool like the others. We swindled him but he showed us up.' Raccamond," he said intensely to Jules, "think of the name: it's going to be synonymous with ruin. I'll show you all up. William Bertillon, who has been secreting funds in anonymous coporations abroad for years, so that he could fly and leave nothing in the till; Jean de Guipatin, Comte, a sort of Bourbon, out of our best families, goes to all the fashionable weddings and helps two thieves to pick the pockets of their clients. You're as bad as they are, Monsieur le Comte. You know what they are doing and you say nothing: you stick with them. Prince Campoverde, standing with swindlers, in the hope that they'll give you a share. All standing together, all standing against me. But I'll show you all up. I'll ruin you all. I'll go straight to the Prosecutor with my books and you won't have time, Monsieur le Comte. The place will be closed and the funds will be sealed to those who have a right to them, not to a lot of parasites trading on their titles."

This went on for some time. Everyone was indicted, everyone in a great conspiracy against poor Raccamond, the gentle fool. The silence of them all at length embarrassed him, and by degrees he returned to a more perspicacious state.

Campoverde understood nothing at all of all this and looked at Raccamond with revulsion. Jean de Guipatin, in his deep soft voice, the lofty accent much diminished, said kindly, "Aristide, it would be foolish to behave like a jealous woman: blot out the whole show for self-justification and a sort of pitiable notoriety; you would be like a woman who jails her husband for alimony or shoots her husband and so abolishes all husbands, present and future. You can realize that you would be committing suicide yourself, and no one would take you for the instrument of eternal justice."

"You threaten me with a boycott?"

"Yes. If you do this, I will let everyone within earshot hear about it and the way you went about it, your belly growing bigger and bigger, your appetite getting more monstrous, until you wanted everything in the bank for your own. And the fact that you accepted a gigantic salary, knowing very well where it must come from; and that you bribed clerks, put in your men, stole books, stole clients, everything.

"Now," said Jean, shaking his head, "you are on the wrong track. I have no pride; I am humble. I know what I am, a very simple and rather stupid young man who is accepted under protest, because he has a father who is one of the richest men in France. You have not the intuitions which humility gives. You cannot distinguish reality from the wild melodramatic rendering that your jealous ambition paints you. That is why I would lay a bet on any odds of your coming to grief. You haven't the coolness necessary to success. Mr. Bertillon is superstitious and he averred that you had the evil eye on you, or something like that, wasn't it, Jules?"

"He's unlucky," said Jules crossly.

"You see?"

"All right," said Aristide, "now I know where I stand. And you too, Prince Campoverde?"

"Oh, as for me," said the young man laughing, "a fortuneteller told me I'd make my fortune with this bank, and there it is: I won't leave it. Who would?"

"You won't give me the two million francs guarantee, then?" asked Aristide.

"No." Jules leaned back in his chair, gradually coming to himself.

"But you'll keep to the other agreements?"

"Those? Oh, sure, sure. Yes, of course."

"And you'll show me the gold?"

"Any time you like."

"And you'll give me six months' salary while the restitution is going on so that I can travel round and put my affairs in order?"

"Yes."

"Will you pay it to me now?"

"Yes."

Aristide's color came back: he recalled the scene—Carrière being paid his money on the nail. Jules saw this through half-closed lids; he picked up the telephone and before William could make a move, ordered briskly, "Henri Martin? Send one of the boys up with—how much is it, William?" William started to protest, but Jules hushed him with a gesture, "How much is it?"

"One hundred and twenty thousand francs. Aristide must give a receipt for that."

"Only for half," said Aristide at once. "Otherwise my income-tax statement is askew. Give it to me, half in cash, half in a check on my London corporation."

Jules gave the necessary orders: William wrote out two receipts, one for the cash and one for the London corporation. When it was paid, Aristide, suddenly restored to equanimity and even amiability, said, "When do we start for Amsterdam, Mr. Bertillon?"

"I'll go by plane tomorrow," said Jules offensively. "You

700

can go by train when you like. No, wait, the day after.
I have to get a witness in Amsterdam and he may be busy
tomorrow."

This was arranged. Jules immediately secretly sent a
telegram to Alphendéry asking him to travel to Amsterdam to be his witness in an opening of the vaults.

"Why Michel?" asked William.

"Just to spite Aristide," said Jules, with hatred.

Scene Ninety-five: Léon's Grand Passion

ALPHENDÉRY and Léon met in Amsterdam. "See if you
think I'm right, Henri. One morning when I walk in, I find
Jules surrounded by Señor This and Señor That and Rear-
Admiral Something; I inquire what's going on. 'Why,' says
Jules, 'are you still here? I thought you'd left us?' The
same evening I go out with William as usual, and William
got drunk, a very rare thing for him, but he shouted his
address getting into the taxi, and William said, 'Well, cheer
up, Alphendéry, we're good for at least nine months
and we'll all be cozy: I saw to that!' Bluff, a put-up job,
indiscretion? I don't know, Henri. I heard the bell ring:
I jumped."

" 'M, 'm," considered Léon frowning at Alphendéry with
one eye, " 'm. . . . Go on, my boy, and—and—and you
said?"

"I went into Jules and said, 'I'm transferring my
money.' "

"How's that, how, transfer?"

Alphendéry explained patiently, "I gave them all my
gold back to show to Aristide Raccamond."

Consternation shook the face of Henri Léon. "You
gave it back? No."

"Yes, they asked me—to show to Raccamond—I said
to Jules, 'I'm transferring it out.' Well, it took me three
days to get them to sign the transfer back. I sweated those
three days."

"My boy—I respect you—very nice of you," Léon's
voice had taken on a deep note of love, since he realized
that Alphendéry still had the money, "but—fouh—very

701

dangerous—elfin type like, any man with—that type. You were lucky to get it back." He nodded impressively, his eyes calculating the worth of the man in front of him. He suddenly beamed, coughed a laugh. "And so you said, 'I'll go and play along with Léon, eh?'"

"Or Ralph Stewart. Stewart thought I could swing the big accounts."

Léon looked anxiously at him. "Big accounts, eh? Baron Koffer? He likes you, eh? Well! No, no, you come to London with me. You get my account; you give it to Stewart. Good account; you get commissions. I give you ten per cent commission on all you make for me. . . . Michel, want some—er, some cognac, cognac, eh, eh, waiter?"

"No, and neither do you: you're already drunk with Léon."

Léon peeked suspiciously, then a radiant smile painted his whole face with youth. "Very good, 'drunk with Léon': drunk with—hi, hi, hi, that's the best I've—'drunk with Léon.' You're good, my boy, you're good. You stay with me, eh? We'll make dough, boy, you won't be able to see our heels for dust. Yes? Yes! Some cognac, waiter. We'll celebrate."

Scene Ninety-six: The Secret Vaults

WHEN Jules, Claire-Josèphe, and Aristide had assembled at the Amsterdam bank on the appointed Saturday morning they found Alphendéry already there, talking to the bank manager whom he had come to know. At this unexpected sight, Aristide trembled and lost some of his wooden dignity. He scarcely acknowledged Alphendéry, wherefore Jules said with malice, "Mr. Alphendéry is my witness."

Raccamond, outraged, said in a high tone, "But I thought your wife and these others—"

"My wife is here to witness to her own gold; the gold broker, Mr. van Eyk, is here to see his two subordinates make the count, merely as a matter of business; Mr. Heuting, the bank manager, is here as a matter of routine.

I represent myself; Mr. Alphendéry is my witness. You are here in your own interests." He turned sharply from Raccamond, asked the bank manager to lead the way downstairs, and said no more, except curtly, when the vault was opened, "This section contains the gold of certain clients, gold held in private numbered accounts; this section holds my wife's gold; this section holds gold belonging indiscriminately to the bank and myself. I guarantee the bank, as it were, it being a private institution and belonging to me."

With suspicious, careworn, hungry eyes, Raccamond watched the counting of the gold. Alphendéry, seeing his eyes wander once, said cheerily but in a tone only to be heard by Jules, "You'd better watch: we're going t~ this expense and bother for you alone." He laug~ good-naturedly pawed Aristide's arm, eviden~ to make him feel more friendly.

Aristide shook his arm free and l~ gold. He had a notebook with him ar~ worth. When the counting was thro~ appointed and truculent tone, "An~ longs to the bank?"

"Yes."

He turned pompously to the g~ounts," gold here actually belongs to Mr~ "I can

"Certainly," said the broker w~

He was not moved. "And ~ by anxiety. longs to private clients?" ~ ~ itself (or to

"This gold is held priva~ ~out four million said the broker, after lookir~ ~ted at least twice say no more." ~about the gold said

Raccamond turned fret~ ~e numbered accounts, The gold said to belong ~ ~s soon as they were free Jules, indiscriminately) ~ch with reasons, jolly with paper francs, not more ~ense: he said, "Good God! as much. He was inte~ in times like these? Think to belong to Claire-J~ch ~ ~ven one bar of gold. The and he taxed Jules a~ ~like to be able to do what Jules of the bank. Alphen~ laughter at Raccam~ What are you as~ yourself lucky to ~
German bankers~." 703
Bertillon has just

"I didn't come here to hear you," said Aristide in grand gloom. "I understood that you were not with us any more."

Alphendéry laughed and said, "I am not either: I just came as a personal friend, you know. I am working with Mr. Léon and—others—you know now. And not much of anything. My heath is not too good." Jules winked at him and Alphendéry made his good-bys, intimating that he had an appointment with Léon.

This made Aristide restless enough. He said with spite as soon as Alphendéry had gone, "I don't believe you've severed your connection with that man: it doesn't look like it. A man doesn't show his gold to a mere friend. I believe you're still working in secret with him. On every side I see your evident bad faith. What am I to believe? And this gold that belongs to your wife—and to alleged private clients?"

"Take it or leave it," said Jules airily.

"No. I thought there was much more, much more. I am not satisfied. You must show me more gold than

bit his lip. "I've gone farther with you than with any man: do you think I'd have done the same with own brother? You jump over yourself with Raccamond. If you're not satisfied now, you

price that I set—" said Aristide obstinately, "four millions in gold. If you had shown

"Banging to the bank I would have been low," but what you have shown me is only not enough. You must show me

Let's put Why do you say you are doing it your object is s. I get nothing out of it."

"My object is n guarantee you want to swal-fair and square fasbank you want to get hold of. gold. If there isn't an, stide: everyone knows what give some of that gold to see business done in a family duty to the clients to see the rest of the guarantee," Claire-Josèphe look the bank; it is your out speaking. He took it for as epted your personal
istide quietly, with-
He looked upon

704

Claire-Josèphe as a silly, meek woman with a head full of frivolities, impressed by all businessmen. He continued, "Besides that, the only thing you can do at the moment is to buy in the greater part of your positions, so that in any case, the gold you have shown me almost if not quite covers them."

"If you're so honest," said Jules, "why not buy in the lot? If it's only a question of fair and square."

"We have to be reasonable," said Aristide, troubled. "We can't make that big disturbance in the market. Let us buy back or sell out gradually. The position is—" he paled at the thought, "colossal." He seemed shaken. "Colossal! I have not slept since I saw the London books. How is it possible for you to have taken on this immense responsibility so lightheartedly. I cannot understand it. Either there are books I have not seen, or you and your brother are the most bizarre businessmen I have ever seen. No thought of the future. Why, you could be ruined by a move in the markets, while we're standing here talking." He wiped his forehead, not ashamed, even pleased, with the sweat of fear that had come out on him. He began to tremble somewhat, though. "It is terrible, terrible," he cried in anguish. "I have not had a moment's peace since I learned of it. And it's been going on for years! We have walked on the edge of a volcano—it can blow up any moment. God! I don't dare face the facts—if it weren't for my clients. . . . If anything went wrong, before we have time to straighten the accounts, there would be nothing for us but to commit suicide." He looked at Jules. "I know you, Mr. Bertillon, you could never stand it. You don't seem to realize where Alphendéry brought you with his wild, fanatic—unspeakable—speculation."

Jules looked calmly at him: "Yes, Alphendéry should never have done it. That's what comes of trusting a man too far. You can't trust anyone to keep his head."

"The commissions!" cried Aristide.

"What?"

"The commissions back, half-commissions, he must have got from the brokers. What else would induce him to speculate like this? You've been robbed, Mr. Bertillon. You ought to send an officer of the law after him. You don't seem to see the abyss, the profoundity of self-interest. Why, the whole bank has been run by Alphendéry for his own profit! You have not counted. And your brother either a party to it or blind." He wrung his hands. Jules laughed.

"Nobody twists me round his little finger," said Jules impatiently. "Don't be melodramatic, Aristide. I was lax, all right, but I wasn't robbed. Be sure of that. I have never been and I never will be. That's all. Forget the subject, will you? You have Alphendéry on the brain. Forget him, too. I'll meet you in Paris tomorrow, Aristide. Now, don't go near the Amsterdam office, you hear. I don't want them to know we've been up here without calling in: they wouldn't like it." Aristide said nothing. "Do you hear, Raccamond?"

"They have no supervision. I'm a director: it's my right if I want to inspect it."

"You keep away from my bank, understand that," shouted Jules suddenly. "It's my bank. If you're a director, you're my director . . . you're under my orders. Stop getting round like a field marshal: you make me sick. You don't seem to realize that all this is mine, arises in me, is nothing without me. If I shut up shop tomorrow, you'd be on the street. The whole crowd of you forgets that. You all posture, but I'm the one who charms the comtesses. I'm the one that gets the rake-off and if I divide with you, it's because I want to and not because anyone forces me to. Remember that. I can fire you tomorrow and give no reason. Remember that. And I can have you locked up, if I want to. I don't give a two-penny darn for your so-called books. I'll deny them. I'll take you for a ride into Belgium if you're not careful and have you arrested there. Your accounts! They're half in the red; I'm out of pocket over them. They don't pay their margins and we have to foot it lightly because it's the Princesse; they lose money and yell and we have to 'make reparation' because it's the Comtesse, and we mustn't offend her. They've got an overdraft and they won't pay up, and we've got to forget about it because it's the Duchesse. And you call that business. Those are the accounts you brag about! You'd make a nice figure taking your accounts to another house: no one would take them. I can only afford to keep them because of my 'practices' that don't suit you. Why, you're living on my charity, all of you, half the time and you go round inflated with righteousness, like a cow that's eaten a bad weed; you shriek and dance thinking you're the whole

706

show. I'm the whole show. I'm the Barnum and you're the only freak in the works." He laughed suddenly, angrily, looking at Aristide's dignified and rebelling attitude. "Cheer up, Aristide. I'm king. I wouldn't be in business if I couldn't be that. I'm not going to be anyone's partner, and I'm not going to work in with anyone. I'd rather shoot myself. That's my nature. So don't push me too far. Take what you can get, take what I offer you, and be thankful. I'm not mean. I'm willing to give you a fair share. But understand how things are in my bank."

Aristide pressed his lips together. "Then you're immoral," he said thickly, articulating with some difficulty. "All this is just to tickle—your vanity. I understand now. There is no bank. You just think it's a booth in a bazaar. But I'll settle the affairs of the bank without you. I've got your books and I can force you. It's not just your toy!" he said loudly. "It's a public institution . . . there's public money in it, the money of the people. I'll put it right without you. I'll clean it out and if you won't co-operate I'll force it from you and run it honestly: that's my duty. I see where all this has been leading to. I'm not satisfied with your attitude or your gold and I'm going to crush the bank like matchwood unless you give me a written promise to co-operate with me."

"Help!" cried Jules. "I say, Aristide, you're crazy. You better go slow."

"Otherwise I go straight to the police."

Alphendéry encountered them in the hotel lobby. He intervened, "We have more gold—elsewhere . . . you can see that if you want to." He spoke with authority. "Aristide, don't you realize one thing, that we may cover the position today to suit you, and tomorrow the crash in prices will come that we've been waiting for? You would have made us cover too soon, at a loss. We would lose everything. What is the use of waiting so long, if we don't wait till the end? You don't seem to understand that this was not an imbecile operation done for the sake of being evil."

Aristide turned his back on Michel and spoke to Jules.

"If I saw enough gold, I would say yes," Aristide explained, "I'd wait till the collapse came. Then I'd insist on your covering. But the danger is too great. You must have made immense profits: where are they?"

"In my gold deposits."

"I don't believe you."

"Go to hell then."

Alphendéry said eagerly, "You can see them, Aristide: some are in Belgium, some Switzerland, some London."

Aristide saw that Alphendéry believed this; at last he said, "I will consider it. In Paris I will let you know my decision. As it is now, I am very disappointed."

They parted. Jules looked after him, said negligently, "Don't worry: I'll get him. He'll never get back to Paris."

But that was the last of it, and Aristide did get back, and reported to Marianne with horror the small amount of gold he had seen. He came to the bank the following morning, primed with indignation, moral superiority, and masterful intentions. Marianne had warned, "Don't travel with them any more. Ask to see the gold receipts of the brokers—they are dangerous men and may take you for a ride, as they say. And not too much about the Parquet . . . that's your trump card but you don't want to play it. You don't want to go to the Parquet; you want to get the bank in your hands. You can do it now. Bertillon is weakening. He's neurotic. The game is ours. A high tone, a little more bluff, and he'll take you in as partner. After that, no more threats. Work along with him. You'll soon get to be known as the man that saved Bertillon's and, even by your Comtes, as a strong man. They will work in with you."

In the meantime, Alphendéry had learned that Jules really had no other gold that he would show Raccamond. (He only had the gold shipped to Oslo which he would not mention to anyone.) He remained in Amsterdam with Henri Léon, and two days later appeared in the Bank in Paris, full of joy, the messenger of miraculous news. For his sake (said Alphendéry), Léon offered, of his own accord, to put his vaults in Switzerland at Jules's disposal, to convince Raccamond that Bertillon was a Midas. Aristide insisted on seeing seven and a half million gold francs: he had seen four million.

Léon had in two vaults in Switzerland, under a private number, the equivalent of more than twenty million paper francs of his own. Léon was willing to write a letter to his Geneva bank announcing that a gentleman, with the keys and the private number of the vault, would visit the bank, in Léon's company, and that this gentleman was to be shown round, shown the gold, and to be treated as

Léon's agent. Léon would be in attendance, as witness, but only as a witness. For business reasons, Léon wished the person presenting the keys to be treated as the owner of the vault. Léon did immense business with the bank and believed that they could only obey this order. Alphendéry had believed up to this moment that Léon was, as he loved to paint himself, a "mean bastard," a man who couldn't play straight, who had to get his rake-off even out of his sister's dowry or a whore's pocketbook, a man who hedged even happiness, who courted women on the deposit technique, and dealt with fellow Balkans because he loved to outcheat them, as he had when a boy at home. Alphendéry now found out that Léon was capable of an act of generosity, almost unprecedented in the business world. Why was it? Jules refused to see anything surprising in Léon's offer, but Alphendéry puzzled for days. Was it for some superstitious reason? Was it to appease the old White Rabbi of Botoshani, whose denunciations had frightened Léon on several visits? Was it because, in some way, Léon associated himself with the fate of Jules, like himself a meteor following the orbit of great planets? Was it in dislike of Raccamond and his ways? It might have been that Léon, like many others, hated to see that delightful fellow, Bertillon, in a mess; and it might have been Jules's astonishing luck.

Alphendéry was now sure that Jules was saved, and that he himself, after this one act of grace, could leave the bank forever and take up one of the jobs offered him by Stewart and Léon. He would not feel that the friendship for William or love for Jules was spoiled, or that he was leaving them to a dark and shameful future. It was the ideal, unhoped-for, incredible solution.

Jules said carelessly, "Yes, I'll accept the offer."

But Raccamond would not go to Geneva. "It is only some trick," he said, and though they argued he stood firm. Jules was disinclined to be in Léon's debt, also.

Scene Ninety-seven: Man of Destiny

Now Aristide was walking about with his three agreements in his pocket and his books and papers, "the evidence," in a safe at home; but he felt he was a startling personality and should be heard from every day, one way or another. It was difficult for him to wait for his reign to begin; there were weeks, months, six months, and much work to be done. And it had to be done underhand, in the dark; it had to be slowly painted on people's minds, the picture of his importance. He could not understand why now he got nothing but rebuffs, although he was in the right, with the law on his side, and all the evidence that anyone could ask for. That he was a blackmailer, he never for a moment admitted; he was an injured man serving himself and others. Now that he was ventripotent with destiny, he brooded at the relative secrecy of the whole business. He had shouted, clamored, and his cries had fallen on deaf ears.

Alphendéry had returned to the bank; he was there every day and in his old post: was he being used to manipulate the accounts and restore the shares? Aristide knew nothing of Alphendéry's occupations still. He went to Jules and asked.

"Alphendéry is doing my private business. Go and get clients, Raccamond."

"No. If he remains I must advise my clients to withdraw their accounts."

Jules's pale thin face as it hardened looked like an old man's or a corpse's. "Another house won't take them. What are you going to transfer, may I ask?"

"Mme. de Sluys-Forêt," proclaimed Aristide forcibly.

"Do so."

"You can't pay her out!"

"Try me."

"Ah, you don't think I'll do it, but I will."

Wearily Jules replied, "I wish you'd get out. I really do. Take your clients with you."

Aristide rushed out of the room, crossed Alphendéry

in the corridor, passed him without speaking, and pale and emotional, ran down to the board room. He came close to Jacques Manray and although the board room was full of people said to him in a dramatic *sotto voce,* "You will see the denouement soon. A man like me cannot stay here." He sank down in the armchair alongside Jacques and watched the roomful of people. Some of them looked at him curiously, but immediately looked away: the market was rising and they were all excited. At last, perhaps, prosperity had begun again.

Aristide said to Jacques, "When one of Alphendéry's orders comes through signal me." He leaned back again, breathing huskily.

"I don't know them from the others," Jacques explained helplessly.

"You don't?" He was suspicious. "Who knows them?"

"Mr. Alphendéry is the only one."

Aristide fell farther back in his chair, his eyes open. This was only what he expected. Alphendéry had been brought back to outwit him. Alphendéry had never gone to Zurich anyhow. He had found out that Alphendéry had arrived immediately in London. The whole house was against him and intended to outwit him. They would not get away with it. Never!

"Jacques," he said, "show me every order that goes up. I am going to confirm them."

"Mr. Raccamond, what has come over you? I can't do that. It would make a scandal. The clients see all we do here."

"But not upstairs, not upstairs, that's where Alphendéry comes in." He started. Alphendéry came into the room at that moment, from the other end. "I'll show him up; I'll tell everyone what he does," he said aloud.

Jacques turned round. "Mr. Raccamond, ask Mr. Bertillon about Alphendéry, not me; I know nothing and neither do you. I'm busy, do let me send these orders up, Mr. Raccamond. You see the market's rising and everyone's going into it. Do give me a chance."

"I'm going to withdraw my clients," said Aristide, "every one: they won't have my clients. I'm going to take them out. I'll ruin them."

Jacques said nothing. At the same moment providentially, Alphendéry went out of the room again and upstairs. Aristide rushed out of the board room and stood at the bottom of the staircase slowly veering round as Alphendéry mounted, his lips moving. He watched him go along the gallery. He was bowed and trembling. The clients, who in the midst of their fortune-making had had time to look at him when he brushed past, turned to each other and repeated the current rumor: that fellow Raccamond had general paresis and was now in the stage of megalomania.

Aristride took a taxi home, there telephoned Mme. de Sluys-Forêt, and with his books went straight over to her house. He showed her the books he had stolen from London and Brussels. She must withdraw her account at once. The market was going up. Bertillon had sold out all the accounts; he would have to buy them back at higher prices, and a multimillionaire would not be able to pay the losses. She must withdraw her account at once before the bankruptcy. He might close his doors any night, perhaps after the market closing tonight! Bertillon had no guarantees in France. Some of his money was tied up in lawsuits and that was all he had in France. He paid Carrière's famous drafts out of clients' accounts; his own gold, his own bonds, he kept abroad. Aristide named the places.

Mme. de Sluys-Forêt was very much startled. She rang up Bertillon while Aristide was there and asked for an immediate interview. She was flustered. She called out her car and went immediately to the bank. Aristide proposed to accompany his client, but she firmly refused. Aristide could come and see her the next day.

This first real victory excited Aristide beyond measure. He followed the lady back to the bank, made sure that she was upstairs, and while he was there heard Jacques Manray answer the telephone: "Mme. de Sluys-Forêt. Yes, I'll send you what she has on the books still, as soon as I get a moment. O.K. I'll ask Henri Martin." Aristide, justified, flew into an ecstasy of terror and self-righteousness. He laid his hand on Mouradzian's arm and dragged him out of the doorway in which he was standing watching the course of the market.

"Mr. Mouradzian, come with me quickly. I must speak to you. I have something monstrous, absolutely monstrous to reveal to you. Not here! Not here!"

At his air, Mouradzian was frightened. "What is it?"

"Not here, not here, come to the Bar Florence with me."

At this moment a client called Mouradzian, and he could only whisper, "If it's serious, later in the Cinzano Bar. I'll be down that way, say, twenty minutes."

Aristide looked round. He suddenly thought, "If I tell Mouradzian all now, he'll withdraw all his people, and mine will be ruined. I won't get my money." He had thought this many times before; but he had no sequence in his motives: he thought of things, forgot them, remembered them in nightmares, forgot them in excitement, remembered them in an off hour and forgot them again, because he lived in too many torments! What a life! Not a life for him. And all to make a miserable living—for he was crushed with debts. And on top of all this, he had to protect the clients, some of them millionaires, some of them making easy money chirping in public or pulling long faces on the screen. He was crazy to bother about others the way he did: who thanked him for it? The other men were calm enough.

Mouradzian! He told him months ago what he suspected and did Mouradzian care? That crooked Oriental simply went on doing business. With a chasm opening under his feet. He did not care for his clients, only for his salary, his commissions, even if he was commissioning them into a swindler's den. Ah, ah, all the same Aristide was not like that. He would rescue his clients, willy-nilly; he was not so blindly egotistic. "I will go to them all, this afternoon."

He thought, "Mr. Pharion is abroad, he is in Spain—I can't get him. He has a paying account, too. I can't transfer it. What am I to do?"

He ran to the telegraph office and sent telegrams to Pharion and to his biggest client, Weimar, now at Cap Ferrat, thus conceived:

CONFIDENTIAL: HAVE SECRET INFORMATION THAT MERCURE BANK WILL CLOSE SATURDAY AT LATEST. TELEGRAPH INSTRUCTIONS TO TRANSFER YOUR ACCOUNT TO CRÉDIT IMMEDIATELY. KEEP IN TOUCH WITH ME.

RACCAMOND

Aristide rushed down to the Cinzano Bar and there found Mouradzian waiting.

"What is the matter, Mr. Raccamond? You seem sick

713

to me: You're not yourself at all. What could you have found out to put you into this state? Calm yourself; whatever it is, calm yourself."

Aristide sat down, planked the books beside him, put his face in both hands, on the café table. "I am ill, horribly ill. I haven't slept for weeks. A catastrophe is rushing upon us, there's a sword suspended over our heads as we sit here, as we breathe—but it isn't that only. I suffer horribly in my mind: I have suffered this way for weeks, carrying the whole terrible, terrible secret myself. Protecting others, carrying it myself. I can't bear it any longer. I am not myself, Mr. Mouradzian, excuse me, bear with me, when you hear—" he turned to Mouradzian, his mouth trembling, his eyes wide open, pale.

"But what, what then? Take something first: a coffee for me, waiter, and Mr. Raccamond, a—"

"A cognac," said Raccamond. "Listen, friend, I will tell you everything. You are in danger; there are many people in danger. We are threatened with ruin!" He stared terrified at Mouradzian, who quizzed him: these Frenchmen are such actors, half neurotic, half cunning. "Perhaps we are ruined as we sit here! Mr. Bertillon is nothing but a swindler!"

Mouradzian's look questioned him and the books. But Aristide would not unseal his secret so soon. First the drama. "Bertillon is our enemy. It's hard to believe the worst of Mr. Bertillon, I know. He is charming, disarming, in fact, I still think he is better than the game he plays. He is superior to it but he has been dragged into it. I firmly believe that it was not Bertillon who began this crookery, but the other, this vile Boche Alphendéry. Bertillon could not have thought of selling out to begin with: he isn't the type. Someone showed it to him, engaged him in it. And to begin with I denounce this German. They're all like that: they think treason with jolly-Robin airs; they get you along with them, they propose some little trip, some little evening, and when you're fond of them and believe in their good natures and simple hearts, they hit you on the head and plunder you. They would if we weren't too smart. But we, the cunning ones, are not so smart. We're led. They're clever fellows, such men. They don't use a poniard like an Italian, or a sword or wordplay like the French; they're not of our Latin race. They employ the basest methods, the kiss of Judas. I'm

714

certain that this so-called Alsatian Alphendéry is a secret agent. He's too smooth and simple on top, too friendly. He paws you, laughs into your eyes. He's a German agent, probably; dupery is second nature to him. He has no position in the bank. He is paid from abroad. 'Clients,' he says. What clients? I can imagine. He has 'big clients,' they say. Who are they? No one has seen them here. We don't know their names. And then, you know, Henri Martin, the cashier? That's the proof of what I'm saying."

"What do you mean?" questioned Mouradzian, completely astonished.

"You know he was a spy in the war?"

"No."

"Yes." Aristide triumphed. "Now what is he doing there in the bank? Did you ever see a spy who ceased to be an agent of some sort? He is perhaps there to watch Alphendéry."

"No, no."

"And Alphendéry goes about telling everyone, brokers, rich clients, he told the Princesse, the Comtesse de Voigrand, Dr. Carrière, that he is a communist. A blind, eh? A blind for his real politics? It's clear to me."

Mouradzian almost imperceptibly raised his shoulders: he drank the rest of his coffee. "And what have you in the books there?"

Raccamond suffocated, paler still. A group of drinkers at a corner table had begun to watch him. Mouradzian caught the low-spoken words of one of the men: "He's in some trouble," one said.

A second man replied, "No, I would say a settling of accounts. Look out!"

"Here? This is not a café where——"

"Mr. Raccamond," Mouradzian said briefly, "people are looking at us. Come to the point. What is this horror? It's a house that employs spies?"

"No, no, no: I'm not saying that. I said such a man could be a spy. No—they have a bloc *contre-partie* account. All your clients are sold out. Look at these books."

He opened them cautiously, showing some pages, but not letting the books out of his hands. Mouradzian looked at him surprised and then gave up trying to take the books. "But if you won't let me see. . . ."

"It's not that, Mr. Mouradzian. This is all the guarantee I have: they have signed agreements with me. I could only

715

force them to with these books. These books are my life, the life of all of us. You see . . . I forced them to sign an agreement to restore all the positions."

Mouradzian stared. *"What! All at once?"*

"No, no," he waved his finger, "obviously, not all at once. . . ."

"You have the agreement?"

After some hesitation, Aristide produced it. The other broker's man read it carefully. "Yes, you are right. It is an acknowledgment in a way." He studied Raccamond. "Why do you tell me now? It appears that you settled everything already."

"I think they are trying to scuttle us all; they have brought back Alphendéry . . ."

"Alphendéry is your refrain! What harm is there in that? He is the only man there who could do it with delicacy, without disturbing the accounts or the markets."

"Yes, but they promised to do it under my direction. They promised me a partnership at the end." He went on with gloomy solemnity. "But now, I wouldn't take it. They couldn't force it on me. You see, Alphendéry is there to side-step this agreement." Mouradzian edged away and turned to face his man. "When did you get the books?"

"Over a month ago. I have struggled day and night since to protect the accounts and get my guarantees. It wasn't easy—they held on like leeches. I forced them to the wall. They showed me their gold; I know where it is. . . . I have been struggling alone all this month, without anyone behind me, against the whole pack. The Comte de Guipatin is with them; Prince Campoverde is with them. I showed them the books. It made no difference to those aristocrats. All the same. You and I as senior men are left standing alone against them all. They are all out to rob us and share the booty."

"You took your time about telling me, I must observe," said Mouradzian.

Raccamond took him by the lapel. "Mr. Mouradzian, don't bear me a grudge. It took me time. I could not believe my eyes. I heard the rumors long ago. I got the confidence of the accountants in the foreign branches, with a view to controlling the accounts. Anxious themselves, they were glad to show me the accounts. Then I began to divine the cancer in the bank. But still I did not want to believe. . . ."

"Why not? I don't understand you at all."

"Listen, Mouradzian: I am a fool, but I'm a good fool. That they sold out my clients, robbed me after all my work for them, when they were, as one says melodramatically, living on the sweat of my brow—why, I couldn't adjust myself to the idea straightaway. It's not business—it's—drama; it's the sort of thing you see on the stage, rather. You know, I nearly killed myself with worry; I didn't sleep. My God! I don't seem to have slept a wink since the day my man—the accountant first telephoned me. And then think of it, I didn't really have the right to bruit abroad such a thing without getting confirmation: I would be destroying the reputation of a house. I had to get all the details. That's why I asked the accountant—a poor fellow I got the job for, I knew him before—to confirm or not in the Brussels office to begin with. Because, you know, I had already seen that the Brussels office was important; I sensed it. And I saw orders go through. Then it was said, of course to throw dust in our eyes, that Alphendéry's clients dealt with Brussels. . . ."

Mouradzian, who had a client with an anonymous account at Brussels, said nothing for a moment; then, "So you got all the Brussels books with the accounts?"

"No, not all. I got those showing some of the anonymous accounts, books 1A. and 1B. There are others. But what I have here is the bloc account that the bank runs under the name of the London Finance; the rest of the books are here. I got them from the London office and they complete the story of the *contre-partie* account. You see, there's no question. I have caught them on all the facts. They knew it, too. They signed everything I asked. I cornered them. They had nothing to say to me. They simply agreed to everything."

"To restore the shares?—To make you a partner?—And—"

"I have an agreement to make a guarantee fund of two million francs. I am to manage the guarantee fund with Mr. Jules Bertillon. But I have had no dealings with them since, and Alphendéry is back at his old game. What does that look like to you?"

Mouradzian called the waiter and asked for the bill. "Are you staying here, Mr. Raccamond? I have to leave you."

"Where are you going?"

"To the bank: I have business to do. Plenty of business. I am going, meantime, to see Mr. Jules Bertillon to ask him if this is true." He made a gesture including the books, Raccamond.

"You're so naïve as to think he'll say yes?"

"I've known him longer than you, Mr. Raccamond. Ever since I came to Paris, fifteen years ago, I've heard these rumors about the Banque Mercure—and about other banks. It's possible that it is so. You have those books and it looks like it. But I have never tried to compare accounts. I have simply made profits for my clients on the whole. They are a good house. They don't try to sell bad stuff to the clients. They have never pushed shares, they have never given out tips or recommendations, they have never encouraged clients to destroy themselves by overplaying. They simply do stock-exchange business when the clients want it, like any other bank. They don't solicit business. If they live by *contre-partie,* how do you account for it? Nevertheless, it's my duty to find out if Alphendéry is gambling again, and I will find out something from Mr. Bertillon's attitude rather than from what he says. I am used to doing that. . . ."

Raccamond stared lamentably at him. "Then, Mouradzian, you don't believe me? You think I'm lying? And what about these books that I brought with me—I got them with difficulty—from Brussels and London? I have his books: they speak louder than words. What more do you want? They are not all here. I have a few more at my house. Will you go home with me? What more do you want to convince you? You are reckless. If anyone came to me and said to me, 'Mr. Raccamond, this is a short-selling *contre-partie* house, in a rising market,' I would fly and get out my clients' accounts—I wouldn't hesitate. You are rash. You will see. Every word I have spoken is the truth. . . ."

"I will go with you and see the books," said the Armenian, "and I will go and put some offhand questions to Mr. Bertillon. Perhaps, if necessary, I will tell him everything. I am old in this business, Raccamond, and I believe nothing easily. You may be right and you may be mistaken."

"You will regret this," Raccamond cried, "I have told you the truth."

"Yes," said Mouradzian, "I am inclined to think so.

But you seem very selfish to me, Raccamond. When you found this out, a month ago, you say, you first thought of saving yourself and getting your foot well into the house. Not a word to us of what you thought you had discovered. I believe you: we are used to these things. But supposing it is true—what then? As I said to you two months ago, it is not Mr. Bertillon who would ruin the house but a man like you, who runs round the streets showing the private accounts of a house to anybody, who tries to get complete control and then to get clients to withdraw their accounts; who tries to steal the clients of other men, then tries to form a team of those men, then betrays them in favor of himself and his clients, and then falls back on them and tries to organize a general rout when everything else has failed. You walk about the bank looking like a madman, you get the employees round you telling them all sorts of bogey tales; then you blackmail the boss, then you betray him to his enemy, then you give items to the newspapers, then you make a scene in some café or restaurant. You support all the enemies of the bank, you give away its game, and you are yourself its worst enemy—and you're the one who shrieks loudest that it will be ruined. You are its ruin. If I think of moving my clients, it is to save them from you. Aren't you ashamed? You tell me your chief client is in the bank this afternoon withdrawing her account. You have telegraphed another fellow that the bank will close this week. It's lunacy! Of course, I will fathom it. How can I trust your word. You are neurotic, you are shouting, foaming at the mouth—you talk hysterically. Perhaps you don't know what you're saying.

"No, I can't take your word. Who behaves like you? If you're so goodhearted, so innocent as you say, you shouldn't be in business. You can't enter medicine either, where a certain amount of swindling is essential to money success; you can't be a schoolteacher. Can you be an artist? There one has to falsify, compromise. Since you have such a sense of smell, since you go by smell, you had better be a perfumer. No, you are fit for nothing at that rate. But, of course, all this is nonsense. You are not so naïve as that. Go home and calm yourself, my friend: I will come and see you this evening and we'll look at your books and see what to do. Go home, my friend: you look ready to drop. . . ."

Raccamond, anxious, said with avidity, "All right, come this evening. But I have many visits to make before that. It is my duty to sound the tocsin among my clients: I must give the warning. Otherwise I am ruined."

Mouradzian looked grave, sat down. "Mr. Raccamond, if you provoke a run on the bank, where will we all be tomorrow?"

"How about my clients?"

"Think of the employees of the bank too. If Mr. Bertillon is restoring the position slowly, all can be cured. If you yield to this hysteria, Mr. Bertillon will not be able to meet the demands of the clients, Carrière, and yourself. Sixty employees will be without bread tomorrow: you and I and the other men will be ruined. At our age all our work will have to be begun again. We will have to get new clients; our old clients will be ruined. And by whom? Not by Bertillon. By you. By your hysteria. I don't understand at all why you wish to do this! You have your agreement. Let it stand; let it work."

Raccamond cried, "But he is swindling me: he doesn't intend to fulfill it."

"You know that? Give him a chance and give them all a chance."

Bitterly Raccamond cried, "For the others, I don't give a damn: let them sink or swim. They've all been in it; even the accountants have known what was going on. They've all been against us. Let them go."

"Good. Well, go home and I will come straight after you. I just have some orders to receive from London, and I will be with you."

"Yes. Oh, it's frightful. But you will see, you will know I haven't lied."

"Good. Good afternoon."

"And, Mr. Mouradzian, remember—remember I warned you first. You remember, two months ago—and now. I thought of your big clients."

"Thanks for that," Mouradzian said dryly.

But scarcely had Mouradzian left before Aristide had another idea: Mouradzian had only gone to warn his own clients and to get out his accounts before Aristide had a chance: he had repeated, "Go home, Aristide, rest, calm yourself." Just so. Aristide rushed to a telephone booth and began telephoning his clients one after the other, gasping out his warnings, saying he had terrible evidence against the bank, making appointments with them (for they were alarmed, even so) to show them the books. When Mouradzian got to his house, Aristide had not yet reached home.

Jules's conversation with Mme. de Sluys-Forêt began sweetly and ended brusquely, and the Princesse refused to be enchanted by Jules's delicate conversation and insisted on having her account paid out that afternoon. She told him all, in the meantime, how she had been warned by Raccamond and that he was going round to clients showing them the books and Jules's promise to retire from the stock-exchange business. She had hardly gone before a telegram arrived from Pharion, Aristide's client in Spain:

TRANSFER OUT IMMEDIATELY MY BANK AND STOCK-EXCHANGE ACCOUNTS TO THE CREDIT.
FRED PHARION

This was followed by a telephone call from the Comtesse de Voigrand: "Your strip-jack-naked customers' man Raccamond has been here: I assure you he's in a lather, and he's running round the town shrieking from the housetops that you're crooks and bankrupts. His own words. He's mad. Why don't you shut him up? He's stolen your books, hasn't he? Of course, I'm not taking any notice of him. Is Jean de Guipatin there?"

She wanted to sell her gold, held with Bertillon Frères. The market was going up, and she would buy gold back later on. Jules and Jean dropped their eyes shamefacedly when Jean gave this message. The comtesse was taking her precautions. Jules said, "You had better take the train at once to Amsterdam. Claire-Josèphe will go with you and see the gold out . . ."

"I am sorry," said Jean de Guipatin. He did not even try to pretend that his client was loyal to Jules. "Jules, why don't you let me drop this fellow in his tracks? I can get a couple of gangsters tonight who will grab him, take him out in a taxi, and there'll be another mystery of the *milieu* for the criminal division to amuse themselves with. It's all I can do. I don't dare try to dissuade old Voigrand. He'll ruin you, Jules. You'll never get out of this mess alive, financially speaking, if you let him go on."

"Right, we'll get somebody to drop a brick on his head," said Jules, without conviction.

Jules often spoke of murder, blackmail, and embezzlement, but he hadn't the strength or the moral conviction necessary to pull them off. He wanted to dazzle without getting tangled in all sorts of systems: he feared murder, not as murder, but as a machine from whose wheels one could perhaps never escape.

While they were still there talking about Raccamond, Mouradzian crept in.

"Mr. Bertillon, Raccamond has stolen your *contre-partie* books and is showing them to everyone. You must stop him. He will ruin us. He started as an egotist and he is ending as a man amok; he is blind to his own interest."

"Yes, we know, Mouradzian; what can we do with him?"

"I am going to his house tonight. I will try to get the books. But if I had someone to back me up I could perhaps do it. He has his wife and she is the real motor there. He is lost without her. If we could get them apart —I am afraid, just the same, we can do nothing. I will try to get the books for you."

"He is mad; he is ruining himself, too."

"No, I am wrong in that," emended Mouradzian. "He had got himself a provisory position with the Crédit. The rest of us—we can starve. He does not care. You may be sure his charges don't interest me. I am a man of the world."

But by this time Aristide trusted no one. When he arrived at his house, he found Mouradzian there, and he gloomily ate the supper, which Mouradzian refused, at once fatigued and blown up with his maggots, like a fly. After supper he showed Mouradzian the books as promised, but without allowing him to have them out of Aristide's grasp. Although Mouradzian saw that Aristide's charges were true he was able to do no good. He explained to Marianne that Aristide would only ruin them all if he provoked a run on the bank, and Marianne seemed impressed by his conversation. Instinctively she liked the hard-working, hardheaded, honorable little fellow. Mouradzian came away with the hope that the wife would urge her husband now, not to further desperate scenes, but to moderation.

"You have Bertillon in a tight place," Mouradzian had said. "Know how to manage the colt you have caught. Don't make it worth his while to do you an injury or to default with all his gold abroad!"

"Listen, Mr. Mouradzian," she had said. "He is over-tired now; in the morning I will give him good advice."

But in the morning he was feverish, screaming, tossing her arms away when she tried to hold him back.

"Let me go: I must go to the Crédit and get a position there. I must make sure the Princesse transfers her account there and I get the credit. They are sharks, all those men; you have no idea how I have to fight to keep a single account. Let her only walk into the Crédit, and everyone, even Paul Treviranus, will try to pretend she is his client . . . I must go."

He dressed, his eyes starting: she had to let him go, and he refused her counsels, her advice, her anxiety. She was terrified: she realized what support she would lose if she lost Aristide.

In the morning, during his absence, an inspector called from the tax department. She managed to find out in the end what it was: "Mr. Raccamond has been denounced as a tax evader: a private denunciation." He would not say, he did not know, from where the blow came. But where could it come from? Only from the bank! When Aristide arrived home in the late evening, she only told him this because of the urgency of the matter.

"Let's go to Maître Olonsky at once and transfer the property to my name."

"I can't do it; I am all in, Marianne."

"Let us do this just the same, my dear. Will you sleep tonight, thinking that tomorrow night the officers will be here to make an examination? Make our living safe . . . our future must be protected. You are one of the few men, besides, who does not have his property in his wife's name, to reduce assessments. Bertillon has his apartment in his wife's name, his car in his chauffeur's; even Claire-Josèphe has her fur coat in her maid's name. . . ."

"How do you know?"

"I found out."

723

He worried. "But it will look like fraud, dated today and no compensation!"

"No, Olonsky will arrange that: he's an old hand. He knows so much on our family that he couldn't blackmail us; people would take him for a fantastic dreamer and discredit his whole story. . . ."

"Marianne! You know who did this to me?"

"I should say so: the Bertillons, of course."

"Yes! I'll kill them for this. Tomorrow morning, I take those books to the police."

She had hard work getting him away from his vengeance, but in the end he went to the lawyers with her, and it was carried out exactly as she had suggested in the first place. The lawyer behaved with admirable bonhomie. He knew of Aristide's anxiety to avoid the police and government officials and how he avoided half his income tax. At the end, Marianne found herself in possession of Aristide's three-story townhouse in the Rue du Docteur-Blanche, of the gold coins (of various countries) in the safety vault at the Crédit, of the bank accounts in three banks, with Aristide's future salary (six months' to be paid at the end of six months), all assigned to her, "on account of the following moneys received on loan and without previous security over a period of ten years"—a list of supposed loans followed. He appeared to own merely the cottage at Biarritz in which their son lived, and for this arranged a first and second mortgage, the first held by the shell company which theoretically paid Aristide's salary abroad and the second by Marianne through the company she had formed for the cinema gazette. The furniture in both houses was chattel-mortgaged through two clerks in Olonsky's office. Aristide held only his car, the first six months' salary which Bertillon had already paid him, the commissions coming to him on future business by his customers in the Mercure Bank and the Crédit. . . .

When this series of transactions was completed, it was two in the morning, Aristide was speechless with fatigue and fear; the lawyer, tired, gave them drinks and Marianne a perplexed but congratulatory smile. Marianne noticed Aristide's collapse and said, "We must also draw up a release of these properties to my husband, in case anything should happen to me."

"I did not understand your last remark," said the lawyer

severely: "I know of a transfer, your consideration is complete; we say no more." A warning to Marianne, that head of gold, not to melt, in other words. But at home she carefully wrote out and gave to Aristide the following release: "The bank accounts, gold, house-properties, mortgages and other estate which have been transferred to my name today on account of loans, I leave to my husband: taxes and encumbrances are to be paid from the rest of my estate, that is, from that part of my estate which I owned before this date," and signed it.

Aristide, in whose eyes she had seen bogeys, nude bogeys of poverty and complete ruin took it carefully and folded it into his billfold. He did not even smile. He sat thinking for a while and then said, "Yes, I feel freer and safer."

She smiled. Aristide was not really made for the commercial world: he liked knitting people together in all sorts of relations, that was his talent and that was why he was in business. A child could rob him. She was glad she had no such intention, for he was helpless.

But he tossed and moaned all night. He feared the tax inspector who was coming in the morning. When he shrieked she waked him up.

"What are you dreaming of?"

"Bertillon," he said once.

"Go to sleep—forget him."

"I can't, I can't. He tried to ruin me. I'll ruin him . . . he'll never get away with this." He didn't sleep all night. In the morning, however, he was up, feverish and malicious. "This is his last day as a banker, that forger and liar!"

She had never seen him so wicked and resentful. She respected him for this thirst for vengeance. She did not try to detain him, nor did she say one word of all that Mouradzian had poured into her ears. Aristide rushed straight off to the Financial Investigation Division with his books.

"Mr. Bertillon is going to close the bank today; he is going to ruin everyone: I know it. Here are his books. These books show that he has robbed and cheated the clients in various ways for years. You must send an inspector and a magistrate immediately and close the bank and arrest Bertillon. He has all his money abroad. I have seen it. If you give him any notice, he will fly—literally, for his brother is an airman and still has a pilot's license and a licensed plane. . . ."

"How do we know all this?" asked the police inspector.

"My client Pharion asked for his account to be paid out, and they refused to pay him out, only yesterday," said Aristide. "Another thing, be careful you arrest the right man: there are four brothers Bertillon in the bank daily, and the three others would give themselves up for Jules."

"What is his description?"

"Tall, thin, yellow-skinned, with excellent manners and a sweet smile," complained Aristide. "A man born for swindling. But the employees will tell you."

"No, you can come with us and identify him."

"Not in the bank. Please think of my situation . . . I will wait outside with an officer and identify him."

At eleven o'clock in the morning William came running to Alphendéry's room. "Michel, there are police downstairs; they want to arrest Jules."

Michel did not even answer: he seized the telephone and asked for Maître Lemaître's number. "Maître? Alphendéry here. Come immediately to the bank—take a taxi and come *at once!*" He dropped the telephone and rushed downstairs where Jules was arguing without making any impression on the magistrate and police officers. "What are you doing here?" asked Alphendéry boldly. "You have no warrant. You are making a scandal."

They riposted, thinking themselves in the right and Alphendéry a bluffer. Jules stood to one side, now that reinforcements had arrived. He was exhausted and had no fight in him.

"It is a lie that we will not pay out accounts," Alphendéry blustered. "You have no evidence. We can just show you that we have paid out Mme. de Sluys-Forêt every sou of 630,000 francs and every bond and stock. Do you want to speak to her on the telephone? Who gave you this information? Someone who is trying to ruin us. I know the name. Raccamond. He is a customers' man who has run amok and has been trying to drag us in the mud for weeks. We are a respectable bank standing here for twenty years, doing business, no complaint allowed against us, paying out every sou owed, with a brilliant, respectable, and rich clientele, and all you can do, you

726

miserable crowd of legal pedants, is to set up hue and cry on the complaint of the first blackmailer who falls on all fours in your bureau!

"The trouble with you all is that you love theatrical scenes. You are divided against yourself. There is the magistrate who tries to dispense justice and, no doubt, with reasonable impartiality; and there is the eye of the magistrate who is all the time thinking, 'I am playing in a boulevard play; this is the second act. How is everyone taking it? Am I in the grand style? Would Racine have written the way I talk? Have I got the opponent buffaloed? Am I really a magistrate?' Whence it follows, that you don't dare give the other fellow a moment to explain himself, for fear he will be talking like Racine and you like a ninny that has made a mistake. What are the police and government officials without a little browbeating?

"Listen, Messieurs, come upstairs and I'll show you a safe full of gold. Here, groom, go and get Mlle. Bernard; tell her to go at once and open the gold safe. Mr. Bertillon and I and some gentlemen wish to see the gold there—a little party of pleasure."

Some were inclined to back down at this. The party tramped upstairs and walked in on the astounded Mlle. Bernard sitting guard over the gold safe. She opened it as she saw them come in.

"Take out the bags and show the gentlemen," commanded Alphendéry. She opened a few of the wash leather bags and poured out the coins before them.

"Give one to this gentleman," said Alphendéry. Mlle. Bernard did so, reaching up from where she brooded over the coins. The magistrate, intimidated at the sight of so much wealth, took the bag and, feeling it with immense pleasure, sighed and returned it to the girl.

"I see."

"You can ring up the Banque de France and find out if we have not just deposited two million francs there. . . ."

"Ah, ah," said the magistrate, trying to be cunning, "but if all this is so—of course, I see the gold—why do we have so many complaints against you that you don't pay out accounts?"

"You only have had one," stormed Alphendéry, "and it was from a liar. Do you want to know the bottom of the matter? This lunatic—he is a neurotic, but a neurotic is a lunatic—this lunatic telegraphed a client to Spain telling him to order out his account. The client telegraphs us ordering out the account. But did you ever hear of a banker paying out a large account on an unconfirmed telegram? Of course not. And do you wish to know what we are going to do? We have that telegram sent by your plaintiff Raccamond. It says that we are going to close our doors last Saturday. But this is Tuesday! You see? This Raccamond is an excitable, jealous, mad sort of fellow, the typical blackmailing employee, with a brainstorm on top of it all. And this is your evidence? This is the man you trust? You came up here without sufficient reflection, Magistrate!"

At this moment, Maître Lemaître walked in. He had lost no time for he knew Alphendéry did not cry wolf for fun.

"You have no powers here," said the *maître*. "No complaint has been lodged, no evidence given. You are trespassing here. You should be sued for causing a scandal and injuring a man's business. Mr. Bertillon has never failed to pay a sou and you can look for that from the beginning of the bank until now."

As soon as Maître Lemaître entered, however, the police and the judge, already partly convinced, changed their minds entirely. Lemaître was one of the most distinguished men in France and had salon influence. They felt that if he supported Bertillon, Bertillon was either right or rich. That is right.

"Nevertheless," sulked the judge, "this complaint we had."

"Ah," cried the lawyer, properly angry, "if you make a descent on a business every time someone complains, we can shut all the commerce in France from this morning on."

"No, dear *maître*," said the magistrate, "we did not act on caprice. The warning given us by the accuser, Mr. Raccamond, would not have been seriously considered by us, despite his books, which call for no emergency action. We believed his assertion that Mr. Bertillon refused to pay clients and was about to depart today, only because this bank promised to open its books in London for our inspection in the complaint against X for concealing evidence in the case of Henri Parouart. We heard from London this very morning that on the pretense that an inquiry against X is not permitted in English law, the Banque Bertillon has not honored its word. We are well acquainted with the complaints of Mr. Parouart. We know his character and if you are afraid of a petty swindler, all must be wrong. The conjunction of this vicious behavior on the part of this bank with the complaint of Mr. Raccamond determined us to act at once. But now we shall proceed, since there is no urgency to a *mise en moeurs* or general inquiry."

Maître Lemaître escorted them to the prison car they had brought with them, for the arrest of Bertillon. On the pavement, a figure of vengeance, astonished and mortified, stood Raccamond, waiting to see Bertillon carried off to jail. Swindled again, thought Raccamond. He is as cunning as a fox. He went to the nearest bar, entered the telephone booth, and rang up Bertillon.

"Jules Bertillon speaking. What? Is that you, Raccamond, you miserable rat. Wait till I get hold of you . . . I'll screw your neck. Just come near here! We've got a reception committee here for you. Listen, just hear one thing—take your clients and get out of here."

Someone took the telephone; a voice said, "Raccamond? You're completely discredited; you needn't work for your twelve months' advance salary. You can go to the Crédit or whatever it is at once. Don't come near the place. We'll pay out your clients. We don't want to see your mug again. And listen, any more comic-opera stuff like you stage-managed this morning and you'll find yourself thinking things out in the cooler. Tell that charming wife of yours we're going to sue you both for defamation. You'll never get another job after that, Aristide, Carrière or no Carrière." A string of foul words followed. William jammed down the phone.

Ah, ah, ah. So they were gloating over his defeat. . . . But he was not beaten. He was going to make out a complaint in regular style against them for abuse of clients' confidence. He would have them in the end. He took an absinthe and then hailed a taxi and went to Maître Olonsky's.

Mouradzian learned that his instincts were right and that Raccamond had failed. The magistrate dismissed Raccamond's charges, and the famous books, the Aladdin's lamp of power, were retained in the file.

That evening he went to see Aristide Raccamond.

"Well, bad news about the Bertillon case: I sympathize with you."

"He has influence on his side: the courts are full of corruption. This examining magistrate is evidently bought."

"Tough luck. That makes no difference to you. He goes scot-free and you're in a hole. He dismissed you, evidently."

Raccamond drew back, looked carefully at his enemy. "No, I left. I got twelve months' pay, I still have his agreement, and I have withdrawn all my clients."

"I understand he's suing you for telegraphing that he was going bankrupt."

"Who told you?"

"I heard. What made you do it? Never put anything on paper; make the other fellow do that. Simple maxim. And now, what's the future, Raccamond? You have plenty of support, of course. Carriére still. . . ."

"Yes, he's introduced me to the Crédit: he's a friend of mine. I'm glad to be out of the bank."

"You did well," said Mouradzian heartily. "You could not do any better."

Raccamond hunched his shoulders. "I had an instinct against the place: everyone told me it was a bucket shop. The way they think—they thought I was trying to blackmail, when I was trying to conciliate, to avoid a scandal for the good of all parties. I did not want to ruin them, I only wanted to save the clients and the jobs of the employees."

"Yes, yes, of course."

"Who will be in the London office?"

Mouradzian guessed cruelly. "Alphendéry, they told me. He never seems to be able to draw himself away: but I understand that this time it's a part-time job; he's also working as a secretary for this grain merchant, Léon. Did you ever meet him?"

"Yes."

"A remarkable man, Alphendéry: I'd like to work in with him, to see how he does things. Everyone whispers that he made Bertillon's fortune for him. Queer how these rumors are born and get about, isn't it?"

Scene Ninety-eight: Interlude

WHEN Alphendéry telephoned him Maître Lemaître explained that he never ate out, but asked Alphendéry to breakfast with him at seven-thirty the next morning. When Alphendéry arrived the lawyer was ready to go out, with his satchel on a chair. They first gave a glance to politics, spoke of the end of the Meerut process, commenced in June, 1929, and the longest now in the history of India. It interested French people on account of their own social troubles in Indo-China.

Then Maître Lemaître broached the topic of the bank's troubles. "Do you consider Mr. Bertillon has been in a normal state of mind, the times I have seen him lately?"

Alphendéry said very rapidly, "I am a most devoted friend of Jules Bertillon, and I want to see him get out of this mess; also I have the highest respect for you, *cher maître,* but I don't see how you can go very far unless you have all the facts."

"Exactly," said Lemaître with satisfaction.

"The books Raccamond has are the books of the London Finance, a subsidiary, in fact, a ghost company, formed by Jules, or some unknown associates of his, in Luxemburg, to cover transactions which function like a *contre-partie* carried out by the bank against the operations of some of the clients."

Lemaître smiled a broad smile: "I knew it. Raccamond showed the books, and all he has filched, to my friend Luc, of course, and he came running to me this morning, with them, to try and dislodge me from your legal department. But not only is it my duty to ask Jules Bertillon for his interpretation—but I had a personal reason: I wanted to form an opinion on Bertillon's mental processes."

"I love Jules," said Alphendéry, "but he is a constitutional liar. I warned him to tell you the truth, but he can't tell the truth. See, all of us had acknowledged the truth to each other; but he had to lie to you. Don't take it as an offense, please, *cher maître;* he is psychologically twisted in this direction. Like a good many businessmen, he can only survive on the comforting thought that he is diabolically smart and that his game, however transparent it really is, is opaque to all other minds."

"I know them very, very well," said Lemaître consolingly. "Almost no clients of a lawyer tell the whole truth: there is no miracle in that. But with Bertillon——" He looked with half-factitious hesitation at Alphendéry to draw him out as he saw him embarked on the sea of confidences.

Alphendéry saw the maneuver and, glad to unburden himself said, "Jules Bertillon is not only temperamental, he is as unstable as fire. His two or three chief characteristics are—that he is generous, thus distinguishing himself from the solid businessman who builds up a fortune out of every grain that comes his way. Jules feels that money will always flow into his pockets—he belongs to the fabulous race of the great swindlers, though he is not a great swindler. Second, he finds it impossible, almost degrading, to tell the truth; he believes every question is a challenge to his ingenuity, and he would feel flat and in cold standing water if he told the plain truth; that seems to him the cue of plodding dullards. Next, he is very neurotic, and can stand no strain. Fourth, he can only think when he is succeeding; when he is failing, he seems as threadbare as those hanging round the draggled skirts of finance. Last, he is a fisher in troubled waters; he does not rise and fall with the business world, like most people I know—optimistic, belligerent, stupidly boastful when markets are up; depressed, canaille, naïve, invertebrate when markets are down. With him it is the opposite—the world seems to crown asses when markets are up and when markets are down and everyone is talking about suicide, then Jules feels grand and he chortles at the distress of the others, and thinks it heaven's cue for him to jump in and take the principal part."

"I am more than grateful to you for your portrait," said Maître Lemaître. "I had guessed part. It lacked confirmation. Now I know how to proceed."

Then he leaned forward and said in a low and rather sad tone, "Make the best arrangements you can with Bertillon. I have absolute knowledge—and you know how cautious I am, Monsieur Alphendéry!—that this bank cannot last much longer under any circumstances. A combination of circumstances, of personal and professional enemies, which the unfortunate amount of scandalous publicity has brought you, has brought you near a wall you cannot scale. I advise you to give Raccamond certain assurances to keep him calm, and then prepare yourself quickly for a decent bankruptcy or for any other arrangement. In fact, it is now too late for you to go bankrupt. If that advice had been taken a year ago there would have still been time. In any legal matter, I am willing to be consulted." He leaned forward and said very earnestly to Alphendéry, "I know, for sure, that the tax authorities will close the bank for examination of its books, for a few days." He was silent, looking at Alphendéry curiously, but friendly; then continued, "Are you going to try to restore some of the shares? With Luc, who is the dearest friend of a friend of mine, and by influencing Lallant, as I know how, we can bring pressure to bear on Raccamond and explain to him in divers ways that to spread scandal now will mean danger to him. We can hold him off for six months and by then—he will be non-suited." He smiled.

"The Bertillons have been going through their papers," Alphendéry said cautiously, "preparing for—eventualities."

Actually the night before, the two brothers and Alphendéry had been through gold brokers' confirmations and extracted all those mentioning sale of gold, or withdrawal of gold, and leaving only those showing buying or deposit of gold, or transfer to the banks or vaults. True, the checkup of the gold brokers' books would show another reckoning different from both the affirmative receipts and the reckoning just made by Alphendéry but that would take a very long time and their time was short; their object to make the gold-holdings seem larger, and call in Raccamond. They had all three decided that the only thing to do was to cool him off, soothe his vanity, load him with importance and statements, and get him off on some mission while they decided what the future of the bank and of themselves would be.

Alphendéry smiled, turning the subject, "Raccamond has gone back to witchcraft. He met me yesterday in the street and said, 'I know you claim you don't love profit. I am sure you feathered your nest, just the same—but that was a side issue: you love scheming for its own sake. If you were a poor man, a pauper, you'd do the same. How can these brothers equal you? You never rest; you never tire; it is in your blood. As long as your blood beats in your temples, this swarming of schemes will stream through your head. Your head is not a brain, it is a beehive—it is a beehive that turns and turns—' He put his hand to his head; the sweat was pouring from his forehead and neck. He stooped, exhausted by his passion."

Alphendéry had stared at him, pitifully, shaken by so much hatred and fear of himself. He said in an undertone, gently, "My own fault—"

Lemaître laughed keenly, "Yes, you inspire passions of all kinds."

"I fear passion," said Alphendéry.

"I don't think so," smiled the lawyer.

Scene Ninety-nine: Judges Like Serials

MEANWHILE everyone was making preparations. Richard Plowman complained once again that he could never see his dear friends Jules and William, although Claire-Josèphe was now always at home, more accessible than ever. "I am glad you have left the bank," he said to Alphendéry. "You were keeping the brothers apart; now William and Jules are always hobnobbing—even I never see them. You meant well . . . don't misunderstand me. Personally, I think you're a charming fellow—but now they are united, there's a shoulder-to-shoulder air about them that I, personally, find altogether sane and most promising for the future."

This puzzled Alphendéry, although he put it down to Jules's aviation and oil monopoly and other projects.

He made a friendly call on Maître Lemaître, who said, "I hear that Legris are ready to ditch him: this Raccamond created too much of a stink and there has been an investigation of Legris and Company from the Bourse of Amsterdam. . . . Then Carrière's opponent in the elections knows that Carrière still has his foreign accounts with Bertillon, and he is only too anxious to get at their books and show up Carrière as a tax evader. Oh, a nest of trouble is being put together assiduously. I like Bertillon, although I think he's short in the thatch and although he lied to me outrageously. I don't want him to sit in the Santé."

"You're tenderhearted for a lawyer, *maître*."

"Well, no. None of my clients is an angel, not even the injured parties, but Bertillon is outside the law—he does nothing legal. His affairs must be in the most unspeakable tangle; I don't want to be mixed up in it. I'm his lawyer. Let him fly. I don't want to defend him. I like him and I've considered it from all angles—let him take some of the books with him and fly. That would be the best for all of us, including you. And as for you, I hope you are leaving Paris, Mr. Alphendéry."

"Yes, tonight," said Alphendéry. "I am not even waiting to get my back salary."

"You are right. There is very little time left to us. Tell Mr. Bertillon. Not from me, but let him understand. Maître Luc, although Raccamond's lawyer, told me the same. He wishes Bertillon would fly. Bertillon has our sympathy. He will end badly. Why? Why go to the bitter end? The game is ended. If he could wait another five years, he might beat Carrière at his own game; he might make another fortune on exchanges, on tourists, on anything—but he can't: he hasn't the youth, the elasticity, the freshness. I know men, Mr. Alphendéry, and Mr. Bertillon has spun his thread. He needs refreshment. There, I only do this for you, as a friend, and Bertillon is your friend. There, write to me: I disagree with you entirely on everything. Thus we have much to say to each other. Put every agreement with Mr. Léon on paper and have it witnessed! Ah, ah, you won't though. Well . . . good luck."

Alphendéry told all this to Jules, "But there are two million tied up for Raccamond, and the money not yet released from the Parouart case," said Jules. "I have five million here and there in various companies, the Spanish oil, the French aviation—I've put up a million for each already—you don't know the half—" he smiled between sheepishness and cunning. "I can't go away and leave all that money behind."

"It's that or the Santé," said Alphendéry calmly. "Think who sent you the message, Maître Luc."

"Raccamond's lawyer."

"Just so—his lawyer asks you to fly. Raccamond doesn't want you to fly. But Luc is a friend of Lemaître, and Lemaître is a friend of yours. There's the sequence."

"Those lawyers are always playing safe: they don't understand a type like me," said Jules fretfully.

"Take their advice, Jules, and as for what's lying round here—leave it. Collect what you've got in Legris in Amsterdam, clean out the branches, leave enough to pay the boys here, and a few sacks of gold in the safe. That will puzzle them. When they descend on the bank they'll find money there. Strange escapade, they'll call it, not a fugue. The great point in all these things is mystery: the liquidators want mystery till they've laid their hands on the carpets and bookcases, just what they wanted to fill up the spare room at home; the journalists want mystery—it's a substitute for a bad serial; the judges want mystery—they don't have to make up their minds; the expert accountants want mystery—it's their job. Start the idea of mystery in the minds of all and you have a smoke trail that will not clear away but that will go on thickening for years. When it finally clears, you will doubtless be clear, too—"

"Transparent," chuckled Jules, amused, his eyes fixed in the distance.

"Still, there will be a crowd to believe in your innocence and see a secret hand, a hidden force, a fatalism even. Carrière, Raccamond will be blamed, not you . . ."

"I'm not trying to shift the blame—I like blame," cried Jules petulantly.

"You'll get enough to satisfy you: then you'll be glad of the mysticism of people—in the end you'll find people suing Jean de Guipatin or Mlle. Dalbi, or Campoverde or Mouradzian—and in the end you'll be glad. You're a shadow, Jules; you're not a focus for blame. There's something unhuman about you; people prefer a grosser-grained, a fatter-boned culprit—me—or Raccamond—or William. You'll see."

"Pttt!" cried Jules. "You're imaginative, Michel. Will you like your new job?"

"Léon is a petty tyrant—but I'll get along all right. I may not stay there long."

"Ah, you'll come back to me, Michel; you'll be back

736

with me before you know it. You need me. I give you rein. You'll find out."

Michel laughed. "Maybe! Who knows?"

Scene One Hundred: Last Days

THEY were in Plowman's London club.

The old man raised his kind face with a flash of indignation, perhaps covering some doubts. "Bomba, I am surer of Jules than of my own son. I have been through tight places with him for twenty years. He knows he can depend on me. It's a sign of sanity that instead of taking out his gold and selling it, he is calling on the bank balances of the branches—no doubt he's in a temporary jam. He's a big gambler, and a safe one. No doubt, he needs some margins."

"Ralph Stewart tells me that he has been rather slow paying his options lately and that has created a certain impression in the city, you know. No man in business should let them wait an hour. Why is it? Is he rash? Is he strapped?"

"I don't know. He has his reasons, no doubt. Jules has been in business for twenty years: he has always come through. I don't ask him questions." He hesitated, "The slow payment—I know—that's William. That's his idea. His idea is always to keep people waiting."

"That's true enough," sighed Theodor Bomba. "When I was there I had trouble enough getting ordinary office cable charges and salary lists paid. I pressed him not to ruin the bank's name for quick payment—it was when Carrière was pressing—for the sake of a few centimes' interest gained. Now I am away—Alphendéry has gone. Jules has gone up in the air, if you want my plain opinion. William thinks of hoarding, scraping, and saving and—quite the opposite of other days—he is full of levity and freaks. Jules is alone. Someone should stand with him. I was speaking to Alphendéry—he is in London now doing business for Henri Léon. A smart fellow. Feathers his nest in time, eh?" Cunningly, he looked into the old man's face.

The old man raised his fading blue eyes, faintly blood-shot. "Don't urge Alphendéry to go back. Don't go back yourself. I am staying away. I'll tell you why. I think you're a friend of Jules. The brothers are reunited now. Never before did the four brothers dine together in the evening. Now they do it nearly every evening. Claire-Josèphe spends most of her time out riding or motoring with her little ones. A thing that has not happened for year and years. She used to spend her whole time out with friends and at the dressmakers'. It makes me so happy." He wiped away a senile tear. "Of course, I suffer from it. When the family is so close, the old family friend is a little *de trop*. But for their sake and for the good of the bank, I am glad to be exiled a little. And then—since the death of dear old Frank Durban—" another pair of tears—"I have become a philosopher." He teetered. "The clients are impressed," he went on energetically. "They comment upon the activity of the brothers. They feel there is a firm leadership, a syndicate of brothers. Divided we fall, united we stand!"

"So there was a syndicate of brothers in Claude Brothers! Raccamond got them, too."

"Raccamond is mistaken, but he's a good man—he'll make a good manager: I've been begging Jules to take him back. What a sense of organization! You see," he said with pathetic charm, "he is ambitious, but he worships Jules. I know men, my boy—I'm old. . . . As for Alphendéry—better as it is. I always combatted the theory that he was the brains of the bank. He's subtle—never spread it himself. To a man as sensitive as Jules, to undermine his sense of responsibility and importance is fatal."

Theodor Bomba smiled.

Plowman put his hands in his pockets and whistled to the cash, as it were. "Jules is," he spoke softly with all his heart, "the greatest genius I ever met, the greatest natural, untaught, original genius."

"He has great charm, and he has genius, no doubt," cut in Bomba. "Well, you are convinced your money is safe? Then I am. For where a man's money is, there his brains are."

Rumors clustered thicker as the days went on. Stewart said that Jules had pyramided with him and that other brokers in the city were calling for their margins from Jules in vain. People began to smile when Alphendéry mentioned Jules and say, "I see you've left him; well, I suppose that's all right. You always knew what you were doing," with a broadening smile. Others snickered and asked him if his friend Jules Bertillon was still in cahoots with Montagu Norman. Although William could get no information at the bank in Paris, everyone Alphendéry spoke to in London and in Amsterdam (by phone) knew that Jules's aviation company was fantastic, not worth the paper its letterhead was printed on, that big interests who saw themselves defeated by the proposed aviation combine were out to crush him, that the taxation authorities had decided to close the bank. Jules could get no credit in London. Paul Méline no longer dragged Alphendéry through Shorters' Court in the busy hours, to show that he had the Banque Mercure account; Ralph Stewart no longer whispered about what Bertillon was doing this week.

Alphendéry, with all these things flying round in his head, sickened and went to bed for a week.

How then was Jules? Jules was in a deep blue funk. All of the rumors were right. Jules had sunk five million francs, by now, in the aviation combine, to please Jean de Guipatin and young Campoverde. With these two were associated Juarez de Machuca, Hervé Dumas, young Lucé, Daniel Cambo, and young Mouradzian, all of whom had been named as directors in the Aviation Combine. Jules was now "betting on blue blood." "Enough rads, Reds, and proletarians," he proclaimed.

These young bluebloods were supposed to bring money into the venture from their various high-toned families and associates, but Jules was the only one who had done so: the others were chary, wary, their families asked questions and, for the most part, it turned out that they were the least trusted, the most ridiculed member of the family, the younger son without a pension or a father's blessing, or any hope but some doting aunt. And doting aunts don't like aviation.

But Jules was in no state now to put pressure on these ambitious and naïve young aristocrats, snuffing up politics, position, and money with wide nostrils and long necks. He sat in his bank, transformed into a junior version of the Jockey Club and gossiped with these youths and entertained all the retired admirals and gaga generals they liked to bring along. He had felt he was in clover: he was almost ruined.

There was some anxiety in Claire-Josèphe's young heart, too. When Jules transferred the gold from Amsterdam and elsewhere to Oslo, he had failed to segregate the gold bars which belonged to her personally, as part of her dowry. She saw him pouring money out for these ventures, and into the stock markets; she had moments of black panic, when she saw herself and her children ruined and Jules a runaway. She felt that afternoon had fallen on Jules's world, too; it was not shining and sunny any more; it did not love him. All he could do was to hide his head or change his hemisphere! The family atmosphere was streaked with lightning.

Thereupon Jules called his brothers and Maître Olympe to his apartment one evening and said, "I'm through. I'm going to leave the bank with the doors open, and run. I'm on the verge of a nervous breakdown. At present you may not notice it but I do. Every minute I snap at someone—I lose my temper. Every hour of the day is a battleground for me, a fight against screaming! Something's gone wrong. Maybe it's me. I want to run away from you all, even you people. You see where I am? If you don't put your heads together and save me, there'll be a scandal, and you'll all have to face the music. . . . Our money is all abroad now. It is all in two spots—Oslo and Esthonia. You must all follow me there, unless you have made up your minds about some other spot. . . . Things are bad here. There's no one to stand the gaff for me—I let Alphendéry go too soon. We're short of money. Carrière takes all the profits we make on plain trading. I've dropped twenty million francs in markets and clients and ventures since the beginning of the year. We were ruined before the Kreuger windfall came and that only helped to stop the gap. I've had to pay some of Raccamond's clients out of my own pocket. Now since Raccamond ran round to the branches with his story, they've become very cagey: Bomba won't send me any money from London; Brouwer won't let me touch the Brussels balance; the same in the other spots. They're determined to cover themselves if I go down! They seem to forget whose bank it is! However, there I am. I haven't enough money to run the bank. And I can't stand another struggle for clients, and I can't pay out the ones I've got. As for the employees:

740

I'm sorry. I always intended to give them six months' pay each, when I folded up, but I can't. That's flat. I'll give one of them six months' pay, to stay round when the inspectors come, but that's all I can do. The others must fight with the liquidators. It's a dirty deal—but what the deuce! I've got to think of myself first."

The next morning, Jules flew off in William's airplane, and William flew in a borrowed plane to the field where Jules's was, and burned it. This was the only aviation which resulted from Jules's aviation venture. As soon as William received the following telegram from Jules:

THE SKY'S THE LIMIT
MERCURE

he telephoned his mother and Claire-Josèphe and told them to call for him in the Rue Pillet-Will at five that afternoon. He stayed until four-forty-five, giving orders, running things as usual, and then sauntered downstairs. It was Saturday afternoon. There were only the inveterates in the board room watching the figures jump; the rest of the bank was beautifully dark and quiet. In the great circular lobby he found Daniel Cambo writing a letter while he waited for him.

"Are you going to the bouts tonight?" asked Cambo.

"No. I'm driving down to Lourdes for the weekend. You know how old women are—as my old lady gets older she gets more superstitious. I thought I'd give her a treat and show her the Basilica."

"It's nice weather," said Cambo. "Don't know what I'm going to do. Mme. Gerson is out of town. Just get drunk, I suppose."

William stuck his head in at the board-room door. "Well, will you close up, Jacques?"

"Yes."

William looked up at the glass pane still sparkling on the first floor, outside Jules's room. The luster was always on in that room while the bank was open, whether Jules was there or not. William nodded upstairs. "I forgot to turn off my brother's light. Do you mind turning it out, Jacques?" He freshened and said good-humoredly, "Well, never mind. I'll do it myself." He disappeared by the private staircase and in a minute the light had gone off. Thus Cambo saw him coming down the main staircase again.

"Can't we get rid of you, eh?"

"Sure," amiably responded William.

Daniel Cambo accompanied him to the footpath and found the car waiting there, an unusual thing, for William usually rejoined his car at one of the gates of Paris, to avoid the city traffic. William casually remarked, "The old lady wanted to drive down and pick me up, so I let her. Well, tootle-oo: see you Monday." His white teeth appeared in a charming smile.

An affectionate smile appeared on the merchant's face, and he mimicked the nancy-boys with a wave of his hand, "Tootle-oo!"

They drove off.

When the police found that all the Bertillons were absent for three days, they came in and closed the bank, supposing it had failed; but as they were in the dark and were afraid of moving too fast, they simply put up a notice: CLOSED BY TAX AUTHORITIES FOR INSPECTION OF BOOKS. WILL REOPEN ON FRIDAY.

Scene One Hundred and One: Post-mortem

NO ONE knew anything, and the poor employees stood around in consternation like a family of fowls when an airplane passes overhead. It was discovered that no one knew anything about the bank. What was its name? Everyone called it the Banque Bertillon. It had a plate which said BERTILLION FRÉRES, but it was really the Banque Mercure, S.A. Some said the general manager was William Bertillon, some said Alphendéry, some Aristide Raccamond, some Jacques Manray, and one even said Urbain Voulou. As to the money behind the bank, some said it was Claire-Josèphe's, some said Jules's, and others thought that there was big anonymous money behind it, while others inclined to the idea that it was nothing but a branch of Legris and Company of Amsterdam.

This difference of opinion existed about every question of office and interest in the bank. This was what had excited Aristide Raccamond to his "reorganization," and this was what now roused the magistrates to admired frenzy. "How could you possibly work in a bank and not know who was the manager?" they asked Jacques Manray. "You were there thirteen years."

Manray respectfully but manfully replied, "Mr. Jules Bertillon was everything: he decided everything, everything was his. When he was away the bank seemed asleep, at least above stairs. What did it matter who we were? We had our jobs and we did them and we were paid for them. Everyone seemed to be in some secret, in Mr. Jules's secret. We each had our secret. We all thought we were important: that's why we were satisfied and asked no questions. Besides, it was his money, and that was how he ran things."

"What secrets are you jabbering about?" asked the little, rude magistrate Dame.

Jacques flushed, and this pleased Dame and disposed him more favorably to Jacques. Jacques explained: "For example, Brossier, the young man who went abroad, was allowed to look after the gold safe, and only the Bertillons and Brossier knew what was in it. Only the Bertillons and I knew about certain arrangements with clients; only Mlle. Gentil and the Bertillons knew whose were the anonymous numbered accounts. In this way we all trusted Mr. Bertillon, because we knew one or other of his secrets. But he is all secrets; he has plenty and to spare. I am sure even his brother does not know them all."

"What were the secret functions of some of the others, for example?"

"I don't know. I only know they all had some secret up their sleeve and they thought they were intimate with the bank. We gossiped a little between ourselves, but we were all loyal to our job. What did it pay us in the end?"

The client-creditors gave bewildering testimony. They all had set ideas, all quite different about the functions of different officers of the bank, about where their accounts were really held, about the promises made by Bertillon to them and by them to Bertillon. They only all agreed that Jules Bertillon was the bank and that the rest was makeweight, except for two possible backers, Richard Plowman, the retired banker, and Alphendéry, said to represent banking interests.

The accountants gave complicated and conflicting statements about the accounts. Jacques Manray dumped some hundredweights of paper in Jules's great room and gave the examiners the freedom of the files. Jules had never been stingy in the matter of records and had already deluged the courts with thousands of papers from different countries in the Parouart and Carrière cases. These were all partial records which appeared to be complete records, and the examiners had got foxier and foxier and then paler and paler, but at last they had come to no conclusion of any sort. They, after all, had a restricted knowledge of French financial business and almost no knowledge of business done on foreign exchanges. Thus, finding one of Jules's companies incorporated in the State of Delaware, U.S.A., the judge said severely to Manray, "But you tell me Mr. Bertillon incorporated this company, of which you were an officer, in the U.S.A., and now I find it was incorporated in De-la-Ware. How do you explain that error?"

"But Delaware is one of the U.S.A.!"

The judge scowled. "I will confirm that." He consulted a gazetteer, raised a surprised hand. *"Tiens, tiens, tiens!* So it is. I never heard of anything so extraordinary. Yes, you are quite right. To think of that!" He laughed with contentment, thinking of the *apéritif* hour. "I must tell my friends that there is a state in the U.S.A. called De-la-Ware. *Tiens!"*

This convinced the magistrate that Jacques was telling the truth, and after that his sessions were agreeable.

Some of the clients tried to sue the employees for knowing the state of affairs and not immediately reporting it to the police; but this, it was explained, would only result in the world being turned upside down, and the complaints were dismissed.

As soon as a preliminary study of the papers was made, an immense peace settled on the accountants and liquidators. None of them had the least idea of the business, and they would certainly be still studying it in 1940. Besides, it began to resemble a treasure hunt. It appeared that Jules was not bankrupt. He had plenty of money. There was all the gold he had shown Aristide. He had often said to Campoverde, "I have gold here, there, and everywhere. I don't know what to do with the stuff." Richard Plowman had himself seen gold in four different countries. Then apparently he had money sunk in and not withdrawn from his London, Amsterdam, Delaware,

744

Luxemburg, and other affiliated corporations. They drew up a partial list:

Amstel Starr Corp.—100,000 guilders fully paid up.
Anglo-Belgian Billbroking Co.—
                              5,000,000 francs paid up.
Amsterdam Foreign Investments Co.—
                              100,000 guilders paid up.
Edinburgh Nominees, Ltd.—£20,000 paid up.
Five Brothers Simla (Luxemburg) Holding Co.—
                              5,000,000 francs.
Geneva International Economic Research Founda-
                              tion—5,000,000 francs.
German Bondholders' Overseas Insurance, S.A.—
                              2,000,000 francs.
Leman Trust Co., Geneva—1,000,000 Swiss francs.
Lollard & Co., Amsterdam—200,000 guilders.
Leadenhall & Co., London—£20,000.
London Bank Deposits Insurance Co.—£20,000.
London Reinvestment Guarantee Banking Corp.—
                              £20,000.
Delaware Blue Dome Holding Co.—$250,000.

There was no earthly reason why Jules should have run away. The above companies were solvent and, as far as they had ever been, in life.

As soon as this list was drawn up, each one of the creditors, who had been angry and discouraged, suddenly found himself to be a Hercules of retribution, a Tantalus of need. The lawyers swarmed round and everyone settled down to a splendid feast. They had a great deal of information by now.

Aristide's badly drawn complaint against the bank was dismissed with the opening of the courts but the flight of Jules created still graver charges. Alphendéry was not a communist and the bank was not the agent of Red Russia. No widows and orphans had been ruined.

A pitiful story was told of a young girl awaiting marriage whose portion was lost, but that was Henrietta Lorée. Paleologos, who tried to sue Mlle. Bernard for not running to the police with her boss's iniquities, was discovered to have bought himself two of Jules's Swiss corporations to conceal his assets. Dr. Carrière, who was considered the nemesis of the bank, had an account in the bank, had never paid any serious consideration for his sterling contract, fraudulently kept a great quantity of capital and bonds abroad to avoid paying taxes, and kept his accounts in Amsterdam. He was the account Brussels A1, which thrilled the accountants every month when the statements were sent out: he paid nothing for this service. Aristide Raccamond himself had a corporation formed in London, inoperative and with small capital, from which he pretended to pay himself half his salary every month, in order to avoid income tax. Arturito Mac-Mahon before his death regularly received ten thousand francs a month from Jules for sending his Argentine friends to the bank. Comtesse de Voigrand sent her coupons to Switzerland by the bank's messenger, in order to receive payment there and avoid French taxes.

But these were only a few of the discoveries. Beyond them lay a sea of mysteries that they had little hope or desire ever to solve.

The reason for the mystery lay not only in the incapacity of the judges, or in the bounty of evidence, but also in a few little touches added by rational members of the bank's staff.

Newchurch, the loyal London accountant, at William's request a few days before the debacle, took the fifty odd books remaining in the London *contre-partie* account and deposited them for five years, rent paid in advance, in a great London warehouse, under the name of "John Murray." Newchurch then threw away the key and the receipt into the Thames, "so that I won't be tempted to remember anything about it," he explained to William, "or anything else improper. In five years they'll take them out, find them indecipherable, not know to whom they belong, as the name is a fiction, advertise them, and burn them. It's easier."

As soon as Theodor Bomba heard that Jules had been away from the bank five days and that William was not to be found and that the William Bertillon plane was missing from its hangar, he judiciously took home and burned every paper, book, and receipt, every calendar, blotting paper, scribbling block, and check stub in the London office. He left nothing there but the certificate of incorporation, showing that fifty thousand pounds had been paid up.

Jules, in a weekend trip to Amsterdam, made two

weeks before he left, had taken the account slips, showing the buying and selling of gold by the bank through Van Eyk of Amsterdam, and taken out and destroyed all the slips which showed the sale of gold; so that when the accountants came to look at that, it appeared as if the bank had millions in gold in vaults somewhere in the world.

Mlle. Gentil, of her own accord, destroyed the cards referring to the account held fraudulently abroad by the Comtesses de Voigrand and de Chaise, Mesdames de Sluys-Forêt, Eloth, and Margaret Weyman, and Messieurs Dreyer, Cambo, Plowman, and others.

Jacques Manray, on the advice of his wife, threw away a number of letters complaining of the late delivery of stocks and others insinuating that the bank had had to buy back these same stocks, and other things of the sort.

William took away the books of nearly all the private corporations set up by the brothers for their own family and private purposes. Those two he left showed deposits of nearly five million dollars in the Delaware Blue Dome and the Geneva Research Foundation.

Jules destroyed a number of letters that no one had ever seen, not even William. Alphendéry, at the news, tore into little pieces and gave to Léon's office manager to burn at home his own personal analyses of the bank's short positions, over a series of years.

Fifteen millions of francs were on the books of the airplane company just formed by Jules, Jean de Guipatin, Maître Olympe, and others. This was intended to unite the few pitiful obscure French airplane companies then existing into one large company which was to supplement the inadequate capacity of the larger producers and eventually sell out to the French War Department—and hold them up, of course! Five of these millions had actually been paid in by Jules, from the bank, not merely by a "transfer on the books." The Spanish oil company was actually under way at the time the bank closed, with a capital of fifteen million francs.

How to believe that with all this money lying round, the bank was bankrupt, Jules really in flight, and the creditors really out of pocket when they paid their lawyers?

Madame de Sluys-Forêt insisted on the judge calling in Ras Berri, the seer, as a witness; he was now doing a rushing business "and must know something about a thing so sympathetic to the spiritual world as gold." The chambers were now thronged with both credulous and creditor. Mountains of gold gleamed in the dreams of this moneyed rag, tag, and bobtail by day and by night. By night they thought up new persons mysteriously connected with Jules, and by day they pursued them.

Thus, Daniel Cambo was interrupted while he was congratulating himself that he had never put a centime in Jules's bank and marched off to the magistrate, for the Princesse Bérésina had had a vision, in which Cambo appeared as the secret villain and Bertillon's agent. Richard Plowman had to dry his morbid tears and try to convince the magistrate that in his last visit to England to visit his daughters, he had not also taken the opportunity to conceal Jules's assets for him. Some highborn and cultured ladies came down to scream against Jacques Manray for his complicity, and some very statesmanlike gentlemen pilloried Mlles. Dalbi and Bernard, for the sake of their lost money. Now everyone whispered that Jacques Carrière had made Jules lose his nerve and that if he would withdraw his claim, Jules would return and pay them off; again, some argued that Jules's later conduct showed Carrière to have been perfectly justified and as innocent as the poor young girl who had lost her dowry in the bank.

But soon, since there was no one responsible to question and the facts of the lawsuits against Jules and the details of all that preceded the closing of the bank began to run together and were woven into one dirty mass of conjecture, anxiety, doubt, self-excuse, greed, and recrimination, the supposed guilt of the Bertillons faded relatively, and the fierce well-fed hatreds of the clients began to turn against each other.

The Belgian clients hated the French clients who had an unfair advantage; the French clients were indignant that the Dutch clients had been paid off one hundred per cent; the English clients pursued the Belgian clients for trying to sue in two countries at the same time; the Swiss clients complained that no one listened to them, until it was found out that the "Swiss" clients were an assortment of the French, Belgian, and Dutch clients who kept their money abroad.

All the clients banded themselves together in national

protective associations, and thus the next European war began in little.

When one day someone had the new hypothesis that Legris and Company were the real criminals, and Jules was only a cover for their operations, the national protective associations began to make complaints against Legris. Most of them got hopelessly trapped in some incompatibility of claim or procedure in the tangle of countries and interests.

Within a few days, the news came that the family in its entirety was in Constantinople and moving east. The employees, poor things, taken unawares, believing in Jules to the last, despite the many rumors and the scandal created by Carrière and Raccamond, were still more cruelly harassed by the bullying examining and committing magistrates and police officials. Their salaries, jobs, and the work of their years in the bank were all gone. The news, after Jules's sensational and daring gambling, his speculations, his splendid show, his lone-hand game, his ineffable dudery, the lavishness of his domestic and business establishments, created a great stir. The police lighted on another nest of documents, avowing and mystifying, which they saw would keep them going for three years. The managers of two of the branches (London and Brussels) refused to close their offices or to allow it to be said their were bankrupt, for they had money to cover all their debts. Jacques Manray stayed downstairs to see the crash through, in hope of getting the six months' salary due to him from the liquidators: Urbain Voulou fled the first morning when he came to work and found a policeman guarding the door. All the other employees bestowed themselves as best they could, with relatives, some abroad, to avoid questioning, not because they had anything to tell but because they feared the miseries of the boring and interminable procedure of examination and the rough airs of the police officers.

Poor Armand Brossier, who had so worshiped Jules and his gold, turned bitter, and now went about reviling Jules, a wicked, deceitful, and thieving man, forgetting Jules's benefits and only thinking of his future: where was he to get a job now, with his sick air, to keep his wife and two children?

Mouradzian, the loyal, who had ridiculed all detractors to the last, and whose fidelity and hard work in the last few months had helped Jules through some pinches, was also much embittered. Here was a man whom he had helped like a brother, whose reputation he had protected, and whose business he had supported; he had asked no questions, had been proud of the house and of Jules even when they were being slandered, and, jumping to his own conclusions, he had thought Jules would be as fair to him. But Jules was a Westerner—no long tradition of keeping engagements lay behind him—quite the contrary. Being the son of a restless, uneasy new civilization, a new society, he had no traditions whatever except those of a bandit. This Mouradzian had never guessed. It was a sad awakening for him. He never forgave Jules and for months after, contrary to his habits, went about abusing him forcibly. His great account, Paleologos, the plum of accounts, had lost a great deal of money in the crash; he, Mouradzian, was blamed. . . . Nevertheless, he immediately got into another house and in six months was doing big business again. Small, unhealthy-looking, weak, and unhandsome as a rat, he had great powers of recuperation and survival like a rat. . . . Those who never blamed Jules at all were an ill-assorted collection—Jean de Guipatin, who had assisted Jules at the last, and alone went to the bank every day after it was closed and during the investigation, answering all the questions put to him, crushing insults with the lofty "I am the Comte de Guipatin," arranging things as best he could to excuse Jules's flight and save appearances.

"Mr. Bertillon had a nervous breakdown. You will find if you look through the accounts that we are quite solvent."

On Maître's insistence, two million francs had been left in cash in the bank, and this was enough to surprise the investigators and hold off condemnation for weeks. Otherwise, it was found that the Silva-Vizcaïnos, the MacMahons (of Argentina), and others owed the bank nearly a million francs. An immense sum was reported by young Prince Campoverde to be in the vaults of a London bank: he had the assurance of Jules. . . . Jean de Guipatin gave them pointers to possible treasure-troves and thus managed to prevent Jules being indicted for some weeks. Everyone read the details of Jules's domestic organization, likewise, smacking their lips: it was a real detective story.

Jules's yacht was burned a few nights after his departure, in Le Havre yacht harbor. The great automobiles were missing. The furs, jewels, clothes, and silver and gold plate were missing, and most of the servants had disappeared. One maid still lived in the apartment in the Avenue Raphael, and it was found that a great many of Claire-Josèphe's clothes were in her name (to avoid taxes). The furnishers came to claim the furniture in the new Porte de Saint-Cloud apartment owned by Claire-Josèphe, and not yet inhabited. The apartment run by Jules for tax-evading purposes was, and had always been, half empty. The concierge said that Mr. Jules Bertillon had never slept there, but Mr. "Michel Bertillon" had once or twice. The floor in the great apartment house, Avenue de la Bourdonnais, occupied by the twins and their wives was empty and ransacked and all sorts of bills owing to jewelers, tailors, and purveyors of luxuries, as well as the first papers in a suit in divorce between Tony and Aline left there one cocktail party by mistake, were found there. Most of the furnishers were angry; the jeweler murmured philosophically, however, "Mr. and Mrs. Bertillon and their family made me a profit of half a million francs in the last few years; I won't join their creditors and howl for the last twenty thousand."

The concierges had all been handsomely paid and, though they helped the police, they all said the best things they could think of about the Bertillons.

It was a cleanout. When the Bertillons went, what a golden cloud of providers, suckers, aides, and leeches was dispersed!

The Duchesse de Marengo, friend of Prince Campoverde, went to a competing fortuneteller, who informed her that she saw "the pillars of a great door, a bank door, and inside a vault and in the vault a heap of gold bars." This news cheered up the Duchesse's friends for some weeks, and they had nothing much to say against Jules. But on the whole it was a bad finish, and things only got worse as time went on. The myths about the gold increased and the bitterness against Jules developed on two counts: first, in those who thought he had taken away with him all the vast riches they attributed to him; and second, in those who till this last had calculated that Jules was a smart thief and would come back and who were now coming to the conclusion that he had got away with

751

practically nothing at all! They had cried: "What a cracks-man!" And now grumbled: "What a muff!"

Brokenhearted were Achitophelous who had left Henrietta's marriage portion in the bank; a Chinese student, who had put in a check for collection the day before it closed; the printer who did all the elegant stationery for the Bertillons; the powder-puff manufacturer to whom Jules had been giving a stipend for years; the editor of a boulevard sheet, *Under the Skin;* old Richard Plowman, loyal to the very end and loyal even now, but in misery to see how his boys ended.

When Theodor Bomba came to him in the Athenaeum and told him the news, "The bank is closed, William's plane is missing, and so is the whole family," Plowman had nodded, tried to smile. "I suppose Claire-Josèphe has the money in her name!"

Old Richard Plowman, gallant and not so dumb! thought Bomba. Richard Plowman caught his breath. "Poor Alphendéry! Poor you, too! You both warned me. I wouldn't believe anything. Well, I believed in the boys; one makes mistakes." His breath failed him again.

"Don't worry, Mr. Plowman, you'll hear from them . . . it's probably only a fugue. Jules is ill: it's not so bad as it looks."

"Oh, no, no, I know: there's nothing really wrong. Probably. . . . Claire must have taken the train and the twins. I suppose William and Jules took the plane."

When Plowman rang up a few days later, to say, with a broken voice, "They found the plane burned in a paddock," Bomba went straight over to his house and thought the old man was dying. But later editions of the paper announcing that no remains were found, that apparently the burned plane was only a blind, a herring across the trail, Plowman revived again, smiled feebly, and murmured, "Well, I suppose they got away with it all then, thank God!"

He followed them (in their surmised newspaper wanderings) from Constantinople, to Tripoli, to Spain, Portugal, the Argentine—everywhere they were reported in the next few weeks. Indeed, the police were not very serious: they seemed to have got up a lark with the journalists. In the end it turned out that the whole family had very simply gone to Esthonia, from which no extradition is permitted for any reason. When Plowman heard this in the end, he believed it at once. "They thought everything out: they're safe there!" It was clear he expected a telegram from them at any moment.

"I will go and join them when they send for me; they'll be feeling bad," said Plowman. "If they send you their address, tell it to me at once." He had no pride. He behaved like a kind and all-forgiving father. Besides, thought Bomba, there is no doubt that he thinks they have kept his money for him: I can see that shining through!

Scene One Hundred and Two: The Money Just Went

AFTER a momth's wandering and wondering, the meteoric Jules was discovered in Reval, Esthonia. He was not by any means in hiding, simply living in the finest hotel in the finest way, with his mother, children, brothers, and their wives. When the reporters found him he was lounging in a silk pajama suit on a chaise longue, reading the stock-exchange sheets.

"Are you Mr. Bertillon?"

"No, I am Mr. Clément Népomuk."

"Oh, pardon. We thought you were Mr. Bertillon."

"Well, yes, I suppose I am Mr. Bertillon as well—Mr. Clément-Népomuk Bertillon."

"Oh! Have you any brothers, Mr. Bertillon?"

"Yes, I have Mr. Simla Bertillon, Messrs. Paul and Francis Bertillon, Mr. Aristide R. Bertillon, Mr. Michel A. Bertillon, and so on."

"What a lot of brothers!"

"Oh, yes, ours is a large family. I have many more; but why mention them all? That is enough."

"Haven't you a brother called Jules Bertillon?"

"Oh—him! I've quarreled with him. I prefer not to talk about him. A flighty sort of guy."

"Have you heard about his late adventure in finance?"

"Of course."

"How would you account for the bank's closing—knowing your brother as you do, we mean?"

"Oh, I should just say it closed from absence of

753

liquidity: a not uncommon weakness with banks nowadays."

To other reporters he gave different stories: he was Mr. Jules, Mr. Jacques, Mr. Simla. A fourth came along and heard he was Mr. Mercure. To a fifth he was Mr. Jules Bertillon himself. This reporter, happy man, was able to ask directly, "They found two million francs in your bank, Mr. Bertillon. What happened to the rest?"

Jules crossed his legs. "You know how those things are! The money just went!"

And as all this was done not with impertinence, but with an extreme charm and insouciance, the thing created a ripple of laughter and convinced people that he had got away with the swag, which amused the public and annoyed the creditors very much. Esthonia is a poor country. There are several ways of creating a national income: there is baccarat, divorce, and the harboring of runaway bankers. Runaway and bankrupt bankers in particular always live high and keep their families in comfort, so that even if the itch gets them and they take a flier beyond frontiers, they leave their dependents in the safe refuge. As to Esthonia itself—that has been thought of: the corsairs of international finance are not allowed to go into business in Esthonia.

Scene One Hundred and Three: The Employees

ALL of Jules's creditors had desperate sessions with their solicitors, lawyers, attorneys, and other legal advisers. In about two months there were sixty-eight lawyers retained by individuals and corporations, and it was perfectly clear that the only people who would divide up the assets of the Banque Mercure, S.A., were these same sixty-eight lawyers—and the liquidators.

The liquidators entered and inspected the furniture, appropriated the bookcases, Persian carpets, typewriters, books, and fine chairs. "Look, I'm taking that carpet," said one. "My wife had been asking for a carpet piece to fill up the corner of the room for years."

"You're up-and-coming," said his mate, "but I'll let you have it; as for the bookcase, I'll take it."

Manray observed this with a jealous eye, and waylaid the liquidators in their goings and comings. "I want my pay: employees have a first claim for wages."

"Yes, yes, tomorrow: wait till we've made an inventory." But the days passed and Jacques, angry, trailed one of the liquidators and found him in his apartment. "What about my wages?"

As he spoke his eye fell on the beautiful desk on which the liquidator was writing—broad, polished, with carved garlands. "I haven't time to attend to that yet; we have our procedure which must be followed."

"Where did you get that desk?"

"What do you mean?"

"You pay me my wages or I'll make a stink. I'll let the creditors know you've taken Mr. Bertillon's desk." His eye traveled over the other pieces of furniture in the office apartment, elegant pieces, part of a suite, odd members like the desk, all splendid.

"My dear fellow, there is no intention of robbing you: you must wait till we finish our examination."

"You're paid for this, aren't you?"

"You came to make trouble."

"Listen, Mr. Liquidator, I did come here to make trouble. I want my wages. I can't wait till your examination is finished: it won't be finished till your boy has been through the university and your girl has got herself a rich husband. I should like to have learned the liquidation game early myself. You pay yourself your salary and you have sticky hands . . . And I'm going to the creditors and I'm going to the newspapers; I'm going to make a hell of a lot of trouble. I'm not in a joking mood; I'm out of a job, and I'm behind in my salary . . ."

"Who wants to rob you? Listen, I'll pay you out of my own pocket."

"I don't care how you pay me, as long as you give me my pay."

The liquidator, conciliating, picked Jacques' wages out of his pocketbook and handed them over, Jacques gave him a receipt and went out. He would be lucky if after weeks of pounding the pavement and marking time on door mats, he landed any sort of clerk's job in another bank or stock-exchange house. Banks and stock-exchange houses are superstitious. Then again, the competitors of Jules Bertillon were naturally the only houses to which he could apply—Peney and Denari, Cleat, Placket, and Co., the Crédit, and so on. And in all these houses Raccamond had already left his traces, spreading scandal with his famous account books, pretending that he possessed all the clients of Bertillon, representing himself as the moving spirit in Bertillon's. Jacques Manray, the manager, engaging as anyone, but a little irritable and angry, would have difficulty in so much as swallowing their first insulting jokes and rebuffs.

Well, it had to be done. Jacques dissolved and reformed slowly; but an acid was at work and by hints, allusions, and exclamations within himself, his love for Jules began to fade. When he had excused himself and Jules a few more times (and it didn't do to excuse Jules too much or the bastards would say he had been hand-in-glove with him and duped the clients with his eyes open) and been sneered at by the customers' men of other houses who hated the "inside man" and been treated like dirt by the bosses who despised him for a lump who had not even known how to get his own cut, and who despised him more and more as time went on and it came out that even Jules had not got away with much money—and this had gone on for a few weeks, Jacques had no love left for Jules at all.

"Although," said his wife, "I suppose if Jules Bertillon came back to you tomorrow, you'd forgive him everything and go and slave for him again, and let him fleece people over your head, and let him make another fortune and still ask for nothing but your miserable wage. I know you."

"You never met Jules," said Jacques Manray, with regret. "Perhaps I would, perhaps I wouldn't. Jules could make anyone forgive him murder, I used to say, but I don't know now. Things have gone so black with us the last few months that I don't think I could forgive Jules any more. He left a couple of million lying round the bank —he could at least have given me three months' salary. Now it is all in the hands of a swarm of crooked lawyers and the liquidators. It's always the same. I have to answer the questions, face the police; and Jules is there acting charades in his tiptop hotel in Reval. It comes down hard on me; he's let us all in for a bad time. He might have known we couldn't get jobs so easy after a crash."

"I don't know why you go and answer the judge. Why don't you let some of the others do it."

"Mlle. Gentil is down there—she's having a tough time: she kept the stock records. Henri Martin is down there, but he's in with the police. Armand Brossier is—he hates Jules now: he says he'd kill him if he could get him within hand's reach. François Vallat is there; he used to buy theater tickets and get identity cards for the clients—he knows about as much about the bank as Etienne the doorkeeper. He's nearly going crazy, he's got no place, and he really knows nothing, and his wife's ill now. The police keep after him—you'd think they like to pester timid people. . . . Don't you worry, they're having enough trouble. Poor Mlle. Dalbi has to go down. She tells all she knows and you can see, poor kid, that all the time she's thinking, 'William Bertillon will never forgive me.' Meanwhile 'Old' Berthellot is foxing away back there in Choisy-le-Roi, refusing to give any evidence, and his wife's nephew that he got in in his place doesn't know what's become of the books. Of course, those were the books I burned myself. It's a mess and everyone's in it."

Scene One Hundred and Four: What Avatar?

THE Bertillons took a beautiful country house and flourished in exile. For Jules yearned out of his harbor of refuge, like many another erring Frenchman, for his native lands and its fleshpots. It took the force and argument of the whole family, combined with the fact that his grandfather was now the richest of them all, to prevent him from casually taking a yacht, cruising round the Baltic, German Ocean, Channel, until he reached ports of France, and visited them, with his flag flying, to remind him of the days when his yacht *Purpure* caused a stir in the fashionable world of the waterfront.

"That's how the police catch half the light-fingered gentry that run from France," William reminded him unpleasantly. "Why, the Pyrenees aren't full of gypsies and contraband stars—they're full of crooks: toughs, horny-souled guys supposed to be pachyderm to the world, and really sighing and gasping for a breath of air trademarked Marianne. The boats and yachts that appear in hordes off Mentone and Biarritz aren't smugglers or dago refugees—they're French bankers trying to see a *bistrot* through a pair of field glasses. Don't you be such a mug as to join them. I thought you had some distinction. You're just like the flock of ordinary muffs."

"Well, what the devil! Do you think I'm going to sit in this hayseed paradise for the rest of my life?"

"Yes, the police have heard that one too," consoled William. "Every Frenchman thinks, 'Good God! I'll never see my country again. I'd rather go back and sit in the cooler for a few years, do my time, and then be free to start pickpocketing again in the sweetest country on earth.' Why," he cried wrathfully, "refugees from Guiana have only one thought—to get back to the country that sent them there, and the first thing you know is that they're bobbing round Paris or Marseille where everyone is under suspicion in the nature of things. You're not going to be such a fool. Go to America, go to England. Wait till the comic act has been played off and then go quietly to a place where you can sleep without bromides."

Jules wrathfully got up and went outside to kick the lawn. Then he disappeared into the town. While there he telegraphed Theodor Bomba in London:

IF FREE TAKE YOUR VACATION IN THIS TOWN: SOME INTERESTING VIEWS TO SHOW YOU.

MERCURE

Then he went home smiling and they all knew he had started a secret game again. They frowned on him and he sulked; and William, who was most anxious about him, suddenly became sunny and brotherly. But Jules knew William, and Jules said nothing. William kept a weather eye open and the next day intercepted a telegraph boy at the gate. Theodor Bomba had cabled back:

MERCURE STILL MY BRIGHT STAR: NOT FREE BUT COULD BE WITH UNIVERSAL SOLVENT

ENOUGH FOR FARE. WILL SEE VIEWS WITH
YOUR EYES. EVER DEVOTEDLY,
THEODOR BOMBA

William tore this to pieces and went in to lunch with content.

But Jules thought William looked too lardy with content and immediately after lunch telephoned the telegraph office, found that a telegram had been sent, and asked for a copy. In a few days Bomba arrived in Reval and was lodged in a hotel of medium standing. Jules strolled down and saw him there, and was followed by the suspicious William.

"Glad you came. I can't sit here and enjoy myself. I've got to be doing something. I'm no wood violet. But the police here, though kind, are watchful and I've got to go over borders to do any business. I say, will you go to Oslo for me and see about some office space I've been telephoning about? I want to take it just for six months and I've sent the chap my references, under the name of Mr. Jules Simla, but he won't do anything unless he sees my representative or me. I said I'd send my private secretary or my brother. But William is grouchy—he wants to sleep here the rest of his life and the twins are just pups. Don't tell Dannevig."

"Dannevig? He's bankrupt."

"Bankrupt! Where did you get that bedtime story?"

"Why he was in Schiltz and Company, wasn't he? When they went down he was sued along with the other directors, he was thrown off the grain exchanges and later declared a bankrupt. Everyone knows he's bankrupt. He's sold his car and his house: I know for a fact that the bank he's been doing business with for fifteen years refused some bills countersigned by him and he was furious, but they stuck to their ground."

Jules twinkled darkly and the cunning Bomba immediately assumed an expression of great foxiness and winked. Jules said shortly, "He sold his house and immediately rented it back from the same man. Ptt! People are easily fooled. . . . Now, Bomba, are you going to work with me? I need a man and I need secrecy at the beginning. Later on, people will be glad to know it's me."

Jules rather feverishly pushed some visiting-cards (the lawyer's and the landlord's) and some correspondence across the table. He added to them a couple of pages of new letterheads with the title, OSLO DEPOSITS CORPORATION, beautifully engraved, and with the address tentatively printed underneath.

"There you are, there's the name and the address: there's the letter with the name of the renting office, the landlord's lawyers, and so on. When can you go? I'm still being watched by detectives; the crowd is still convinced I've got their money hidden somewhere. If you're afraid, I'll telegraph to Alphendéry—" he looked at Bomba with an appealing imperiousness which touched Bomba's heart, as much as his cupidity and jealousy.

William, listening at the door, following the light and shade of his brother's conversation as if he had been in the room, bit his lip to see Jules so little himself. The secretly admired and loved brother begged for Bomba's courage as he had never begged for William's loyalty. He thought to himself, "This damned hue and cry has ruined Jules's nerve: will he ever be himself again?" He distrusted the business which began with the leech Bomba. He would rather have seen Jules magnificent in ruin, rash, splendid, wild, mad, as he had been for a day or two at first, than humbly crooked, raggedly proud, menially enterprising like any twopenny swindler, like a Parouart, some jail-shocked confidence man grubbing for a crust. He did not like to cross him openly, for he knew his brother's irritable temper and pride, and he feared that he might run away altogether to get away from the family and get into danger, confide in someone less reliable than Bomba who, after all, was bought and loyal for a salary.

So he was pleased when Bomba swept the papers into his hand and said, "Sure, I'll go and if I can't do it at the last minute, I'll telegraph Alphendéry myself, if you want me to. Alphendéry got out before me, and if I'm recognized in Oslo, Alphendéry would not be. I'll keep in touch. Pay my checks into the Oslo Banking Company . . ."

Curious evasion, thought William, and looked calmer still, in his fear. In whose pay was Bomba?

But Bomba was erratically loyal, according to his needs for friendship and drama: and the same afternoon William had a telephone call from him.

"I must see you—about Jules's new business," in a little voice, shot with secret pride, intimate with virtue.

He came and put the papers in William's hand. "Keep them, William: I don't want to go into this business yet and I don't think Jules should; I see Jules isn't in form. You keep in touch with me and tell me when I should move. Jules insists on giving me a stipend. If I didn't accept it, he'd think it pretty strange, but if you like I'll return you *half:* I don't want to fatten on a man who isn't in trim: it's not good nature, simply bad luck!"

Bomba then was one of these temperamental, Sarah-Bernhardt crooks. William breathed freer. "O.K. Thanks. I'll keep in touch with you." He put the papers in his pocket. "And we'll forget this, in any case; let him secrete a few more ideas first. You'll be in the swim, evidently. No need to think I'm sabotaging you . . ."

Bomba crinkled his eyes. "Ah, someone gave me away! You have paid me back in your coin—calm and confidence. Thanks, William. I'm your man. Don't hesitate to call on me. And what shall I do about the half-salary?"

"If you get it—" said William, shamelessly, "you can send me half back until you do some work. I'll chalk it up against what you owe the firm."

"Still the old William: he grumbles but he has a heart of gold." And Bomba could be seen to be already regretting his generosity! William smiled maliciously.

"My heart may be of gold; it has never been *touched.* I'll be seeing you around, Bomba, one of these days. Good-by for the present."

"Then it's friendly warfare." Bomba tried to be gay.

"It's my brother Jules that counts and nothing else—that's all," William said stiffly as he held open the door.

He went immediately to Jules, irritated, going beyond his plans. "Where are you going to get the money to pay Bomba?"

"Oh, hang that: a man can't sit about without making some money. We've got to eat. I can't retire."

"No. Now don't lose your temper. No one's asking you to retire. Only keep cool. You made such a brilliant exhibition of yourself lately that your only move is to stay undercover and let someone else begin quietly for you. Leave the theatricals, the façades, the leeches, the Bombas until later, will you? Listen, Bomba had a moment of pity for you, which I profited by. Cut him out. Pay his fare back and give him a couple of crowns if you like, but don't start paying him. I'll do this business for you. I'm

761

cool. I'll go to Oslo and I'm really your brother, so there'll be no aliases, or anything phony at the beginning. Understand. I don't give a damn about the extradition: I'll take my chance because, you poor muff, I see you're going to land yourself in a high-class penitentiary otherwise."

"You give those papers to Bomba right away and see how much he'll need for expenses," said Jules in the royal manner of old. William liked that tone.

"I'll see to it," he said coolly and got up to go. "Now stop fooling around with your harem of Bombas. I'm your chief mate, and don't forget it." He went in to his mother, whom he loved very much, and asked her not to irritate Jules; Jules was getting ideas, and if they were not careful might fly away from them, get into some mess. "I suppose I'll have to shake myself and tail him if he goes off. I have nothing else to do after all; you and the twins can look after Claire and her children. He thinks I'm a dumbbell and I think he's goofy: that's how well we get on. But everyone else is after his skin. That is no way for our Jules to live. He'll go crooked or go under."

The fresh small mother, young for her age, said irritably, "Jules is crazy: he never went straight. I don't know who he takes after—not after my side."

William did not contradict his mother, who, in some mysterious way, was right, even when she was totally wrong (and she was always wrong on Jules). His eyes fell, and he thought in a flash of "our Jules" who was only his Jules, the irresistible, tender, harmonious creature that Jules had always been, different from the characterless, twin egotists, from the wastrel Clément, and from himself, a natural "Dutch uncle." He saw him also in a flash, for years ahead, an irritable anxious baffled impish vampire, using his charm and his connections to no purpose, flying out in a dozen illegal ways, sitting presently in some birdlime of the law. He sighed.

"Do you feel well, Will dear?" The buxom little mother smiled confidingly at her eldest son.

"Yes. Should you like to go to Oslo, Mother? It's pretty tedious here."

"Oh, yes. Your grandfather is getting so old and dear Claire is busy with the children. Let's run away by ourselves."

They went off the next week while Jules champed at Reval.

Campoverde, having burned his fingers badly and lost his father's estate in high finance (money which had been made in armaments, artificial silks, and gold mines), could not think of anything better to do than to go into finance for himself. He had hoped to inherit some of the Bertillon invisible estate, and for over a year had risked his family money to get near to Jules, whose type of banking and financing he had guessed pretty well from the very first. He was an ace aviator, always went in for the Italian high-speed trials, and always came off honorably: thus a little flier in finance was a mere morning spin to him. He had stuck to Jules at the last and held his hat ready to catch the money when Jules's pocket burst open.

When the crash came Campoverde first consulted the distinguished Mme. Quiero, was assured of Jules's wealth, and thereupon immediately began to get a team of men together to work with him. He had something on the Legris firm and would open a business in Amsterdam. Although he looked drawn and occasionally faint from the long anxiety he had gone through and the family explanations with his father, the gleam of the financier was in his eyes, and he recovered from the crash like a young dog from a hurt. He had sat now for a few months and listened to them all, stories of how Jules began, what he had done all along, how he made his money, what connections he had, how he had swindled them all, as they saw it, and he made careful notes in a large black-leather book at home of all he heard. His impatient haughty young blood was fired: Jules was a good scout, a thoroughbred, but harum-scarum; what Jules had done badly, Campoverde would do well. He was younger, he had the same ingenuity but more strictness, the same worldly disillusion and social relations but more method and less mad generosity. Campoverde saw his way very clear. . . . In a little while when all was set on foot, he would get in touch with Mouradzian, who had believed in Jules to the last, and now lamented daily, detested him, but who had already got together another fine clientele, all Orientals, all rich, all ingenious, all disabused. When he returned from his present visit to Constantinople, Campoverde would buttonhole him.

Jean de Guipatin remained and Campoverde had doubts about this soft aristocrat: true, he was loyal to Jules and had stayed to the very last, after William had fled, had seen the wreck of the bank through its worst batterings, had answered clients and employees and police officials alike; but Jean de Guipatin was the liberal and even radical younger son, not the sort the hard young Campoverde wanted. Campoverde wanted the sportsmen, the heirs apparent, the clubmen, the beaux, and the monarchist-royalist-fascist crowd, men of the new world. His life was going to be built in the new world. He was born during the war and he knew nothing soft or broadminded: he only knew his own wants, his own age, and his determination to belong to the governors of the future. . . . But he discovered something. After Jean de Guipatin had routed the police, he was away for some time—with his mother, it was thought. But it was now discovered that he had gone to Esthonia to see Jules. To start a new business? To discover the whereabouts of the missing gold? Who knew. Therefore, tentatively, Campoverde wrote a friendly boyish letter to Guipatin and mentioned that he had some plans he would discuss with him, when he returned. Perhaps also Jules had funds he could not use himself, and might secretly back Campoverde. But Campoverde would never allow Jules in his bank as a partner. . . .

The next news was that Cornelis Brouwer was also in Esthonia! And then Jan Witkraan from Amsterdam. And last of all Dick Plowman, the old backer of Jules. What was on foot? Another bank perhaps! Campoverde languished a little at the thought that Jules might become his competitor before he was properly established. Once established, he felt he could beat Jules.

The news about Brouwer and Witkraan was true. But as for Dick Plowman, he only went to Esthonia to see the country. He was found by Brouwer staying in the same hotel as himself. Brouwer naturally asked Jules how he got on with Plowman now and was surprised to find that Jules did not know Plowman was in Esthonia. He exclaimed in shocked surprise, "Plowman? Why he's never been near me, never even wrote me a note. I can't understand it," and it became evident that Jules had the feeling that all members of his class should rather applaud him than otherwise for what he had done, even if they had lost money in the venture.

"Why," Jules went on indignantly, "he knows I never meant him any harm. He knows that I'll pay him back when I get my affairs in order. It's just in trust. He can trust me. He always did. And I know he's not broke. I know quite well he's rich. Imagine," he went on with some wrath, "Dick used to tell me he kept every cent with me, and now I find he had nearly half a million sterling in various banks of the Big Five in England and two hundred thousand crowns with Dannevig's trust company. That's not honest; he wasn't open with me. . . . Then I've heard of a safety vault, too. It's funny, isn't it? You'd swear a man's your friend for years. Why, he used to live at our house. Then you suddenly find he's been lying to you all along."

He brooded a little, though, over Plowman's silence. Plowman, after making what inquiries he could about Jules and setting a detective to watch for him, in case Jules went to any bank vaults, or made any move to export gold or bonds, went back to England. He had already entered his name along with the French creditors. This to him unexpected enmity disturbed Jules and made him feel that his star had fallen. He was an unquiet, bad-tempered person; he had lived in a fairy world and thought he would be fate's spoiled darling to the end of time. He began to nourish a stout grudge against Plowman, whom he now thought of as going about telling his tale to people and ruining what little amiability they had for him.

But Plowman went to see Alphendéry, when he returned from Alsace to Amsterdam, in his new employ with Henri Léon. He went out to dinner with the two and, when Léon had gone routing to the telephone, said in a low voice, "I was in Esthonia but I didn't see Jules. He rang me up but I didn't speak to him." He stopped speaking and looked bitter and sad. "I always looked on Jules as my own son. Well, a good many sons have given their fathers bad hours." He tried to laugh. His face was old, almost as if he had had a stroke; it grimaced away, out of his control.

But Rhys of Rotterdam, the next day, lunching with Léon and Alphendéry, had no sympathy. "Really I don't think he's entitled to any pity. I don't think the financial district of the world gives a sou for Plowman's hurt feelings or his pocketbook, and Jules Bertillon needn't worry about that. When a man's been in banking in every quarter of the compass, all his life, the way Plowman has, and he allows himself to be stung that way, by a very obvious flimsy promoter like Bertillon—and after how many warnings!—I have no sympathy for him, I assure you. He ought to be ashamed of himself."

Alphendéry laughed. "You never met Jules: he was irresistible. Even if he'd told people the whole story, I believe they would have trusted him."

"I've heard that said. That's what damned him. It all came too easily. He must have been a knockout of a young fellow, though. I can easily see how poor old Plowman might get soft that way. His own sons are such hunting-and-shooting gawks. His own fault. Our sons are our wives' revenge on us. . . ." Rhys turned his healthy little face to Alphendéry seriously. "Mr. Alphendéry a personal question . . . no need to answer it. Will you ever have any idea of going to Esthonia for a visit?"

Alphendéry laughed. "No, I'm through with finance for ever and a day. I'm in tangible goods now. You are afraid I will go in again with Bertillon?"

Rhys's beryl eyes glinted pleasantly. "Yes, I *am* afraid. You see, you are too fond of him."

"I have other dreams now: I'm getting older. I've given my whole youth to this sterile business. I'm not a boy any longer. I never thought the day would come when I would feel as independent and—cold as I feel today. . . . Myself first, the rest nowhere; that's not blatant—that's what finance has brought me down to . . . Maybe I'll get out of it some day."

Rhys nodded, then grew serious. "Mr. Alphendéry, I must ask you: is there any truth in the statement in some French papers that you are a communist, a Soviet agent?"

"Fairy tales have nine lives. No. And I never was."

"I'm glad of that," said Rhys portentously. "I should have felt very differently about the whole thing. Yes, indeed . . ."

At the end of a year, the creditors' case for the opening of the bank vaults, refused by the banks, was fought to the highest courts in Holland and, despite the assurances of Mme. Quiero, when they were opened, nothing was found there. . . . Campoverde who to the very last had depended on his family's money being there, and who had ridden the storm very well, was greatly dashed by this news and began to consider suits against everyone in general, including Jacques Manray, Richard Plowman, and Alphendéry. But Maître Lemaître, become his lawyer, drew a piece of paper to him and figured for a while on it, then pushed the paper to Campoverde. He read:

Banque Mercure S.A. Creditors are paying at this moment:

> Eighty-five Belgian lawyers,
> Sixty Dutch lawyers,
> Ten English lawyers,
> Thirty French lawyers,
> Twelve North American lawyers,
> One South American lawyer:

Grand total: two hundred and eight fat oxen on the Bertillon pastures.

"How much of the totals aimed at (not of those accessible) will be paid over to the members of my profession, before one red living centime is returned to them?" asked Lemaître. "Prince, I counsel you to take no counsel. Go into business yourself, and make money that way. Do not attmept to get it back. You will only lose your health, time, and money. Bertillon might go into business again, make another coup; then you would have a chance of getting your money back. Now it is pure fantasy. Drop it. It would be better, in fact, to go into business with Bertillon. That is a better play for you. You have the funds, you have the capacity, that is your ambition. Bertillon yielded up all his secrets to you. Go ahead, consider yourself paid, and try to get back your family's money one of these days, as interest. . . ."

And after some slow thoughts and sleepless hours, Campoverde decided to take this cheap advice.

When Campoverde opened his bank in Amsterdam in the very offices once occupied by Jules, with Jan Witkraan as his manager and Mouradzian as his Paris customers' man, Henri Léon and Alphendéry went to wish him good luck and make the usual fuss. Alphendéry had a telegram which he smoothed out on Campoverde's desk, when the visitors had left him for a moment:

ALPHENDÉRY, AMSTRAMGRAM, AMSTERDAM. JULES LEFT HERE WITHOUT WORD: HAVE YOU SEEN HIM? PLEASE TRY TO TRACE HIM.
WILLIAM

But Jules did not turn up and although everyone made extensive inquiries in every quarter of the financial universe, he was not seen. This was strange, contrary to Jules's usual glorious, Hollywood way, and those who loved him began to hope that he had really been able to renew himself and start a new life elsewhere in a new name, without the shadow of the old. Who knows? Adventurers are flying every day and rising again under new governments and speaking new languages. His old friends, and even the most pertinacious of the creditors, hoped that he went and made immediately a shining new fortune with which he would come home presently to flash in their eyes. For he had by now benefited by the immorality as well as by the mythomania of the financial world and had begun to be relacquered in the minds of the rich. For others, though, it is true, he still remained a rankle and a hurt, the charmer who deceived.

Montpellier, France, 1937